The Wielder Trials

The Wielder Trials

Book 2 of the Wielder Series

Franca Ogbonnaya

Published by Tablo

Published in 2020 by Tablo Publishing.

Publisher and wholesale enquiries: orders@tablo.io

20 21 22 23 LSC 10 9 8 7 6 5 4 3 2 1

THE WIELDER TRIALS

Book Two of The Wielder Series

by

Franca Ogbonnaya

Books in The Wielder Series

Betrayal of Blood

Book One: The Novice Wielder

Editing & Proofreading: Bobbi Beatty, Silver Scroll Services, Calgary, Alberta,Canada.

This is dedicated to my family. Thanks so much for all your support.

PROLOGUE

How is a god born?

In silence or in fire? Or as the waters of life rise up or as the Earth is rend asunder?

Surely, the rest of the world shall not survive the labor pains.

A thousand years shall pass before one lost child of the seas shall go mad and attempt to ascend.

This will mark the end of all that is and all that is to be.

Unless…unless the mad child is stopped by the One and the Three.

Ah, we see you, listener. Your eyes ask, of whom we do speak?

These four individuals come from different worlds. One is the lost heir; one is the teacher.

The third will be the catalyst, and the fourth…will be the sacrifice.

From the Hidden Tome of Prophecies

CHAPTER 1

Malie was hungry. It had been too long since he had last eaten. Maybe she had finally forgotten about him. That would be ideal but too much to hope for.

The giant sea serpent sighed as he tried to make himself comfortable in the transparent, reinforced tank now too cramped for his coils. Malie could barely recall what it was like to swim in the free waters of the Heldiar Sea. He, along with his four siblings, had been plucked from his nesting ground an eternity ago. That thought made him open his one good eye to look at the other four empty tanks resting against the irritating pure white marble walls of the large underground chamber.

His broodmates had been dead for years. The Alkynaia weren't supposed to survive in captivity, but he had.

If one called this surviving.

Footsteps . The alkynaia froze as a familiar figure in a flowing, crimson gown glided down the white marble stairs leading into the large chamber. She was followed by a group of attendants and her Specialist Wielder Guards, two of them dragging a protesting young girl in prison garb.

It looks like food has arrived, thought Malie with disgust as he watched the proceedings. He stirred to get a better view of the ceremony he'd witnessed countless times over the years, one that never failed to fill him with loathing…and fear.

The group moved towards the grey stone altar occupying the middle of the room.

"Bring her forward," ordered Queen Kallesa as she used runes to open a small built-in compartment at the altar's base. Already the young wielder was pleading for her life, swearing she had always revered the Immortal Queen of Namira. Malie shook his head in pity. Her cries for mercy would do no good. He knew what was to come.

"You would serve me better by keeping still my dear," said Queen Kallesa, ironically cheerful as she attached an ancient looking armlet to the girl's right arm. The guards in their deep-violet uniforms looked wary but didn't dare let go of the struggling girl as the queen continued her preparations. They knew better.

She activated a small fire rune on the bracelet, and for a long moment nothing happened.

The frightened girl looked at the queen, hope dawning momentarily. Queen Kallesa held up a hand.

"Any moment now."

"What—" the girl's words were cut off and her eyes widened as unrelenting pain wracked her frame. She began to scream as the queen nodded, a satisfied smile on her face.

"Place her on the altar and hold her in place," she instructed. The guards darted to carry out her orders. Queen Kallesa waited as the girl experienced seizures so violent the guards strained to keep the wielder from falling off the altar. Pain tore through the poor girl. The bracelet began to glow. Finally, the seizures stopped, and the girl's pained expression was replaced by a vacant look as her breathing slowed.

The queen glanced at the timepiece on the wall and nodded. "Just like clockwork. Three minutes of fits and three minutes of gasping for breath," she observed with a sardonic laugh. "This never gets old."

Malie watched the attendants waiting nearby. Though they were the clean-up crew, they still appeared uncomfortable with the murder before them. And yet none of them ever lifted a finger or tried to intervene. And neither could he.

The young woman took one more gasp then went still in a way only a corpse could. Queen Kallesa waved the guards away, their nervous expressions now transformed into looks of hunger for the armlet, now glowing a golden brown. The ancient jewelry was now filled with the earth wielder's element. The queen's smile widened at the expressions on the guards' faces.

"Not today, my dear Specialists." The two purple-clad guards dropped their disappointed gazes. Queen Kallesa chuckled, turned back to the girl, and tugged on the armlet. Her smile dimmed when she realized the jewelry was stuck. That was unusual. She tugged again, and suddenly the dead girl's eyes snapped open, the orbs glowing white. The attendants and guards cried out in fear.

"The prophecy will be fulfilled. She and the Three are coming for you!" The dead girl spoke in a voice not her own.

Queen Kallesa's eyes widened, but she refused to let the armlet go. She tugged harder and began to wield fire in one hand. But before she could release the burning sphere, the light left the undead girl's eyes and the armlet loosened, falling into the queen's hand. She stepped back slowly as if expecting the dead body to speak again. She turned to face the others, her face a picture of rage.

"What in the Abyss are you idiots standing around for?! Throw her useless body into the snake tank before I toss you all in there!"

They hurried to comply as she put on the glowing armlet, her hands trembling softly. Once the jewelry was attached, the glow spread from the armlet, up her arm and through the rest of her body. Anyone watching closely would have seen the crow's feet around her eyes disappear and her red, flowing hair shine from within. She smiled as the earth element renewed her, turning back the hands of time. The queen waited until the armlet stopped glowing before returning it to the rune-locked compartment.

She turned back in time to see an attendant lift the heavy glass lid above Malie's cage before dropping the body into the tank. There had only been one occasion when the attendants had been too slow to dispose of the body and Queen Kallesa had blasted one of them into oblivion. That had taught them to move faster.

The alkynaia watched the attendants, motionless. He had learned early on not to attack her servants. There was no point…not yet anyway.

"You must be very hungry by now," crooned the queen. Malie turned his one baleful eye on her. "Come now, you'll take a bite for me, won't you dear?"

The alkynaia just stared at her, refusing to regard the corpse that had settled on his coils. Moments passed and the queen's smile slid off her face.

"I wonder what would happen if I boiled you alive in your little tank?" The sea serpent only continued to stare.

In the queen's right hand an orb of fire appeared that gradually increased in size, and still the snake refused to be cowed.

This is it , thought Malie. *Just kill me, you miserable excuse for a wielder* .

"Your Highness."

Queen Kallesa spun around. The guard who had just entered the room paled at the expression on her monarch's face. "I apologize for the interruption, but you asked to be informed when the Chief of Intelligence and the other ministers arrived."

The queen stared at the guard for a moment before letting the flame dissipate.

"Indeed, I did." She smiled, to the collective relief of the rest of her servants. "We'll continue this conversation later," the monarch hissed to the serpent as she left.

Malie didn't relax until he was alone with the corpse. He squeezed his eyes shut. She had been about to kill him, and he was more than ready for it. He glanced at the dead body in his tank.

You did not die in vain. Your sacrifice is appreciated . Now it was time to eat.

#

Queen Kallesa strode briskly, her guards rushing to keep up with her. Visitors of the past had marveled at the long broad hallway with its colossal, ornately decorated marble blue columns spaced widely enough to allow one glimpses of the spectacular royal gardens. To her though, it was nothing more than gaudy and human inspired. *And the gardens? Ugh* .

She ignored the bows of the courtiers who darted out of her way. Right now, she was tempted to immolate anyone who looked her in the eye. They had no idea how fortunate they were as she strived to keep her anger in check.

Conversation ceased immediately as she entered the conference room. Queen Kallesa waved away the bows as she glided regally to the head of the ancient round grey marble table. All those present remained standing until she sat.

"Lensworth, report."

The Minister for the Namiran Intelligence Agency, Nathan Lensworth, cleared his throat and spoke. "We have located fifteen more wielders from families attempting to cross into Malaquey. They have been taken to the hostel."

The queen frowned. "Fifteen is a pitiful number."

Lensworth nodded. "And I'm afraid it's the largest number we've discovered in six months. The only places that would have wielders in significant numbers would be the three colleges in Malaquey."

She raised an eyebrow. "Are you suggesting we openly raid the three colleges in the heart of Malaquey?"

The minister flushed. "No, Your Highness. I apologize for speaking out of turn."

"Splendid." The queen turned to face another official. "How is the progress on the new ships coming?"

Master Engineer Tresh Stamets nervously stepped forward. "The shipbuilders are working as fast as they can, Your Highness. We will have one fully completed warship in four months."

"Make that two ships in three months or I'll have to get a new master engineer," threatened Queen Kallesa with a cold smile. Stamets went pale but nodded.

"Minister Lensworth." The intelligence officer looked wary. *Good* . She loved abruptly switching from one official to another. It made them so uncomfortable.

"Yes, Your Highness."

"Did you identify the merchant ship that convinced the Dyhaeri and Alkynaia to destroy four of my brand-new warships?"

The official answered carefully. "We need more time, Your Highness. I have sent word to our spies in Malaquey's major docks. Sailors have loose lips, so in time we will get the information we need."

The queen stared at him until sweat formed on his brow. "No word yet on how the Malaquey government will respond to our excursion into their territories?"

"It is too soon to tell, Your Highness."

She turned away and stared at a tall open window for a long moment. Five months ago, she had received an unexpected prophecy from a dying wielder. A month after that, she had ordered four of her new warships to cross the sea border into Malaquey waters. Their orders were simple. Find any wielders, preferably female, around the ages of fifteen and sixteen years old. Snatching wielders for her private use was an order none of her naval officers dared disobey. But this had been the first time in decades the Namiran navy had ventured uninvited into Malaquey waters.

And it had ended in disaster. Somehow, three of her new warships had been destroyed by a Malaquey merchant ship with the aid of the Alkynaia and a lone cursed Dyhaeri wielder.

How in the Deep had that occurred?

"Prepare a statement and send it to their king. Tell them we accidentally strayed into their waters because we saw a ship being attacked by Alkynaia. However, when we tried to intervene, the serpents turned their attention on us, allowing the other ship to escape. Make sure you get the name of that merchant ship and its crew manifest." She lazily waved a hand. "You're all dismissed."

The officials looked at each other, clearly wishing to discuss more, but Queen Kallesa was not in the mood. She kept her gaze on the window long after they had left. Her mind was occupied with the words and memories of her latest subject.

Nothing in the dead girl's memories was useful.

The queen gripped the armrest as her hand began to heat up, the smell of burning wood forcing her to clamp down on her rage. Over the past four decades, she had modified the ancient armlet so when it took the subject's powers, it also took the memories. This was why she had been able to gain so much information others could not, such as where wielders were hiding in her kingdom, timetables and locations of those smuggling wielders into Malaquey, the identity of spies, and technological secrets that had been hidden from her.

But Queen Kallesa's mind kept returning to what had occurred five months ago, the real reason she had sent those warships into Malaquey waters. A wind wielder had been captured hiding close to the border. But once the armlet had sucked out the element, memories, and life force of the wielder, Queen Kallesa had tried to remove it, only for the corpse to open its eyes and speak with another's voice. She could still remember the words.

A wielder awakes late but still in time. She of sixteen cycles has the strength and the ability to bring the Three together. She is the catalyst. The Dyhaeri, the lost ones, the chained ones, and the Alkynaia will aid her and the Three. She and the Three will send the Immortal One to the Abyss.

Queen Kallesa had grabbed the corpse. "Who is this girl? What is her name and element?!"

The dead wielder had grinned at her and said in an otherworldly voice, "Kallesezza, betrayer of blood and cursed of your people, your time is coming to an end."

And those had been her last words. Of course, Kallesa had been forced to kill the attendants and guards who had witnessed the odd event. They had heard her true name after all.

Even when the queen had put on the armlet, she had only gotten the power and some stupid memories, nothing that had made sense. She suspected the first strange wielder to speak in such a way had been an untrained Seer.

But to find two in five months? That couldn't be a coincidence.

She was still tempted to kill those who had been in the room today, though she knew that was unnecessary. They knew the price of spilling her secrets. However, maybe things were looking up. That merchant ship must have been carrying the wielder mentioned in the prophecy. Why else would the Dyhaeri and Alkynaia have helped her? She suspected if she found this girl, then she would find the remaining Three.

"Who are you?" she asked of the universe.

#

Britea inspected her reflection in the tall mirror as she nervously straightened out her uniform. She wore a white cotton, short-sleeved, buttoned shirt tucked into a long storm-grey skirt, the hem of which was a pale water blue to represent her element. She was grateful for the long black woolen stockings, especially now that the chill of winter had arrived. Britea had braided her curly, deep-chocolate hair into a single plait and hoped it looked tidy enough.

The finishing touch was the storm-grey jacket with its pale blue-edged cowl. As she put it on, a now familiar numbness in the center of her chest began to grow.

This was her third day at the college, and already she was so overwhelmed. In less than two hours, she would be meeting with the warden to decide on her classes. She had arrived on the weekend, so the last two days had been spent dealing with minutiae rather than preparing her schedule.

First had been getting fitted for a uniform. Fortunately, the college tailor had already had something in her size. Next up had been getting a timetable and a list of rules a mile long such as the daily waking, resting, and lights-out schedule. She would have been completely overwhelmed if not for her roommate.

"You ready?"

Britea turned to face Danai. The older student was already dressed in her own storm-grey jacket and long skirt, both of which had fire-red edgings. On Danai, the outfit made her look regal.

"I…I think so."

Danai smiled kindly at her. "Don't worry. With time, you'll get used to being here. So, what's the first thing on your agenda today after breakfast?"

Britea checked the list on the notebook on her desk. "Orientation with Warden Asteros, register at the library, and the rest says, 'Class levels to be decided.'"

Dania frowned. "They probably want to test your general knowledge first, before sticking you into a class. They did that with me."

"How did it go?"

"I'll tell you on the way to breakfast."

The girls joined the others leaving the girls-only wing on the west side of the college grounds. A long, wide hallway connected the dormitory to the main building. Its walls were old but polished light oak panels. Enormous portraits of former female teachers hung from some of the panels. Britea wondered if there were portraits of male teachers in the boys' wing on the east side. *Probably.*

From her brief perusal of the college map, she knew they were heading north to the massive dining hall. The classes and the library were close by, but she was yet to memorize that part of the map.

"I first came here when I was sixteen years too."

Britea looked at Danai in surprise, and the older student chuckled. "That may be why Warden Asteros picked me as your mentor. You already know Weltonians have their own system of training, yes?"

Britea nodded.

"Well, I started wielding at an early age with my people's training but…but I wanted more. For me, it was my Time of Seeking."

Britea dredged up her memories of her grandaunt's stories. "That's when Weltonian youths travel the world to find their place in it."

Danai looked impressed as she nodded. "Correct. A Time of Seeking can last not less than a year and as many as five. This is my fourth year in Syla." She paused, remembering, then continued. "When I first arrived, Warden Asteros and the headmaster were a bit concerned about how I would fit in because to them, I was already a fully trained wielder. So, I was given a general test of knowledge, arithmetic, social studies, and a bunch of other stuff. My scores were satisfactory, I guess, and I was placed in a class of my peers. After that, I was put through a mild version of the Wielder Trials so they could assess my ability."

Britea stared at her. "Wielder Trials? What's that?"

"The mild version or the real thing?" responded Danai with a question of her own.

"Both."

"The mild version is just a series of tests any qualified wielder can pass to show the instructors how well you can wield."

"But I'm not qualified," said Britea.

"True, but Kahl taught you, yes?"

On the second day of her stay at the college, Britea had found herself telling Danai about Kahl, the Dyhaeri, and the *Windrider.* The older student had been speechless for several moments before she'd started firing questions at the novice wielder about the Dyhaeri. That had continued late into the morning until both had become quite sleepy.

"For less than fifty days, so that doesn't make me qualified."

Danai nodded. "Yet you adapted quite well. Just think of these trials as mild compared to what Kahl put you through and you'll be fine. Once the instructors have your scores for both the tests and the trials, they'll decide your class levels and instructors. At this college, there are three types of instructors: educational, wielder, and combat."

Britea almost faltered in her steps. "We have to do all three?"

"No, general education and wielding instruction are a must, but combat training is optional here."

"That's good to know." *Wait, was combat training compulsory at the other two colleges?* Britea was too nervous to ask.

Danai smiled at the relieved expression on the younger's girl's face. "Combat isn't that bad. Anyway, whatever classes you end up in, I'll help anyway I can."

"Thanks. I'll appreciate that," said Britea faintly. As if she wasn't worried enough already, now she had to anticipate trials.

Oh joy.

"So, what does general education cover?"

"History, social studies, arithmetic, economics, ancient languages—which is optional—geography, and the sciences. The sciences are subdivided into engineering and biology. Some students do both; however, you're allowed to choose one or the other."

Britea felt a bit dizzy with all the information. "It all sounds so complicated."

Danai gave her a sympathetic look. "You'll get used to it."

Britea hoped so. "So, how many years will I have to spend here?"

Danai grimaced before answering. "That depends on your current level of education."

Britea just stared at her.

"Training usually takes six years."

Britea felt faint at the figure. *She couldn't go home for six years?!*

Danai continued. "Most students, on average, are twelve years old when they start, which is the usual age one begins to wield. By the time they graduate at eighteen, they must have passed all the compulsory general education subjects, and most importantly, they have to become accomplished wielders, meaning, they're fully in control of their ability and ready for the Year of Discovery."

Britea was speechless for a moment, overwhelmed and saddened by what she was hearing. But then she realized something alarming. "But…but you only have one more year before you leave!"

Danai tried to smile reassuringly, but it was tinged with sadness. "Aye. There is that. Cheer up, little sister. Let us not fret. My leaving is still a year away." She patted Britea's shoulder reassuringly.

Britea's chest felt uncomfortably tight. She had thought she had just met a friend only to realize Danai would be taken from her soon. She tried to swallow past the lump of dread in her throat.

The two students reached the dining hall and joined the queue of students as they picked up trays. Britea looked at the trays of food. She didn't feel hungry, but she knew she had to eat something. In the end, she got two slices of toasted bread with scrambled eggs and a mug of warm tea. She glanced over at her roommate's tray, which had a lot more on it. She couldn't help but wonder how Danai stayed so trim.

"Danai, over here!" The two turned to see three students waving at them from one of the many tables in the hall.

"These are my mates. We're all in the fifth-year class. They were away over the weekend. Let's sit with them."

Britea said nothing as her nervousness increased. She had stuck like glue to Danai for the last two days, so she was yet to really meet anyone.

"Morning, future Weapons Master Riverun. Can't wait to face off with you in the yard." The friendly but mocking voice belonged to a male student with light olive skin, shoulder-length, chestnut-brown hair, and broad shoulders. He wore a similar storm-grey uniform as the girls, but his had edgings of wind white. Britea stared at him and gulped. Even though he was sitting, she suspected he was a giant. To her, he was the perfect representation of the warriors she had read about in Erina Seaworth's romance novels.

"Britea, meet Navos Odell, my sparring partner in training and crime." Britea's eyes widened at the fact that Danai was a fighter, *and* she fought a giant like Navos.

"You…you both fight? Using weapons?" She suddenly realized she sounded stupid, but she was trying to picture slender, graceful Danai fighting this giant warrior, and her respect for her roommate grew.

"Oh yeah. It's one of the courses offered at here, but you can decline that class. I wish these knuckleheads had done that," said a petite freckled girl with light reddish hair escaping in ringlets from the loose bun at the back of her head. "I'm Lexia Detran by the way."

Britea smiled as she noted the girl's storm-grey uniform also had air-white edgings.

"And the third individual wolfing down his meal as he reads is Shran Alton," Lexia said.

The third student lifted his head from his book for a brief moment. His straight, short black hair and almond-shaped, light-green eyes emphasized a narrow face, and he pushed back spectacles perched on the bridge of his nose as he studied her. His uniform had dark earth-brown edgings.

"I apologize in advance for both my coming questions and my ongoing distraction as I have a presentation in less than four hours."

Lexia rolled her eyes. "One he's been studying for the past two months."

Shran continued reading. "It has to be perfect," he said without looking up.

"Mmhmm," said Navos.

Shran shook his head. "Fine." He looked up at Britea.

"You're Weltonian like Danai?"

"Please excuse his bluntness," said Lexia with a sigh.

Shran frowned. "Do recall I did apologize in advance. So, you're Weltonian?

"No," said Britea as she sat down. "I'm from Weldaros, a small village—"

"Located in the western part of Malaquey. The closest port is Xantos, and travel by sea takes just under three months."

Britea gaped at Shran, who had turned back to his book again. Danai came to her rescue.

"His presentation is on the changing geography of Malaquey, and he has both a terrific memory and poor manners."

"You can say that again," muttered Navos dryly as he dug into his meal.

"So, what's your story? This is the first time I've seen you. Were you at one of the other colleges?" asked Lexia.

Britea's nervousness returned in force. She looked at Danai helplessly. "I'm new to wielding. I just discovered this ability less than two months ago."

Shran raised his head and stared at her, while the other two students paused with food or drink halfway to their mouths. Navos looked wordlessly at Danai who nodded.

"You're a late wielder?" whispered Lexia. Britea nodded silently.

"Which is exceptionally rare. Less than seven percent of the population are wielders and of those, more than ninety-five percent wield from the age of twelve and a half years which means—"

Navos sighed. "We get it, Shran. Please, could you stop sounding like an epidemiology textbook for one hour?"

Shran closed his book. "But she," he said, indicating Britea, "is extraordinary—"

"And she needs to eat her breakfast before it gets cold," pointed out Danai. Shran shut up at her gentle words. The group of five enjoyed silence for a few minutes until he raised a hand as if asking for permission.

Britea braced herself as Danai wearily nodded.

"So, how did yours manifest?" asked the earth wielder.

Everyone looked at Britea as she replied. "I got into an argument with my sister and before I knew it, I wielded water at her."

Shran's eyes widened.

"Did she get hurt?" asked Lexia.

"No, just a little wet and mad as hell." The other wielders chuckled in relief.

"How did you find your way to the college?" Shran asked, shooting another question at her.

Britea felt Danai go still beside her as if in warning.

"My dah got passage for us both on a merchant vessel. It was a long journey."

Danai relaxed at her reply, which seemed to settle Shran's curiosity for a bit.

"Any other wielders in your family?" asked Navos.

Britea shook her head slowly. "Not that I know of."

Shran frowned. "Maybe an ancient ancestor you're unaware of was a wielder. It's not unusual for many wielders to be unable to trace their family tree. The talent does tend to skip several human generations, except for the Dyhaeri and the Weltonians." Britea couldn't help but glance at Danai, who was calmly drinking her tea.

"So, what's your schedule for today?" Lexia asked Britea, smoothly changing the topic.

"I'm to check in with Warden Asteros first, then my classes are to be determined afterwards."

"Well, you can join us for lunch if you want," said the petite redhead.

"Thanks," said Britea.

"We'll be absent, I'm afraid," said Navos. "Danai and I will be at the training yards, and Weapons Master Caren prefers that his class eats lunch under his supervision."

Britea frowned. "Why?"

"He's a fanatic about eating the wrong foods, plus it allows more time for training when we don't have to go back and forth from the main dining hall," replied Danai.

"Let's be honest. He's a control freak," snorted Lexia.

Navos chuckled at her words.

"Can I ask a question?" began Britea hesitantly.

"Sure. Don't be shy," said Lexia.

"What are the Wielder Trials? Danai told me that because I'm presenting to the college late, I'd have to take a mild version of these Trials. So, what are the real ones like?"

Navos bounced in his seat. This was obviously his favorite topic. "The Wielder Trials are the best thing about being here. It first occurred two hundred and fifty years ago, and it's held every two years. High-level wielders are picked from the fifth and sixth years to compete in a variety of events to thrill the senses. This year, it will be held once again here in Syla. Even Shran is taking part."

"Mmhmm," agreed Shran solemnly without looking up from his book. "I shall only be taking part in the general knowledge round. However, this competition is very important because it's also a recruiting opportunity for Malaquey's military, not to mention the money and prestige earned from winning."

Britea shot a startled glanced at the bookish older male novice.

"The money is, of course, kept in a trust to generate interest and is only given to the victors after they complete their Year of Discovery," added Lexia dryly.

"Sounds intense," said a stunned Britea.

"You have no idea," said Navos. "And guess what? The Trials are in just five months. I so hope I'm picked for a team!"

Lexia rolled her eyes at his enthusiasm.

"Britea, are they any other wielders in Weldaros?" asked Shran suddenly as he looked up from his book.

"Um, not that I know of..."

"So, you may be the first wielder your village has had for some time."

"I...I don't know." Britea wondered why Shran was so hung up on her lineage.

Shran studied her. "Don't you think that's strange? Do you know if any Weltonians settled on Weldaros generations ago?"

Britea stared at him inquiringly as she spoke the first thought in her head.

"Um…there are Weltonians on my mother's side."

Now all four wielders were staring at her.

"That would explain it," said Danai.

Shran read the question on Britea's face. "Researchers have been trying to determine the first human wielder for the past century. It's believed the first humans to settle these lands a millennia ago were almost devoid of magic, but gradually, over time, they began to exhibit the abilities of the Dyhaeri. One factor that may have caused this development was the existence of the Weltonians, seafaring nomads who were no stranger to magic—"

"To cut his long thesis short," interrupted Lexia, "it's surmised that some Weltonians settled on land and interacted with the landlocked humans, giving rise to the few human wielders." Shran glared at Lexia for cutting him off.

"So, it's possible every wielder is part Weltonian," said Britea.

"Exactly," said Shran as he stopped frowning at Lexia to grace Britea with a smile.

"Just don't say that too loudly," said Davos. "There are some wielders of nobility at this school who'd feel insulted at the possibility of such a connection. Me, I can take the punches. Others, not so much," he looked pointedly at Britea.

"Excellent advice," said Danai, with an odd expression on her face as she studied Britea. "On that note, maybe you should join us for combat training."

Britea was struck speechless as Lexia muttered, "knuckleheads" under her breath.

#

"Enter."

Britea took a deep breath before entering the warden's office, and her anxiety increased when she saw the warden wasn't alone. Standing by his desk was a middle-aged, slightly overweight woman in black robes and a long dark skirt. Her cowl had air-white edgings. That made her look back at the warden's outfit. He was in black robes without colored edgings. She wondered what it meant.

"Good morning," said Britea.

The warden nodded. "Britea D'Tranell, meet Instructor Eowise Shelley. Together, we'll determine which classes you're to start with."

The older female wielder smiled brightly as she waved at Britea, making the young girl smile a bit. The instructor's demeanor was nonthreatening, almost motherly, and Britea felt herself warming up to her.

"Please be seated." The warden waited until both had found chairs. "How are you settling in?"

"Danai has been very helpful, and I'm just trying to get used to my surroundings."

"Good," he nodded at Eowise.

"Britea, you may address me as Instructor Shelley. What do you know of the Wielder's Creed?" asked the female instructor.

"It…it states that any wielder must submit themselves to one of the three colleges for training. Only Weltonians are exempt from this rule."

Eowise nodded. "Are you aware there's a second, more detailed Creed for wielders?"

Britea looked from one instructor to the other. "N…no. What is it?" Her alarm grew when both older wielders stood and began reciting.

A wielder must be trained by a registered college. Only Weltonians are exempt from this rule.

A wielder must never use their talent to harm or kill except in self-defense.

A novice wielder must never fight fellow students. This will be punished severely.

A novice wielder must never wield without supervision. This will be punished severely.

A wielder must always endeavor to serve the people of Malaquey by fulfilling a Year of Discovery.

A wielder must never divulge the secrets of the college or wielder training to outsiders. Outsiders include non-wielder members of the family or the public.

After graduation and the Year of Discovery, a wielder may take up paid work that does not break any of the aforementioned rules.

A fully qualified wielder must check in with a college once a year. Only Weltonians are exempt from this requirement.

Any wielder who breaks the laws in such a way that endanger the public will be tried by their senior peers and sentenced accordingly.

Britea remembered to close her mouth as the two wielders sat down. Eowise resumed talking as she gave her a printed sheet of the Creed. "You must memorize this to the point that if I wake you in the middle of the night, you will be able to recite it perfectly. The Creed is what we live and die by. Do you understand?"

Britea gulped. Though the female instructor smiled, her eyes were deadly serious.

"Yes, I do Instructor Shelley."

Eowise's smile widened. "Good, your general knowledge test starts now."

#

"That's enough for today," said Eowise. "We will resume your assessment tomorrow." The novice nodded wearily before leaving. Both older wielders waited until the door had closed.

"So, what do you think?" asked Warden Asteros.

"Her general knowledge is impressive, especially in history. It's still too early to decide which class to put her in though, and we're yet to assess her wielding. Do you want me to handle that part as well?"

"It may be best that you do, especially considering she was trained by a Dyhaeri."

Eowise shrugged. "I doubt that will be a problem. After all, she didn't train for long, and it's highly unlikely she learned much in that time." As she looked down at Britea's file, she missed the odd look the warden sent in her direction.

"I would like to be present for her wielding assessment, though, if you don't mind."

"Of course. I'll see you later at lunch then," said Eowise, rising and leaving the office.

CHAPTER 2

Britea was mentally exhausted as she closed the warden's door. Though Danai had warned her of the tests to come, she had hoped they would give her some time to prepare.

That instant quiz had caught her completely unaware. Well, at least she had a day to prepare for the rest.

Yeah, like that would be enough .

"I need to find the library," muttered Britea to herself as she checked her list and the small map attached to it. She peered down the empty hallway suddenly feeling afraid of wandering. She wished Danai was with her, but the senior student had already done so much for her, and besides, she had her own schedule to keep.

Well, standing here wasn't going to get her to anywhere anytime soon . Britea looked at the map once again.

She was just outside the warden's office, which was in the southern part of the college grounds. To get to the library, she had to walk to the northeast. As she began to walk, she tried to make note of her surroundings. The oak-paneled hallway soon led to a larger, more exposed walkway with dark-brown stone columns. The gardens on either side contained large ponds surrounded by midnight-blue stone benches.

Britea idly wondered if people came here to relax or to train. Looking at the pond made her want to wield, but she knew that would be frowned upon. The blue sky was clear, but her teeth chattered at the mild chill in the air. Autumn was fast approaching, and she wondered if her father was getting ready to set sail with the *Windrider* .

The walkway was strangely deserted, probably because everyone was in class. To be honest, the thought of joining a class was scary. *Would she be put in a class with much younger students or one with older, more arrogant wielders?*

She shook her head as she neared the library. The custodian at the front desk frowned as Britea approached, and she glanced at the name on the plaque on the desk.

"Custodian Mitra. My name is Britea..." her voice trailed off when the librarian put a finger to her lips. When she resumed speaking, she made sure to lower her voice. "I'm a new student, and I'm here to get a library card."

The librarian nodded silently as she produced a form for completion. In less than three minutes, Britea was registered and in a possession of a library card. Now she had the chance to marvel at the Syla College Library.

And it was impressive.

A soundless "wow" escaped from her lips as she took in the towering bookshelves in the massive chamber. She had never seen so many books in her entire sixteen years. This was her idea of dying and going to heaven. It took a few minutes before she remembered what she was supposed to be doing.

She found the social studies and history section and pulled out a few heavy hardbound books. After a few minutes, she started with the book titled, *The Social Structure of the Malaquey Republic, 11th Edition* ,by Thozas Belling.

Britea tried to think of possible questions from Instructor Shelley.

Let's see . How is Malaquey governed?

Well, everyone knows the current monarchy consists of His Majesty Wilhem of House Taros, his wife, Queen Ariande, and their three children, Wiltran, Crystal, and Aren .

Next possible question . Why is Malaquey's government unique? *Answer: even though it's a monarchy, the king's power is counterbalanced by his elected ministers and lords. They can veto any orders the monarch makes, though that's rare.*

What other powers do the elected officials have? *The ministers can also use their veto when choosing the heir to the throne in the eventuality of the king's demise. This veto power has only been used once in the entire history of Malaquey, and historians state such a decision prevented a civil war.* Britea sighed when she realized she'd have to find the name of that particular monarch and the time frame.

What of the military? *The Malaquey military has three divisions: navy, army, and...wielders?* Britea blinked when she read the text. She had never considered wielders would be part of Malaquey's military. Britea was starting to learn that many things about wielders weren't part of the curriculum in schools outside Malaquey. At that thought, she realized something had been bugging her since she had left the warden's office.

The Wielder's Creed. The secret one she had just learned, especially the part that stated no wielder should discuss matters of the school with outsiders. But the *Windrider's* assigned wielder, Ken Lanfor, had. Britea had never met the wielder, but the *Windrider's* First Mate Melina had had a lot to tell Britea about wielders thanks to what she had heard from him.

Had he committed a crime? Should she report him? Britea shook her head. That wasn't her call. Besides, she had never even *seen* him.

"Novice D'Tranell?" The whisper almost made her jump in her seat. The stern-faced librarian was right behind her. "You are to report to Warden Asteros' office at once."

Britea gaped at her. *Why the summons?* She was too scared to ask. "Um...can I borrow these books?"

The librarian smiled. "Of course."

#

Britea was winded by the time she got to the warden's office. It was a long walk, and she had tried to run while weighed down by the heaviest books she had ever seen. That hadn't stopped her from wondering why she had been summoned. *Was it her dah? Was it the Windrider? Had something awful happened?*

She took a deep breath before she knocked on the door.

"Come in."

Britea entered to find the warden was once more not alone. Three official-looking individuals in the navy-blue uniforms of the Malaquey Navy stood in the middle of the room: one woman with iron-grey hair and two men, one middle aged and the other a handsome young man with a blond ponytail. Warden Asteros was seated.

"Britea, these officers are from naval intelligence: Lieutenant Commander Elizea Trent, Lieutenant Commander Peras Nell, and Lieutenant Harto Flay."

They're here about Kahl, thought Britea. Strangely, she was worried they could hurt him even though he was far away. Kahl had risked a lot by helping her and the crew of the *Windrider* escape the Namiran raiders. She hoped he was somewhere safe.

Elizea smiled at her, but that didn't allay her fears.

"Ah, so you're the young wielder we've heard so much about."

"They've been to the *Windrider* already," said Warden Asteros. Britea saw Lieutenant Flay frown at the warden as if annoyed he had spoken.

Even Elizea's smiled dimmed a bit. "Yes, we have, and they had an interesting story to tell us. So, we're here to verify it."

"But you must have the Namiran prisoners," said Britea.

"You mean the ones you and the Dyhaeri conveniently saved?" asked Harto in a tone that made her narrow her eyes.

"What do you mean 'conveniently'?" She spoke more sharply than she'd meant to, but something about the young lieutenant set her teeth on edge.

His gaze was intent as he replied. "They attacked your ship. You were within your rights to leave them to die, and yet, you didn't? Why?"

"They were seeking aid, so we helped them."

Harto's eyes narrowed, and he opened his mouth to speak, but the older male official started coughing. They all looked at him.

"I believe we started this off poorly. Let me get a drink of water, and then we can start afresh." He shot a look at Harto, who seemed to back down. Peras took a sip of water while Elizea directed Britea to a seat. The three naval officers remained standing.

Britea didn't like the position she was in. She suspected they were trying to scare her.

And it was working.

"Now, why don't you tell us about the events on the day you first wielded?" started Elizea.

Britea was startled by the question. *What did that have to do with the Namiran attack on the Windrider?*

Nevertheless, she complied.

"It was a day after a wedding in my village of Weldaros, and my sister and I were having an argument. I felt an odd sensation build up in my chest, and when I lost my temper, I wielded at her." The naval officers looked at her sharply while the warden looked bored.

Britea continued. "But at the last minute, the water veered in two directions away from her and hit the wall behind her. That's when she ran screaming for our parents."

Harto narrowed his eyes. "And that was the first time you'd wielded? No one taught you before you boarded the *Windrider* ?"

Britea glared at him. *Was he calling her a liar* ? "Yes, Lieutenant. That was the first time, and to answer your second question, I had no instruction before I boarded the ship."

"And afterwards?" asked Harto.

"I—we—met Kahl. He offered to teach me when he learned I had just wielded for the first time. Our daily lessons began on deck, with Nathan, the ship's artist, sketching everything," Now she was grateful they had done that. "I continued training for forty-eight days until I reached the Fifth Tier of Wielding. Even Kahl's mother observed for seven days. Soon after, Kahl warned us of the Namiran raiders' approach. He tried to help us escape and then..." she faltered as she remembered the dying screams of Namiran sailors as they were being torn apart "...then you know the rest." She rubbed at her eyes, willing herself not to cry.

Elizea looked sympathetic as if she knew what the young wielder was reliving.

"Do you know why the Dyhaeri, Kahl, wanted to teach you?" asked Peras gently.

"At first, I thought it was just because he'd happened to come across an untrained wielder, but then later he said it was because the high priest of the Dyhaeri had ordered him to teach any untrained wielder he encountered."

Elizea raised an eyebrow. "This was part of Kahl's assignment? Teaching the untrained?"

"No, he said he was just a scout given an additional task."

"Didn't you find it odd?" asked Harto.

"We all did; however, he helped me and I'm grateful for his tutoring."

"How old is he?" asked Peras.

Britea's brow furrowed. Surely, they'd already gotten this information from the *Windrider's* crew and her dah. "He's seventeen years or cycles old, according to his people."

"Did you ever go below the surface to the Dyhaeri community?" asked Harto.

"No." But she wished she had.

Elizea frowned as if she knew what she was thinking. "What else did he teach you apart from wielding?"

"Not much, apart from his history—"

"Give us every detail," demanded Harto.

Britea glared at him. "He told me of the disastrous first contacts between man and Dyhaeri. Especially of how the Dyhaeri had rescued humans from the Alkynaia, only to have the human leaders reciprocate by trying to capture Dyhaeri to enslave them or keep them as pets."

Harto blinked, but she wasn't done.

"He also said that was how the war between the humans and the Dyhaeri began, continuing until the Sea Treaty Agreement was reached, requiring a wielder on every vessel that crossed the Heldiar Sea. Any more questions?"

Elizea and Peras shared a glance as Harto's face reddened.

"I'll lead the inquiry from here," the female naval officer said firmly. Harto's face went blank.

"Britea, we're not your enemy, but we do need to understand why the Dyhaeri and Alkynaia decided to attack the Namirans."

Britea stared at Elizea. *Was she implying Kahl and the sea serpents were the aggressors?*

"Excuse me if I sound stupid, but didn't the Namirans commit an act of war by crossing over into our waters?"

"The royal court received an urgent message from the Namiran government stating four of their warships had been trying to aid a Malaquey merchant vessel when the Namiran ships were attacked by the Alkynaia. Only one of their ships escaped," explained Peras.

Britea's jaw dropped. "And you believed them?" Behind the naval officers, she saw Warden Asteros give her an encouraging nod.

Peras smiled. "We're just trying to understand what exactly happened that day. It has the potential to turn into an ugly political mess."

Now she knew what was going on and she was angry. Her own government was looking for a scapegoat because for some reason, they were scared of the Namiran queen.

"Ma'am and sirs, the Namirans were chasing us when there were no Alkynaia in sight. We sailed into the Sorrow's Pit hoping to throw them off, and they stayed outside the boundary, waiting for us to come out. The Alkynaia appeared to us then, and I bargained with them." She saw Harto regard her with disbelief, but she continued. "The price was was Namiran lives or ours, and I chose the Namirans to be taken by the Alkynaia. Am I under arrest for defending the *Windrider*?"

"No, you're not," said the warden to everyone's surprise. "However, because you wielded without recognized supervision in an event that resulted in the deaths of Namirans and the destruction of three Namiran ships, these fellows are here to ensure you didn't kill anyone by wielding."

"I didn't."

"In fact, you and Kahl saved four Namiran souls with your wielding, as I'm sure Lieutenant Flay is aware. And he does know the Wielder Creed."

Britea stared at the young officer in surprise. *He was a wielder?*

Harto was less than pleased at the warden's words. "Warden Asteros, that is none of her concern."

Britea blinked. *Why was he hiding the fact that he was a wielder?*

Harto continued. "Besides, she has not yet been cleared of wrongdoing—"

"What does the last part of the Creed say?" snapped the warden.

For a moment, Britea thought the question was directed at her, then Harto answered.

"Any wielder who breaks the laws in such a way that endangers the public will be tried by their senior peers and sentenced accordingly."

"And Britea has not knowingly broken any of *our* laws. So, why don't you do your own jobs and leave wielder matters to me?"

Harto was pale by the time Warden Asteros finished speaking. Elizea and Peras looked a bit embarrassed for him.

"Of course," said Elizea "I just have a few more questions for the novice."

Britea struggled not to sigh.

#

Britea gently closed the door behind her, though what she really wanted to do was slam it shut. But she suspected that would anger the warden, who had only been trying to help her.

As for the naval intelligence officers? She squeezed her eyes tightly as she tried to control her rage. Their questions had only gotten more embarrassing, especially when they had asked more than once if she ever spent any time alone with Kahl. Did they have a relationship? Were they close?

What. Dumb. Questions.

Had those idiots met her dah at all? Had they not seen the sketches? All the lessons had been above deck with crew present!

At one point, she had been ready to wield the water from a glass jar into their stupid faces. She suspected the warden had seen the rage in her eyes because he had ended the questioning then, stating she had classes to prepare for.

They both knew she was yet to be assigned classes, but she was grateful for the save because she had been *this close* to doing something stupid.

Britea walked slowly as she tried to understand what had just happened. The navy had access to the Namiran prisoners, and yet they had still come seeking more answers.

Why?

As her rage dissipated, she began to worry about her dah and the crew of the *Windrider.* She hoped they were not in trouble.

Of course, they weren't. They had to be fine.

Britea was so lost in thought that she almost walked into a small group of students as she rounded a corner.

"Hey, watch it, you idiot!"

"Oh, I'm so sorry," Britea hastily apologized as she looked up at the three female students.

The one at the forefront was clearly the leader, with her perfect alabaster complexion, wavy midnight-black hair, flashing blue eyes, and water-blue edged uniform. To her right was a stunning blond with brown eyes and air-white edges on her uniform, and to the leader's left was an equally pale, beautiful girl with straight coffee-brown hair, her uniform also with air-white edges.

Britea found her gaze straying back to the leader, whose features looked familiar.

"Do I know you?"

The leader frowned. "I certainly doubt it. One such as you would never have access to the circle I run with. The question is, who are you?"

Britea was a bit stunned by her haughty tone. "I'm…I'm new."

The blond rolled her eyes. "Nice name, 'I'm new.'" Her friends laughed as Britea's confusion turned to anger.

"My name is Britea D'Tranell. I just joined the college over the weekend."

"So," said the brunette, "she's a nobody. She definitely looks like one."

"Wait," the blond said as she studied Britea with narrowed eyes. "I've seen you before. Lianne, this was the peasant girl I saw at the front door a few days ago. She's the one who kept us from getting in on time." Her tone was frigid.

Lianne turned back to Britea as she crossed her hands.

"Let me guess, you got rejected from one of the other colleges and came here? Or you're another Weltonian loser trying to learn something?"

Britea's eyes narrowed. "No, I'm just a late wielder form Weldaros."

The three girls stared at her in shock.

"A late wielder?" asked the brunette in disbelief.

"You're lying," said Lianne.

Britea glared at the leader. "Why would I do that? What do I gain by lying?"

"Little, I suppose," said the blond, a sly glint in her eyes. "However, you can prove you're being honest by wielding for us."

Britea blinked. That was the most stupid suggestion she'd heard in a while. The three girls looked like they were waiting for a trained pet to perform.

"No."

Lianne blinked. She was probably not used to being denied.

"What?"

"I said no. I wear the uniform with my wielding marker, so that should be enough for you. Besides, according to the Creed, we're not allowed to wield without supervision."

Lianne went pale with rage. "Do you know who I am? I'm Lady Lianne Arkei, related to—"

"King Wilhem," finished a stunned Britea. "You're Lady Selina's sister?" No wonder she looked familiar. Lady Lianne Arkei bore a striking resemblance to the arrogant but beautiful wielder who had looked down on Britea when they had met at sea.

The young noblewoman was even more incensed at Britea's words. "How do you know my sister?"

Britea's shock disappeared, only to be replaced by a cold rage as she recalled how the older sister had humiliated her. "Oh, we've met." She didn't bother to hide her anger.

Lianne walked up to her, eyes blazing. "You will wield, at my command."

Britea stood her ground. "No."

Lianne's right hand balled up in a fist. Britea braced herself and she tightened her hold on her bag of books. She could already envision swinging it at the noblewoman.

"Shouldn't you all be in class?"

The startled students turned to face the newcomer. He was of average height, lean with iron-grey hair in a plait framing a scarred face with chestnut-brown, almond-shaped eyes. He wore a walnut-brown leather jacket over form-fitting, similarly colored pants with knee-high boots. Britea's gaze was drawn to the earth-brown edgings of his jacket. *Wait, his outfit wasn't that of a student! Was he an instructor?*

"Master Caren," began Lianne. Britea's eyes widened when she heard the name. Lianne continued. "I was just explaining to the new wielder the rules around here when she insulted—"

"I asked if you shouldn't all be in class?" interrupted the instructor in an even but commanding tone. It didn't take Britea long to see the students were intimidated by the oddly attired master.

"We were on our way to class," the blond one hastily answered, "but she," she pointed a finger at Britea, "delayed us so—"

"Which class?" demanded Master Caren in the same mild tone.

"History," replied Lianne with a sullen look.

"Then get to it."

The three glanced at Britea, clearly wondering why she wasn't being admonished. Master Caren kept staring at them until they finally beat a hasty retreat.

Master Caren turned back to Britea.

"I'm Britea D'Tranell and I'm…new."

Caren smiled, his scarred features softening. "I know. I'm Weapons Master Pietor Caren." He looked at her bag. "Your stance needs some work, especially if you *were* trying to swing a bag that heavy at your opponent. But, I'm sure you know fighting between students is a grave offense, so, it is fortunate that didn't occur today."

Britea felt her face go red. She felt it would be wise to keep silent.

"Warden Asteros told me all about you."

Wait, what? Should she be worried?

"I trust I shall see you applying for the combat and defense class?"

"Um, yes?" said Britea, hoping her reply would make him leave her alone.

His smile widened. "Good. Then let's proceed in that direction."

"You mean now?" asked a startled Britea.

"No time like the present," answered Master Caren cheerfully as he indicated the path they would take.

Filled with dread, she fell in step.

"You've had your first assessment for class placement?"

"Yes, Master Caren."

"'Sir' will do."

"Yes, sir," said Britea nervously.

"How did it go?"

"Not as well as I would have liked, sir."

Master Caren nodded. "Good."

She shot him a stunned look.

"You've realized your limitations, and I can see you're preparing for the next engagement." He glanced again at the heavy bag she was carrying.

"Uh, I got books from the library," she hastened to explain.

The weapons master chuckled. "Clearly. What is the Creed?"

Britea was thrown by the sudden question. "It's…uh, the…" She struggled to recall the recitation "…any wielder must submit themselves to one of the three colleges for training. Exemptions: Weltonians. That is the Creed the public knows."

Master Caren glanced at her, and she hurried on. "But for wielders both new and old, there is a more extensive Creed." She took a deep breath and recited:

A wielder must be trained by a registered college. Exemptions: Weltonians.

A wielder must never use their talent to harm or kill except in self-defense.

A wielder must always endeavor to serve the people of Malaquey by fulfilling a Year of Discovery.

A wielder must never divulge the secrets of the colleges or wielder training to any outsiders.

Outsiders include non-wielding members of the family or the public.

After graduation and the Year of Discovery, a wielder may take up paid work that does not break any of the aforementioned rules.

A fully qualified, trained wielder must check in with a college once a year. Exemptions: Weltonians.

Any wielder who breaks the laws in such a way that endangers the public will be tried by their senior peers and sentenced accordingly.

Master Caren stopped walking, clasped his hands behind him, and looked at her. "When did you learn that?"

It took a moment for Britea to catch her breath. "I heard it this morning in Warden Asteros's office."

"And you memorized it that quickly?" If she wasn't mistaken, Britea thought he sounded a bit impressed.

"I also read more about it in the library when I went to register afterwards."

"Hmmm," Master Caren muttered before he resumed walking.

"Recall is essential both in peacetime and during battle. Considering your recent experience at sea and with the three young ladies, I strongly urge you to register for combat and defense."

Like I have a choice? thought Britea.

Master Caren frowned at the expression on her face. "Speak your mind."

Oh, not likely! She quickly thought of something else. "Sir, why should I fear the Arkei family?"

The weapons master raised an eyebrow. "What do you know of them?"

"I met Lady Selina Arkei when she boarded the *Windrider* for a brief visit. She wasn't very nice."

"And how do you view her younger sister, Lady Lianne?"

"She's not nice either."

The instructor laughed. "That's a mild way of describing that family. The Arkei are a powerful family and enjoy close proximity to the royal court. Their influence can create opportunities or close doors, and they can build reputations as well as destroy them. You want some advice?"

Britea nodded warily.

"Know your opponent, but also know when not to engage. Fortify yourself with knowledge, and never, ever wield without supervision except in dire situations. Understand?"

"Yes, sir."

"And now, welcome to combat and defense."

Britea looked up and realized they had reached two heavy, dark-oak doors. Already she could hear sounds beyond the two doors that filled her with both dread and excitement. She watched as Master Caren opened the doors and waved her in.

She stepped down stone steps that led to a large exposed courtyard filled with students of different ages sparring and wielding. A long running track with eight lanes curved around the massive field. In the center was a green lawn that had been divided into two sections and separated by a wide white line. On the left, paired students were practicing either hand-to-hand combat or sparring with weapons. On the right, several students in a row were wielding at wooden or stone targets. She flinched when a wielder used air to carve a chunk out of his stone target. Through it all, the students paid her no mind as they continued their routines.

"Today, you will watch and observe. If you get bored, feel free to study on the benches over there." He showed her where four students sat on elevated benches close to the track. The students appeared as dazed as she felt. Britea suspected they were new recruits. *Did Master Caren regularly go around poaching students?*

"Any questions?"

"I noticed you had different ages in this class. Are Danai and Navos here?"

The weapons master smiled at her. "This class is unique in more ways than one. First, we don't have enough students for six different combat and defense classes. So, we created one general class. The youngest students are around your age and start by training in endurance." He pointed at students running around the track.

"Then, as their stamina improves, we pair them with older students who help train them."

Like I was trained by Kahl.

"And yes, Danai and Navos are here, sparring somewhere on the field. Any more questions?"

Britea felt she had asked enough for now. Besides, she could always bother Danai.

"No, thank you, sir."

He nodded to her before she made her way over to the benches while trying to find Danai and Navos. To her relief, she saw the two in the left section of the courtyard. They stood on a surprisingly smooth dark floor laid on the grass and bowed to each other while an older wielder in a uniform similar to Master Caren's looked on. Danai was barefoot but wearing a close-fitting, sleeveless black top with baggy trousers. A horizontal red stripe crossed the front and back of her tunic. Navos wore similar attire except his top had a white stripe to indicate his element. Britea sat down beside the other nervous recruits. She didn't want to miss the show.

"Good day," said the young man beside her. He had light brown hair and wore a grey uniform with air-white edgings.

"Uh, yeah, hello," she said briefly, keeping her eyes on Danai and Navos, who were still facing each other.

The instructor watching them issued a command. "No wielding allowed. Begin."

The two student wielders nodded without looking at him, then Navos charged without warning. Danai twirled out of the way, bent low, and aimed a strike at the back of his right calf. Navos stumbled but managed to swing at her. Danai dove to the ground as if doing push-ups, then twisted her lower body to swing both legs, one after the other, at her opponent. Navos caught her legs and smiled, but Danai, who was now upside down, used her hands to push herself closer to him. The sudden movement made him stumble backwards. Danai didn't let up, and before he knew it, she was sitting on his shoulders using her body weight to topple him to the floor. She pulled her right hand back to deliver a punch but stopped just before the blow would hit his face.

"Time," intoned the instructor. Danai grinned at a groaning Navos as she got up and helped the bigger wielder up.

"Amazing. Way to go, Danai," said Britea in wonder.

"You know her?" asked the male student beside her.

"Yes, she's my roommate." She turned in time to see his stunned visage.

"Oh, that must be scary. I hope you're all right."

Britea blinked. "Excuse me?"

"Oh, where are my manners? My name is Henrick Walters, third-year general studies, tier three, maximum wielder."

"Britea D'Tranell." They shook hands. "What did you mean about my roommate?"

"I heard she's difficult to live with and quite rude and uncivilized due to her Weltonian heritage. To be near her is to invite bodily harm."

She had only known Danai for three days, but she felt Henrick must have her mistaken with someone else. "Who told you that?"

"Oh, Lady Lianne Arkei and her friends warned several of us to stay away from her."

That name made Britea see red. "Lady Lianne is an idiot and has no idea what she's talking about."

Henrick and the other three students stared at her.

"But why would Lady Lianne lie? She's related to the king and—" said one of the students.

Britea couldn't take it anymore. "Just because she's royalty doesn't mean she's right. Have any of you ever had a conversation with Danai or even met her? No? Then, do that first before making false assumptions."

The students looked at each other. "You're Weltonian, aren't you? That's why you're taking her side."

Britea sighed. "No, I'm not. Besides, what does that have to do with anything?"

Henrick watched her thoughtfully. "But—"

A bell rang, interrupting the student.

"Time for lunch everybody!" yelled Weapons Master Caren. This was greeted by whoops of joy. Britea breathed a sigh of relief as she went in search of Danai and Navos.

After a few moments, Henrick followed her.

#

"Hey, look who turned up," said Navos as Britea hurried up to them.

Danai was surprised to see her. "What are you doing here?"

"I ran into Master Caren in the hallway, and, well…it's a lot more complicated than that. Anyway, he advised me to join the combat and defense class. I thought you two wanted me to join?"

Danai chuckled. "I was joking. Master Caren must think you have potential though, or you wouldn't be here. Welcome to the club. Let's get some food."

The three students joined the growing line.

"So, how's your day been?" asked Navos as they snatched their choice of food and found an unoccupied round table.

"I had my first assessment this morning…" Britea's voice trailed off when she saw who was headed in their direction. "What does he want now?"

The two older students looked up to see a nervous young male student approaching them with his tray of food.

Henrick Walters.

"Friend of yours?" asked Danai with a smile.

"I—"

"May I sit with you? Britea suggested maybe I should."

Everyone looked at her as she felt her face heat up.

"Yeah, grab a seat, friend. I'm Navos."

"Danai Riverun," said the female fire wielder before taking a sip of water.

Henrick introduced himself while Britea watched him closely.

"So, Master Caren recruited you as well?" Britea asked.

"Um, yes. He walked into class, had a few words with Instructor Melvin and the next thing I knew, the weapons master is calling my name and ordering me to follow him." He paused for a second then asked, "Did the three of you have a similar experience?"

Navos shook his head. "Nah. I came to his class and asked if I could join. He asked me to wield, then asked me about my martial arts experience, and just like that, I was part of the class."

Henrick and Britea looked at Danai.

"I was advised to join the class a week after I arrived, and I must say, I'm glad I did. It's quite enjoyable."

"That move you used against Navos was pretty impressive. Which martial arts form was it?" asked Henrick.

"Weltonian calisthenics."

Henrick and Britea stared at Danai while Navos laughed at their stunned expressions.

"You're not the only one who was surprised to learn that. And even after three years of sparring together, she still gets me with those moves most of the time."

Danai just smiled and kept eating.

"Calisthenics?" mused Henrick. "Well, I expect being seafarers, your people must run into a lot of pirates."

Danai shook her head. "No. More like run away from. Once we sight pirates, we sail away like the wind. We also try not to venture into areas they frequent. My people only fight if there's no other option."

The younger male student seemed a bit confused. Britea wondered what kind of preconception had been shattered by Danai's casual reply.

"So, Britea, you get placed yet?" asked Navos.

She shook her head. "No, I have a few more assessments coming up."

"I don't understand. Which assessments are you talking about?" asked Henrick.

Britea sighed inwardly. "I'm a late wielder; I just got here over the weekend. Warden Asteros has me preparing for assessments so they know which classes would be suitable for me."

Henrick blinked at her, and she waited for the usual reaction of disbelief.

"You're a late wielder?'

"Yes." She knew she sounded a bit testy, but the last hour had been stressful enough, and she was getting so tired of this reaction.

"That's rare. How did you find out? Did anyone get hurt when your ability manifested?"

Danai raised an eyebrow and shared a silent look with Navos.

Britea forced herself not to snap. "It was spontaneous, and no, no one got hurt. Instead, I got to join this college to learn more about wielding." She hoped Henrick got the hint and would stop asking her more questions.

"Seven more minutes!" Only Henrick and Britea were surprised at the instructor's loud announcement.

"Eat fast, my friends," said Navos cheerfully. "Just don't choke."

#

Weapons Master Pietor Caren sighed happily as he let himself into the private quarters reserved for instructors.

"Ah, you're back," said Warden Sammel Asteros when the instructor walked into the kitchen. The warden was putting the finishing touches on a meal of spicy vegetable fried rice with chicken soup and warm bread. "How was your day?"

The weapons master grinned. "It was brilliant, actually. How was yours?"

"Not so brilliant, I'm afraid." Sammel carried two trays of warm food to the dinner table. "I had to deal with some pushy naval intelligence agents."

Pietor's smile disappeared as he followed with a tray of warm, tasty-looking bread. "But they took your report seriously, didn't they?"

"That's not the impression I got when they left."

"Hmm. Let me change and wash up quickly, and then you can tell me all about it. By the way, the meal looks good."

"Yeah, thanks. It's your turn tomorrow."

Pietor ran to his room to wash up and change, and then the two wielders sat down to dinner. As they ate, Sammel described what had occurred earlier in the day.

"I hate to say this, but it doesn't look like they're taking the attack on the *Windrider* seriously," said the weapons master.

Sammel nodded. "I spoke to Headmaster Clayre about it, and he said we should leave it alone. It's not our responsibility."

Pietor raised an eyebrow at the bitterness in his friend's tone. "You're worried something worse is on the way."

The warden sighed. "I have no idea, but I feel Namiran warships in our waters is an ominous sign. I don't buy their excuse that they just happened to wander into our territory to save the *Windrider*."

"Neither do I. The sad thing is our opinions clearly don't matter in King Wilhem's court."

The front door opened before Sammel could say another word.

"Evening, my fellow wielders," announced Eowise breathlessly as she entered the dining room. She paused when she saw the food on the table. "Oh, save a plate for me." The female instructor rushed off to change.

"No hurry, dear," shouted Pietor. "I'll make sure there's nothing left before you get back.

"Don't you dare!" yelled back their housemate. Both seated wielders chuckled, and soon enough their colleague returned in a loose, long light-blue cotton shirt with loose dark-blue pants.

"So, what gossip have I missed?" she asked as she heaped food on her plate. Sammel repeated what he had said earlier.

Eowise frowned then smiled as she took a bite of her food. "This is divine. Now back to the visitors from the navy. Are they that stupid?"

"Not only that, they seem blind as well," added Pietor.

"The Namirans are obviously lying to us; even our latest novice saw through that official report."

"Hmmm, speaking of which, I recruited her to my combat and defense and class." Sammel and Eowise stared at Pietor.

"She just got here. We barely know what she's capable of," protested Sammel.

Eowise nodded. "Just because she fought in one sea battle doesn't mean she's a warrior."

"That's precisely why I picked her," said Pietor with a grin. "At her age, I doubt I would have even dared think of negotiating with an Alkynaia or dream of wielding in tandem with a Dyhaeri. Yet she did so and adapted admirably. I think she may be more capable than we give her credit for."

Sammel gave him a wry look. "Just like you thought with Danai? Tell me, has she finally agreed to participate in the Wielder Trials?"

Pietor sighed. "Alas no. However, she has agreed to help train the contestants. But she has so much potential and her skills in hand-to-hand and wielding are quite impressive."

"I was a bit surprised when you first told me about Danai's skill at physical combat," said Eowise after taking a sip of water. "Especially when one considers the pacifist ideology of the Weltonians."

"Mmhmm," agreed Sammel.

"Danai is a determined young lady," said Pietor. "I can give you that much, and if I can convince her to stop holding back, she would be a perfect candidate for the Naval Wielder's Division. The problem is that despite my obvious hints, she has no inclination of applying for military training."

"As Eowise pointed out, the Weltonians are largely pacifists, so you've got no chance of changing her mind," said Asteros.

"So, now that we've destroyed Pietor's dream of creating an Admiral Danai Riverun, I guess Britea will be the next candidate?" teased Eowise gently.

Pietor smiled at his roommates. "From what our esteemed Sammel here told me, she handled herself quite well when the *Windrider* was attacked, and she's no pushover, especially when confronted by Lady Lianne Arkei and her two hangers-on."

Eowise sighed in dismay. "Oh, by the Maker, what did those three rich brats do now?"

Pietor described what he had witnessed.

The female instructor shook her head. "I predict more troubling encounters between Britea and those three airheads."

"Maybe we should put them in separate classes," suggested Sammel.

"No." The other two turned to Pietor. "Britea is going to run into others like the Arkei family in the real world. She might as well learn how to deal with it now, so she's better prepared."

Sammel looked at Eowise, who nodded. "Fair enough. Let's talk about a happier topic, shall we?"

CHAPTER 3

Kahl slid sideways on the wet deck as he tried to dodge the blow Mat aimed at his head. This was their fifth day on the *Peacekeeper* , but to Kahl, it felt like eons.

On the second day, the Weltonian captain, Lanead Riverun, had told them in excruciating detail that for the foreseeable future, they were to learn how to interact with humans.

Mat had been shocked, then enraged, at the idea, and Kahl was still trying to figure out how to cope with the news. He had been relieved when Lanead had suggested they start with daily early morning sparring. At least that was familiar.

But now he was wondering if he had been a bit hasty in his relief because he was half convinced Mat was trying to kill him.

Kahl swung his spear to the left to deflect another strike from Mat's trident.

"Hold!" yelled Kahl. "I yield for respite!"

That was the prearranged signal indicating he'd had enough, but for one split second, he expected Mat to ignore him. But then the older Dyhaeri dropped his weapon, breathing heavily. His cousin looked away from Kahl, frustrated.

Slow clapping made both of them turn to see Lanead approaching.

"When I suggested sparring, it was meant as a way to let off steam and stay battle ready. The intention wasn't for you to attempt murder." The captain glared at Mat.

Kahl looked at his cousin, expecting him to attack the Weltonian, but something in Lanead's gaze made Mat drop his.

"I may have gotten carried away."

"Really? For the past three days?" asked Lanead sarcastically. "I was told you both were responsible, level-headed Dyhaeri, but that's not what I'm seeing. My advice to you two is to sort out whatever it is preventing you from working as a team because once you start your assignment amongst the humans, you'll only have each other. Your animosity is only going to get you killed in enemy territory."

Both Dyhaeri stared at him. Lanead spoke as if he had something against the humans. But wasn't he also human?

"Now, for wasting my time, you're both on below-deck duty for the next two hours."

"What?" gasped Mat. Kahl blinked. *What did that mean?*

"Report to Tracee."

#

After being handed a mop and a bucket of soapy water, Kahl had a fair idea of what below-deck duties were.

Tracee looked at him sympathetically. "The quicker you clean this area, the sooner you'll be above deck." Mat glared at his own mop with such anger Kahl was surprised it didn't instantly combust.

"Thanks," said Kahl before Tracee left. He started working from one corner of the cargo hold. To his relief, it didn't smell that bad, and he didn't see any sign of rodents. Not that he had ever seen one aboard the *Peacekeeper.*

Kahl was all too aware of his cousin at the other end of the hold. They had been here five days and shared the same cabin, but Mat refused to talk to him. Their only communication was their sparring.

Working with his back to his cousin, Kahl first heard a muttered curse, then he heard Mat pick up his bucket and walk over to Kahl's section of the hold.

They worked in silence for several minutes before Mat broke the silence. "You still haven't told me why you did it."

Kahl glanced at his cousin. Mat refused to look at him as he continued mopping. "What are you talking about?"

Mat went still, then slowly turned to glower at him.

"You have the gall to not know how you betrayed me and our people?!"

Kahl took a deep breath and chose his next words with care. "I've done a lot in the last two months. So, yes, it would help if you were more specific."

The cousins glared at each other.

"Fine," said Mat through gritted teeth. "Why did you train the human girl?"

"I was ordered by the high priest to do so."

"Did he give you a reason why?"

"He said the Sea Mother willed it. And for the record, the king was also aware of the assignment."

Mat glanced to one side. "Why am I not surprised those two were up to something."

Kahl frowned. "You do realize they are our leaders, right?"

"That doesn't mean they can't make mistakes or stupid decisions."

"Fair point, but would you say the same about the Sisters?"

Mat shuddered. And for good reason. The Sisters were seers, blessed by the Sea Mother with foresight. However, due to the nature of their calling, they lived as hermits far from Light-Under-the Sea, the cousins' underwater home. And they only appeared to deliver dire warnings to the king. There was a saying in their culture: "To see the blind, all-knowing Sisters is to know doom is around the corner."

"That's right, they also knew about it. At least that's what I got from the little they said at my sentencing."

Mat scowled. "You mean *our* sentencing. I wouldn't be in this mess if you hadn't used the information I gave you."

Kahl held up a hand. "Yes, that's on me. I apologize for using you to get what I needed. But I had no choice."

Mat shook his head. "Wrong. You had a choice. You could have told me what was going on!"

"And considering how much you hate the humans, you would have helped? I didn't think so."

"So, now we'll never know because you didn't ask," said Mat through gritted teeth.

Kahl looked away, feeling guilty. He knew there was strain between them now. Growing up, they had been as close as brothers, and now that relationship was at risk.

"I'm sorry. I betrayed you. Of that I'm guilty. I just wanted to help them, and I didn't think I could risk telling anyone my plans for fear they may try to stop me. Even my mother was unaware."

Mat sighed and shook his head. "Damn. With commitment like that, it's no wonder you were able to involve the Alkynaia and still escape without being eaten. You would have made a great marine."

His cousin's praise made him feel uncomfortable. "Um…about the Alkynaia. It was Britea who ended up bargaining with the sea serpents and getting us out of that mess."

That caught Mat's interest. "So, Britea is her name. That reminds me. I never did get the full gist of how the encounter with the snakes and the Namirans went down. Start from the beginning."

Mat was silent as Kahl recounted the desperate race between the *Windrider* and the four Namiran warships and the unbelievable conclusion when the Alkynaia had sided with he and Britea.

Silence filled the hold for several moments after Kahl had finished his story.

"Britea sounds like a very brave…human and a strong wielder," said Mat reluctantly.

"She is."

Mat chuckled dryly. "She wanted to fight the others and I when we came to arrest you. I thought she was insane…maybe she is insane. Bargaining with the Alkynaia? That takes guts. Most of the time, the snakes come out on top with a full belly."

"True," agreed Kahl.

The cousins mopped the cargo hold in silence for several moments.

"I'm still mad at you though." But the heat was lacking from those words.

"I know," said Kahl with a small grin. Mat saw his expression and wielded a bubble of dirty, soapy water at him.

"Hey!" protested Kahl as he retaliated in kind. Before long, both Dyhaeri were wet and laughing at themselves.

"This is absolutely ridiculous," said Mat smiling for the first time in days. "I can't believe we're cleaning the hold of a human ship. If someone had predicted this a month ago, I would have called them a lunatic."

"Makes you wonder why the king sent us here, doesn't it?"

Mat's smile disappeared at the mention of their sovereign. "He's just punishing us, Kahl, forcing us to learn more about humans."

"No, I don't think that's it. Remember it was the Sisters who suggested this, not him. And he even brought us here, *personally.* "

Mat sighed. "What are you trying to tell me?"

"I don't know. I just feel there's more to the captain and the *Peacekeeper* than meets the eye. He's different."

"Hmm, I thought so too. Every Weltonian I've ever met has been a bit…scared of us. Almost reverent in some cases, but Lanead is a different fish. He was angry at the king, and he definitely wasn't afraid of him—or us."

"Care to ask him about it?"

Mat snorted. "And get my head taken off? Nah, let's just finish this assignment and go home." His tone indicated he still had doubts about the authenticity of the *assignment* .

"But what if we don't get to go home? Lanead said he's preparing us for the royal court."

"All right, let's pretend that's true. There's only one court we could be going to."

"Malaquey Royal Court," added Kahl.

More than forty years ago, the Dyhaeri could swim in both Malaquey and Namiran territories. But ever since Queen Kallesa had ascended the throne in Namira, the Dyhaeri had been warned by King Jahlaniin to avoid Namiran territory. Only specially trained marines ever snuck in, and at great risk. Over the years, some had even never made it back to base.

"And how much do we know about the Malaquey royal family?"

"Their king is Wilhem of House Taros; he's a direct descendant of the monarch who agreed to the peace treaty offered by Queen Zaleria over two millennia ago."

"Well done, I'm glad to see someone was paying attention in class," said Mat dryly.

Kahl rolled his eyes. "The question is, why would King Jahlaniin want us at the royal court?"

"To gather information, perhaps."

"No, there's more it. We stand out, so everyone will just gawk at us, and they'll be too afraid to speak around us."

"Oh, you're so wrong," disagreed Mat. "You'd be surprised at how talkative humans get once they get over their initial fear. I bet there's a lot we could learn in just a few hours at court...that is if we're *really* going there."

Kahl shook his head. Mat still thought the assignment was fake. Why would the king lie? The younger cousin looked at the empty stairs leading out of the hold, and even though he knew they were alone, he still lowered his voice.

"Have you noticed the Weltonians on this ship aren't very talkative?"

Mat nodded. "I've noticed it on other Weltonian ships too. They also stayed out of sight whenever I came around. I always found it odd how quiet they were. Now, on the other human ships? They couldn't stop whispering and making remarks they thought I couldn't hear." He shook his head. "Some of what I heard was quite..." he struggled to find the right word.

"Interesting?" added Kahl helpfully.

"No, disturbing." Mat saw the question on his cousin's face. "And I'm definitely not going into detail!"

"Fair enough." Now Kahl was curious, but he decided not to probe. The two Dyhaeri mopped in silence for a bit before Mat sighed.

"You need to work on your offensive stance."

"Huh?"

"All you did was defend your position. You didn't attack once in the last three sparring sessions."

Kahl blinked. "Excuse me, but you seemed determined to take my head off!"

Mat shrugged as he smiled calmly. "Perhaps, but that doesn't excuse you from not landing a hit now and then. From tomorrow, our sparring will be different. Take note."

Kahl gave his serene-looking cousin a troubled look. *Why did he feel like he was going to have more bruises and sore spots in the coming days?*

#

Lanead stepped silently away from the top of the stairs leading below deck. He knew just where to stand to avoid being seen while still being able to listen in on the conversation between the two Dyhaeri.

To be honest, he had expected them to start fighting the moment they were assigned the punishment. Imagine his surprise when all he heard was what sounded like an overdue argument. He still didn't know what to make of the two young Dyhaeri. He wished King Jahlaniin hadn't gotten him involved, but there was no going back now.

The younger one, Kahl, seemed to think this assignment was important, while Mat viewed it only as punishment. Lanead felt sorry for them. They had no idea how dangerous their real assignment was.

Lanead shook his head as he turned. Tracee was waiting for him.

"Cancel the second punishment. Once they finish, I suspect they'll be hungry."

Tracee nodded. "I'll let the cooks know."

#

"Novice D'Tranell. Today we will begin your wielding assessment. Before we start, what is the Creed?"

Britea took a deep breath before reciting the words. Instructor Eowise Shelley watched her keenly. She nodded once Britea was done. Warden Sammel Asteros was silent as he stood in the background. The three of them stood beside one of the large pools in the college gardens.

"Good. You seem to have a good memory."

"Thank you, ma'am," said Britea as she wondered if the Dyhaeri had a Creed of their own. *Did they have to recite it a dozen times a day as well?*

"At the end of the wielding assessment, I shall discuss the summary of your assessments for the past three days." Britea was so glad it was almost over; two days ago had been the social studies tests, and the day before had been the arithmetic test. She was exhausted.

"First tier of forms, begin."

For a moment, in her panic, she almost forgot what to do. Then it came to her. She started wielding and concentrated on her forms. Drawing from the calm pool before her, she wielded an orb the size of an orange; six identical shapes joined the first. She held the seven orbs in the air for ten breaths, then picked a different shape: a triangle this time. Seven of those hung in the air. She repeated the first tier five more times with different shapes.

Instructor Shelley kept a neutral expression. "Second tier."

Britea complied, and the forms came easily to her. She created two different shapes this time. An orb and a triangle floated before her, and she began to rotate them around each other as she twisted the shapes into a rod and a star before changing the shapes a third, fourth, fifth, sixth, and seventh time while keeping them moving through the air.

"Third tier." Three different shapes this time, moving in different directions now, increasing in speed with each subsequent wield until the seventh and final set. One rotated around her left wrist while the remaining two rotated around each other.

"Fourth tier." Britea frowned as she concentrated. Now it was getting a bit harder. She took a moment to collect more water and form it into a watery shield that covered only the top half of her body. She glanced at the instructor and was surprised to see a frown on her face. Even Warden Asteros looked a bit pensive.

"What of the lower half? It too is vulnerable." said Instructor Shelley.

"Um, right, yes, instructor," said Britea as she hastily constructed a second shield to overlap the first one and extend down to her ankles.

"Not bad," said Instructor Shelley. Then she suddenly wielded a spear of air at Britea's shield. The young woman gasped when the tip of the weapon penetrated her defense.

"Did you not practice projectile deflection or shield hardening?" asked Warden Asteros.

"N…no. There was no time."

Both instructors glanced at each other with relief. Britea wondered why they seemed happy about her lack of training.

"Stop wielding."

The young novice complied. "Am I not doing the fifth tier?" she asked.

The instructor smiled kindly at her. "In due time. For now, we need to concentrate on the first four tiers. You definitely need more practice with the fourth tier. Now it's time for your placement in both general education and wielding classes."

Britea felt her heart rate rise. She was sure she was going to be with the *babies* of the college. *Please, no.*

"Based on your scores in history, social studies, and arithmetic, you will be assigned to a class of your peers, and that will be the third-year class." Britea could not hide her relief. After talking to Henrick, she'd found out that the third-year class was made up of sixteen-year old students like them. She had been dreading being placed in the first-year class.

The instructor wasn't done. "As for wielding, you will be starting with the most junior novices in the first-year class." Britea blinked. Surely, she had heard wrong. *Those novices were twelve or thirteen at most!*

"But, but I can wield up to tier five!"

"Indeed, you can," said Instructor Shelley. "But you still need to strengthen your skills in the first four and learn discipline. Look, we have no idea how Dyhaeri teach their wielders, but I suspect it's a lot different than our way."

"Why do you say that?"

"Because we never train our students up to tier five in just forty-eight days."

"Which is what Kahl did," muttered Britea.

Instructor Shelley lifted an eyebrow. "That may be so, but there's a lot of material in the wielder curriculum. We need you to understand it the *human* way; thus, we will start from the beginning, understood?"

"Yes, ma'am," said Britea, trying to hide her disappointment. Well, at least she wasn't getting kicked out of the college.

#

Britea felt her anxiety grow as she walked beside Instructor Shelley to her assigned general education class. *What would the other students be like? Would they be friendly or belittle her?*

To be honest, she was terrified of facing the other students. She couldn't explain why she felt this way.

"Your class is currently in history. The instructor is Kacia Felgreen; be sure to speak to her after class to get a list of the reading material you'll need for exams."

"Yes, ma'am," said Britea nervously.

Instructor Shelley looked at her, and her expression softened. "I know this is new for you, and you've not had much time to adjust. That will come with time. You'll be fine."

"Thank you, ma'am."

The instructor rolled her eyes. "Please, call me Miss Shelley. Ma'am makes me think my grandma is right behind me."

"Yes, Miss Shelley," said Britea with a small smile as they stopped before a wooden door. From within, she could already clearly hear a female voice.

The instructor knocked loudly before opening the door. The voice within stopped.

A short, plump woman with red curly hair and spectacles frowned as they entered. She wore a black gown with earth-brown edgings on the cowl. Judging from the expression on her face, she wasn't pleased at being interrupted.

"Instructor Felgreen, pardon the disturbance. However, I have a new student for you."

The instructor's frown was replaced by a curiosity as she adjusted her glasses to study a shy Britea.

"Class," said Instructor Shelley, addressing the silent students. "This is Britea D'Tranell. She will be joining you."

Britea forced herself to look at her fellow students. She was relieved to see Henrick Walters waving at her with a smile. That brought a grin to her face and gave her courage to look at the other members of her class. Her smile disappeared when she saw three girls glaring at her.

Lady Lianne Arkei and the blonde and brunette who always flanked her. Their eyes were filled with cold hatred.

She barely heard Instructor Felgreen tell her to take a seat. Somehow her legs managed to obey, and she quickly sat down in an empty seat beside Henrick.

No, no this could not be happening!

She looked up as Instructor Shelley exchanged a few quiet words with Instructor Felgreen before leaving. Britea wanted to run after her, but it was too late.

"Novice D'Tranell."

Britea almost jumped at the brisk tone of the history teacher.

"We were just discussing the early history of the first recorded wielders of this part of the world. I want you to name the era and name of the first known master wielder."

Britea's mind went blank with terror at being put on the spot. "I…I…"

Instructor Felgreen frowned at her. "Do you know what I'm talking about?"

"I'm new…um, I don't know much yet—"

"Not much? Why am I not surprised? She is a farm girl after all," said Lianne to the amusement of much of the class.

Instructor Felgreen glared at the noblewoman while Britea wanted to sink into the floor.

"That's quite enough. Do you wish to answer the question, Novice Arkei?"

"Of course," said the young noble smugly. She stood up. "The first recorded master wielder was Headmaster Lance Cen-Taros. He founded Syla College in 1384 AC. The current ruler, King Wilhem of Taros, is related to him, as, by the way, am I."

Britea suppressed her exasperated sigh. This girl never ceased to remind everyone of her relationship to royalty.

"Headmaster Lance Cen-Taros was the brightest and bravest of his generation; he is why we have a strong Malaquey today." The students around her began to clap before a loud sigh from the instructor silenced them.

"Is that your final answer, novice?" Britea frowned and turned to see a puzzled expression on Lianne's face.

"Yes, it is. Lance Cen-Taros was the most learned and powerful wielder of his generation—"

"That wasn't the question. I asked you who the first recorded master wielder of this part of our world was. Let me give you a hint. You need to look further back in our past."

Britea found herself recalling something she had just read the day before when she was fervently preparing for her assessments.

Lianne had a haughty expression on her face. "I stand by my answer. Look it up, instructor."

"No, no. You're wrong," said Britea distractedly. The class went silent as Lianne stared at her first in shock, then in fury.

"What did you say?"

Instructor Felgreen ignored the enraged noble. She was now looking at Britea. "Stand up, novice, if you wish to defend your answer."

Britea complied quickly. "I mean, the question is about the first recorded master wielder, and it's not your ancestor, as much as you wish it to be."

Some members of the class gasped while Lianne went white with fury. Britea was thinking too much to be bothered by their reactions.

"What's the answer then, Novice D'Tranell?" asked the instructor, who looked a bit impatient.

"The first master wielder recorded in our history wasn't human. She was Queen Zaleria of the Dyhaeri. In 184 AC, she led the battles against the humans when the old, combined kingdom of Olderia declared war on the Dyhaeri. She never lost a fight. Back then, humans had no wielders, only the Dyhaeri did. It was only after the Dyhaeri won the war and the peace treaty was signed that humans began to wield, and even then, it was the nomadic Weltonians who were the first human wielders." As she paused, she noticed the livid light in Lianne's eyes.

"I'm sorry," said Britea insincerely with an innocent smile, "but Queen Zaleria of the Dyhaeri would have wiped the floor with Headmaster Cen-Taros." Lianne took a step forward but froze when Instructor Felgreen started laughing.

"Good answer, Novice D'Tranell. Welcome to history." She smiled at the rest of the class as Lianne and Britea resumed their seats.

"I'm sure you're all wondering why I take such delight in your lack of knowledge." The smile disappeared to be replaced by a serious expression. "Nay, it is not delight but horror."

What? thought Britea.

"You may feel somewhat arrogant because you're the few who have the ability to wield. Novice Walters, what's the percentage of wielders in the general population?"

The male student answered without hesitation. "Seven percent."

Instructor Felgreen continued. "To simplify it for those of you lacking in math, out of a hundred people, only seven can wield. Now, compare that to the Dyhaeri. Every one of them are wielders."

Britea discreetly looked around. No one appeared surprised by this news.

"I want you all to recall that humans have only been on the Olderian continent for the past two thousand, one hundred, and eighty-four years, while the Dyhaeri have existed in this part of the world for over twenty millennia." She waited for them to absorb her words.

"So, for those of you who feel privileged and think themselves powerful because they can also wield, let me give you a piece of advice. Don't be an idiot."

From the corner of her eyes, Britea saw Lianne's enraged expression. She probably felt this was directed at her.

"For each of those twenty millennia, the Dyhaeri have wielded, so they have more knowledge of this ability at their fingertips than our three pitiful colleges combined. Many of you will do a Year of Discovery at sea, and you will run into the Dyhaeri. I want you to remember how insignificant your skill with wielding is so you don't cause a diplomatic incident, which is why history is your most important subject at this school. If you don't learn from the past, you will destroy the future of those around you."

Britea gasped at the petite teacher's choice of words.

"Do you understand?"

"Yes, Instructor Felgreen," answered the class as one.

"Turn to page thirty-four of *History of the Crossing* ." Britea felt lost as the other students pulled out books from under their table.

"Here, you can share with me," whispered Henrick.

"Thanks," said Britea with a small smile. She could feel Lianne's glare without having to turn around.

CHAPTER 4

Britea was out the door the second Instructor Felgreen dismissed the class. She tried not to run even though she felt Lady Lianne Arkei's eyes following her. No one had to tell her she'd made a powerful enemy.

Which was why she was looking forward to her next class.

"Britea, wait up!"

She looked over her shoulder to see Henrick hurrying after her. She slowed down so he could catch up.

"That was a clever answer by the way."

Her face went red at his praise, and she tried to brush it away with a weak laugh. "Nah, I just got lucky. I'd read about Queen Zaleria recently when I was preparing for my assessments."

The smile slid off Henrick's face then, and he took a quick glance around and lowered his voice. "May I offer some advice?"

Britea felt uneasy now. "Sure."

"I know how hard it is to accept how the nobles…how they treat us folk. I'm from Frantia. It's a small village north of Malaquey. To the highborn, we're worth less than the dirt beneath their feet, so you don't want them as your enemy. If you want to get through training, it's best if you try not to draw their attention."

She almost stopped in her tracks but forced herself to keep walking.

"I didn't exactly pick a fight with Lianne during history class."

Henrick smiled dryly. "You might as well have. After you humiliated her, everyone could see she was upset. Nobles like her don't let insults slide."

Britea couldn't help but laugh. "But I didn't insult her."

"It wasn't just your words but your tone. You weren't afraid of her."

Now Henrick was upsetting her. She stopped walking, and moments later, so did he.

"And why should I be afraid of her? Because she was born rich and I wasn't, or because she's descended from royalty and I *ain't*? Just because our stations are different, doesn't give her the right to look down on us and treat us terribly."

Henrick stared at her. "Remember, it's people like her that make the rules in Malaquey. Her family can have you blacklisted before you even graduate." Henrick lowered his voice once more, then looked around again to ensure they were alone. "We shouldn't really be discussing this, Britea. It can get us into trouble."

She stared at him in shock. Not sure how to respond, part of her wanted to yell or punch something, but instead, she closed her eyes briefly.

"You know what? Let's get to class."

The two novices walked in uncomfortable silence.

#

Britea's spirits brightened when her small group of students neared the outdoor combat and defense class. On the way to class, a few other students from the higher classes had joined Henrick and Britea. She had searched for Danai, but her roommate had been nowhere to be seen.

However, once they entered the training sector, she saw Danai and Navos already there with a few other students.

"New recruits, form up in the right corner of the field!" Weapons Master Caren's voice boomed as Britea and Henrick hurried into position with the other recruits. Britea found it interesting that the new recruits appeared no older than her or Henrick.

"Everyone else, report to Instructor Talios for sparring assignments." Whoops of joy filled the air at this announcement. Britea gazed enviously at her older colleagues. They all appeared so strong and confident.

"Face front!" yelled a female instructor dressed head to toe in walnut-brown close-fitting leathers with earth-brown slashes on the tunic. Weapons Master Caren waited until they were in position before addressing the new students.

"Yesterday, you had the privilege of observing. From today, you train. Instructor Lexar will guide you."

The female instructor stepped forward. "The change rooms are at the rear of the field. You have two minutes to grab your gear and return to this spot. The last five students back will do thirty push-ups as punishment." Before she had even finished speaking, there was a mad dash for the change rooms.

Britea just barely avoided being one of the last five as she raced back to Instructor Lexar. The five unfortunate students began their push-ups as the female instructor addressed the novices once more.

"Today, we run. Seven laps around the field."

Wait, what? thought Britea as she and the rest of the new students stared at their torturer.

The smile left the instructor's face. "What are you waiting for!?"

That yell had them running.

#

"Two more laps to go!"

Britea glanced down at her forearms as they pumped up and down with each stride. Her ebony skin glistened with sweat, and she was hot and exhausted. She was grateful for the full, billowing pants. At first, she'd thought they would be a hindrance, but the design kept her legs cool and made the experience a bit more bearable.

"Start slowing down in the last lap, people!" yelled Instructor Lexar.

Britea gradually began to reduce her speed. By the time she came to a complete stop, she wanted to lie down on the floor and never get up. Some of the students had given in and collapsed on the ground, but somehow, the rest remained sitting or standing.

And she was one of them. She walked slowly towards the table upon which glass jars of water had been placed. She prayed to the Maker that the liquid was cool. Eventually, those who had been prostate on the floor stood up and made their way over to the table.

Britea forced herself to drink the water slowly. The last thing she wanted to do was vomit in front of her colleagues.

A slow clap had most of them turning to face Instructor Lexar. "Well, that wasn't a bad start, though my baby brother would have left you all eating his dust."

Many of the students were upset at her words.

The female instructor raised an eyebrow. "I see questions on some of your faces. Let's hear them."

Britea blinked and looked at the other novices. They looked stupefied by the instructor's approach.

A student tentatively raised his hand. "Instructor Lexar, when do we get to spar like the others?"

She smiled dryly. "When I'm satisfied with your running."

Someone in the group protested, and she shot a dark look at that corner of the crowd, silencing the disgruntled novice. “So, you wish to spar? Have any of you wielded while blocking blows from your assailant?”

No one answered.

“Have any of you wielded when exhausted and found it so hard to even move a muscle, let alone run or walk?” She paused and waited for an answer. The group remained silent.

“None of you have been in this situation? That is why you need to run and exercise. Racing round the track doesn’t only exercise your pitiful muscles, it also helps you develop mental discipline. Only when that is attained will you be allowed to try physical sparring and wielding at the same time. Any objections to that?”

No one said a word.

“Mark my words, some of you may not be able to tolerate this class. There is no shame in dropping out. Just do it fast so you don’t waste my time.” She smiled coldly at them. “Now, grab your lunch before the next round of exercises.”

As Britea walked away with her classmates, she began to realize what she had undertaken. Strangely though, she didn’t regret her decision.

“You all right?” She turned to see a tired Henrick had fallen into step beside her.

“Yes, just exhausted and hungry.”

“Same.” Both novices joined the buffet queue. Britea had just collected her meal when she heard someone complaining loudly to the other recruits.

“I don’t agree with her! I came here to learn how to wield, not to run in circles!”

She looked at the speaker, a lanky, brown-haired male, as he continued.

“We all know the real work starts once we graduate and do our Year of Discovery. That’s when the rewards come in. I even heard that in some places, you get paid a lot. I joined combat and defense because the navy recruits directly from this class, and they pay the most. Running around and doing a bunch of weird exercises isn’t going to teach me to wield better, so I’m wondering if this class isn’t a total waste of my time!”

Britea stared at him. Not even two weeks ago, she, Kahl, and the crew of the *Windrider* had barely escaped being captured by the Namiran raiders. They had only managed to get away because of the unusual bargain she’d made with the

Alkynaia. Britea had traded the lives of the Namiran crew of the four warships for the safety of the *Windrider* crew. She still had nightmares of that day.

Britea knew why she'd joined this class. Before the bargain, when she'd been sure she was about to die, Britea had realized how vulnerable she was. And she had been reminded of that with her interrogation by the Malaquey Navy and with her run in with Lady Lianne Arkei. She never wanted to be weak again.

Apparently, some wielders didn't appreciate what was being offered in Master Caren's class.

"Hey! What are you looking at?!"

Britea was yanked back to the present when the recruit yelled at her, and she realized she was still staring at him.

"I'm sorry. I wasn't looking at anything really."

His face went red.

"I mean…I didn't mean *you're* nothing!" Britea hastily explained before continuing, unable to stop herself. "But you are wrong."

Henrick raised an eyebrow. The lanky student was shocked into silence.

"We all heard Instructor Lexar. If this class isn't for you, you're free to leave. However, I'm staying because I don't have the luxury of paid protection or safety."

Britea didn't hang around to discuss it further. She strode angrily away from the group to the bench she had occupied yesterday. To be honest, she was feeling a bit homesick; at times she regretted coming to the college in the first place. But she was here now, and she was going to make the most of it.

"Mind if I sit with you?"

She looked up into Henrick's kind brown eyes. Britea really didn't feel like talking, but his expression was so earnest she decided not to be cruel.

"Sure. Sit with the girl determined to make enemies everywhere she goes."

Henrick looked at her quizzically. "Why do you say that?"

"I humiliated Lianne and her group of sycophants in class, remember? And now here I am, annoying my fellow classmates in combat and defense."

"Ignore Laris," said Henrick. "He talks about himself all the time. He thinks he's important because he's the first wielder in his family since forever."

Britea narrowed her eyes. "You sure know a lot about everybody."

Henrick didn't back down from her gaze. "And you would too, if you watched, listened, and waited for the right moment."

"Spoken like a spy," said Britea after a moment.

He blinked and peered down at his food as if embarrassed. "You think so?"

"Hey, hey! How are the two new warriors?" boomed Navos as he planted himself beside Henrick with an overflowing plate of food he attacked with gusto.

"Wow," Britea said, watching how fast he could shove the food down as Danai sat down beside her.

"We're…uh, fine," said Henrick weakly as he gaped at the older wielder beside him eating at an inhuman speed.

Danai laughed softly. "We just finished sparring a bit later than the others. That's why we're late."

She smiled at Britea. "How did your assessments go this morning?"

Britea felt a bit insecure as she replied. "I got put in the third-year class for general studies but for wielding…" she paused and Navos slowed down to frown at her expression. "I got put in the first-year class."

"Why?" asked a curious Henrick. Britea chose her words with care.

"Instructor Shelley said it was because of how I wielded." She sent a silent apology to Kahl for having to hide his tutoring. "When I first wielded, I did so in fear and anger, so even though I'm sixteen, she feels I need to start from the beginning."

Henrick nodded. "Makes sense. If you need help, I can tutor you in the wielding tiers. Of course, we'd have to ask the instructors for permission."

Britea forced herself to smile as her instincts screamed *no* . "Thanks, I'll keep that in mind."

"Are you in her class, Henrick?" Danai asked, drawing his attention away from Britea.

"Yes."

Navos took a sip of water. "Good to know our Britea has a friend there."

"And enemies," muttered Britea.

She sighed when Danai and Navos gave her questioning looks. "Lady Lianne Arkei and her two friends are in my class, and I may have…embarrassed her in front of the whole class."

Danai muttered something dark under her breath. Then she raised her voice and added. "Pearl Ceres and Valerie Mern. Those are her lackeys. Best stay out of their way."

"Why and which is which?" asked Britea.

"The blond is Valerie, and the other is Pearl," answered Danai with a weary sigh. "As to why you should stay away from them, just take my word that those two are trouble."

Britea frowned. "In what way?"

Danai wore a pained expression on her face. She glanced at Henrick before she replied.

"From my experience, they tend to…well, start trouble, then pin it on someone else and manage to look innocent the whole time."

Henrick's eyes widened before he suddenly found great interest in his food.

Britea was still staring at her roommate. "You mean they lie?"

Danai was saved from answering when Navos started laughing.

"Britea, you're a breath of fresh air. That's a blunt way of stating the obvious, but it's a lot more complicated than that."

"They like playing games with new or unpopular students," continued Danai in a hard tone. "The kind of games that can get someone hurt or expelled. So please, don't play with those girls."

Henrick was focusing on his food, but Britea bet he was taking note of everything being said.

"Five minutes!" The warning rang through the air.

Navos groaned as he tried to eat faster. "I swear, this class is going to give me heartburn."

Britea grinned.

#

Dancing and Etiquette Class for Third Years , read the sign on the door. To be honest, Britea had been surprised when she'd realized this was actually part of the curriculum. Then she had been curious. *Why was this class part of her education?* She studied her fellow female students. She had been puzzled when the boys had split off and gone to a separate class as she had made her way here. Britea heard laughter, and she turned to her right. Lianne and her friends were chatting, clearly looking forward to the dance class.

Great. She bit her lower lip in frustration. Of course the nobles would know more about dancing then she did. Come to think of it, she hadn't been keen on dancing even in her own village. Give her a good book any day, and she could forget the world existed.

"Good day, class," greeted an attractive, slim female instructor wearing a stylish, cowled jacket over a black flowing skirt with air-white edgings.

"For those of you new to us, I am Instructor Helene Droye. In this class, you will learn the fine art of communicating with your body. When you graduate, many of you may find employment at the royal court or in noble houses. This class will help you learn how to behave in such surroundings."

Britea frowned. Most of the other students were excited at the idea. Only a few seemed to share her lack of enthusiasm.

"Now, before we get started, can the new students step forward?"

Britea was the only one to do so.

"Ah, Britea D'Tranell," said Instructor Droye. "Welcome to my class. What manner of dance do you know?"

Lianne muttered something behind her and the group of girls surrounding the noble laughed.

"What was that?" asked Instructor Droye brightly.

"Oh, I was wondering what dances she knows. We're all dying to know," said Lianne innocently. "And it'd be nice if she could perform for us."

The dance instructor nodded and smiled. "That sounds like a delightful idea."

Britea clenched her fists so hard she almost cut the skin of her palms with her fingernails. "I don't know how to dance." She felt angry and humiliated.

Lianne gasped as if stunned. "But I heard farmers and peasants love to dance all the time when not working the fields. Surely, you must have learned something growing up in your village?"

"As I said," repeated Britea through gritted teeth, turning her head to glare at a smug-looking Lianne. "I don't dance."

"No, no, we'll have none of that," said Instructor Droye. Both girls turned to her. "Dancing is a wonderful way to both relax and communicate. We will teach you." She nodded at Lianne. "Lady Arkei is an accomplished dancer and shall partner you to help you learn the steps."

By the Abyss, no!

"I shall do my best," said Lianne with a smile that didn't reach her eyes.

Britea shot a desperate look at the instructor, certain the senior wielder could see through Lianne's fake sincerity. But there was no sign Instructor Droye was aware of the bullying taking place right in front of her.

"Right. Now that's settled. To your places everyone."

#

Britea was both relieved and exhausted as she read the plaque on the dark-oak door: *Beginners Wielding Class for First Years* . The dance and etiquette class had been awful, and Lianne was to be her partner for the foreseeable future. Throughout the entire class, Lianne had kept mentioning how peasants were so uncivilized. Several of her questions still reverberated through her mind.

"Do peasants eat off the floor?"

"Oh, I heard when they wish to empty their bowels, they use holes in the ground. Is that true?"

"Do they wear shoes?"

"I heard farmers' daughters have to sleep in the barn to make sure the livestock don't escape into the wild. Is this true? Do you sleep on the hay or the dirt? Do you even know what a bed is? I'm surprised you know how to read. However did you manage that?"

And on and on it had gone. Lianne kept asking if this or that was all true, but Britea had held her tongue as her rage had grown.

And through it all, Instructor Droye was oblivious to it all. Of course, Lianne never said anything when the cheerful instructor was nearby.

As the time had passed, the verbal barbs had gotten more and more cruel, made worse by the fact that the nearby students giggled or laughed when they overheard. No one had come to her aid.

Right now, Britea felt like screaming. It was times like this that made her think of running away from the school. But then Lianne and her friends would win. Britea closed her eyes and took a deep breath.

Stay calm and put her out of your mind. Move on to the next class. She looked up again at the plaque on the door. Britea really didn't want to be in the most junior class. She had wielded up to the fifth tier! She had moved an entire ship!

With Kahl's help, you idiot! thought Britea, as she realized immediately how childish her behavior was. But the truth was, she was scared. After what had happened in dance and etiquette class, what if this one was worse?

Standing here is not going to make this next class go faster. Get on with it. You've faced Namirans and sea serpents. You can do this! She took another deep breath and opened the door. The sounds of excited children filled the air as Britea entered the class. The first thing she noticed were the four enormous transparent cauldrons at the front of the class. The one closest to her was filled with leaves, the second with clear water, the third with fine sand, and the fourth with red coals. She finally turned to face the class, and her heart sank when she saw her fellow junior wielders.

It was as she had feared. She suspected the oldest student was thirteen, the rest much younger. For a long moment, they didn't notice her as they chatted and laughed with each other. Then one of them saw her.

"Good day. Are you a new teacher?" asked a fresh-faced boy of about twelve.

Britea winced internally. "No, I…I'm a new student."

The boy stared at her, and gradually, the rest of the class began to take note of the conversation.

"I'm to join you for training."

The junior wielders looked at each other in consternation.

"But you're old!" exclaimed one of the students.

"How old are you?" asked a young girl.

Britea blinked, a bit intimidated by the boldness of the students. "I'm—" The door opened abruptly behind her, saving her from answering.

The whole class stood up as Instructor Eowise Shelley marched into the class.

"Good afternoon, Instructor Shelley!" chorused the class while Britea stood to one side feeling useless.

"Good afternoon, class." The instructor gave Britea a brief glance. "This is Novice Britea D'Tranell. She's new to the college and to wielding, so she'll be joining us for training. Britea, take a seat at the back."

Feeling curious eyes on her, she quickly escaped to the rear of the class. The instructor waited for her to be seated before addressing the class once more.

"Stand and recite the Wielder's Creed."

Britea found herself scrambling to her feet as the younger voices began to speak in unison. She found herself impressed by how well the junior wielders had memorized the words. The instructor in the meantime was walking around the class as she watched the students closely.

"Very good," said Instructor Shelley when they were done. She suddenly turned to a young boy in the second row.

"Describe the first tier."

The male novice remained standing as the others sat down. "The first tier is the first and easiest level of wielding. Seven times shall one wield the same shape."

"Well done, Zaren. Class, what does the first tier represent?"

"Stability," came the chorus.

"And though the first tier is the easiest, it is also the most important. Without mastering it, you cannot proceed to the second tier." The instructor's gaze lingered for a moment on Britea before moving on.

"Which is why we shall practice it in every lesson, even when you graduate to a higher class. As we proceed, I will remind you that you can only wield in class under supervision and never in your dorms or the rest of the school grounds. Is that understood?" Once again, she glanced briefly in Britea's direction.

The special attention was beginning to feel odd.

"Yes, Instructor Shelley," chorused the class.

"Now, I will demonstrate the first tier for air." The instructor took a bunch of leaves from the cauldron before her and closed her fist around them. She held out her right fist, and as she opened it, a small tornado of leaves formed on her palm.

"Ahh," exclaimed the students in wonder. Britea couldn't help but be impressed. The senior wielder's control was perfect. Instructor Shelley let the students watch for a bit longer before she collapsed the wield.

"Now, each of you will try. Form lines behind your respective elements."

The students eagerly surged from their seats, while Britea tentatively followed. While she felt nervous about being in this class, she couldn't help but wonder how different she was from the girl who had faced Namiran warships and bargained with an Alkynaia serpents less than a month ago.

Instructor Shelley poured a thimble of a clear liquid over the cauldron with glowing coals, and she was rewarded with a huge blaze of fire.

"Novice Blade, you may start. First tier please."

A young boy of twelve eagerly stepped forward and instantly wielded a large orb of fire. Students behind him jumped back.

Instructor Shelley sighed. "Much smaller, novice."

The boy grinned as he complied.

"Repeat six more times, same shape." The instructor said, nodding and writing a note on a clipboard before ordering him to take a seat. Britea caught the disappointed look on the young student's face. He obviously wanted to wield some more.

I know how you feel, little brother. She had wielded only once in weeks, and she was itching to do more of it.

"Novice Masters."

Once again, the instructor made a note as the next wielder created a small orb of fire. Britea looked at the second student and could see the young novice straining to create a tier-one form. Some students snickered, but that died quickly when Instructor Shelley sent a quelling look in their direction.

"Once more, Novice Masters." The embarrassed junior novice tried once more, and her second wield was slightly better than the first.

"Well done. Have a seat." The female student looked relieved as she fled to her seat.

"Next!"

Britea grew more nervous when she realized she would be the last person in the class to wield. *What if she failed?*

The very next moment, she berated herself silently for such thoughts. *Of course, she knew how to wield the first tier!*

"Are we boring you Novice D'Tranell?"

It took only a heartbeat for Britea to realize she had unconsciously turned away from the class. "Um, no Instructor Shelley. I'm sorry for not paying attention." She felt her face grow warm with embarrassment.

The senior wielder stared at her for a long moment before turning back to the curious junior wielders.

"Next!"

Britea made sure to keep her eyes on the students before her. It didn't take long for her to notice something odd.

First, there were no signs of euphoria. Britea had experienced that the first few times she wielded until Kahl helped her through that tricky phase by ensuring she ran up and down the deck after wielding. With more wielding the euphoria soon became nonexistent.

These juniors must have either been practicing for quite some time now, or they were so young the euphoria did not affect them.

Second, a significant number of the children were finding it difficult to maintain the first-tier wields. Very few were as powerful as the first eager student, Novice Blade. Many of them needed to attempt it up to three times to properly wield the easiest tier.

Why am I in this class again?

However, she was smart enough to keep her thoughts to herself. As the students before her practiced, her eyes were drawn to the book in the instructor's hand. *Was she making note of those who may be harder to train? Or those to kick out of the college?*

"Next!"

Britea was pulled from her thoughts at that, only to discover it was almost her turn. She took a deep breath to steady her nerves, and then it was just her, the cauldron, a class full of curious children, and one very stern-looking instructor.

She blocked them out of her mind as she spontaneously wielded a large orb of water. Instructor Shelley frowned disapprovingly, and Britea quickly reduced it to half its size. Some of the students exclaimed in surprise, and a few even clapped.

Surprisingly enough, the instructor didn't shush them, but neither did she make any notes in her book.

"Same shape and size six more times, Novice D'Tranell."

Once she had completed the task, the instructor ordered the class to return to their seats. Britea had hardly gotten back to her seat before the instructor continued talking.

"Before we move on, is anyone experiencing euphoria?"

Silence greeted her question, so she moved on. "Excellent." Britea felt a sudden pang of loneliness as she recalled a certain young Dyhaeri who had helped her overcome wielder's euphoria. She wondered how Kahl was.

"Now, on to your assessments." Instructor Shelley looked at her notebook.

"Some of you wielded adequately but many of you need to practice your first-tier forms more often. Starting from today, you will be paired up. Those with stronger wields will help the weaker ones."

Britea glanced around as the students began to mutter excitedly. Apparently, this was not the norm.

"But let me make a few things clear. Being a stronger wielder doesn't make you better than your partner. What matters most of all is control, and if you don't learn that, you will fail this class. Is that understood?"

"Yes, Instructor Shelley," chorused the class.

She smiled at them and began to assign partners.

Britea found herself biting her fingernails as she wondered who she would be partnered with. She began to count the students.

There were forty-three of them including herself.

Wait. Forty-three students. That meant someone wasn't getting a partner. *Who?*

The instructor smiled grimly as she looked at Britea then. "You'll be partnered with me."

Seven Hells!

#

Britea was mentally and physically exhausted by the time she got back to her dormitory. She was so tired she just shrugged off her jacket and kicked off her shoes before collapsing on her bed.

She knew it was almost time for supper. She would just lie here for a minute.

Barely a moment later, her eyes closed as she drifted off into a deep sleep.

#

She jerked upright, her heart pounding.

"Wow, easy. It's only me, your friendly roommate."

Britea tried to calm her heart down at Danai's voice. "I just wanted to sleep for a little bit."

The older student chuckled. "It's almost time for lights out, sister."

Britea's stomach chose that moment to growl. She winced at the sound. "I'm going to die of hunger."

"Not on my watch." The aroma of delicious food filled her nostrils. She stared at Danai in amazement. The fire wielder uncovered a small bowl of chicken soup on the table between them. Beside it was a sandwich, an apple, and a cup of water.

"Be sure to thank Navos when you see him. The cooks are used to him asking for second and third helpings, so that's how we could smuggle this out of the dining hall for you."

Britea felt ashamed. One of the rules was all food should be consumed in the hall and not kept or stored in their rooms. She hoped Danai and Navos didn't get into trouble for this.

"Come on, eat before it gets cold."

"Thanks so much for this." Britea dug in.

Danai busied herself getting ready for bed. "So, how was your first day in wielding class?"

Britea made a face as she took a sip of water. "It was…awkward. But the class before was way worse."

Danai tilted her head. "Which class?"

Britea sighed as she pushed her bowl away. "Dance and etiquette."

Danai's eyes narrowed. "What happened?"

Britea thought about telling her about Lianne's inane questions. Then she shook her head. She could not keep running to Danai with every problem.

"I can handle the dancing class."*I hope!* she added to herself. "I just feel like I…I don't belong in either class."

The fire wielder snickered to Britea's surprise, annoying her. "You just don't understand, that's all."

"What do you mean?"

Danai hesitated, then took a deep breath. "When I first arrived here, they didn't know what to do with me. From my assessments in general studies, they could see I wasn't stupid. So they put me in a class with my peers, but as for my wielding…well, I think it confused them."

Britea frowned.

"A lot of Weltonians are wielders, unlike the landlocked humans. I don't know why. It's just always been like that. So, we also tend to start wielding earlier."

"How old were you?"

The hesitation this time was longer. "I was nine years old."

Britea's eyes widened. "What?" The average age was usually twelve!

Danai nodded. "Yes. I was nine and I got a lot of teaching by the time I was sixteen years old. But I wanted more. So, when I arrived here, I showed them how good I was. So, they placed me in an advanced wielding class with students who were a few years older than me. It was a disaster."

Danai saw the expectation on Britea's face. "Lady Selina Arkei. She was the belle of the class. Students flocked around Selina because of her status. Once it was common knowledge I was Weltonian, she made it her mission in life to make me miserable." She paused, lost in her memories before continuing. "It got worse when she was assigned to me as a mentor. I don't know which instructor suggested that. But to keep a long story short, things got out of hand, and I was moved to the wielding class just below hers. I'm thankful for that because I met Navos, Lexia, and Shran in the new class." She shrugged. "So, don't feel bad about being in the junior class. They just learned from the mistakes they made with me."

Britea was speechless for a long moment. Once again, she battled with telling Danai that she too had just been partnered with the younger Arkei. Instead, she went in another direction. "I…I'm sorry about what happened with Lady Arkei."

Danai waved away her apology. "What are you sorry for? You didn't create her. She's responsible for her actions, and sadly, her sister is just as vindictive as she is."

Britea looked down as the wooden boards, suddenly realizing how far from home she was in this very strange place. By the Maker, she missed her cat. Moments like this made her wish she had never left Weldaros.

"What's on your mind?" asked Danai as she noticed her roommate's expression.

Britea eventually looked up. "Do you ever miss home? The sea?"

Danai stared at her, startled by the question, then understanding dawned. "I do, sometimes. This place can get overwhelming."

"My dah will be gone in less than three days, so I've thought of running away at times."

Danai stood up and came to sit down beside her. She held out a hand and Britea took it. "I know what that feels like, but you can't run away. This place isn't perfect, but it will help you nurture your gift and provide opportunities for you and your family in the future. Do not throw this chance away."

Britea felt tears in her eyes. "But what if…what if I fail? What then? What if I'm not supposed to be here?"

"You took the first step when you boarded the *Windrider,* the second step when you allowed a Dyhaeri to train you, and the third when you helped save everyone on board that vessel with your wielding."

"That was all Kahl and Natia the Alkynaia," countered Britea.

"Yeah, but I'm pretty sure you had a big part to play in that. If you hadn't been on the *Windrider,* Kahl would never have offered to teach you and…"

"The Namiran warships would have sunk the *Windrider* ," finished Britea.

Danai nodded. "Now, you understand. Tell you what. I have an idea."

"What?"

"Letters."

Britea's brow furrowed in confusion. "Excuse me?"

"Start writing letters home, to your mah, your dah, your sister, or your friends. It will take a few months to get there, but I promise, it'll help. And when I go into town on my days off, I can take them with me to give to any Weltonian ship. My next day off is in two weeks. Maybe you could even come into town with me if Warden Asteros agrees."

Britea felt a smile grow on her face. "I hadn't thought of that. Thanks!"

"No problem. And I'll let you in on an open secret. Some Weltonian ships can sail much faster now. They had to improve their engine design because of the attacks from the Namiran raiders." The fire wielder got up and returned to her side of the room. "Now get some sleep. We have an early start tomorrow as always."

"Thank you, Danai."

"Anytime, sister."

As Britea got ready for bed, she was already excited about what she would write to her family.

Then another thought entered her mind. *Could she write one to Kahl?*

CHAPTER 5

"Incoming!"

Kahl bounced on the balls of his feet as he tried to anticipate his cousin's shots. After a week of physical sparring, Mat had suggested they also incorporate wielding sessions. Both Dyhaeri had approached the Weltonian captain with the request, and he had warily agreed.

Kahl didn't blame the captain for his caution. Mat was a high-level wielder, as was Kahl, but battle wielding on the deck of a ship was enough to scare anyone. For the first two days, the deck crew was suspiciously absent, probably for fear of being accidentally hit by errant shots.

But once they had realized the Dyhaeri aimed at the water and took care not to hit the rigging or masts, the crew had gradually returned to the deck.

While the exercise was taxing, Kahl had to admit it was also a lot of fun. He forced his mind to return to the present and dove low to avoid a fast-moving orb of air. He responded with one of water, and his cousin laughed gleefully as he leapt over the watery missile, simultaneously firing another orb of air at his opponent.

Kahl quickly sidestepped the attack then felt an impact on his left shoulder.

"Another hit to Mat!" yelled the young female crew member keeping score.

Kahl groaned, held a hand up, and waved it in a circle.

"And his opponent concedes!"

A smattering of applause peppered the deck. Kahl sighed as he watched his cousin take a bow for his admirers.

He had no idea how Mat did it. He would have thought his cousin's charms would work only on fellow Dyhaeri, but surprisingly, they also worked on Weltonians. It had been no secret when Mat had first boarded that he hated being on a human ship and surrounded by humans. His cousin hadn't been at all friendly, and Kahl had expected the Weltonians to take offense.

Instead, the crew had given both Dyhaeri plenty of space and left them to their own devices. Only the captain had spoken to them, gruffly barking out orders from time to time.

And now Mat was warming up to the humans.

Then a dark thought crossed Kahl's mind. *Was Mat's change of heart genuine, or was he just being a good marine?*

"Outstanding." Lanead's dry voice pulled Kahl back to the present.

"Kahl and Mat, with me." The captain gave the other crew members a look that made them suddenly realize they had places to be and things to do.

The grey-haired Weltonian waited until no one was in earshot. "I'm glad to see you're both finding constructive things to do in your spare time; however, it's time for your real lessons to start."

Both Dyhaeri shared a wary look before turning back to the Weltonian captain.

"What lessons?" asked Mat calmly.

"Lessons on appropriate behavior with humans."

Kahl blinked. He didn't think he had heard right.

Mat opened his mouth to say something, then shut it.

Lanead raised an eyebrow. "Speak your mind plainly."

Mat took a deep breath. "I thought you were joking when you first said that."

Kahl shot his cousin a concerned look. The gruff Lanead didn't seem to have a sense of humor.

"But…but why did you let us waste our time for the past three weeks?" Mat continued.

Lanead smiled. "Do you call reconciling with your cousin a waste of time?"

Mat's complexion looked embarrassed. "No, but…"

The captain's smile disappeared. "I needed you two in the right frame of mind before the real training started. To be honest, I thought it would take longer for you two to come to your senses, but thank the Mother you both have some brains after all."

It took a moment for Kahl to realize the captain was referring to the Sea Mother. He thought the humans only worshipped the Maker and His Lords.

"So, what could you possibly teach us about the humans we don't already know?" asked Mat causally.

Lanead's smile was dry. "Let's start with current affairs. Who is the current monarch of Malaquey?"

"King Wilhem of House Taros," replied Mat without hesitation.

"Who are the members of his immediate family?"

"Queen Ariande and their three children."

"Their names?" pressed the Weltonian captain.

At this, Mat hesitated. "The crown prince is called Wiltran…I, uh, don't know the names of the last two children."

Lanead looked at Kahl, who shook his head. He hadn't even known the queen's name.

The Weltonian sighed. "Princess Crystal and Prince Aren. Now, how many elected officials make up the ministry, and can you name at least three of them?"

Mat's face flushed. "You've made your point, captain. I know nothing at all about the Malaquey kingdom, and to be honest, I'm not sure how that information is important to us."

Kahl caught his breath, stealing a glance at Lanead, Amazingly, the captain looked thoughtful.

"Fair enough. Thank you for your honesty. Do you have anything to add, Kahl?"

For a moment, Kahl was unsure of what to say. Then he had a thought. "Well, actually I am interested." Both the Dyhaeri and Weltonian stared at him. "We do share this world with them, so we should learn about each other."

Mat gave him an odd look.

"So, we'll start with that. Come with me." Lanead turned away, clearly expecting the two Dyhaeri to follow. It didn't take long for them to realize they were headed to the captain's cabin. This was a first for the cousins.

Neither hid their curiosity as they entered the cabin. It was quite spacious and tidy. A table filled with pinned down maps occupied the center of it. Several routes were marked on the maps. Lanead bypassed the table and instead went to a bookshelf at the rear of the cabin. He selected two books and handed them to the Dyhaeri.

"I've given you the 14th edition of Ana Stral's *Who's Who in the Malaquey Royal Court* and the 11th edition of Thozas Belling's *Social Structure of the Malaquey Republic.*"

He waited for them to flip through the books for a few moments.

"You both have a week to read as much as you can before your test."

Mat and Kahl shot him identical shocked looks. "What!?"

Lanead smiled dryly. "Any operative worth his or her salt needs to memorize the social structure of their assigned countries. This is basic espionage training. I hope for your sakes you read fast. Now, go on and start studying."

The cousins shared a befuddled look and left his cabin.

#

Once the two Dyhaeri reached their cabins, Mat nearly threw the book to one side. Was Captain Riverun really going to test them about human society? He can't be serious! But Mat soon found himself rethinking his own reluctance when he saw how eager Kahl was to read the human book he had been given.

At first he wanted to ask his younger cousin what he was doing. But a part of Mat wondered if he, himself, was just being a stubborn idiot.

But surely the king wouldn't send him and Kahl to Malaquey as undercover agents! He was a junior lieutenant in the marines and his cousin was still a very junior scout. They were certainly not qualified for such a sensitive operation.

Then a horrifying thought crossed his mind. *What if the king and the Seers were planning to turn them into humans? Just like how Princess Sle'niazza and Princess Kallesezza had been transformed decades ago?*

He closed his eyes briefly at the dizzying thought.

No. He was overthinking this.

But what if…

Mat stared at his younger cousin, who was completely oblivious to Mat's thoughts. If what he feared was about to happen, then Mat had better surpass Kahl in this test and any others to come. That way he might be able to convince the king and the Seers to spare Kahl from such a transformation. Mat would even take the pain of being stripped of his Dyhaeri heritage to save his cousin.

With his newfound goal, Mat sat down on his bunk and started reading.

#

Kahl waited nervously as Lanead marked their tests in front of them. They were once again in the captain's cabin. The week had passed quickly, and the test had come and gone. He glanced at Mat, who was watching the Weltonian captain with narrowed eyes.

He had been surprised by how hard Mat had prepared for the tests. Kahl hadn't expected his cousin to take it seriously. But he was relieved they were together in this training. It made him feel less lonely and unsure.

I wonder how Britea is doing. He forced himself to push that thought away. He had been thinking about her a lot recently and wasn't sure why. Training her had made him happy even though he suspected he may never see her again.

A sigh from the captain brought him back to the present.

"Well done to both of you. The results are better than I expected with so little time to prepare."

"So, how'd we do?" asked Mat so fast Kahl quirked an eyebrow.

"Pretty good, but Kahl had a slight edge: eighty-nine percent to your eighty-seven."

Kahl's eyes widened in surprise. He was oddly giddy with relief. He turned to smile at his cousin, but his smile slid away when he saw the dark expression in Mat's eyes.

"I see. When's the next assessment?"

Lanead gave Mat a curious look. "You seem eager. Well, fear not. You'll have another in a week."

Mat opened his mouth to speak, but he thought better of it and stayed silent.

Kahl was perplexed at his cousin's behavior.

"Next up is social etiquette in the human royal court."

What? thought Kahl with no small amount of alarm.

Lanead tried not to smile at the alarmed expressions on the faces of the two Dyhaeri before him. He shouldn't have fun tormenting them but he couldn't help it.

"We're really going to be assigned at court?" asked a pale-faced Mat.

"That depends on King Jahlaniin," replied Lanead as he handed a book titled, *Etiquette Do's and Don'ts, Seventh Edition* by Tobeyi Avias to Kahl.

Mat stared at the book as if it was a poisonous viper. "Captain, may I have a word?"

"Certainly," said Lanead. He wasn't surprised to hear Mat complaining. That's all he had done since coming on board, though the captain had to admit the older Dyhaeri's attitude had been improving lately.

"Alone."

Kahl shot his cousin a startled look.

The Weltonian's expression changed to one of puzzlement as Mat looked pleadingly at Kahl. After, a long moment, Kahl nodded, a hurt expression on his face as he stood up and left the cabin.

Lanead sat up and braced himself. "All right, what's on your mind?"

Mat was still in his seat for a moment, choosing his words carefully. "I know why Kahl and I are here. The king needs agents in the Malaquey court."

Lanead waited.

"But he's wrong to think he needs two agents. One is sufficient."

Lanead's eyes narrowed. Now this he had not foreseen. "What are you suggesting?" He tried and failed to keep the hard edge out of his voice. He was darkly satisfied when Mat flushed at the tone of his voice.

The young Dyhaeri stared at the ground for a moment as if gathering courage, then looked up and met Lanead's gaze. "I'm the one you need."

Lanead blinked. "What?"

"Kahl may have done some stupid things, but that's just inexperience. We both know he doesn't have the experience for espionage. It would be a suicide mission."

Lanead was still trying to recover. Here he was thinking Mat was about to sell out Kahl, not try to save him. "I got the impression this was a two-person assignment. You can't do this on your own Mat."

Mat closed his eyes briefly for a moment. "I have never asked this of a human, but you need to convince the king that all you need is me. I cannot let Kahl sacrifice his Dyhaeri heritage for this mission. It's not right—"

Now Lanead was *really* confused. "Hold on. His Dyhaeri heritage? I don't understand."

For a long moment, it seemed like Mat was having difficulty speaking. "For this mission to succeed, I suspect the agent would have to be made fully human to blend into the Malaquey court. It has been done before—"

"I know," interrupted Lanead curtly as a familiar dark rage almost overwhelmed him. He forced himself to shut that part of himself off.

Mat stared at him. "Are you all right, captain?"

It took a while before Lanead could trust himself to speak. These poor boys had no idea what was going on, and already Mat had jumped to the worst conclusion.

And that made Lanead angry. "I'm fine." He tried to force a smile. "No one is going to transform you or Kahl into humans to carry out this mission."

Mat looked skeptical. "Respectively sir, I disagree. As Dyhaeri, we would stand out among the humans."

Lanead knew there was no point in arguing. "You don't believe me. Tell you what. I'll find someone you'll believe, and afterward, we'll concentrate on your lessons. You're dismissed."

Mat stared at him. "Yes, sir." The Dyhaeri left the cabin, a confused expression on his face.

Lanead spent several seconds looking at the vacant seat in front of him. It was days like this that made him wish his wife was here. Sonei had a calming influence that was almost magical.

Well, no point wasting time. There was only one thing to do.

His mind made up, he got up and strode over to his wardrobe. It didn't take long to find what he needed. He changed into a one-piece, specially made Weltonian dive suit. As he walked out on deck, a crewman saw him.

"Tell First Mate Tanet I went for a swim. Shouldn't be long."

"Aye, captain." Lanead ran to the rail and dove off the port side of the *Peacekeeper.*

#

Once in the water, Lanead held his breath as he drew wet soil from the depths towards him. His element was earth. As a child, he had been taught by Weltonians and two particular Dyhaeri how to create an airtight earth bubble. Soil usually contained moisture, and water was breathable when broken down. Once the wet ocean soil reached him, he spread it paper thin while keeping the soil vibrating so it locked in the moisture. Next, he wielded the thin layer of wet earth to his dive suit and made it airtight before he began to expand it, thus creating a pocket of slightly moist, breathable air. The earth particles were spread so thinly Lanead could see through the earth capsule.

As soon as the bubble was to his satisfaction, he began to descend. When he reached his destination, he wielded continuously, causing small tremors in the ocean floor that sent vibrations in his chosen direction. Any Dyhaeri nearby would recognize the pattern of the vibrations.

It was the call for an urgent message.

He knew someone would answer, and he hoped he had calmed down by the time they arrived.

Lanead waited only five minutes before three Dyhaeri in their bubbles swam up to him. He smiled when he realized they were also earth wielders. That meant what had to be done next would be easy. He motioned for them to combine bubbles. As expected, they looked a bit shocked at the suggestion. Usually, he would use sign language to communicate, but right now, he couldn't care less. He had a message to deliver. He motioned again and the three Dyhaeri reluctantly agreed.

Once all four were within the air-filled bubble, he didn't waste time. "Tell High Priest Myltan to get his holy arse to the *Peacekeeper* as soon as possible or the lessons don't continue."

The three Dyhaeri marines were speechless with shock. Finally, one of them spoke.

"You wish for us to word it exactly as you said?"

Lanead smiled coldly, showing his teeth. "Word for word. Got it?"

The three Dyhaeri nodded hastily.

#

Kahl tried to read the same page again for the umpteenth time, but he was unable to concentrate. What had been so important Mat felt he had to speak to the captain alone? At first, Kahl was worried, but then that feeling soon turned to anger.

What was Mat hiding from him? That question made him laugh though there was no humor in their current situation. Here he was, berating the cousin he had betrayed not so long ago.

Yet he wanted to know what was on Mat's mind.

The sound of the door opening made him look up from his bed. He was both relieved and annoyed to see it was Mat.

"Oh, you're here."

Kahl frowned at his cousin's body language. He looked stiff and worn out. "Mat, what's going on?"

At first, the older Dyhaeri refused to acknowledge him, then he sighed as he sat down beside Kahl.

"Nothing. I just had some questions for the captain." Mat's attitude implied he didn't want to talk about it.

Kahl was silent as he struggled with the decision to let the matter go. Then he shook his head, shut the book, and dropped it on the small table beside the bunk bed.

"What exactly did you have to discuss with Captain Riverun?"

"I said, it's nothing."

"No, it's not. Does it have anything to do with why we're here?"

Mat glared at him. "Yes, but I don't want to talk about it."

Kahl matched his stare. "Oh, no. You're going talk about it. Keeping secrets is what got us into this mess in the first place."

An incredulous look appeared on Mat's face. "You're one to talk."

Kahl held up his hands. "I agree. I was the one that kept the secrets and got you into trouble. All I'm asking is you don't make the same mistake I did. So, what's going on?"

His cousin stared at him for a long moment. "I went to ask the captain to try to convince the king only one of us is needed for this mission in Malaquey."

"Why?"

Mat grimaced as he replied. "I assumed for this mission to work, any agent placed in Malaquey would have to be transformed into a…a human, to blend in. Like what was done to the condemned princesses."

Silence reigned for several moments.

"Oh, I see."

Mat nodded wearily. "I asked Captain Riverun to pick me for the assignment."

"You did what?!" yelled Kahl. Mat's eyes widened at his cousin's declaration.

"I was only doing it to protect you—"

"I didn't ask you to!" Kahl closed his eyes as he tried to calm down. "Mat, I love you like a brother, but I am not a child. I can make my own decisions. Besides, I broke the rules, so if the punishment is that I become human to make amends, then so be it. By trying to take that decision away from me, you dishonored me."

Mat stared at him. "You've grown."

Kahl almost bristled before he realized his cousin wasn't mocking him.

"I'm sorry. I thought I was looking out for you, as a brother should. Besides, your mother would be heartbroken if you were stripped of your Dyhaeri heritage."

"Aunt Neilara would also be unhappy if anything happened to you, cousin."

Mat laughed dryly. "Maybe."

Both Dyhaeri sat in silence for several heartbeats.

"So, did he say when they'd do it?" asked Kahl somberly.

"Well, actually, he said that wasn't the case." Mat rubbed his face wearily. "Lanead said no one was transforming us into humans, but I find that hard to believe."

Kahl was puzzled. "Why would he lie?"

"I don't know. He is human after all."

Kahl rolled his eyes. "He strikes me as an honorable person, Mat. The king wouldn't place such trust in him otherwise."

Mat shrugged, "I still wonder what kind of relationship exists between the captain and our leader."

"Same here." Kahl's eyes were drawn to the new textbook on the table. "We might as well study until we find out more." He was startled when Mat startled laughing.

"What?"

"Your resilience is amazing. When this is over, you're definitely joining the Marine Corps."

Kahl just sighed. "Let's just study."

#

Lanead was pacing the deck when the high priest finally arrived. Though the captain was still angry, he had to admit the religious leader had arrived on the *Peacekeeper* in a timely fashion. Startled mutters from the Weltonian crew peppered the deck when they saw who had graced their ship.

High Priest Myltan and three Dyhaeri guards. The high priest acknowledged the respectful nods and gestures of the Weltonian crew. Lanead was grateful his wife had insisted every crew member be able to recognize the ranking members of the Dyhaeri. The courtesy and deference his crew were showing now illustrated the wisdom of that rule. Many other Weltonian factions were not so diligent in such things, and though there were times he wished he could be just as oblivious as them, his birthright wouldn't permit it.

"Captain Riverun," said High Priest Myltan as he bowed to the Weltonian captain, startling him with the unusual respectful gesture. The three Dyhaeri marines exchanged worried looks at the deference shown to this human. Even some of the crew were gaping at this act.

"Please," said Lanead, "don't do that. I'm just a low-ranking Weltonian captain." He tried to keep his tone cordial while hiding the panic and anger as he recovered from the shock.

"Of course," said the sly priest.

Lanead swallowed his rage. He knew the priest was just trying to get back at him for the stunt he had pulled earlier.

"If we could please talk privately in my quarters."

Haigh Priest Myltan nodded, told his guards to wait for him here, and then indicated Lanead should precede him.

Lanead waited to speak until they were alone in his quarters.

"You look well." The captain sat down behind his desk.

The Dyhaeri looked around the cabin and remained standing. "So do you. It has been quite a while since we last spoke."

Lanead grimaced. That had been several years ago, and that conversation had ended in a shouting match. "Well, I thought it best to keep my distance until matters improved."

"Oh, is that so? Is that why you terrified three of my marines to get me here? A simple request would have been sufficient."

Lanead sighed. "So that's why you have an honor guard this time? Are they worried I'm going to tear you to bits?"

The priest waved the question away. "The guards are not because of you. Some of our Dyhaeri scouts have disappeared recently, so High Commander Neilara felt it was prudent to safeguard senior officials journeying beyond the border."

The news disturbed Lanead. "Are the Namirans involved?"

"That's a possibility."

He tried not to think about the fate of those unfortunate Dyhaeri. Lanead shook his head and said, "Anyway, I called you here for something else entirely."

High Priest Myltan waited.

"Mat-rallenin is certain he and Kahl are going to be transformed into humans for this mission in Malaquey."

The priest blinked. "Where in the Deep did he get that idea?"

Lanead shrugged. "I have no idea, but that's why you're here. You have to speak to them, give them at least some inkling of what's been happening. They can't go to Malaquey without any intel."

An angry glint appeared in the high priest's eyes. "Like you did with Danai?"

"Keep her out of this," growled Lanead.

"I'm afraid I can't." High Priest Myltan rested his hands on the desk and leaned towards the captain. "We warned you, and how did you respond? You spirited her away to Malaquey in hopes of foiling the prophecy, even though we both know she has a part to play in what is to come."

"I don't want to go over this anymore," said the captain through gritted teeth. The Dyhaeri and Weltonian looked each other in the eye, neither willing to back down for several moments. Eventually Lanead looked away first.

The senior priest sighed and backed away from the table. "I will speak to Mat and Kahl and try to ease their minds." He turned to go then paused. "A word of advice. The time will come when you must speak to Danai about who she really is. I hope, for all our sakes, that you tell her the truth rather than attempt to shield her from her destiny."

On his way out the door, he looked over his shoulder and added. "Especially since a person with your experience knows one can't hide from fate."

He was gone before Lanead could utter a word.

#

Kahl finally gave up on studying. His mind was in a turmoil and he was unable to concentrate. He looked at the top bunk. Maybe Mat had the right idea. They'd been trying to read the human book on etiquette for hours until Mat had declared he needed a rest and had thrown the book to the side.

But one thought continued to dominate Kahl's mind. *Would it be such a bad thing being a human?*

"I could see Britea," Kahl whispered to himself. Then he shook his head. *Who was he fooling?* For the mission to work—whatever that mission was— he couldn't afford distractions. But Kahl was getting the distinct impression he and Mat were being left in the dark about the true purpose of the assignment. All they had received so far were hints, riddles, human books, and tests.

He was beginning to feel more than a bit frustrated.

A loud knock at their door interrupted his train of thought.

"Who is it?" demanded Mat from the top bunk before Kahl could say a word.

"First Mate Tanet. You have a visitor."

Mat stuck his head over the side of the bunk to share a startled look with his cousin. *Who would be coming to visit them?*

"It's got to be my mother," whispered Mat as he jumped down.

Kahl darted upright. "I hope nothing terrible has happened."

Mat froze at his words. "Well, let's find out, shall we?"

Kahl's anxiety multiplied when he saw who was waiting for them outside their door.

High Priest Myltan.

The Dyhaeri clergy took in their stunned expressions. "I believe you two have questions."

Mat was the first to recover. "Um…yes?"

"Walk with me."

Kahl and Mat exchanged puzzled looks before following the high priest. It took only a moment for them to notice the three Dyhaeri marines standing by the bow of the vessel deep in conversation with two Weltonians, one of whom was First Mate Tanet.

The high priest led them to the ship's stern, which at that moment, was deserted. "How has your stay been on the *Peacekeeper?*"

Kahl watched an uneasy expression cross Mat's face.

"Eventful."

The high priest raised an eyebrow. "I hope I don't have to remind you two to treat Captain Riverun with respect?"

"No, sir," said Kahl. Mat nodded in agreement.

High Priest Myltan regarded them for a long moment. "Good. Your mothers are well, and our home is safe for the time being. Now, onto the crux of the matter. What do you know about your assignment?"

There was a moment of silence before Mat spoke. "Not much, to be honest. I thought being banished to the *Peacekeeper* was simply punishment. I wasn't aware at first that we were to be assigned to the Malaquey Royal Court. Then, just in the last week, I discovered that was our new mission."

High Priest Myltan smiled dryly. "The royal court is not your final destination, but we will have to go there first."

Kahl frowned. "If I may ask, high priest, what is the true assignment then?"

The priest was silent for several heartbeats. "The situation within Namira is worsening. For four decades, we have observed and waited for the Malaquey government to respond, but all they have done is take in refugees and attempt diplomatic negotiations, which have all failed. As Dyhaeri, our policy is not to get involved in human affairs." He looked at Kahl, who felt his face grow warm at the scrutiny. "However, it appears our approach of noninterference is about to change, and we need you two to help us."

"H…how?" stammered Kahl while Mat gaped at the high priest.

"You're both young and handsome. I believe you can accomplish much more than an ancient one like me."

Mat and Kahl shared a brief look of disbelief before the older cousin raised his hand.

"Yes?" said High Priest Myltan.

"Permission to speak freely, sir?"

"Granted."

Mat took a deep breath. "Sir, we are the two least qualified Dyhaeri to deal with the human mess. So why did you really choose us? Lies and half-truths will only get us killed, so please, cut the Alkynaia crap and tell us what we need to know to keep us alive among the humans."

Kahl's jaw dropped. He half expected the high priest to punish Mat for his insolence.

The Dyhaeri priest stared at the angry Mat for a moment, then suddenly started laughing. This alarmed both cousins.

"It's all right. It's just that it's been a long time since I had a reason to be amused," said High Priest Myltan when he finally recovered. "The Seers chose you. They said only you two could make this work, that your inexperience and temperaments were key factors…" he paused thoughtfully before adding, "Especially when considering your human counterparts."

Mat's face paled at the mention of the Seers. "Does this have to do with a prophecy?"

Kahl's mind flashed back to when his mother had muttered something about a prophecy. "Which one?" he asked without thinking.

The high priest narrowed his eyes. "Who mentioned a prophecy?"

Mat and Kahl shared a look.

"I'm waiting for an answer."

Kahl decided to take the plunge. "Well, it's logical to suspect that considering you mentioned the Seers. So, my question is, does this involve a short-term prophecy or one we've been anticipating for thousands of years?" Mat nodded in agreement,

The priest gave the two younger Dyhaeri a startled look. "You are perceptive, but I'm afraid I can't reveal anything at this point." High Priest Myltan sighed at their frustrated expressions. "In time, more will be revealed, but for now, know you don't have to become humans for this assignment."

Even as he felt a flicker of disappointment, Kahl saw his cousin's shoulders drop with relief.

"My advice to you is to learn everything you can from Captain Riverun. His experience is invaluable and will help you survive." High Priest Myltan turned to go.

"Wait!"

The high priest turned to face Kahl.

"You mentioned our human counterparts? Who are they? Are they soldiers at the Malaquey Royal Court?"

"Good question," agreed Mat, but Kahl ignored him and concentrated on the high priest's expression, which gave nothing away.

"That too, in time will be revealed. For now, you two have to learn a lot about the Malaquey government, so we can better assess the political situation and what they plan to do about Namira's Queen. Good day my sons. I will send your regards to your mothers." He left before Kahl could protest. The young Dyhaeri was determined to go after him but found Mat blocking his way.

"Let him go. He's said all he's willing to share."

"But don't you want to know more?!" demanded Kahl.

"Oh, I do. I want answers, but I think we'll have to discover the rest on our own."

Kahl turned to see High Priest Myltan exchange a few words with Captain Riverun, who had emerged from his cabin.

"I wonder who our human counterparts are."

"Probably soldiers like us. I can't wait to meet them," said Mat dryly as the cousins watched the high priest and his guards dive off the starboard side of the *Peacekeeper.*

CHAPTER 6

Piotra looked out the dirty, stained window. *Where in the Deep was his contact?*

His morning had started as normal. Wake at the crack of dawn, run down to the docks of Virtoria for another day of hauling cargo for minimal pay, and leave an important message in a hidden compartment in the wall in the worker's toilets. He had checked later in the day, and the parchment had disappeared, so his contact must have picked it up.

But the appointed time for the meeting had come and gone, and his contact in Malaquey Naval Intelligence was yet to appear here in one of the rundown shanties at the edge of town.

This part of the city had once been the jewel of Virtoria decades ago; it had been home to one of the most acclaimed wielding colleges in Namira. But now it was the poorest sector, home to the vagrants and criminals. Unless one had nefarious purposes, it was best to avoid it after dark. However, Piotra had lived here long enough to know which areas to sidestep. He had also discovered hardly anyone loitered near this particular abandoned house, almost as if the locals were scared of it.

Which made it an appropriate place for clandestine meetings. But something had felt off when he had approached the meeting point earlier that evening, and his feeling of unease had only grown the longer he waited. With his nerves screaming at him to leave, he turned and did so.

Only to run into the Namiran Military Patrol. And from their expectant expressions, the four officers had been waiting for him.

"Evening, officers," he tried to say calmly as he wondered why their patrol schedule had changed. He had memorized their route, and they hardly ever patrolled this abandoned part of town. It had been another reason why he had chosen this location for the meeting.

"You're out quite late, friend." The patrol officer's smile was chilling.

Piotra tried to keep his voice calm. "I…I was checking out this house. I heard it was on the market, and quite cheap too. So, once I got off work, I came over to investigate."

The leader faced him while the remaining three surrounded him. "It's not surprising it's dirt cheap, considering it used to belong to traitors of our beloved monarch."

"Oh, I see," said Piotra, trying not to tremble. There was something odd about this patrol. The others he had met in the past usually asked for money right off the bat. "Well, it's getting late. I better head home. Please have a pleasant evening." He turned to leave.

"Leaving so soon?" asked a female patrol officer, blocking his path. He noticed something different about her coal-black uniform. She had a pistol. *Where was her truncheon?* He glanced at the other three. No truncheons in sight, just pistols.

This wasn't a real patrol. He had to get away from them. "Um…I need to get home. I start work early tomorrow."

The leader chuckled coldly. "Good excuse. Almost believable, if one didn't already know you're a spy for Malaquey intelligence."

Piotra froze as he stared at the fake patrol leader in shock.

"I must admit, I am impressed you chose the house of the late Master Tren Baths, the former headmaster of the destroyed Astral Wielding college. No one would have thought to look—" He was abruptly cut off when Piotra wielded sand into the faces of the four officers.

As they yelled in pain and fury, Piotra took to his heels.

"Find him! Take him alive!"

Piotra realized he was in a bigger mess than he'd first thought. The four pursuers soon became several more, which meant backup hadn't been far away. With his heart beating painfully against his ribs, Piotra wielded small balls of hard-packed sand behind him as he weaved his way through the dark alleys. He felt a moment of grim satisfaction at the shouts of pain as his sand balls struck targets. His inattention almost made him crash right into someone lunging at him from a side alley. Veering to the right, he barely avoided the outstretched hands of a young man in a Namiran military police uniform.

By the Maker! He had to reach safety. They must not catch him. A plan began to form in his mind as he changed direction and turned right to run towards an enormous, also abandoned, building.

"He's headed for the old school!"

Suddenly finding new strength, Piotra outpaced his predators as his new destination came into sight. It was a looming structure, which in its heyday would have been an impressive work of architecture filled with bright wielder students. But the ravages of time now had its once proud walls peeling, its windows cracked and dirty. Piotra ran for the damaged double front doors, wielding a blast of sand at the doors so they sprung open at his approach. He ducked inside and started up the damaged stairs. Having explored this place extensively in the past, he knew which would bear his weight and which wouldn't.

It wasn't long before the supposed military police were inside too. Screams of pain soon followed as the unwary officers stepped on rotted wooden steps and crashed through.

But Piotra didn't have time to gloat. His pursuers would learn fast.

After what seemed an eternity of running, he reached the roof. He had almost reached the edge when the fake patrol leader and several of his officers burst through the door.

"Halt in the name of the Immortal Queen! You have nowhere to go!"

Piotra paused and turned to face the Namiran officer. Though winded, he couldn't help but laugh.

The fake patrol leader's expression went from triumph to shock. "What are you laughing at? You're under arrest for treason. There is no escape!"

Piotra raised his hands and inched slowly backwards, nearing the roof's edge. He wasn't surprised when no one raised their pistols to shoot at him. Someone important really wanted him alive.

He didn't have to guess who that may be.

"You're wrong. I do have options, and I do have somewhere else to be."

The counterfeit patrol leader looked behind Piotra and suddenly realized what the spy was about to do.

"Stop!" But he was talking to empty air as Piotra casually stepped backwards off the edge of the roof.

#

Such a waste, thought Minister Nathan Lensworth as he studied the vacant eyes of the broken body of Piotra Velztra. Nothing of any worth had been found on his person apart from a worker's temporary identity card that bore his name. Probably a fake name at that.

The head of Namiran Intelligence eventually held up a hand to stop the sham patrol leader from trying to explain for the umpteenth time why he had failed such an important mission.

"So, Lieutenant Kato, let me get this straight. Instead of grabbing the suspect, you decided to gloat?"

"I…I just wanted to be sure we had the right person—"

The minister gave the unfortunate officer a look that shut him up. That was the weakest explanation yet. True military police were known to grab their victims without any ceremony, but this fool had thought to show off his powers before his juniors instead. He knew this masquerading idiot had been promoted too soon.

It was time to rectify that mistake.

"Well, do you know who else is going to be, shall we say, disappointed, by this blunder?" The junior officers moved away from Lieutenant Kato.

The officer was confused for a long moment. "Um…I…"

Minister Lensworth decided to just tell him. "Her Immortal Majesty."

Lieutenant Kato went deathly pale.

"Since you were in charge of this operation, you shall have the honor of reporting directly to her." He watched the officer's eyes fill with horror, glancing around him as if searching for support. None of his fellow officers dared make eye contact. "You will be escorted to the palace to ensure you arrive safely."

Lieutenant Kato was still speechless when two of his colleagues grabbed his arms and marched him off. The minister went back to studying the body. He wondered what had been so important that the spy had jumped to protect it.

"Orders, sir?"

"Bury him. He deserves that at least." Then he turned and walked away.

#

Minister Lensworth strode down the empty but grand marble hall. After searching the abandoned wielder's college and finding nothing useful, he had made his way back to Flintwood Castle. The granite-faced guards at the double doors leading to the throne room nodded at him as he approached.

"Her Majesty is expecting you. I'll announce you."

"Thank you," said the minister, waiting to be announced.

It took only moments for him to be shown in. For once, no courtiers were in attendance, but the stench of burnt meat filled his nostrils, and he noted the still smoking corpse of a nearly unrecognizable Lieutenant Kato in the corner of the throne room.

As for the queen, she was lounging on her throne, reading a book.

The minister approached at a steady pace, neither too fast nor too slow. He wasn't keen to anger her. Once at a distance he knew to be safe, he stopped and waited.

Several minutes passed, during which he remained mute.

"Wise of you to send him first before making your own appearance."

The minister wisely continued to keep quiet.

"It seems I'm becoming a disposal unit for the dredges of our military and intelligence agencies. I'm disappointed you think that's all I'm here for." Queen Kallesa closed her book with a snap that almost made Minister Lensworth cringe.

"However, you're not completely useless. At least you found this spy in our midst." Minister Lensworth relaxed a bit. "Though, I am surprised he turned out to be a wielder."

Turning to fix her livid green eyes on the intelligence minister, she added, "And you know how I hate surprises." She delivered her last words with a hiss.

Mindful of the burnt body beside him, he said, "That fact wasn't relayed to us by our informant, Your Majesty."

The queen glared at him for a long moment. "Well, I suppose it's not entirely your fault. Any news on the merchant ship responsible for the destruction of four of my new warships?"

For once, he was grateful for her habit of abruptly changing subjects. "Our informant asked for more time. He is yet to gather enough data on all those involved—"

"Time is a luxury we cannot afford," cut in the queen in a calm, icy tone. "Inform our spy of the consequences of not sticking to the agreement. Maybe that will be an incentive."

The minister swallowed nervously. "By your command." He turned to go.

"Oh, Lensworth, I have an idea."

He tried not to flinch at her words. Her ideas usually resulted in someone dying horribly. Ensuring his face was a mask, he turned and asked carefully, "Yes, Your Majesty?"

"Maybe you also need an incentive. I think from now on, a division of my Specialists will work with you."

Minister Lensworth felt the blood drain from his face. Surely, she wasn't talking about *them* ?

The queen laughed softly at his expression. "Oh yes, the Specialists will work with you from now on."

#

Britea stared at the blank sheet of paper before her, then glanced at the closed envelope beside it. It had been easy writing letters to her parents, and even one to her sister.

But each time she tried to think of what to put in this next letter, she found herself at a loss for words. Well, to be honest, this was the first time she'd written to this particular person.

"Better get on with it." She sighed to herself as she picked up her pen. The more she hesitated, the more anxious she became. *What if he thought she was a fool?*

Still, she found herself reaching for the blank parchment.

Dear Kahl,

Was that too forward? Britea shrugged and continued.

I hope this finds you and your family well and happy. I have been at Syla College for two weeks now, and it has been an interesting experience.

She thought about telling him about the bullying, then decided against it. She hadn't even mentioned that to her family. *Why make him worry unnecessarily?*

I have been fortunate enough to make a few friends. They are helping me with my general studies but not wielding. Only instructors can do that here. I can't really talk much about it.

Because there is nothing to talk about , she thought. She was still in the most junior wielding class. Not that she minded. It hadn't taken long for her to see the wisdom in Instructor Shelley's decision. But she hoped a certain student never found out. Lady Arkei always found ways to make her life unbearable. At least for now it was just a few snide words here and there, though the noble was always careful not to do it in front of the instructors. Britea had a feeling that things would escalate at some point though.

I am still trying to adjust to the school. It is very different from Weldaros. My village seems so small compared to the college and even smaller compared to Raven's Fall. My roommate, Danai, feels it's time for me to explore the town. We got permission from our instructor yesterday, so wish us luck.

Britea leaned back and reread her letter. For a first attempt, she thought it was all right. She wondered if she should ask him to write back. Then she shook her head. That would be up to him.

Kind wishes from Novice Britea D'Tranell of Syla College, Raven's Fall, Malaquey.

Britea folded the letter, stuffed it into a separate envelope, then wrote out Kahl's full name on it.

"You ready to explore?"

She looked up at an excited Danai. Her roommate was dressed in a soft cream blouse with puffy sleeves that ended at the elbows. Dark reddish-brown, close-fitting leather pants, and thigh-high black boots completed the outfit. Clearly not a college uniform.

"What?" asked Danai when she noticed Britea's expression.

"You're…you're not in uniform. I thought we would be in…" Britea's voice trailed off as she thought of the few clothes she had. Back in Weldaros, she hadn't minded what she wore. But here, she'd soon realized how she compared to others—especially Lady Arkei and her cohort of nobles.

"Ooh." Understanding shone in Danai's eyes. "I'll change back into my uniform, and then we can match."

Britea jumped up. "No, no. It's all right. It is your day off after all. I can buy some clothes in town later for other outings."

Danai frowned. "Are you sure?"

"Absolutely," said Britea firmly.

"All right, but I'll only accept your decision if I get to take you shopping."

Britea smiled with relief. "Deal."

#

A black coach was waiting for them when they left through the grand entrance. Britea spied a coat of arms painted on each side. It took the shape of a shield divided into four sections representing each of the four elements: a single orange-red flame for fire, a small whirlwind for air, a blue wave for water, and a rock for earth.

The Wielder's Shield.

"This is one of the college's coaches," explained Danai when she caught her roommate's curious expression. "The official recommendation is to book one at least three weeks in advance if you wish to be dropped off in town. However, I always find one available at a moment's notice, especially if you don't mind sharing a ride with other students."

"Does everyone use the coaches?" asked Britea.

Danai scoffed. "Nah. A lot of the nobles would rather die than use them. It's for us folk who don't have the same resources. Some call it the Pauper's Coach, but I don't care. Their opinions don't matter to me." She turned and greeted the man high above them. "Good morning, Trevor."

A short, stout man alighted from the driver's seat. "Top of the morning to you as well, Mistress Riverun. Looks like it's just you two for Port Trident."

Danai gave him a surprised look. "No one else is joining us?"

"Not today. And you must be Novice D'Tranell? I haven't had the pleasure yet."

Britea finally remembered her manners and said, "Good morning to you too. This is my first time going into town."

"Welcome to Syla College," said the portly man with a smile. "Stick close to Mistress Riverun. She won't steer you wrong."

"Thanks for your overly kind words, Trevor," said Danai, embarrassed.

"Ah, you know them to be true. Now, let's be going. Daylight is wasting!"

#

Once they were underway, Britea found she had questions. "How often do you go into town?"

"Every two months. My parents were adamant I keep to that schedule. At first, I thought they were just being silly." Her expression darkened but she continued. "Then I realized how important these regular visits are."

"Oh," was all Britea said. She suspected the first few months had been tremendously hard for Danai. She tried to find something else to talk about. "What about Navos, Lexia, and Shran? When do they visit town?"

"They have their own schedules. Besides, sometimes Lexia and Navos want to get away from the college on their own. Shran or I wouldn't be welcome on their special outings," Danai said with a wink.

Britea blinked. "Wait, Lexia and Navos are…" her voice trailed off.

Danai smiled at her expression. "Yes, they're dating. She may seem exasperated with him sometimes because he's in defense class, but may the Lords of Light and Shadow help anyone who gets between them."

To be honest, she *had* thought it was a bit odd the towering Navos paid so much attention to the petite Lexia. Now Britea realized there had been times when the two wielders had sat close together, exchanging fond glances, even when Lexia was scolding the gentle giant.

"So, what do you want to do in town today, apart from delivering your letters and shopping?" asked Danai.

"I don't know really. I didn't plan on doing much. I guess we could look around, if you don't mind," said Britea. She touched the small purse in her right pocket. It contained her allowance for the week. Apparently, the royal court gave the poorer students a weekly allowance.

Danai observed her movements. "Word of advice. In the market place, make sure your hands are in both pockets, so the pickpockets won't know which one to target. Plus, it'll discourage them from stealing in the first place."

Britea frowned. "What if I want to look at something by holding it in my hand?"

"First, try to limit touching anyone's wares, especially if you don't intend to buy it. The merchants of Carlellis aren't friendly. Second, if you really need to examine something closely, lean against the stall with the pocket containing your purse, and make sure no one is crowding either side of you. If there's a crowd around a stall, avoid it at all costs. Whatever they're selling will certainly be there tomorrow, or you might find something even better elsewhere."

"Thanks, Danai," said Britea in a subdued voice. "This place is so different from Weldaros."

"Don't be so glum, dear sister," Danai gave her an encouraging smile. "I felt the same way when I first arrived. You'll learn fast. You'll see."

#

The noise at Carlellis Market seemed even louder than the first time Britea had gone through it when she'd disembarked in Raven's Fall. The coach slowed to a crawl as it joined a queue of similar vehicles trying to reach the center of town. This gave her time to properly observe the market.

It was large, overcrowded, and noisy, and it smelled terrible. Small stalls covered with straw-brown canopies dotted the edges of the charcoal-grey brick road; merchants hawked their wares with loud voices and frantic gestures. Some even brought samples of their goods right up to the coach windows, and though Britea politely declined, the hawkers still shoved their products in her face. Danai had to speak harshly to the more insistent ones many times until they backed off, shooting dark looks at the senior wielder.

The shops, however, were more impressive. For one, they were clearly bigger than the stalls. They were also located further from the main road, and they had a pedestrian walkway in front. Though all the shops had dark-blue canopies, some shops had just one floor while others had two or three floors. They had been built side by side with barely any space between them. Many shops even shared a wall. Britea frowned. That could be a security risk if someone tried to break into a shop from another one.

Her attention was soon caught by lone stoic figures in dark-red uniforms standing resolutely in front of many of the shops. Britea peered closely at them. They were diligently watching anyone who approached the shops. "Those people in dark-red uniforms, who are they?"

"The Crimson Merchant Guard. The Merchant Guild pays for them. The more guards you see, the richer the owner of the shop. However, the astronomical cost of those guards is always transferred to the customer." Britea took note of her roommate's cynical tone and was about to say something, but then she noticed something else as the coach pushed ever deeper into the market.

"These shops…they're different from the ones at the entrance."

"In what way?" asked Danai with a knowing smile.

"They keep getting bigger for starters," said Britea, pausing when they reached the largest shop yet with three guards at the entrance.

"The bigger and more expensive shops are at the center of the market while the cheaper ones are at the outskirts," explained Danai. Britea nodded as she stored that small bit of information away for later. The wielder coach soon came to a stop beside other packed vehicles. As Britea alighted from the coach, she felt a sudden sense of being watched. She glanced around only to see several people walking across the square, going about their business. No one looked in her direction. She shook her head. She was probably just being self-conscious.

"Here we are, ladies," said Trevor. "I'll be heading back to the college in exactly four hours. Please don't be late."

Danai smiled at him. "Thanks, Trevor. We'll be there." She set a timer on a chronometer and tucked it into her pocket before turning to her roommate.

"Let's go exploring!"

"Oh, yes!" replied an excited Britea.

#

At first, Britea was content to listen to Danai as she named the different parts of the large market. Grocer's Lane was east, and it had several small roadside stalls and at least four large shops with bright green canopies that sold fresh and preserved foods. Britea nodded when she realized it was close to the docks, which lay northeast. Directly opposite Grocer's Lane was what Danai grimly stated was Armaments and Armor Lane. These shops were bigger than the rest. They had black canopies and they all had at least three crimson-clad guards. Britea felt a shiver run down her spine as they walked past the imposing row of heavily guarded shops

The next important sector was Fashionista Lane in the northwest area of the market. As she and Danai stepped into that area, she understood the reason for its name. For one thing, the road here was a bright, pinkish-purple, brick-laden road. A few roadside stalls displayed small vividly colored hats and unique clothing accessories, belts and scarves, and other items she had never seen before. Britea wondered how they kept stock dry when it rained. Secondly, the bigger shops had bright pink canopies and brightly colored signs advertising clothes, jewelry, and accessories. Most of these shops also had crimson-clad guards. Even the roadside stalls had one or two sentries.

Her jaw dropped when she tried and failed to count the various buildings. Carlina, her older sister, would die and go to heaven if she ever came here. Then her gaze happened upon a small shop with grey walls and a distinct blood-red canopy.

Carlelli's Books and Writing Materials . A bookstore. And it didn't have any guards.

"Please, can we look in there quickly? If you don't mind?" asked Britea in one breath.

Danai laughed softly. "Of course. I'm looking for a good book myself."

Britea smiled with relief. She had been worried Danai might be irritated because she probably had better things to do. Britea knew the school had an extensive library, but nothing beat owning your own books. The few she had brought with her were her favorites, and she was ever so careful with them.

Her thoughts returned to the present as the two wielders entered the bookstore. A bell rang above them as Britea pushed the old but well-preserved wooden door open.

Though small on the outside, the interior appeared vast.

"Hmm, that's odd," said Danai in a low voice.

"Good day. How can I help you?" Both wielders turned to face a middle-aged, pale-skinned woman dressed in a brightly colored emerald gown. A frightened expression replaced the smile on the woman's face when she saw Danai.

"You...you're here?"

Danai and Britea shared a confused glance. "I'm sorry, but have we met?" asked Danai.

The woman shook her head, then smiled. "Forgive me, but for a moment, I...I thought you were someone I'd heard of...I mean, that I knew." Her laughter sounded a touch hysterical.

Britea was beginning to feel uneasy and could see from Danai's expression that she felt the same way. Maybe they should leave.

The shopkeeper laughed again. "Where are my manners? I'm Erina Seaworth."

All thoughts of leaving disappeared when Britea heard the name. "Erina Seaworth? The author of *Lost Histories of the Deep, Volumes One and Two?* And *Wielder's Tales, Volumes One and Two?* And *Doomed Love Stories of Time and Legend!?"* Her voice was rising as she listed all the books. It was Britea's turn to be stared at.

"I have all your books!" squealed Britea in delight. "You are such a talented writer!"

Erina blushed. "Well, thank you. I'm so glad you like my work," she looked uncertainly at Danai.

The fire wielder nodded. "I've read some of your work too. I never thought I would meet you. It is an honor." Then to Britea's amazement, Danai placed her right hand on her chest and bowed to Erina. What happened next stunned the two wielders. Erina began to cry.

Danai and Britea shared a startled look.

"I'm so sorry," apologized Danai. "I didn't mean to mock or insult you."

The writer waved her left hand as she used a handkerchief with her right to blow her nose. “No, no. You didn’t insult me. I am truly happy with your gesture of respect. To think that I would receive it from one such as—” she paused before taking a new tack, “one as noble as you.” Britea suspected she had been about to say something else.

“So, pardon me for asking, but why the tears?” asked a worried-looking Danai. The writer stared at her and Britea for a long moment, then sighed dramatically as if she had made an important decision.

“Have a seat, both of you, and hear my tale. Oh! And I have tea and biscuits.”

CHAPTER 7

Britea and Danai sat down at a tiny wooden table nestled beneath a grimy window, and despite their pleas that they weren't hungry, Erina insisted on serving tea for the two wielders. She carefully poured the tea into three cups as she began to tell her tale.

"When I was a little girl, I was fascinated with books and stories and writing. I wrote so much my parents despaired at the cost of writing materials, but still they encouraged me, and for that I was very grateful. But as I got older, my hunger for knowledge only grew. As you know," she looked pointedly at Danai, "Our Weltonian history doesn't exist on paper but is only passed on orally."

Britea blinked; she hadn't known that. Mama Chloe had never mentioned that.

Danai appeared a bit uneasy as she answered. "Aye, that I know."

Erina smiled sadly as she continued. "So, you can imagine my family's shock when I began to put our history to paper."

Britea saw Danai go pale. "That's…that's not allowed."

Erina nodded as she sat down. "I know, but I persisted. I was warned to stop but I couldn't. It was as if some part of me was compelled to write everything down. At first, I kept it a secret at my parents' urging but…" she paused as if unsure of how to proceed. Both Britea and Danai kept quiet, sensing her inner turmoil. Erina took a deep breath.

"Then one day, I couldn't keep it secret any longer, and I presented all my writings of our history to a Council of Elders meeting." Danai's eyes went wide. Britea could tell from her expression that Erina had done something wrong according to Weltonian ways.

"What happened?" she asked when she could stand the suspense no longer.

"Instant exile." Britea saw Danai wince.

Erina smiled and patted their hands. "Do not despair for me. Now, drink your tea before it gets cold." Britea and Danai glanced at each other and reached for their tea cups; Erina also took a sip from hers.

An uncomfortable silence followed until Danai cleared her throat and turned to Erina.

"Don't," commanded the Weltonian author with a firm smile. "Never apologize for something that happened way before you were born."

Danai's face flushed as Britea stared at her. "But it's unfair what they did to you."

Erina gave Danai an odd look. "You don't agree with the elders?"

"Not on some things and certainly not on that."

The Weltonian writer shook her head. "I broke the law, and I deserved to be punished. Which is why I'm here, selling and writing as many books as I can before the Sea Mother calls me home."

Britea was a bit startled by that. "The Sea Mother? Don't you mean the Maker and His Lords of Light and Shadow?"

Erina laughed softly. "The Sea Mother and the Maker are one and the same."

"What?" Britea gasped in shock while Danai sighed wearily and rubbed her forehead.

"It's best if you don't speak of it in public," warned Danai grimly before turning to Erina. "Why did you tell us your story of exile? We're just two strangers passing by."

The writer grinned and tapped her finger against her nose. "I know a secret. A prophecy. I'm not supposed to tell, but when I saw you two…well, I just had to talk to you. Oh! Let me get you my catalogue of books." She leapt up and hurried to the back rooms.

Britea waited until she was out of earshot. "Is she insane?"

Danai hesitated before replying. "Perhaps, though I doubt she means us any harm. Her…exile may have affected her mental state." Pity filled her eyes.

She's all alone , thought Britea. She felt guilty for fearing the exiled writer she had always idolized from afar and remembered to smile when Erina returned with a thick book.

Both she and Danai were soon enthralled when they discovered it contained descriptions of countless books. To Britea's relief, from then on Erina talked only about the books and said nothing more of her exile or of gods. Eventually, the two wielders picked up a total of four books between them, but when it came time for payment, Erina tried to waive the payment.

Danai put her foot down and paid for all the books.

"Okay, but next time is free for you two." Erina insisted.

Britea looked at her gravely and walked over to her, arms wide open. Erina didn't hesitate to give her a hug, and the writer's eyes looked suspiciously wet after Danai hugged her too.

"Please, come again," said Erina when she had gained enough composure to speak. Both girls promised they would as they left. The two wielders remained silent for a long moment as they strode down the lavender-paved streets.

"I don't think she's dangerous," said Danai thoughtfully.

Britea nodded, relieved. "I'd like to visit her again. I'll definitely need more books."

"Uh huh," agreed Danai.

"You didn't have to pay for my books, you know."

"Consider it a sisterly gift," said Danai with a smile.

Britea knew better than to argue. "So, where to next?"

"There's a small shop at the end of the street, not too expensive, and they have some decent clothes. I also want to pick up a few gifts for my parents."

Britea wished she could do the same, but she suspected she wouldn't have enough money to get gifts *and* pay for delivery to far away Weldaros. Soon enough they reached a small shop aptly entitled, *Lara's Attire for the Frugal Wallet.*

"I like the name already," whispered Britea to a smiling Danai. The shop's baby-blue walls and watermelon canopy made it feel cheery and welcoming.

Two crimson-clad guards noted Britea's wielder uniform. To her surprise, they treated her with respect and regarded Danai warily. This didn't faze the older wielder. She just greeted them cheerfully. "Morning, Boren and Kliev."

"Morning, milady," chorused the guards hesitantly as the two girls walked into the shop. Britea made a note to ask Danai about their odd behavior later. A bell hanging over the polished white door musically announced their presence.

"Good morning! Good morning!"

Britea was caught off guard at the overly cheery greeting of a striking, rugged young woman in a close-fitting, canary-yellow gown. Her dyed pastel-blue hair seemed to defy gravity with its wavy vertical flow that seemed determined to reach the ceiling.

"Morning, Lara," said Danai with an easy smile. Lara squealed and ran forward to hug the young Weltonian. Britea's eyes widened when the shopkeeper lifted Danai off the floor.

"Put me down," said Danai with a laugh. Lara obliged.

"How's my favorite troublemaker? Did Boren and Kliev give you any trouble this time?"

"No, no. They definitely remembered me." Danai turned to Britea. "I brought a friend. Britea D'Tranell, meet Lara Firbright." The shop owner focused her eagle-eyed gaze on her new target.

"Well, hello there. I don't recall seeing you before."

"I'm from Weldaros. I'm a late wielder, so I just enrolled at the college a few weeks ago." Then it clicked. Britea stared again at the gravity-defying waterfall of blue hair and said, "You're also a wielder."

Lara shared a smile with Danai. "Oh, she's a smart one. Yes, sweetie, that is what I am. Although I'm not as talented as our Danai here. I'm just a lowly tier-two air wielder." She studied Britea. "Your face has a question written all over it."

Britea blinked. "Why are you…I mean, I know it's none of my business, but…but don't all wielders serve in the royal court, the military, or the government?"

Lara laughed softly. "Danai hasn't told you yet of what really awaits low-level wielders who manage to graduate?"

Britea glanced at her roommate, who shifted uncomfortably.

"Well, let me enlighten you. Surviving college as a low-ranking wielder is one thing, but making the necessary connections to further your career after you leave is another. I learned that early enough. Once I'd realized I had neither the necessary family connections to make it to court nor the wish to kiss someone's—"

Danai coughed in warning.

Lara didn't blink as she modified her words "…behind to nab a cozy, high-paying job in government, I started saving my monthly college allowance money. Then, when I graduated two years ago and began my Year of Discovery, I invested my money and opened this shop once I'd completed my service to the state."

Britea had no idea what to say, so she took a moment before settling on. "You…you seem quite happy."

Lara smiled brightly. "I really like you. So ladies, what can I do for your today? Do remember that for wielders, everything is thirty-five percent off."

Danai gasped. "Lara, you're robbing yourself."

"That's just for today, darling. Give me a little credit. It's my shop after all." Thus began a shopping whirlwind. Britea almost fainted at the price tags but then began to breathe easier when she saw a rack of discounted clothes. She soon found an emerald-green dress that caught her eye. The outline of a peacock was embroidered near each hem. It was so much more beautiful and softer than anything she currently owned—or had ever owned.

"Good choice," said Lara when Britea asked if she could try it one. "Use the room at the back." As Britea walked away, she heard Lara ask Dana about Navos, Lexia, and Shran.

It took a while for Britea to make up her mind. The fit and color made the dress perfect, but even when she took thirty-five percent off, it still cost forty-five silvers. That was more than anything that she had ever owned. She felt guilty spending that much, but she really wanted to have just one pretty dress. All her other clothes had been passed down from Carlina.

"Are you happy with it?" asked Lara. Danai had already picked out a leather cap and two brightly colored scarves.

"Yes, I really like it." Lara nodded, took the dress, and examined it closely.

"So, with thirty-five percent off, that would make it twenty-nine silvers and twenty-five cente." Britea winced at the price, but Lara wasn't done. "Oh, imagine that. This fashion is so last week, I believe that makes the cost twenty-five silvers."

Britea blinked. "But…but it's twenty-nine silvers and twenty-five cente?"

Lara's smile widened. "And now it's twenty silvers."

Britea shook her head in shock. *Why was Lara driving the price down?*

"Just pay the twenty silvers, sister," said Danai with a weary groan. Britea shut her mouth and did as she was told.

"Thank you kindly," said Lara as she gently wrapped the dress and put it in a velvet bag. "So, you're off to the docks after this?"

"Yes," replied Danai. "I wish we could spend more time gossiping, though, because boy do I have tales for you."

Lara giggled. "Don't worry, I'll make the time to come down to the college to see my old—and new—troublemakers," she nodded her head at Britea.

"Thank you so much for the dress. I am so very grateful."

"Save your money, sister, work and study hard, and listen to Danai here. She's a survivor and a fighter."

"And Lara loves to exaggerate," countered Danai.

Lara wielded a yellow feather at the Weltonian. "Get outta here. Give your mother a hug and a kiss from me, and come back any time, my sisters."

#

Britea was full of curiosity when they left the shop. "I have questions."

"Fire away," said Danai easily.

"First, what happened with Boren and Kliev?"

"When Lara opened her shop for the first time, I was one of her first customers. Unfortunately, the guards correctly identified me as Weltonian from my attire but incorrectly treated me like a criminal."

"They did what?" gasped Britea.

"I tried to explain I was a friend of Lara's and a student at the college, but they laughed and tried to detain me. Suddenly, they found themselves surrounded by six-foot flames. Lara ran out, saved their hides, and fired them on the spot. I intervened on their behalf, and she gave them back their jobs after I asked her to forgive them. Since then, they've behaved, well…differently whenever I show up."

Britea tried to imagine the terror the men must have felt. "I can imagine. And you and Lara? What was all that about lower-tier wielders?"

Danai sighed sadly. "She's right. Lower tiers, from one to three, tend to have a harder time graduating. Plus, finding a well-paying job is harder to obtain for lower tiers and those from poor families. Tier four and higher have a chance to further their education in the Army or Naval Wielding Divisions, but it's a tough competition."

Britea felt disquiet at her words. "You two seem quite close."

Danai smiled at the change of subject. "She was my roommate before you, and she stopped me from running away when the bullying got to me."

Britea stared at her.

"I was where you are now. She saved my sanity, and she too was bullied by Lady Selina Arkei. They were in the same class. When Selina and her group realized Lara was protecting me, they went after her and left me alone. Yet, somehow, she always seemed to keep her head up, using her eccentricity to cope with the constant bullying."

A thought struck Britea that made her stop in her tracks.

"What is it?" asked Danai.

"Lara graduated two years ago and has completed her Year of Discovery. She even owns a business, but Selina is *still* on her own Year of Discovery."

Danai smiled evilly. "Selina failed a couple essential general education exams, and she was forced to repeat a few semesters."

"Oh," was all Britea could say.

"Yes, though of noble lineage, the Arkei sisters have rocks for brains."

"I definitely agree," Britea said with a laugh. Danai joined in, and they nearly doubled over.

#

The main road and paths gradually became charcoal grey again as they left Fashionista Lane and headed for the docks. The smell of rotten fish slowly surrounded them.

"I can't believe I missed all this when I disembarked," said Britea.

"It depends on when you arrived. You got here just as the weekend was ending, so there were far fewer fishing boats about. It's definitely the worst time for shopping though. There are way too many people then."

Britea wrinkled her nose as the stench of rotten fish got stronger.

Danai laughed at her expression. "You'll get used to it after a while."

"Uh uh," disagreed her younger roommate. Britea found herself searching for the *Windrider* even though she knew it must have departed over a week ago. She hoped her dah didn't get seasick this time. She forced her mind to return to the present. Ships of varying sizes and purposes were docked in the harbor, some offloading passengers and cargo, some departing. This was nothing like Port Xanthos, the closet seaport to her village. Xanthos was downright comatose in comparison to Port Trident.

"There he is," said Danai softly, pride evident in her voice. Britea looked straight ahead, expecting to see a man. Instead, she saw the most colorful ship she'd ever seen. Its bright iris-colored sails were rolled up, but the ship's hull was of burnished, gleaming, rich-brown cedar. Even the murky waters of the harbor could not dull its brilliance.

"Welcome to the *Wandering Star*. It belongs to my mother, Sonei Riverun."

Britea stared at the Weltonian ship in mute amazement as they approached the gangway.

Danai hailed the Weltonians carrying cargo onto the ship. The crew stopped and shouted back greetings. They were clearly happy to see her.

At first, Britea was unsure how to behave until Danai yelled, “She’s one of us, brothers and sisters!” And just like that, they welcomed her as a Weltonian. Their kind smiles and greetings almost brought tears to her eyes.

“Whose voice is it that I hear?” The owner of the voice was a tall stately looking woman, with almond skin and thick walnut-colored curls held back by a cerulean hair band. Her matching silk blouse, close-fitting indigo leather pants, and battered thigh-high boots gave her a daunting air. Britea took one look at her face and knew immediately who she was.

Danai’s eyes brightened as she ran up the gangway and flung her arms around her mother, who eagerly returned her only child’s hug. Britea stood to one side as she watched them reunite, oddly not feeling awkward.

The two finally separated. “You look a bit thin, daughter,” said Sonei with a small frown.

Danai shook her head with a laugh. “I’m fine, mah. By the way, Lara sends her love.”

“Why didn’t you bring her with you?” asked Sonei.

Her daughter sighed. “She has to mind her shop. Anywho, I’d like you to meet Britea D’Tranell of Weldaros. She’s also one of us.”

“Indeed. I heard you announce it to every ship in the harbor,” said Sonei dryly. She walked over the Britea and held out a hand. “A pleasure to meet you, daughter of my sister.”

Britea was a bit startled by the greeting and timidly held out a hand. “I...um...it’s a pleasure to meet you too.” Sonei laughed and drew her into a gentle embrace.

“Enough with the formality. We are all sisters in the eyes of the Mother. Come inside, my girls.”

Once seated, Sonei didn’t waste time questioning Danai and Britea while also trying to tempt them to stuff themselves with a parade of aromatic dishes.

“So, Britea, you’re Danai’s roommate. That’s fabulous. I hope your studies are going well?” Before she could answer, the captain turned her attention to her daughter. “Danai, how’s your martial arts? I hope you’ve been practicing? Are the Arkei girls still pestering you? You really should consider setting their pretty petticoats on fire.”

“Mah!” exclaimed Danai in exasperation. Britea’s eyes were as round as dinner plates.

Sonei laughed. “I jest. But seriously, do something about them or I might.”

Now Danai looked worried. "It's fine mah. I can handle it."

Sonei shrugged.

"I brought you and dah a few gifts," said Danai, changing the subject. Sonei hugged her daughter again after she'd seen the presents.

"Your father will love this."

"Oh, mah, could you please help Britea deliver her letters?" The two Weltonians looked at Britea, who blinked at them before remembering she had two letters in her pockets.

"Please, if it isn't too much trouble. How much will it cost?"

Sonei waved away her question. "No payment is necessary. Two letters for Weldaros, yes?"

"Umm…one is. The second one is for…" She took a deep breath. "…is for Kahl."

Sonei and Danai went still at the name.

"He…he's a water wielder and a—"

"Dyhaeri," completed Sonei. She stared at her daughter questioningly. Danai shrugged, so Sonei asked the questions for them both. "Child, how is it you're writing a letter to a Dyhaeri?"

Britea wondered what she was allowed to tell as she looked at the worried eyes of the older Weltonian woman before making her decision.

"My dah and I met him on our way to Raven's Fall. I'm a late wielder, so he trained me. Then we ran into Namiran raiders." Sonei's face went pale. "It's because of him that the crew of the *Windrider* and my dah and I are still alive. I just want him to know that…that I thank him for all he did and I'm all right."

But is he all right as well? thought Britea with no small amount of dread. She still saw how his even his own people regarded him.

With anger. And suspicion.

She hastily wiped away a tear.

"You're worried about him," Sonei observed.

Britea's head jerked up to see Danai and her mother looking concerned. "Yes, that too."

Sonei gazed at the two letters in her hand for a long moment. Britea suddenly feared she had said something wrong.

"I'll make sure these letters get to their owners. Do not fret, daughter of my sister."

"Uh...thank you." Britea dried her eyes. "May I ask why you address me like that?"

Sonei and Danai shared a sad smile. "Weltonians, though being of one people, are of different factions, and our biggest fear is that of exile. Many believe those who are exiled are never to be spoken of again and should be forgotten, but a few of us believe the opposite."

Sonei took Britea's right hand. "Your ancestors may have moved to land generations ago, but to me, they will always be family. That I will not hide."

Britea looked at Danai who nodded proudly. Now she understood why her roommate had been furious about how Erina Seaworth had been treated. "Thank you."

"You're welcome." A mischievous light entered Sonei's eyes. "Now, tell me if my dear Danai has managed to meet an agreeable young man at that college."

Danai groaned. "Mah, please!"

#

All too soon, it was time to leave. But not before Sonei gave them bags full of food to take back to the college. It was so much Danai had to refuse a large portion of it.

"Mah! We'll be late for the coach. Besides, we do have food at the college."

"Not as good as this I bet," countered Sonei.

Danai planted a kiss on her mother's cheek. "Thanks again. We'll be fine." Britea thought she looked ready to cry.

There was a suspicious wet sheen in Sonei's eyes too. "I'll see you two again soon." The older Weltonian woman looked at Britea and said, "And your letters will get to their final destinations."

"I am truly grateful," said Britea.

"Off with you now. Be careful on your way back, my dears," gently warned Sonei as both girls left.

As they walked, Britea tried to adjust the heavy bag of treats. "Your mother is really nice, and her ship is stunning."

Danai smiled at her. She was carrying two heavy bags. "Thank you. I think so too."

They soon reached the central square, and Britea was relieved to see the college coach had arrived. Just a few more steps and she could set down this heavy—

"Well, well, well, what do we have here?" Britea came to a sudden stop when a familiar person stepped out and blocked her path.

Her heart rate sped up as she stared at the face of Lieutenant Harto Flay. Even in casual clothes, he was no less intimidating.

"What business do you have in the market today, Novice D'Tranell?" demanded the Malaquey Naval Intelligence officer.

"We're shopping. What business is it of yours, and who in the Deep are you anyway?" Danai countered as she came to stand in front of and to the side of Britea. A startled expression briefly flashed across Harto's face before he replaced it with a stern countenance.

"This is wielder business and a matter of national security. I would advise you not to get involved."

If he thought that would scare Danai off, he was in for a surprise. The fire wielder dropped her bags, folded her arms, and pinned Harto with a steady stare.

"Fifth-year wielding student, tier five. I am fully aware of the Creed, and you are clearly out of order. Once again, I'll ask. Who are you?"

"Lieutenant Harto Flay, Malaquey Naval Intelligence." Britea replied before he did. Harto glared at her as she continued speaking. "He was one of the three who questioned me about what happened on the Heldiar Sea. He's also a wielder like us."

Danai's eyes hardened. "Which college?"

Harto went pale with fury and his gaze bore into Britea. "You discussed this with an outsider!?"

Danai's eyes blazed with suppressed fury. "Am I an outsider because I'm Weltonian or for another reason?" Her tone indicated that he should choose his answer carefully. "You still haven't told me which college you studied at. Did they teach you to harass other wielders just for kicks and giggles?"

"I ask the questions here, not you," replied Harto coldly.

"Don't worry about it," Danai's smile was pure ice. "I'll eventually find out anyway."

Harto backed down from the confrontation with Danai but turned his attention back to his initial target.

"Why did you tell her?"

"Danai is my friend," Britea declared through gritted teeth, the rational part of her thinking she should explain further. After all, Warden Asteros had appointed Danai as her mentor and roommate, and he had even advised Britea to confide in her. But right now, she was too angry to be reasonable.

Danai kept glaring daggers at Harto while he tried to ignore her.

"You divulged state secrets."

Britea spoke without thinking. "That's hilarious coming from you given that right now, you're interrogating us right in the middle of a busy market. Now who's leaking state secrets?"

Harto seemed to remember where he was and looked around him, as if checking for observers.

Danai smirked. "She got you there." Her smile widened when she saw some people approaching behind the intelligence officer. "Well, as entertaining as this is, it looks like we have to leave you, Lieutenant Flay."

"No, you're not going anywhere—"

"Is there a problem, ladies?" asked a gravelly voice behind Harto. He turned to face three crimson-clad merchant guards flanking the short, stout man who had asked the question.

"We're perfectly all right, Trevor. This kind man was just reflecting on the weather. Weren't you?" asked Danai sweetly, at odds with the warning light in her eyes.

After a long moment, Harto reluctantly nodded. "And now that I have my answer, I will not delay you any longer."

"Why, thank you!" said Danai with an uncharacteristic girlish giggle. The three guards remained until Harto walked away, then they nodded at the girls and the coach driver before returning to their posts. Britea breathed a sigh of relief as Trevor helped the two students with their bags.

"Thanks, Trevor," said the two wielders at the same time.

"No worries. When that young man deliberately blocked your path, I suspected something was wrong. And Danai taking on that fight stance of her had me running for the merchant guards."

"I thought they only guarded the shops," said Britea in an effort to change the topic.

"They also patrol the streets. If there's violence or mayhem, shops can get damaged, people stay at home out of fear, and merchants lose money if order isn't maintained in the market," explained Danai.

"I see."

With their bags packed away, Trevor went to untie the horses. Britea made to enter the coach first, but something made her glance over her shoulder. She was startled to see Harto standing several feet away from them. He was staring at Danai with an odd expression on his face.

"What's wrong?" asked Danai. Britea glanced at her roommate. "Harto."

Danai whipped around, but the officer had disappeared.

"He was there, watching you."

"That lieutenant is trouble," said Danai in a worried tone.

"We have got to go ladies!" announced Trevor from his seat atop of the coach.

"We're ready!" said Danai as she climbed into the coach.

#

Harto tried to control his thoughts as he rode home. He clicked his tongue, and the stallion between his thighs galloped faster. Yet he couldn't stop thinking about what had just happened.

His sole mission today had been to check on a special ceremonial dagger he had commissioned as a birthday gift for his uncle. After checking the progress of the work, he had been preparing to go home…until he caught sight of a certain novice wielder.

Britea D'Tranell. He had been stunned to see her in the market. He was surprised Warden Asteros had allowed her out. First, she was a late wielder, and how sure were the instructors she was in full control of her abilities? Second, she was at the center of a major diplomatic incident concerning the Namiran government. And now she had gone and discussed it with a Weltonian!

Danai was the name of the Weltonian lass. He had to admit she was attractive, and the way her body filled out that outfit…he shook his head briefly. He needed to concentrate on the matter at hand.

Weltonian wielders didn't study at the colleges. Centuries ago, the Namiran and Malaquey governments had given up on forcing them to enroll. Thus, the adjustments to the Creed.

But there was one at Syla College and she had been there for four years! And he was just finding this out?

There was a mystery there, but he wasn't sure if it was connected to the diplomatic mess Britea D'Tranell had created. If there was a connection, he was going to find it.

Harto pushed his heels into the sides of his horse, and the loyal steed ran yet faster. The lieutenant enjoyed riding and would have been a racer if not for his abilities.

Moments later, the tree-lined road to the Flay estate came into view. He slowed so the hidden sentries could get a good look at him. Before he even reached the stable, the grooms were out and waiting. The head groom, an elderly gentleman, stepped forward.

"My lord, welcome home." Harto tried not to sigh at the title. He dismounted.

"Evening, Claren." He waved away the groom's outstretched hand. "I'll brush Thunder Ice down."

The head groom smiled dryly. "Of course, sir."

It was an ongoing game between the two. Claren had been serving the Flay family for years before Harto was even born; he had taught the young Flay heir how to ride and groom his own horse. Yet, every time Harto returned from riding, the head groom still tried to care for Thunder Ice.

"Your mother and uncle are home, my lord. They arrived a few minutes ago."

He cast a wary look at Claren. "Any special guests and their offspring?"

"Not at the moment, sir." Replied the head groom dryly.

Harto brightened at that news. "I'll be quick." Besides, he really needed to talk to his uncle about this Weltonian, Danai.

#

Once he was sure Thunder Ice was brushed down well, he changed the drinking water and ensured the horse had fresh hay and food. Harto patted the stallion's rump on his way out.

He walked up to the impressive red brick mansion, hiding his unease as he nodded at the male servant who bowed as he passed. Harto didn't know why it made him uncomfortable. Perhaps that explained why he found Danai's disrespect refreshing.

The grand foyer was empty apart from one of the maids who stood with a tray containing a pitcher of ice-cold water and a clean glass.

"Welcome home, Lord Flay."

"Thank you, Mara."

She blushed as he said her name. Harto had made it a point to learn everyone's name, face, and background in his mother's household so as to better identify any spies.

He took a sip of the refreshing drink. "Where are Lady Flay and my uncle?"

"In the lower parlor, my lord. I believe they are waiting for dinner."

"Please let them know I'll be joining them shortly." He placed his empty glass on the tray and turned away as she bowed her head. He ran up the stairs to wash and change.

A few minutes later, he felt renewed from sluicing off the dust of Carlelli Market. As he dressed, he studied himself in the mirror. He was tall and well-built, with a thick mane of blond hair. Many members of the fairer gender had assured him he was a fine-looking gentleman. But he took most of their comments with a grain of salt. He knew they were only after his family's vast wealth, and he suspected their pursuit would be worse if they really knew who he was. A feeling of melancholy filled him.

"Not now. I have work to do," he said harshly to himself. He didn't have time to feel sorry for his situation. Many others were worse off. He pushed his thoughts away and left his chambers.

#

"Ah, there's my beloved son," said his mother brightly as he strode into the lower parlor. She already had a glass of wine in one hand. He smiled and kissed her on the cheeks. He was a bit disappointed to see his uncle wasn't in the parlor.

"Where's Uncle Peras?"

"He wanted to wash up, and where is my 'How was your day, mother?'"

Harto grinned at her. "How was your day, mother?"

"As usual, though I did run into Lady Arkei. She's arranging a little homecoming party for her oldest daughter, Selina, and we're invited."

Harto tried to hide his grimace. "That sounds lovely." He knew 'a little coming home party' was going to be an outrageously expensive get together of gargantuan proportions.

"When is this little party?"

Lady Shalina De'tre Flay narrowed her eyes. "You're not going to get out of this one, Harto. I've already promised you'll be there."

Harto sighed. "Mother, you know I hate those gatherings."

"You're one of the most eligible bachelors in Malaquey."

"No, I'm not."

"By now, you should be betrothed to a girl of good standing and noble blood. Now, if only Princess Crystal was several years older…" a speculative look crossed her face. "Hmm, maybe if we wait another seven years, then she'd be ready to marry you."

Harto closed his eyes in despair. "Please, not this again."

"I only want what's best for you—"

A loud sigh interrupted her. "Shalina, please, for the sake of the boy's sanity, can we stop throwing eligible brides at him?"

Harto couldn't help but grin at his mother's brother, Lieutenant Commander Peras Nell. He had been a father figure to Harto after Lord Flay had passed away many years ago while in service to Malaquey Naval Intelligence.

"Welcome back, Uncle Peras." The two men hugged while Shalina took a sip from her wine glass.

"How was your trip?"

Peras sighed. "Boring and not very productive."

"Gentlemen," interrupted Shalina. "Can we talk shop later? I'm starving as we stand." She led the way to the smaller dining hall for family.

There was no time for conversation as the servants brought out the lavish spread. The starter was a small bowl of spicy tomato soup, and the main was fried sea bass with delicious crispy skin on a bed of fluffy white rice surrounded by a tangy mushroom sauce that went perfectly with the sea bass.

"The meal was lovely as usual, Valhar. Please extend our compliments to the cooks," said Shalina.

Next was the dessert: a Namiran dessert of coffee cake with a generous dollop of rich whipped cream. The servants withdrew from the dining hall after serving it. They had been there long enough to know when their presence wasn't needed—or wanted. By the time Harto finished his portion, he felt as stuffed as a roasted fowl and as heavy as a log.

"I need to stop eating like this," he groaned.

Peras smiled. "Why didn't you pass your dessert to me? I had such horrible food while I was away."

"Sorry, uncle, but that dessert was to die for."

"So, what was the purpose of your trip this time?" asked Shalina. Her eyes were serious; Harto knew this was a side of her she never showed the outside world.

Peras's smile slid off his face. "Two of our people didn't report in."

Harto and his mother went still.

"It's possible they're dead."

Shalina leaned back from the table looking exhausted and haunted.

Harto felt like throwing up. "There's no way we can verify if…if she has them?"

"If she does, or did, I hope they're dead by now," replied Peras gravely. He pushed his empty dessert dish away.

"So, what happens now?" asked Shalina.

"Harto and I will discuss it with the minister of intelligence, but I believe they're reluctant to risk sending any more agents to Namira. Too many have been caught, and none have made it back alive." Peras rubbed his face wearily. Harto noticed the grey hairs that were increasing in number in his uncle's once night-black hair.

"I saw Novice Britea D'Tranell in the market today. She wasn't alone."

"Who was with her?" asked Shalina.

"What were they doing?" asked Peras at the same time.

"Apparently, they'd been shopping. Britea was with a Weltonian girl by the name of Danai Riverun, and get this: Danai has been in training at Syla College for the past four years, *and* she's a tier-five wielder."

Both Shalina and Peras shared a puzzled look. "You're sure she's Weltonian?" asked Shalina.

"Absolutely. She confirmed it. Uncle, you didn't know about this?"

Peras wore a disturbed expression. "No…no, I didn't. That doesn't make sense. The last Weltonian students I know of were those who created the college eight hundred years ago. Why would one join now after all this time?"

"Why didn't Headmaster Clayre report this to Malaquey intelligence?" asked Harto.

Shalina snorted as she poured a generous amount of wine into her glass. "And why should he? It's not as if he's hiding her now, is it? One Weltonian joins the college for the first time in eight hundred years. So what? Besides, it's wielder business, and we know how well they handle their affairs. Just recall what they did to my Namira." She took a big gulp of wine. Peras and Harto shared a worried look. This was her fourth glass this evening.

"Mother…" began Harto tentatively.

She held up a hand, stopping him. "I know."

He fell silent. She reluctantly let go of the glass of wine and stood up. The men stood as well. "Stay and talk my boys; I will be going to bed. It's been a long day."

Harto kissed her on the cheeks, as did her brother. They waited until she had left the room before taking up the conversation again.

"I wonder if we made a mistake telling her about the missions," said Peras.

Harto shook his head. "We didn't. Namira is her home. She may not be an agent in the field, but she's a fighter, just like us." He clenched his fists in frustration.

"Why won't Malaquey do more against that witch queen? Why won't they help us?!"

Peras gave his nephew a stern look. "King Wilhem gave thousands of us shelter when he didn't have to in addition to protecting us and letting us become part of the Naval Intelligence Agency. Many of his lords argued against it, but he convinced them."

"I know but—"

"But nothing!" snarled Peras, frightening Harto. "It's because of King Wilhem that your mother and you can live in this fine house with specially trained Namiran servants and guards, and yet you're ungrateful?!"

Harto looked down, full of shame. "I'm sorry, uncle."

Peras sighed and then clamped a reassuring hand on his nephew's shoulder. "I apologize for my outburst, my lord."

Harto shot his uncle a stunned look. "Please…please don't call me that."

Peras smiled sadly at him. "Someday, you will reclaim what's rightfully yours. But in the meantime, you need to be patient." The older man stood wearily.

"We both need to sleep. We have an early start tomorrow."

"Yes, uncle." Yet after Peras left, Harto sat alone for a long time, thinking of a homeland he had never seen.

CHAPTER 8

Malie's one remaining good eye snapped open. Something was about to happen. He didn't have long to wait before the doors opened and several humans walked in. His scales trembled in fear and rage as he recognized their uniforms: violet tunics, wine-colored pants, and flowing, hooded black capes with blood-red edgings.

Her Specialists.

Malie had watched them *experiment* on his broodmates when they had outlived their usefulness. The queen and her Specialists had been the cause of their deaths.

He wondered if today he was going to join his siblings.

The sea serpent kept still as the queen descended the stairs. Her purple-clad guards knelt and bowed their covered heads as she passed them. She reached the white stone altar, then turned and raised her right hand.

"Reveal yourselves, my children."

The kneeling Specialists pushed back their hoods but remained kneeling.

Queen Kallesa's smile broadened when she saw the hunger on their faces. "Today, is a special day, my children. Today, I grant you another taste of what awaits us all. Bring in the captives."

Malie turned his head in time to see three prisoners being dragged in, each of whom had two Specialists guarding them. His eye widened when he realized they were Dyhaeri. Two males and one female. Something was wrong.

They looked terrified and defiant at the same time. *Why weren't they wielding?* Then he saw the odd golden bracelets on their bruised arms. Malie heard one of them gasp. He turned his head slightly to see the female Dyhaeri staring at him, shock on her face.

"We have here three Dyhaeri scouts who wandered too close to our waters." The queen smiled coldly as she approached the prisoners. The Dyhaeri cringed at her closeness but stayed silent. Malie noticed the single female Dyhaeri looked livid.

"As is commonly known, all Dyhaeri are wielders. So, who better to use in this important ceremony?" Her Specialists nodded, keeping their hungry eyes on the unfortunate three Dyhaeri. Queen Kallesa used her fire runes to open the altar compartment and withdrew two armlets this time. Malie felt his heart sink; he knew what was going to happen next.

The queen beckoned to the two Specialists holding one of the male Dyhaeri. They dragged him forward. He struggled in silence, but he was no match for the two guards. However, they were unable to lift him onto the altar.

"Hold him in place." Queen Kallesa stepped forward with the two armlets.

"Betrayer of blood!" The female Dyhaeri shocked everyone in the chamber, including Malie, with her shout. "We didn't enter your borders! You snatched us from our own territory!"

Like she did to my siblings and me , thought Malie as he watched the words stop Queen Kallesa in her tracks. The queen stared at the indignant female Dyhaeri for a moment, then she slowly strode over to her.

"You have no honor! You are a liar and kinslayer! May the Dark Sister take you!"

Queen Kallesa cruelly gripped her face. "What is your name?"

"I will not share my name with a traitor!"

A dangerous glint appeared in the queen's eyes. Her fingers glowed brighter and brighter as she slowly began to burn the Dyhaeri's skin, yet the captive refused to cry out, though her tears flowed freely.

Not a sound escaped from the Dyhaeri's lips. Malie noticed some of the Specialists looked a bit squeamish. Long moments passed before Queen Kallesa stopped. The Dyhaeri almost passed out from pain.

"She goes first." The queen's voice was dark and cold. "Let's not waste her abilities, shall we?"

Queen Kallesa began to attach the armlet to the badly burnt Dyhaeri, and though weakened, the female Dyhaeri began to speak in her language. Malie pressed his head against the side of his glass tank to better hear the words.

"...how is a god born? In silence or in fire? Or as the waters of life rise up or as the earth is rent asunder? Surely, the rest of the world shall not survive the labor pains. A thousand years shall pass before one lost child of the seas shall go mad and attempt to ascend. This will mark the end of all that is and all that is to be. Unless the mad child is stopped by the One and the Three.

Ah, we see you, listener. Your eyes ask, whom we do speak of?

These four individuals come from different worlds. One is the lost heir, another is the teacher, the third will be the catalyst, and the fourth will be the sacrifice."

Queen Kallesa shot her an unreadable look and activated the armlet. The Dyhaeri cursed the queen as the device began to glow blue. The prisoner held eye contact with the queen even as her body began to jerk from the growing pain. The Specialists let go as her body flopped to the hard concrete floor, yet the dying Dyhaeri never once broke eye contact with the Immortal Queen.

"May…your name…fade…into obscurity." Those were the Dyhaeri's last words as life left her body. The cold hatred in the queen's eyes was unnerving. Silence fell as she stared at the dead body for what seemed an eternity. Malie glanced at the two surviving Dyhaeri; a combination of sadness and pride shone in their faces as they looked at their dead comrade.

Queen Kallesa finally growled a name, and one of the kneeling Specialists stood and ran forward. Malie could see he was terrified of his monarch even as he tried to ignore the dead Dyhaeri.

"Paren, are you ready for my gift?" The Specialist flinched as if she was offering him poison. Malie's eyes narrowed at his expression; some part of the human must still realize the queen was a maniacal, terrifying leader. *So, why did he still serve her?*

"Y…yes, my queen."

The queen snapped her fingers, and two other Specialists took hold of his arms. One exposed Paren's right arm, and he began to breathe heavily. The queen tore the blue glowing armlet from the dead Dyhaeri and attached it to herself. She closed her eyes in a long moment of bliss as she fed on the power of the dead captive.

Queen Kallesa finally opened her eyes and attached the second armlet to a perspiring Paren. She drew a fire rune into the second armlet and then the transfer of power began. The Specialist grimaced as the power flowed into him, then his expression was replaced by one of ecstasy.

Malie saw the looks of disgust and horror on the faces of the remaining two Dyhaeri. He didn't blame them. Each time he witnessed this ceremony, he felt like throwing up, especially when he knew what followed. His attention was abruptly returned to the ceremony when Queen Kallesa suddenly stopped the transfer. Paren cried out in despair. His hunger for more shone in his eyes.

"Shh." The queen placed a well-manicured finger on his lips. "Soon, we will have all the power we need. This gift will get you there." She glanced at the others. "We will all get there."

She called forth another name, and a second eager Specialist ran to take Paren's place. The queen repeated the process until the power in the armlet was depleted. Then the next Dyhaeri was dragged forward, and Queen Kallesa waited for the captive to say something. He just glared at her.

"No final words like your stupid comrade?"

"May your name fade into obscurity." The two remaining Dyhaeri said it at the same time, repeating it like a chant. Malie thought it was interesting how the queen's face turned a funny shade of red. She had definitely walked into that one.

He could see she itched to burn both Dyhaeri to the ground, but she needed to complete the ceremony. She attached the armlet even as the Dyhaeri kept chanting. Queen Kallesa punched one of the Dyhaeri hard in the gut, but he continued chanting the moment he recovered. Even, when the queen triggered the armlet and the pain started, he didn't stop.

A furious Queen Kallesa shared the power she collected with more of her acolytes, then repeated the procedure with the last Dyhaeri. He was unfortunate to receive a few hard slaps across the face from the angry queen, but that didn't stop him from chanting the infuriating words.

She appeared slightly mollified when the third Dyhaeri was dead. "Store the Solarian bracelets." Malie's internal ears quivered at those words. He noticed how reluctant the acolytes were to handle the strange jewelry. He suspected those had been what the queen had used to inhibit the Dyhaeri's wielding abilities.

"And now, my children, it's time to practice." She turned her cold green eyes on Malie. The sea serpent's heart rate rose in terror. Part of him hoped he died this time, but the rest of him knew she would keep him alive for more pain and torment.

It didn't take long before Malie's screams rent the air.

#

"And what is this used for?" Lanead pointed at a small spoon in the carefully arranged cutlery set.

"For stirring tea, but not sipping," promptly replied Kahl. Behind Lanead, Mat rolled his eyes. The cousins were in the captain's cabin. Their topic today was court etiquette.

"Mat, please pay attention," continued the captain without turning.

Kahl fought to suppress a smile. Mat thought learning about how humans interacted at the dinner table was a waste of time, but to his credit, Mat was learning faster than Kahl.

"And this one?" The captain pointed at a small three-pronged instrument.

"That's for desserts."

"All kinds of desserts?"

"Um...no, for the baked ones, like cakes or pastries."

Lanead nodded. "Very good." He began to clear the table to Kahl's surprise. "I think you have learned enough about the humans' eating habits."

"Thank the Mother," muttered Mat. Kahl ignored his cousin. He'd seen the mischievous glint in Captain Riverun's eyes.

"That's because it's time for your next lesson in court etiquette."

Mat frowned at the glee in the captain's voice. "Which is?"

Lanead stood and hummed a tune on the way to the door, beckoning for the two Dyhaeri to follow. They did as bid. Once on deck, Kahl noticed two things. One, most of the crew were present, and two, they were decked out in the most colorful, ridiculous outfits he had ever seen.

"Welcome, my young princes, to a royal ball!" announced Lanead gleefully. At his words, a group of crew members in one corner began to play stringed instruments. The dancers separated into rows of men and women facing each other. As the music played, the two lines moved forward, curtsied in time with the beat, then danced backwards, each individual twirling round at the end.

Kahl's jaw dropped while Mat gaped at the dancers. The Dyhaeri marine was the first to recover.

"No. By the Deep, no..."

"Oh yes," said Lanead, his eyes twinkling. He danced backwards into the two moving rows of female and male dancers who swayed as they faced each other. As the beat changed, partners were chosen, and soon, couples were twirling around the deck-turned-dance floor.

Kahl and Mat kept watching in equal parts amazement and horror as the Weltonians danced.

"There is no way we can learn this. We'll need months!"

Mat nodded, his countenance grim. "You couldn't pay me to learn those steps. It seems...painful."

Lanead finally left his partner, who joined her group of dancers when the couples separated to form the two swaying lines.

"So, what do you think?"

"No," said the two Dyhaeri at the same time.

The captain's grin grew wider. "Excellent answer. But, we all have to do things we don't like." He went to stand beside the puzzled cousins and added, "There is no way you can learn these steps in the time you have left."

"And how much time is that?" demanded Mat. Kahl shot his cousin an exasperated look. *Could he not sound less aggressive?*

"I don't know, but the high priest gave me the impression you'll be moving out soon."

"So, why are we watching your crew dancing?" asked Kahl respectfully.

"Because, I don't want you gawking like tourists when the Malaquey nobles try to bedazzle you with their flashy clothes and fancy steps."

Mat stared at the captain when his tone turned hard.

"Most of the nobles at court are vipers. They're only interested in furthering their personal goals and have no love for the poor and unfortunate. To deal with the nobles, it is best that you appear aloof and unimpressed by their performances, and if they ask you for a dance…" Lanead gave Mat an expectant look.

"Refuse," said Mat thoughtfully.

Lanead nodded.

Kahl frowned. "But won't that be rude?"

"And why would you refuse?" Lanead didn't even acknowledge the younger Dyhaeri. Kahl felt uneasy as he watched the exchange between the captain and his cousin. This felt like some sort of test.

Mat looked at the Weltonians dancing, seemingly reluctant to reply.

"Come on, don't be shy," coaxed Lanead in a deceptively calm voice.

"Because then we'd be performing for the Malaquey court."

Lanead sighed. "Mat, you might just survive court life after all." He glanced at Kahl. "You, on the other hand, better learn fast."

Kahl blinked. This lesson was…confusing.

"This is the crew's down time. You can watch or not. It's up to you." The captain wandered off.

Kahl watched him go while trying to sort out his maelstrom of thoughts. At times, he could swear the captain was saying one thing while meaning another.

Was he trying to prepare them for court by behaving like a noble? Had the captain lived in Malaquey for a long time? And why? He was Weltonian.

He turned to put his questions to Mat, but to his amazement, his cousin was among the male dancers trying to mimic their steps.

"What in the Abyss…?" He ran up to his cousin. "What are you doing?"

"Learning." Mat executed a sharp turn and almost fell as he tried to keep in time with the dancers.

"But…but you said you didn't want to learn!"

"I know. It *is* interesting though and fairly complicated." Mat tried another step, then grinned as he almost got it right. "This is fun!"

Kahl stared at him. His cousin was actually smiling with joy. He watched Mat for a while then smiled in return. Then a thought crossed his mind.

I never asked Britea if she likes to dance. Maybe I should learn…in case I meet her again.

"You're right, it looks like fun."

#

From the helm above, Lanead observed and smiled as he watched the two Dyhaeri laughing while trying to learn how to dance.

Let them be innocent a bit longer.

#

Britea knew something was wrong the moment she stepped into the social studies class. Students had clustered around Lianne and her two lady friends; their voices dropped to a whisper as they frequently glanced in her direction. None of the looks were kind.

What now?

She hoped never to find out. Britea had been at the school for six weeks and was still settling in. She knew things would have been a bit smoother if not for Lianne's antics.

"What's going on?" whispered Henrick as Britea sat down next to him.

She was mildly surprised. "I should be asking you. I thought you knew all the secrets."

"Not really. That group has been gossiping like mad since I walked in, but I have no clue what about. I must say though, it sure picked up when you appeared."

"Is that so?" Britea tried to hide her despair. She had an inkling of what they were talking about. At that moment, Lianne turned her pretty head and looked at Britea; her smile was absolutely malicious.

"Good morning, class," said Instructor Teron Dawn as he breezed into class. Those not seated hurried to their spots.

"Good morning!" chorused the class.

"Today we're going to discuss the structure of the Malaquey government." Britea forced herself to turn to the front of the class, all the while aware of the girls behind her.

"We all know who the king is…" he paused and regarded the class. "I hope." This was met by a few nervous giggles.

"So, we'll start from the bottom of the rung this time, shall we? First question: which group of people occupy the lowest rung but hold the most power in Malaquey?"

Britea blinked and shared a puzzled look with Henrick. That question didn't make sense. She glanced around, and everyone including Lianne appeared dumbfounded.

"Come on. You lot are supposed to be smart. Give me an answer?"

"The Merchant's Guild?"

Instructor Dawn laughed. "Wrong answer, even though it is true that, collectively, they make more money than the king himself. Now, think again."

The students began to murmur among themselves; some began to open books as if searching for the answer.

The instructor shook his head. "You won't find it in any textbook. Let me give you a hint. When you go into town, you see them, you walk among them, most times you probably ignore them, and most of you *are* them."

Something clicked in Britea's mind. "The common people." From the corner of her eye, she saw Lianne glare at her.

Instructor Dawn clapped. "And at last, one bright mind amongst the dullards speaks. Yes, it's the common people, and why is that?"

Britea thought fast as she recalled a quote she had read in an old book in the library about revolutions. "Those that are ruled may not have wealth or property, but they possess two things their rulers should never take for granted: discontent and numbers. One may suppress them or murder them, but combine their thirst for revenge with their overwhelming majority, and you get the perfect recipe for a bloody revolution."

The instructor raised an eyebrow. "Ah, someone's been reading the memoirs of Helia Weldrass. Can anyone tell me who that is and why she's important?"

"The rebel leader who caused the Great Civil War of 399 AC, which led to the splitting of the Olderian Empire into the Kingdom of Namira to the south and the Republic of Malaquey to the north," answered Britea once again.

The instructor grinned. "This one is quick on her feet. Don't get left behind class. Now, I know this isn't your history class. But, to know how our current government works, you need to know this fundamental truth. Never take for granted the power of a mob. When Helia protested the plight of the working class, she led a mob that later grew into a well-trained army. That's how they brought down an empire."

He looked at each student before continuing. "As our nation grows, our leaders have tried to keep in mind that the common people need to be taken seriously…always. If, for instance, a wielder didn't adhere to the Creed and attacked civilians, there would be nothing stopping those same civilians from storming and burning this college to the ground."

He paused to let his words sink in.

"In three to four years, some of you will be on your Year of Discovery. That's when you need to be on your guard and be on the best behavior of your life."

Britea wondered if Lianne even knew what the word meant.

"Now, will someone apart from Novice D'Tranell explain what our government is?"

"It's a constitutional and democratic monarchy," replied Henrick.

"Meaning?" Instructor Dawn searched the class.

"While the title to the throne is inherited, it's not guaranteed unless the elected governors and ministers agree with the monarch's selection of the heir," answered another student.

"Exactly. Some of you are wondering why I'm bringing this up. Well, that's because in exactly one month, we will witness the election for the local minister for the district of Syla."

Britea's eyes widened.

"That's right. Our district. This class is going to be at the ballot boxes to observe democracy at work, something our neighbors in Namira still lack. Now, I see disinterest in some of your faces, which is why I am declaring this exercise an assessment. Anyone not at the election site will fail this class."

There were cries of dismay at this. Britea tried to hide her smile as Lianne complained loudly that she had plans. The instructor was unperturbed.

"Furthermore, after I've confirmed your presence at the polling station, you will each write an essay of nothing less than twelve thousand words on how it impacted you."

"What?!" yelped a student behind a stunned Britea. "How are we going to write that much? There isn't much to write about elections!"

Instructor Dawn's smile was serene. "Then you better find something. Now, let's discuss how the far-off districts and towns govern without the eye of the Malaquey court on them."

#

"Take one step forward! Look at your partner. Curtsy slowly." Britea felt her lower back and knees ache as she tried to copy the dance instructor.

"No, no D'Tranell! You need to appear as graceful as a swan," chided Instructor Helene Droye before moving away to check on another pair of students.

"Or stay as awkward as a cow," commented Lianne, standing opposite Britea. The words were met with snickers while Britea went hot with embarrassment.

"What was that you said, Lady Arkei?" asked the instructor airily.

"I was just saying how hard Britea has been working to learn this particular move," lied Lianne smoothly as she gracefully turned and curtsied.

The instructor nodded, approval on her face. "See how clean that move was Britea? You would never find a more perfect dance partner than Lady Arkei. I see placing you beside her *was* the best idea. Learn all you can from her."

Lianne returned the instructor's smile with an innocent, wide-eyed expression.

Britea forced herself not to glare at the teacher. Of all the classes, this was her least favorite. One, she thought it was wholly unnecessary, and two, Lianne was the instructor's pet and could do no wrong. It was here Lianne was at her most cruel because Britea was her partner. It had been clear from the beginning that dancing at court was a far cry from dancing at village-square parties. Britea wished she had protested when Instructor Droye had asked Lianne to teach Britea. At first, she had been stunned when the noble had accepted, then that had turned to dismay when the cruel pranks had begun. Lianne would *teach* her a dance move, and when Britea performed it, the other students would laugh at her because she did it incorrectly.

Because Lianne had taught her the wrong steps.

She dared not report her to the dumb instructor, so she tentatively asked Danai to teach her how to dance. Danai agreed and even got Navos and Lexia to help. So now Britea was stuck continuing to pretend Lianne was teaching her how to dance.

Britea glanced at the large chronometer on the wall. Twenty-five minutes to go, then a twenty-minute recess before her junior wielding class. By the Maker, she wished she was there already!

"Worried about your next class, peasant?" asked Lianne with a cruel smile.

Britea swallowed back the angry retort. "We all have places to be soon." She willed the clock to move faster.

"Oh, is that so?" Lianne's eyes glittered. "I heard a strange rumor about your wielding."

Britea barely caught herself from stumbling. "What?"*Oh no, she knows about Kahl.*

"I hear you're stuck in the junior classes because you still can't wield even a tier-one form." Lianne waited for a reaction. Her eye's narrowed when Britea didn't say a word.

"Are you deaf as well as stupid? Did you not hear what I just said?"

Britea blinked. She had been so relieved the rumor was about her junior class that she hadn't realized she was supposed to be upset. "Oh, that. Uh…yes, I'm in that class."

Lianne glared at her, clearly unhappy with her reaction. "So, what are you doing there?"

"You'd have to ask Instructor Shelley," Britea saw Lianne go a bit pale. *Ah, so the noble did fear someone* . "I'm sure she'd be delighted to answer your questions." She didn't bother hiding a grin at Lianne's disgruntled expression, which only further infuriated the noble.

"I'll have you kicked out of this school if it's the last thing I do."

Britea had always wondered about Lianne's anger, and she could no longer hold her tongue. "What did I ever do to you?"

Lianne was taken aback by the question for a moment.

"Ever since we've met, you've been nasty to me. So, I'm asking you why."

Lady Arkei's cruel smile returned. "Oh, is the poor peasant girl about to cry?" She said it loud enough for the nearby students to hear. "Is it because she can't wield even tier-one forms and will soon be kicked out of the college?"

Britea was getting irritated with the speculative looks being sent her way. Her eyes soon strayed to the pitcher of water on the teacher's desk.

"Maybe if she demonstrated, then we would all know she wasn't a fraud." There was a challenging light in Lianne's eyes.

Britea could feel the heat rising and she was sorely tempted to wipe that smile off Lianne's face with a giant tier-three orb of water. To the Deep with the Creed.

Then the bell rang.

"Well done, class. See you all tomorrow!" The instructor left the class before the students, clearly in a hurry.

Lianne smiled coldly. "As I thought, all peasants are cowards and frauds." She turned to walk away. Britea felt something snap within her. She had tried to keep out of trouble, she had tried to be nice, and she had tried to ignore every insult thrown her way.

"Helia Weldrass was a blacksmith from a small village," said Britea, a challenging tone in her voice. Lianne and the other nearby students stopped in their tracks.

"Meaning?" asked Valerie as she and Pearl walked over to stand on either side of Lianne.

"Meaning, she was also a peasant, but she led an army that brought down an empire. I'm just shocked you've forgotten that lesson already, Lady Arkei."

Lianne's face went pale with fury as other students *oohed* and nodded approvingly in Britea's direction.

"Are you trying to threaten me?" demanded Lianne.

Britea walked up to her. "I don't have to. It's clear that you, a noble, are already threatened by me, a peasant."

"Watch your tongue—" began Pearl.

"Or what?" challenged Britea without looking at her. "What are you three going to do to a single peasant girl you're clearly scared of?"

"Tell them, sister," encouraged a female student

"Fight me? Wield at me? Or just scold me?"

Lianne clenched her fists and Valerie grabbed one of them, only to have her friend shove her away.

"Come on, Lianne" goaded Britea. "I'm standing right here."*In most battles, let your enemy be the first to attack. Then you respond as needed.* She could hear Weapons Master Caren's voice in her mind.

Pearl and Valerie backed away from Lianne. The looks on their faces said they knew something terrible was about to happen.

Britea kept still. Lianne had to make the first move.

"You'll pay for this..." began Lianne, and from the corner of her eye, Britea saw the pitcher of water began to vibrate.

"What are you all still doing here?" The students all jumped when Warden Asteros suddenly walked into the class. His expression changed when he saw Lianne and Britea facing off. "I want an answer, now." The warden's voice was hard and unforgiving.

Britea decided to take the plunge. "Lianne was just about to show me a dance step. She's been an excellent teacher during my time in this class."

The warden's eyes narrowed as he stared at Britea for a long moment. Then, he turned his thousand-yard stare on Lianne. She nodded quickly.

"Yes, it was just dancing, nothing more."

The warden glared at the two, then at the other scared students, who kept silent. "Fine. Get to your recess, and no dancing on the way. Is that clear?"

"Yes, warden," chorused the class as they fled from his presence. Britea made sure she went in the opposite direction from Lianne and her friends. She knew the warden had seen through her lie. At the same time, Lianne was going to be even more mad at her for saving her noble hide.

This was far from over.

#

The short recess came and went like a dream, and then it was time for the last class of the day: junior wielding class. Britea released a sigh of relief as she opened the door. Most of the students were already present.

"Hello, Britea!" She smiled as she responded to the numerous greetings from the juniors. To be honest, she was more relaxed in this class than the others. None of the novices looked down on her, and at times, some of them even asked her for advice. She had wondered why, but one look at the stern face of Instructor Shelley had given her the answer. But Britea wasn't scared of the senior wielder. For the past six weeks, she had been partnered with the instructor and had learned how to hold tier-one and two forms for far longer periods. She knew there was a lot more to learn, but she found herself liking the pace.

"Good afternoon, Instructor Shelley," chorused the class as said instructor stormed in as if on the warpath.

Uh oh, thought Britea when she saw the expression on the teacher's face. *Who had been crazy enough to upset her?* Instructor Shelley's eyes scanned the class before settling on Britea.

By the Deep, it was me!

"Britea D'Tranell, may I have a word?" Her voice was calm, but her eyes were steel.

With her heart racing, Britea silently stood up and followed the instructor outside the class.

The door had barely closed before the instructor began.

"What happened at your dancing class today?"

"I—"

Instructor Shelley held up a finger, cutting her off. "And don't tell me it was just Lady Arkei teaching you how to dance!"

Britea bit down on her lower lip and looked at the floor. That had spread fast.

"Novice D'Tranell, you will tell me the truth!"

Britea's heart slowed down as anger replaced her fear. "The truth? Do I have your permission to speak freely then, Instructor Shelley?"

The instructor folded her arms. "You do."

"I hate dancing. I always have, even in Weldaros. My feet are too clumsy, and I know I'm not much to look at, so I didn't bother learning. I understand why I'm in the junior wielding class, and I truly appreciate how you're trying to ease me into your method of teaching. But what I don't see is the point of the dancing classes. It's not going to stop an enemy from trying to kill me, and it certainly won't help me further my wielding education. So, why do I have to do it?"

Instructor Shelley gave her a thoughtful look. "Is that why you tried to pick a fight with Lianne?"

"She started it! Ever since I entered that class six weeks ago, she's been calling me names, making fun of the fact that I'm the daughter of peasants, and goading me about my so-called wielding ability. Today, she called me a fraud and a coward and swore she would kick me out of this school. So, I got tired of taking it and reminded her of when Helia Weldrass, a blacksmith, brought down an empire."

"Then what happened?"

"She asked if I was threatening her, and I said there was no need to since she was already scared of me."

To her surprise, Instructor Shelley grinned. "I bet she didn't like that one bit."

"Um…no," agreed a stunned Britea.

"Tell me what else happened." The instructor was silent as she listened to the rest of the encounter.

The female instructor sighed as Britea finished her story. "Is Instructor Droye aware of the bullying?"

"No," replied Britea "Lianne is always careful to do it out of eye and earshot."

"I see. Starting from today, you need to be more careful…"

Britea stared at her. *Why was she being made to feel at fault here?*

The instructor continued "…however, while I commend you for not giving in to the urge to wield an orb of water in her face, I still must stress the risk you took in goading her to wield first."

"She would have been punished—" began Britea.

"Or she could have killed you!"

That shut her up.

Instructor Shelley continued. "The Arkeis are one of the oldest and most influential noble families in Malaquey. She would have made up some excuse, said it was an accident, and her family would have stepped in to prevent her from getting the harshest punishment. You need to be smart with the enemies you make, my dear. At times, we wait, and then when the time is right, we react. Accordingly. Never, ever mistake restraint for weakness. Do you understand?"

"I understand," said Britea, subdued.

Instructor Shelley placed a gentle hand on her chin and lifted her head upwards. "Consider this a lesson. Now, let's return to class. We'll talk more about this later."

The whole class turned as one, expectant looks on their faces.

"Juniors, I have news. Starting now, Britea will be my assistant instructor."

Britea snapped her head around to stare at the instructor. "What?"

"There will be times when I will be called away, so Britea will fill in for me. What do you all think?"

"Yes!" yelled the happy students. Britea was left speechless. Instructor Shelley lifted a large book and handed it to her. She glanced at the cover. *The Basics of Teaching Wielding, Volume 1* by Pras Val-Taros.

"Study every page. After each class here, you and I will practice for an extra hour." Instructor Shelley waited for a response.

"I…I…thank you?" Britea was still not sure what to make of it all.

"Good. We'll start today."

CHAPTER 9

"Master Engineer Stamets, I must say, the ships are coming along rather nicely." Queen Kallesa smiled at the relieved expression on the terrified Namiran's face. She turned back to examine the bustling covered shipyard as a small army of workers swarmed over the almost completed hulls of three oddly shaped behemoths. The one closest to her was the prototype. Once it had been tested and demonstrated adequate mobility and speed, it had been taken apart to make copies of its parts for the two other special ships. Then the two new ships were assembled simultaneously.

"How soon will they be ready for a test run?"

"Three months…" his voice trailed off when he saw the smile disappear from her face. "Two months, Your Highness," he said, quickly correcting himself.

The smile returned. "Maybe you're not as incompetent as I had feared. However, in the meantime, a squad of my Specialists will stay and keep watch."

The engineer went so pale she hoped he would faint. "I…is that necessary, Your Highness?" His eyes darted to the silent guards clad in violet encircling the queen.

Queen Kallesa arched a brow at his question. For a moment, she was mildly surprised at his boldness.

Master Engineer Stamets bowed deeply. "Forgive me, Your Highness. I spoke out of turn." The silence lengthened. "I…I wasn't thinking."

The queen sighed. She was in an unusually good mood today. "Do stand up, Stamets. I tire of looking down at you."

The engineer straightened instantly. Queen Kallesa snapped her fingers, and a squad of her Specialists peeled off and positioned themselves around the scared Namiran.

"I shall be checking on your progress twice a week, Master Stamets. Don't fail me." Her cold smile made the poor man sweat. She turned away as the engineer walked away surrounded by his new, eerie guards. The queen leaned on the railing, taking in her new, unique ships.

#

"Captain Riverun?"

Sonei stopped writing in her logbook to acknowledge her first mate.

"The Dyhaeri are inbound."

"Thanks, Erike. Prepare to drop anchor. I'll be out shortly." She closed the book and opened the special compartment of her desk. Within it were two letters. Selecting the top one, she rose and left her quarters. Many of the crew were on the top deck going about their duties. None stopped to gawk at the approaching Dyhaeri. The Weltonians had encountered so many Dyhaeri they were no longer an oddity.

Sonei collected the spyglass from First Mate Erike as she moved to the portside of the *Wandering Star*. Immediately, she spied movement in the water. She frowned.

"That's odd. There are three of them."

"Why is that?" asked her first mate, who appeared worried.

"Maybe they're scouts." She tried to suppress her own concern. "It's probably nothing to worry about."

Erike gave her a dubious look.

In a heartbeat, the three Dyhaeri reached the anchored ship. The Weltonian crew momentarily stopped what they were doing as the Dyhaeri scaled the portside and landed on the deck—and for good reason.

First, there were three Dyhaeri. In the crew's experience, only one Dyhaeri ever boarded. Second, the Dyhaeri radiated a tense, almost hostile body language.

Most times when Sonei encountered Dyaheri, they usually acted nonchalant, as if human-Dyhaeri interactions were boring. But these three Dyhaeri were agitated…she might even say they were scared.

Sonei decided to forgo the usual greeting. "May we be of assistance? We do not seek to trade." Erike looked sharply at her. She ignored him.

The three Dyhaeri watched her for a long moment before the apparent leader waved at the two behind him, and the tense atmosphere dissipated.

"I thank you for your kind words. We don't need assistance…at this time."

Sonei's eyes narrowed. Something had happened, but she knew she would have better luck wringing water from a stone then getting information from the Dyhaeri.

"Is there a wielder on board?" asked the Dyhaeri as he settled into the familiar greeting.

First Mate Erike stepped forward. "Air wielder present and accounted for."

"Fine, you may cross our waters." The three turned to leave. Sonei and Erike shared a stunned look. Usually the Dyhaeri spent more time on board, asking about the ports they had visited and the current political atmosphere in the human territories. But this current aberrant behavior was alarming.

"Wait!"

They turned as one to face Sonei.

"I have a letter for Kahl."

The lead Dyhaeri looked surprised. "From who?"

"From Britea D'Tranell," the Dyhaeri's expression turned to one of confusion. Apparently, he didn't recognize the human name.

"Are you able to deliver it for us?" asked Sonei. The three Dyhaeri looked at each other in silence. After a long moment, the leader sighed.

"Wait here. There's someone else who needs to know about this." The three dove off the portside before Sonei could say a world.

"Something has them spooked," said First Mate Erike.

"Whatever it is, it can't be good," agreed Sonei.

#

Their wait wasn't long, which made Sonei wonder just how many Dyhaeri were nearby. More hands gathered on deck as four Dyhaeri climbed over the portside this time. Sonei's breath caught when she caught sight of the half-spear attached to the fourth Dyhaeri approaching her. The Dyhaeri was attractive, but the fierce expression on her face and the weapon at her back disturbed the Weltonian captain. Dyhaeri scouts were rarely armed.

"You have a letter for Kahl? Who are you?"

"I'm Captain Sonei Riverun of the *Wandering Star.* I promised Britea D'Tranell..." The female Dyhaeri's eyes widened at the name. *Ah, someone recognizes Britea. But how?* Sonei continued. "...that I would get the letter to her friend."

The female Dyhaeri extended her hand.

Sonei was suddenly reluctant to give it to her. To be honest, when her daughter's friend had requested Sonei deliver the letter, she had been stunned and a bit curious. Of course, not curious enough to actually read the letter.

"And you are?" asked Sonei. The female Dyhaeri raised an eyebrow as if surprised at being interrogated.

"So that when next I see Britea, I can say whom I delivered the letter to."

To the captain's surprise, a wry smile appeared on the Dyhaeri's face. "I am Commander Almeita, Kahl's mother."

"Oh," said a surprised Sonei as she hastily gave the letter to the Dyhaeri. Sonei could completely understand her attitude now. If some stranger was delivering a letter to her Danai, she would have been even more suspicious.

Commander Almeita studied her son's carefully spelled name on the envelope. She stared at the closed letter for so long Sonei knew the commander was tempted to open it. Then, with a deep sigh, she returned it to the Weltonian captain.

"It is best the letter remains with you."

Sonei was disappointed. She pictured the eagerness on Britea's face when she had asked for it to be delivered.

"And your reason being?" asked the female captain. First Mate Erike shot her an alarmed look, which she ignored.

The commander smiled dryly. "Because right now, my son is on the *Peacekeeper,* whose captain is Lanead Riverun. I believe, he is your—"

"My life mate," finished a stunned Sonei. "Wait, what is Kahl doing on my husband's ship?"

The female commander shook her head. "You will have to discuss it with him. But I have words of warning for your people." The three Dyhaeri behind the commander stared at her.

"Commander Almeita," one of them urgently whispered. The commander lifted a hand without looking at him, and he felt silent.

Sonei was almost speechless at the abrupt change of topic. "Warning?"

"A number of my people have gone missing, and I hear some Weltonian ships have been attacked near the Velreen Strait. Crews were taken captive. I fear the Namirans are hunting us both."

The gathered Weltonian crew began to mutter, worried.

"Thank you for your warning," said a shaken Sonei.

Commander Almeita nodded solemnly. "Be safe, daughter of the sea." Then she and the other three Dyhaeri ran to the portside and dove back into the emerald-blue waters.

"Erike."

The first mate turned to his captain, who had a steely look in her eyes.

"Haul the anchor and maintain full speed to the designated meeting place."

"Aye, captain." Erike barked orders to the gathered crew, who promptly disappeared to their posts. Sonei stepped towards the railing and stared out at the deep blue sea.

#

"So, what do you think?"

Kahl and Mat stared at the drawing on the table before them, then shared an uneasy look. They were currently in the deserted mess hall so they could stay out of the way of the busy deck crew. Captain Lanead had taught as many lessons here as he had in his office. At first, Mat and Kahl had been uneasy at being cooped up in such a small space. However, in time, the two gradually adapted to the close quarters,

"Come on, I don't have all day," complained Diev, the diminutive Weltonian as he impatiently tapped his right foot.

Kahl tried to think of a polite way of sharing his opinion.

"It's hideous," said Mat. Kahl rolled his eyes. Trust his cousin to state the obvious.

To their surprise, Diev nodded.

"I thought so myself, but I hear this is the latest fashion at court."

Kahl turned his attention back to the drawing. It depicted a male human in a white puffy shirt, open from the neck to halfway down the chest, with billowing sleeves. The lower gear was just as ridiculous, with indigo-blue pantaloons covered in frills from midcalf to ankle. The figure wore pointed-toe sandals.

"I'm not wearing that," said Mat. "How in the Deep can one move with that much material attached to the ankles? And the footwear is nothing short of torture!"

"You should see what the women are wearing," said the Weltonian tailor dryly. "Well, since we're in agreement, I would like you to consider these designs." He brought out more drawings from a large leather folder.

These were quite different. The first showed a simple short-sleeved, button-up, night-blue tunic with a scoop neck. The tunic extended to midthigh, sweeping over long leather pants. Knee-high black leather boots with a slightly raised heel completed the outfit.

Mat and Kahl nodded at the same time.

"Nice," said Kahl.

"Adequate," said Mat reluctantly.

Diev grinned at them. "That shall be for the balls and state dinners you attend. Now, what of these?"

The next set of drawings had the model in a reinforced indigo-blue leather jacket over long pants of the same color. The boots this time extended to above the knees and had greaves from below the knee to the shin.

Kahl was speechless. He knew this outfit.

Mat looked sharply at the smiling tailor. "That looks like a Dyhaeri marine uniform. Where did you get this design?"

"My great-great-great-great grand ancestor. She saw Dyhaeri marines only once, but their uniforms stuck in her mind. Tell me, is that still the same design?"

Mat kept staring at Diev. "Yes. But why are you showing this to us?"

"Because this will be your dress uniform when you meet with the Malaquey Navy. You need to be taken seriously, and this outfit will achieve that."

Mat held up a hand. "You said your ancestor saw Dyhaeri marines once? When and why?"

A loud knock at the door interrupted them. A Weltonian sailor opened the door. "Diev, a ship is inbound!"

"Well, look at that. I'll see you two later." The cheerful tailor quickly gathered up his drawings and scurried out without answering the question.

Mat had a thoughtful expression on his face. "Ever get the feeling we don't know as much about Weltonians as we should?"

Kahl nodded. "All the time. Come on, let's see who's approaching."

#

The deck was a hive of activity. Kahl took note of the expressions on the crew's faces, and they were all excited.

"Must be someone they know?"

"Uh huh," agreed Mat as he strode to the starboard side. Both cousins waited side by side as Mat shaded his eyes to better observe the approaching vessel.

"It's a Weltonian ship. Even our captain is on deck, and I believe this is the first time I've seen him smile."

Kahl nodded. But he found his mind turning to something else entirely.

"Mat, did your mother ever mention a prophecy?"

His cousin turned to him. "Which one? Bear in mind there are several hundred, if not thousand, taught at school."

Kahl couldn't help but grimace. Prophecy had been his worst class. He had barely passed it. History had been different because tomes and tomes of written words of the past existed, and it was all a simple retelling. But literature based on possible futures? That was a nightmare to read, let alone understand or interpret.

"I can see you thinking, cousin. What's wrong?"

Kahl sighed. "I don't know. It's just something my mother said when she found out the high priest had ordered me to train Britea."

Now Mat was interested. "Out with it."

"She said…" he paused. "I can't describe it. It was like she just blurted out what she was thinking even though she didn't mean to."

Mat kept quiet, waiting for him to go on.

"Then she said. '…it must be the prophecy? But this doesn't make sense.'"

Mat raised an eyebrow. "That's it?"

"I'm afraid so."

"And you didn't question her?"

"I did, but she just changed the subject."

Mat was silent for a long moment. "I can't help you there, little cousin. My mother is even more secretive than yours." As he spoke, his gaze followed Captain Riverun. The man seemed to be vibrating with happiness as he stared at the approaching ship.

"Maybe we should ask him."

Kahl whipped his head around to stare at Mat. "Are you insane? We just got on his good side, and you wish to ruin that now?! And why would he know anything about it?"

Mat rubbed his jaw. "Because he's quite informal with our king. Which is odd because Lanead is a mortal, and he's, what, in his early forties? Younger? We both know humans live, at most, to just under a century, and though King Jahlaniin has swum these seas for over eleven hundred cycles, there is still some kind of relationship between them. I say we ask him."

"Mat, I don't think that's a good idea. Besides, maybe it's none of our business…" began Kahl uncertainly.

His cousin turned to stare at him. "Captain Riverun sent a message to the high priest, who came running. Doesn't that make you wonder even a little?"

Kahl found himself agreeing. Lanead was vastly different from other Weltonians. He turned to watch the captain, who was enthusiastically welcoming a lithe, auburn-haired woman. Kahl suspected she and the captain were close. His face flushed when they kissed to the cheers of the gathered crew. Kahl averted his eyes to give them privacy.

Mat kept looking, a curious expression on his face.

Kahl finally answered. "Fine, but I think we should wait for the right time to ask him."

"Or we could ask him now."

"What?! Why?"

"Because they're headed our way." Kahl turned to see Captain Riverun and the female Weltonian bearing down on them.

#

"I'd like you to meet Sonei Riverun, captain of the *Wandering Star.* I am fortunate to be her husband."

The stately, curly-haired woman smiled at her husband then turned back to face the two Dyhaeri.

"I'm Mat-rallenin."

Kahl introduced himself when her gaze turned in his direction. "I'm Kahl, Mat's cousin."

Sonei stared at him for a long moment. "Do you know a girl named Britea D'Tranell?"

Kahl's jaw dropped as Mat gave him a sharp look. Even Lanead looked askance at his wife.

"Um…yes, I do. How do you know her?"

Sonei pulled out an envelope from her jacket. "I met her at Port Trident. She wrote you a letter."

Kahl stared at her outstretched hand. As if in a daze, he took it from her.

"Is she all right? Did she seem well? Is she safe?" He realized he was babbling when Mat, Sonei and Lanead looked at him with concern.

Kahl tried to calm down. "I apologize. It's just that when last we saw each other…well, the situation was precarious to say the least." Lanead's gaze flicked to Mat, whose face was blank.

Sonei's expression softened. "She appeared well and happy, though eager for you to get her letter, and I believe she is quite safe at the college."

Kahl felt the pressure ease in his chest. "Thank you. I am grateful for the delivery. If you would all excuse me." He gave the two Weltonian captains a bow and walked away, letter in hand. Mat watched him go, then looked at the captains. Clearly, he wanted to talk to them. Eventually though, he just sighed.

"I'll stay with him. Until later," he said nodding at the two Weltonians before hurrying after his dazed cousin.

"Lanead," began Sonei in a deceptively calm voice.

"Yes, wife," replied Lanead, answering warily.

"We need to talk. Right now."

#

Lanead knew his wife was upset, and she had every reason to be. But this had not been his fault.

Not all of it anyway.

"I can explain," he started once they were alone in their quarters. His beautiful, stern-looking wife folded her arms and kept silent, though her eyes warned him to hurry up.

"Jahlaniin arrived on the *Peacekeeper* four weeks ago and warned me they'd found the final player in the prophecy and that we had to start the training at once. High Priest Myltan and the Sisters were also part of it. And there was no way I could send word to you without risking the message being intercepted."

Sonei bit her lip as if conceding the point. "And let me guess, the final player is Britea D'Tranell?"

"Yes. I never thought you'd meet her." Lanead looked thoughtful. "Wait, how exactly did you meet her?"

Sonei closed her eyes briefly. "Our daughter is her mentor and roommate. She brought her to the *Wandering Star* to introduce her. Danai was hoping I could deliver Britea's letters to her family in Weldaros and…and to Kahl." She paused to let that sink in before continuing. "Of course, I was curious as to how Britea had come to know a Dyhaeri. Then she said she was a late wielder, and I still thought it was just a coincidence…until she said a Dyhaeri had taught her how to wield."

Lanead went pale. "The Sea Mother is devious."

His wife prayed urgently. “Sea Mother, please forgive him.” Sonei glared at Lanead. “Don’t say things like that! You’re just begging for bad fortune.” Sonei ran a weary hand through her curls. “When I first heard the prophecy, I prayed Danai was not to be part of it, but it looks like this is her destiny. Do Mat and Kahl know what is to come?”

Lanead shook his head.

Sonei sighed. “I hate this. They’re still children, and I feel like they’re being led to the slaughter!”

“You know what the Sisters said. If they know before their time, they all die. That includes Danai. The only thing we can do is prepare them as best as we can.”

Sonei chewed on her fingernail, a sign she was really stressed. “So, it’s begun.”

Lanead walked over to her and rescued her poor fingers.

“We can move closer to Port Trident, so we can get there quickly if she needs us.”

“Before we decide on that, there are some things you need to know.”

Something in her tone made him worry. “What?”

“Kahl’s mother warned me that more of her people, and ours, have been disappearing. They suspect the Namirans are involved.”

Lanead’s worry turned to fear. “Queen Kallesa has never been this bold before. And how are the Dyhaeri planning to respond?”

“She failed to share that with me.”

“Typical.” He replied dryly. “Anything else?”

Sonei sighed wearily. “I received a summons from the Weltonian Elders Council. They’re demanding you and I present ourselves for extensive questioning. I think they’re rather upset with us right now.”

His anger at that erased his fear. He suspected he knew why the Elders Council was being nosy, but he had to be sure. “What did the summons say?”

Sonei gently grasped his hands. “Danai for one. They demand to know why she’s *really* at Syla. They came close to accusing us of using her to sell our Weltonian wielder teachings to the Malaquey. They also think she’s been too long at the college and are demanding she return to her rightful place in the faction.”

Lanead closed his eyes briefly as he tried to rein in his temper. The coolness of his wife’s hands was doing a fine job of preventing him from blowing his top.

“What else?”

"They're upset we've been helping Namiran refugees escape from Namira. They wish to avoid Queen Kallesa's ire. They reminded me once again of how she tried to cleanse the seas of Weltonians both before and after she became queen."

"I think we need to get word to the council about Queen Kallesa's increasing excursions outside her territories, but I suspect…" He paused and tried to count to ten to keep his temper reigned in "…the elders already know."

"Hush." She gently kissed his lips, then drew back as he reached for her. "You're upset, as am I. I told them to take a hike and that I would get back to them after I completed my trips for the year."

"Wow." He stared at his wife. "That was brilliant." According to Weltonian law, no captain could be called in for questioning during their trading trips unless it was a dire emergency or the captain had committed a heinous crime such as murder. The trading trips were the lifeline of the Weltonian people; without them, they would starve.

"Once I get back from Weldaros, our ships could trade in Port Trident, or close to it," said Sonei. "That way, whenever Danai needs us, we'll be ready. The Elders Council be damned."

Lanead grinned. "Agreed."

His wife's smile was fierce; he loved this woman. Without her, they would have never made it this far. When Sonei kissed him, he forgot everything else.

#

Dear Kahl,

I hope this finds you and your family well and happy. I have been at Syla College for two weeks now, and it has been an interesting experience.

I have been fortunate enough to make a few friends, and they are helping me with my general studies. As for wielding, the instructors have been helpful too. I can't really say much more about it.

I am still trying to get used to the school. It is very different from Weldaros. My village seems so small compared to the college, and even smaller compared to Raven's Fall. My roommate, Danai, feels it is time for me to explore the town. We got permission from our instructor yesterday, so wish us luck.

Kind wishes from Novice Britea D'Tranell of Syla College, Raven's Fall, Malaquey.

Kahl felt both happy and sad as he reached the end of the letter. He was glad to hear from her but sad the letter wasn't longer.

"How is she?"

Kahl was startled by his cousin's atypically soft voice. "She is well. She wrote this only two weeks after being at the college. That was over a month ago." He didn't want to describe the whole letter.

"That's interesting."

Kahl heard something in Mat's voice. "What is it?"

Mat hesitated for a moment, which made Kahl frown. His cousin hardly ever hesitated before speaking his mind.

"You may not believe me, but I'm glad she's all right."

"Thank you," said Kahl cautiously, "but I sense a 'but' coming on."

"The *Wandering Star* got to us in less than five weeks. Either we're a lot closer to Port Trident, or the Weltonian ships have more advanced cranite engines than the Malaquey Navy."

Kahl felt both relieved and annoyed that Mat was worried about something else other than Britea.

At least be thankful he doesn't disapprove of your friendship with Britea.

"Kahl," his cousin said hesitantly, as if he was about to break bad news.

"Yes?"

"Are you going to write back?" Mat's gaze was on the letter in Kahl's hands.

Kahl studied it as well. Replying hadn't been on this mind, but now that Mat had mentioned it, he thought. *Why not?*

"Yes, I will."

Mat closed his eyes and sighed as if in pain.

"What's wrong?"

His cousin sat down beside him. "At the end of the day, she's human. And you know how long humans live compared to us."

Each of Mat's words was like a lead weight dropped on his chest. His eyesight blurred as he stared at the letter in his hands.

Britea would be dead by the time I reached my first century. If I live that long.

"You don't have to be so morbid," protested Mat.

It was only then Kahl realized he had spoken aloud.

But the truth was the truth. The average Dyhaeri could live up to one thousand five hundred to two thousand cycles if they were in perfect health. The royal lineage was known to surpass that age due to blessings from the

Sea Mother. King Jahlaniin's sire, Queen Zaleria, had been three thousand, nine hundred, and forty-seven cycles before she answered the final call from the Sea Mother.

But then yet other Dyhaeri had a much shorter life-span due to the nature of their professions.

Dyhaeri patrollers statistically had the highest mortality rates, after Dyhaeri marines. They were more likely to die before reaching a hundred cycles.

And it wasn't because of illness or accident.

Mat's father had been a marine, and after his ninety-fifth cycle, he had disappeared close to Alkynaia territory when Mat was just three cycles old. Of course, the sea serpents had been the prime suspects.

Kahl had only been thirteen cycles old when his own father had died when he had run into Alkynaia on a routine patrol. That occurrence had been witnessed, so there was no doubt about his cause of death. Kahl's father had been ninety-nine cycles old.

Generations of Dyhaeri were taught early that life in the Heldiar Sea was beautiful and utterly dangerous. "Live each day as if it was your first and last. No one knows when the Sea Mother will call her children home," was the familiar refrain. After all, the ultimate reward was to swim in the Gentle Seas of the Mother once the physical form was shed.

"We only have one life, Mat," said Kahl slowly. "I don't know if I'll ever see her again, even if we get to Raven's Fall. Whatever mission we're undertaking may be too dangerous for us to interact. However, I will write her back, so she knows she's not alone." He sighed. "I know you're trying to be helpful, but I don't want to live a life of regrets and 'what-ifs.' I'll see where this friendship takes me, however long I live."

He turned to see Mat staring at him.

"Kahl, have I ever told you you're a lot wiser than me?" That broke the tension, and they started laughing. The two cousins stood side by side, soothed by the gentle movement of the *Peacekeeper* as they watched the night sky overhead.

"You know if this spy thing doesn't work out, you could always write a book on the philosophy of meaningful relationships before reaching one's first century."

Kahl playfully punched his cousin in the arm. "Now who's being morbid?"

#

Lanead woke up reluctantly as the pounding in his skull transformed into urgent knocking on his cabin door.

Were they under attack? No, the horns would have been sounded, waking everyone not working. *So, what was it?*

Before he could say a word, he noticed the space beside him was empty. His wife was already up and had thrown on a dressing gown before striding to the door.

"What is it?" she asked as she opened the door. Her husband jumped up and shoved his clothes on when he heard the urgency in Sonei's first mate's voice.

"They're here," said the pale, rattled Weltonian crew member.

"Who?" asked Sonei and Lanead at the same time. The crew member shook his head as if trying to compose himself.

"King Jahlaniin, High Priest Myltan, and…and the Sisters."

The last two words made blood drain from Lanead's face.

#

Britea,

I was very happy to get your letter.

Kahl paused. That was a good start. Wasn't it?

I'm also glad to hear you're settling in well at the college and making new friends.

He felt a stab of jealousy at the thought of her meeting a human male, then he pushed the feeling away. After all, they were hardly friends, let alone more than that.

His heart called him a liar.

When last we parted, I was assigned new duties with my cousin.

He realized he couldn't tell her anything about his new *duties.*

We have been well and learning new, exciting things about other places. It has been an enlightening experience. I even got to read a lot of interesting books.

Kahl chuckled at that bit. That was new, but it had resulted in he and Mat often discussing how the Malaquey government functioned. It was similar to that of the Dyhaeri. Then his mood turned serious as he tried to think of how to end the letter.

I hope this letter finds you well, and I pray you succeed in your studies. May we meet once more in happier circumstances.

From Kahl.

He had just reread his letter and folded it into an envelope when the door swung open and a flustered Mat barged in.

"What—"

"The Sisters are here! With the king and High Priest Myltan."

Kahl almost knocked over his chair as he darted up. "Why?"

"I don't know. I was just getting a breath of fresh air when I sensed their presence. The Weltonian crew is awfully agitated right now. Didn't you hear the chaos outside your door?"

"I was busy," said Kahl, trying not to look at the letter in his hand.

Mat raised an eye brow. "Uh huh. Come on, let's find out what's happening. I bet it's the Namirans again."

Kahl had no choice but to follow his excited cousin.

#

Lanead tried not to sweat as he stared at the individuals gathered in his suddenly small captain's office.

King Jahlaniin, High Priest Myltan, and last but certainly not least, the Three Sisters of Fate. The three Seers worried him the most, and right now, they were staring at him and Sonei with their uncannily bright silvery eyes. Lanead couldn't help but notice that the king and the high priest tried to keep some distance between them and the Sisters.

"To what do we owe the honor?" started Sonei while Lanead was still trying to find the words.

The king of the Dyhaeri looked worried as he spoke. "She knows of the prophecy."

Lanead fell his legs go weak. There was only one *she* who could scare King Jahlaniin: Queen Kallesa of Namira, formerly Princess Kallesezza, co-heir to the Dyhaeri throne.

"How?" demanded Sonei. In contrast to the king, his wife was angry.

"The how hardly matters," replied the middle Seer.

"The *what now* is what we should be deciding," said the Seer to the right.

"Anything else is a waste of time," said the closest Seer.

Lanead and Sonei shared a glance. The Sisters of Fate were right.

The captain of the *Peacekeeper* sighed. "So, what's the plan?"

"We make for Malaquey at once. The boys must be put in place," said High Priest Myltan.

Sonei went pale. "Right away?"

"Yes," said the Sisters simultaneously.

Lanead narrowed his eyes. "I assume you'll give the lads time to say goodbye to their friends and family."

"There is no need..." began one of the Seers.

"There is a need," interrupted Lanead harshly, his fear of the Sisters erased by his anger. "At the end of the day, we're sending children to do the work of entire armies. They're going in blind and may not survive. At least let them see their families one last time!"

The Sisters of Fate stared at him for a long moment.

"Captain Riverun is right," said King Jahlaniin. Everyone turned to the king. "They go home tonight and leave first thing in the morning."

#

Kahl wondered if his cousin felt as frustrated as he did. They had come on deck only to find the door to the captain's office blocked by ten Weltonian crew members. He recognized one of them as First Mate Tanet.

"Evening Tanet. Is all well?"

The usually jovial Weltonian was a bit pale. "That depends, Kahl."

The Dyhaeri waited for him to elaborate, but he said nothing else.

"Why is the king here?" asked Mat.

The first mate shook his head. "I don't know. Guess you'll have to wait to find out like the rest of us."

Kahl wanted to ask more questions, but Mat laid a hand on his shoulder.

"Thanks for your time. We'll wait and ask him ourselves then." The first mate was visibly relieved when the two Dyhaeri walked away.

"Something must have happened," said Mat.

Kahl suddenly thought of his mother. "Do you think our mothers are safe?"

Mat looked worried. "If they'd been hurt, we would have known."

Kahl fell silent. When his father had died, he had known immediately. Still, he couldn't help but worry.

The two cousins waited for several minutes until the door opened. The visitors and two Weltonians emerged. Lanead saw the cousins immediately. A fleeting expression of regret passed over his face before he waved them over.

"You're both going home tonight," began the Weltonian captain before either could say a word. "To say your farewells to your family. In the morning, we set off for Port Trident."

Kahl stared at him as Mat started firing off questions.

"What's changed? I thought we had at least two more months of training?"

"You've learned enough," said one of the Sisters with a finality that sent shivers down Kahl's spine.

Mat backed off.

"Moonlight is wasting people," said King Jahlaniin solemnly. "Let's go home."

#

Light-Under-the-Sea loomed large in Kahl's vision as their group neared the underwater Dyhaeri city. Part of him was happy to be home, but the rest of him was scared. He stole a glance at his cousin, who wore a serene expression. Clearly, he was looking forward to returning.

All too soon they reached one of the air-water portals. Kahl was startled to see more sentries than usual outside. That was odd; it was as if they were expecting an attack.

The sentries nodded respectfully to the king but barely spared Mat and Kahl a glance. They each passed through the portal and switched off their full-body bubbles as their feet gently touched the dry floor of the underwater city. Kahl looked around a saw a few Dyhaeri he recognized. He waved at them but was stunned at their almost hostile expressions.

"You're both to attend the briefing tomorrow morning," announced the king, drawing Kahl's attention from the passing Dyhaeri.

"Why?" demanded Mat.

The king just looked at him, and after a moment, the younger Dyhaeri dropped his defiant gaze.

"We'll be there," replied Kahl nervously.

"Seek no trouble this evening," said one of the Sisters as they walked away with the king and the high priest, leaving the cousins staring at their receding forms.

"What in the Abyss is that supposed to mean?" asked Mat once their elders were out of sight.

"I don't know, and right now, I'm too tired to care," said Kahl. "I'm going home. What about you?"

"I'll check up on a friend and my squad mates before heading home. Give my greetings to Aunt Almeita for me."

"Be sure to greet Aunt Neilara for me as well."

Mat smiled as he sauntered off. Kahl watched him go, suddenly worried and not knowing why.

#

Mat was looking forward to catching up with his squad mates, but first he had to call on someone first. He met very few Dyhaeri on his way to his destination, but he noticed they took one look at his face and hurried on. He shrugged it off and walked on. It didn't take long to reach Ciera's home.

He patted his hair down, then sent an air rune floating into the doorway to ask for permission to enter. Several moments passed before a reply floated out. It wasn't what he had expected.

"Request denied."

Mat stared at the gaping rune, unable to think for a moment. He spent several moments deciding on his next more before he sent in two messages. "Is something wrong? Is Ciera well?"

The wait this time was longer; however, the response was different. Ciera emerged and she was furious.

"Ciera, I—"

"You're not welcome here."

Mat stared at her. "What did I do?"

"You have the nerve to ask? Everyone knows what you did! You broke the law and were exiled, yet you dare to show your face at my door?!"

Mat was confused. "I made a mistake…"

"So, you admit it!"

"But, I didn't break the law—"

"Then who did?" demanded Ciera. "Who let the Alkynaia swim in our waters? Who made that possible?! More of our people have been disappearing each day, and it's your fault!"

Mat's jaw dropped. The court had twisted and embellished the story of Kahl's *adventure* and made Mat the scapegoat. He knew, though, that trying to correct the story would only add fuel to the fire and put a target on his cousin's back.

"Ciera, I can explain. Whatever you've heard isn't true."

Her eyes narrowed. "Where have you been for the past seven weeks?"

"Training, for a new assignment—"

"Lies," hissed the female Dyhaeri. "The rest of your marine squad has been present this entire time and you weren't with them.

"I wasn't training with my squad—wait, what do you mean by the rest of my squad?"

She held up a hand. "It doesn't matter. I will not associate with someone who has caused the deaths of fellow Dyhaeri at the hands of the Alkynaia. Never darken my door again."

Mat was left gaping in shock as she walked away, slamming the door behind her.

What in the Deep had happened while he had been away?

#

Kahl sighed happily as he gazed at the food in the cooling cupboard. The Weltonians had tried their best to feed them, but nothing could compare to his mother's cooking.

He had initially walked in only to realize, to his dismay, that his mother wasn't home. He suspected she was out patrolling. His sadness had turned to joy when he realized he could raid the cooling cupboard to his heart's content.

After throwing together a cold seaweed sandwich and grabbing a peach-flavored tea, Kahl closed his eyes in bliss and savored each bite. Once he had washed his dish, he decided to explore the family library for something to read while he waited. He browsed the books and was planning to pick one on human history when his eyes fell on the *Hidden Tome of Prophecies*. He recalled his mother not letting him read it when he was seven cycles old.

When he had asked why, she had said it was too dark for him. He recalled his father keeping it high on the bookshelf out of sight and reach.

As he had gotten older, he had forgotten about it…until now.

He reached up and pulled down the thick, worn copy. Kahl casually flipped the pages, glancing at some of the headings.

The titles ranged from "Natural Calamities" to "Starvation,""Wars,""Extinction," and "Plagues." It seemed to be filled with doomsday prophecies.

"No wonder she didn't want me reading it," Kahl said softly to himself as he carried the book to the kitchen. He sat down at the table and continued flipping through the book until an underlined passage caught his eye. He turned back to the page.

The heading was "Birth of a God."

Why had this been marked? And by who?

He continued reading.

How is a god born?

In silence or in fire? Or as the waters of life rise up or as the earth is rent asunder?

Surely, the rest of the world shall not survive the labor pains.

A thousand years shall pass before one lost child of the seas shall go mad and attempt to ascend.

This will mark the end of all that is and all that is to be.

Unless…the mad child is stopped by the One and the Three.

Ah, we see you, listener. Your eyes ask, whom we do speak of?

These four individuals come from different worlds.

One is the lost heir, another is the teacher, the third will be the catalyst, and the fourth…will be the sacrifice.

"Interesting," said Kahl as he settled in to read more.

"You're home!"

His head shot up to meet the gaze of his stunned mother. "Mother, I'm sorry, I was hungry—"

She lunged at him and hugged him tightly, cutting off his words.

"When High Priest Myltan sent word you were back, I thought something terrible had happened." She seemed on the verge of tears even though she looked happy. "You have been well?"

"Yes. Captain Riverun and his people treated us well. Were you out patrolling? Is all well?"

Almeita smiled. "Yes, it is…" Her voice trailed off when she saw what he was reading. Kahl thought she even went a bit pale.

"Oh, you remember this old tome you kept saying I should wait to read until I was older?"

"Yes? Why are you reading it now?"

Kahl narrowed his eyes. He could swear his mother sounded scared. Surely, that was impossible. Nothing frightened her.

"I was bored and remembered it. I hope you're not angry…"

She waved his apology away. "Of course not. It's just very old. So, what do you think of it?"

Kahl looked closely at her. She seemed back to her old self.

"You were right. It is very dark. I would've had nightmares if I'd read this as a child. It's filled with curses, death, and wanton destruction. It makes for interesting reading though."

"That it does."

Kahl missed her brief expression of relief when he closed the tome and put it aside.

"Where's Mat?"

"Oh, he went to check on a friend and his squad."

"His squad?" Almeita stared at him in alarm.

Kahl was stunned at her reaction. "Why, what's wrong?"

"They disowned me."

Mother and son turned to face a despondent Mat.

Kahl hurried over to his shocked cousin. "What happened?"

"You better sit down for a bit, my dear. Kahl will make us some tea," Almeita said to Mat as she took his hand and guided him to the table. She shot her son a sharp look when he tried to ask more questions. Instead, Kahl quickly poured the still-hot water over some dried peach tea leaves and added a pinch of ground red seaweed to make a calming brew.

Almeita pressed the warm cup into Mat's hands when it was ready, and her nephew took a sip. Kahl sat down beside him.

Mat was silent while he sipped, but the story finally emerged. He had gone to see Ciera, who had blamed him for the disappearance of the Dyhaeri. Mat also told them she had mentioned his squad, so, knowing something was wrong, he quickly sought them out.

"Half are missing, including Liera-tan and our captain. They think the Alkynaia took them, and they blame me for it."

"Why would they…" then Kahl's voice trailed off. "They think you made the pact with Natia. But that's not what happened! It was me!" he stood up. "I have to tell them—"

"Sit down," ordered Almeita in her commander voice, and Kahl found his legs automatically obeying. "You'll only make things worse."

"Aunt Almeita is right. They're too angry to listen. I almost got trounced, but one of the older members stopped them and warned me to stay out of their sight. Now I know why everyone was looking at us so oddly."

Kahl felt so guilty he wanted to throw up.

"I warned them this would happen. Someone most likely heard a rumor and spun a web of lies from it. The truth has been blown way out of proportion." Almeita's expression was one of annoyance. Mat looked at his aunt, his eyes bright.

"You know what's going on?"

Kahl stared at his mother. She seemed to be struggling to reach a decision.

Eventually, she sighed. "It's not the Alkynaia. Namiran ships have been seen close to the last locations of the missing scouts. Only a select few know this. We've been ordered to keep it quiet."

Mat's eyes went hard while Kahl's jaw dropped. "By whom? My mother?"

"No. She was against it, but the Sisters insisted we keep the information to ourselves until the time was right, but I wonder if the Sisters," her tone was harsh, "foresaw that this secrecy would cause such internal strife."

Mat's expression closed off.

"Why are we hiding this information, mother?" asked Kahl.

"To prevent panic," said Almeita. "But now I think the time for that has come and gone."

"Why were we really chosen for assignment at the Malaquey court, Aunt Almeita?" asked Mat softly.

She stared at him and her son for a long time. "We need you two to gather intel about their defenses."

Kahl went still. "What? But, they aren't the enemy!"

Mat stayed silent as he watched his aunt.

Almeita took a deep breath. "We hope they're not the enemy. It's just that for so long now, we've isolated ourselves from them, so if we ask for help, we're not sure if they will answer."

"Why do we need their help?" finally asked Mat.

"A time of great strife is upon us. We need to know who will stand with us when the time comes, which is where you come in."

Kahl shared a quiet look with his cousin. He wondered if Mat was also thinking of what the high priest had told them almost a month ago. At the time, he had stated the Sisters had chosen them for this assignment. But Kahl was getting more and more frustrated that they weren't being told everything. He suspected his cousin felt the same way.

Almeita stood up. "Both of you stay here. I need to speak to the king about what just happened with Mat's squad. Do not leave the house."

Kahl waited until she had gone and looked at his cousin. "I'm sorry about Ciera and your squad. This is my fault."

Mat sighed. "No, it's not, and I'm not mad at you, Kahl. Seriously, I'm not. I'm just shocked at my mates. We trained together for ten years. They should know by now I would never betray them, but they turned their backs on me. And Ciera…" his voice trailed off.

Kahl laid a comforting hand on his cousin's shoulder. The two Dyhaeri sat quietly for several moments.

"I wonder," began Mat.

"Wonder what?"

"If our human equivalents are as scared shitless as we are."

#

Kahl stared at the packed hall. It was still in the early hours of the new day, and he, Mat, and their mothers had arrived early to get good seats for the morning's briefing. The events of the night before were still fresh in his mind. His mother had gone to see the king and had returned later with High Commander Neilara. Kahl had been worried Mat and his mother would start arguing, but to his amazement, they had been quite cordial with each other.

Just before they had turned in for the evening, Aunt Neilara had promised them both all would be well in the morning. Kahl had been too exhausted then to ask her to explain.

His mind returned to the present when Mat nudged him with his elbow. Then he saw what had drawn his cousin's attention. Directly across from them was Mat's former squad, and with them was Ciera. The pretty Dyhaeri was currently glaring at Kahl and Mat while the marines refused to acknowledge their former teammate. After a few moments, Mat turned away from them. Ciera wore an ugly smile of triumph at his reaction.

Kahl was relieved when the king finally strode to the circle in the center of the auditorium.

"Morning's greeting to you all." The crowd politely murmured their reply before falling silent.

"Thank you for attending to this morning's gathering, which I realize is earlier than usual. But the news I have cannot wait." Everyone was paying attention now.

"It has come to my attention that rumors have abounded regarding our missing brethren, and those rumors have grown into something more dangerous than the enemy that stalks us."

Kahl glanced at Ciera, who was again glaring in Mat's direction.

The king continued. "It is true that several of our brethren have been taken, but not by the Alkynaia…" Confused muttering broke out at his words. Ciera's expression turned to one of surprise, and she turned to concentrate on King Jahlaniin's words.

"…but by the Namirans!"

Kahl gave his mother and aunt grateful looks. He had no doubt they had been the ones to convince the king to reveal this information.

The crowd's muttering grew to frightened yelling. Kahl saw Ciera's face lose all its color. She glanced at Mat, but his cousin was staring intently at the Dyhaeri king.

The king waited for the cries of outrage to diminish. When they didn't, he raised his right hand, and the noise quickly died down, but the tension remained.

"We all know of the Namiran queen. I fear she has become capable of much more pain and misery than we thought." He paused for emphasis. "This is why I am sending a delegation to the Malaquey government to determine if they are willing to stand with us."

Kahl and Mat shared a stunned look.

"He's not going to expose us, is he? Wouldn't that put the mission at risk?" whispered a nervous Mat.

Kahl felt his heart rate go up. "I don't think he'd be that stupid…"

"The chosen delegation includes High Priest Myltan, Mat-rallenin, son of Neilara, and Kahl, son of Almeita!" The king pointed his left hand in their direction, and the attention of the whole auditorium was turned to them. Ciera's jaw dropped. The marines had identical expressions of shock on their faces.

"You were saying?" asked Mat dryly.

CHAPTER 10

"Today, you'll be learning how to create a shield with your element."

Britea felt both excitement and dread. This was a one-on-one training session. The junior wielders had been dismissed, and it was just her and Instructor Shelley left in the empty classroom. For weeks, it had been all tier-one wielding, and now she was finally moving on to the next tier.

Thank the Maker.

"Many people think a large thick shield or barrier is unbreakable, but that's not true. Such a shield requires high-level wielding and lots of concentration, which isn't sustainable in long battles. That's why the lower tiers are used for shield recreation."

Britea looked at the instructor quizzically. The older wielder smiled knowingly and continued.

"Think of the links in the ancient chainmail our ancestors used to wear in battle. Thousands of small steel rings that individually are weak but together are strong. That is how the lower tiers work together if used properly."

Britea nodded. The explanation actually made sense.

"Start with a tier-two wield. Pick two small shapes easy to hold in place." Britea effortlessly created an oval shape and a square shape. Each was smaller than the palms of her hands.

"Now, overlap the two, and multiply it by a thousand." Instructor Shelley nodded when Britea complied.

"Good. I want you to shape it into a full-body shield now."

Britea strained to mold the shapes into a shield but could only make it extend from her head to the upper third of her thighs.

"Not bad, but someone could aim a blow here…" Instructor Shelley wielded a blast of air at Britea's legs, making Britea lose focus so the water shield lost its shape and splashed on the floor "…and you'd be dead."

Britea looked at the older wielder in shock.

Instructor Shelley's face was stern. "Always expect the worst from your opponent. They'll most likely lack honor, and they'll aim for the vulnerable parts of your body. Start again."

Britea regarded the wet floor and began to wield the spilled water. Once she had withdrawn what she could, she glanced up to see the instructor watching her oddly.

"That was…most… considerate of you. I'm sure the cleaners will appreciate your thoughtfulness. Now create your shield. A thousand overlapping pieces please."

Britea obeyed while she racked her brain for ways to extend the shield to cover herself completely. Then it came to her. *Stretch the pieces* . She did just that and soon she had a head-to-toe shield. She looked at the instructor, who was now staring at her.

"You're adaptable."

Britea wasn't sure if she was pleased or upset. "Thanks, Instructor Shelley."

"Hold your shield as steady as you can." Without warning, the instructor wielded a lance of air at Britea's shield.

Caught off guard, Britea wobbled and the shield shattered, this time soaking Britea. As she wiped her face, she saw the instructor regarding her thoughtfully.

"Your shield work is going to need a lot of practice. Start again."

#

Britea had no idea how she got to the dining hall before supper was over. But she was relieved because she was starving and oh, so tired. She thanked the servers as she collected food from the buffet line. The hall was already half empty; even Danai and her friends were nowhere to be seen. Britea decided to sit by herself.

Halfway through her meal, she heard someone call her name. Britea turned to see a familiar face.

"How's your day going?" asked Henrick as he sat down beside her.

"It's been a long one, and I'm exhausted," replied Britea.

Henrick nodded. "I can see that. So, the junior wielding class is that hard? It wasn't like that for me."

Britea snorted. "I bet." She wasn't really in the mood to talk, but she didn't want to offend him either, so she tossed the conversation back in his court. "So, what about you? Any juicy stories?"

Henrick wore a pained expression. "Now, you're making me sound like a gossiping fishwife."

She couldn't help laughing, and Henrick smiled. "At least I made you laugh."

Britea nodded, feeling lighter already.

"However, you're yet to answer my question. Why is the junior class hard for you?"

Britea sighed. "It's not hard, it's just that I want to be in the senior class, but Instructor Shelley doesn't think I'm ready, and she's right."

"In what way?"

"There are basic patterns to wielding the first three tiers, and I don't know them. The twelve-year olds in my class know more than me. I have to admit, it's a bit embarrassing."

"And there are no wielders in Weldaros, so there was no one to teach you," mused Henrick

"That's right."

"But you already knew the first tier before coming to Syla."

Britea gave him a sharp look.

He smiled sheepishly. "One of the juniors in your class has a brother in my dance class. He told us how you wielded a large orb of water and Instructor Shelley told you to shrink it."

Britea blushed. Henrick sounded impressed.

"So, who taught you before you got here?"

Her irritation returned. Henrick was politely persistent, but a quiet voice warned her not to talk about Kahl.

"I guess I'm a natural." She tried to sound nonchalant.

"Uh huh," responded Henrick skeptically.

Britea tried to change the topic. "When did you start learning to shield?"

The male wielder was surprised at the question. "Shielding? I'm not doing that until my fourth year."

She stared at him.

"Wait, are you learning shielding in the junior class?" he sounded doubtful.

Britea reasoned that Instructor Shelley hadn't actually told her to keep her lessons a secret. "Um...yeah."

His eyes widened. "The entire junior class as well?" She heard the alarm in his voice.

"No, just me."

Rather than being mollified, he seemed upset. "The fourth-year curriculum states that's when shielding lessons start. Why did you get the go ahead?"

Britea was wondering the same thing. "I don't know."

#

Britea was relieved when she finally reached her room. Every muscle ached. Training hadn't been this hard with Kahl. She chuckled when she remembered how he had made her race him on the deck. Then, just as suddenly, her mood sobered.

Was he all right? Had he gotten her letter?

She tried to push the thoughts away as she entered her room.

"Welcome back."

She smiled at her roommate, Danai. The older wielder was seated at the desk, pen in hand hovering over a parchment.

"You're wrung out."

Britea sighed. "Tell me about it." She dropped her bag of books on her bed and tried to remove her boots.

"How was your day? I didn't see you at dinner," said Danai as she returned to writing.

"Instructor Shelley had me practicing shielding with tier-two forms." Britea watched the Weltonian wielder go still, then carefully lay down the pen and turn her chair around.

"Why?" Her hazel eyes were darker than usual and seemed to be aflame with anger.

Britea was startled by the change. "I didn't think to ask."

Danai looked down as if she was trying to control her temper. "Shield work doesn't start until the fourth year."

"Henrick said the same thing."

Danai closed her eyes briefly. "You told him?"

"I didn't know I wasn't supposed to!" Britea felt stupid as she replied.

"Now, the whole school may know."

"Henrick isn't the type to gossip."

Danai gave her a sad look. "You don't know that."

Britea had nothing to say to that.

Her roommate continued. "Let's forget about Henrick. The question you should be asking yourself is why Instructor Shelley is teaching you shield-wielding already."

Britea shrugged.

"You have to ask her," said Danai, quiet intensity in her voice.

"But what's the harm in teaching me shielding?" asked Britea.

Danai was quiet for a long moment. "In the early years of the colleges, shielding was taught in the junior classes. Then students created a game called, 'The Wielding Duels.'"

Something in her voice told Britea there was nothing safe about the duels.

"The duels were done in secret of course, but it came to light when students started dying. At first, students dueled for fun, then some took it too far. That's why the Creed underwent a lot of changes in the early years. That's also why anyone who wields against another wielder for no justifiable reason gets expelled or worse."

What could be worse than being expelled? But Britea was too afraid to say that aloud.

"Unfortunately, making the duels taboo only encourages the less honorable to continue that sick game," Danai sounded bitter. "I was almost drawn into one by a certain lady, but at the last moment, I came to my senses and walked away."

Lady Selina Arkei. "She didn't hit you when your back was turned?" asked Britea, horrified.

Danai smiled grimly. "There are rules in the game even she's not stupid enough to break. Besides, she had an audience, so she taunted me and called me a coward as I walked away with my hands clenched by my sides so I wouldn't lose control."

"You think Instructor Shelley is training me for the duels?"

Danai's eyes went wide. "I surely hope not!" A worried countenance appeared on her face. "But, it may be for something worse."

"Like?" asked a scared Britea.

"The Naval Wielder's Division or the army."

Britea blinked. "Wouldn't that be a good thing?"

Danai let loose an exasperated huff. "I don't know, but the thought of being one of those wielder soldiers gives me chills." Britea gave her a questioning look.

Danai's looked grave. "There is a reason very few humans can wield. All we do is destroy, a prime example being the Immortal Wielder Queen of Namira. There have been several reliable accounts of how she used her ability to kill innocent people just for the fun of it." She paused thoughtfully and ran a hand through her short hair. "We're lucky to have the monarch we currently do, but what if the next one turns out to be like the Namiran queen?"

Britea shuddered at the thought as she recalled the Namiran warships chasing her ship on the way here and the Immortal Queen behind them.

"If you were a member of the Naval Wielding Division and our next king or queen ordered you to drown a small fishing village, would you do it?"

"Of course not!"

"Then you would be committing treason, and the punishment for that is death."

A grim silence filled the room.

Danai turned back to the parchment on the desk and picked up her pen. "I don't know if Instructor Shelley is training you for that, but if I were you…I'd ask her."

#

Danai's words stayed with her throughout the next day. *Was she being prepped for the Naval Wielder's Division?* She didn't want to be a soldier.

Her distraction earned her extra laps around the field in combat and defense class. The only bright part of her day was when she found out Lianne was no longer her dance partner.

She still hated the class though.

By the time she got to junior wielding class, her stomach was a ball of knots.

Britea kept wondering how she was going to ask the question.

"Novice D'Tranell."

She tried not to jump when Instructor Shelley called on her as she entered the class with the junior novices.

"Yes, Instructor Shelley."

"You will monitor the juniors in their tier-two wielding." She handed a book to Britea. "Only tier two. I have to attend an urgent meeting."

The instructor turned to address the class. "Novice D'Tranell is in charge until I return." She left before a stunned Britea could react.

A long moment passed before one of the students coughed. She turned to face the expectant class. The silence grew as she tried to say something wise.

"Um…is everyone ready for tier two?" She felt like slapping herself. That sounded so lame.

"Most of us are," scoffed Chelton Blade as he glanced slyly at Vindell Masters. Some students laughed.

Britea's gaze sharpened when she noticed how Vindell's shoulders dropped as if she was trying to make herself smaller. Chelton was doing exactly what Lianne had tried to do to Britea.

"Enough of that." Her firm tone had the class shutting up immediately.

Britea waited until everyone was paying attention to her. For some reason, she didn't feel as nervous as before. "We're going to do this in pairs—"

"But we did that last time!" protested Chelton.

Britea tried to hide her annoyance.

"We want to learn something different! Tiers one and two are for babies!"

Britea fixed a stern look on him while she marveled at how Instructor Shelley made teaching seem so easy. She also wondered if the instructor had been insane to leave her alone with these scary students.

"Today's exercise will be tier-two wielding, and once Instructor Shelley gets back, please feel free to tell her what you really think about the curriculum." Something in her eyes or her tone made Chelton back down.

"Will someone explain what tier-one represents?" Silence reigned for a moment, then Vindell hesitantly raised a hand.

"Yes?" Britea tried to keep her voice gentle.

"Stability?"

"And tier two?"

"Flexibility."

"Well done, Vindell." Britea let the smile slip from her face as she faced the rest of the class. "You all need to master stability and flexibility before you can attempt to control tier three. That is why we're here at this college. Is that clear?"

"Yes, Instructor D'Tranell," chorused the class.

Britea winced at the joined voices and her new title. "Novice will do just fine." She glanced at Instructor Shelley's notebook. Picking it up, she sighed with relief when she found the detailed section for today's lesson entitled, "Pairing up weak and strong students for learning tier two." The list of students assigned to each other was below the heading.

"Now we'll pair up. First up are Chelton and Vindell—"

"I don't want to be paired with her, and you can't force me to," announced Chelton loudly. Beside him, Vindell's face reddened in embarrassment.

Britea felt a spark of anger, and she almost ordered him to pair up with Vindell before a thought came to her.

"All right. I'll pair up with Vindell while you'll stand aside and watch."

Chelton gaped at her. Vindell's head shot up. The other students were now staring at Britea.

"That's not fair!" protested Chelton. Britea ignored him and called out the other pairings. No one else complained.

"You can't leave me here doing nothing!" Chelton continued.

Britea beckoned to a stunned Vindell to follow her. Chelton trailed them both as he kept complaining. "You're supposed to be teaching me!"

"Novice Blade, look around and tell me what the other students are doing," said Britea calmly as she checked the contents of the cauldrons.

"They are standing around—"

"In pairs waiting to wield, which I too will be doing in a bit with our fellow classmate, Novice Masters. You had the opportunity to partner up," Britea paused and looked at him. "So, while we're practicing tier-two wielding, you will stand in the corner doing nothing. When Instructor Shelley returns, I'm *certain* she'll be interested in the reason why." Her last words made him go pale.

Britea turned to the rest of the class. "Please watch as I demonstrate a tier-two form." She wielded two watery shapes: an orb and a square. She let the two forms rotate around each other. "As I call out the names of each pair, you will step up and repeat what I just did."

Britea watched the students perform the wield. She used the marking scheme in the instructor's notes to score each pair of students. Before long, she realized it wasn't that hard.

She was about to observe a fifth pair when Chelton walked up to her. "I'm sorry, Instructor D'Tranell."

Britea stopped the next pair from wielding and turned to correct him, but the young novice continued.

"Please, I'll wield with Vindell." The student in question stared at Britea in fear; she wasn't keen on practicing with Chelton.

Britea tried to give her a reassuring look. "I'm not the only one you have to apologize to."

Chelton's face went red, and then he stared at a scared Vindell.

"I'm sorry, Novice Masters," muttered Chelton.

Britea nodded encouragingly at the female novice.

"A...apology accepted," stammered Vindell.

"Splendid," said Britea with a smile that hid her relief. "You two will go next after Saria and Odenn."

The rest of the wielding went smoothly, but as she got to the end of the list, she began to worry she would be the temporary instructor for the whole period.

Just as the last two students were wielding, the door opened and Instructor Shelley appeared.

"Apologies for keeping you all waiting."

Britea gladly gave the senior wielder her book of notes back.

"How were they?"

"They behaved well and did as instructed." Britea didn't dare acknowledge Chelton who released a sigh of relief.

The instructor looked at the students and at Britea. "Maybe you also have a knack for teaching." The bells rang at that moment signaling the end of the period.

"Read Chapter 19 of *How Not to Wield* by Drav Septon. There might be a quiz later."

There was a collective groan as the younger students filed out of the class.

Instructor Shelley turned and noticed Britea had stayed behind. "No after-class training today. Consider it a rest period." Then she noticed Britea's questioning expression.

"Is something the matter?"

Britea hesitated, then shook her head. "No, no...see you tomorrow, Instructor Shelley." She hurried out of the class but felt the instructor could see right through her.

She would ask her about the reasons for her early shield-wielding training later...maybe tomorrow, maybe never.

CHAPTER 11

Britea stifled a yawn as she stood in line for breakfast. She had no one to blame but herself for staying up late studying; even Danai had advised her to go bed earlier.

But the history book she had been reading was so interesting.

It had now been a week since she had taught the students on her own. Instructor Shelley was still testing her shielding, but Britea had yet to work up the nerve to ask her about the shield-wielding.

Maybe she would ask her today.

Yeah, right!

On the bright side, Lianne and her friends hadn't bothered her again. That should have made her feel better, but instead it gave her a feeling of impending doom.

Once she had gotten her meal of warm bread, fried egg, and vegetables, she honed in on her roommate and the others and strode over.

"Morning, sleepyhead," said Danai as Britea sat down.

Britea grinned sheepishly. "I know, I know."

"Why so tired?" asked an interested Navos.

"Stayed up way too long studying," replied Danai dryly.

"Nothing wrong with that," commented Shran without looking up from his book.

Lexia rolled her eyes. "Please, can we talk about something else other than studying?"

"Hey, did anyone hear what happened in town the other night?" asked Henrick.

Britea was just as mystified as the rest.

Henrick explained eagerly. "Rumor has it some of our students were in a brawl with some locals in town and damaged a lot of property in the process."

The group exchanged worried glances. "This happened recently?" asked Shran finally glancing up from his book. "And how did you get the news so fast?"

"My roommate said he heard it from someone related to one of the guards who had to break up the fight."

"Sure," said Danai skeptically.

Henrick's enthusiasm was dampened by her tone. "I think it's true. I'm not the only one talking about it this morning."

Britea put down her cup of tea to ask a question.

"Attention, students!" The amplified voice of Warden Asteros startled every student in the noisy hall and brought talking to a halt.

"You have five minutes to complete your meals and then make your way to the Great Hall. Any latecomers will be punished." The stern-looking senior wielder left as the stunned students started muttering.

Britea turned to the others to see them already standing.

"Make a quick sandwich and bring your mug with you," advised Shran. He had already tucked away his book and shoveled the rest of his food into his mouth.

"I hope you have a strong stomach because you'll have to eat fast. It takes nine minutes just to get to the hall from here," added Lexia. Her plate was already clean. Even Danai had little food left on hers.

Navos and Henrick rolled their fried egg up in their flat bread, and she followed suit as Shran had suggested. Britea's heart rate increased watching their anxious reactions.

"This can't be good," said Navos as they waited for her.

"Why not?" asked Henrick.

"The hall is rarely used. So, why now? And who's insane enough to upset Warden Asteros?" replied Navos.

No one had an answer.

"The Great Hall is northeast of the dining hall, isn't it? Right next to the outdoor defense class?" asked Britea as she turned and stood.

"Yes," answered Danai as they set off at a brisk pace. Some students were already leaving while the rest were still trying to finish their food quickly.

"So, what is the hall used for then?" asked Britea as she fell in step with the Danai and the others.

"Graduation of final-year students, important announcements, the general knowledge rounds of the Trials, and grand balls usually," answered Danai.

Britea frowned. It sounded like a place saved for only the most serious of occasions. Then she registered Danai's last two words. "The school hosts balls?"

"Once in a blue moon. Most of the faculty isn't too fond of it. They say it tends to take students' concentration away from their studies," said Lexia strangely cheerful.

Britea looked at her. "You sound happy about that."

"Oh, indeed I am. I absolutely hate dancing."

"Hear, hear," agreed Danai. "Well, that stupid, refined dancing anyway."

Britea had never been to the Great Hall since there had been no need to until today. Once they had passed the doors to the outdoor combat and defense class, they climbed several steps up to the Forever Bridge, a wide exposed stone bridge that led to the Great Hall. Henrick happily explained it was a thousand feet long.

Thank the Lords it was warmer this morning, or it would have been a chilly walk across the bridge. Still, it was an impressive walk, and she could hear the distant sounds of the ocean hitting the rocks. Britea looked over the side and was scared by the drop. They appeared to be several dozen feet above the ground.

"The school was built on a gradual elevation," said Lexia when she noticed her puzzled expression. "You may not realize it, but starting at the entrance, every hundred feet there are a few stairs. Add them all up and you'll realize the school has risen off the ground completely at this point."

"Impressive, isn't it?" said Henrick. "I also hear that when the tide comes in at night, the water flows right beneath this bridge. One could even lean over the side to touch the water. I wish I could see that one day."

Britea at first wondered why he said that until she remembered the curfew after lights out at night. Students were strongly discouraged from wondering the hallways at night. She could not help but marvel at the school's architect as she ate and walked. Whoever had built this school must have been quite skilled. She wondered who it had been.

As they got closer to the hall, Britea could not ignore the feeling of dread in her stomach—until she stepped through the enormous gleaming black double doors of the Great Hall.

It was impressive. The sizable hall was circular in shape with several rows of elevated white benches set up close to the light grey walls. Several waist-high, dusty-blue round marble tables were arranged in a circle with the center left empty. There was also a foot-high stage at the opposite end of the vast chamber. The floor was lined with smooth, shiny, aged mahogany, and the high, domed ceiling was festooned with colorful murals that caught her eye. Her mouth dropped as she realized it was a glass roof.

"That's…"

"…incredible," completed Henrick. "This is only the second time I've stepped into this hall, and it never ceases to blow me away."

"No wonder," said Britea, continuing to gaze at the murals above. They depicted humans wielding the four different elements, and in their midst was a beautiful, green female Dyhaeri watching them.

Who was she?

"All right people, let's find a decent seat," said Navos. Reluctantly, Britea dragged her gaze away from the murals and followed her friends to a table close to the stage. As she sat, she couldn't help but notice the odd porcelain bowls set on the floor beside each chair.

It didn't take long for the hall to start filling up. Britea gulped down the last of her now lukewarm tea while she watched the students stream in. She saw Lianne with her usual two hangers-on, Valerie and Pearl. The three talked animatedly and chose a table close to the stage. It was already occupied by three junior wielders. The smile left Lianne's face as she stared at them, and the juniors scattered before she even said a word. Britea felt her blood boil as she watched the three noble ladies. Lianne was smiling brightly now as the other two fawned over her.

"I wonder if this is about the upcoming Wielder Trials," mused Henrick. Britea was grateful for the distraction; it was taking a lot for her not to give in to her anger.

"Nah," disagreed Navos. "This is something else."

The double doors shutting with a loud bang killed the chatter in the room. Silence reigned as the most senior instructors at the academy walked towards the stage. For a scary moment, Britea wondered where they had appeared from. *Had they used the distraction of the slamming doors to sneak into the hall?*

She recognized a few faces: Headmaster Zalei Clayre, Warden Sammel Asteros, Instructor Eowise Shelley, Weapons Master Pietor Caren, and Instructor Kacia Felgreen. Accompanying them were five other senior wielders in instructor colors.

One thing was certain; they all looked very solemn.

Once the group faced the students, the headmaster began to speak.

"I should be saying good morning to you all, but there is nothing good about what I'm about to say and do."

Britea glanced at Danai. Her roommate had a puzzled expression on her face. It mirrored the expressions of the others.

"A few days ago, in Raven's Fall, there was an incident. Three of our final-year students decided to get into a fight with the customers of a tavern. From the description of the events, these students were clearly in the wrong and deserved to be told to leave the tavern." The headmaster's expression went even more grim. "But instead of leaving peacefully, they decided to wield and caused bodily harm to the bouncers and five of the customers. They also destroyed quite a bit of property. More people would have been injured if the local guardsmen had not intervened. I have heard from the healers that at least two of the injured will never walk properly again and will always require assistance."

The doors behind the students opened and there were sounds of a scuffle as three bound and gagged male students were dragged in by the school guard. Close behind were six local guardsmen and a dozen civilians, two of whom were supported by relatives.

Headmaster Clayre continued. "Today, the students will meet their fate."

Britea felt the blood drain from her face as students began to talk in hushed voices. Her friends remained silent, their uncertainty mirroring her own.

The students were brought before the headmaster and forced to their knees. They were terrified and they held out their hands in supplication, but the head of the academy stared coldly at them until they were unable to meet his unyielding gaze.

"What is the Creed?" No one said a word. Then the headmaster glared at the entire assembly.

"All of you, speak it now!" His barked order had the entire school and the instructors reciting the Wielder's Creed as the civilians and local militia watched in silence. At first, their voices were in disharmony but by the second sentence, every wielder recited in synchronicity.

Headmaster Clayre even joined in reciting the Creed. "…any wielder who breaks the laws in such a way that endangers the general public will be tried by his or her senior peers and sentenced accordingly." Then he held up a hand for silence.

He turned to face the offenders. "This is what you were taught from the moment you stepped into this school. One would have hoped after years of drumming this into your minds, you would have at least learned that." He wielded air and the gags fell off the perpetuators.

"Do you have any idea who I am?!" demanded one of the students whose rage had replaced his fear.

"Sir, please! We were drunk! It won't happen again!" Wailed another of the students on trial.

"Silence!" barked the headmaster. His fury cut off any further words. "Look at the victims of your arrogance and stupidity!" He pointed at the crippled civilians.

"Due to your antics, they may never find work again. They may not be able to feed their families. Can you give back what was stolen by your wielding? No. This is why the precious gift you have squandered will be rent from your bodies."

The three male wielders went pale. The first one began to threaten while the remaining two begged for mercy. Then the warden and the weapons master approached. The three students tried to run, but the school guards held them down.

While a terrified Britea watched, a part of her wondered why the students weren't trying to wield to escape. Then her gaze was drawn to the bonds on their wrists. From afar, they appeared to be ordinary handcuffs, but then she saw an intermittent flash of gold light between the manacles.

Her eyes went back to Warden Asteros and Weapons Master Caren. The warden placed one hand each on the heads of two of the struggling students while the weapons master placed one hand on the warden's back and his second hand on the third student's head. The students were now all pleading as the instructors' hands began to glow. Their pleas turned to screams that seemed to go on forever. Britea was dimly aware of Henrick being violently sick beside her, and she was sorely tempted to throw up as well. From the sounds of retching around her; other students were just as affected. *I guess that's why the bowls* , she thought, disgusted.

When the sentence was finally complete, the three students looked like rag dolls, barely able to support themselves even with help from the expressionless school guards. The headmaster nodded at the guards, who then bore the nearly unconscious students away. The warden and weapons master returned to their positions behind the headmaster, and the school's director turned to the silent civilians and the local militia. Many of them were as pale as the students.

"Those three will never wield again. We have taken what they thought made them special. Just as they caused you a loss of irreparable magnitude, so have they reaped the irreversible consequences of their actions."

One of the local militia stepped forward. "We are pleased." He and the civilians stared at the gathered students, a grim satisfaction on their collective faces, then they left quietly with the two crippled individuals.

The headmaster turned to the silent, shocked students. He clasped his hands behind his back.

"This is a difficult but valuable lesson. I trust none of you will forget it in a hurry. You're dismissed to your classes."

Britea's legs felt like rubber as she tried to leave with the rest of the students. *How in the Deep did he expect them to carry on as normal?* Her mind returned to the present when she realized most of the students were trying to run from the hall as if to distance themselves from the horror they had just witnessed. To keep from being trampled, she hung back and soon found herself separated from Danai and the others.

"Hey, farm girl." Lianne's voice stopped Britea in her tracks. She stopped and turned.

The noble was right behind her, a smug smile on her face. Britea stared at her, wondering how she had stayed so calm during the sentencing.

"You're next." Lianne sailed past her while Britea stood there, speechless.

#

Britea spent the rest of the day in a daze. She wasn't the only one. The general mood was subdued in all her classes, and every teacher made sure to touch on the topic of sentencing wielders.

Some of the teachers seemed saddened, but many were stern. The general consensus was if those wielders had not disobeyed the laws, then no one would be having this conversation.

Even Weapons Master Caren had a conversation with the class once he had them seated on the floor of the training field. "Some of you may consider yourselves above others because of your rare talent," stated the weapons master as he remained standing with his instructors hanging back as silent observers.

"Well, let me state the obvious. We are not special. Neither are we blessed." Some students were shocked at his words. "We simply possess an ability few others have, and whilst they may look at us with envy, there isn't much stopping the public from ripping our throats out if we step on the wrong side of the law." He paused to look at every student in the eye before continuing. "Take, for example, the death of the wielding society in Namira."

Now everyone was paying attention.

"How do you think the destruction of their academies came about so easily? Lies spread throughout the country about the arrogance of the Namiran wielders. Whispers circulated about how they flourished while the poor suffered.

Unlike us, Namirans wielders did not do a Year of Discovery. Maybe that contributed to their demise, maybe it didn't. But what we know for sure is that once a new queen was crowned, those whispers grew into declarations, and she used the people to capture and hand over wielders to her for judgement."

Britea felt her lower jaw drop. No one had ever told her this. *Why was this not public knowledge?*

She looked around. The older students wore solemn expressions while the newer ones mirrored her astonished mien.

Weapons Master Caren nodded. "I see your astonishment and disbelief. And yes, what I say is true. This is why we must obey the laws and never forget where we are on the social ladder. Wielders are at the bottom of the ladder, boys and girls. We are the servants of Malaquey; we aren't its betters no matter which family or clan you come from. So, we must use our gifts to help our people and never forget we hold no power over even the poorest of Malaquey citizens. He let his message sink in. "Is that clear?"

"Yes, sir!"

The weapons master considered each of them in silence. "Get up. We shall begin wielding drills for everyone today."

Some students responded with cries of joy, but Britea felt far from relieved. Then, unbidden, she saw Lianne's face, and a sense of dread filled her. She was almost relieved when one of the instructors yelled at her to get into formation.

#

"Welcome to Port Trident."

Kahl tried not to gag from the horrendous smell. He glanced at his cousin, who had gone an interesting shade of pale, fading his usually striking emerald visage.

"Some call it Port Smelly," continued Lanead cheerfully.

"Does the rest of Raven's Fall stink like this?" asked Kahl when he felt less queasy.

"No, but the rest of the city has a different aroma, which may just be as unpleasant."

"Oh joy," said Mat lifelessly.

Lanead patted him reassuringly on the shoulder. "Cheer up. It's only going to get more interesting from this point on. I'll escort you boys and High Priest

Myltan off the ship once we dock." He left the two Dyhaeri to their thoughts. It had been late afternoon when the *Peacekeeper* had finally come within sight of the Malaquey port.

Mat was the first to break the silence. "We need to be careful here. Assume everyone is an enemy."

Kahl stared at him. "But Malaquey is our ally."

"So were the Namirans once a upon a time," continued Mat in the same serious tone. "We also have to protect the high priest."

Kahl glanced over his shoulder to make sure no one was listening. "I thought we were here as spies."

"Uh huh, but spies have to multitask. Don't forget that. Let's get our gear."

Kahl lingered for a moment to stare at the ships in the harbor growing closer. He had never seen so many human vessels in one place. Just last night he had realized he was visiting a human city for the first time. That thought had briefly replaced his trepidation with excitement.

"Kahl, we have to go," called Mat.

"On my way!"

#

Kahl straightened the tunic of his modified indigo-blue marine uniform. Diev had been true to his word, and uniforms had been ready days before they were within sight of the harbor. The dress uniform was comfortable and even had a magnetized section between the shoulders to hold their tridents. However, to not alarm the Malaquey Army, said tridents had been telescoped and placed in the Dyhaeri's respective rucksacks. Kahl had to admit he and Mat looked handsome and somewhat deadly in their uniforms even without the tridents.

Once they had left their cabin and made their way above deck, he realized the deck was more crowded than usual, and the Weltonians appeared to be waiting for them.

"Is everything all right?" asked Mat.

First Mate Tanet stepped forward. "We just wanted to say goodbye. May the Sea Mother keep you safe." Thus began good wishes and short prayers of safety from the Weltonian crew. This made Kahl misty eyed as he tried to thank everyone. Even Mat's expression softened as he thanked the crew as well.

The crew of the *Peacekeeper* had been kind and courteous at every turn. Sometimes Kahl could close his eyes and almost believe he was surrounded by fellow Dyhaeri instead of humans. He wondered if Mat felt the same way.

It didn't take long for the vessel to dock, and High Priest Myltan joined them on the gangway. He wore a sky-blue leather outfit almost identical to the marine uniform but less severe. The high priest held his ceremonial staff in his right hand, and a rucksack was slung over his left shoulder. Kahl wondered if he had weapons tucked in it too.

"Good. You both look like guardians. Keep silent and let Lanead and I do the talking."

"Yes, sir," replied the cousins simultaneously.

Captain Riverun was already waiting for them on the gangway. He had changed into a brightly colored outfit in various shades of purple. Kahl wondered for a moment how anyone could take him seriously in that outfit, but he wondered if maybe that was the point.

The Weltonian captain nodded to them before leading them off the ship. Already waiting on the dock were a dozen Malaquey naval soldiers, and none appeared happy to see them. One stepped forward, and Kahl observed the markings on his uniform. Recalling what Lanead had drilled them on helped him to recognize the rank of a lieutenant commander.

"I'm Lieutenant Commander Peras Nell," said the human with iron-grey hair. "Welcome to Malaquey." His smile was polite, but Kahl's eyes were drawn to a young blond man staring at them with open suspicion. He held the rank of lieutenant. Kahl glanced at Mat, who was carefully eyeing each Malaquey soldier.

High Priest Myltan bowed his head. "May the Sea Mother keep and protect you. Thank you for welcoming us to Raven's Fall. I trust you are our escort to the palace?"

"Yes." The lieutenant commander noted Kahl and Mat, who just stared silently at him. "And these are your guards? I was expecting more."

The high priest smiled at him. "They are more than sufficient for the task at hand. Shall we? There is much to discuss."

"Of course." The human officer began to turn away until Captain Riverun coughed. Commander Nell froze then turned around. Kahl saw an irritated expression flash across the officer's face before it was replaced by a neutral expression. "Yes?"

Kahl glanced at Lanead, expecting him to be insulted, but the Weltonian just smiled brightly. "I'm Captain Riverun of the *Peacekeeper,* and I wish to petition King Wilhem on behalf of my people.

"You may present your petition to the local judiciary, and they will decide if it merits the king's personal attention..."

"Captain Riverun's interest lies with ours," interrupted High Priest Myltan. "It would be best that you listen, but certainly not out here on the docks."

Lieutenant Commander Peras Nell and the high priest locked gazes as the air became thick with tension. Eventually, the human was the first to drop his gaze.

"Of course, he may join us in the carriage."

As their small group walked to the carriage, Kahl took note of the bustling human dock. He tried not to stare, but he couldn't help himself. The stench aside, the port was certainly busy and crowded. He noticed haphazardly constructed stalls beside well-built buildings, and those humans who weren't staring at their entourage were busy hawking their wares, shouting themselves hoarse. The Malaquey officers had to make way so they could get to the coach. Kahl thought this would be the perfect opportunity for an ambush. He looked at his cousin, whose loose gait told Kahl he was ready for an attack. He tried to imitate Mat as he looked around, only to meet the suspicious gaze of the blond lieutenant.

Fortunately, they reached a carriage with the Malaquey royal seal without incident. Kahl stared at it. He had seen pictures of this vehicle, but how was he going to climb into that without making a fool of himself?

The lieutenant commander saw his expression and smiled smugly. "This is how we get around here in Raven's Fall."

He had barely finished speaking when Mat wielded a blast of air to open the side door, and while everyone stared at him, he wielded a cushion of air below his feet to levitate to the level of the door. He peered into the coach, then turned to face the high priest.

"It appears safe," he said while glancing sidelong at the lieutenant commander, who simply glared at him. Mat grinned and levitated backwards into the coach with bent knees and arms folded across his chest.

Show off. Thought a smiling Kahl as the high priest also wielded a hot pocket of air beneath his feet to enter the coach. Kahl instead jumped onto the steps, grabbed the handles beside the door, and hauled himself in with what he hoped was one fluid motion. He could feel the Malaquey officers staring. There were six seats within: two sets of three facing each other. The high priest was already seated in the center of one set, and Mat sat on his right, so Kahl took his left.

Commander Nell entered next and took the seat opposite Mat, Captain Riverun followed and sat in the center, then a sixth person entered the carriage.

Kahl wasn't surprised to see the male blond lieutenant who had been glaring at them.

"Please meet Lieutenant Harto Flay."

The blond officer inclined his head as Commander Nell introduced him. "I am honored to meet you."

Kahl narrowed his eyes. *Why did he dislike this human already?*

Harto smiled but it felt insincere. "I don't believe I caught the names of your guards."

"Mat-rallenin and Kahl," the high priest said as he pointed at each Dyhaeri in turn.

Kahl saw a light of recognition flash in the eyes of the younger human officer at the mention of his name.

"You must be skilled wielders for the high priest to only need two of you. What level wielding have you each reached?"

Kahl wanted to ask how any of that was his business, but Mat rubbed his hands. That was a Dyhaeri code meaning, "Say nothing." Harto spotted the movement and inclined his head again. "Are you cold?"

"I'm fine, thank you." Mat pasted a polite smile on his face, but it didn't reach his eyes.

"High Priest Myltan, what brings you to Raven's Fall?" suddenly asked Commander Nell.

Kahl wondered at the abrupt questioning.

"Matters of security involving both my people and yours, lieutenant commander," answered the high priest calmly. "Specifically, the Namiran government."

"Our people are being hunted," cut in Lanead gravely.

Harto stared at him as if stunned by his audacity.

"I refer of course to both Weltonians and Dyhaeri," calmly continued the captain. "We've unearthed reliable intel indicating the queen is looking for more wielders, having almost sucked Namira dry."

An uneasy expression passed over Harto's face. Kahl found that reaction interesting.

"That is unfortunate." The lieutenant commander wore a neutral expression.

"Maybe if the Weltonians and Dyhaeri had stepped in to help us more than forty years ago, Namira wouldn't be in this state!"

Everyone stared at an angry Harto.

"Lieutenant, apologize!" Commander Nell barked.

Instead, the younger officer defiantly continued glaring at the Dyhaeri, clearly not intending to take back his words.

The high priest held up a hand. "Not all fault lies at our door."

Even Commander Nell turned to stare at the high priest. "Meaning?"

"Meaning if the late King Olnanier had listened to the warnings of both the Dyhaeri and Weltonians about marrying a pirate queen, Namira wouldn't be dealing with the ramifications of that union."

The lieutenant looked stunned. He turned to his superior, who looked pained.

"That can't be true—"

"Lieutenant Harto Flay!" barked the lieutenant commander. "Not another word!"

The agitated lieutenant momentarily appeared ready to rebel. He visibly struggled to assume a stony expression. "Yes, sir."

The rest of the carriage ride continued in agonizing silence.

#

As dusk fell, Kahl tried to take note of the surroundings outside the carriage. As they traveled, he noticed how unsteady the movement of the human vehicle was. It almost made him queasy, but a glance at Mat and the high priest revealed calm visages. Kahl tried to distract himself by looking out the window.

It was foggy here, probably due to the proximity to the sea. Before long, they reached a cobblestone road. Sticking his head out the window, he realized they weren't alone. Officers in Malaquey uniforms rode before and behind the carriage.

As he pulled his head back in, he could feel Harto was watching him closely. Kahl chose to ignore him. No sense in causing hostility in close quarters.

Besides, he was still feeling a bit nauseous. He decided to close his eyes and lean his head against the carriage wall behind him.

"Is he all right?" asked Commander Nell.

"He's just resting," answered Mat calmly. "It was a long trip."

Kahl kept his eyes closed.

"And where exactly did you sail from?" asked Harto. He sounded a bit sullen.

"From our territory in the Heldiar Sea," answered Mat in the same even tone. If Harto was smart, he would remember Dyhaeri territory was vast; asking any further questions would make him look stupid.

Harto said nothing, and Kahl reluctantly began to think the Malaquey officer had some brains after all.

No one spoke for a long moment, and Kahl's queasiness slowly eased. In fact, he was almost lulled into sleep by the rocking movement of the carriage.

Then it gradually came to a stop.

"We have arrived," said the senior Malaquey officer as Kahl's eyes shot open. He soon realized everyone was looking at him.

"Had a good nap?" asked Commander Nell cordially while Harto frowned.

"It was pleasant, thank you," said Kahl as the door was opened by a middle-aged man in a rich red uniform with golden braids. He was carrying a stool, which he placed just under the steps of the carriage.

"To aid your dismount," said the commander by way of explanation. Kahl knew if he looked at his cousin, he would only see boredom. He scurried down the steps and found the stool helped. He glanced around; they had arrived in a large circular courtyard with a huge fountain in the center. Now parked beside an awe-inspiring architectural wonder of glowing white, fronted by enormous circular columns, they had arrived at the royal palace of the king and queen of Malaquey. Though he could not see the royal guards, he had no doubt they were being observed closely. A noise behind him had him turn in time to see High Priest Myltan descend, followed by Mat, Lieutenant Flay, Captain Riverun, and Lieutenant Commander Nell.

"Considering the lateness of the hour, His Majesty the King has retired for the evening to his private quarters. However, he has made plans to see you tomorrow after you have broken your fast. I will convey you to your quarters." The commander turned to Lanead. "You, however, will be staying in the servant's quarters."

"That won't be necessary," interjected the high priest. "He can stay with us. Please relay my thanks to His Majesty, King Wilhem, and do lead the way."

Commander Nell opened his mouth to argue, then shut it and forced a smile. "Of course. Follow me."

#

Kahl tried not to stare, but the palace was unlike anything he had ever seen. White marble columns with grey veins outlined the palace entrance, and the grand double doors were of a smooth, aged gleaming oak. He wondered how well the doors would hold against elemental wielding. Inside was just as grand as outside. The carpet along the wide walkway was a rich red almost identical to the servants' uniforms. As they walked deeper into the palace, he could hear music and loud conversation.

"What is that?" asked Mat.

Harto gave him an odd look. "The music? Have you never heard music before?"

Mat shot him an unfriendly smile. "More than you have ever heard. My question is, why the noise? I thought since the king had retired to his quarters, the palace would be quiet. Are his nobles having a party without him present?"

Lanead had a wry expression on his face but kept silent.

Kahl saw a wary look appear on Harto's face.

"Yes," answered Commander Nell smoothly. "That does happen. Our king doesn't stand on ceremony."

"Ah, I see," said Mat. Kahl knew his cousin had seen through that flimsy excuse.

Their small group eventually reached an area where the beautiful white marbled walls were replaced by marbled walls of seafoam. Kahl had no idea why, but this particular green was irritating. He looked at the high priest, but he seemed unperturbed. Mat's eyes narrowed though as he took in the color change.

At the end of the hall, double pine-green doors were guarded by two Malaquey Navy officers. At a nod from their commanding officer, they pushed open the doors to reveal a vast room with full-length glass windows. It also had four king-sized, velvet-covered beds arranged in a circle around a sizable round pool that had been carved out of emerald-green marble. There was no other furniture.

"These are the old Dyhaeri quarters. I hope they are acceptable. Truth be told, they've hardly been used since the last time your people graced our land over eight hundred years ago," said the commander in a deceptively calm tone.

Kahl gave him a dark look. *Was he deliberately trying to start a fight?*

"Dire times are upon us, gentlemen," said the high priest. "Which is why we're here now. I trust we'll meet again on the morrow?"

Commander Nell was surprised by the gentle but abrupt dismissal.

"Um…yes. Do you need refreshments?"

"We'll be quite all right until morning, when I will have to speak with your chefs about our ongoing dietary requirements. Good evening to you both," said High Priest Myltan firmly.

The commander and his junior officer exchanged a glance and left.

The three Dyhaeri and one Weltonian waited for the doors to close before speaking.

"Kahl, wield nine noisy waterfalls in a perfect circle, please," commanded the high priest in their language. Kahl quickly obeyed, wielding nine-foot tall spouts in the pool as he wondered why.

When the high priest was satisfied, he stripped down to his underclothes. "Join me for a chat."

The cousins hesitated for only a moment before joining the captain in doing likewise. Once in the pool, each of the four wielded a bubble around them and entered the center of the waterfalls.

At the high priest's signal, the four combined their bubbles. "Now we can talk."

Kahl felt his face grow warm as he realized the wielding was to prevent eavesdropping.

"Don't worry, you'll get the hang of it," said Mat.

"You'll have to," concluded a solemn Lanead.

"All right, an analysis of our hosts?" asked the high priest.

"They're scared and angry," said Kahl.

Mat nodded while the captain grunted in agreement.

The high priest sighed. "It is as I feared. Regardless of what the commander said, King Wilhem must be awake and aware by now that we have arrived, yet he chose not to greet us."

"So perhaps we aren't wanted here in the first place," said Mat, a thoughtful expression on his face.

"That may be so; however, it is imperative we are always on our best behavior. We gain nothing from antagonizing our hosts." The high priest looked Mat squarely in the eye in emphasis.

Lanead scoffed. "Too late for that." High Priest Myltan shot him an admonishing look and the Weltonian captain rolled his eyes. "You and I both know the Malaquey court cares not for matters they're not in control of. They still believe if they bury their heads in the sand, nothing will bother them."

"We simply have to explain the situation to them," countered the high priest.

"Good luck with that."

Mat and Kahl shared a glance. *Why was the captain being so fatalistic?*

"Are Lieutenant Commander Nell and Lieutenant Arrogant Flay our human counterparts then?" asked Mat suddenly in a change of subject.

The captain grinned while the high priest sighed. "No and please don't ask him about that, or you'll cause a diplomatic incident."

"Speaking of incidents, why did Harto become so upset when you mentioned King Olnanier having been warned about marrying Queen Kallesa?" asked Kahl.

"Yes, I was meaning to ask about that. For a Malaquey officer, he seemed overly angry about it," noted Mat, folding his arms.

The captain and the high priest both stared at them. "Neither of you caught it, did you?" queried the Weltonian captain eventually.

Mat and Kahl exchanged puzzled looks.

"The lieutenant commander and Harto are Namiran refugees," explained the high priest.

"What?" asked a stunned Mat. Kahl was speechless.

"They have assimilated well with the Malaquey officers, but I can still pick up traces of their accents," said Lanead. "Many Namirans over the years have become citizens of Malaquey, but that doesn't replace their love and yearning for their homeland. And that is why you three need to watch your backs when I leave after our audience with the king."

"Why are you leaving?" asked Kahl when he'd finally found his voice.

"I have several errands to run, my friends, and so little time to complete them." The captain's expression became grave. "Please be careful, especially with…" he hesitated, "…with the nobles."

Kahl had a distinct feeling the Weltonian captain had been about to say something else. But what?

"Of course, we will be."

"Now, let's get out of this pool and eat. I'm starving," said High Priest Myltan.

#

Harto waited until he was alone with his uncle.

"Uncle, was the high priest telling the truth—"

"Are you stupid, Lieutenant Harto Flay?" interrupted the lieutenant commander in a barely controlled tone.

Harto was rendered speechless for a moment. "No, but—"

"You came this close to causing a diplomatic incident. And not once but twice! You blamed the Dyhaeri delegation for the existence of Queen Kallesa outright, then followed it up by calling the Dyhaeri high priest a liar!"

Harto took a step back from the fury on his uncle's face. "I just didn't believe—"

"That is not the point! While we wear this uniform, we serve Malaquey. It would do Malaquey and Namira no good to alienate the Dyhaeri. You graduated in the top ten of your class, so I know you must have passed your diplomacy course at the Royal Malaquey Naval Academy! What in the Seven Hells were you thinking!?"

Harto looked away in shame. "I'm sorry. I will endeavor to apologize tomorrow."

Commander Nell stared at him for a long moment, then sighed and kept walking. Harto quickened his pace to keep up.

"But what he said about King Olnanier, surely that wasn't true—"

"He *was* warned against the union," cut in the lieutenant commander. "Weltonians and Dyhaeri alike contacted him, and he rebuffed them both. That is why Namira is in the state it is."

Those words stopped Harto in his tracks. It took a few seconds before the commander realized his nephew had fallen behind. "Keep walking. We need to present our report to His Majesty."

A disturbed Harto obeyed. "But…but does mother know?"

"Yes, and so did your father, but otherwise, only a few are privy to this information."

"How exactly did they warn him?" asked Harto. He felt a desperate need to learn more.

His uncle appeared reluctant to reply.

"Uncle? Please, I have to know."

The senior officer stopped walking. He looked up and down the long hall to ensure they were alone.

"A year before the royal wedding, three Dyhaeri and a Weltonian showed up unannounced at the royal residence in Namira. They found the king alone in the royal gardens. How they got past the guards, no one knows. In the privacy of the garden, the visitors warned the king about the pirate who would later become our queen. But, for some unknown reason, he refused to listen to them, and he called the guards on them. Your grandfather was one of those guards, so that is how your father and I know of what happened that day."

"Did these Dyhaeri or the Weltonian harm anyone?"

"No, they left peacefully, though your grandfather said they scared the daylights outta him."

"Why?" asked Harto.

"Their eyes were pure silver, completely covered in a silver milky film, yet they seemed to see all."

"Do you know their names?"

"Afraid not. I presume my dah was too scared to ask for names. Now, let's not keep His Majesty waiting. We will talk of this anon."

Harto nodded silently. As he continued on, he looked back once in the direction of the Dyhaeri quarters.

CHAPTER 12

"Good morning, High Priest Myltan. I am Ernaz Calle, the court herald for the king." The short, stout man bowed. Kahl had to stifle a giggle. The herald wore a frilly white shirt framed by a form-fitting rich, red brocade pant suit topped with knee-high black leather boots. His shoulder-length corn-silk hair was done up in red ribbons that had been arranged artfully around his powdered face. It gave Kahl the impression of a walking, talking, red dahlia. He was sorely tempted to check out Mat's expression, but his instinct warned him his cousin was struggling not to laugh as well.

"Good morning to you too. How shall we proceed?" asked the high priest calmly. Beside him, Lanead wore a somber expression.

"First, I will introduce you to the court. So, while I have your title, High Priest Myltan, I do not have the full names and titles of those who accompany you."

"Please, don't introduce me, I'm just a lowly Weltonian." Lanead said, bowing and stepping back. The court herald dismissed him with a sniff, and the humor in Kahl died. A quick glance at Mat revealed his cousin was frowning.

"Present them as Guardian Mat-rallenin and Guardian Kahl," said the high priest.

Ernaz Calle was appalled. "Guardians? Bodyguards? I might as well call them mercenaries for hire or thugs! Surely, these two have some standing in your world?!"

Mat and Kahl shared a puzzled look. *What was he going on about? Why was he overreacting?*

The high priest seemed just as nonplussed. "Yes, they do have some standing in the social order of our world—"

"Such as?" interrupted the herald as he motioned for the high priest to hurry up and explain.

"They are defenders of our world, a position that has been passed down through countless generations." Ernaz now appeared impressed as the high priest continued.

"Important duties have been entrusted to them, and many depend on them to make the right decisions."

Kahl and Mat stared at the high priest with identical startled expressions. This was the first time they had heard such lofty but disturbing words from him. Beside them, Lanead had a sad smile on his face.

"Ahh! I have it. Princes they are and princes they shall be called." The stout herald walked away before Mat or Kahl could protest. Ernaz motioned to the silent guards, who swung open the huge double doors, exposing the inner court where a sea of richly dressed guests awaited.

"High Priest Myltan of Light-Under-the-Sea accompanied by Prince Matrallenin and Prince Kahl!"

Kahl exchanged an exasperated look with Mat before they all stepped forward as one group.

Kahl tried not to fidget in his own close-fitting yet comfortable indigo leather uniform as their small entourage descended the steps into the morning court. All conversation stopped as the entire court turned to face them. The high priest took point, the captain beside but respectfully a pace behind him. Kahl and Mat took up the rear, and thus began the long walk to where the king and queen sat upon their seats of power.

Last night had been a miserable affair. After their discussion, the four companions had supped on the snacks the thoughtful Weltonian cooks had packed for them. They had tried to sleep then, but the beds were unyielding and uncomfortable. In the end, they had all slept on the floor. Kahl wondered why the Malaquey didn't have mattresses that adjusted to one's shape like the Dyhaeri did. He dismissed the thought; there were more important things at stake.

Kahl's mind returned to the present; he glanced at his cousin, who was taking care to observe the nobles lined up on either side of them. Kahl did likewise and noticed that mingling with the nobles were many Malaquey naval and army officers.

Was this normal? Then he realized some of the officers had different colored bands on their left arms. The colors varied: white, blue, red, and brown.

"Mat, the bands."

"I see them," Mat whispered back in Dyhaeri.

"They represent the elements they wield," said Lanead, also in Dyhaeri.

Kahl almost broke his stride, but Mat somehow managed to keep his composure.

Lanead knew their language?!

"Stay steady, boys," said the captain, briefly glancing behind him, a wry smile on his face. Kahl glanced at the high priest, who didn't seem bothered in the least.

Mat and Kahl shared a quick glance before resuming their surveillance. Kahl tried to figure out what the bands meant. Red had to represent fire, blue was water, and white could be air, which meant brown had to be earth.

Among the Dyhaeri, runes were used to represent one's element but were not displayed as marks on uniforms. Was this a human characteristic? But Weltonians didn't identify themselves with such markings either. Maybe it was only used among the Malaquey soldiers.

Finally, they reached the gold-gilded double throne, which was also surrounded by Malaquey officers, each of them with those strange colored bands on their uniforms. One of the officers was Lieutenant Harto Flay. His uniform displayed a brown band.

Kahl frowned. He was certain that had not been on the officer's left arm yesterday.

The herald who stood before the king and queen of Malaquey inclined his head at the high priest, then began the royal introductions as per protocol.

"His Highness, King Wilhem of House Taros, which has ruled since the separation. May his line rule forever more." The herald bowed to his king, then turned to the woman seated beside him. "His wife, Queen Ariande."

Kahl waited for more to be said of the queen, but nothing followed. *Was she not as important?*

The king and queen raised their right hands, and the entire court, Captain Riverun included, bowed or curtsied. High Priest Myltan, Mat, and Kahl remained standing.

Murmurs flowed throughout the court, and the Malaquey officers frowned when the Dyhaeri's behavior was noticed. The high priest ignored them and raised his ceremonial staff.

"I carry the blessing of the Sea Mother, which has been bestowed upon King Jahlaniin and all Dyhaeri. We from Light-Under-the-Sea come in peace. May all transactions be favorable today and always."

"By the Sea Mother," intoned Mat and Kahl loudly. Mat amplified their voices using a tier-one air-wielding maneuver. Some of the court nobles were startled by the effect, but Harto and his fellow wielders glared at the small Dyhaeri delegation.

King Wilhem stood and the muttering died down. He strode down the dais; some of his wielders tried to form a barrier between him and the high priest. He simply raised a hand, and reluctantly, they fell back.

"Let's disperse with titles and posturing please. The Dyhaeri people deserve our respect, as well as the Weltonians. We are amongst friends." He nodded at Captain Riverun. Kahl saw the expressions of those closest to the throne—richly dressed, middle-aged men—harden at that.

Kahl went back to observing the human king. He seemed a bit younger than Captain Riverun but with additional and deeper lines creasing his weary face and a hint of grey in his coal-black hair. He wore an elaborate slate, fur-lined coat over a charcoal brocade jacket and black trousers, none of which hid his warrior physique and the calluses on his hands.

The king continued. "I'm sure what you wish to discuss is best aired in private."

"Of course, Your Majesty." The high priest nodded in agreement.

"Please, come with me," said the king as he pointed to indicate they should precede him. Kahl saw shock appear on human faces of those close enough to hear him. Clearly, this had not been intended. King Wilhem waved off all but one of the human wielders who stepped forward. It looked like Lieutenant Flay would be joining them.

Why was Kahl not surprised?

"But your Majesty!" complained one of the richly dressed men.

"Not now, Minister Havcroft. We'll speak later," said the king with a firm smile. King Wilhem turned to his wife and nodded at her.

Queen Ariande turned to the perplexed ministers. "Sirs, your petitions may begin."

As Kahl walked away, he glanced back to see some of the ministers were clearly tempted to follow them, but the queen deftly drew their attention back to her.

"She is my partner and rules better than me most days," said King Wilhem as they accompanied him to a large private study.

"I see," said the high priest politely as the king ushered them in.

The study wasn't empty. Inside were two senior Malaquey naval officers, one of whom was a woman Kahl didn't recognize. The second was Lieutenant Commander Peras Nell.

This should be interesting , thought Kahl.

"I believe you've already met Lieutenant Commander Peras Nell, so let me introduce Lieutenant Commander Elizea Trent." Now that Kahl knew to look, he glanced at the arms. The bands were absent. So, Harto was the only human wielder in this room.

"I apologize for not personally meeting you last night, but circumstances beyond my control prevented me for doing so."

The high priest studied the king. "I hope you didn't take ill?"

King Wilhem was silent as he removed his heavy fur cloak with help from the Commander Nell.

"Yes, I was ill."

His officers looked sharply at him.

"That was unfortunate. I trust you are on the mend," continued the high priest.

The king bade them to sit as he too sat down. "I appreciate the concern, and yes, I do feel better, but do me the courtesy of keeping this between us." He looked at his still standing, mortified officers and said, "A word of advice, never lie to a Dyhaeri high priest. They pick up on that sort of thing." He turned back to the visitors.

"So, gentlefolk, what brings you to Malaquey?"

The high priest smiled thinly at the straightforward question. "The same problem that troubles you. The Namiran kingdom and its current leader."

King Wilhem frowned. "I have no quarrel with Queen Kallesa."

"Not yet," continued the high priest, "But once she runs out of wielders to hunt at home and in the seas, I suspect those in Malaquey will interest her a great deal."

"We have a treaty with Queen Kallesa," said King Wilhem.

"Which will not last, Your Majesty," Captain Riverun interjected.

The king stared at him for a long moment.

"You seem quite certain. Would you care to share your reasons?"

The captain and the high priest shared a look before the Weltonian captain turned back to the king of Malaquey. "The Namiran shipyards have been very busy of late. Rumor has it she's building ships no one has ever seen. However, we have no idea what makes these ships unique. We do know she calls them warships."

King Wilhem's eyes narrowed. "We are aware of that, but one cannot fault her for building new ships after three were destroyed by the Alkynaia recently." His gaze settled on the high priest. "Though the attack occurred in our territory, the Queen of Namira sent us word they were trying to aid one of our merchant ships when suddenly the Alkynaia and Dyhaeri attacked them."

Kahl's first thought was to deny this, but something held him back.

The high priest looked calm. "The Queen of Namira is lying to you. They pursued one of your merchant ships, which had sought refuge in Alkynaian waters. The Namirans followed them in, and the Alkynaia attacked them."

"But why didn't the sea serpents attack the merchant ship?" asked the king.

The high priest smiled. "You already know the answer to that, Your Majesty. The question that remains is whether your forces are preparing for war."

King Wilhem blinked, and by the expressions of the silent Malaquey officers, it was clear this question had not been expected.

"Surely you know it's only a matter of time before the situation in Namira worsens," said Lanead. "Her people rising up against her isn't going to happen anytime soon. Over the course of decades, she's manipulated the common people into believing wielders are dangerous, and only her and her select group of wielders can be trusted. Wielder families have sold out their own flesh and blood, especially if they've been suspected of informing or spying. Those ill-fated wielders are never heard from again. So, if you keep thinking she won't attack Malaquey at some point, then your head is buried in the sand, Your Majesty."

Harto glared at Captain Riverun. Though the Weltonian's voice had been polite, his words had been blunt.

The king smiled and nodded. "I appreciate your honesty, believe me. It's refreshing. However, I am interested in peace, and I do not plan on invading Namira anytime soon just because the Weltonians and Dyhaeri are a little concerned."

"We do not seek or want war, Your Majesty," said the Dyhaeri high priest. "But it would be best if you prepare for it."

King Wilhem stared at the high priest for several heartbeats. "How do you propose we do that?"

"I would like to start by inspecting your wielding schools."

The king didn't try hide his surprise. "Why?"

"Though your wielders are few in number to ours, they can still be a formidable force…as long as they're being trained properly."

Kahl watched as Harto and the other two naval officers exchanged worried looks.

"The Royal Malaquey Naval Wielding College and the Artra Army Wielding College will be out of bounds," declared the king after a long silence. The officers were visibly relieved by the king's words. The high priest waited expectantly and the king continued.

"However, there is still Syla Wielding College, which is an hour's ride from here. I trust their teaching will be up to par and they are ready for you inspect." The king set his jaw as if expecting an argument.

High Priest Myltan smiled and nodded. "Understood. Then, with your permission, I will leave anon to inspect Syla Wielding College."

#

It had been all Harto could do to keep his expression neutral when the king had agreed to the high priest's suggestion. He had stayed silent as the meeting had ended and the Dyhaeri delegation, and Captain Riverun, left the king's private study.

The king stared at the closed door for a long moment before turning to the three naval officers. "Well, that was interesting."

Commander Nell opened his mouth to speak was beaten to it by Lieutenant Flay. "Your Majesty, why did you let them inspect our wielding college?" blurted out Harto.

Peras gave his nephew a reproving stare, but Harto ignored him.

"He also agreed to inspect Syla College quite quickly, as if that was what he'd wanted all along."

The king shrugged. "I'm just as curious as you are. If I was a visiting dignitary who wished to assess my ally's readiness for defense, I would demand to inspect the military wielding colleges, not the weakest of the trio." His expression grew troubled. "Though I must admit we cannot take for granted the high priest's request. His own king has ordered him on this venture. There must be something of import behind it."

"Or someone," added Lieutenant Commander Elizea Trent.

A spark went off in Harto's mind. "Britea D'Tranell."

The king gave him a blank look, and Peras and Elizea looked puzzled.

"She's that novice wielder that arrived on the *Windrider* ."

King Wilhem's expression cleared. "The one who'd been briefly trained by a Dyhaeri—"

"—whose name was Kahl, the same name as one of the high priest's bodyguards or princes or whatever they're calling them. And now they're interested in Syla College where she's a student?" continued excitedly. He noticed their skeptical expressions and frowned.

"Surely, it's obvious to you too! They're here for her!"

King Wilhem and Peras shared a skeptical look while Lieutenant Commander Trent sighed.

"We looked into her; the girl is the daughter of a farmer and no more. She is of no importance. I doubt they're here for her."

Harto wanted to protest, but a part of him wondered if maybe he *was* off base.

"Then, Your Majesty, it may be best if we assign someone to the Dyhaeri delegation while they inspect Syla College," Harto suggested.

King Wilhem smiled. "Are you volunteering for the job?"

Harto was about to reply when he saw his uncle shake his head as if warning him not to.

But why didn't his uncle want him near the Dyhaeri? The events of the day before were still fresh in his mind. This was his chance to find out what the high priest knew of the days when Namira was a free country.

"Yes, Your Majesty. I volunteer."

At his reply, his uncle's features tightened in frustration for a brief moment before easing.

"Splendid," said the smiling king of Malaquey.

#

Kahl stared at the outfits on the bed and sighed. After being given a tour of the palace grounds, a royal steward had handed the high priest an envelope containing an invitation for them to attend a royal ball held in their honor this evening. Kahl had hoped the high priest would decline the invitation, but his hopes had been dashed when High Priest Myltan had stated they would be attending.

Captain Riverun was long gone. After the meeting with the king, he had gone to attend to his other errands, but not before warning them to watch their backs. Kahl was actually missing him now; Lanead had begun to feel almost like a concerned father.

"Can't make up your mind?"

Kahl turned to face his cousin, who was soaking in the pool in the center of their quarters. High Priest Myltan had gone out on the balcony to get some air.

"I'm just worried that whatever outfit I choose, I'll look like a fool."

Mat laughed. "Nah, you'll be a dashing young Dyhaeri noble as long as you keep a polite and intrigued smile plastered on your face."

Kahl gave his cousin an amused look. "You were really listening to Lanead's teachings."

Mat sighed as he climbed out of the pool and reached for a towel. "Say what you want, but he knew a lot. I wish he was still with us." He paused to give his dark green locks a shake. "So, picked an outfit yet?"

Kahl turned back to the outfits, then he touched one. "I'll go with the night-blue one."

Mat dried the rest of his lean form and nodded. "Excellent choice. We'll wear matching outfits and see if anyone can tell us apart."

"Do you think Lieutenant Flay and his superiors will be at the ball?" asked Kahl as he began to dress.

"Ha! That's a bet I'm not taking. He and all the other wielders be there just to keep an eye on us." Mat picked up his own outfit, identical to Kahl's. "I wonder how high he can wield though." A mischievous glint appeared in Mat's eyes. "Maybe we should try to join their wielding sparring sessions."

"Wait until we get to Syla College," said High Priest Myltan, coming in from the balcony. He had a thoughtful expression on his face.

"And why is that?" asked Mat.

"Call it instinct. Something's not right in this court. It's subtle, but it feels eerily familiar."

Mat and Kahl gaped at the high priest, who initially didn't realize they were staring at him. When he finally did, he switched gears and said. "Enough of that. Let's get ready for this ball, shall we?"

#

Mat glanced at Kahl as they stood before a full-length mirror. Their outfits were stunning; both had been crafted of vert-silk. A material exclusively made by Weltonians, it felt like velvet but was much lighter and comfortable and kept the body cool or warm as needed. The Weltonian dressmaker had made long-sleeved, thigh-long tunics buttoned from hem to collar, and the straight-cut pants were of the same dark-blue hue. Their regal outfits were topped with walnut leather shoes. Not a frill in sight. Thank the Mother.

The color of their outfits made their green skin paler, and with their pine-colored locks combed back, Mat had to agree he and Kahl appeared quite handsome.

"I've never been to a ball," said Kahl in a nervous whisper.

"Neither have I," said Mat cheerfully. He clapped his cousin on the shoulder. "Come on, I'm sure it won't be that bad."

"Just recall all that Captain Riverun taught you, and we'll be fine," said High Priest Myltan, who was waiting beside the door, his hands clasped behind his back. He was also dressed in a similar but lighter green outfit of vert-silk; it nearly matched his skin tone, and made him appear ancient and regal. For this occasion, he was leaving his ceremonial staff behind. He had, of course, bound it to the floor of the pool with runes as a precaution.

Right on time, there was a knock on the door.

"Show time," muttered Mat.

His cousin tried to smile, but it came out as a grimace. He couldn't quite pinpoint why he was so worried. This was just a ball, or a dance party, for humans. How hard could it be?

#

"My, what a lovely suit you're wearing! I must have the name of your tailor!" Mat tried to keep his expression pleasant as the human lady's shrill voice threatened to pierce his eardrums. It took all his will power not to wield her into the next dimension when she touched his chest for the umpteenth time.

This evening was worse than any battle drill he had endured as a marine, and he had been through thousands. Once they had stepped into the crowded ballroom, everyone had wanted to speak to them. It only worsened when the nobles realized the delegation wore vert-silk. Apparently, the stuff was so expensive only the royals and the richest of nobles could afford it, so to see three Dyhaeri clothed in it from neck to ankle was unbelievable.

Which was precisely why most of them had insisted on touching their outfits to see if they were really vert-silk. High Priest Myltan was lucky to have avoided such travesty because he had been taken to the king's dais to sit with the queen and her children while Mat and Kahl were forced to mingle with the guests.

Somehow, while mingling, Mat and Kahl had gotten separated. Mat had just escaped one group of overly inquisitive humans, mostly females, only to be trapped by a certain Lady Nara Gedea. She would have been pretty if not for the overwhelming make-up she wore. And then there was that cloying perfume threatening to suffocate him.

"You look absolutely dashing! Your style is so unique, it thrills my senses!" shrilled the woman as she tried to touch him again. Mat moved backwards this time to avoid her hand.

"Why thank you, Lady Gedea. You are a vision as well." As he suspected, she blushed, and Mat had to resist rolling his eyes.

"So, tell me, Prince Mat-ralini," Mat tried not to wince as she mangled his full name. "What is a typical day like for a Dyhaeri prince?"

Mat was getting tired of the honorific and tried to resist cursing the court herald for insisting on calling him and Kahl princes.

"Please, just call me Mat. I hold no titles, really."

Lady Gedea gasped. "But that would be so inappropriate, Prince Mat. And you must be a prince to afford this vert-silk and be in the attendance of the high priest of your people. You must be jesting with me. I'm sure you're a highly placed prince among your kind."

Great, now she thinks I'm lying.

"No, kind lady. I am just a marine in service to my king." He smiled politely.

She blushed deeply and fluttered her eyelashes. "Ah, now I recall that indigo leather outfit you wore earlier today as well, so masculine and fitting your magnificent physique to perfection! I do love a prince in uniform. You and I simply must have dinner alone, and then you can tell me all about your thrilling life under the sea!"

Now, Mat felt physically ill. *Was she flirting with him? Was she even really listening to him?*

He glanced around for a means of escape and saw his poor cousin was surrounded by at least seven nobles, most of them women.

"Please excuse me, Lady Gedea. I must seek out my cousin. Matters of state." He bowed hastily and made off before she could recover.

Mat ignored the admiring glances from most of the women—and some of the men. The Weltonian tailor had done too fine a job. He felt as though everyone wanted a piece of him. It made him self-conscious. As he got closer to his cousin, pieces of the conversation began to drift in his direction, and he began to realize his appearance was the least of their problems.

"So, you're saying not everyone is invited to feast in the king's court or to attend his balls?" asked Kahl, sounding puzzled.

"Of course not," laughed one of the women who had put her hand possessively on Kahl's right arm. "Why would we invite the poor into this sanctuary? The stench alone would make us all ill." The other human nobles nodded in agreement.

"But surely, since he rules them and taxes them, they should be guests at his balls. And why are they poor? Surely the king has the power to redress that situation," pressed Kahl. Mat closed his eyes briefly; his cousin was this close to causing a diplomatic incident.

Kahl was behaving as though King Wilhem was similar to King Jahlaniin. The Dyhaeri king treated everyone the same and attended briefings and plays alike with the Dyhaeri people. Also, due to the cardinal rule that all must share both the workload and the bounty or harvest, there was no poverty. That was their culture, but Mat knew from his observations and teachings that the humans were divided into factions based on wealth and station. The rich and powerful looked down on the weak and poor. Kahl too had experienced it briefly with Britea and the crew of the *Windrider*, but he still had not seen all Mat had witnessed for years observing humans and their selfish behaviors.

"Are all your poor guests at your king's balls?" challenged one of the male nobles.

Kahl stared at him. "We don't have balls."

They stared at him.

"What my dear colleague means is we don't call them balls," interjected Mat loudly. They turned to him. "We call them gatherings, and we have a wonderful time while our king is in attendance. He's not a great dancer though." The face he made caused a round of laughter. He saw Kahl glaring at him, but for once, his cousin wisely kept silent.

At that moment, the gentle background music picked up tempo.

"Oh, it's time to dance!" said one of the young noblemen. "Come! You must show us your native steps!"

By the Deep, no! thought Mat as he pulled Kahl away from the group. "I'm afraid I must decline. Due to religious reasons, we cannot." The adoring group was so disappointed he tried not to laugh. "And since the head of our religious order is in attendance, it will be our necks on the line if we disobey. Please, enjoy your dance. We shall enjoy watching."

The group left them, eager to take to the ballroom floor.

Mat kept a smile on his face as he prepared to chew out his cousin.

"Can you believe they don't invite everyone to these? I mean what kind of—" began Kahl, irritated.

"*Start smiling, keep your mouth shut, and listen,*" interrupted Mat in their native language.

Kahl gaped at him for a long moment before remembering to do as he was told.

"For a usually quick study, you, my dear cousin, can be an idiot. This is the human world. They are not like us and certainly don't follow our culture or ways. We are here to observe, not debate their way of living. So, listen and try not to cause a diplomatic incident because you find their behavior towards the less fortunate shocking."

Kahl narrowed his eyes. "Are you saying we're not to speak up at all? Just smile and nod, even when we should speak up?"

Mat suppressed a curse. "Sea Mother give me strength," he muttered under his breath. "Look, maybe I didn't explain it as well as I should have. But yes, most times you have to keep your mouth shut. Only speak out when absolutely necessary."

Kahl didn't look convinced. "Then how will I know when to—"

"I hope you're both having a good time."

Both turned to find Lieutenant Harto Flay right behind them.

#

Harto kept a polite smile on his face even though he wanted to grin at the startled expressions on the faces of the two Dyhaeri before him. From their body language, they appeared to be arguing. It was one of the few good things that had gone right this evening. Harto had made sure to get ready for the ball hours before the event, then waited until one of the guards had informed him that the honored guests were in the ballroom. Harto had immediately questioned the spies he'd inserted in the walls of the Dyhaeri chambers. He had gritted his teeth in frustration when they had nothing significant to report. The problem lay in the fact that the Dyhaeri spoke in their own language when alone, and none of the spies were fluent in the native tone of the undersea folk.

He had decided it was time to approach the problem directly.

"Thank you. The event has been quite pleasant," said Mat, pasting on an equally insincere smile. Kahl was still visibly upset about whatever they had been arguing about. Too bad Harto couldn't understand their language; however, Kahl seemed the weakest of the trio.

"I don't fault you for not dancing. I find these events to be quite tedious to be honest."

Mat looked skeptical, but Kahl seemed interested. "Why is that?"

Harto plucked at his frilly white sleeves and pointed at his chocolate velvet puffed-up pantaloons. "This outfit makes me feel like a fowl being sent to the slaughter. This event," he gestured at the dancing nobles, "is just to pander to the court and those who circle the throne to further their own goals. It's just a waste." Harto pretended not to see Kahl's stunned expression.

To be honest, Harto was speaking from his heart. He hated balls because he spent half of them avoiding mothers and their daughters, and he felt guilty living in the lap of luxury while so many of his fellow Namirans were starving. Today, he had been granted a reprieve because most of the court wanted to catch a glimpse of the Dyhaeri princes, as they were calling Mat and Kahl.

Oddly enough, he was a bit grateful for the Dyhaeri distraction.

"You're the first person here to say that," began Kahl as he stepped closer. Harto hid a smile. Now was the time to get some information. "I wondered why—"

"Ha! You expect us to fall for that nice-guy act? Especially after you just eavesdropped on Kahl and the other nobles?" Mat cut in. Kahl and Harto turned towards him. Kahl said something animatedly to his cousin in their Dyhaeri language. Though Harto couldn't understand it, he suspected Kahl was pleading with the fuming Mat.

Mat stared at his cousin briefly before turning to Harto.

"My dear cousin was just asking me not to cause a diplomatic incident, but for you, I'm willing to make an exception."

Kahl covered his face with his palm, muttering what were likely curses under his breath.

Mat continued his rant as he began to tick off points with his fingers. "Less than a day ago, you called our high priest a liar to his face. Then, you and your

Malaquey Naval Intelligence cohorts have treated us with hostility since we set foot in your port, and don't get me started on the spies hidden in the walls of our chambers."

Harto could barely hide his shock, and he noticed Kahl was watching his reaction closely.

Mat continued as he moved closer to stand just a few feet from Harto. "And now you think you can get us to tell all by pretending to be disgusted by your excessive human lifestyle?"

Harto was getting angry now. "That's rich coming from one wearing vert-silk."

Mat waved those words away. "It was a gift. It would have been rude to say no. Now, back to you. What was the point of engaging with us? What do you want?"

The two adversaries from different worlds just glared at each other while Kahl looked on, alarmed.

"Why did your people destroy the Namiran warships trying to aid the *Windrider?*"

"The Dyhaeri didn't destroy the warships. The Alkynaia did," countered Mat before Kahl could say a word.

"Witness reports state Dyhaeri were in the area," hissed Harto.

"So what? In case you forgot, the Heldiar Sea is our home; we're always in the area!" The two stood close enough to swing at each other. Kahl felt he had to do something before matters got out of hand.

"Lieutenant Flay, those Namiran warships were hunting the merchant ship. I would know—"

"Kahl," hissed Mat in warning, but Kahl ignored him.

"—because I was there. The *Windrider* sailed into Alkynaia territory because they were desperate to escape the Namirans. Maybe if the Malaquey Navy had been nearby, your own people—that you are sworn to protect—wouldn't have had to risk their lives to remain free."

Now Kahl and Harto were glaring at each other. To Mat's surprise, the Malaquey Naval Intelligence officer dropped his eyes first.

"You do have a point, but the Namiran government swears the Dyhaeri were involved."

"Oh, there you are!" A shrill feminine voice stopped Harto in his tracks. The three males turned to see a trio of women in expensive dresses bearing down on them. Leading them was Lady Gedea. Harto heard Mat mutter a foreign word, most likely a curse. He had seen how Mat had extracted himself from her presence. It had been amusing to watch.

But Harto's smile disappeared when he saw the two women with Lady Gedea. These were the two he had been trying to avoid all summer.

"Prince Mat and Prince Kahl!" said Lady Gedea loudly. "I would love to introduce you to a very, very good friend of mine." She turned to the attractive older woman dressed in a modest silver and black high-necked gown with wide skirts; her greying hair had been coiled up on the top of her head, making her appear regal. "Lady Adria Arkei, and of course, her beautiful daughter, Lady Selina Arkei."

The daughter wore a scarlet dress with voluminous skirts and shimmering lines that seemed to coil around the dress. The bodice was tight, enhancing her exposed, pale décolletage. A neck collar adorned with a central emerald and a pair of emerald-green earrings completed the look. Her waist-length raven hair flowed freely but was swept off her face by a matching emerald-colored velvet circlet.

"Oh, Lord Flay. What a pleasant surprise," said Lady Selina with a bright smile when she noticed the Malaquey naval officer.

Harto tried to keep his expression pleasant. "My ladies, you are a treat for the senses," he said, bowing as the three women tittered away at his praise.

Lady Gedea turned back to Mat and Kahl. "My friends simply demanded to meet you. They are directly related to the king."

Lady Adria smiled. "Distantly related. I have never met Dyhaeri royalty. Please, tell me if the ball is to your liking."

Mat smiled politely, but Kahl silently regarded Lady Selina as if she was an alkynaia.

"It has been an educational and pleasant experience." Mat settled for a partial lie.

"Oh my!" exclaimed Selina. She had glided up to Kahl and was examining his outfit while he remained frozen, his muscles tense. "Your outfit is entirely vert-silk! When I heard the rumors, I couldn't believe it. You simply must come to our estate for a weekend. We throw the best balls and parties..."

"Have we not met before?" Kahl cut in to the surprise of the onlookers.

Selina blinked then laughed airily. "I would definitely remember meeting a Dyhaeri prince."

Harto saw a puzzled look briefly flash across Mat's face. *What was going on here?*

"On the *Windrider*? You came on board, did you not?" continued Kahl.

Selina looked a bit confused, but then suddenly her expression cleared. "Oh! That ramshackle boat! The one that poor excuse of peasant wielder—quite an ugly one by the way—was on…" her voice trailed off when she noticed the glare Kahl was directing her way.

"Wait! You were teaching that ugly, fat peasant upstart!"

Kahl's expression turned murderous.

"Ah, it's time we said hello to our cousin, the king," interrupted Lady Adria firmly as she laid a gentle had on her daughter's arm. Selina glared at her mother for a moment, then looked away. Lady Adria continued before turning to leave. "It was nice to meet you. Please, enjoy the ball."

She practically dragged her daughter away, leaving Lady Gedea to stare at their receding backs. The lone noblewoman glanced back at the Dyhaeri and Harto, visibly torn between the desire to flirt with them or rub elbows with Malaquey royalty. She eventually ran after the two Arkei nobles.

Harto, Mat, and Kahl stood in awkward silence for a long moment.

"Well, that's the shortest conversation I've ever had with them," said Harto finally.

Mat ignored him and placed a hand on Kahl's shoulder. "Excuse us. My cousin and I should eat."

He missed the surprised expression on Harto's face. The Malaquey naval officer watched them leave. Just from this one conversation he had learned two important things: one, Mat and Kahl were related, and two, Britea was someone special to Kahl.

He could use that.

#

"And that is how you dine at court," stated Instructor Helene Droye in a voice so loud it made Britea wince. The class had just gone through all the court etiquette so as not to appear as uneducated savages.

Oh yes! That is so important, isn't it?

As if the instructor could hear her thoughts, her gaze swept over the class. "Some of you may realize how important this is, but the rest of you think this is all a waste of your time. I'm here to tell you it isn't. Do recall it's only the favor of the royal court that keeps this school open and the common people appeased."

Britea was more than a little scared of what had occurred four days ago when the entire school and faculty had been witness to the stripping of powers from three final-year students. She was finding it hard to sleep at night thanks to the nightmares, and the constant reminders weren't helping. At least she had Danai. She had been not only supportive, but equally shaken by what they had witnessed. It had been the first time Danai had witnessed such a sentencing as well.

Britea looked around, and most of the students appeared…indifferent. She frowned.

By the Lords of Light, it seemed like the sentencing had already become a distant memory for most of the students.

"Now, clear the tables and push them to the walls. It's time for dancing."

"Not this again," Britea heard someone mutter, and she heartily agreed with the sentiment. She stood up, hoping she wouldn't get paired with Lianne again. The lady and her two friends had been staring at her for the past four days and whispering whenever she passed them.

She suspected it was just an intimidation tactic, but thanks to what Lianne had said to her at the sentencing, it was working.

"Instructor Droye?"

Britea went still when she heard her arch enemy's voice.

"Yes, dear?"

Why did the instructor only call Lianne 'dear'? Wasn't that inappropriate?

"May I be excused? I really need to see the healers. Valerie and Pearl have agreed to accompany me for support."

Britea's eyes narrowed. Surely the instructor could see through that farce.

"Of course, dear. You poor thing. You should have said something earlier. Please take your time, and rest after your visit until your next class."

The three girls happily left the class as Britea stared open-mouthed at the instructor.

Clearly, the woman had favorites!

"Everyone else to your places!"

Britea hid her annoyance and took her place on the dance floor. At least she didn't have to partner with the bully princess.

#

"And that's it for today class," Britea said, watching the junior students cheer after completing their tier-two wielding exercises. It was the start of the weekend, and Britea shared their joy at the thought of two free days.

Once again, Instructor Shelley had left her in charge, but this time was different. The instructor had told Britea to continue teaching until the bell rang, and then she could leave as well. No one-to-one teaching today.

"That was some wonderful wielding, and some of you are improving. I'm glad." She looked at a smiling Vindell, who had again been partnered with Chelton. The two were now getting along. Who knew? They could be friends before graduating from this class. "See you all next week."

"Thank you, Instructor D'Tranell," chorused the class as they stood up.

Britea sighed. "Hey, it's novice!" The kids grinned at her and skipped from the classroom. Vindell and Chelton were the last to leave, chattering happily to themselves. She chuckled to herself as she tidied up the now empty class.

Usually she and Instructor Shelley would do that before their one-to-one lesson, which was why she usually arrived late to the dining hall. Well, today, she would be on time.

Once the state of the class was to her satisfaction, she took her bag of books and left. Britea was tired. It had been a long day, and she was looking forward to sleeping in her bed. But first, she had to drop her books off in her room and then head for the dining room. Britea held her coat tighter around her as she entered the large exposed hallway beside the pools and central gardens. Only a mild frost covered the green hedges, but though it was cold and damp, the pools remained unfrozen. Apparently winter in Raven's Fall was mild with more chilly rain than snow.

For once in her life, she missed the snow of Weldaros. Winter there was harsh, but it was fun, what with building snowmen and having snowball fights with her sister and their parents. Britea smiled as she thought of the plans she and Danai had made; apparently her roommate's parents were in town, and Danai had invited Britea to spend the whole day on board her mother's vessel.

Oh, she was looking forward to that indeed .

Britea turned down a second corridor, which led to the girl's dorms, and came to a complete stop. Chelton stood in front of her, and the junior wielder looked scared. A bruise marred his left cheek.

"Chelton, what happened? Where's Vindell?" At the mention of his friend's name, his face scrunched up as if he was about to cry.

"They have her."

Britea went down on one knee until she was level with him. "Who has her?"

"Three girls grabbed her as we neared the dining hall, and one of them hit me. They had their hoods down, so I couldn't see their faces." Despite his best efforts, a tear escaped the corner of one eye.

"We have to report this to the warden." She reached out a hand for him, but to her dismay, he drew back.

"No! We can't do that. The one that hit me said *you* had to come and find Vindell right now. If you call anyone else, Vindell will get hurt!"

It's a trap. The words sprung into Britea's mind. She had a good idea who was behind it, and she knew she should be running for the warden right now, or looking for Danai and the others for help. *But at what cost?*

"Please, Instructor D'Tranell!"

Britea made up her mind. "Where do they want me to go?"

#

Britea ran towards the stairs that led up to the stone bridge connected to the Great Hall. She tried to ignore the sane part of her that was warning her to run in the opposite direction. The Forever Bridge was the perfect place for an ambush, the one area so rarely used so no one would hear her calls for help. It had taken a lot of work to convince Chelton not to follow her. Britea just hoped he had done what she had asked him to do.

At least she wasn't out of breath when she reached the top of the stairs. In her mind, she thanked Instructor Lexar, who had insisted on daily running in her combat and defense class. The last few months in that class had conditioned her legs and lungs. But Britea was still scared and unsure of what she would come upon up there. As she pushed open the doors, she realized the weather had changed. Now the wind was picking up, and even worse, it was raining. In the distance, she heard thunder in the night sky.

Great. Britea shivered as the first cold drops of rain landed on her chestnut hair and on her face. *Give me snow over this!* As she walked across the windy bridge, she realized the roar of the ocean was closer now. She looked over the side, and sure enough, the tide had come in, and the water was right beneath the bridge.

The rain fell heavier still as she approached the center of the bridge and the sizable group of people on it. There had to be more than forty students present.

As Britea edged closer and they made way for her, she studied their faces. These were students from her general education classes, some that had once seemed friendly but now regarded her with malicious glee and expectation. She was relieved when she realized Henrick was not one of them.

Britea soon reached the center, and her heart seized when she caught sight of Vindell. The junior wielder was on her knees on the wet stone floor while a hooded feminine figure stood over the little girl, one hand pressing down cruelly on her shoulder.

"What is this?!" Britea had to shout to make herself heard over the loud winds.

The hooded female drew back her cowl to reveal the pretty features of Lady Pearl Ceres. Already her coffee-brown locks were damp from the falling rain.

"Britea of Weldaros, I name you as an imposter in our fair college. Your wielding talent is a sham and a lie..."

Britea's mouth dropped open.

Pearl continued. "To maintain the purity of this esteemed college, I challenge you to a duel that will only end when one of us yields!"

Britea's gaze darted around her as the onlookers cheered Pearl on. Her eyes finally rested on two hooded females standing slightly apart but in front of the spectators. She caught the smug smiles on their faces. Lady Lianne Arkei and Lady Valerie Mern. It had to be.

"What say you, peasant?!" yelled Pearl, drawing back Britea's attention.

Britea thought fast. "We...we can't do this! It's against the Wielders Creed. We'll both be punished if we duel—"

"There stands a coward!" bellowed Pearl. "She hides behind a Creed that does not include her since she is no wielder! How many of you have seen her wield?"

"I haven't," said one of the hooded females. It *was* Valerie. The noble dropped her hood and stepped forward to stand on the other side of the kneeling Vindell.

"Neither have I," said one of the onlookers on Britea's right.

"Nor I," said Laris. Britea recognized him. He had been kicked out the combat and defense class in his second week when he had challenged Instructor Caren, and she knew he wasn't her friend.

Others began to say the same thing. Britea knew she couldn't convince them because she attended the junior wielder's class, and apparently, Lianne and her friends had had plenty of time to convince her peers that Britea was a fraud.

"Please, let us settle this another way—" began Britea.

"She teaches us!" shouted Vindell, surprising everyone. "She *is* a wielder—"

Valerie slapped the kneeling twelve-year old girl, and Britea felt something cold snap inside her. "Shut up you, little brat, or I'll wield the foul air out of your lungs." The words made Vindell sob. Even Pearl gave Valerie a startled look.

"Touch her again and I'll rip your head off your shoulders," growled Britea.

"Aha!" Valerie laughed. "The savage speaks! Well, if you wish to do that, you first have to get past Pearl." The blond wielder moved back to stand beside a smiling Lianne.

A part of Britea was screaming, *No, this was against the Wielder Creed!* But the other part of her was past caring and was actually looking forward to the fight.

She turned to Pearl, conscious of the fact that the students surrounding them were backpedaling to give them more space.

"So, let's begin—" she had barely formed the words when Pearl abruptly wielded a spear of air in her direction.

Britea grabbed the droplets of rain and formed interlocking ovals of water to create a full-length concave shield. She caught the surprised expressions of Pearl, Lianne, and Valerie as the onlookers cheered on the fight. They clearly had not been expecting her to know how to wield a shield.

Surely, now that she had showed them she could wield, that was enough, right? But then she saw the determined countenance on Pearl's face and knew the fight had just begun.

The female wielder formed three air spears and flung them at Britea.

She responded by reinforcing her shields as Instructor Shelley's words rang through her mind. "A good defense at times is the best way to wear down the enemy. That is why we practice this all the time. Then, when they appear to be weakening, you strike."

"Why won't you fight back?" taunted Valerie as Pearl continued trying to break her water shield. "Is that all you can do? Hide like a coward?"

Britea knew Valerie was trying to distract her, so she ignored her and kept her shield tight. Kahl and Instructor Shelley had taught her it was harder to hit a moving target, so Britea made sure never to stay still. She risked a glance at Vindell and to her relief, the junior wielder was now by the wall to her right. Apparently, Lianne and Valerie had forgotten her.

A hard ding on her water shield reminded her to keep her eyes on the menace before her.

"Come on, fight me!" yelled Pearl in frustration. Britea hid a smile.

"If you can't break this *simple* tier-one water shield, then who's the fraud?" challenged Britea.

This drew *oohs* and *aahs* from the crowd, and Pearl's face flushed with anger as she threw more air spears at Britea. Each bounced off as Britea kept reinforcing her shield by fashioning a second layer of small ovals from the small puddles now forming on the bridge. This was a trick she had learned from watching Instructor Shelley during one of their one-to-one session, but it was tiring. Her heart was beating too fast, and she felt as if there wasn't enough air in her lungs. The cold rain felt like sharp pinpricks on her skin, but she had to keep wielding until Pearl gave up. At least the rain was her friend.

Then she saw Lianne look silently at Valerie and nod.

Something was about to happen.

Valerie stepped away from Lianne and joined the onlookers to Britea's left.

Britea now had a double-layered shield, and it was getting heavier the longer she maintained the shape. She tried to stay on the balls of her feet, ready to run in case Valerie started attacking as well. Pearl didn't seem to notice what was going on, but that didn't mean she wasn't pretending.

She continued raining spears and arrows down on Britea, over and over and it was getting harder to maintain the double shield, but she had to until reinforcements came.

Where in the Deep was Chelton?

Then Valerie made her move, but not on Britea. She blasted a burst of air at Vindell who was now huddling in the corner. Acting on impulse, Britea dashed the few feet to Vindell and took the brunt of Valerie's attack, fighting off the double assault. It made her stagger backwards, but miraculously, her shield stayed intact.

"Hey! Not fair!" shouted one of the spectators. Lianne shot a murderous glare at the person, and he fell silent.

Behind Britea, Vindell cowered.

"Just stay behind me. It'll be all right!" shouted Britea as both nobles rained air projectiles on her watery shield. It was time to change her strategy. Already she could feel her barrier weakening. She waited for a slight pause in their attacks, then she yanked on the pool of water beneath their feet while keeping her shield up. It was almost comical to see them stumble and try to keep their balance. Some students started cheering Britea on.

As the girls recovered, Britea transformed her shield into a convex shape as another snippet of Instructor Shelley's teachings came to her.

"A convex shield is harder to hold but is highly effective in repelling attacks."

"Why? What's the difference?" a tired Britea had asked.

Instructor Shelley had smiled patiently. "It means it can cast attacks back at the wielder."

"That the best you got, ladies?" taunted Britea, hoping they didn't detect the exhaustion in her voice. Identical looks of fury appeared on the faces of her attackers. In response, they linked hands and hurled a single giant air spear in her direction. Britea connected her convex shield to the puddle of water at her feet and braced for impact. What happened next was not what she had expected.

She had hoped that when the spear hit her reversed shield, it would simply cause a blowback that would make her attackers fall, nothing more. Instead, while the air spears did indeed rebound and blow back, the force was far stronger than she had imagined, pushing back both her attackers and many of the students who had been standing nearby. Some students dropped to the ground crying out in pain, but others flew over the side of the bridge. One of those who had gone flying was Pearl, who had been closest to the stone bridge railing.

"No!" screamed Britea.

Valerie, terrified, took one look at her and ran to Lianne, who was already fleeing from the bridge with the other frightened students. Britea ran to the railing. Close behind her ran Vindell. They both peered over the edge, trying to see through the rain. To her immense relief, she saw Pearl clinging for dear life to a large stone pillar. The other students were also hanging on to the same pillar. How none of them had fallen into the raging waters below was a miracle that Britea thanked the Lords, the Maker, and Sea Mother for.

She wielded a watery rope and wrapped it around Pearl's waist. Pearl just stared at Britea in shock.

"Hang on!" Britea pulled her upwards and deposited her roughly on the bridge and reached for the next student.

"You there! Stop wielding!" The command had come from the opposite end of the bridge, but Britea ignored it. She had people to save. She pulled up another student.

"I command you two to stop," Britea glanced sideways and noticed a pale-faced Pearl had wielded an air rope and tied it around one of the remaining three students.

"One more wield, and I will put you down!" ordered the voice harshly.

"They're trying to save them!" screamed Vindell as she put herself between Britea, Pearl, and the newcomer. Britea retrieved a third student while Pearl saved the last. The unlikely partners scanned the column and surrounding waters to make sure no one had been missed.

Only when she was satisfied did she turn to face the new arrivals.

Her heart sank when she beheld the thunderous expression on Warden Asteros's face. Behind him were at least four academy guards and one exhausted-looking Chelton, whose face brightened when he saw Vindell and Britea.

"Please tell me that what happened here is not what I think happened?"

Britea and Pearl looked at the floor, too scared to answer. Both were shivering from the cold rain and the close brush with death. The four rescued students behind them were lying on the hard stone floor, exhausted but alive.

"Take them all to the infirmary and ensure they're healthy enough for judgement," ordered Warden Asteros.

Britea let a gentle hand guide her. She just wanted to lie down and pretend this was all just a bad dream, but the cold feeling in the pit of her stomach told her it was all too real.

CHAPTER 13

Britea tried to stay still while Healer Thomena Storm rested a hand on her patient's forehead.

It had been over an hour since the duel on the Forever Bridge, and Britea's whole body ached as if she had spent the whole day tilling her parents' farm in Weldaros. Her forearms hurt the most, and she found massaging them helped to reduce the discomfort.

She wondered how the others were doing. The four rescued students had been taken to another huge ward while she and Pearl had been given over to the care of Healer Thomena Storm.

Britea still shivered even though she had since changed into a warm patient's gown and dried her hair as best she could. Healer Storm muttered a few healing runes, and a gradual warmth ignited in Britea's forehead and spread down to her arms. She released a sigh of relief when her shivering gradually stopped and the pain in her muscles receded a bit.

The healer nodded. "That should keep you comfortable for a bit. Now, sip this tea. It will help keep your warm and treat your sore muscles. Make sure to sit up in bed for an hour with the blanket wrapped around you."

"Thanks, Healer Storm." Britea tentatively took a sip of the tea and was pleasantly surprised to taste honey, cinnamon, and a slight hint of lemon. Even the soreness in her arms was easing. Using her wielding power to pull the students back onto the bridge after the duel had taken a lot out of her. The middle-aged healer smiled at Britea and moved on to a sulking Lady Pearl Ceres, who was pacing up and down the other side of the huge, empty ward. Her bed was more than twenty feet away from Britea's.

"Novice Ceres—" began the healer.

"I am Lady Ceres to you! I demand to speak to the headmaster right now! She tried to kill me!" she pointed dramatically at Britea.

Britea was too tired and worried about her future at the academy to respond, but that didn't prevent her from sending a glare in Pearl's direction. Saving the haughty noble's life had not changed her attitude towards Britea.

Wonderful.

Healer Storm's gentle expression hardened. "Young lady, as long as you're my patient, you will address me with respect and obey my orders. Sit down on the bed so I can assess your auras."

"But I demand—"

"Nothing. You will demand nothing. Whether or not you realize how grave your actions were, I certainly don't appreciate being yanked away from my dinner to fix you up after your stupid duel!" The expression on the healer's face had Pearl backing down and walking backwards to her bed.

Britea hid her smile behind her teacup as she sipped the delicious tea.

"That's better," said the healer as she repeated the warm rune treatment with Pearl, also giving her a cup of the medicinal tea. She repeated the same instructions she'd given Britea. Once she observed both charges were drinking their tea, she issued an unexpected pronouncement.

"You're both to stay here over the weekend."

Both Britea and Pearl shot her startled looks.

"Here are the rules. One, no wielding in the wards. I will put you to sleep if you even attempt a tier-one form." Her stern expression warned them she was not bluffing. "Two, do not try to leave the ward. There are guards outside and a very angry Warden Asteros down the hall."

Britea felt ill at that reminder. The healer walked over to a desk that was close to the entrance but also close enough to keep an eye on them. Britea realized she was going to miss the outing with Danai. She groaned softly in despair. *Why had this stupid duel happened today?*

"You're not going to get away with this."

Britea pinched the bridge of her nose in annoyance and turned to a fuming Pearl. The noble's haughty expression flamed the embers of Britea's anger. "Really, you have the gall to say that? Who in their right mind kidnaps a twelve-year-old junior wielder just to force someone into a duel? Let me give you a hint: I'm looking at one of the idiots who hatched that stupid plan."

The expression on Pearl's face went from indignation to shock to outrage, and she clenched her right hand. Britea was half convinced the noble would wield right now. In fact, she hoped Pearl would. A discreet cough from the healer's desk made Pearl unclench her right hand.

Pearl hissed, "I am Lady Pearl Ceres. My family is one of the oldest families in Malaquey. You'll pay for what you tried to do to me, and Lianne and Valerie will..."

Britea shook her head in disbelief. "Valerie threatened to wield the air out of Vindell's lungs."

Pearl stared at her, at a loss for words finally.

From the corner of her eye, Britea noticed the healer go still before glaring at Pearl with a hard glint in her eyes.

Britea continued. "Was that part of the plan? I saw the shock on your face when she said that. Are those the kind of people you're friends with? A noble who would threaten a child?"

Pearl was still lost for words. Fortunately for her, the doors opened at that moment, and Warden Asteros entered the ward with Instructor Shelley at his side.

Britea felt a lump form in her throat when she noted their stern expressions. Pearl jumped off her bed and stalked over to the warden, not noticing the glare he sent her way.

"Finally! I demand she be punished for—"

"Novice Ceres," said the warden in a voice that could have cut glass, "Sit down."

Pearl finally registered his countenance and obliged without another word. Britea was too petrified to take any joy in the spectacle.

The warden stared at both students for a long moment. "I just spent the last two hours doing a roll call of the entire college. Would you like to know why I was doing roll call late at night with the aid of the entire faculty?" His tone was calm, but beneath it was tightly controlled anger.

He waited for an answer. Britea and Pearl kept silent.

"Fine. I'll answer. Because two stupid students decided to duel during a storm at high tide on the Forever Bridge to the Great Hall."

Part of Britea wanted to protest, but another part warned her to keep her mouth shut.

"You see, I had to be sure only five students fell over the railing during that idiotic duel. I *was* to accompany the headmaster to the royal court this evening for an important meeting. Yet there I was, about to get into the coach, when someone ran up to me to warn me that an event that has been outlawed since this school was created was secretly taking place!"

Thank you, Chelton.

Britea was grateful he had obeyed her when she had begged him to go to the warden for help. She was also glad the warden hadn't mentioned his name.

"The good news is no one died this evening."

Britea sighed with relief. She had been so afraid she had missed someone.

"But the bad news is that now one of you is going to receive a punishment so severe you'll wish you hadn't gotten out of bed this morning while the other one might, at the least, be expelled." Britea felt her heart skip a beat when Pearl shot her a triumphant look.

No. The warden couldn't mean her?! She had done nothing wrong!

"I completely agree with your decision, Warden Asteros," began Pearl with a smile as she confidently stood. "Britea deserves to be removed from the college—"

"Did I give you leave to speak?" asked the warden coldly. Pearl looked confused.

"No, but—"

"Then shut up and sit down," added Instructor Shelley in a hard tone. Pearl paled and collapsed back on the bed. Clearly, she was still in denial about her part in all this.

"Before I make a final decision, I want to know exactly what led to the events on the bridge. Make no mistake, I have already questioned the two junior wielders involved and several others caught up in this unfortunate incident. So, I'll start with Lady Pearl Ceres." The warden looked at Pearl. "What were you doing on the bridge?"

For a moment, Pearl, who had been so ready to speak earlier, was now hesitant to speak. The warden and Instructor Shelley waited.

"We…I mean, I, wished to challenge Britea's position in this college. None of us had seen her wield, and she's in the junior's class! I was sure she was a charlatan who had entered this school on false pretenses; thus, I was trying to expose her for what she really was and save the integrity of this noble college." She stood tall, back straight, as if expecting to be praised for her actions. What she got instead was silence.

Britea stared at her in disbelief. That speech sounded so rehearsed.

Instructor Shelley startled Pearl and Britea when she started clapping slowly.

"Bravo, Lady Ceres. So brave of you. Tell me, did you write that speech yourself, or did someone do that for you too, like they did the duel?"

Pearl's face went different shades of red as she shifted between outrage and shame.

The warden shared a look with Instructor Shelley before addressing Pearl. "And when you witnessed Britea wield, you kept attacking. Why?"

Britea watched as Pearl struggled for an answer. "I…I wanted to be sure."

"You battered her shield with air arrows for fifteen minutes until another student joined you, then you both continued for another five minutes," cut in Instructor Shelley.

Britea whipped her head round to stare at her instructor. *It had been that long? And how did the instructor know that?*

The female instructor's smile was chilling. "Oh yes, we questioned the four other students who fell over the side of the bridge. They were more than willing to tell all. Who can blame them? After all, they came very close to death, thanks to you."

Britea's eyes widened. So that was why they had separated them. Smart move.

Pearl went pale with fury. "This was her fault!" She pointed an angry finger at Britea. "If she hadn't used that shield—"

"And why did she have to use the shield?" interrupted the warden. Pearl fell silent. "Was it because she was being attacked? While you held one of her students hostage?"

"She doesn't deserve to be here!" cried Pearl.

"What do you base that assertion on?" demanded Instructor Shelley.

"She is…I mean…" Pearl struggled for words before falling silent. Britea clutched her mug in anger. Pearl and her friends had known what they did was wrong, but they had done it anyway—and justified it to themselves! By the Lords, she hated bullies!

A discreet cough behind him had the warden and Instructor Shelley turning to face Healer Storm.

"I heard Novice D'Tranell ask Novice Ceres if a certain Lady Valerie Mern had really been planning to wield the air out of a student's lungs. The targeted student's name was Vindell." The warden's expression was grave, and Instructor Shelley's countenance hardened. Britea gulped in fear; she glanced at Pearl. The noble looked frightened now.

"Thank you for that information, Healer Storm," said Warden Asteros before he and Instructor Shelley turned their attention back to Pearl. "What have you to say about that?"

Pearl stared at the floor. "I have no idea what Healer Storm is talking about."

Britea glanced at Instructor Shelley's face and thanked the Lords the instructor's ire wasn't directed at her.

"That's very interesting, Novice Ceres. But I do wonder about your *close* friends."

Pearl peered at the warden, a cautious expression on her face.

The warden lowered his voice. "I also spoke to Novice Arkei and Novice Mern, your two inseparable friends. I asked them about their whereabouts during this duel. Would you like to know their answers?"

The color drained from Pearl's face, but she said nothing.

The warden continued. "They said they were in their rooms studying."

Britea heard the derision in his voice. She glanced at Pearl, who had gone sheet white with shock.

"I asked if they had any inkling of what you had been planning. Both your friends denied any knowledge whatsoever, and when I reminded them duel punishments come with expulsion, Lady Arkei stated she would support the college's decision. Do you still have nothing to say?"

Peal fixed her gaze on the floor and shook her head silently. Britea thought she heard Pearl's breath hitch.

"Which brings me to you, Britea," began the warden somberly.

She snapped her head back to face the solemn warden. "You know the Creed, and you have seen firsthand the penalty for wielding without permission. You both could have been killed, as well as the other four students. What do you have to say for yourself?"

Britea stared at the warden and Instructor Shelley. "I didn't start this fight."

"We might agree on that, but how you ended it almost resulted in the deaths of Lady Ceres and the four students in the next ward."

Britea wanted to scream in frustration, but then she saw Instructor Shelley hold up a hand, forestalling whatever the warden may have been about to say.

"Britea's defensive tactic, while a bit extreme, may be understandable considering she was facing two attackers instead of the standard one in a typical duel."

Huh?

A thoughtful expression crossed the warden's face before he delivered his decision. "Fair enough. Britea, your punishment is kitchen duty for the next six months."

"What?!" exclaimed Pearl while Britea was struck silent with shock.

The warden ignored Pearl's reaction. "You will help prepare the meals before breakfast, lunch, and dinner." He turned to an irate Pearl. "As for you, I'll prepare your expulsion papers for your trip back to your home at Arders-Heights."

Pearl went pale with horror. "No, no, you can't…I…my family—"

"Will not be pleased," said Instructor Shelley with a grim smile before leaving the ward with the warden. Healer Storm returned to her desk.

Silence followed their exit. Britea sighed with relief. So what if she had kitchen duty? It would be just like life on the farm, helping her mah in the kitchen while Carlina did nothing. For a moment, she missed her home terribly.

A soft cry broke the quiet. Britea looked across to see Pearl curled up on her bed, her shoulders heaving.

For a moment, Britea felt sorry for her.

But, I didn't start that fight.

"Time to sleep," announced the healer from her desk. Britea placed her empty cup on the small table next to her bed. As she tried to sleep, Pearl's sobs followed her into a restless slumber.

#

"She sleeps."

"She must awaken and hear our warning."

"She is tired, but more is to come."

The feminine whispers made Britea sluggishly open her eyes. *Who was by her bedside?* She turned and all sleep disappeared in an instant when she saw the three female Dyhaeri with glowing silver eyes. A hazy glow enveloped them as they hovered beside her bed.

Wait, what?! screamed her tired brain at the impossibility before her. She opened her mouth to sound the alarm, but one of the Dyhaeri stepped forward and lightly placed a finger on her lips.

"We wish you no harm, but you cannot allow that human child to leave this school."

Britea could hear the words in her head but didn't see the mysterious Dyhaeri's lips move. Yet, Britea knew without a doubt the words came from her.

Britea stared at the healer, asleep at her desk. She glanced over at Pearl, who had also finally fallen asleep.

"Whom do you speak of?" Britea finally asked in a whisper. She had no idea why she was whispering when she should be shouting their presence to the rafters.

One of the Dyhaeri pointed at Pearl. "Her."

Britea gaped at the three Dyhaeri before her. It took a moment before she could find the words.

"I…why?"

Another of the three female Dyhaeri tilted her head. "You wish her harm?"

"No! No, I don't…but…" She wanted to complain about what Pearl and her friends done to her, but somehow Britea suspected the three Dyhaeri already knew that.

And they didn't care in the slightest. Then a worrying thought crossed her mind.

"Wait, will something terrible happen to her if she gets expelled from the college?"

The three Dyhaeri stared at her, then smiled at each other. "She'll do," they said in synchronicity and turned to leave.

"Don't go!" Britea tried to get out of the bed, but she was so weak and sore. "Tell me what it is! Let me warn her!"

One of the Dyhaeri turned while still somehow keeping in step with the other two, who continued to the door.

"Keep her in school, Britea D'Tranell. One warning is all you'll receive. Ignore it and many will fall."

"Who will fall?! Please, help me!"

She truly woke then, sitting up in a cold sweat.

"Novice D'Tranell, are you all right?" asked the healer as she walked between the two beds, checking on her patients. Britea stared at her in shock. A few seconds ago, she could have sworn Healer Storm was asleep. Pearl was also awake and feverishly writing on a sheet of paper.

The Dyhaeri she had just seen…that…that had only been a dream?

"Do not ignore it." The whisper in her mind made her shiver.

The healer frowned and stepped closer to touch Britea's forehead. "You look like you've seen a ghost. Bad dream?"

Britea tried to calm her racing heart. "I…something like that."

"Healer Storm." Both turned to face Pearl. She had obviously been crying and she appeared frantic. Jumping out of bed and holding out the paper she'd been scribbling on, she said. "I need to get a letter to Lady…I mean Novice Lianne Arkei. Please, it's for my family."

The healer's eyes narrowed. "You know you cannot leave the wards until Primeday or until Warden Asteros says so."

Pearl nodded quickly. "I am aware. However, perhaps you could send one of the guards stationed just outside the door. Please, this is very important."

Healer Storm scrutinized the letter in the novice's outstretched hand for a long moment, and then with a sigh, she took it. "I will make sure it is delivered. Back to your bed, Novice Ceres."

Pearl briefly glanced at Britea before returning to her side of the ward. Britea wondered at her expression. It had been a mixture of anger and desperation, but it hadn't seemed to be directed at her. Britea checked the chronometer on the wall; it was close to the seventh hour of the day. She'd somehow slept all night.

She shuddered at the thought of the…the dream she had just had. She was wide awake now, slumber being the furthest thing from her mind after that experience.

Britea glanced over at Pearl's bed. The noble was sitting on her bed with her arms around her drawn-up knees. She looked miserable. Britea wondered why she feared returning home so much. She had thought nobles had no one and nothing to fear.

The sound of the main ward door opening and closing had Britea and Pearl turning towards the sound. The healer had not returned alone.

"Novice D'Tranell, you have a visitor. You have half an hour." Britea was both surprised and worried to see her roommate, Danai.

"Danai—"

"Are you hurt? What did they do to you?" Danai shot a dark look in Pearl's direction as she hurried towards Britea. The noble turned away from them.

Britea smiled with relief as she hugged her roommate. She had been worried Danai would be mad at her. "I'm fine, just a bit tired. I—" she began before remembering something. "Shouldn't you be getting ready for your weekend out?"

"I'm not going anywhere until I'm sure you're all right," Danai sat down on the bed after extracting herself from the hug. She lowered her voice. "I only found out about the duel when Warden Asteros summoned me to find out what I knew about the bridge incident." Her expression darkened. "My outrage convinced him I knew naught of it," she said pointedly while waiting expectantly.

"I had no idea!" whispered Britea urgently. "I'd just left my junior wielding class and was going to drop off my books in our room before meeting you and the others for dinner when Chelton ran up to me and told me they'd kidnapped Vindell!"

"I believe you," whispered Danai. "Now, tell me the rest."

Britea stared at her. "I thought the warden told you what happened."

"Not in so many words. His first question was 'What do you know about the duel on the Forever Bridge?' Once I'd convinced him I knew nothing, all he said was you were in the infirmary, and no one was allowed to see you until morning."

"Oh."

Danai gestured impatiently with her hands. "Well, give me the rest of it."

Britea filled her in on the whole thing in a whisper, intermittently glancing at Pearl's side of the room. The noble had laid down and turned her back to them. Danai's expression hardened when she heard of Valerie's threat to Vindell when the junior wielder had tried to support Britea.

Danai was silent for a long moment when Britea was done, then glanced over at Pearl. "How did she react when Valerie threatened to harm Vindell?"

"She looked shaken."

"But she didn't say or do anything, did she?" pressed Danai. "And Lianne?"

"She was smiling the entire time."

Danai's expression was unreadable as she glanced once more at Pearl's back. "Not surprised. Lianne always did get others to do the dirty work and reap the punishment while she comes out smelling like roses. You, on the other hand..." continued Danai dryly as she turned back to Britea "... are full of surprises. I guess Instructor Shelley's one-to-one teaching was useful after all."

Britea thought about the three Dyhaeri she had dreamt of, or hallucinated, and hesitated.

Danai noticed her reaction. "What? There's more, isn't there? Out with it."

Britea rubbed her jaw, knowing she was going to sound insane. "I...I had this strange dream last night about..." she tilted her head in Pearl's direction." Danai nodded and kept silent as if realizing this part was difficult for Britea.

"I saw three Dyhaeri, females with glowing silver eyes."

The light in Danai's eyes grew. "You saw the Seers?" She sounded alarmed.

Britea felt hope dawn. "You know of them?"

Danai motioned for Britea to keep her voice down. "Only what Weltonian folklore says of the three Dyhaeri sisters cursed with seeing the future."

Britea tilted her head. "Why do Weltonians know so much about the Dyhaeri?"

Danai shrugged. "We share the seas with them, so it only makes sense to know thy neighbor." Then her tone turned serious. "So, what did the Seers want? That is, if it really was the Seers."

Britea wanted to ask more about the Seers but decided to finish describing her strange dream sequence instead.

Danai looked concerned when Britea was done and was silent for so long Britea began to fidget. "Well?"

Her roommate sighed. "If you really saw the Seers, then you can't ignore their warning. My mah always says this famous Weltonian saying: 'A fool that ignores the Seers' foretelling is a fool twice dead.' I'd never thought about it much or taken it seriously before now, but nothing about you has been simple in the time I've known you." Danai looked once more at Pearl's bed several feet away, then turned back to Britea. "You have to tell the warden."

"I can't! I'm stuck in the ward until Primeday. By then, she may be gone." She had made sure not to mention Pearl's name throughout the description of her dream so she'd have no reason to perk up and pay attention.

Danai bit her lower lip, thinking hard. "Then I'll tell them."

"But…but you had somewhere to go today, and I don't want you to draw the warden's ire."

Danai waved Britea's protest away. "I'll tell them—"

"What exactly?" cut in Britea with a whisper. "That I dreamt of the Seers? Do they even know about the Seers?"

Danai hesitated. "I don't know."

Britea threw up her hands in frustration. "Then we'll both end up looking crazy. There has to be another way." The two friends sat in silence for several moments, both lost in their thoughts.

"Maybe there is something that can be done—" started Danai.

"Visiting time is over." Both turned to see Healer Storm standing nearby. "It's time for breakfast."

Danai hugged Britea once more. "I'll find a way, don't fret," the Weltonian whispered in her ear before hurrying from the ward under the healer's watchful gaze.

"Your food will be here in a few minutes." Healer Storm returned to her desk.

"Lianne will get me out of this. She'll come for me; you'll see." Britea turned to Pearl, now sitting up, a confident expression on her face. "You'll rue the day you crossed our paths."

Britea frowned at her smug countenance and found herself hoping, despite herself, Danai was unsuccessful. She was still trying to think of a suitable response when the doors opened again to admit a guard clad in the standard charcoal uniform. He walked over to Healer Storm's desk and spoke with her for several moments in barely a whisper, making both girls itch to know what he was saying.

The conversation ended, and the healer stood up and motioned for the guard to follow her. They came over to Pearl, who now seemed a bit worried.

"Where's Lianne?"

The guard exchanged a look with the healer.

"Bryan has a message for you," said the healer, and she nodded for him to speak.

"I tried to deliver your letter as you requested. I met Lady Lianne Arkei as she was preparing to disembark for her family's home." Pearl went pale with shock, but the guard wasn't done.

"She refused to take the letter. In fact, she stated, and I quote, 'I do not associate with breakers of the Wielder Creed and breakers of academy rules. Whatever punishment she gets is what I'm sure she deserves, so the warden's decision has my blessing.'"

Britea's jaw dropped. Part of her knew she should have expected this, but she was still appalled at how Lianne treated her friends. *By the Lords, what would she do to her enemies?*

The guard handed Pearl the sealed letter. Britea saw the telltale glint of tears appear in her eyes.

Pearl took the letter with trembling hands and stared at it in disbelief. "Was Valerie with her?"

Bryan nodded. "Yes, I believe they were traveling together."

There was silence for a long moment until Pearl replied. "I see," was all she said in a broken voice.

"Is there anything else you need?" asked the healer softly.

Her shoulders slumped, Pearl shook her head slowly and stared at the floor. The guard and the healer left her alone with her thoughts.

Britea sympathized with Pearl. She looked defeated. While part of Britea coldly reminded her Pearl would have been rejoicing and mocking her if their positions were reversed, for some reason, Britea could not find it in her heart to hate her.

Pearl suddenly glared at her; the wielder's eyes were bloodshot now and filled with a frightening intensity.

She's looking for someone to blame, realized Britea. *She's close to the edge and ready to break.*

"I didn't abandon you. I'm not Lianne." Britea tried to sound calm.

Pearl stared at her for an eternity, and somehow Britea knew she wanted to lash out. They stayed locked in that long stare for what felt like hours. Eventually, Pearl looked away first, lying down slowly and presenting her back to Britea once more.

Only then did Britea relax and let go of the tier-one shield she had been ready to wield.

#

Danai paced up and down in front of the warden's door. She had knocked already, and the warden had asked who it was. Once she had announced her name, there had been silence for a moment before he had ordered her to wait.

That had been several minutes ago. Danai had forgone breakfast. She was too keyed up to eat, so though she was a bit on edge, she was glad for the wait.

Britea had been right; she couldn't mention the Seers, or both she and her roommate would be admitted to an asylum. *So, what in the Deep was she going to do?*

"Danai."

She turned to see the warden had opened his door a fraction. "You can come in now."

He opened the door wider to allow her entry.

"Thank you, sir." She walked in and was surprised to see Instructor Shelley and Weapons Master Caren. The two instructors were seated at the central desk. They looked up from the documents before them, their expressions stern.

"This had better be important, Novice Riverun," said the warden as he returned to his desk.

For a moment, Danai was unsure how to begin.

"Novice Riverun, what is it?" asked Instructor Shelley.

Danai took a deep breath. "I just came from the infirmary. Britea told me about what happened on the bridge and…and your decision."

Master Caren tilted his head while his colleagues regarded her with impatient expressions. "You have something to say about the judgement."

Danai asked both the Sea Mother and the Lords of Light and Shadow to give her strength. "I think the punishment for Novice Ceres was too harsh."

The room suddenly felt colder, and she saw the harsh looks on the faces of the senior wielders.

"Please, hear me out." She raised her hands in supplication. Instructor Shelley shared a silent look with the two senior wielders. Master Caren shrugged and the warden sighed. Danai suspected they were communicating without speaking, but she hoped she had not angered them.

Instructor Shelley turned back at her. "Go on."

"What Pearl and Britea did was against the Creed, though Britea isn't at fault for that. She was simply defending an innocent. But you're going after the wrong person." Now she had their attention.

"Valerie made that threat, and Lianne is clearly the mastermind. They should also be punished, and Pearl's punishment should be reduced."

The warden' smile was without humor. "And you might be right, but Pearl has decided to show some honor and not rat out her two friends."

"Who were suddenly in a hurry to leave the academy this morning for the weekend," added Instructor Shelley dryly.

Danai found that interesting. "Be that as it may, expelling Pearl will put Britea in the crosshairs of the Ceres household."

The weapons master's expression cleared in understanding while Instructor Shelley and the warden frowned at her.

"Please think of what will happen when Britea graduates. If Pearl is expelled, the Ceres will ensure many doors will be shut to her. Someone like me can always return to my people and live comfortably among them, but she'll have to contend with the ire of the Ceres family forever. In the end, Lianne will have won, destroying two lives and appearing innocent of the mess she created."

Her speech was followed by several moments of silence. Danai could see the senior wielders thinking it over.

The warden rubbed his chin. "Be careful who you say that to. You don't want to be accused of spreading rumors and facing their wrath yourself."

It's not a rumor and you know it. "I understand."

Instructor Shelley wearily pushed back her chair. "All right, suppose I agree with you. Don't you think reducing Pearl's punishment sends the wrong message? She and others may try this rubbish again if they think they can get away with it."

"Not if you play your cards right," replied Danai as an idea began to form. Master Caren and the warden looked interested.

"We're listening," said Instructor Shelley.

#

Britea's eyelids grew heavy, but she forced them open. Breakfast had been hours ago, so she was hungry and her muscles still ached. She felt so tired. The healer had not seemed surprised she was so sore and tired, explaining it was because of the duel. Britea wondered if it had been holding up that water shield for almost twenty minutes that was the culprit. The hands on the wall chronometer said it was approaching midday. She had kept an eye on Pearl through the morning, but she kept her back turned to Britea. She suspected the noble was asleep.

Britea wanted to sleep as well, but after last night's dream, she wasn't so eager to sleep.

Was this how it was going to be? Dreading sleep because of dreams? She wished she had a book to read right now. That would have kept her awake.

Her thoughts turned to Danai. Britea was worried about her. What if the warden got mad at her roommate for trying to help?

Ugh! This was a fine mess indeed! Britea tried to distract herself by thinking of something else.

The Seers. She was curious about them. Why would they appear to Britea? Who would fall if Pearl was sent home? Was the school in danger? Was Pearl in danger?

What was going on?

"Sleep. Rest."

Britea's eyes snapped shut, and she fell into a mercifully dreamless slumber.

#

"Wake up, Novice D'Tranell." Britea groggily opened her eyes, and for a moment, wondered why a healer was in her room. Then she recalled where she was, and the sleep cleared faster.

"Uh…did Novice Riverun come while I was sleeping?"

"No one came while you slept, child," said Healer Storm as she placed a bowl of chicken soup, a piece of freshly baked bread, and a cup of water on a tray on Britea's lap. "Be careful with that. The soup is still hot."

"Thank you, Healer Storm." The aroma of the soup was making her mouth water. She blew air on the spoon of soup before taking a sip. She sighed with happiness it tasted so good.

"Wake up, Novice Ceres," said Healer Storm so softly Britea could barely hear. Pearl mumbled something back. The healer sighed and sat beside Pearl's tucked-in form.

"You have to eat. You expended a lot of your energy reserves during the duel."

Pearl mumbled again and shook her head as she lay on her bed.

"All right, I'll leave the food here for when you're ready." Healer Storm put the tray of food on the table beside the bed and returned to her desk.

The food on Britea's tray disappeared rapidly once it cooled enough to eat. She took her tray to the healer's desk. Healer Storm thanked her for not making her retrieve the tray. As Britea returned to her bed, she glanced over at Pearl. Her meal was untouched.

Britea stood undecided for a moment, then slowly walked over to Pearl's bed. When she got closer, she could hear sniffles coming from the noble, who had curled into a fetal position.

The sobs stopped as Britea neared.

"I'm not hungry, Healer Storm. I just want to be left alone."

Britea felt uncertain why she stood by her enemy's bedside, but she could not help but feel sorry for how broken Pearl sounded.

"It's me."

Pearl's body went rigid, then she slowly sat up and turned to face Britea. Her eyes were more bloodshot than ever, and tracks of tears snaked down her cheeks.

"You." Her voice was filled with loathing. "What do you want?"

This was a bad idea, thought Britea. "I just wanted to check and see how you were feeling. I…I think you should eat. You'll need your strength."

Pearl looked puzzled for a moment, but then she narrowed her eyes. "You came to gloat, didn't you?"

"No, no. I take no pleasure in your predicament—"

"Then what are you doing beside my bed?" hissed Pearl.

Britea stared at her. She was still asking herself the same question. "I just wanted to learn."

Pearl frowned. "What?" Britea's words had caught her off guard.

"Do you know how scared I was when I found out I could wield?" Britea blurted out. "I had to leave my family and the only home I'd ever known and travel for more than three months at sea to get here. And that doesn't even begin to cover everything that happened during that trip."

Pearl opened her mouth to say something, but Britea didn't let her speak. "And yet when I got here, the first thing you, Lianne, and Valerie did was to try to make my life hell. Why? What did I ever do to you to deserve this?" She waited for Pearl to answer.

The noble stared at her, at loss for words.

"Novice D'Tranell." She turned to see the healer standing quietly nearby. "You best return to your side of the ward."

"Yes, Healer Storm." Britea looked at the silent Pearl once more and went back to her bed. As she walked away, she heard Pearl pick up her food tray.

#

Hours passed while Britea stared at the ceiling. She was bored and again wished she had a book to read. She sat up with a sigh and glanced at the time piece on the wall. Two more hours until supper time. She glanced over at Pearl to find the noble was flat on her back also staring at the ceiling. At least Pearl had eaten, but the two had exchanged no more words.

Britea turned with relief when the ward doors opened, hoping it was Danai. Her eyes widened with surprise when she saw five students she knew quite well.

Danai, Navos, Lexia, Shran, and Henrick.

Healer Storm gave them a stern warning that visiting time was only thirty minutes. Her five friends rushed to her side. Britea saw Pearl sit up and regard them with longing. She must be missing Lianne and Valerie.

"Hey, little warrior," said Navos in a loud whisper as he got closer. He engulfed her in a bear hug, then each of the others, even studious Shran hugged her. Britea found herself a bit teary eyed at the show of kindness.

"How are you?" asked Lexia in a worried tone.

"Much better. Healer Storm has been giving us tea and food and taking care of us." At her inclusion of Pearl, the five looked over at Pearl, who quickly turned away from them.

"Hmm," muttered Shran darkly. "Is she giving you any trouble?"

Henrick kept staring at Pearl, his expression a bit unreadable, but then he turned back to Britea.

"No, no, she's being staying on her side of the ward."

A warning look flashed on Danai's face. Britea got the impression she couldn't ask her how the visit with the warden had gone, so she asked another question that had been bothering her. "How are the other students?"

"You mean the four novices that got blasted over the bridge?" responded Danai.

Britea could not help but wince. "Are they all right?"

"They were discharged after breakfast," replied Danai.

"And now the entire school knows what happened," whispered Henrick excitedly. "Though the junior wielding class has been talking about it non-stop since last night."

"What are they saying?" asked a concerned Britea,

"Britea, the Hero of the Oppressed," said Shran in a solemn tone. Britea gaped at him.

"What?"

"It's true," said Navos proudly as he assumed a pose theatrical orators took before launching into a ballad: back straight, head titled back, left hand extended, indicating Britea with his right hand on his chest and a heartfelt expression on his face. "You stood up to three rich, pampered brats—pardon me—nobles." His voice was just loud enough for Pearl to overhear him. Britea saw her hunch her shoulders. Lexia elbowed him, and he lowered his voice slightly but the damage was done. "As I was saying, here stands, or sits, Britea, the defender of the defenseless. She ran onto the Forever Bridge to rescue the student she'd taken under her wing for she saw in her the baby sister she'd never had. Britea, our hero, would risk her life for her sister-of-another-mother even if it meant her own death."

Britea felt her face grow warm, she put her hands on her head in dismay. "That sounds awful."

Navos gave her a mock affronted look while the others laughed.

"Excuse me while I continue my tale. And, though the odds were against her, she wielded a shield a hundred feet high and two feet thick—"

"It wasn't even seven feet high!" protested Britea. Navos winked at her and continued.

"—that bounced back the air spears and air arrows and every other weapon hurled in her direction as she protected her protégé and herself. And when the villains decided to throw one last volley that would surely break her, Britea the Valiant…" Britea rolled her eyes.

"…transformed her shield so it would reverse their attack and toss them off the Forever Bridge. But those stupid students who'd come to gawk and cheer on the villains got caught in the blast, and lo and behold, ten of them fell towards the waters below, along with one of the villains—"

"There were only four of them," said Britea, groaning and trying not to laugh. Navos winked at her as the others giggled, caught up in his enthralling storytelling.

"What does Britea the Brave do? She releases her shield and strives to save the doomed villain and the fifteen students who'd fallen to their certain death—"

Britea held up a hand. "Pearl helped me save the students as well."

Navos continued without losing stride. "—and so honorable was Britea of Steadfast Heart that her enemy was at her side in an instant, and for once, the two worked as one to hold off the manacles of death once more and thus were the twenty fallen students saved from oblivion. The end." He bowed as his friends clapped and whistled. Britea tried to get them to keep the noise down. She glanced behind her and to her relief, Healer Storm actually seemed amused.

"Thank you, thank you," said Navos. "I'm here all semester and will accept coin for any further performances." His friends booed him while Lexia stood on her tiptoes to kiss his right cheek.

"Navos, that was awful, yet so good it made me laugh. But seriously, please tell me this is not what everyone is saying?" asked Britea as she wiped the tears from her eyes.

"More or less," said Shran, shrugging. "The number of people you fought and the number you and Pearl saved grows more with each retelling. You know what students are like. Most have too much free time on their hands."

"Says who?" complained Danai.

"Me for now," answered Shran.

Lexia and Danai exchanged a look. "Typical."

"So, when can you leave?" asked Henrick.

"Healer Storm said not until Primeday."

"You get to spend one more day in the ward," said Danai as she passed Britea a bag of books. Britea squealed with delight.

"See, Shran? Someone else who loves books as much as you do," teased Lexia.

"I approve," agreed Shran with a small smile.

Britea was so happy. She had been so bored. She was about to bring the books out but Danai put a hand on her arm. "Let's chat for now. You can read those later." A hidden message shone in Danai's eyes.

"Um…sure. So, what's everyone doing for fun this weekend?"

#

All too soon, visiting time was over and her friends had gone, promising to return the next day.

Britea was eager to see what was in the bag. There were at least five books in the bag, and she almost wept with relief when she saw the assignments in politics and math she was yet to complete. She had completely forgotten about those!

Two of the books were novels she was yet to read. Well, now she had a few hours to do just that, after she had done the assignments of course. As she opened one textbook, a folded piece of paper fell out. On it was written a short note in Danai's hand writing. *Read this first!*

That was ominous. She opened it and read the contents, her heart rate speeding up as she realized Danai had spoken to the warden, Instructor Shelley, and the weapons master. Her eyes widened when she read the last part. *They wanted her to do what?*

"So, you have friends."

Britea stilled. Pearl's voice was right behind her. Surely there was no way she had seen the note.

Right?

Trying to act casual, she tucked the note back into her textbook. She turned to find the noble was standing by her bedside, her arms folded across her chest. She looked cross.

Please, not another fight.

"Yes, they've been nice to me."

Pearl kept staring at her to the point that it made her uncomfortable. Britea glanced at the healer's table, shocked to find she was absent.

"She's probably in the bathroom. Don't worry, I'm not here to fight."

Britea wanted to believe her, but Pearl's body language said otherwise.

"I see. What do you want then?"

For a moment, Pearl seemed indecisive, then she sighed. "You said earlier you came from so far away to learn to be a wielder…well, good for you."

Britea waited, clutching her textbook in her hands, taken aback by this version of Pearl. *Was this the start of an apology?*

"I don't really hate you. It's just that you and I are from different worlds. It may be all rainbows and a simple, easy life on your farm…"

Britea blinked. Pearl thought farm life was easy? Clearly, she had never been to a farm!

"…but here in Raven's Fall, life is anything but simple. You have to be ruthless or you don't survive. Here's some free advice: being kind is weak, and it will destroy you."

Britea watched her turn and start to walk away. Part of her warned her to keep silent, but she couldn't stop herself. "You're wrong." Pearl stopped and looked at her over her shoulder.

"Being kind costs nothing and might even gain you real friends."

Pearl's expression turned cold. Britea's heart sank. She had just reminded her of Lianne and Valerie.

"Keep thinking that and see how far you get." As Pearl returned to her bed, Britea wondered if the Seers had made a mistake.

CHAPTER 14

Lanead read his daughter's note and frowned.

Britea, a friend of mine, is in the infirmary, so I had to stay until I knew she was safe. I promise I will come tomorrow. Love, hugs, and kisses to you and Mah."

Britea D'Tranell was in the infirmary. Well, that was certainly ominous. And why would Danai have to stay until she was safe? Those words didn't inspire confidence in the safety of Syla College. Apparently, trouble had a way of finding Britea D'Tranell, and now his daughter was connected to this mysterious girl.

He was tempted to march over to the college gates and demand to see his daughter. If she was that worried about Britea, then maybe he should do some snooping around. Lanead took a look at the pile of notes on his desk.

That is, if he ever got his paperwork done.

"Captain?" First Mate Tanet stuck his head through the open door.

"Yes?"

"Lieutenant Commander Peras Nell is here to see you. He's alone." That made Lanead pause.

"Alone?"

"Yes, sir."

"Give me five minutes then show him in."*This should be interesting.* Lanead stashed away certain documents and maps he didn't want the Malaquey intelligence officer to see. He left only lists for provisions and repairs for both the *Peacekeeper* and the *Nightflyer* on the desk. Lanead assumed a concerned expression just as the officer appeared in his doorway.

"Lieutenant Commander Nell." Lanead stood up to shake his hand. "Welcome on board the *Peacekeeper.* Is all well?"

Peras smiled. "Of course." He casually surveyed the office and then gestured at the open door with a tilt of his head.

"I've spent so much time at sea that when I get to land, I prefer to have the door open for the fresh air," explained Lanead. He wondered why the Malaquey officer was concerned about privacy.

"Understood," said Peras as he sat down, his gaze skipping over the documents strewn here and there on Lanead's desk. "I see you're quite busy."

"Aye, a captain's work is never done. Each time we dock, I have a list a mile long of provisions to buy, goods to sell, and repairs to be made. It gives me nightmares."

"Hmm," said Peras in agreement before moving on. "To be honest, this is not a social call."

Here it comes. "I thought not. It's not often a senior officer from Malaquey intelligence graces our decks."

"Unless you're running contraband."

Lanead frowned. "Such as?"

"Namiran refugees for one," Peras appeared relaxed, but his eyes told a different story. He stared intently at Lanead.

"There are no refugees among my crew, Lieutenant Commander," said Lanead carefully.

"I didn't think so, but perhaps you've been helping them escape from Namira? Wielders perhaps?"

The tension in the room grew. Lanead wanted to ask the officer why he was concerned about Namiran wielder refugees, but he chose his next words with care. "When Weltonians come across poor souls seeking help on the waters, we always help. It is our mantra. We help whether they be from Malaquey or Namira or Dyhaeri. We've even been known to help the occasional Alkynaia..." That last bit made Peras raise an eyebrow. "...and we ask not what their business is, so I know not if any Namiran wielders have been pulled from the Heldiar Sea."

Both men stared at each other for a long moment.

"I don't suppose you could inform me of the whereabouts of your rescued souls?" asked Peras after being the first to look away.

"I'm afraid not. Once they reach safe harbor, we don't keep track of their movements," replied Lanead.

Peras cocked his head to one side as if surprised by his honesty. "You're not like other Weltonians I've met."

And how many have you met, I wonder, and under what circumstances? Better yet, where are they now?

"Is that so?"

Peras nodded. "The high priest of the Dyhaeri vouches for you, and when you walked into court by his side, you had such confidence. You weren't swayed by the palace or all the rich and powerful nobles. Even the two young Dyhaeri guards gawked at everything and everyone, but not you."

Uh oh.

"You just sauntered through as if you owned the place and were quite familiar with it. Yet I've gone over the records, and this is the first time you've ever registered in the visitor log book. Why is that? Did you perhaps work in the palace as a child or when you were much younger?"

Lanead smiled. "You know the answer—"

"Humor me and answer the question," cut in Peras.

Lanead maintained eye contact as he replied. "I have never worked in the palace or the royal court."

Peras waited as if expecting more. Lanead stayed silent.

The Malaquey officer laughed dryly. "The mystery continues."

Lanead was tiring of this thinly veiled interrogation. "Was there anything else I could help you with?"

"Oh yes. What is your connection with the Dyhaeri high priest and King Jahlannin?"

Finally, he's asking the right question. "The king requested a trade agreement. He asked that I transport his high priest safely across the waters to Malaquey."

Peras was once again startled by the frank reply. What Lanead had said was the bare minimum of the truth, so if the commander asked for more details, that would make things more complicated indeed.

"And what exactly do you get out of the bargain then?" asked Peras, leaning on the table, watching Lanead's every move.

"Continued safety on the Heldiar Sea and early warning of impending danger."

Lanead found it interesting his answer disturbed the intelligence officer, who leaned back in his seat at that.

"That is a…a good trade, especially considering the Namiran navy has been active lately."

"Sure is," agreed Lanead. They stared at each other yet again.

"The harbor master informed me you're to depart in a few days."

"Yes."

"And your destination?"

Lanead smiled. "The welcoming sea and whichever friendly port we seek refuge in after that." He waited for more questions.

Peras' expression mirrored Lanead's insincere one. The officer stood up. "Then I wish you safe travels. I'll see myself out." He paused upon reaching the doorway as if he had forgotten something. "I hear your daughter, Danai, is at Syla College, training to be a wielder. I find her presence there quite odd since the college hasn't trained a Weltonian student in over seven hundred years."

Lanead froze, trying to keep a pleasant expression on his face. "And what of it?"

Peras smiled coldly. "I bet she's just as unique as you are. I look forward to meeting her." He left before Lanead gave into the temptation to do him some serious harm.

Lanead sat back, exhausted, as if he had been in a wielding duel. But he had no time to reflect on that conversation. He and Sonei were going to the college at once.

#

Danai bid farewell to Lexia as she turned down the corridor to her room, which was now empty since Britea had to spend another night in the infirmary. She hoped everything went as planned and Pearl would get to stay at the college.

She was mystified, though, as to why the Seers, or the Sisters as they were also known, were paying such attention to Britea and Pearl. To be honest, Danai thought most Weltonian folklore was just tales to scare children into doing their chores or being good.

At first, she had wanted to dismiss Britea's "dream." But the poor girl had been so scared, and besides, why would she specifically dream of the Seers? It wasn't like they were in any human storybook. Britea came from an isolated farm. Danai only knew what the Seers looked like because her father had insisted she learn about them.

He had also warned her not to speak of them to anyone. She winced. She didn't think Britea would be one to blab though, and she *had* accurately described them. Besides, she had been the one to suggest not telling the warden about them since it would make them sound crazy.

Danai rubbed her forehead as she reached her room. She was exhausted and looking forward to a blessed and hopefully dreamless sleep.

"Novice Riverun."

She froze abruptly before turning to see a female guard behind her. Danai scolded herself silently. She was so exhausted she'd failed to hear the guard's approach.

"Yes, ma'am."

"Your parents are here."

Her fatigue fled from her. "What? Why?! Are they all right?"

The guard held up a calming hand. "Warden Asteros has granted them a short visit. They appeared quite anxious to see you."

Danai was already moving, still alarmed. "Of course, thanks for telling me. Where are they?"

"Visitor's Lounge B," the guard replied.

They spoke no more after that. Danai was too full of trepidation and questions by the time she reached the second of the four rooms by the main entrance set aside for college visitors.

Her concern only grew when she saw her parents with Warden Asteros. The three wore grave expressions.

"Is everything all right?"

The warden smiled. "No reason to be alarmed. After recent events, your parents were eager to see you. I only granted this because it's the weekend, and you did forgo your outing to help other students." He turned to her parents.

"We're grateful for this visit," said Sonei. Lanead clasped the warden's hands in a firm shake.

"The pleasure is all mine." The warden nodded at the Riverun family and left.

Danai turned to her parents. "Why are you here tonight? I was planning on coming tomorrow morning!"

Sonei and her father exchanged a look.

"What is it?" asked Danai.

"Your message left a lot out," said Sonei. "My friend is in the infirmary and I cannot come until she is safe? You expect us to read that and say, 'Oh, let's wait until morning to hear the rest of it?'"

Danai rubbed the back of her neck. "I guess the wording of my letter did sound alarming."

Lanead gave his only child a wry look. "You think?"

"All right, I apologize. I was in a hurry because of what happened."

"And what exactly did happen, Danai?" asked Sonei as she folded her arms.

Danai stared at the floor. "I'm not supposed to discuss wielder matters…"

"Your father is a wielder, and we're your parents, so what happened?" interrupted her mother.

Danai recognized that tone. If she didn't tell her, she could just picture her mother marching up to Warden Asteros to get all the details. The embarrassment would kill her.

"My roommate got tricked into a duel with one of Lady Arkei's friends." The mixed expressions of horror and disapproval on her parents' faces hastened a detailed description of what had occurred.

Both Sonei and Lanead looked worried when she was through.

"Was she hurt?" asked her mother.

"No, just completely exhausted. She was ordered to stay in the infirmary until Primeday."

"Good," said Lanead. "I hope those girls get expelled."

"Doubt that's going to happen," said Sonei before Danai could utter a word. Her husband gave his wife a puzzled look.

"Don't forget who Lady Arkei's mother is. That trio will get away with this."

Lanead sighed. "You're probably right."

Danai chewed her lower lip. She definitely wasn't going to tell them about what she and Britea had planned. Besides, she had a burning question. "Dah, do you remember when you told me about the Seers?"

Now both parents gaped at her. Lanead in particular seemed a bit concerned. He glanced around as if searching for eavesdroppers.

"Yes?" he asked in a cautious whisper.

"Of what…what importance are they to the Dyhaeri?"

Sonei narrowed her eyes. "Where is this coming from?"

But Danai was more startled by the brief look of fear that had flashed in her father's eyes. If she had not been watching him, she would have missed it.

"Dah?"

Lanead tried for a casual tone. "Did you see them, my daughter?"

"No. It's just something I was curious about."

Lanead seemed like he wanted to press, but something held him back.

Danai wondered if he would have spoken freely if they were back on the *Peacekeeper.*

"We can talk more when I visit tomorrow…" Her words faded away as she saw that odd look her parents shared again. "What's going on? There's something you're not telling me."

Sonei bit her lower lip in frustration. "A high-ranking Malaquey officer visited your father today. That is the second reason we're visiting you just before your planned visit."

Danai now noticed her mother was tenser than usual. "Who was this officer, and what did they want?"

Lanead reluctantly launched into a description of his encounter and the officer's parting words.

Danai was quiet for a long moment. "It's not exactly a secret that I'm studying here. I've been here for years. I'm actually surprised the Malaquey intelligence officer is making so much of it."

"Have you met this man before?" asked Lanead.

"No, but Britea and I ran into one of his junior officers in the market the other day. A Lieutenant Harto Flay."

Lanead's expression changed when he heard the name.

Sonei turned to her husband. "That was the other officer with Lieutenant Commander Nell when they came to the docks."

"What were they doing down at the docks?" said Danai.

"It doesn't matter," answered Lanead.

"Dah—"

"Danai, please listen. Do not come down to the docks tomorrow. We will visit you instead."

"But—"

"Please, don't make us worry about you," begged Sonei. "We know you're more than capable of taking care of yourself, but these are trying times, and you need to be cautious. Besides, your friend, Britea, is still in the infirmary, and I'm sure she could use your company."

Danai stared at her parents. She wanted to protest, but eventually she nodded. "Fine, I'll stay here—this time."

Her parents smiled at her but failed to hide the worry in their eyes.

What were they so scared of?

"Ah, that reminds me," said Sonei as she removed an envelope from her bag. "Your roommate has a letter from Kahl. I was planning to give it to her when you both came to visit."

Danai was speechless for a moment as she accepted the envelope. "Wait. You hung around waiting for him to write a letter back?"

"Yes," answered both parents. Danai's eyes narrowed. That sounded true, but why did she have the feeling more was being left unsaid.

"He was quite eager for it to get back to her," continued her mother.

Danai too was wondering what kind of relationship Britea had with Kahl. It was rare to hear of human-Dyhaeri friendships. Even Weltonians kept to themselves. Maybe it was time she asked Britea a few more questions once she was out of the infirmary.

#

"You didn't tell her about the Dyhaeri visiting the Malaquey court," said Sonei once she and her husband were back in their carriage. Weltonians piloted the coach, so here they could talk freely.

Lanead yawned, relieved now that he had been assured Danai was safe. "I don't trust the walls of Syla College. Who knows what listeners they hide? Besides, it's best she's not drawn into this mess any further."

"We can't keep protecting her, Lanead," said Sonei quietly.

Lanead grasped his wife's hand. "I know, but let's try a little longer."

Silence was their companion all the way back to the docks.

#

Solisday.

Britea woke up early. The infirmary, as usual, was silent. She glanced over at Pearl's bed. The novice was facing her this time but was still asleep. Britea tiptoed to the washroom at the other end of the ward. Even though she had socks on, she could still feel the cold of the cement floor.

She still felt tired, but not as much as the day of the duel. All she wanted now was to return to her dorm room. Britea knew she was lucky she wasn't being expelled, but that didn't mean she liked the predicament she was in.

Instructor Shelley had gone easy on her, but she wondered how the instructor would really treat her once this whole debacle was over.

Britea returned to her bed after freshening up. She didn't feel like sleeping, so she tried to finish her assignment on the recent regional election that had been held last week; her class had attended the election and observed. Though Lianne and her friends had also had to attend, they had managed to leave before the election was over.

Britea had found the election both noisy and interesting. Now she was supposed to write an essay of at least twelve thousand words about how the election would affect her. She had started the essay a week ago, right after the election, but it was taking her forever to finish it. The deadline was in two days.

She was still working on it when Pearl woke up. The noble ignored her and made her way to the washroom as well. Putting Pearl from her mind, Britea struggled with the essay and tried not to think of the arithmetic assignment waiting for her.

She was relieved when it was time for breakfast. As she bit into a piece of buttered toast, she snuck a look over at Pearl and was relieved to see the noble was eating at least.

Once her plate was empty and had been taken away, Britea forced herself to continue with the election assignment. Instructor Dawn had suggested a particular textbook they could use to aid them in writing the essay, but the book bored Britea to tears. She bit her lower lip as she tried to concentrate. She was sure the instructor would turn this into a quiz in the near future too. When she felt a kink in her neck, she stretched and noticed Pearl's bed was empty again. *Probably in the washroom again* . Britea bent back to her work. She had to get this finished.

"Britea, you have visitors."

What? She had been so engrossed in her work she hadn't heard anyone approach. Beside Healer Storm were the last students she had expected to see. Vindell and Chelton.

Before she could say a word, the two junior wielders hugged her at the same time. Britea was speechless for a moment. "I…are you two all right?"

"Yes! We just wanted to see if you were getting better," said Chelton once they had let her go.

"Are you well, Instructor D'Tranell?" asked Vindell.

Britea laughed. "I keep telling you, my name is Britea. I'm no instructor."

Both junior wielders smiled and sat beside her when she motioned them towards the bed.

"You're the only one in this ward," stated Chelton. Britea froze and darted a quick look in the direction of the washroom. She prayed Pearl stayed there a bit longer. The last thing she wanted was for the junior wielders to be scared.

"Um…no, the other patient is just occupied at the moment. So, what have you two been up to this weekend?"

Chelton and Vindell happily told her of their opportunity to go into town with some older students for a brief excursion. Britea smiled as they talked and tried not to look towards the washroom. To her relief though, Pearl didn't emerge.

Eventually, after what seemed like an eternity, the healer came to tell the junior wielders that visiting time was over. This was met by pleas to stay a little longer, but the healer stood firm and gently told them they had to let Britea rest. She hugged them once again and waved at them as they left the ward.

Once the door closed, an irritated looking Pearl emerged from the washroom.

"I thought they'd never leave," said the noble. Britea was speechless for a moment. So Pearl had stayed in the washroom to avoid the junior wielders. Britea stared at the noble.

"What?" scowled Pearl when she noticed Britea's expression.

"You stayed in there so they wouldn't see you?"

Pearl's face reddened. "So, what of it?"

Britea opened her mouth to thank her.

"Never mind," said Pearl abruptly "I just didn't want to listen to them whine." She lay down again, this time with her back to Britea.

Britea's gratitude was replaced with irritation. Just when she thought Pearl had a heart, the noble went ahead and destroyed the illusion. Britea shook her head and resumed her boring assignment.

#

Britea read her assignment once more and scowled at it. She had no more to give.

"Done with your scribbling?"

Britea looked up to see Pearl pacing up and down her side of the ward. She had been doing so for the past half hour. Britea had ignored her so she could complete her work.

"Yes."

"What is it?"

Britea stared at her in surprise. Was Pearl trying to strike up a conversation?

"An essay on last week's regional election and how it impacts us."

Pearl laughed dryly as she kept pacing. "Oh that. Yes, I do believe I still have to complete mine." She sounded bitter. "There's no point now since I'm getting kicked out of this fine college."

Britea didn't know what to say.

"What, nothing to say?"

Britea shook her head.

Pearl continued pacing. "You're odd. If our roles were reversed, I'd be rubbing it in. But you just sit there and do your homework and even try to be nice to me. There must be something wrong with you."

Britea narrowed her eyes. Now this was the Pearl she remembered. "Why are you scared of going back home?"

That stopped Pearl in her tracks. "None of your business." The pacing continued.

Well, she had tried. Britea glanced behind her, and sure enough, Healer Storm was watching them closely with a neutral expression.

"Would you like something to read? You look bored," said Britea turning back to Pearl. The pacing slowed and Pearl stared at the other books on Britea's beds.

"I doubt you have anything interesting." But her eyes lingered on the books all the same.

Oh, she was definitely bored.

"I have Erina Seaworth's *Doomed Love Stories of Time and Legend.*"

The pacing stopped as Pearl stared at her. "You read Erina Seaworth?" Surprise filled her voice.

"Yes, do you?" asked an equally stunned Britea.

"Of course! She's an amazing writer! I just don't know where she gets her ideas from."

Britea saw the glow in Pearl's eyes. She obviously loved to read, so why was she dumb enough to associate with Lianne?

Her mind returned to the present when she realized Pearl was still looking at the book Britea held.

"Here. I've finished reading it." Britea rose from her bed and strode over to Pearl, stretching out her hand and waiting for a stunned Pearl to take the book.

Pearl hesitated, then after a long moment, she took the book from Britea. "Um…thanks." Her tone was uncertain.

"You're welcome." Britea smiled and returned to her bed and the waiting arithmetic assignment. When she looked back, Pearl was sitting on her own bed and had already dived into the novel.

#

Danai, Navos, Lexia, Shran, and Henrick showed up after lunch. When Pearl saw them, she hastily escaped to the bathroom, clutching Britea's book.

"She sick or something?" asked Lexia as she watched the noble scurry away.

Britea hoped not. "I don't know."

"It looked like she was running away from us," said Henrick thoughtfully.

Danai gave Britea a questioning look. She shrugged. Pearl had been quieter since she'd opened the novel. Britea wondered if Lianne and Valerie liked books. Probably not.

"So, what have you been up to?" asked Lexia as she sat down beside Britea.

"Homework," groaned Britea. "I just finished the political essay on last week's regional election. Now I have math to look forward to."

"Good luck," said Lexia as she eyed the books. "By the way, her friends are back," she inclined her head towards Pearl's empty bed.

"Lianne and Valerie?" Dread filled Britea when her friends nodded.

"Yeah and with juicy gossip from the royal court," added Henrick excitedly.

"As usual, Henrick was the first in the know, and he refused to say a word until we all gathered to visit you," said Danai dryly.

"So, out with it please. The suspense is killing me," said Navos. Even Shran had a curious expression on his face.

Britea was also curious. "What did they say?"

"Just for the record, I got this story from someone more reliable than Lianne and Valerie." At their impatient looks, Henrick hurried to explain. "I heard the Dyhaeri high priest and two Dyhaeri princes are guests of the king."

"No way," exclaimed Lexia. The others just gaped at him.

"Are you sure?" asked Danai. In contrast to the others, she appeared worried.

"My source, Dariuz, my roommate, said his uncle, who happens to be a minister at the royal court, and his cousins always tell him about the goings on at the palace. So this time, they told him the nobles have been trying to nab invitations to the upcoming balls because apparently at the first ball they attended, the visiting Dyhaeri were completely clothed in vert-silk."

Britea was mystified. "What's that?"

"Only the most expensive material on the planet, exclusively made by Weltonians," explained Shran, pointing to Danai.

"Hey!" protested her roommate as they all stared at her. "I don't own the merchandise. I've hardly even seen it even though *I 'm* Weltonian."

"How costly is this stuff anyway?" asked Lexia. Shran, Navos, and Henrick stared at her. The redhead sighed. "Why are you all looking at me like that? I hardly keep up with fashion. Now, why is everyone so crazy about the silk stuff?"

"Britea, what's the average daily minimum wage in Raven's Fall?" asked Shran suddenly.

She stared at him. "Forty-five silvers a day. Why?"

"A yard of vert-silk costs fifteen thousand silvers. You need at least six or seven yards to make an ensemble consisting of a long-sleeved tunic and full-length pants." Henrick looked at Shran questioningly. "I know this because my parents are tailors and were extremely nervous when given just a yard of vert-silk to make a scarf and some gloves. They didn't waste a strand."

Britea tried to calculate how much seven yards of vert-silk would cost and was almost dizzy at the total amount.

"Danai, where does it come from?" Lexia asked.

"Divers collect the gel from inside the hatched egg shells of young Alkynaia," answered Danai grimly. "The gel only appears after the young are hatched, and if left exposed to the sea water for too long, it hardens and becomes useless. So, one has only a short time to collect the gel before it changes. And you can imagine how dangerous it is because of the presence of the sea serpents. That's why it's so expensive."

Navos whistled. "Talk about a high-risk job." The others nodded in agreement, for a moment silent as they tried to imagine diving in perilous sea-serpent territory.

"So," drawled Henrick. "I wonder why the Dyhaeri are in town?"

Danai looked relieved at the change of the subject. "Beats me. I'm just as curious as you are."

"They're probably here about some trade deal," speculated Lexia.

"For the first time in eight hundred years?" Everyone looked at Shran. "The last time the Dyhaeri visited the court, officially, was in 1384 AC to witness the opening of this college. That's why there's a mural of their Queen Zaleria on the glass ceiling of the Great Hall."

Britea gaped at him. She had been meaning to find out what that beautiful mural represented.

"And how do you know all this?" asked Henrick.

Shran frowned at him. "Obviously, I read. It's in the history books."

"But I find it hard to believe the last Dyhaeri visit was eight hundred years ago!" said Lexia.

"Maybe officially. What if they just visited briefly at other times?" suggested Navos.

"That no one has heard of?" asked Danai skeptically.

"It doesn't matter anyway," said Henrick. Britea stared at him. "I doubt we'll ever know why they're here. The king would never make matters of state public."

"Visiting time is over," announced Healer Storm. This was met by sighs of disappointment. Britea's friends promised to visit after she was released as they were shooed out of the ward.

Moments after they left, Pearl stepped out of the washroom. "Finished gossiping about me to your friends?"

Britea's eyes narrowed at the edge in her voice. "We were just talking about what happened at court this weekend."

Pearl scoffed, walked over to Britea, and dropped the novel on her bed, shooting her a skeptical look. "A word of advice: try to lie better."

Britea's temper flared. "I'm not lying. Apparently a Dyhaeri delegation visited the king at the royal court."

Pearl smirked. "Do you know how outrageous that sounds? The Dyhaeri haven't visited our rulers since forever. Did you and your friends hatch this story just to see how gullible I was? And here I was, thinking you were a nice person. You just may survive here after all."

She marched back to her bed. Britea wanted to protest, but she realized there was no point in arguing.

#

Primeday.

Britea tried not to fidget as she and Pearl waited outside the warden's office. It was still early; there was at least an hour and a half before breakfast yet.

That morning, she had woken up with a knot of dread in the pit of her stomach. Pearl had been awake before her, and she also looked frightened. Britea knew what her own punishment was, but she hoped the warden had changed his mind about Pearl just as Danai had written.

Britea's mind returned to the present as she glanced at Pearl. Her fellow novice was deathly pale, and she had barely said two words to Britea that morning. Britea had realized the noble must have had a lot on her mind so had wisely left her alone.

Four guards had escorted them to the warden's office. Britea had been surprised by that. They surely weren't planning on running away.

"Enter," announced a loud voice from within. Britea hesitated at first, then stepped forward when it became apparent Pearl was frozen. Tentative footsteps sounded behind Britea as she entered the room.

Britea's heart rate increased when she saw those present. Warden Asteros, Instructor Shelley, and Weapons Master Caren again. The three sat behind a long desk.

Their expressions were stern.

"Novice Ceres and Novice D'Tranell, please step up to the desk." Both girls silently stepped forward.

Warden Asteros didn't waste time. "Before us are two envelopes. One contains the punishment detail for Novice D'Tranell. Britea, pick it up."

She complied and stepped back.

"The other letter is for Novice Ceres. Do you know what it contains?" he asked Pearl, who was on the verge of tears.

"My expulsion letter," she said quietly.

"Before you leave, do you have any last words?" asked Instructor Shelley.

Britea blinked. *Wait, this wasn't how this was supposed to go* . She opened her mouth to speak until she saw the weapons master glance at her and almost imperceptibly shake his head.

She stole a quick glance at Pearl, who was staring at the floor. "Yes, I do have something to say."

The noble sniffed then she turned to Britea. "Novice D'Tranell, I am sorry for being mean to you."

Britea was speechless. This she had not expected.

Pearl turned back to the school officials. "I also apologize to the college for the shame I have brought to the school. That is all I have to say."

All three senior wielders managed to keep their expressions neutral. Then the warden spoke. "We wielders are few and should be brothers and sisters in arms, not opponents at each other's throats. That is why the consequences for dueling are so severe. You knew this, Novice Ceres, and yet you went ahead with the duel. Whether you planned it alone or with others, today, you'll pay the price." He paused, then looked at Britea. "As the victim in this whole ordeal, do you have anything to say?"

Britea looked at the senior official. *What? They were asking her to say something?*

She thought fast. "I…I also apologize to the school for how I handled the matter. But I think Pearl's punishment is too severe."

Pearl shot her a startled look, which she ignored. "She knew what she did was wrong, and she has apologized for it. But for her to learn from this experience, she deserves a second chance, as do we all." Britea glanced at Pearl and was a bit startled at the wild light in her eyes.

Instructor Shelley narrowed her eyes. "Wise as your words may seem, how does withholding punishment teach her anything?"

"Give her the same punishment detail as I. She would certainly learn something from that."

The elders shared a thoughtful look.

"You two wait outside. We'll call you back in shortly," ordered the warden.

Pearl barely waited for the doors to close before she turned on Britea. "What in the Seven Hells are you doing?!"

"I'm trying to help you—" started a shocked Britea.

"I don't need you to save me!" hissed Pearl. "I didn't ask for your help, and I certainly didn't ask for your friendship!" She began to pace. "All you've just done is further humiliate me! You think the three foremost officials in this school are going to value the word of a farm girl from the Lords-forsaken regions of Malaquey? They're still going to send me packing!"

Britea watched her warily. A minute ago, Pearl had been apologizing, now she was upset because Britea had intervened? What was wrong with this girl?

"If that's the case then, when we get called in, you can tell them you'd rather be expelled than accept the punishment detail."

Pearl gave her a baleful look and scoffed in disbelief.

Britea wasn't done. "And then you get to go home."

Pearl faltered. Britea narrowed her eyes at the telltale sign of how terrified the noble was of her own home. *Why was that?*

No more was spoken as they waited in silence for several minutes.

"Come back in!" The shout from within had them reaching for the double doors at the same time. Pearl pushed ahead of her and entered, a silent fuming Britea not far behind.

Once more they walked up to the desk, behind which sat the three senior officials.

"Novice D'Tranell's suggestion has merit. It is quite telling the victim was gracious enough to have mercy on you, Novice Ceres. Even, your…friends weren't here to plead on your behalf. Why is that?" asked Weapons Master Caren.

Britea saw Pearl hang her head dejectedly. That must have hurt.

"We will accept Novice D'Tranell's suggestion…" began the warden.

Britea couldn't help but feel a bit smug when she saw the astonishment on Pearl's face.

"…but with conditions," continued Instructor Shelley as she stood up.

"You two will do the punishment detail…for seven months instead, but from now on, you are both responsible for each other until the completion of your punishment."

"What?" exclaimed both novices at the same time.

Instructor Shelley smiled coolly at them. "You will study together, train together, and work together. Should one of you end up mysteriously hurt—physically, emotionally, whatever—there will literally be the Seven Hells to pay. You are to take care of each other, regardless of the circumstances you may find yourself in." Then she glared at Pearl. "And if I catch one whiff of you dueling or using your ability to harm someone, I will personally strip you of your wielding powers myself. Is that clear?"

Pearl swallowed nervously and nodded hastily.

"I can't hear you," insisted the instructor coldly.

"Yes, ma'am!" answered Pearl immediately. Britea even found herself saying the same thing. She didn't want to risk having the instructor's ire directed at her.

Warden Asteros silently picked up the second envelope and wielded fire to destroy the contents, and then he smiled. "Instructor Shelley will take you back to your dorms to get what you need for class. From there, she will escort you to your first punishment duty. Do take note of the new seating arrangements in your classes because that will be permanent for the next seven months."

Britea thought about her wielding studies, but the saner part of her mind squashed that thought before it fully took form. This was neither the place nor the time to inquire.

Instructor Shelley walked around the desk and to the door. “Girls, with me.” She left the room then, with the two subdued novices trailing her.

Out in the hall, Britea glanced at Pearl, and she was at least grateful that her fellow novice looked just as terrified as she felt.

Seven months as partners? By the Deep!

CHAPTER 15

"Her name is Britea D'Tranell, and she's from Weldaros, a village in west Malaquey. The rest of her family consists of Valden and Samera D'Tranell, her parents—farmers—and one older sister, Carlina. This Britea seems to be the first wielder to appear in their family."

Queen Kallesa twirled ribbons of fire around her fingers as she listened to her intelligence officer's debriefing. Today's briefing was in the queen's shipyard office. The building was the tallest in Her Royal Majesty's shipyard and had floor-to-ceiling windows that enabled the queen to observe the cloistered shipbuilders at work. Outside the only entrance stood a pair of her elite guards. No one would disturb the queen without a very, very good reason.

"Apparently, from our source in Malaquey intelligence, she was trained by a Dyhaeri named Kahl during her voyage to Raven's Fall."

The twirling stopped and the Namiran queen turned to stare at Minister Lensworth.

"She was trained by…by a Dyhaeri?"

Her minister nodded, noting the disbelief in her voice.

"At first, I thought our source was lying, but cross checking with other sources indicates this is the truth. *Windrider* sailors have been spreading the tale of two wielders from different worlds simultaneously fighting off eight Namiran warships and bargaining with an Alkynaia army."

Queen Kallesa looked at him skeptically.

Minister Lensworth sighed. "Sailors are known to exaggerate their encounters, my queen. However, this may be the girl you're looking for."

The Namiran queen said nothing and went back to watching the shipbuilders while twirling her ribbons of fire.

"Perhaps. Where is she now?"

"She's studying at Syla College at the moment. There is also news of a Dyhaeri delegation visiting King Wilhem."

The queen looked sharply at Lensworth. "That is unusual. Do we know why?"

"They appear to be interested in inspecting the wielding colleges, my queen. It would seem King Wilhem balked at allowing them access to the military wielder colleges and gave them Syla College instead."

The queen laughed dryly. "Now they're interested in human wielders? Ha! Someone, somewhere, is plotting and planning against me and using this *inspection* as a diversion." She was thoughtful for a long moment. Minister Lensworth wisely stayed silent.

"Find out more about this girl: what her hobbies are, what she eats, where she goes, and who her friends are. Everything she does or says, I want to hear about it." Then she noticed the minister's expression. "What is it?"

"She's at Syla College, Your Highness. Out of the three Malaquey colleges, Syla is the only one with none of our spies. We've tried for decades to plant one, even among the kitchen staff, but to date, we've been unsuccessful."

Queen Kallesa rolled her eyes. "Not that old excuse again. Find a way, Minister Lensworth, before I lose my patience. You're dismissed."

"As you wish, my queen." He bowed and left as fast as he could, leaving the Immortal Monarch to her thoughts as she watched the building of her nearly completed ships.

#

"Today is the first day of your seven-month punishment," said Instructor Shelley briskly, the pace of her words matching her stride as they rushed to the kitchen. Britea and Pearl tried to keep up without breaking into a run.

"You must complete the tasks you're assigned before you go for your meals and classes. If you're late for your classes, your instructors will punish you, as is standard." Britea's jaw dropped. This was worse than she had expected. She glanced at Pearl, who looked frightened and furious at the same time.

I bet she blames me for this.

"Refusal to complete a task at hand will result in additional punishment, and arriving late to your tasks will also result consequences. Do I make myself clear?"

"Yes, ma'am," murmured both girls.

Instructor Shelley stopped suddenly. "I can't hear you!" she barked.

Britea and Pearl almost ran into her. "Yes, ma'am!" Their scared replies were much louder this time.

Instructor Shelley glared at them over her right shoulder briefly before again marching down the corridor. Pearl scowled at Britea for good measure before following.

Britea sighed and tried to keep up. A growl escaped her stomach, reminding her she was hungry. It would soon be time for breakfast, but she doubted they would get a chance to eat before their first set of punishments. Instructor Shelley turned down a corridor leading to the kitchens, which were just behind the dining hall. Britea had never been in the kitchens. A sign in capital letters on the right corridor wall stated, "NO NOVICES BEYOND THIS POINT!"

Britea wondered why.

As they got closer, she began to overhear sounds that could only belong in a kitchen. Instructor Shelley pushed open the double doors, and they walked into a world of heat, mouth-watering aromas, and ear-splitting noise. It took a while for Britea to make sense of the chaos as individuals in white uniforms scurried here and there, chopped up ingredients, or washed giant utensils and pots used to make the meals of hundreds of students and instructors.

"Welcome to the most essential department, the one that keeps everyone in Syla College fed."

"Good morning, Instructor Shelley." The three turned to face a diminutive man outfitted in a white uniform and a ridiculously tall chef's hat. "How can we help you today?" His bushy mustache bobbed with each word he spoke.

Instructor Shelley smiled at him. "Chef Blane, thank you for having us. I have two helpers for you for the next seven months: Novice Pearl Ceres and Novice Britea D'Tranell."

The chef frowned at the two novices. "Punishment detail?"

"I'm afraid so," said the instructor with a grin.

Chef Blane transferred his frown to her. "You know I don't like novices in the kitchen. They're not responsible enough."

Instructor Shelley's smile brightened. "That's why I bring them to you."

"Fine," growled the chef. The instructor bowed and walked away without a word to the two startled novices. The chef turned in the opposite direction; he took a few steps then stopped in his tracks and barked, "You two, with me!" Britea and Pearl silently followed as the denizens of the kitchen ignored them and carried on preparing the day's meals.

Chef Blane led them to the far-right corner of the kitchen and pointed them towards a large pile of dirty, unpeeled potatoes next to three large bowls of clean water. "First you wash this lot til every speck of dirt is removed, and then you peel them."

He produced two short knives and handed them to the two novices. Britea took hers first, then noticed Pearl was staring in horror at the knife in the chef's hand.

"Is something wrong with you, girl?" asked the chef, clearly irritated.

Pearl drew herself up and glared at him, and Britea just knew she was going to say the wrong thing.

"I am Lady Pearl Ceres. I do not do kitchen work. You must find me something else to do—"

"This is your punishment. You peel or you go home!" shouted the chef. Nearby staff stopped working for a moment, glanced in their direction, then resumed their duties as if nothing had occurred.

"If you didn't want to be here, then you shouldn't have been dueling on the Forever Bridge! If it were up to me, only you would be in here peeling potatoes, certainly not Britea the Brave!"

Britea felt her face heat. So the story had made it to the kitchens. It had seemed at first as though the chef hadn't known who they were. *This was so embarrassing* .

"Now take the bloody knife, or I call Instructor Shelley back. Your choice!"

Pearl was silent for a long moment before she finally reached across to snatch the peeling knife. Britea saw the rage and humiliation in her eyes, and for one moment, was worried Pearl may attack the diminutive chef.

Chef Blane ignored the baleful light in Pearl's eyes and walked away.

For a moment, both girls just stood there. Then Britea decided they had better start.

"Well, at least we don't have to fetch the water." Britea put her knife down on a nearby table. She rolled up her sleeves past her elbows and tucked them in as tight as she could manage, then scooped up as many potatoes as she could and dumped them in the nearest large bowl of water. She turned to collect the next set and realized Pearl was still staring at the peeling knife in her hand.

"Hey, you going to stand there all day, or are you going to help me?"

Pearl slowly looked at her. The anger in the novice's eyes almost made Britea take a step back, but she was getting tired of this.

"And if I don't?" growled Pearl.

"If you don't?" Britea couldn't believe this. "Pearl, a few minutes ago, you were *this* close to being expelled," she said, putting her thumb and index finger nearly together. "I don't know what's going on with your family," fear flashed briefly in

Pearl's eyes, "but I know you don't want to return to them, so why are you trying to get yourself kicked out of school?"

A look of uncertainty appeared on Pearl's face. "You don't understand."

And frankly, I don't care. Britea was sorely tempted to utter those words, but prudence stilled her tongue since Pearl still held the peeling knife.

"Fine, so I don't. But we still have this punishment detail to do, and if it doesn't get done in time, things will be even worse for both of us."

Pearl stared at the pile of dirty, unpeeled potatoes with disgust. "I…I don't know how to wash those…or even peel them. I've never even entered a kitchen before."

"I'm not surprised," muttered Britea. "Look," she said more loudly this time, "just tuck in your sleeves like I did and follow my lead, all right? We'll get by."

Pearl slowly set down the knife and tried to roll up her sleeves like Britea had. It took a few tries, but eventually, she managed. But she refused to scoop up the potatoes as Britea had; instead, she gingerly picked up one potato at a time to drop into the water.

Britea groaned in frustration. "At this rate, we'll be here all winter." She doubled up her own efforts collecting more potatoes and dropping them into the first bowl. Pearl ignored her and continued picking up each potato as if she was afraid the tuber would bite her fingers.

It took several trips, but Britea got most of the potatoes into the bowl of water before she remembered something important.

"Hang on. We need washing towels," said Britea.

"What?" asked Pearl.

Britea walked over to a young girl. "Please, can we have two small washing towels for the potatoes?" The girl gave her a startled looked then turned to the chef.

"Give the smart one what she wants!" barked Chef Blane. He stood on a high stool using a gigantic ladle to stir the boiling concoction in an enormous pot.

She prayed the tiny chef didn't fall into that pot because it looked like he would with the smallest misstep.

The silent girl nodded and went to a table to collect two clean, folded washing towels. She gave them to Britea.

"Thank you."

The girl smiled.

"What do we need those for?" asked Pearl, gingerly dropping a single potato into her bowl of water.

"You use it to wash the potatoes, like this." Britea demonstrated as she took one wet tuber and began to scrub the skin with the wet towel. "Then you transfer the potato into the next bowel of water to rinse it and repeat."

Pearl watched Britea rapidly wash three potatoes at the same time, rotating the potatoes in the water as she scrubbed at the surfaces and then expertly flipped each clean potato into the second large bowl of clean water. "You truly are a farmgirl." There was no scorn in her voice this time, but maybe there was a hint of wonder?

Britea snorted. "I never denied that, did I?"

Pearl hesitated before replying. "No, you didn't." She collected the last few remaining potatoes and dropped them into her bowl, which was now full of wet, dirty, unpeeled spuds. She hesitated before dipping her now dirty hands into the first bowl and tried to emulate what Britea was doing.

"How...how did you get so good at this?"

"At washing potatoes? Sitting with my mah in the kitchen, watching and wanting to help. She didn't let me until I was six years old, and even then, I had to do it properly, or I was booted from the kitchen. She didn't let me near the peeling knife until I was eight, and then I had to peel one without cutting myself before she would leave me unsupervised."

Pearl shot her an odd look. "You sound like you enjoyed it."

Britea's eyes stung as she relieved those happy memories. "Aye. They were some of the best days of my life." She swiped away her unshed tears with her sleeve.

"You miss your farm life," declared Pearl, sounding a bit surprised.

You certainly don't miss your noble home. "I do. You did get one thing right: life on the farm and in the village *is* simpler than your city life, but," she gave Pearl a hard look, "it's never easy." She went back to washing the next three potatoes.

Pearl wisely kept silent and tried to keep up.

It seemed to take ages before they got all the potatoes washed to Britea's satisfaction. Several of Pearl's needed rewashing. Britea tried to rein in her impatience as she showed the clueless noble how to properly remove the dirt from the potatoes.

At the end of it all, Britea looked at the three large bowls of clean, unpeeled potatoes and grimaced. While she knew how to clean and peel, she had never washed so many at once. At home, they had only cleaned enough for their small family of three. This pile was for hundreds of students and instructors, and now they had to peel this lot? *Lords save them!*

"And now it's time for peeling," said a weary, hungry, sweating Britea. Pearl also looked exhausted. Her fine dark hair was plastered to her scalp with sweat, yet she didn't complain. Both reached for their peeling knives.

"That's enough for now." They turned to face Chef Blane. He had a tray with two plates of steaming porridge with delicious-smelling, freshly baked bread. "Breakfast started ten minutes ago. Here's some grub. Eat up fast and get to class. I expect to see you two an hour before dinnertime." Britea wondered why he was going easy on them, but she was too distracted by the warm food before her to ask.

"Thank you, chef," chorused the two hungry novices as they grabbed their breakfasts and sat at a nearby table to eat. The chef walked over to the bowls of washed potatoes. Britea tried not to laugh as she realized the bowls of water were only slightly shorter than the master of the kitchens. The chef hemmed and hawed as he examined the potatoes.

"Not bad at all, but we all saw Britea did most of the work." Pearl went red, but then the chef looked at Pearl and continued. "However, it appears you were trying to learn. I'll let this pass for now. I expect equal efforts from you both next time. Now, hurry and get to class."

Both novices went back to concentrating on their food.

#

Britea and Pearl each had to dash to their dorm to change. The heat in the kitchens had been so great that their clothes were soaked through. Britea was relieved she still shared a room with Danai. At least the punishment had not included rooming with Pearl. There was only so much she could take.

To Britea's chagrin, her room was empty. Danai was probably on her way to her fifth-year class. Hopefully Britea caught up with her at some point.

She was a bit surprised to find Pearl waiting for her in the corridor. The noble was pacing up and down and frowned when Britea appeared.

"We're stuck together, remember? Now, hurry before Instructor Dawn gets mad. I haven't even done my assignment!"

They ran to the social studies class. To their relief, Instructor Dawn was yet to appear, but as Pearl and Britea entered the classroom, it fell silent.

Most of the students stared at them in shock, including Lianne and Valerie. Henrick, who was at the back of the class, smiled when he noticed Britea and Pearl. He even waved at them. He was the only one who appeared happy to see them.

"What are you two doing here? You're supposed to have been expelled!" exclaimed Lianne in a loud, outraged voice. From the loud whispers of the other students, it was all to evident Lianne had been spreading that rumor.

Britea found herself rooted in place, dumbstruck for a moment. Then she looked at Pearl. The noble was pale and staring at Lianne as if she was really seeing her for the first time.

"Good morning, class," said Instructor Teron Dawn as he walked briskly into the class.

"Good morning, instructor," chorused the class." But Lianne was already out of her seat and walking up to the teacher.

"Sir, I do believe there has been a mistake. These two shouldn't be here."

The instructor frowned at Lianne before scrutinizing the two silent novices standing just inside the door. "Novice D'Tranell and Novice Ceres, yes, I was expecting you two. Take those two seats at the front of the class."

Lianne became more flustered as Britea and Pearl walked pass her.

"Instructor—"

"Novice Arkei, do return to your seat before you earn your own punishment detail." That made the furious novice march back to her seat.

The instructor seemed to be in good humor this morning. He rubbed his hands. "I'm sure most of you are wondering what in the Deep is going on after all the fracas of just three days ago." He looked around the class. "Well, let's refresh our memories, shall we? Three days ago, two of our students were involved in a duel, which is outlawed, not just at Syla but in Malaquey as well. The penalty for this is usually expulsion, but, due to certain circumstances, we have decided to set an example."

He pointed at Britea and Pearl. "These two come from vastly different worlds, so they will share the same punishments and the same assignments and will be the best of study partners for months to come." He turned back to the rest of the stunned class.

"Do not think this punishment is light, not when they have to work in the hot, busy kitchens before each meal, and probably after the meals as well, and still get to their classes on time while being observed by the entire school."

Britea felt like sinking into the floor. She glanced at Pearl. The noble was staring straight ahead.

"Lift your chin, Britea, and keep your back straight," hissed Pearl in a voice only Britea could hear. Britea found herself unwittingly obeying.

"Don't let her see you defeated," continued Pearl. "Lianne takes joy in other people's pain. I swear, she will pay for this."

"And now on to my next favorite topic," continued the instructor.

"Take out your assignments." There was a flurry of activity as the students began to place essays on their desks. Britea took hers out before realizing Pearl wasn't moving.

"Pearl?" she whispered.

"I told you, I didn't finish mine," replied Pearl in a strained whisper. Britea glanced at the instructor. He had started collecting the essays.

"Just submit what you've done already—"

"I barely wrote a paragraph! I was planning to finish it over the weekend, then the duel happened, and—"

"Novice D'Tranell and Novice Ceres, you two better be discussing the assignment," said Instructor Dawn as he collected Britea's essay from her desk. He frowned at Pearl's empty desk.

"Where's yours?"

Novice Ceres sighed. "I failed to finish mine, sir, because I was in the infirmary."

The instructor studied her for a long moment. "And yet Novice D'Tranell, who was in the same infirmary, was able to complete hers in time? Novice Ceres, stand at the front of the class." When Pearl stayed put, he added. "Now."

Finally, she obeyed. Lianne whispered something to Valerie and both laughed. Instructor Dawn glared in their direction and the laughter died.

Britea turned back to the front where Pearl was furious as she faced her peers.

"Novice Ceres is going to tell us what she was planning to write in her essay."

Britea was very glad she had gotten hers done. There was no way she would have survived an impromptu verbal essay before the entire class.

Pearl looked at the floor for a brief moment, then faced the class and stared right through them.

"Novice Ceres, you may begin when you're ready." Instructor Dawn perched on an empty desk with a notepad in one hand as if he was about to take notes.

"Last week, I attended a regional election with my fellow classmates," began Pearl in a strong, clear voice. "At first, I couldn't be bothered to learn the name of the political entities because their policies have no impact on my way of life. I was more interested in being with my dear friends, Lianne Arkei and Valerie Mern, and planning on how we would get away early, so we could plan for the weekend ball at Lianne's home. After all, we only cared about what to wear and who to flirt with."

Britea glanced at Instructor Dawn, who frowned and made a note on his pad. Britea covered her face in embarrassment. This was going to be a disaster. She could not bear to watch.

"However, I had no idea how stupid the three of us privileged brats were." Britea's hand dropped from her face when she heard the gasps of outrage from Lianne and Valerie.

Pearl wasn't done. "Being born noble and rich means nothing, especially when one is alone and afraid and hanging for dear life from the railings of the Forever Bridge!" Pearl was glaring at Lianne and Valerie as she spoke. The two nobles looked like they were contemplating murder.

Britea glanced at the instructor, whose frown had deepened.

"But I digress," said Pearl as she tore her gaze from her former friends. "We were talking about the election. A single vote represents one voice of one individual. That voice can easily become lost in the void because it isn't loud enough. But when you have many voices screaming for the same thing, you cannot help but hear them, even if the rich and privileged hide in the highest of glass towers. Those voices as one can shatter any foundation. This is why you cannot ignore the significance of elections." She paused to look a few of the students in the eye before continuing.

"Being able to vote is a luxury many of us take for granted, probably because we don't see its importance and its influence in changing the balance of power in this nation. Namira lost that balance a long time ago, so we must never lose sight of how powerful one's voice is. Which is why we must listen to them all." She ended her spiel by looking at Britea.

Silence filled the air, and then someone clapped. It was the instructor. Soon most of the class joined him, apart from a fuming Lianne and Valerie.

"Bravo! Now, that would have gotten a top grade," said the instructor with a smile before turning to the class. The smile disappeared. "If only those words had made it onto paper. Return to your seat, Novice Ceres. While you have earned kudos, you have also earned an extra assignment."

Pearl darted to her seat beside Britea, her hands shaking. Britea reached across and grabbed Pearl's hand. Soon the shaking stopped.

"That was quite good," whispered Britea.

"Thank you," replied Pearl before releasing Britea's hand.

Britea glanced behind them, and sure enough, Lianne and Valerie were glaring at them.

#

Instructor Felgreen made Britea and Pearl stand aside until the entire history class was seated. Britea had a horrible inkling of what was about to happen.

"As you all know, these two," she pointed at Britea and Pearl, "decided to be idiots and duel on the Forever Bridge." The entire class stared at them. Britea glanced at Pearl, who was pale and staring ahead defiantly. The instructor continued. "History has shown us armies decimated from within because of discontent and infighting. Now, that will not happen in this school. Both of you will sit at the front in every class and answer every question." Instructor Felgreen's smile was so cold Britea shivered.

So, this was what they had to look forward to. Being humiliated in every single class.

Britea wished she had called in sick.

#

"Oh, my dears!" Instructor Droye appeared to be on the verge of tears as she made Britea and Pearl stand in a corner of their dance and etiquette class. "When I heard the news, I was so disappointed! I had such high hopes for you, Britea, that you'd learn etiquette, but then you had to go and get involved in a duel. And Pearl, what were you thinking?!" Britea saw several of their peers trying not to laugh. Not so Lianne and Valerie. They were openly smirking.

Beside Britea, Pearl muttered a prayer. "Lords of Shadow and Light, please kill me now." Britea was herself wishing for the same fate.

And so it continued in every class. By the fourth class, Britea was getting more irritated than embarrassed at how she and Pearl were introduced each time. Well, at least she and Pearl would go their separate ways when Britea had to go to the combat and defense class.

But to her dismay, as she and Pearl exited their economics class behind their amused classmates, they ran into Instructor Talios. She was second in command to Weapons Master Caren. Instructor Talios usually taught the senior members of the combat and defense class, and Britea had heard from Danai that she wasn't one to take lightly any day of the week. She wore form-fitting training leathers dyed as dark as coffee with a red fire slash on her right arm. A wielder of fire. Her chestnut, almond-shaped eyes were framed by an oval face and night-black hair currently in a pony tail. Her features were stern as she regarded the two students.

"Novice Ceres, your extra curriculum class of additional etiquette has been switched to combat and defense." Pearl's eyes flashed.

"I didn't sign up for combat," said the novice through gritted teeth.

The female instructor's answering smile was cold. "Oh, but you did, the moment you decided to challenge Britea to a duel while holding a hostage." They stared at each other for a long moment before Pearl looked away. Britea released the breath she was holding.

"Follow me." The instructor turned away. Pearl and Britea shared a tired look and went after her.

"I didn't know one could take extracurricular etiquette," said Britea as they followed behind Talios. She was a bit tired of the silence and wanted to talk about something, anything, and besides, they had a long walk to the combat and defense training yard.

Pearl glanced at her. "It was either that or something even more boring. After you've been here for two years, you're encouraged to take additional classes. I sure didn't want more economics or history or geography, so I asked for more etiquette. It's easy. I learned it all even before I started wielding."

"But why is etiquette so important?" asked Britea.

Pearl scoffed. "You sound like you think it's rubbish."

"Isn't it?"

"Spoken like a farm girl," sighed Pearl. "Etiquette is the language of the Malaquey court. Without it, you're defenseless. When we graduate, we'll be employed by members of the court—"

"After our Year of Discovery…" cut in Britea.

"Yes, let's talk about that, shall we?" said Pearl dryly as she glanced at the instructor walking several feet in front of them. She lowered her voice "In truth, the Year of Discovery is a small concession to the common people, a way of keeping them in line. So, in the grand scheme of things, it matters not." Britea almost faltered in her steps while Pearl continued talking as if she had not noticed.

"Your real work lies with the government and the Malaquey nobles. Without etiquette, you won't survive. So, I suggest you learn as much as you can because you've got a lot of catching up to do, my friend."

Britea frowned at her, disturbed at how the Year of Discovery was considered nonessential by the nobles of society. This was contradictory to what the instructors had been trying to teach them.

Were the nobles right and the teachers wrong?

She refused to believe that, plus she didn't like Pearl's condescending tone, but part of her realized that Pearl, in her own way, was trying to help. Besides, Pearl had just called her a friend. *Was she mocking her?*

"I'll teach you. We *are* partnered now," continued Pearl.

"Thanks. I appreciate the offer." Britea still didn't really know how to feel about learning etiquette, which she still thought was a waste of time.

"So, you learned shielding in combat and defense?" suddenly asked Pearl suddenly.

"Uh...no."

Pearl frowned at her. "Who taught you then?"

"Instructor Shelley." Pearl almost stopped in her tracks.

"One-to-one teaching? Is that why no one has seen you wield?"

Britea rolled her eyes. "The junior wielders saw me wield in class. Why don't you believe them?"

"We…I thought they were just trying to protect you."

Britea looked at her closely as she heard the wistfulness in Pearl's voice. *Was she missing Lianne and Valerie?*

There was no more time to analyze it though. They had reached combat and defense class.

#

As they entered the class, Britea felt more settled. She had just realized this was fast becoming her second-favorite class, the first being wielding class. It took but a moment for the other students to realize who was in their midst. Most of them hailed Britea like she was a heroine warrior coming home, but Pearl got some hostile looks.

To Britea's relief, Master Caren simply nodded at them, not subjecting them to the same humiliating introduction as the other instructors. He did leave them in the *loving* care of Instructor Talios though.

"Change into practice outfits and run back to me," ordered Instructor Talios.

Britea showed Pearl where the practice uniforms were.

"Everyone likes you here," said Pearl. "They clearly hate me."

"I don't think so…"

"Oh, don't try to sugar coat it, Britea. Your friends have good reason to dislike me." Pearl sounded resigned.

Britea had no idea what to say, so she kept silent. Back in the courtyard, the rest of the class had already been paired off for wielding sparring, hand-to-hand combat, or weapons training.

"Ten laps around the field!" the instructor barked at them.

Britea rubbed her hands in glee. That was easy. Then she noticed the concerned look on Pearl's face.

"You have to finish the run together," stressed the instructor. "Now get to it."

Halfway into the first lap, Britea realized they had a problem. Pearl was falling behind. Looking back, Britea could see the strain on Pearl's face and could hear her labored breathing. Britea slowed considerably so Pearl could catch up.

"I…know…what…you're doing." Pearl said, panting hard as she tried to continue running. "Don't…I don't need…your…help."

Britea said nothing and just matched her speed. Pearl could only glare at her. They had barely started the run, and she already looked too tired to argue.

The run seemed to last forever, and several times Britea worried Pearl would keel over; however, the noble was determined to finish the assignment. At the end of the last lap, Britea was barely winded, but Pearl dropped first to her knees, then to the floor in an exhausted heap. Her labored breathing was so loud some nearby students giggled until Britea glared at them, causing them to stop mid-giggle and concentrate on their activities.

Britea turned to help Pearl up, only to find the noble studying her with a puzzled, tired expression. "You…defended…me?"

Britea shrugged, feeling self-conscious. "They didn't have to laugh about it."

Pearl wearily shook her head, clearly too fatigued to utter more.

"My elderly grandmother could run faster than the two of you." Both girls were startled by the instructor's silent approach. "Congratulations to you both for running slower than a tortoise." Britea lowered her eyes in embarrassment as Pearl continued breathing fast.

The instructor studied them for a few moments. "Rest up for the next two minutes, then be prepared to recite the Creed when I return."

Britea was relieved, but Pearl snorted once the instructor was out of hearing distance. "Is…is this what you do at every class? Just run?!"

"Hey, it's endurance training. How do you think I could withstand your wielding as long as I did?"

Pearl stared at her from the ground. "So, this class *did* help you?"

"In some ways," replied Britea, thrusting out a hand Pearl grasped without hesitation, and in a blink, the noble was on her feet. She swayed a bit but thankfully maintained her balance.

Britea saw the intensity on Pearl's face as she watched the other students. "You've never been in this class before, have you?" asked Britea.

"No, as I said, I saw no need for it…" Pearl's voice trailed off.

"But now?" Britea had a feeling Pearl's perceptions were slowly shifting.

"Now, consider me…. intrigued," the noble sounded reluctant.

"The Creed!" yelled Instructor Talios, who had once again crept up unannounced. The loud command had both girls stiffening, and they began to recite as one.

#

Britea and Pearl were relieved when Instructor Talios informed them the kitchen had given them a reprieve for lunch because of the distance between their current class and the kitchens.

But when Britea and Pearl collected their food, Britea noticed that Pearl appeared uncomfortable.

"Is something wrong?"

"I expect you'll wish to join your friends. That's fine by me. I'd prefer eating alone anyway," said Pearl as she turned towards an empty table.

Britea was sorely tempted to leave Pearl alone, but it didn't feel right. "Hey, come sit with us."

Pearl tilted her head. "Are you sure they want me there? Especially Danai?"

Britea instantly felt guilty. She had not considered the bad blood that already existed between Danai and Lianne's older sister.

"I…I think she'll be fine with it. Besides, we're supposed to stick together."

Pearl stared at her for a long moment, then sighed. "Fine, lead the way, Britea the Considerate." Britea rolled her eyes at the last words.

Sure enough, Danai, Navos, and Henrick were already seated and waving at her to join them. Their expressions faltered when they saw Pearl in her wake.

Please, don't be angry, prayed Britea as she smiled nervously.

"Um, can Pearl join us? She's new to this class."

Navos and Henrick shared a puzzled look. Danai studied Pearl, who didn't break eye contact.

"Sure, why not?" said Danai with a smile. Britea failed to hide her relief as they sat down. She chanced a glance at Pearl, who was also visibly relieved at the invitation.

"So, how you finding the class so far?" asked Henrick. Britea narrowed her eyes. He sounded a bit nervous.

Pearl peered at him, her expression uncertain. "It's quite…different from what I'm used to."

"Oh," was all Henrick said before concentrating on his meal.

"Anyway, welcome to our side of the school," said Navos with a smile as he dug into his meal. Pearl stared at him in shock as he polished off his plate in record time.

"Uh…thank you."

Danai smiled dryly at her stunned expression. "We have less time for lunch than the rest of the school, so we have to eat quickly."

"Surely that isn't healthy," complained Pearl as she stared at Britea, who had almost finished her meal.

Britea shrugged. "I'm used to it."

"Soldiers don't get time on the battlefield," pitched in Navos between bites. "That's what Master Caren says."

"Oh, I see," said a subdued Pearl as she looked at her barely touched plate.

"You have eight minutes left!" bellowed one of the male instructors.

Danai's smile widened as Pearl tried to eat faster.

#

Junior wielding was the last class of the day, and Britea had been dreading it all day. Instructor Talios had informed Pearl at the end of combat and defense class that she would be joining Britea in the junior wielding class.

Pearl had wisely kept her objections to herself.

Now the two novices stood just outside the door. Britea could already hear the junior novices chatting within. Beside her, Pearl stood silent. A quick look at the noble showed she seemed just as nervous as Britea was. That was surprising.

Britea had been expecting snide remarks from Pearl about being in the junior wielding class, but she had said nothing.

"Are you two waiting for an invitation?" Both turned to see Instructor Shelley.

"I..." began Britea before finding she had nothing to say. Pearl kept her gaze lowered. The female instructor studied Pearl for a long moment.

"I had my misgivings about having both of you in this class." Britea stared at the instructor in horror.

"However, it is necessary. Every week for the next seven months, you will spend two days in the junior division and the remaining three in Pearl's class." Pearl looked up in surprise.

"Instructor Melvin is expecting both of you the day after tomorrow. He is less kind than I am. Now, enter the class."

Britea shared a troubled look with Pearl and opened the door.

At first the class was joyful when they saw Britea, but their expressions changed to fear when they beheld Pearl. All except Chelton, whose eyes were filled with fury, and Vindell, who shivered beside him as she refused to take her eyes off Pearl. Now Britea knew why the instructor hadn't wanted them both here.

Instructor Shelley didn't waste time. "You all know who these two are. I won't go into details."

Britea was thankful for that.

"But there is something we need to do. Vindell come here." The little girl sat frozen for a long moment and tried to hide behind Chelton.

The instructor softened her voice. "It will only be for a moment."

Everyone waited until the girl was able to stand. Chelton went to stand as well.

"No, Chelton," ordered Instructor Shelley. "Vindell has to walk this road alone...for now."

The trembling junior novice trudged to the instructor's side, putting the adult between her and Pearl. Britea glanced at her peer and was shocked to see a wet sheen in the noble's eyes.

"Sometimes events in our lives define us and affect our growth. What happened on the Forever Bridge is one of those. However, we cannot live in fear." Instructor Shelley regarded the pale young student beside her before continuing.

"You will see Pearl for half of each week, and you will talk with her even if you don't wish to. In this way, she will cease to be your nightmare." The last word made Pearl's eyes widen and her face pale.

The instructor wasn't done yet. "It will be hard; however, you must conquer your fear because as you get older, you will come across worse people than her." Instructor Shelley glanced at a shocked Pearl. "Is there anything you wish to say?"

Silence filled the room for a long moment before Pearl spoke in a shaky voice. "I'm sorry, Novice Masters, for the pain I caused you. I ask for your forgiveness."

Britea's jaw dropped. This day was continuing to be full of surprises.

Instructor Shelley turned to Vindell. "Does this suffice?"

"Yes, it does. I accept," responded the younger novice quickly as if eager to run away.

The instructor smiled sadly at the young girl. "You may return to your seat." Vindell fled back to sit beside a scowling Chelton. He had certainly not forgiven Pearl.

"Britea and Pearl, take the two empty seats at the back and to the right." Britea was only too happy to sit down. She glanced over at Pearl, who looked downcast.

The noble was certainly taking this punishment harder than Britea was.

#

Britea was bone tired by the time she and Pearl were released from the kitchens after the evening meal. Once again, they'd had to report to the kitchen an hour before the evening meal, and a mountain of fresh, dirty carrots had been ready for them to wash and peel.

That had been tedious. Again, she'd had to teach Pearl how to wash and clean the carrots; however, Pearl had cut herself so many times Chef Blane had ordered one of the kitchen staff, who was also a healer, to stand beside them and heal each cut.

Pearl had cried at her difficulty in peeling the carrots, and Britea had tried her best to comfort her, but it was obvious this punishment was going to be more challenging than she had thought. The chore had taken them so long they'd had to eat their supper in the kitchens while cleaning the carrots.

Britea's mind returned to the present as she struggled to put one foot ahead of the other. It seemed an eternity passed before she reached her room.

Danai was already back; she was lying on her bed reading a novel. She sat up when she saw her weary roommate.

"You look awful."

"I feel it too," said Britea as she shrugged off her school cloak. She glanced at her still sweat-drenched shirt. "I need to wash, but I'm worried I'll fall asleep in the bath."

"You won't," Danai stood. "I'll stand outside the door and talk to keep you awake."

"Thank you so much," said Britea. To be honest, she was close to tears. She had never been this tired in her life.

After a refreshing bath, she felt a bit better and more awake. She changed into a loose white nightgown before exiting the bathroom. True to her word, Danai was still standing beside the door, reciting from the book in her hand.

"You see? You didn't collapse," said Danai with a smile.

"Thank the Lords." Then a thought crossed Britea's mind. She suddenly hugged Danai, who responded with a laugh.

"Are you feeling okay?"

"I'm just glad to be out of the infirmary. Thanks so much for convincing the warden to give Pearl a chance."

"That was thanks to both of us," said Danai as they separated. Then she saw the hesitant expression on Britea's face. "What's wrong?"

"You're not mad at me?"

Danai was surprised by the change of topic. "Whatever for?"

"For inviting Pearl to sit with us."

Danai snorted. "At first, I was stunned, then I remembered how kind-hearted you are and how it's only in your nature to help those less fortunate—even those who look down on you."

Now Britea stared at her. "What makes you say that?"

Danai began to tick off points with her fingers. "You joined forces with Kahl to save a merchant ship, you bargained with the Alkynaia for the lives of the crew, and then—just last week—you ran without hesitation into a duel to save your junior classmate when anyone with sense would have run in the other direction, screaming for help from the instructors. Plus, when others would have rejoiced in getting their nemesis expelled, you tried to save her from that fate."

Britea felt embarrassed now. "That's different. The Seers wanted us to save her."

Danai smiled. "My point is most other folks would choose the easier path, which is to do nothing and not get involved. You, my little sister, have a heart of gold."

Britea wanted to reply but found herself yawning. "This heart is about to keel over with exhaustion."

Danai chuckled. "Well before you pass out, what exactly was your punishment detail?"

Britea stifled another yawn. "Kitchen duties and paired learning with Pearl for seven months." She noticed the dumbfounded look on Danai's face. "What?"

"That was not what I suggested!"

"Come again?"

"I told the warden to give Pearl the same punishment as yours because maybe she would learn something from it. I did *not* recommend you two being paired together or increasing the duration of the punishment!" Danai was horrified.

Britea was too tired to be upset, so she just shrugged. "It's fine. I'm just hoping it goes by fast. Now, please excuse me while I pass out." She mimicked a log falling in the forest as she dropped onto her bed.

Danai laughed and gave her a folded letter. "By the way, this came for you yesterday, courtesy of my mah."

"Who is it…" Britea's words trailed off when she saw the name on the back of the envelope. She sat up quickly as sleep disappeared from her eyes.

"I'll leave you to it," said Danai with a knowing smile as she returned to her own bed.

"Thanks again," said Britea in a daze as she began to read a letter she had never thought she would receive.

Dear Britea,

I was very happy to get your letter.

I'm also glad to hear you're settling in well at the college and making new friends.

Since last we parted, I have been assigned new duties with my cousin. We have been well and learning new, exciting information about other places. It has been an enlightening experience. I even got to read many interesting books.

I hope this letter finds you well, and I pray you succeed in your studies. May we meet once more in happier circumstances.

From, Kahl

CHAPTER 16

Britea hummed as she scrubbed the large oily saucepan.

She and Pearl had presented themselves to Chef Blane again an hour before breakfast, and he had put them to work without delay washing pots and pans. Britea gave Pearl a quick tutorial before turning to the seemingly daunting task at hand.

Usually, she hated washing pots and pans. Give her a thousand potatoes to peel instead. But today, she was walking on air because of the letter she had reread so many times already that she had memorized each word.

"You seem awfully cheerful washing pots. Is this another favorite hobby?" asked Pearl with a scowl. The noble was trying to wash a pot while holding the sponge with two fingers as if trying to limit her contact with the pot. The result was a pot that remained dirty.

Britea was so happy she wasn't going to let Pearl take away her joy. "No, I actually hate washing pots."

"So, what's making you so sickeningly cheerful?" asked an irritated Pearl.

Britea was tempted to talk about Kahl, but she recalled the words of caution from Danai not to talk about her relationship with the Dyhaeri. "Oh, it just seems like a wonderful day."

Pearl gave her a jaundiced look. "I swear, if you could bottle up your enthusiasm and sell it, you would make a mint."

Britea simply smiled. "By the way, you really need to grip the sponge like I am and give the pot a good scrub, or we'll miss breakfast in the hall."

"But my nails will be ruined!"

"They'll grow back. Come on, put your back into it."

Pearl growled in frustration. "Seriously, tone down the happiness a bit please."

Fortunately for them both, Pearl reluctantly did as Britea suggested, and they finished the pots five minutes before breakfast. Chef Blane shooed them out of the kitchen, and the two novices hurried to the dining hall.

They ended up at the back of the line and were among the last to get food.

"Ugh, we get the dregs from the bottom of the pans," whispered Pearl as she scrutinized the congealed porridge in her bowl.

Britea glanced at Pearl's plate then compared it to hers and frowned. Britea had two wraps bursting with scrambled eggs, a small bowl of fresh fruit, and a large cup of tea. There was plenty of food left, but Pearl had only chosen a bowl of porridge. Come to think of it, the day before in the combat and defenseclass, Pearl had hardly eaten anything.

No wonder she had been so tired.

"Shouldn't you get some more food?" whispered Britea.

"Of course not. I have to maintain my figure," said Pearl as if that was a most reasonable response.

"Well, look what trash decided to invade our dining hall." The silky voice had Britea and Pearl freezing in their tracks. It had come from behind them. Lianne, Valerie, and two other girls Britea didn't know stepped around them to face both novices.

"Ladies," began Lianne. "This is what failure looks like. Worn out and pathetic after one day working in the kitchens. Imagine what they'll look after seven months working as servants for the rest of the school."

Britea kept her eyes on their hands. She wouldn't put it past them to start wielding in the dining hall.

Pearl, meanwhile, was gripping her tray of food so hard her knuckles were snow white, but not out of fear. Her barely contained fury was palpable.

"Lianne and Valerie, I see you found two more brain-dead ladies to join you. Daphne Kellen and Therese Chade, I recall you two begging to be friends with us once a upon a time."

"Well, now you're the nobody," taunted one of the new girls. Pearl shot her a cold look.

"Watch it, Therese. My family was nobility long before your great-great-grandfather married his way into the Chade line. He had to change his surname, did he not?"

The new girl went red with embarrassment.

"Enough of this." Lianne waved her hand as if bored. "I'm hungry." Then before anyone could move, she grabbed Pearl's bowl of porridge. "This seems quite bland," she said digging her fingers into the congealed food and swirling it around before dropping the bowl back on Pearl's tray. Therese stepped closer to Lianne and gave her a silk handkerchief to wipe her fingers with.

"There. I'm sure the dirt under my nails has improved the taste. Enjoy." Lianne smiled at Pearl and Britea's appalled expressions, then walked away with her giggling trio of friends.

Pearl was staring at her bowl as if it was something vile.

Britea looked over to the breakfast trays. The cooks were already clearing away the remaining food. "Pearl, let's get you another bowl of porridge before…"

"I am going to kill her!" growled Pearl.

"No," Britea insisted. Pearl glared at her. "Let's just wait until after breakfast, and then we can talk about it." Britea held her own tray with one hand while she dragged Pearl back to the breakfast buffet line.

Unfortunately, the porridge was gone, so this time Britea convinced Pearl to grab an egg wrap and a small bowl of fruit. Pearl balked on tea and took water instead.

Britea searched for her friends and was relieved to find they were at a table far away from Lianne and her group. As she walked beside Britea, Pearl kept muttering about what she was going to do to Lianne. The threats became more creative by the minute.

Danai was already seated with Navos, Lexia, Shran, and Henrick. She, Navos, and Henrick weren't surprised to see Pearl, but Lexia almost choked on her drink and had to nudge Shran, who as usual, had his head buried in a book.

Shran looked puzzled as Britea and Pearl approached them.

"Good morning," said Pearl civilly.

"Hey, everyone," Britea said, trying to sound cheerful. "Pearl's sitting with us again today. I hope that's all right."

Lexia frowned and opened her mouth to say something.

"Glad you two made it out of the kitchens," said Danai before glancing at Lianne's table in the far corner of the hall. "And past a certain group."

Pearl's face colored while Lexia frowned at Danai. "Wait, we're all friends now just because *she's* being punished?"

Pearl shot Lexia an angry look. "I don't need your sympathy."

"It's not sympathy. Just honesty," responded Lexia archly.

"Britea is our friend," said Shran calmly. "So any friend of hers is a friend of ours. Let's not act like Lianne." Lexia stared him before backing down. Navos rubbed her back gently, a sad smile on his face. Henrick was frantically watching the interaction, clearly anxious about the outcome.

"Pearl, please sit down," said Danai gently. Britea looked at Pearl and was certain the noble would refuse, but to her immense relief, Pearl sat down beside Henrick.

Britea exchanged a relieved look with Danai.

For a moment, awkward silence reigned as they concentrated on their breakfast.

"So, how's everyone doing?" asked Britea.

"Henrick was telling us about the ball at the royal court last night," said Shran as he dove back into his book. Pearl raised an eyebrow and glanced at Henrick, whose features reddened.

Maybe Henrick should withhold his gossip for now , thought Britea. She tried to catch his eyes to warn him, but Pearl was already speaking.

"You? Were at the court last night?" The disbelief in her voice was obvious. Lexia narrowed her eyes, and Britea sighed inwardly; this was turning out to be a disaster.

"No, no not me," corrected a flustered Henrick. "My roommate came back last night. He had special permission from the school to stay an extra day so he could attend the ball."

"Who's your roommate?'" asked a skeptical Pearl.

"Dariuz Solarn."

Pearl's expression cleared. "Oh, him."

"You know him?" asked Danai in a neutral tone.

"He's the nephew of Lord Nalin Solarn, Malaquey Finance Minister, and Dariuz just happens to be the *only* wielder in both Lord Solarn's close and extended family. From time to time, he gets extra days away from school so his uncle can show him off. Dariuz hates it."

Silence greeted her words. Pearl sighed at their expressions. "Truth be told, I've never gotten a chance to stay home for an extra day, so I guess being a wielding nephew of the finance minister has its perks. So, what happened at the ball?" Pearl sipped her water while trying to appear bored.

Britea smiled behind her cup of tea; Pearl was interested even if she was reluctant to show it.

"Apparently, the finance minister tried to introduce his entire family to the two Dyhaeri princes—"

Pearl almost choked on her drink. Lexia hid her laughter while Danai tried to hide her smile. Shran looked up briefly and went back to his book. Navos ate as if he was starving.

"Pearl, are you all right?" asked a concerned Henrick.

She waved his concern away. "Wait, did you just say Dyhaeri princes? Is this a joke?" She sounded more dismayed than angry.

"It's not a joke." Now Henrick sounded offended. "You can always ask Dariuz about it if you don't believe me."

"Oh no, thanks, but say I believe you—which frankly I don't—" Henrick rubbed his forehead wearily "—why are the Dyhaeri visiting the royal court now?" asked a dubious Pearl.

"That's what we're trying to figure out," said Navos, pausing with his fork halfway to his mouth. "None of us have come up with an answer."

Pearl watched them all closely, then looked at Britea. "You're not trying to make fun of me, are you?"

"No, we're not," answered Danai. Pearl's eyes narrowed before she turned to Henrick.

"So, did Dariuz meet the Dyhaeri princes?"

Britea could tell Pearl still didn't believe Henrick.

"Well, he said they tried to, but lots of people were trying to chat with the princes. Then the Dyhaeri princes and their high priest had to leave the ball early to rest."

Pearl's eyebrows threatened to disappear into her hair line. "High priest?" she sounded almost shrill.

"Change the topic," said Shran without looking up from his book.

"I wanted to ask Britea about her punishment detail," jumped in Lexia. Danai sighed and gave her peer an exasperated look.

"It's a valid question!" Lexia retorted.

"Peeling potatoes, washing carrots, and scrubbing pots and pans," replied Pearl instead with a barely suppressed shudder. Lexia smiled smugly at her.

"I bet you never did either of those before. So, what do you think of them?" There was a challenge in Lexia's tone.

Pearl looked at her cautiously. "It's harsh, but what scares me most is combat and defense class." Lexia went still, then turned slowly to face Navos.

"She's in combat and defense? And you didn't tell me?!"

Navos sighed. "I didn't want to upset you."

"Well, I'm upset right now!"

Pearl seemed amused by the bickering of the couple before her. Britea looked at the others. Shran was still buried in his book while Henrick looked like he was trying to hold his laughter in. Danai had a smile on her face.

Britea blinked. This was not the reaction she had expected. To her immense relief, the rest of the meal was relatively peaceful…while Lexia gave Navos the silent treatment. Britea, hoped the two made up before the day ended.

#

"Which cutlery set do we use for dessert?" asked Pearl patiently. Britea stared at the cutlery before her.

"I don't know."*By the Lords, she hated dancing and etiquette class!*

Pearl gave an exasperated sigh. "Did you not pay attention when Lianne was mentoring you?"

Now, that almost made Britea explode. She knew she was smart and took to most things quickly, but for some reason, she found this class difficult. That had only been compounded by the way Lianne, Valerie, and Pearl had treated her. She wondered if Pearl had forgotten that part already.

"How sure was I that she was telling me the right thing?" shot back Britea with an angry hiss.

Pearl glanced over at Lianne and Valerie, who were practicing the latest dance steps while Instructor Droye complimented them on their technique. Their two new friends danced beside them. Since the incident at breakfast, Lianne and her friends seemed to be ignoring Britea and Pearl, but Britea doubted they had been forgotten.

"You're not wrong, I suppose. She *was* trying to make you fail this class. All right, let's start from the top. Arrange the cutlery like this: medium on the outside, large in the middle and small beside the plate. The medium set is for the starter, the largest one is for the main course, and the last and smallest set is for the dessert." Then she noticed Britea's sour expression. "What now?"

"How is any of this of any use if Namira invades us tomorrow?"

Pearl's gave her a puzzled look. "Where in the world did that thought come from?"

"You didn't answer the question," said a mulish Britea.

Pearl rolled her eyes. "Fine. Etiquette will not deter a Namiran invasion; however, etiquette and diplomacy work together, and the latter can prevent wars."

Britea reluctantly saw her point of view, but Pearl wasn't done.

"But the main goal of this exercise is to help you pass this class and learn something useful you can take with you to improve your chances of getting a job with a prominent house after your Year of Discovery." Pearl gave her a questioning look. "You ready to begin now?"

"Yes," said Britea. She correctly identified the cutlery this time.

"You do know one can use cutlery as weapons, right?" said Pearl, a grave expression on her face.

"During the invasion or the diplomacy?" asked Britea seriously. Both girls stared at each other and started laughing.

They failed to notice the dark looks Lianne, Valerie, and their two new friends sent their way.

#

Dear High Priest Myltan,

You would honor my family and I greatly by attending an afternoon soiree tomorrow at my humble residence at Golden-Leaf Hills.

Please let us know if there are any dietary requirements.

Malaquey Finance Minister Lord Nalin Solarn

Mat dropped the letter on a pile of other open letters. The three Dyhaeri were discussing the influx of invitations in their quarters at the royal palace. "This is the third letter from the minister of finance inviting us to another event and the fifteenth letter overall from different members of the court."

"We've only been here less than a week," said Kahl in a puzzled tone.

"Not only that, but Minister Solarn has been trying to schedule a meeting with us since that first ball. His persistence is disturbing," added Mat.

"Mat, why does the finance minister want to meet with us?" asked the high priest. Mat stared at the senior Dyhaeri and Kahl translated his cousin's expression as, "How in the Deep should I know?"

"I have no idea."

The high priest smiled sadly. "The sea holds numerous secrets, especially the countless sunken ships full of treasure." He watched their expressions clear. How many times had humans asked them to bring up treasures from the depths of the sea?

The answer? Too many times.

"He wants to talk about human treasure," scoffed Mat.

"Perhaps. It could, though be something else, like opening up trade negotiations with us. If he achieved that, it would be quite a feather in his cap since there is no existing trade between Dyhaeri and Malaquey or Namira."

Kahl raised an eyebrow when the priest didn't mention the Weltonians. Though the Dyhaeri didn't trade with them either, they did at least have a better relationship with the Weltonians than the other humans.

"I also heard, from the lieutenant commander, that the finance minister is quite intent on introducing his nephew to us," continued the high priest. "Now, I wonder why."

"So, are we going to this soiree then?" asked a concerned Kahl.

The high priest shook his head to Kahl's relief. "We're heading to Syla College tomorrow."

Kahl tried to keep his excitement hidden; he couldn't wait to see Britea.

"Finally," sighed Mat. "High Priest Myltan, permission to speak freely?"

The high priest nodded.

"These balls and events we've attended at the royal court have been pure torture. I'd take any marine drill over attending another blasted ball." The high priest may have given his permission to speak freely, but that didn't stop him from staring at Mat. But he wasn't done yet.

"Can we please skip the ball tonight? Tell them we need to meditate for our next destination because I swear I'll wield a certain member of the court into the nearest fountain if they ask another stupid question!"

The high priest sighed. "I know exactly how you feel my son, but which question made you so upset?"

Kahl was curious too. He was surprised to see his cousin's green complexion darken in embarrassment.

"It was about mating rituals and…" he took a deep breath "…certain organs." He said the last part so fast Kahl wondered if he had heard right. He suddenly recalled how Mat had fled from a certain female human noble who had cornered him at every ball. Lady Nara Gedea.

"Oh," was all the high priest said after a long moment. "We're definitely not attending the ball tonight."

"Thank you, high priest," said Mat with heartfelt gratitude.

"And I and Lieutenant Commander Nell shall seek Lady Gedea out tonight and explain in detail how asking such questions is sure to incur the wrath of the Sea Mother."

Mat and Kahl stared at the high priest in amazement.

"I don't wish to cause a diplomatic incident," said Mat, a worried expression on his face.

"Do not worry. All will be fine," said the high priest with a fatherly smile and a hard glint in his eyes. Kahl almost shivered with fear even though he knew the senior Dyhaeri's ire was directed towards the unfortunate Lady Gedea.

"I guess we better start packing," Mat said, breaking the resulting silence.

#

"Have you packed your daggers?" asked Lady Shalina De'tre Flay.

"Yes, mother," said Harto as he took a bite from his apple pie.

He, his mother, and his uncle were enjoying a late but decadent dessert at the Flay estate. Harto and his uncle had left the ball early because of Harto's trip to Syla College tomorrow.

"And your spare sword?" pressed Harto's mother.

Peras sighed. "He's been a naval officer for more than two years. I'm sure he knows where his weapons are."

Shalina scowled at her brother while Harto rolled his eyes. "I'm just checking. You'll be accompanying those Dyhaeri after all. Who knows what they're capable of?"

"I doubt I'm in danger from them," said Harto.

"You still need to watch your back," said Shalina, sipping from her second glass of wine that night. "I met with Lady Adria yesterday, and she was worried about the Dyhaeri."

"I'd take anything she or her daughter says with a pinch of salt," said Harto through gritted teeth.

Shalina narrowed her eyes at her son. "Do recall the Arkei influence is quite significant in the Malaquey court. We cannot afford to antagonize them."

"Neither can we afford to upset the Dyhaeri," said Peras. "You should have seen how terrified Lady Gedea was after the high priest spoke to her."

"What happened?" asked a curious Shalina. Harto kept silent; he was aware of the details.

"Lady Gedea has been stalking Prince Mat-rallenin, apparently inviting him on several occasions to dine...privately with her." Lady Shalina gasped.

"That is hardly appropriate." Harto knew the reason for his mother's disapproval. Lady Gedea had attained a reputation of relationships with much younger men. Due to her high standing in the court, hardly anyone paid any attention to it, but Harto had heard rumors that not all of her partners had been willing.

"Prince Mat has refused her each time, but things got a bit dicey when she started asking him about Dyhaeri mating rituals and certain body parts."

Harto saw his mother's jaw drop. For a brief moment, she was flabbergasted. "Is that woman insane?!"

Peras smiled thinly. "The high priest brought the matter to me and asked me to accompany him to confront Lady Gedea. I was only too happy to comply." The lieutenant commander took a bite of his dessert before continuing. "When we got to the ball this evening, Lady Gedea was already present and asking for Prince Mat. The high priest asked to speak with her, and once we'd taken her aside, he asked her if she knew how deep the Abyss was."

Harto smiled as he recalled what had happened next.

"So, what did she say?" asked an intrigued Shalina.

Peras changed his voice to sound shrill in mimicry. "Oh, I have no idea!"

His sister laughed.

He continued, clearly enjoying the role of storyteller. "The high priest smiled coldly and said, 'It is a bottomless cold hell, and it is where the Sea Mother and Dark Sister send ignorant, arrogant, crude individuals who refuse to take no for an answer.' At this point, Lady Gedea finally realized she was in trouble, but the high priest still wasn't done."

Peras went on to describe how the high priest had told her that as of that moment, she had been identified as a predator, and it was only the grace of the Sea Mother that was preventing him from sending her into the Abyss. He concluded by stating that would be her only warning.

Shalina was speechless for a moment. "How did she respond?"

"She asked me to beg the king's forgiveness and fled from the hall. I doubt we'll be seeing her at any more court events for a long time."

"Good riddance," said Shalina. "That woman always made my skin crawl with how she preyed on younger men. Only her social standing prevented action being taken against her."

"And yet she's close friends with the Arkei family, is she not?" pointed out Harto.

Shalina sighed. "I doubt the Arkei family is influenced by that woman, and after this public disgrace, I'm sure they'll cease to interact with her."

Harto closed his eyes briefly in exasperation. His mother had completely missed the point.

"Is something the matter, dear?" she asked.

"No one in the Arkei family is a saint. Their daughters are the most conceited individuals I have ever met. I still fail to see why you insist I keep attending their social events."

Shalina gave her son an impatient look. "You have to marry at some point, my dear boy."

"I'm not marrying an Arkei girl even if she's the last female alive," said Harto stubbornly.

"Can we please spend this evening in peace?" asked Peras as he regarded his sister and his nephew.

Harto nodded reluctantly. "I'm sorry, mother and uncle. It has been a trying week."

Shalina touched her son's right hand softly. "Forgive my nagging. I just don't want to see you alone. Your uncle is right. Let's change the subject. I think you should pack an extra set of weapons."

Harto opened his mouth to argue then saw the pleading look on his uncle's face.

"Yes, mother."

#

Instructor Eowise Shelley hurried into the packed meeting room near the instructor's residence. Looking around, she saw she was one of the last to arrive, so she walked over and sat beside Weapons Master Pietor Caren. On the dais, Warden Sammel Asteros was standing, waiting for the Headmaster Zalei Clayre to appear.

"Thank the Lords you made it," said Pietor in a low voice.

"I had a quiz to supervise. Do you know what this is about?"

"No, but whatever it is has Sam worried. He hasn't been himself since the headmaster summoned him. I thought it was about the duel fiasco, but it looks like something else is afoot."

Eowise was about to speak when the headmaster emerged from a door to the left of the dais. The warden bowed to him and took one of the high-backed chairs on the right side of the dais, leaving the headmaster facing the silent, expectant instructors.

"Good evening, everyone. I apologize for the late meeting and for what you're all about to hear."

Eowise shared a nervous look with Pietor.

"Last weekend, I was summoned to court by King Wilhem. As most of you have already heard, the high priest of the Dyhaeri and two Dyhaeri princes are guests of the royal court." The instructors began to mutter amongst themselves. From the whispers, many had been unaware.

The headmaster let the whispers die down before continuing, obviously reluctant to share his news.

"The Dyhaeri delegation has requested an inspection of our wielding colleges, and Syla College was chosen."

This time, the whispers erupted in an uproar. Pietor swore while Eowise glanced at the warden. The senior official wore a grave expression.

"When are they arriving?" asked Pietor.

"Tomorrow." The headmaster looked exhausted as several instructors began to complain that this was extremely short notice.

The warden stood and held up a hand, and the protests died down. That was Sam's role, to be the moderator at these meetings. Once there was silence, he resumed his seat. The headmaster nodded at him in gratitude and continued.

"I pled with the king to give us more time to prepare, but he and Malaquey intelligence want this done as soon as possible. So, the Dyhaeri delegation will be here tomorrow afternoon, and the inspection will begin the day after. Any questions?"

One of the instructors was quick to stand, his hand in the air.

"Yes, Instructor Melvin?" prompted Headmaster Clayre.

"Why are they inspecting us? We're hardly military! Why not the Royal Malaquey Naval Wielding College or the Artra Army Wielding College?" Other instructors agreed with him.

"Because King Wilhem offered the Dyhaeri Syla College. He does not want the Dyhaeri in the military colleges."

"So, we're chopped liver? Is that it?" queried one of the instructors.

"Definitely not. I heard Dyhaeri don't like red meat or offal," drawled the warden. This was met by laughter and the tension abated somewhat.

Eowise stood next and waved her hand. The headmaster nodded at her.

"How long are they staying?"

Headmaster Clayre looked uncomfortable. "As long as the high priest deems necessary."

"You have got to be kidding," loudly complained one of the instructors. "This will disrupt classes!"

"Only if we let it," said the headmaster. "I'm certain once they see the students learning their lessons well, they will leave us be."

Instructor Melvin waved his hand frantically. The headmaster sighed and pointed at him.

"Why now though? The last time the Dyhaeri visited us was at the inception of this school over eight hundred years ago!"

The headmaster clasped his hands. "I asked the same question of the king, and I was told it was a national security issue." This was met with groans.

"Trust me, I know how you feel about this, but we have no choice but to comply. Do not forget we exist only at the Malaquey royal family's wish." This was met by a wary silence.

"I suggest keeping this news from your students for now." The instructors gaped at him. "Many of our students come from prominent families. Once the news gets out, I expect to see many little lords and ladies suddenly interested in touring the school grounds in hopes of running into the Dyhaeri delegation."

"Makes sense to keep quiet for now," agreed Pietor.

"They'll find out soon enough," countered Instructor Melvin in a disgruntled voice.

"Any other questions?" asked the headmaster. To his relief, there were no more questions.

"Now, on to other agenda items. Preparing for the 126th Wielder Trials."

CHAPTER 17

Kahl felt the carriage come to a stop. A loud knock on their door informed the three Dyhaeri they had reached their final destination.

Syla College.

Kahl's hands felt clammy, and his heart rate was faster than normal. He was scared Britea had forgotten him. *Wait, had she even gotten his letter?*

"Hey, you all right?" Kahl returned to reality and realized both his cousin and the high priest were watching him with worried expressions.

"Just a bit anxious."

Mat raised an enquiring eyebrow.

"I'm sure all will be well," said the high priest with a kind smile as Lieutenant Harto Flay opened the carriage door.

"Welcome to Syla College, High Priest Myltan." The young lieutenant had already placed the stool for their descent.

Kahl waited for the high priest and his cousin to disembark before he followed. Once out, he got a better look of the impressive brownstone structure. They had parked in the spacious, circular, paved courtyard, and they were not alone. He counted at least twenty humans dressed in black cowled outfits. A distinct colored band adorned the hems of the cowls. White, red, blue, and brown. That had to represent each of the wielding elements. But what caught his attention the most were their expressions: a mixture of fear and anger.

He wondered why.

A slightly overweight man stepped forward, his cowl with brown lines on the hem. Behind him was a thin, tall man with stern features. His own cowl had no distinct color.

"Welcome to Syla College. I'm Headmaster Zalei Clayre." He struck out his hand in greeting. Kahl frowned slightly; the human sounded nervous.

The high priest smiled kindly at the headmaster and shook his head. "I am honored to be here. With me are Mat-rallenin and Kahl."

The thin man behind the headmaster turned his head slightly to look at Kahl, his expression neutral.

"This is Warden Asteros," said the headmaster cheerfully as he introduced the thin, tall man.

"The pleasure is all mine," said the warden with a respectful bow in the high priest's direction.

"And we have with us Lieutenant Harto Flay, who is here to watch over us," said the high priest. Kahl and Mat shared an amused look at the Malaquey officer's apparent embarrassment at the introduction.

"Ah yes, we were expecting him. Let's introduce you to the others," said the headmaster a bit too brightly. Kahl frowned when he noticed the thin sheen of sweat on the headmaster's forehead.

This was the head of this school? Why was he so afraid? Kahl glanced at the warden, who was still watching them. He was a picture of calm and efficiency beside the flustered headmaster. Kahl would have taken the warden as the head of this school if someone had asked him to guess.

Once the other instructors had been introduced, the high priest, Kahl, Mat, and Harto grabbed their luggage and followed the headmaster and the warden into the school. Kahl took note of the two guards in charcoal grey standing at the double-doored entrance.

Was that the extent of their security?

The wide entrance hallway had a high white stone roof, dark-brown oak walls, and a warm indigo-blue carpet. It too was empty. The high priest asked where the students were.

"They are currently in their afternoon classes. We didn't wish to disrupt their studies today, so you shall address them tomorrow," answered the headmaster. "The warden will get you settled in shortly; however, before then, may we talk for a while in my office?"

"Of course," answered the high priest.

Kahl took in their surroundings as they walked down the wide oak-paneled corridors. This school was a far cry from the marble-walled Malaquey palace. Kahl suspected the school was older than the palace. It had an aged feel to it. He glanced at his cousin, who was also studying his surroundings. Then he noticed Harto was watching them.

Since the Malaquey officer had joined them that morning, he had mostly kept his own counsel, only saying a few words now and then. He had even ridden beside the carriage rather than in it. Kahl wondered if the young human officer had changed tactics in obtaining information.

Eventually the small group reached the headmaster's office. It was spacious, with a big oak desk to match the walls and a plush chair behind it. Stuffed bookshelves reached the ceiling and surrounded the one window. Two long couches sat before the desk.

"Please be seated," said the headmaster, gesturing at the couches.

Once the high priest was seated, the rest followed. The warden remained standing, casually leaning against the edge of the wooden table.

The headmaster cleared his throat. "The purpose of this brief meeting is to discuss your reason for this inspection."

Out of the corner of his eye, Kahl saw Harto shoot the headmaster a worried look. Interestingly, the warden was tracking Harto's every move. Apparently, he saw the Malaquey intelligence office as a threat.

The high priest nodded. "I appreciate your curiosity. We're here because Namira is becoming more of a menace, and we need to know if your wielders will be prepared for the battles to come."

Silence reigned as Harto transferred his shocked look to the high priest. "We should not be discussing matters of national security. They are on a need to know basis—" hastily began Harto.

"And they need to know," said the high priest firmly as he turned to face the intelligence officer. Harto must have seen something frightening in the elderly Dyhaeri's gaze because he backed down immediately. Beside Kahl, Mat grinned.

The headmaster recovered from his shock in a heartbeat. "You're expecting an attack from Namira? How sure are you about this?"

"Quite. Their queen is running out of wielders to experiment on," said the high priest.

Kahl saw the warden stiffen in shock while Harto looked as if he wanted to stop the reveal but saw the futility of it.

"Experiment?" repeated the headmaster in horror.

The high priest tilted his head and stared at the head of the college with a puzzled expression on his face before glancing at Harto.

"They were not aware of this?"

"As I said, matters of national security are not shared unless there is a need to know," repeated Harto through gritted teeth.

The high priest scoffed and said. "Keeping this secret won't stop her. Neither will it protect the people of Malaquey." The high priest turned back to the headmaster. "Queen Kallesa has hunted down almost all the wielders in Namira over a span of more than forty years. She has also hunted other wielders amongst the Weltonians and even my own people. The Immortal Queen is running out of bodies and will turn to Malaquey next."

Kahl waited for the headmaster to ask the next question on everyone's lips, but he seemed too distressed to speak.

"What is she using the wielders for?" asked the warden as calmly as he could.

The high priest turned to him. "She absorbs their abilities to stay young. That is why she is the Immortal Queen of Namira."

The warden stared at the high priest for a long moment, then he turned his gaze on Lieutenant Harto and hardened his expression.

The lieutenant sighed. "We've suspected this for decades but had no way of confirming it." He paused and turned to the high priest. "How did you verify this?"

High Priest Myltan smiled. "Need to know, my dear lieutenant."

Kahl was surprised to see Harto smile back, recognizing the irony in that answer.

"But we are too far from Namira. Why would she come all the way to Syla College?" finally asked the headmaster.

"When an alkynaia hunts a herd of whales, it targets the smallest one, which is always further away from the herd. Syla College may be that small, unprotected whale."

Now Kahl stared at the high priest in horror. *Britea was here!* He forced himself to put his feelings aside for now though because the senior Dyhaeri was still speaking.

"As you have no doubt been told, we will only leave when we are satisfied about the readiness of this college. Then we may inspect the other colleges if King Wilhem agrees."

A glance at Harto showed a blank expression. Kahl suspected the king was never going to agree on an inspection of the two military wielding colleges.

"If I see any concerns regarding the training of your students, I will discuss it with you and the instructors in private. I am in no way planning on taking over the training of your wielders," said the high priest.

"We will appreciate the input," said the headmaster gravely before trying to lighten the mood.

"Why don't we show you to your quarters so you can freshen up? Was there aught else you needed for now?"

The high priest stood. "Yes. After we drop our luggage, may I trouble you for a brief inspection of your kitchens? I wish to see where our food will be prepared."

As Mat and Kahl stood, they shared a quizzical glance. The high priest had not inspected the kitchens in the royal court. So why was he interested in Syla's kitchens?

They weren't alone. Everyone seemed nonplussed by the request.

"Of course," agreed the headmaster. "Do you have any dietary preferences?"

"Yes," answered the high priest. "Which I will discuss with the cooks in due course."

#

Britea picked up another potato to peel; with a few deft rotations of her left hand and a swift movement of the peeler in her right, she added one more peeled potato to the growing pile in the bowl beside her. She heard the sound of a knife hitting the board and turned to Pearl, who had devised her own way of peeling the potatoes: by cutting chunks off on a cutting board rather than peeling the skin off. The result was smaller potatoes and slower progress.

Some might scoff, but not Britea. She had realized the noble was trying. Pearl was fulfilling her punishment in the best way she knew how.

The girls had been shoved into the far left corner of the kitchen, out of sight and out of the way while they peeled the countless potatoes that had already been washed by the time they had started their punishment detail today.

Pearl paused from her work to wipe her forehead. "The day we get to finish class two hours early only earns us an earlier start on our punishment. Lovely." She resumed her unique way of peeling potatoes. "Did you notice how distracted some of the teachers were?"

Britea chucked another peeled potato in the bowl and picked up a new one. "I thought some of them were behaving oddly, but I assumed I was imaging it."

"No, you weren't. Even in combat and defense, Instructor Talios seemed a bit on edge, and Master Caren was absent today. Something is up."

"Maybe it's the upcoming Wielder Trials?" asked Britea.

"I doubt it. I've seen them prepare for the Trials before. This is different."

"We could always ask them," said Britea cheekily. Pearl shot her a glare.

"I'm not suicidal, thank you very much." She glared at her small pile of peeled potatoes and then at Britea's much larger pile. "Who knew the school consumed this much starch?"

"Less talking and more peeling!"

The two girls almost fell off their stools. "Yes, chef!"

The diminutive lord of the kitchen scoffed and walked away.

"Where did he spring from? He just appeared out of thin air," whispered Britea once he was out of earshot.

"More like where in the Deep is he from?" responded Pearl. "I swear Instructor Shelley seems afraid of him."

"Nah, I think she just respects him," disagreed Britea.

Pearl frowned and opened her mouth to argue when an alarmed exclamation and a crash interrupted her. She and Britea shared a puzzled look.

That was unusual; the kitchen staff rarely dropped anything.

"The chef is going to be so upset—" began Britea until Pearl held a hand up.

"What is it?" asked Britea.

"Why is it so quiet?"

Then Britea noticed the usual kitchen clamor had ceased completely.

"Let's go see," said Pearl as she dropped her peeler in her bowl and rose from her stool.

"No! The chef will be upset…"

"Britea, something is happening that has made the entire kitchen go silent. That calls for an investigation. Come on!"

Britea wavered. To be honest she was curious, but she didn't want to draw the chef's ire.

In the end, her curiosity won out. "Just for a moment." She placed her peeler in the bowl beside her stool and stood. Both girls rounded the corner to see the last people they expected.

Headmaster Clayre, Warden Asteros, a Malaquey naval officer, and three male Dyhaeri.

The lead Dyhaeri wore a moss green, long-sleeved, leather tunic while the two at his back wore indigo-blue leathers that seemed rather familiar to Britea.

The small group was currently surrounded by the stunned, reverent kitchen staff. Chef Blane was respectfully conversing with the lead Dyhaeri.

"By the Lords, who are they?" asked Pearl in a voice barely above a whisper.

Britea's heart rate picked up as they approached the small group. One of the Dyhaeri behind the older one was looking in the direction opposite her, so she couldn't see his face, only his stance. But it seemed familiar.

No, it couldn't be.

Then he turned his gaze in her direction, and she saw a scarred, kindly face she knew.

Kahl's eyes widened when he saw the two girls. "Britea? Is that you?"

His question drew the attention of all, including the Malaquey officer Britea now recognized to her dismay.

"Kahl?" Her words sounded panicked, and she missed the dazed stare Pearl sent her way.

"What are those students doing here?!" objected the naval officer before anyone could say a word.

"It is part of their punishment," answered the chef sharply. That made Britea close her eyes in embarrassment.

Kahl spun to face the chef, eyes wide. The other similarly clad Dyhaeri raised his eyebrows. Britea instantly recognized him as the one called Mat. He had taken Kahl away from her. Her embarrassment gave way to anger.

"Punishment for what?" demanded Lieutenant Flay.

"None of your business," boldly answered the chef. The headmaster cleared his throat before the intelligence officer tried to physically harm the chef.

"Here at Syla College, we discipline our students in a variety of ways, which we do not have to go into at the moment."

Harto looked like he wanted to protest, but the officer bit his tongue.

"Any more questions about food preparation, High Priest Myltan?" hastily asked a nervous-looking headmaster. Britea's eyes darted to the Dyhaeri high priest as her fear returned. *This was the Dyhaeri who had ordered Kahl to teach her! What were they all doing at her school?*

"None at the moment. I've obtained all the information I need for now, so I will not keep you from your duties any longer." The high priest and the other two Dyhaeri bowed to the diminutive chef, who returned the bow.

The headmaster seemed relieved. "Now, if we could all—"

"May I please briefly speak to Britea D'Tranell?" asked Kahl to everyone's amazement. Part of Britea was gleeful at the attention, but the other part wanted to dig herself into a hole and never emerge until the end of time.

Pearl was staring at Britea as if she had never seen her before.

The high priest looked at Kahl, then at the chef. "If Chef Blane agrees."

The short chef was already nodding. "Of course, you may."

Kahl gave his thanks and walked over to Britea under the gaze of all these people. He was completely unaware of Mat trailing in his wake. Harto tried to follow but suddenly found his way barred by the chef. The cold glint in the chef's eyes made Harto pause.

#

Kahl felt his hands go clammy as he approached the two girls. He had eyes only for Britea; she looked more radiant than ever, and more confident, and he thought she looked pretty in her college uniform.

He stopped three feet from her. Then she smiled at him, and for a moment, he was unsure of what to say.

"You're here," said Britea, stunned.

"As are you," said Kahl, and for a moment, he wanted to disappear. That had been such a weak answer. "I see you've settled in quite well."

A reddish hue appeared on Britea's coffee-colored skin.

Oh, he had said something wrong, hadn't he? "I got your letter." Kahl was immensely relieved when she finally spoke.

"It was nice."

Now he was filled with joy. "I got yours as well, and it made me happy."

He missed the odd look the girl behind her gave him, but he could not help but hear Mat's choked laughter. He refused to turn and acknowledge his stupid cousin.

But Britea saw Mat and her features hardened.

Oh no, she remembers him. "Oh, this is Mat." He dragged his surprised cousin forward. "He's my cousin and…and we're friends now," Britea blinked and gave him a puzzled look. Kahl cursed inwardly. He was not handling this well. "And we're working together. That's why we were assigned to your college."

Britea's expression went from confusion to uncertainty. "You…you're not in trouble for what happened?"

The girl behind Britea looked puzzled at Britea's last words.

"No, he's not," said Mat. He held out a hand. "I'm Mat-rallenin. Kahl has told me a lot about you. I am pleased to officially meet you."

Britea stared at the hand for a long moment, then shook it to Kahl's relief.

Mat smiled and leaned in to whisper, "As much as I'd like to continue this conversation, we have to go soon. We don't want to upset the chef, and I doubt you want the entire kitchen staff listening in."

Britea glanced around them, and sure enough, everyone was staring at them.

"Yes, of course." Then she remembered Pearl. "Um, this is Novice Pearl Ceres. She's my friend." Pearl gave her a grateful smile and curtsied to the two Dyhaeri, who bowed in response.

Britea sighed inwardly; she would never curtsy as graceful as Pearl did.

"A pleasure to meet you both, Prince Kahl and Prince Mat-rallenin," Pearl said. The mention of their titles made Britea start.

"And you as well," said Kahl. Then he looked at Britea. "I hope we can talk later."

Britea was feeling self-conscious now. "Of course, Prince…"

Kahl's eyes widened with alarm. "Oh no, just call us Kahl and Mat." Mat rolled his eyes.

"We're still the same as we were when you last saw us," said Mat as he tugged at his cousin's arm. The two walked back to the high priest, though Kahl looked back several times.

Once the entire delegation had gone, the chef simply looked at Pearl and Britea, and they promptly fled back to their corner of the kitchen.

#

"You knew Dyhaeri princes and said nothing?!" screeched Pearl once they were alone.

"Keep your voice down," urgently whispered Britea.

Pearl had a mischievous look in her eyes. "I will if you tell me all."

"There isn't much to tell," said Britea as she tried to get back into the rhythm of peeling potatoes.

"Then tell what there is!"

"I can't."

"Can't or won't?"

"I…I was advised not to talk about it."

"Why not?!"

An exasperated Britea stopped peeling and looked at Pearl. "Would you have believed me?"

Pearl pauses. "You have a point, but the fact remains you're a friend of a Dyhaeri prince!"

Britea was becoming alarmed by Pearl's enthusiasm. "Please, don't tell anyone!"

"Who am I going to tell? Lianne has declared me an enemy, Valerie acts like I don't exist, and they both kicked me out of my room by packing my stuff the morning I was supposed to be expelled…" Britea stared at her, but Pearl was still talking while violently cutting chunks of skin off a potato. "… and I'm definitely not telling my family about this. Trust me, they would kill for information like this."

"Wait, you got kicked out of your dorm room? Lianne and Valerie were your roommates?"

Pearl sighed wearily. "Yes, to both questions. Lianne was given one of the few large rooms with three beds and two tables. I was one of the *lucky* ones to room with her. Now, looking back on it, I wasn't so lucky." Britea waited for her to elaborate.

"But enough about her. I want to hear all about how you met Prince Kahl and Prince Mat! This is the first time I've seen Dyhaeri in the flesh, and by the Lords, they are handsome! Now I see why they were the talk of the royal court!"

Pearl stared at Britea earnestly but then shrunk back in uncertainty when Britea hesitated to speak.

"I understand. I guess we're not exactly friends." Pearl's shoulders drooped, and she painted a dejected picture as she went back to sluggishly peeling potatoes.

Britea felt terrible, but a small voice warned her to be careful. She took a deep breath.

"There really isn't that much to tell." Pearl kept her head down as if she wasn't listening.

"I met Kahl when he boarded the *Windrider* , a merchant ship bound for Port Trident."

The keen expression was back on Pearl's face. "Wait, start from the beginning. How did you get on the ship?"

Britea gave her a quizzical look. "I thought you wanted to know about Kahl."

Pearl brought her stool closer to Britea. "Oh, but I do. However, I really want to know about you." A guilty look crossed her face. "I must admit I've been…thoughtless in my treatment of you."

"No need to apologize. We're past that," said Britea.

Pearl shook her head. "You're something else, do you realize that? If our roles were reversed, I'd hold it against you forever. Lesson one in manipulation," she glanced around quickly. So far, no one had noticed they were chatting more than peeling. "I just got you to tell me your story. Don't fall for that again."

"Now you tell me," growled Britea.

Pearl had the cheek to grin at her and continue talking. "And lesson two: the best way to start a story is to boast of your origins."

"I never hid the fact that I was from a farm, Pearl," pointed out Britea.

"Fair enough," conceded Pearl. "So, then tell me, what village are you from, and how did you get on the ship that would take you to meet a Dyhaeri prince?"

Britea rolled her eyes. "You sound just like Navos."

Pearl grinned. "What can I say? I fall for romantic stories, so please, regale me with yours."

"There's nothing romantic about mine!" protested Britea.

Pearl winked. "Time will tell. Please begin before I die from suspense."

And that was how Britea found herself telling Pearl about how she had met Kahl, her training, the battle with the Namiran ships, the Alkynaia showing up, and Mat taking Kahl away.

Once she was done, Pearl was staring at her with her mouth agape.

"What?" asked a concerned Britea.

Pearl blinked. "Now I understand why you kept this under wraps. If I'd heard this story before I saw the princes, I would have thought you were insane. By the way, bargaining with sea serpents was beyond crazy!"

"Please, keep your voice down before we get reported to the chef." Britea picked up another potato and peeled it. She was finding herself feeling conflicted about having told Pearl about Kahl.

"Who else have you told about this?" asked Pearl, a serious expression on her face.

"The warden knows, and Malaquey Naval Intelligence." Pearl's eyes widened. "Danai knows about it, and now you."

Britea became worried at Pearl's somber appearance.

"That's why Lord Flay was following the Dyhaeri."

"You know that intelligence officer?" asked Britea.

Pearl shrugged. "Not personally, just his reputation in my family's circles. He's apparently one of the most eligible bachelors in Malaquey. Even my mother still hopes he'll cast a look in my direction." Britea giggled when Pearl rolled her eyes in exasperation before continuing.

"I've seen him from a distance and was introduced to him once, but he seemed more interested in escaping from the ball than dancing with any of the girls who'd been paraded before him."

"So, he's a noble like you?"

Pearl shook her head. "Not just a noble, Britea; his family is originally from Namira."

Britea's peeling slowed down. "Really?"

"Yes. The word at court is the Flay family line goes back more than a millennium."

Britea whistled.

Pearl nodded. "And they have properties and lands to match. Or had. You see, most of their property was in Namira, but the Flay family also had property in Malaquey that they'd accumulated over centuries, some were even personal gifts from Malaquey royals."

Britea raised an eyebrow.

"Rumor has it that when the late King Olnanier married Queen Kallesa, the Flay family started buying more land in Malaquey, but only a few Flay family members escaped when the executions started. Apart from Lord Flay, what remains of his family are his mother and her brother. Add in the fact that he's also an accomplished wielder with Malaquey Naval Intelligence and very, very rich, and you can see why even the Arkei family is after him."

"You're a fount of information," said Britea, dazed.

Pearl accepted the compliment with a sad smile before her expression became solemn.

"Back to what you told me. It's a fantastic story." She looked at Britea's stony face and hastened to continue. "Which I believe but would advise you not to repeat."

Britea sighed. "Danai said the same thing."

"And she's right," said Pearl to Britea's surprise.

"What happened out at sea with you, the *Windrider* , the Dyhaeri, the Alkynaia, and four Namiran warships could have led to a war between us and the Namirans."

Britea took one look at Pearl's face and felt sick at the thought.

"This is not the time to draw their attention." Pearl's smile returned. "But Prince Kahl seems to like you a lot."

"He doesn't!" instantly protested Britea. "I mean, does he?"

Pearl laughed softly. "Oh, you have no idea, do you?"

"Hey, you two!" Pearl and Britea almost fell off their chairs. The diminutive Chef Blane was back.

"Enough peeling. Dinner just started. Get to the dining hall."

"Yes, chef! Thank you, chef!" The two girls were up and running for the door, clasping each other's hands.

Behind them, the chef saw that small sign of a growing friendship between two girls of vastly different worlds, and he smiled briefly before barking another command to the two unfortunate kitchen staff standing nearby.

#

The dining hall was packed as usual. Britea and Pearl this time were not the last to get their meals. Britea glanced around and was relieved to find Lianne and her friends were already seated and not paying attention to them.

"Do you think any of the students know about our *guests?* " asked Pearl, stressing the last word.

Britea listened to the chatter from nearby tables. Just mundane subjects. Not one word about the Dyhaeri.

"I doubt it."

"We have to tell the others," said Pearl.

It took a moment before Britea realized who she meant. While Danai, Henrick, and Navos treated Pearl warmly; Shran was indifferent and Lexia was still antagonistic to a certain degree.

"You *want* to tell them? I thought you said not to talk about what happened at sea!"

"Shh," shushed Pearl. "Not that. I meant we have to tell them about the guests in the kitchen. How upset will they be if they found out we knew and didn't say anything?"

Britea thought for a moment. "I see your point."

Then a pained look crossed Pearl's face. "Besides, I have something to say to Henrick."

Britea wondered what it was but had no time to ask as they had reached the others.

"Nice to see you two got off early today," greeted Danai with a warm smile as Britea sat beside her. Pearl shared a shy smile with Henrick and a wave with Navos, who was already demolishing his food. Even Shran looked up briefly before diving back into his book as usual while Lexia glowered at Pearl.

Pearl sat down and cleared her throat until she had everyone's attention.

"Henrick, please accept my apology for not believing what you said about the Dyhaeri delegation."

The male wielder stared at her. "Um, no harm done. I accept."

"What made you believe him now?" asked Lexia in a sharp tone. "Did Lady Lianne corroborate his story?" Britea shared a weary look with Danai. Lexia really didn't like Pearl.

Pearl smiled warmly at the fuming Lexia. "It's actually way more exciting than that. Please ask Britea who stopped by the kitchen this evening." Everyone, including the bookish Shran swung their gaze in Britea's direction.

For a moment, she was speechless. "Um, they're here."

"Who's here?" asked Navos.

"The Dyhaeri. They're at Syla College."

Silence. Then everyone, apart from Danai, Pearl, and Britea, started laughing.

"Nice one, Britea," said Lexia wiping her tears away. "I almost fell for it." Danai was watching Pearl suspiciously.

"It's not a prank," said Pearl. "They're here visiting our school with a member of the Malaquey Naval Intelligence Division."

"That's a bit hard to believe—" started Danai.

"It's Lieutenant Flay, the one from the markets," said Britea.

Her roommate stared at her for a long moment before her eyes widened. "You're both serious about this?"

"Oh, come on, Danai!" said Lexia, who was back to being angry. "Surely you don't believe this—"

"Attention, students!" Headmaster Clayre's enhanced voice boomed through the dining hall, and all fell silent as they looked towards the door where the headmaster stood with a grave-looking Warden Asteros.

"Tomorrow morning, there will be a special assembly at 0730 hours in the Great Hall. Some important guests have traveled far to address us. This will be the first time in eight hundred years they have graced the halls of this college.

I expect to see everyone in the Great Hall tomorrow morning. There shall be no excuses; breakfast will be served after at 0755 hours. Please continue your evening meal."

The chatter in the hall resumed as students wondered aloud who could be coming to see them.

But silence reigned for a long moment at Britea's table as they added up the facts and came up with one astonishing answer.

"In 1384 AC, Syla College was founded," started Shran in a voice just loud enough for their small group to hear. "There were three royal guests at the groundbreaking ceremony: King Adren Cen-Taros, brother to Headmaster Lance Cen-Taros; King Oltair of Namira, and…" he paused and looked at a pale Danai.

"Queen Mother Zaleria of the Dyhaeri, in place of her son, King Jahlaniin. That's why her image is on the mural in the Great Hall," finished the Weltonian.

Lexia glanced at a solemn Pearl, who nodded silently.

"Why are they here?" asked Henrick, also whispering.

"And why now?" asked Navos.

No one could answer as the excited chatter continued around them.

CHAPTER 18

Mat woke to Kahl humming a famous ditty from a Dyhaeri play. The barely awake marine took in the beautiful pastel-blue flower pattern on the roof above him, and his gaze slid to the plain, dove-grey walls. The floor was paneled in rich, dark oak. He and Kahl had been given this room while the high priest had a separate room. Between the two rooms was a spacious parlor filled with three circular indigo couches arranged around a low glass table.

Yesterday they had arrived at the college, and after a brief introduction to the faculty and a short visit to the kitchen, the warden had taken them to their rooms.

Mat had been reluctant to admit the rooms were nice, and the mattress was comfortable. He had been surprised when the mattress had adjusted to his form. The warden had said these accommodations had been specially constructed for Dyhaeri guests by the Weltonian builders who had built the college.

Mat and Kahl had stared at him in shock, but the high priest hadn't appeared surprised in the least.

On this mission, Mat was beginning to feel he was learning something new every day. He wondered how and why these rooms had been kept so well maintained. In contrast, the Dyhaeri quarters at the palace had seemed almost abandoned.

His mind returned to the present when Kahl threw a soft pillow at him. His cousin was already fully dressed and ready to face the day.

"Up and about, my dear cousin! We have students to address today!"

Mat growled at his overly cheerful cousin. "Please stop. Your abundance of joy is making me physically ill." He sat up and stretched.

"Sleep well?" asked Kahl.

Mat nodded. "That was the best sleep I've had ever since we left Captain Riverun's ship."

"Truth," agreed Kahl.

"I find it hard to believe Weltonians built this place eight hundred years ago. I thought they always favored the seas. How did they know so much about building?"

"It's probably in the school's historical annals," said the high priest from the doorway. The remaining sleep disappeared from Mat's eyes as he hastily rose from the bed. The high priest was already dressed in his ceremonial garb of a sleeveless white tunic woven from cotton-like seaweed and long black leather pants. He was just attaching his fire-red rune bands on his bare forearms.

Kahl and Mat were a bit concerned about the change in gear.

The high priest had not worn this outfit while at the palace.

High Priest Myltan smiled at them as if sensing their unspoken thoughts. "Today is about making impressions, my sons. Which of your uniforms would be best to don today?"

Mat thought for a moment. "The same ones we wore yesterday, but I doubt the warden would be happy with us carrying our weapons in the school."

"Agreed," said Kahl.

The high priest folded his arms. "Excellent choice. What is your impression of Headmaster Clayre?"

Mat narrowed his eyes slightly at the abrupt shift in topics. This sounded like a test. "He seems a decent sort, but his authority…" he paused.

"Yes?" prompted the high priest.

"Appears to be lacking?" added Kahl.

"What he said," said Mat, indicating his cousin with a wave of his hand.

The high priest nodded in agreement. "And the warden?"

"Very knowledgeable and a bit scary," said Kahl. Mat was reluctant to agree, but he felt the same way. He saw how the warden had watched each of them, and even the Malaquey officer, like a hawk.

The high priest turned to touch the doorframe of the room. "Very few remember who built these walls several centuries ago, and even less care to acknowledge them…but the warden knows—and acknowledges. What did you think of the kitchen staff?"

Kahl and Mat shared a confused look.

"Um, they're kitchen staff?" answered Mat.

The high priest laughed softly.

"Please, don't make the same mistake most powerful humans do by assuming servants are not individuals as well."

Though said softly, Mat recognized a rebuke when he heard it.

"I'm sorry, sir," both Dyhaeri said.

"Once again, the kitchen staff. Wait, let me put it this way. When we met the instructors gathered outside, what impression did you get from them?"

Kahl answered quickly. "They didn't seem happy we were here, and some were afraid of us." Mat nodded in agreement.

"Now, compare that to the kitchen staff. How did they react?"

It took a moment for Mat to recall. "They were respectful and almost reverent, that is, apart from Britea and Pearl." He saw Kahl shoot a glare his way, and Mat almost couldn't keep himself from rolling his eyes.

"The kitchen staff are all Weltonian," announced the high priest. This time, the two younger Dyhaeri gaped at him.

"I don't blame you for not realizing it. After all, you lived with them for only a few months, barely long enough for you to pick up on the cultural differences I've observed for centuries."

Mat was only a bit mollified by this observation. Now that he thought back on it, he could see the similarity between the kitchen staff and the crew of the *Peacekeeper.*

"But they're working on land. How could they be Weltonians?" asked Kahl.

"That's what I intend to ask the warden about. He seems to know more about this school than the headmaster does. Get ready, my sons, we move out in fifteen minutes." Mat was already dashing for the washroom before he was even dismissed.

#

"No punishment for you this morning," announced Chef Blane when Britea and Pearl showed up for their duty at the usual time.

"Why not?" asked Britea. Pearl glared at her.

Chef Blane laughed, startling the two students.

Seeing their surprised expressions, he scowled. "I do laugh you know. Anyway, the warden said you're exempt for this morning only. He does not wish for anyone to miss the address from our new guests." Then he produced two delicious-smelling, freshly baked fish and bread rolls wrapped in paper and handed them to the stunned students.

"Now git before I'm tempted to find you two work."

"Thanks, chef," chorused the girls as they fled with their breakfast.

"If I had known, I would have slept longer," said Pearl once they were out of earshot.

"Mmhmm," agreed Britea, her mouth full of her own mouth-watering meal.

They soon found themselves in the main gardens near the center of the school. Thanks to the crisp, cold morning, a small layer of frost coated the green lawns and hedges, and the blue pools seemed unnaturally still.

"I wonder which classes they'll be assigned to," said Pearl as she daintily finished her roll. Britea raised an eyebrow.

"Why would they be put in classes? I doubt the high priest needs to learn anything from us."

Pearl shook her head. "No, silly. I'm talking about the princes. How old is Kahl?"

"Seventeen, why?" asked Britea with a frown.

"Steady, I'm not after him," said Pearl with a smile. "And I bet his cousin is close to the same age. I wouldn't be surprised if they get to join our classes."

"Why would they do that?" asked Britea again.

"Think, my dear. For the first time since the creation of this school, we have Dyhaeri visitors. It could be some kind of student exchange program like we used to have with the Namiran colleges." Pearl's face went grave. "Before the Immortal Queen killed all the wielders that is."

They were silent for a long moment.

"I heard rumors about that," said Britea, sitting on a stone bench. Pearl glanced at her. "I even checked the library to see if there were any records, but there's nothing. How certain are you that she killed the wielders?"

Pearl sat across from Britea. "My parents host too many parties, and at every party, there's always ministers of varying positions in attendance. Some of them have loose lips."

"You mean you eavesdropped on their conversations," said Britea, arching an eyebrow.

Pearl laughed. "You're catching on. Truth be told, I didn't always have to eavesdrop. Some of the ministers were so intent on boasting about their positions at court that all one had to do was bat their eyelashes at them, smile at them, dance with them, and then ask, 'So, how's the Namira situation?' They'd stumble over themselves to talk about everything they were learning from the border patrol."

"It's that easy?" Britea asked, scandalized.

"Why do you think I was emphasizing the importance of dancing and etiquette class? That is *the* weapon of the royal court."

Britea was silent for a while to digest that, then thought of another question. "So, what did you learn about the Immortal Queen?"

Pearl was only too eager to answer. "It's said that soon after she took over, the queen took the students and teachers of both Namiran wielder colleges. No one ever knew what became of them, but plenty of corpses in carts were seen leaving her castle every day."

Britea shivered, and not from the cold morning air.

"I've never been to Namira," said Pearl gravely as she stared at the pool across from her. "I heard from one of my grandaunts that their snow-capped mountains are truly beautiful, and they had outstanding winter resorts for the noble elite. I wonder if those resorts are still open."

"It matters not to the refugees still trying to flee from Namira," said Britea quietly.

Pearl was silent for a heartbeat. "You have a point." Then she glanced at the shielded chronometer on one of the garden walls. "Come on, let's get going. I want a good spot in the Great Hall."

The two girls left the gardens and walked side by side towards the stairs leading to the stone bridge adjoining the Great Hall to the school proper. Britea had a flashback of the night she had run over the bridge and into a duel in a heavy downpour. Her chest tightened and her heart rate picked up.

"Does Kahl dance?" asked Pearl suddenly.

"Hmm, what did you say?" asked Britea as she tried to hide her discomfort.

"Are you all right?' asked a concerned Pearl.

"I'm fine," said Britea with a shaky smile, trying to shift the direction of her thoughts. "You were asking if Kahl danced? I have no idea." To her hidden relief, her chest felt less uncomfortable, and her heart rate was almost back to normal.

"You never asked?" enquired Pearl in shock.

"There was no need. Why are you even asking?"

"Oh, just curious," said Pearl with an innocent smile Britea didn't trust.

#

The Great Hall was already filling up with students, most of whom were either curious or complaining of hunger or lack of sleep since they'd had to wake early. Britea was grateful for the small snack the thoughtful chef had given her and Pearl.

Britea looked towards the front, and to her surprise, Lianne and her usual gang were already present. Apparently, they had also taken the headmaster's warning seriously.

"Britea! Pearl!" Both girls turned to see Lexia waving at them. With her were Danai, Navos, Shran, and Henrick. As they hurried over, Britea had the urge to look over her shoulder only to see Lianne glaring at her and Pearl.

Oh, she had definitely not forgotten about them.

"You saved spots for us, thanks," Pearl said to Lexia. The petite redhead smiled coldly.

"I'd rather have you where I can see you, Ceres."

Pearl sighed. "We're still not friends, I take it?"

Lexia shook her head slightly. Beside her Navos sighed, and Henrick and Danai looked embarrassed. Shran, though, was as usual not really listening. For once, he was not reading a book but sitting with a notepad and pencil in hand.

"Hey, Shran, what's all that for?" asked Britea, nudging Shran to get his attention and change the subject.

"Taking notes. If the high priest is addressing us, I want his words in black and white for posterity."

Everyone groaned. He frowned at them. "Need I remind you how significant this visit is? It's the first time in eight hundred years, so we had best pay attention, my friends."

An increase in the noise level had Britea looking to the raised dais, and sure enough, the headmaster, the warden, and several instructors had appeared, along with the three new guests.

#

Kahl was both nervous and excited, and it was getting harder to keep a calm façade around the humans. A quick glance at Mat had him envying his cousin's confidence. The high priest, as usual, had a polite, fatherly smile on his face, reinforced by the ceremonial staff he carried, though he seemed to use it more as a walking stick than for any ceremonial purpose.

That made Kahl raise an eyebrow. He recalled the high priest was also a Dyhaeri martial arts instructor, and his favorite weapon was a staff. Kahl wondered if humans would let him walk around with the staff if they knew of his martial arts prowess.

Kahl forced his mind to return to the present as they followed the headmaster and warden through a door and into a noisy, packed hall.

The clamor worsened when the students waiting in the hall saw them. He heard some of them shout in amazement. Kahl was about to search the students for Britea when his cousin exclaimed softly, "Look at the glass ceiling."

Kahl looked up and was rendered speechless when he beheld a lifelike mural of the late Queen Zaleria surrounded by four human wielders. She had departed for the Gentle Seas when the Sea Mother had called her home many years before Kahl's birth. Those that had met her said she was a kind, passionate, and a more-than-capable capable warrior and monarch.

"Queen Zaleria, The Jewel of the Heldiar Sea. She was here for the groundbreaking. I well recall that day," said the high priest softly. Mat and Kahl stared at him. "Then, I was just a marine like you, Mat. The Sea Mother hadn't yet revealed my eventual path to priesthood. It was a…a complicated time."

Kahl shared a frown with Mat. *Shouldn't that have been a simpler time instead?*

But they had no time to talk about the matter because the headmaster was now addressing the astounded students.

#

"By the Seven Hells, you weren't lying!" gasped Lexia when she saw the three Dyhaeri with the senior school officials.

"I did say so," agreed a smug-looking Pearl. Britea had no words as she and the others were busy staring at the Dyhaeri outfits.

The high priest wore a white sleeveless tunic, black leather pants, and chocolate-brown leather shoes that were nearly moccasin like. His exposed green arms were adorned with red bands that softly glowed when the light fell on them. The look was completed by a ceremonial staff that looked like cherrywood but was probably some unknown substance from under the sea. Runes were etched all around it. Then she glanced at Kahl and Mat. Both wore indigo-blue leather tunics and pants. The shoulders, elbows, and knees seemed to have extra padding, making the two Dyhaeri look dangerous rather than bulky. Their outfits were completed by matching thigh-high leather boots.

Britea caught her breath. Kahl's outfit was identical to one he had worn in a dream she had almost forgotten about. She had dreamt of Kahl in this outfit while she had been aboard the *Windrider* .

Pearl snuck a glance at Britea. "I have to admit, the two princes look very handsome in those uniforms."

"Agreed," said Danai and Lexia at the same time. The three girls looked at each other and shared an impish giggle. Davos and Henrick just shook their heads and shared a weary look.

"Oh, the headmaster is about to speak. Everyone, quiet please," said Shran as he posed with his pencil on his notepad, ready to record.

#

"Good morning, staff and students of Syla College." The headmaster's voice was loud, his stance confident. "Today, we have been greatly honored by the presence of High Priest Myltan, Prince Mat-rallenin, and Prince Kahl of the Dyhaeri people."

Kahl remembered to smile as he searched the student body; there were so many of them. He could not help but notice out of the corner of his eye that his cousin was also causally scanning the crowd. Kahl saw curiosity had replaced surprise for most of the students, though some displayed a mix of emotions. He saw fear and…and anger.

His breath caught in his throat when he caught sight of Britea. She sat closer to the middle of the hall with a small group of students. His smile widened when Britea realized he was looking right at her and smiled timidly. Kahl nodded slightly but then had to force himself to look elsewhere lest he draw unnecessary attention to her. Kahl was worried about the anger he saw among some of the students.

"…they have traveled a long way to visit us, and we shall make their stay here as comfortable as possible. The high priest will now address the school."

Shocked murmurs erupted as the high priest nodded respectfully at the headmaster and took his place at the podium. "Wielders of Syla College, may the Sea Mother keep and protect you all." He paused and gazed over the crowd. Kahl noticed most were puzzled by the greeting.

"Many of you must be wondering why, after eight hundred years, the Dyhaeri have graced your doorstep." Kahl glanced at Lieutenant Flay, who was almost apoplectic. Even Kahl hoped the high priest was not going to discuss the dire situation in Namira. "The answer is simple really. It is time we reconnect with our Malaquey allies, and as a sign of good faith, we wish to share some of our knowledge with you in your wielding training…"

This was met by excited whispers.

"…for you are going to need it in the very near future." The whispers died as the students and instructors stared at him. Lieutenant Flay covered his mouth as if trying to hide his exasperated expression. Kahl glanced at Mat, who wore a neutral façade. The warden, however, appeared calm even though the headmaster had gone pale.

Then the high priest smiled and nodded at the head of the college. "Especially during your Year of Discovery."

The headmaster responded with a relieved smile and a nod. Harto closed his eyes briefly and Mat grinned dryly.

The high priest turned back to the expectant students.

"Mat and Kahl…" The two younger Dyhaeri stepped forward, and the entire school swung their collective gaze to them. "…will be assigned to different instructors who will decide which classes are most appropriate for them to observe." Excited murmurs buzzed again until a young chestnut-haired girl in the front row stepped forward.

Kahl frowned. She looked familiar.

#

"What is Lianne doing?" gasped Britea.

Pearl shocked them all by cursing before answering in an angry hiss. "What does it look like? Miss Entitled is trying to grab attention."

#

Kahl was surprised when the young human female curtsied before speaking.

"High Priest Myltan, I am Lady Lianne Arkei, cousin to King Wilhem of House Taros. Let me be the first to welcome you and your entourage on behalf of the student body of Syla College." She looked at the girls at her table, and they stood up and started clapping and, in a heartbeat, the entire school joined in.

Kahl happened to look towards Britea's table, and he saw anger on her face as she and the surrounding students glared at Lady Lianne Arkei.

There was a story there. *Wait, where had he heard that name before?* It took a few seconds for his memory to provide him with an answer.

Arkei. Now Kahl looked at Lianne in a new light; the resemblance to Lady Selina Arkei was uncanny. Siblings, perhaps? Were they Britea's enemies?

The high priest smiled gently as the applause ended.

"Thank you, Novice Arkei."

Lianne's smiling façade cracked a bit when she was addressed as novice instead of lady. "I appreciate the welcome. Now I shall return the podium to Headmaster Clayre."

#

Britea tried to keep calm as she waited for the headmaster to finish. She was finding it hard to stop glaring at Lianne's back. The noble was lapping up the praise from her friends.

By the Lords, the high priest was going to think Lianne was the queen around here! She just hoped the Dyhaeri saw through her act.

"College, we shall now recite the Wielder's Creed."

Britea was so angry she almost forgot the words, but then her training kicked in, and she recited the words she had memorized months ago. Throughout the recitation, the high priest watched the students closely. Britea found herself wondering if the Dyhaeri had a Creed of their own. The headmaster was beaming with pride as the Wielder's Creed was recited almost uniformly.

"Excellent. Now, head to the dining hall for a late breakfast." The headmaster turned to the Dyhaeri delegation, bowed, and indicated they should precede him. Britea saw Kahl shoot her a quick glance, and then he was gone.

"Come on, everyone, let's get some food before it's all gone," announced Danai. Britea and Pearl fell behind their small group of friends as students around them chatted enthusiastically about the high priest's address.

"What do you think she's going to do?" asked Britea. There was no need for any of them to ask who she was referring to.

Pearl still looked angry. "What do you think?" She spat before taking a calming breath.

"I'm sorry, that was uncalled for. I just get so mad when I see her arrogant face. If Lianne is up to her usual tricks, she'll try to get close to them and flaunt her family's connections. But right now, I have no idea how she'll do it."

Britea suddenly felt weary—and very worried for Kahl.

#

"Request denied."

Harto was speechless for a long moment as he stared at Headmaster Clayre. They were currently alone in his office. After the high priest's address, a member of the school's kitchen staff had arrived to inform the Dyhaeri their breakfast was ready in a private dining room.

Harto had seized the opportunity to speak to the headmaster in private. It had come to Harto's attention he could not handle monitoring the Dyhaeri alone, not with them all being assigned to separate parts of the school. He simply could not be in three places at once.

"Sir," he said, finally finding his voice. "It is of the utmost importance I have assistance from additional intelligence agents—"

"Having one of you in my school is bad enough, yet you expect me to agree to more of your hard-headed military types terrorizing my students and teachers?!" cut in the headmaster, an unyielding expression on his face. "Syla College has taken care of itself these past centuries. Remember, this was the first wielder school ever built and the only one visited—not once, but twice—by the Dyhaeri!"

Harto was now more annoyed than chastised.

"And yet the high priest sees your old school as the weakest of the three!" He regretted the words as soon as he said them, but there was no taking them back. The headmaster's expression was more closed off than ever.

"And who suggested Syla College to them? Hmm?"

Harto was unable to answer.

The headmaster laughed dryly. "Do you take me for a fool, Lieutenant Flay? The king told me about that meeting and how it was your agency's intelligence that was the basis for warning him not to allow the Dyhaeri anywhere near the military wielding colleges!"

Harto had thought it was a good idea at the time but seeing the anger on the headmaster's face now warned him to keep his thoughts to himself.

"So, the grand old Malaquey Naval Intelligence decided the students of Syla College are to be fodder and shields for the brave military wielding division." The headmaster's voice was dripping with scorn.

Harto tried once more. "That is why I am asking for permission to bring more of my fellow officers to observe the—"

Headmaster Clayre held up a hand, and Harto stopped speaking.

"As I said, Syla College will handle this on its own. I expect you'll be needing breakfast." The headmaster sat down and began to concentrate on the paperwork on his desk.

Harto knew he had been dismissed. "Yes, sir," he said before leaving the office.

#

Kahl sighed in contentment as he sipped his warm cup of peach tea. He, Mat, and the high priest had been taken to a small private dining room, and sure enough, the Weltonian kitchen staff soon appeared with warm, covered plates of food.

The breakfast had been a delight: warm fluffy mushroom and bread rolls with a small cup of fresh fruit. It had been far better than the meals at the palace and was so similar to his mother's cooking that for one moment, he wondered if the Weltonians were Dyhaeri in disguise. That thought almost sobered his cheerful thoughts.

"The students don't know what to make of us," said Mat in serious tone.

The high priest nodded. "But what do you know of them?"

Mat was quiet for a long time. "Not much, I must admit. But they—most of them—seem different from those at court."

"Time will tell," added the high priest before looking at Kahl. "You will stay by my side for most of today. Mat will be spending some time with the weapons master."

Kahl tried to hide his dismay; he had hoped he would get a chance to see Britea. Mat on the other hand, seemed intrigued.

"Yes, sir," answered both Dyhaeri. A light knock at the door had the three of them turning. Mat looked at the high priest. At his nod, Mat walked to the door and opened it to see Warden Asteros and Weapons Master Caren.

"Are we interrupting?" asked the warden politely.

"No. Please, do come in," said the high priest.

Mat stepped out of the way as the two senior faculty members entered the private dining room.

"I trust the food was satisfactory," said the warden.

The high priest stood as the duo approached the table. Kahl was already on his feet.

"It was exemplary. I trust you're here to inform us of our assignments."

The warden smiled. "Weapons Master Caren would like one of the princes to accompany him to his combat and defense class."

"Mat will join him," said the high priest.

"Yes, sir," answered Mat. The weapons master nodded at him. The warden looked at Kahl, a question in his eyes.

"Kahl will join me for most of the day. If it's not too much trouble, I was hoping to chat with you, warden, about the college."

The weapons master shot the warden an odd look; however, the warden seemed unperturbed.

"I have some free time right now."

The high priest smiled brightly. "Wonderful."

#

Kahl watched as Mat left with the weapons master. His cousin appeared eager to experience the combat and defense class. He just hoped no one picked a fight with Mat; they would be sure to lose.

"How can I help you today, High Priest Myltan?" asked the warden once he had sat down across them. Kahl forced his mind to return to the present.

"I have questions about your kitchen staff," said the high priest.

The warden seemed puzzled. "I thought you said the food was to your liking."

"Oh, it is, I was just surprised to see the entire kitchen staff is Weltonian."

A glint appeared in the warden's eyes. "Do you have an issue with Weltonians, high priest?" asked the warden in a deceptively soft voice.

High Priest Myltan's face was somber. "Not at all. I consider them kin." Those last words made Kahl look at the Dyhaeri high priest in surprise.

The warden blinked. "Kin?"

"Yes," continued the high priest. "Which is why I must ask if they work for this college under duress."

Now Kahl swung his gaze back to the speechless warden.

"No, they're here of their own free will. You're free to ask them."

The high priest stared at the warden for a long moment, then nodded. "I believe you. On to my next question then. Were they all exiled from the seas?"

The warden shook his head. "That I have never asked. All I know is they're hard workers and are part of the Syla College family. They are safe here."

"Good. I suppose there are no Weltonian staff at the other colleges?"

The warden laughed dryly. "No." Kahl waited for an explanation, but the warden didn't seem eager to elaborate, nor did the high priest seem surprised by his reply.

"Why is that?" asked Kahl without thinking. The high priest frowned at him, but the warden held up a hand.

"That I will partly answer." He glanced at the high priest before continuing. "Weltonians used to study with us when the colleges were first founded, but thanks to bullying and widespread discrimination in Malaquey and Namira, they decided to withdraw completely to the seas about seven hundred and fifty years ago."

Kahl stared at him. "Weltonians are human like you. Why would you hate your own kind?"

The warden looked at him with eyes that seemed too ancient for his age. "Humans have always hated themselves. We have annals that depict many conflicts throughout the centuries. When humans discovered this side of the world, we were running from persecution and war, but instead of leaving all that behind, we brought it with us."

Kahl had nothing to say to that. He wondered at the insecurity of the humans.

"Maybe someday there will be less hate," said High Priest Myltan.

The warden smiled sadly. "Maybe. Was there more you wished to know?"

High Priest Myltan shook his head. "This will suffice for now. Which class will you assign Kahl to?"

Kahl was both relieved and anxious about the abrupt change in topic.

"I think one of our senior wielding classes would be best," replied the warden.

#

"How do you wish to be addressed?"

Mat shot the instructor a worried look. They were walking down the wide, open corridor leading to the outdoor combat and defense class.

"Prince Mat-rallenin or Your Highness?" continued Weapons Master Caren.

"Mat is fine."

The weapons master raised an eyebrow. "You don't wish to attach 'Prince' to your name?"

Mat smiled politely. "Back home, I'm just a marine, but your court herald demanded a title, and based on the high priest's description of our duties back home, Kahl and I ended up being called princes."

The instructor looked thoughtful. "Around here, the title, 'Prince,' means you have royal blood. Are you related to King Jahlaniin?"

Mat appreciated the direct question. "One life, one blood. All are connected. Do not be deceived by possessions or power for all are one. All shall leave this world the way they arrived, naked and with nothing."

Weapons Master Caren raised both eyebrows.

"That is a verse taken from a prayer book by the late High Priestess Iona. The interpretation is that the Dyhaeri are not only related to each other but to every other living being, so yes, I guess I am related to King Jahlaniin." Mat was definitely not going to tell him that several Dyhaeri disagreed with the late high priestess' teachings, though she was still revered by all.

Mat prepared himself for scorn and yet more questions.

"Fascinating," was all the instructor said. A quick look at his face showed he really meant it.

"Um…thank you." Mat said uncertainly.

Weapons Master Caren nodded. "Now, let's talk about my class."

About time, thought Mat.

"What is your weapon of choice?"

"Trident or staff." The instructor waited for him to continue. "And wielding," added Mat rather reluctantly. The weapons master nodded as if he had expected the hesitation.

"Do you mind if I ask about the highest level you've wielded?"

I sure do! "High enough for me to get into the marines," said Mat, and that was all he was planning to say on the matter.

Weapon Master Caren had a wry smile on his face. "I ask this not only because I'm curious, but also to prepare you. Many students will ask you this as well." Then the smile disappeared from his face.

"Wield dueling is not permitted in Malaquey, especially not in our schools."

Mat held up a hand in agreement. "Same goes for home. The high priest would literally have my head if I forgot that law."

"Interesting," said the weapons master, fascinated yet again. "Ah, here we are." They had reached two enormous heavy-looking oak doors. Beyond it, Mat could hear muffled voices.

"Welcome to combat and defense."

#

Danai was warming up for her usual sparring session with Navos when the other students started chatting excitedly.

"What's going on?" she asked one of the students before realizing everyone was staring at the entrance. She turned to see Weapons Master Caren standing there with Prince Mat. The assistant instructors approached them, and the weapons master introduced them. Danai used this time to study Prince Mat. He was clearly quite handsome, and he looked stunning in his leather uniform. She took note of the reinforcements at the neck, shoulders, elbows, and knees that allowed easy movement and offered protection. She found herself wondering if anyone special was waiting for him back home in Light-Under-Sea.

"Is he joining our class?" Danai almost jumped when an excited Navos spoke up beside her.

"By the Sea Mother! You gave me a fright, Navos!" Her friend and classmate gave her an odd look. "What is it?" asked a still-shaken Danai.

"That's the first time I've ever heard you say, 'By the Sea Mother.' Where did that come from?"

Danai mentally berated herself for the slip while she tried to recover. "I'm Weltonian, Navos. I grew up learning about the Sea Mother. When I came here though, I realized not everyone would understand, so I try not to mention Her."

Navos face softened. "You don't have to pretend around me, Danai. I'm your friend."

She smiled and squeezed the gentle giant's arm. "As for your earlier question, I have no idea if he's joining our class or just observing it."

Navos grinned. "But I bet Weapons Master Caren is already thinking about how to make him a permanent student."

Danai chuckled. Master Caren did seem determined to increase the number of students in combat and defense.

"Everyone to the center lawn, now!" bellowed Instructor Talios. The students obeyed with alacrity, and in a few minutes, Master Caren was standing with Prince Mat before the whole class.

"Good day, class. I trust you were all at the address this morning. Joining us today is Prince Mat, who will be observing your training."

This was met by a mixture of excited and anxious murmurs. Danai kept her eyes on the Dyhaeri. He seemed quite calm despite the mixed reception.

Master Caren continued. "You will go about your exercises as usual, and we shall all take our lunch here as usual." He nodded to the small group of assistant instructors, who began to assign exercises to the gathered students.

As Danai waited for her assignment, she glanced around and saw Britea, Pearl, and three other students sent to the track for a run.

"Riverun! Odell!" Danai forced her attention back to Instructor Talios, who was suddenly standing in front of her and Navos. "You two are up for sparring, as usual." Then the female instructor lowered her voice and leaned closer. "Make us look good, will ya?"

"Yes, ma'am," chorused both novices softly before heading to a corner of the yard. Around them were other pairs of older novices. One thing was obvious: most students were nervous.

"We've got this, everyone. Just do what we normally do," encouraged Danai in a voice that carried only to the nearby students. Many of them nodded back and relaxed into a more confident stance.

"Hand-to-hand?" asked Navos.

"Yes. I'd hate to take your eye out with the double sticks," said Danai with a smile. Her preferred weapon of choice was double light swords or a pair of reinforced staffs as long as her arms. It caught many of her opponents off guard.

"You wish," said Navos with a laugh. They nodded at each other, and then Navos made the first feint. Danai danced back while watching his feet. The feet always pointed first in the direction the body would move. One also had to be mindful of the hands. However, enough practice sharpened one's instinct about whether to dodge a punch or a kick.

Navos suddenly rained a flurry of blows towards her face. She danced sideways and kicked at his right shin. He drew back in time—barely—so the tip of her right foot only brushed the hem of his practice pants. She didn't claim it as a hit because she had not touched him.

As he tried to recover from the dodge, she darted behind him and let loose a flurry of her own on his shoulders. Navos hardly made a sound as he spun around and tried to grab her left hand.

Danai let him, at the same time aiming a hard kick just above his left knee. Navos grunted softly and staggered a bit, but he didn't go down.

"Strike one," said Danai as she bounced on her feet. Navos, without warning, swung a haymaker at her chest. Danai flowed to the side and barely missed being hit before using both hands to tug forcefully down on his outstretched right forearm. This pulled him off balance, and he went down hard on his right knee.

She winced inwardly when she heard an audible crack in the knee he had landed on. Navos went pale but uttered not a sound.

"Halt!" yelled Instructor Talios, who had been quietly observing the sparring pairs. The other pairs stopped momentarily, then carried on when they realized the order wasn't intended for them.

"Are you all right?" asked Danai in a worried voice.

Navos tried to stand and went even more pale. "Oh, I think it's just a small sprain. I'll be fine soon."

"No, you won't, not without some healing," said the instructor as she waved at Assistant Instructor Celess, a healer. Three were assigned to this class for injuries sustained during training.

Danai and Instructor Talios helped Navos off to the side and helped him to lie on his back. The healer knelt and assessed his right knee, which was already swelling.

"Not a break, but you'll be very bruised if this isn't treated right now. Do I have your permission to treat?"

"Yes, please," said Navos through gritted teeth. The healer placed her hands on his exposed right knee, and a soft white light coated her palms as the knee swelling began to ease.

Within minutes, it looked almost back to normal. Navos sighed with relief. The color came back to his face again, and he sat up on his own.

"I don't feel any pain. I think I can continue—"

"No," interrupted Assistant Instructor Celess, who was now pale. Instructor Talios helped the healer up. "You need to rest and avoid any training on that knee for two days. Only wielding defense training for you, Novice Odell."

"Thank you, and you get some rest as well, Instructor Celess," said Talios gently. The assistant instructor grinned weakly at her and walked away a bit unsteady on her feet. Danai watched her leave.

Healers were rare, more so even than wielders. For there to be three in the combat and defense class was a treasure most students took for granted. Assistant Instructor Celess was worth her weight and more in gold and was highly sought after by gentry who could afford to pay for her abilities.

Danai turned back to Navos, who was a bit chagrined at not being able to practice.

"I'm so sorry," apologized Danai. He grinned at her.

"Not your fault. I was careless."

"Your stance was off, Odell," said Instructor Talios. She was now back in instructor mode. "When you throw a haymaker, be sure of where your feet are at all times and brace for pushback. That way, when your opponent tries to counter, you'll be as immobile as a mountain."

"Yes, ma'am," chorused both novices.

"What's going on?"

All three turned to face Weapons Master Caren and...Prince Mat.

#

Earlier, Mat had stood to one side as the weapons master had addressed the class. Outwardly, he had looked calm, but inside, he had been a ball of nerves and questions. He found himself once more wondering why he and Kahl had been assigned to the high priest for this diplomatic mission.

He knew there were other marines older and more experienced than he and Kahl, so he suspected their assignment was the will of the Seers.

Though that should have been enough for him, he was still curious and worried.

He wondered how Kahl was doing. Mat had left him and the high priest with the warden.

After the brief introduction, Mat had watched the assistant instructors place the students into smaller groups. Master Caren had explained what each group was doing, and it hadn't taken long to understand the structure. Junior novices started with running and strength-training exercises to improve endurance. As they progressed, sparring hand-to-hand and with weapons was introduced.

Those with previous experience were tested, and if deemed acceptable, were put in the advanced classes while those with no training were assigned to the beginner classes.

Mat had nodded at the explanation. From the little he had seen, the weapons master was quite proficient in his area of expertise.

Master Caren had stated wielding for combat and defense was taught only to older students who had passed the advanced sparring classes. Mat had raised an eyebrow at this. Master Caren had promised to go into detail later.

Mat could not help but compare this to his own training. For the Dyhaeri, combat and defense wielding training began as soon as they began to manifest their ability. Hand-to-hand and weapons training started much earlier, practically as soon as they could walk.

Maybe the difference in training had something to do with the Dyhaeri living in proximity to the Alkynaia, who didn't discriminate between Dyhaeri adults and children when they attacked. A wave of anger washed over Mat as he thought of his late father and Kahl's late father. Both had disappeared on patrols close to the Alkynaia borders. Mat had been eight cycles old when his father died, and Kahl had been thirteen cycles when his father had been labeled missing on patrol. For a while, Mat had envied his cousin for having had more time with his own father, but in the end, he knew his cousin had also suffered a terrible loss.

Mat mentally shed his melancholy and nodded when Master Caren asked him to walk with him as they observed the different groups. Mat spied Britea running on the track. He frowned at first when he noticed she was lagging behind the group, but then he saw her look back at an obviously exhausted Pearl. Mat looked at Britea closer this time and noticed she was not exhausted.

"My grandmother runs faster than you lot! Move those legs!" yelled one of the instructors standing beside the track. Pearl stumbled and Britea stopped, stretching out a hand to help. Pearl shook her head and continued running. Soon, both girls were side by side though far behind those in front.

"Interesting," Mat murmured to himself.

"Excuse me?" asked Master Caren.

Mat wondered if he should keep his thoughts to himself, then decided to speak. "I noticed the novices on the tracks. Reminds me of swimming races our teachers subjected us to. They said it was to build up stamina."

Master Caren smiled. "Same idea, different worlds."

Mat smiled back nervously. Those words disturbed him more than he cared to admit.

Were Dyhaeri and humans that similar?

He kept that thought to himself as he strode beside the weapons master. They were approaching the older students, who were in sparring pairs. Some were hand-to-hand and others used weapons that varied from wooden staves to double sticks or short, carved daggers. A few students seemed self-conscious as if aware they were being closely observed. Mat saw some average fighters and some bad ones, but he was yet to see one who could go toe to toe with a Dyhaeri marine.

"Ah, this bears closer observation," said Master Caren. Mat wondered what the instructor was talking about before realizing the human instructor was staring at a corner of the lawn where two human females were helping a tall muscular male from the floor.

Mat was curious as well. He got closer in time to hear the female instructor scold the human male about his stance.

"What's going on here?" asked Weapons Master Caren.

The three turned and the air left Mat's lungs when he saw the younger female in training gear, a red slash across her chest. She was lithe and had lovely, chocolate-brown skin with grey-green eyes. Her heart-shaped face was framed by short, curly black hair. Her beautiful eyes widened when she saw Master Caren and Mat.

"Training injury, sir," said the female instructor. "Navos has been treated for a badly sprained knee injury. He's out of practice for the next two days at least."

"Understood," said Master Caren as he gave Navos a sympathetic look. "Which means Danai has no one to spar with."

Danai focused her attention on the weapons master. "I didn't mean to injure him. I just got carried away. I'm sorry."

"That's fine. I know you meant no harm. We'll find—"

"I'll spar with her, if she'll have me," blurted Mat. The two instructors and two students gaped at him. Mat's face felt warm. He had to think fast.

"I'm here to evaluate. I think this would be a perfect opportunity."

Master Caren rubbed his jaw thoughtfully while Instructor Talios looked at him suspiciously. Even Danai and Navos were speechless.

"That sounds like a good idea," said the weapons master after what seemed like an eternity.

CHAPTER 19

Harto was having a bad day.

After the disastrous meeting with the headmaster, he had realized he was indeed hungry and had to dash to the dining hall to grab something. Instead, he had found an empty hall. He had forced himself to walk to the kitchens, dreading an encounter with the head chef, who seemed to hate his guts for some reason.

To his relief, he had lucked out. The chef had been busy, so one of the kitchen staff had given him a light meal of warm porridge and a small fruit salad. He had rushed through the meal while sitting on a stool in the corner of the kitchen. As he had eaten, he had tried to look for Britea and Pearl, but the two novices had been nowhere to be seen. Maybe they had made it to class by then.

Once done, he had left the kitchen and headed towards the private dining hall that had been set aside for the Dyhaeri delegation. He had gotten there in time to see High Priest Myltan and Kahl leaving with the warden.

"Where is Prince Mat-rallenin?" asked Harto.

"He accompanied the weapons master to the combat and defense class," replied the high priest.

Harto kept his frustration hidden. This was why he had wanted additional agents. "And yourselves?" He tried to keep his tone polite.

"The high priest would like to survey our library before Kahl is assigned to one of the senior wielding classes," answered the warden calmly.

Now Harto was torn between which Dyhaeri he should accompany.

"Was there anything you needed?" politely asked the high priest.

It took him a moment to decide. "How long ago did Prince Mat-rallenin leave with Master Caren?"

#

This can't be happening, thought Danai in dismay. She couldn't believe Weapons Master Caren was allowing the prince to spar with her. *Surely there had to be some sort of rule against that?*

"However, would you mind changing into one of our practice uniforms? I ask this because yours appears well-suited for battle while hers is not as reinforced."

What? I'm no fragile flower! Danai's mortification gave way to anger.

Prince Mat glanced at her. "Of course. I understand."

Master Caren smiled. "Instructor Brane will show you to the change rooms."

Once Mat had left with one of the assistant instructors, Danai turned to Instructor Talios and Master Caren.

"He didn't have to change his uniform. I can fight him—"

"I did it to give you time to prepare, mentally and physically," interrupted Master Caren in a soft voice that carried no farther than Instructor Talios, Danai, and Navos.

"We don't even know his fighting style," Instructor Talios argued, a worried expression on her face. "Are we certain this sparring should go on?"

Danai inwardly agreed with the instructor. *But did they really have a choice?*

"If anything untoward occurs, I will stop the fight," said the weapons master. "However, you can withdraw if you wish, Danai."

And make myself look like a fool?!

"I'll be fine. It's just sparring, right? You should worry about him," said Danai in a calm voice that belied her rapidly beating heart and racing thoughts.

"They're returning," warned Navos in a whisper. The small group broke apart.

Danai couldn't help but stare as Mat returned. Gone was the Dyhaeri marine gear, replaced now by a form-fitting sleeveless black top that emphasized the muscled torso beneath. He also wore a pair of black baggy pants and was now barefoot. A white slash on his chest represented his air element.

From the corner of her eye, she noticed other students had completed their sparring practice, and the instructors were beckoning to them to gather round, sit on the ground, and watch. Even the junior wielders had returned from running; amongst them were Britea and an exhausted but curious Pearl.

Danai hid a growl. *No pressure, huh?*

Mat glanced at the gathering crowd, and to her annoyance, he grinned at the audience.

"Choice of weapons?" asked Master Caren.

"Stave," said Mat.

"Double rods," said Danai almost simultaneously. Already she was planning her opening attack. She felt her mind calm as she drew on the countless hours of teaching from her parents and instructors.

The practice weapons were brought forward, and by then, the whole class had gathered.

"Three bouts. The winner of each is whoever makes non-lethal near contact to the neck, chest, abdomen, or upper or lower back."

Danai was familiar with the rules. Blows to those areas delivered with too much force could kill an opponent. But did Prince Mat understand the rules?

"Any questions?" asked Master Caren.

"No," said Prince Mat calmly as he stretched his neck to loosen his muscles.

Danai forced herself to do the same, but her muscles didn't loosen. She was too keyed up. "No, sir," she replied as well.

Master Caren nodded. "You will begin when I count down from three to one."

He stepped off the practice area.

Danai kept her eyes on Prince Mat.

"Three."

The Dyhaeri prince began to dance on the balls of his feet.

Danai stayed still.

"Two."

Intensity flashed in Prince Mat's eyes.

Danai glanced down at his feet. He was going to attack first.

"One. Begin!"

Prince Mat flew across the room, the stave pointed at her chest. Startled exclamations erupted from the gathered students as Danai spun out of the way at the last moment. She bent low and swung the short rods at his legs, but the Dyhaeri jumped over them and thrust down with the stave. She used the rods to counter the attack and pushed back. The prince took a step back to balance, and she initiated her attack, swinging both rods at his head and neck. But the Dyhaeri was fast and used the stave to block her attacks.

Then her opponent spun away from her attacks and tried to approach from behind. Danai thrust both rods behind her and heard a resounding *clunk!* as the stave connected with her weapons. She quickly dropped to one knee and rolled to the side. A mere heartbeat later, the stave connected with the packed soil where Danai had been a moment earlier.

"Come on, Danai, beat his green arse!" Danai almost missed the ferocious glare Instructor Talios shot at the speaker, silencing them.

Prince Mat grinned as if energized by the insult. He bounced on his feet for a moment and then started swinging his weapon, trying to rain blows at her feet and head. For the next few endless moments, Danai was too busy trying to block each blow. He seemed determined to hit either her legs or head. *Why was he not aiming for her chest or midriff?*

She had to concentrate to avoid the blows he kept swinging at her head. Danai felt herself giving ground step by step and knew she would soon run out of room. After a particularly hard blow she blocked from the left, Prince Mat rapidly spun the stave with one hand, gathering speed before transferring it to his left hand and bringing it down lightening quick towards her face. Danai shot her rods over her head to block it.

But just as the blow was about to land, he lowered the stave so it was pointing at her exposed chest. He stopped the stave a hair's breadth from making contact.

"First strike," said Prince Mat with a smile.

Danai heard exclamations from the nearby instructors and students.

"First round goes to Prince Mat," announced Master Caren calmly.

Danai tried to tamp down her fury. She was mad at herself for missing that obvious clue.

"Ready for the next—" began Prince Mat but Danai was already running at him. With a yell, she dove towards him. The startled Dyhaeri dropped flat on his back, and she tumbled over him. Prince Mat tried to turn and stand at the same time, but Danai, who was already on her feet, aimed a kick at his head while he was still kneeling. He brought up his stave to block it, but Danai fell to her knees and brought both rods close to his neck, stopping the weapons from touching him.

"Yes!" yelled Navos. Some students started cheering even though the instructors tried to hush them.

"Second strike," said Danai smugly. To her amazement, Prince Mat grinned at her. He was enjoying this. They both slowly stood and stepped away from each other.

"Second bout goes to Syla College," said Master Caren. Danai groaned inwardly. *So now she was fighting for the school?* Even Prince Mat gave the weapon's master a quick look as if he was wondering why he hadn't addressed her by her name.

"Next round decides all," continued Master Caren. "Begin!"

Danai and Prince Mat circled each other, looking for openings. Then Danai feinted left, but the Dyhaeri didn't fall for it. He raised an eyebrow instead and continued circling.

Well then, head-on attack it is , thought Danai as she danced her way towards him, twirling both rods like batons. The more speed, the more forceful the blow. Prince Mat's expression turned grim as he began to spin the stave with both hands, forming a barrier.

Danai was forced to admit the Dyhaeri prince was good. He had not treated her with kid gloves at all. Nor had he played dirty. She watched his stave spin for a moment as she searched for a way through the spinning barrier.

Ah, there was an opening near his feet . She glanced down, and as she'd thought, he noticed the movement. Kneeling suddenly, Danai swept her left rod in a wide arc as if to hit his bare feet. Prince Mat lowered the stave to block her motion. But Danai's move was a feint. Instead, she used her feet to propel her upwards, a maneuver she had learned on the rolling decks of her parents' ships, and aimed the rod in her left hand at his chest.

For a moment, she was certain she would make contact, but Prince Mat darted backwards and to the side. Danai almost lost her footing as she stumbled forward. She almost missed the moment when the Dyhaeri spun his stave at her now-exposed back.

Danai turned as fast as she could and flung herself down to the hard-packed soil as she brought her rods up to block the blow.

There was a resounding *clunk* as the bell for lunch rung.

"Thus ends the match as a draw. It's time for lunch," said Master Caren as the students groaned their collective disappointment.

Danai closed her eyes briefly in relief and failed to notice when the pressure let up on her rods. "Need a hand up, fighter?"

Her eyes flew open to stare up at a smiling Prince Mat, who was offering a hand to help her up.

"Um, thanks," said Danai uncertainly as she grasped his outstretched hand. She grimaced as pain made itself known in her back; the adrenaline was wearing off. But that was forgotten with the pleasant tingling sensation Danai felt when she touched Mat's hand. A quick glance at Prince Mat showed he was calm. She looked around to see if anyone had caught her reaction. Master Caren and Navos still stood nearby, and right behind them stood a Malaquey naval officer she unfortunately recognized.

"That was impressive," said the Dyhaeri, causing her to turn back to him. Danai heard no mockery in his tone. "I didn't catch your name."

"Danai Riverun." It was both comical and strange to see his smile turn into a stunned almost frightened expression.

"Riverun? Are you by chance related to Captain Lanead Riverun and Captain Sonei Riverun?" He asked in a rush.

Wait, how did he know? "They're my parents," said Danai, trying to hide her own shock.

Prince Mat's eyes widened.

"Thank you, Novice Riverun. You may join your classmates for lunch," said Master Caren, who had stepped closer and was pointedly staring at their still-clasped hands.

Her face burning with embarrassment, Danai finally remembered to let go of Prince Mat's hand.

"It was nice sparring with you, Prince Mat…"

"Please, call me Mat," said the Dyhaeri with an easy smile, his apparent surprise gone.

"Um…sure," she ran off with a curious Navos.

#

Harto had no idea what to think.

He had arrived just before the sparring had started. At first, he had thought this could be an excellent chance to observe how the Dyhaeri fought. Then he had seen who Mat's opponent was, and all reason had left his mind.

Danai had been wearing the usual training uniform and was barefoot on the floor of packed sand. A red stripe crossed the front and back of her tunic. So, her element was fire.

And she had looked even more beautiful than the day he had first seen her at the docks.

Harto had forced his mind to pay attention to the weapons master's words. He had been disappointed when he had realized there would be no wielding, but still he had watched silently from behind the crowd of students and instructors as the opponents had chosen their weapons. He had grimaced when Mat had flown across the sand. The Dyhaeri had been fast, his moves precise and possibly deadly if they made contact. Harto had bit back a curse when the Dyhaeri had made the first strike.

However, Danai's reaction had been interesting. Instead of being cowed, she had responded by attacking without warning, and her flurry of blows had made Mat step back until she had tricked him into blocking. Then she had scored a hit.

Harto had stared at her open-mouthed. He had met Weltonians before. They seemed servile and wholly pacifist. Before today, he could have sworn not one would lift a hand to save themselves. But Danai's performance had proved those assumptions wrong.

Was there a branch of Weltonians who were this warlike, or did they hide such talents beneath their pacifist nature?

Harto had begun to take note of her fluid moves, unable to help but be impressed. But soon, Harto had realized he could not identify her type of martial arts. He wondered who had taught her. Harto had folded his arms and held his chin in his right hand as the fight progressed to a brief standoff. Danai's response to Mat's spinning weapon had been brilliant and so simple Harto cursed himself for not seeing it.

What was she doing in this school? With talents like these, she should have been in one of the military wielding colleges! Her talent was wasted here.

"Thus ends the match as a draw. It's now time for lunch," said Master Caren as the students groaned their collective disappointment." Harto shared the students' feelings.

He hung back as the assistant instructors and students dispersed, but he frowned when he noticed Mat and Danai were talking and holding hands. Harto stayed where he was, still unseen as he could not trust his control of his emotions.

Finally, after an eternity, Danai let go of Mat's hand and left with an admiring male peer.

Harto mentally braced himself before stepping forward, clapping loudly.

As intended, this drew the attention of Mat and the weapons master.

"Bravo! What a show!"

Mat's easy smile was replaced by irritation.

"Lieutenant Flay. You finally decided to join us," said Mat in a tone that had the weapons master giving the Dyhaeri a look intended to urge caution.

Harto smiled. Upsetting this particular Dyhaeri was turning out to be a favorite hobby.

"I must say, your technique is intriguing. You and I should spar sometime."

Now the weapon master frowned at Harto.

Mat raised an eyebrow. "Is that an invitation?"

"No duels," ordered Master Caren as he stepped between the two soldiers from different worlds.

"Of course not," said Harto with a smile.

"Wouldn't dream of it, sir," said Mat in a deliberately neutral tone.

Master Caren gave both an exasperated look. Clearly, he didn't believe them.

"Prince Mat was about to change and join me and the instructors for lunch. Will you be joining us, Lieutenant Flay?"

"Definitely," said Harto with a bright smile as he saw Mat's expression harden.

#

Danai and Navos were met with cheers as they joined the buffet line.

"Danai, my girl! That was amazing! I knew you'd beat him!" said one student, clapping her on the shoulder.

"It ended in a draw," corrected Danai, but she suspected her classmate wasn't really listening to her.

"When's the rematch?!" demanded another student.

"Settle down, everyone. We gotta eat," said Navos as he waved away their questions.

This was met by groans of, "Come on! We need a rematch!"

"Go ask Master Caren about it," responded Navos with a mischievous grin. He knew no one had the guts to ask Master Caren for a rematch.

"Thanks, brother," said Danai with heartfelt relief.

"Anytime. Though I'd pay good money to watch a rematch." He laughed when Danai glared at him. The two walked to a nearby table already occupied by Henrick, Britea, and Pearl, and from their expressions, they were eagerly awaiting them.

"Danai, that fight was outstanding," said Pearl, awed. Danai felt herself warming to her former nemesis. Truth be told, she still regarded Pearl with suspicion, but she seemed like a nice person underneath all that arrogance.

"It was unbelievable!" said Britea excitedly. "You were as fast as Mat, and he moved like lightening!"

"It's Prince Mat," corrected Henrick.

"He and Kahl said Britea could call them by their first names," interjected Pearl. Beside her Britea was startled by Pearl's admission.

"Huh? When?" asked Danai.

"When they visited the kitchens. But we need to talk about that fight!" said Britea quickly.

Danai watched her friend and roommate closely; it seemed like Britea didn't want to talk about that encounter.

"I agree with Britea. So Danai, who taught you to fight like that?" asked Pearl.

"My parents," said Danai with a half smile that widened into a full one when Pearl and Britea stared at her in disbelief. Only Henrick and Navos didn't seem surprised.

"I thought Weltonians didn't fight," said Pearl. "People say..." she paused as if unsure how to go on. Danai was sure that whatever she had been about to say was unsavory.

"Yes?"

Pearl shook her head. "Forget them. Their opinions don't matter." She glanced at where the instructors and Mat, now back in his Dyhaeri uniform, were gathered. Danai turned as well and was a bit disturbed to see the Malaquey naval officer seated across from Mat.

"Who's that other guy sitting with them?" Pearl asked suddenly, squinting as she studied the naval officer. "I can't see his face. That looks like a wielder band on his right arm."

Britea looked as well and exchanged a troubled look with Danai.

"Hmmm, looks like Malaquey Naval Intelligence, possible wielder division," said Navos.

"I thought I recognized him. He was standing with the headmaster and the warden when the high priest spoke to us," said Henrick.

"That's Lord Harto Flay!" exclaimed Pearl with a gasp when the officer glanced around him. "Why is he still here?"

"I thought he was just escorting the Dyhaeri. Is he their bodyguard?" asked Henrick.

"After watching Prince Mat fight, do you really think he needs a human bodyguard?" asked Navos.

"Maybe he's here to keep an eye on the Dyhaeri," said Pearl thoughtfully.

"But why?" asked Danai.

Pearl shrugged. "I have no idea, but maybe we can get Britea to ask Kahl about it." Navos and Henrick gave a red-faced Britea a puzzled look while Danai stared at her roommate in shock, obviously realizing Britea had told Pearl about knowing Kahl.

"Why would Prince Kahl talk to Britea?" asked Henrick in a puzzled tone.

"Ten more minutes to finish lunch!" yelled an instructor.

"Less talking, more eating," said Danai, sharing a silent glance with Britea. They had a lot to talk about later.

#

Danai waited until class was over before cornering Britea on the way to the change rooms.

"You told her?!"

Britea flinched. Danai cursed inwardly and laid a gentle hand on her friend's shoulder. "I'm sorry," started Britea haltingly, but then the words came out in a rush. "I just...well, we were in the kitchen when Kahl and Mat showed up. He asked to talk to me, and Pearl was there. Afterwards, Pearl wanted to know how I knew him and then...and then I told her everything."

Danai closed her eyes briefly.

"Please don't be mad. I don't think Pearl would betray me—"

"You don't know that!" Danai took a breath and forced herself to be calm. "I'm sorry too for being so upset. I just don't want you getting hurt. They tried that with the duel. Just because Pearl is acting different now..." she paused, searching for the right words. "Please be careful what you tell anyone, even me."

From Britea's expression, Danai saw those last two words shocked the younger novice.

"But you're my friend. You would never hurt me."

Danai sighed. "No, I would never harm you. But in this school, on your Year of Discovery, and especially wherever you end up working, you always need to watch your back. I won't always be there, or I may be compromised. That's why I'm telling you this." Then she hugged Britea for a long moment. Finally, they separated.

"Come on, let's get ready for our next classes."

#

Britea tried to control her dread. This was her first day in the third year wielding class, and Pearl had been telling her about Instructor Charl Melvin as they hurried to class. The instructor sounded like a harsh man.

"Just wield as he says and keep your head down, and you'll be fine. Even Lianne behaves in his class most of the time. He certainly doesn't take lip from anyone," warned Pearl.

The noble girl took a deep breath as if also trying to calm her nerves. "You ready?"

Britea wanted to say no, but she didn't have a choice. "Yes, I'm ready."

Pearl opened the door and both girls walked in. The instructor was not yet there, but the class was full, and everyone was talking loudly. It took a few moments before the students realized there was a newcomer. Everyone turned to stare as the conversations died down.

"So, when two walking, talking pieces of trash come into class, what do we do?" asked Lianne loudly.

"Shut up, Lianne," someone yelled to Britea and Pearl's amazement. Lianne turned to glare at Henrick. The wielder ignored her look of outrage and motioned to Britea and Pearl to sit by him.

Both girls complied as Lianne got over her surprise and spoke again.

"Anyone who associates with Britea and Pearl is also trash!" Henrick turned as if to retort, but Pearl lay a gentle hand on his arm.

"Let her talk. This is Instructor Melvin's class." Henrick glared at the smug Lianne and her small group of friends, then turned back to Pearl and reluctantly nodded.

Britea was still too scared to be angry. She was trying to recall her wielding forms. She had not forgotten them, but she had no idea what to expect in this class.

"Thanks anyway," said Pearl to Henrick with a warm smile.

Just then, the door swung open with tremendous force as if hit by a blast of air, and in strode Instructor Charl Melvin. The class stood immediately.

"Good afternoon, Instructor Melvin."

The instructor picked up his clipboard. "Good day, class. Now sit," he replied gruffly. He began to call out names without looking at the class, and one by one they answered roll call. Then he got to the end of the list and paused. "Novice Pearl Ceres, stand!" With a resigned look on her face, Pearl rose.

"Novice Britea D'Tranell, stand!" Britea was already moving.

Instructor Melvin slammed the clipboard on the table and glared at the two novices for a long moment.

"To me, it is a travesty you are both still here in the presence of serious students when you should have been expelled for the disgrace you brought to our hallowed halls. Make no mistake, this class is no picnic. I will make you work twice as hard and twice as long as the others. No free passes shall be given to ungrateful brats such as yourselves. Do you have anything to say for yourselves!?"

"No, sir!" shouted both Pearl and Britea. Instructor Melvin reared back as if appalled by their response. Some students even dared to laugh.

Britea felt her heart sink and was sure the instructor would take offense at being made a fool of.

"Hmm, at least you're not deaf or mute. Now, let's see what Novice D'Tranell is made of. Step forward," he said, more calmly now. Britea stared at him, puzzled by his abrupt change in manner.

"Move!" whispered Pearl urgently, and Britea jumped to comply.

"Start with a tier-four wield and work your way down to the first tier."

Britea raised her hands and then stopped; something was missing. In the junior class, there were always cauldrons filled with water or earth or fire. But there were none in this class.

"Well, get on with it!" ordered the instructor harshly. Britea heard a few students snicker. She glanced frantically at Pearl who motioned with her head at the front left corner of the class. Britea caught on and saw a small tap over a sink. She ran to it and turned it on.

As the water began to flow, she quickly wielded four different shapes, flattened them as Instructor Shelley had taught her, and then laid each thin shield over each other while rotating the shields. Tier four was really just creating layered shields. One could shield with tier-one forms for longer periods, but though one could only hold it for a short while, a tier-four shield was a lot stronger. That was why Britea had chosen to use a tier-one shield for the duel.

"Tier three."

Britea turned off the tap with one hand while keeping the four layered shapes in the air. Then she merged the shapes into one big globe of water for a moment before separating them into three shapes—a circle, triangle, and square—all the while moving them in opposite directions. Britea heard startled murmurs from the observing students, but she paid them no need.

This felt so light and easy compared to tier four. She soon found herself smiling.

Instructor Shelley had kept her practicing mostly tiers one and two in the junior class, with the occasional tier three and four during their one-to-one teaching, but Britea had not forgotten what Kahl had taught her.

"Tier two and then one." She effortlessly merged the three forms into a sphere and then split it into two revolving shapes before merging them for the last time into one ball of water.

She looked at Instructor Melvin, who seemed bored. "Drop the wield."

Britea levitated the ball of water to the sink and gently let it collapse into the basin without spilling a drop on the floor.

Instructor Melvin turned back to his clip board. "Return to your seat."

Britea gave Pearl a look of gratitude. Pearl smiled back at her.

Once both girls were seated, the instructor threw the clipboard onto his table where it landed with a clang.

"So, you can wield and create shields. That means nothing if all you can do is make pretty shapes and engage in stupid duels."

Great, he hates me, thought Britea with a sinking feeling.

Instructor Melvin fixed his baleful look on Pearl and Britea. "In this class, we will learn discipline. Disobey me and you will both be expelled faster than you can blink."

Britea heard Lianne laugh softly and knew the female noble was plotting something already.

The instructor turned to the rest of the class. "Now as for you lot—" He was cut short when someone knocked loudly on the door.

The irritated instructor glared at the offending noise while the students exchanged worried glances, wondering who was suicidal enough to disturb this particular instructor while he was teaching.

He marched to the door and yanked it open. Britea saw his expression darken even more. Instructor Melvin spent a long moment staring at whoever was outside before finally speaking.

"Ah, you're here," he forced himself to smile, but it ended up resembling a grimace. "Do come in."

He backed away and in came the last three people Britea expected to see.

"Class, we have visitors. Warden Asteros, High Priest Myltan, and Prince Kahl of the Dyhaeri."

Britea felt her jaw drop as the entire class, including her, scrambled to their feet.

Up close, Kahl looked quite handsome in his indigo marine uniform. He looked at each student, a pleasant smile on his face, and then he froze in astonishment when he saw her. His smile grew brighter then.

Britea had to remind herself to listen to what the warden was saying.

"Class, please be seated." It took so long for Britea to register the command that Pearl had to pull Britea down with her.

"Today," continued the warden, "Prince Kahl will join the class as an observer." The warden stressed that point as he glanced at a disgruntled Instructor Melvin. "I don't have to tell you all to be courteous and remember you represent Syla College, and as an extension, all of Malaquey."

"The prince may take a seat at the back of the class since he shall not be partaking," said the instructor abruptly. "That is, if that is agreeable to you both." The high priest looked at Kahl and nodded before saying, "We'll meet later at supper."

The younger Dyhaeri nodded respectfully before going to take an empty seat close to the window. Britea joined everyone in staring at him.

Never in her wildest dreams would she have thought to be this close to him and yet so far away. She turned back to the front before he noticed her looking. By then, the high priest and the warden had left the class.

"All right, class. You, you, you, and you, prepare the cauldrons." The instructor snapped his fingers at four students, who scrambled to their feet and ran to the tall, wide cupboard beside the blackboard. After opening the cupboard doors, they retrieved four sizable, transparent cauldrons identical to the ones in the junior class. The four chosen students then went on to pull out a few more necessary items. One emptied a bag of soil into a cauldron, and a second student emptied a larger bag of wood chips into another cauldron before striking two flint rocks against each other. Sparks flew into the cauldron, igniting the wood chips.

Britea frowned. That had happened quickly. Maybe the wood chips had been soaked in a fire accelerant.

Meanwhile, a third student turned on the same tap Britea had used earlier and began a tier-one wield, guiding the flow of water into the empty cauldron until it was half full. The fourth and last chosen student quickly cleaned the final cauldron, which was to represent air.

Britea found herself wondering why the cauldrons had not been prepared before class started. She wanted to ask Pearl, but the instructor was already talking.

"Today, in the presence of our esteemed observer…" he said gruffy while inclining his head in Kahl's direction. Britea joined the rest of the class and looked back at the young Dyhaeri. To her surprise, he had unrolled a blank parchment and had a pencil poised, ready to take notes.

Shran would approve , thought Britea with a smile.

"…we shall be learning shielding, which one of you got an unauthorized head start on," Instructor Melvin glared at Britea.

She gulped in fear and tried to disappear into her seat as the rest of the class stared at her.

"There is a reason we withhold this knowledge until your fourth year of training. That reason is that by the time you reach your fourth year, we hope you would have learned some discipline. Novice Tomee, you're up!" Britea watched as a pale student in the middle of the class nervously stood. As he walked to the front of the class, Britea noticed he had water-blue markings on the cowl of his uniform.

"Tier-three wield right now."

The boy complied and soon had three different shapes in the air.

"Layer them like Novice D'Tranell did."

Tomee soon thinned the shapes and overlapped them. Instructor Melvin released a tier-one blast of air that broke the shields, splashing the water on the male novice.

"Pathetic," said the instructor. "Return to your seat. Novice Celene, you're next!"

Britea was speechless with shock as the shaken male student returned to his chair and another scared female novice took his place. Fire-red lines adorned her cowl.

"Tier-three wield and shield!" The girl fumbled as she wielded the three shapes slightly slower than Novice Tomee had.

Instructor Melvin extinguished her shapes with a loud blast of tier-one air that pushed the novice back and had her coughing as smoke surrounded her.

"Return to your seat! I don't have all day! Novice Walton, you're next!"

Britea stole a glance backwards when the instructor was distracted, and she saw a horrified look on Kahl's face. He was clearly appalled by the method of teaching. His expression hardened as he kept glaring at their instructor.

Britea glanced back to see if Instructor Melvin had noticed, but he had already blasted through Novice Celene's tier-three earth shield, and the poor girl had dashed to the sink to rinse the sand out of her eyes.

"May I be next?" suddenly asked Kahl. Startled murmurs arose among the students as Britea exchanged a horrified look with Pearl.

"Oh no, he didn't just do that," whispered Pearl. Britea chanced a look behind her, and Kahl was already on his feet, his parchment and pencil forgotten on the desk before him.

Britea turned back and Instructor Melvin seemed pleased at the subtle challenge.

"Of course. I would love to test your shields."

No, this can't be happening! thought Britea with dismay when she saw the smug smile on the instructor's face. *He'll gladly hurt Kahl.* She wanted to stand, but Pearl had a firm grip on her arm.

"What are you doing?" hissed Pearl.

"He'll try and harm Kahl!"

"Kahl helped you with the sea serpents and the raiders, right? Instructor Melvin is small fry compared to those snakes. Let your prince take care of this on his own." Those whispered words convinced Britea to stay in her seat.

Yet her heart thumped in her chest as she watched Kahl make his way casually to the front of the class. Instructor Melvin had assumed a confrontational stance, and Britea had a sudden flashback to her own recent duel. It still made her feel ill.

Kahl took a position on the far left of the class and faced the instructor. "Tier-three shields as usual?"

"Whenever you're ready, Dyhaeri," said the instructor with a barely concealed sneer.

Kahl effortlessly wielded three different water shapes, then split them into several smaller versions of those same shapes and layered them over each other to form a full-body shield.

"Just like yours," said Pearl in an astonished whisper, sending Britea a quizzical look.

"No, I used a tier-one shield. Instructor Shelley taught me how. Kahl's way is too complicated," whispered back Britea, her panic receding a bit.

Before the girls could say anything more, Instructor Melvin attacked Kahl's shield with a forceful tier-three wield of three different shapes.

Britea almost shouted at the unfairness of it all; the instructor had used tier-one attacks on the other students, but he had switched to a tier three just for Kahl! She glanced at Kahl, and his overlapping tier-three shield was still intact.

A quick glance back at Instructor Melvin revealed a stunned expression when he realized Kahl was still standing. The young Dyhaeri smiled pleasantly at him.

"Would you like to try again, sir?"

Instructor Melvin growled and began to rain tier-three forms down on Kahl's water shield in quick succession. The class watched silently as the Dyhaeri's tier-three shield withstood blow after blow.

To Britea, it felt like hours had passed before the instructor finally started tiring, yet Kahl looked as if he was simply standing there doing nothing…apart from holding up a complex tier-three water shield.

Eventually, the instructor stopped his attack, and the whole class could hear Instructor Melvin wheezing as if he was out of breath. Kahl casually lowered his shield.

"Would you like to take a break, sir?"

The livid instructor's face reddened, but he was too tired to reply. It took several tries before he could speak.

"Rest…for…now."

"As you wish, instructor," said Kahl as he returned the water to the cauldron and strode back to his seat, the entire class staring at him in amazement. He sat down and smiled politely at the stunned students around him. Britea thought he had a twinkle in his eye.

Instructor Melvin, meanwhile, seemed way too tired to issue any more instructions.

"We…will…read…chapter twenty… of *The Fundamental Structure of Wielding*. You…" he wearily pointed to another wary student. "…read aloud." Britea kept her gaze on the instructor as he collapsed into his chair while the students tried not to stare.

"Chapter twenty: 'Ways to Improve Endurance for Prolonged Wielding.'"

Britea and Pearl exchanged an amused smile over their books. What an appropriate topic. They had almost finished the chapter when the bell rang for the end of the class.

#

"You did what?!" Mat yelled before Kahl had finished sharing his first day in the senior wielder class.

"I didn't harm him!"

Mat, Kahl, and the high priest had met for dinner in the small private dining hall. Once they had started eating, the high priest had asked them to debrief. Mat had gone first, and Kahl had been startled to discover that Mat had sparred with Danai Riverun *before* knowing who she was.

Oddly enough, the high priest had not been surprised, but before Kahl could ask him about that, it had been his turn to relay his own experience, and Mat wasn't happy with him.

"Ponder for once, cousin! You humiliated Instructor Melvin in front of the students he was terrorizing! What makes you think he won't take out his anger on them when we're gone?!"

Now that made Kahl pause.

"You're just figuring that out now?!" Mat was sounding angrier by the second.

"That's enough," said the high priest softly, and both Dyhaeri stared at him. He had been watching them calmly as if letting them vent.

"Today was our first day of observation and from your accounts, I believe it went rather well."

Mat blinked. "Sir, you're saying this was…good?"

The high priest smiled. "It could have been a whole lot worse, though I admit challenging the instructor to a duel was not entirely appropriate, Kahl."

Mat gave his young cousin an irritated look.

"I didn't attack him." But that excuse sounded feeble even to Kahl now.

"Thank the Sea Mother for that, or we'd be having an entirely different conversation," said the high priest as he sipped his fruit tea. "I do admit his teaching method seems a bit too…unconventional for my taste, but this is why we're here." He glanced at Mat. "To observe and learn. Tomorrow, you two will switch classes."

"I like the sparring class," said Mat a little too quickly.

Kahl gave him an odd look. "Why?"

"I want to know if the rest of the class fights like Danai."

Kahl raised an eyebrow. "You intend to spar with all the students in combat and defense?"

Even the high priest chuckled at the thought.

Mat gave his cousin a forbearing look. "Of course not. Only some of them. I also want to see how they incorporate wielding in their physical combat."

"You'll have time for that later. Tomorrow, you will switch places. I want the instructors on their toes, because right now, they're determined to show us their best sides. Besides, Britea is also in combat and defense," said the high priest. That made Kahl sit up and smile happily.

Mat rolled his eyes. "Fine." Then his expression changed. "Watch out for Harto. I swear that human dislikes Dyhaeri."

"Or one particular Dyhaeri," added Kahl cheekily.

"Ha ha," said Mat with a glower while the high priest continued his meal, an amused expression on his face.

#

"Are they ready?" asked Queen Kallesa.

"Yes, Your Highness," said Minister Nathan Lensworth as he walked beside the monarch towards the heavily guarded, covered shipyards. Behind them trailed at least twelve Specialists who strode silently as ghosts.

They traversed in the dark of night, a time for nefarious and secret deeds.

Once they reached their final destination, Nathan stared at the two huge, mounted behemoths that had been completed that afternoon. Never before had such feats of engineering been accomplished…that he knew of. He finally brought his gaze down to the thousands of gathered indentured workers who had been manacled to each other for this moment. Many of them, some of whom had been turned in by friends or relatives because they whispered something against the queen, had been classified as enemies of the state and sentenced to imprisonment. The rest had been randomly nabbed from the streets when more workers were need, and a few were even from Malaquey, victims of raids on small border villages.

There had been about fifteen hundred workers at the beginning of the project months ago, but at least a third of them had died on site. None of the workers had been allowed to leave the dockyards, and their quarters were cramped and filthy, most likely leading to the sickness that ended up killing many of them. He glanced at the queen, who smiled as she stared at the completed work.

Of course she didn't care, as long as the work was done.

Nathan felt a sliver of pity for the exhausted, emaciated workers. He knew what was to come.

Maybe it was a mercy.

"Good work," said the queen finally. Standing nearby between two of her Specialists was Master Engineer Tresh Stamets. His shoulders dropped with relief. The poor man had been a ball of nerves since this project had begun. He too had not been allowed to leave the shipyards until the work was completed.

"They will function as expected, yes?" asked the queen softly.

Engineer Stamets nodded hastily. "Yes, Your Highness. However, a test run would be in order—"

"That will not be needed if all goes according to plan," said Queen Kallesa as she gazed at her new toys. She snapped her fingers, and the silent guard behind her marched forward.

"Take care of the workers."

The wielders bowed deeply to her and strode to the workers as Nathan went to stand with the master engineer. The two guards with the engineer joined the other silent wielders.

"What's going on…"

"Just keep silent and watch," whispered Nathan, resigned.

The manacled, exhausted workers watched the wielders approach with dull eyes. That expression changed when the first of them was set on fire by a wielder. The body dropped to the floor and the screaming began. There was nowhere to run with the workers chained to each other. The silent wielders continued the executions, lighting people on fire; wielding the blood in their bodies so they bled from their eyes, ears and mouth; or wielding the air from their lungs. Nathan forced himself to watch as the master engineer vomited until all he could do was retch. The minister of intelligence took no joy in the spectacle and knew nightmares awaited him.

As for the queen, she simply strode beside her new ships, caressing the hull and talking to herself excitedly as the carnage continued behind her.

CHAPTER 20

"He didn't try to break my shields."

Pearl looked up from the large soapy saucepan she was trying to rinse. "Say what?"

Britea turned to her, her hands and forearms still covered in soap. She had been scrubbing a pot twice her size. It was still early morning, and the chef had assigned them to washing several crusted pots and pans. Surprisingly, Pearl had taken to this punishment faster than the others. Britea noticed she used an awful lot of soap though.

"I'm just wondering why Instructor Melvin didn't try to break my shield when he made me wield."

Pearl snorted. "He was probably saving that humiliation for later. I've noticed a pattern ever since I joined his class. First off, he never praises anyone, then he picks the weakest to humiliate them after scaring the living daylights out of the rest of us, and finally he goes after the stronger wielders, who are at that point, too scared to wield properly."

"That's horrible," gasped Britea. "Why is he allowed to teach like that?"

Pearl shrugged. "Damned if I know why he gets away with it. Maybe because we actually learn something from his classes? As I said, I have no idea."

A disturbed Britea went back to scrubbing the huge pot before her. Instructor Melvin's way of teaching was worlds away from Instructor Shelley's. It made her miss the junior wielding class. But the juniors too had Instructor Melvin's brash way of teaching to look forward to. She could not help but feel it would be detrimental in the long run. She had wanted to discuss it with Danai last night, but Britea had been too tired to do so after working in the kitchen twice that day. This punishment was beginning to take its toll.

"I don't like him," said Britea.

Pearl chuckled. "Guess what? No one does. I hear he even annoys his fellow instructors. And now we can add a certain Dyhaeri prince to that list."

Britea sighed and turned as Pearl rinsed her saucepan and gleefully attacked another huge pan with a wide bar of soap. Pearl looked up and her smile dimmed at the worried expression on Britea's face.

"What? Did I say something wrong?"

Britea shook her head. "No, no. I'm just worried about Kahl. Did you see Instructor Melvin's face at the end of that…whatever that was? He looked like he wanted to murder Kahl!"

Pearl shook her head. "I wouldn't worry about it, after seeing how well Kahl wielded and how skilled Mat is in armed combat, it's clear they can take care of themselves."

Britea tried to take reassurance in Pearl's words, but doubt still lingered in the back of her mind.

"Hurry up if you two wish to make it in time for breakfast!" suddenly yelled the diminutive chef who had again appeared out of thin air.

"Yes, chef!" shouted the two novices as they picked up their pace.

#

Danai tried not to fret as she hurried to the weapon's master's office. She had received a note to appear at his office in the morning before her first class. So she wouldn't be late, she had rushed breakfast and had to miss out on the latest gossip.

Apparently, according to whatever version one heard, Prince Kahl had been challenged by Instructor Melvin or the other way around, and the instructor had gotten his behind handed to him. Danai had wanted to ask Britea about it, but the poor girl had been too tired the night before.

Anyway, she could always catch Britea later in combat and defense class. Danai reached her destination and knocked on the aged storm-grey wooden door, then waited until she heard an invitation before entering.

"Good morning, Weapons Master Caren. You wanted to see me?" asked Danai after stepping into the spacious office with its plain dirt-defying white carpet and weapon-adorned dove-grey walls. In the center stood an ancient wooden desk stained a deep navy blue. The weapons master was standing with Instructor Talios in front of the desk.

"Thank you for coming, and promptly," said the weapons master.

Danai tried to keep her face neutral while wondering if she had gotten into trouble for something, maybe something she may have done to Prince Mat.

As if I could hurt him.

"Is all well, Master Caren and Instructor Talios?"

The senior instructors shared a look, then the weapons master spoke.

"You're not in trouble, Danai." He smiled wryly when Danai failed to hide her relief, but then his expression turned serious.

"The Wielder Trials are in four weeks..."

Danai's heart sank. *By the Sea Mother, not this again!*

Weapons Master Caren was still speaking. "Our school would stand a better chance of winning if you joined the reserve team."

"By the Lords, we sure needed you last time," said Instructor Talios wearily.

"We're extremely grateful you've been helping the contestants prepare, but with you as back up, we might be able to beat the military colleges."

Danai stared at them in dismay. Out of all the instructors, she respected these two the most, which was why she hated disappointing them.

"I'm really sorry, but I cannot compete."

The two instructors exchanged a look, and even though she realized they had expected this, she still felt the need to explain even if she could not give them the *real* reason. The last thing she wanted to do was draw attention to the true strength of her wielding.

"I'm Weltonian and I'm grateful to this school for its teaching, but I don't agree with the current spirit of the Wielder Trial games. "*Well, at least that part was true.*

"Why is that?" asked Instructor Talios gently.

Danai glanced down for a moment.

"Feel free to speak, Danai," encouraged the weapons master.

"It used to be a game of unity and bonding, but now it's simply a game of intimidation and humiliation. We lose every time, and the instructors from the naval and army wielder colleges point at us and tell their students we're the rejects, that we're the joke of the wielding society. I'm not going to take part in that."

The two instructors shared another silent look again.

"I doubt Prince Mat feels that way about us," said the weapons master.

"Excuse me, but what does he have to do with this?" asked Danai, puzzled. *And what do you know of how a Dyhaeri views us?*

"Oh, quite a lot. We suspect they'll be here until the Trials commence. I'm thinking of asking him and his cousin to help us prepare for the Trials."

Danai's jaw dropped. For a long moment she was speechless. "Is...is that allowed, sir?"

"There's nothing in the rule book against it, which we know well since we had to adjust the competition after Namira stopped sending teams four decades ago," said Master Caren gravely.

"If you're planning to ask them, why talk to me?"

"He may agree, and we'll need someone to guide him through the rules of the Trials." Both instructors looked at her expectantly.

Oh no, they can't mean…

"Master Caren and Instructor Talios, I am honored by the request, but surely you could pick Navos. He dreams about the Wielder Trials and is eager to be part of them. He knows everything about the games…"

"But he wouldn't be as objective as you would be," countered Instructor Talios. "And Prince Mat respects you, especially after you fought him to a draw."

Danai found part of her looking forward to working with Mat while the other half wanted to run away screaming.

"Surely one of the instructors…" her voice trailed off when Master Caren shook his head.

"Your Weltonian heritage gives you a distinct advantage. Your people tend to have a better, closer relationship with the Dyhaeri then the rest of us humans, plus, I also hope to avoid a duel between him and the Malaquey officer."

Both Danai and Instructor Talios shot Master Caren a startled look. While this was news to Danai, she suspected the female instructor was appalled that a novice was being told about the animosity between Harto and Mat.

"Trust me, that would not be in the best interest of the college or the diplomatic relationship between the Dyhaeri and Malaquey," continued Master Caren.

Danai had to reluctantly agree with the latter statement. "I don't want to fight in the Trials."

"Then don't," said Instructor Talios. Apparently, she had recovered from her surprise. "We can list you as an observer and strategist or assistant coach."

Danai frowned. "Strategist? I'd still be part of the combat team, wouldn't I?"

The weapons master smiled. "Not really. If all goes well, we may also add Prince Mat and Prince Kahl to the team as a strategists or coaches, and then we'll have a team of coaches."

Danai blinked before replying.

"Have you discussed this with the high priest and the princes?"

"We will shortly. Please keep the Dyhaeri's possible involvement in the Trials to yourself as you think about your decision. You're dismissed," said Instructor Talios.

Danai stared at them for a moment. "Yes, Weapons Master Caren and Instructor Talios." She turned and darted out of the office.

She had a lot to think about as she made her way to her first class, which was biology. The sparring match the day before was still at the back of her mind too. Truth be told, it had been enjoyable even though she hadn't won. But what worried her the most was how the Dyhaeri had reacted when she had told him who her parents were.

He knew them, that was for sure. But in what context? This made her think of how evasive her parents had been when she had last seen them. They were scared.

But of what?

As she neared her class, she saw her fellow students chatting idly as they walked in and took their seats. Lexia waved at her. Danai smiled and sat down beside her friend.

"Where were you?"

"I had a summons from Master Caren."

Lexia gave her a worried look. "What's happened?"

"Nothing. He just wanted to talk about the upcoming Trials…and if I would consider joining."

Lexia groaned. "Not you too!"

"I haven't said yes yet!"

"But you will, and it's sad that they keep repeatedly firing up and letting down Navos about the Trials before they turn around and pick you at the last moment."

Danai felt guilty about that. Navos had wanted to be part of the Trials ever since he had arrived at the college, but he had yet to be picked. He had thought this would be his year, but the final selections were almost complete. Danai suspected the instructors wouldn't have approached her again if not for the sparring match with a certain Dyhaeri.

"Good morning, class," said Instructor Yanny Solars. Fire-red lines on his black cowl pronounced him a fire wielder.

The class stood and kept standing as High Priest Myltan, sporting a robin's-egg blue long-sleeved shirt and flowing black pants, entered the class a few steps behind the instructor.

"Good morning, Instructor Solars. Good morning, High Priest Myltan," chorused the class. Danai was impressed at how fast her classmates had recovered.

"Be seated, everyone," said the instructor as he and the high priest remained on their feet. The instructor waited until he had their collective attention.

"Today, the high priest will be joining us for our lesson on the diverse flora and fauna of the Heldiar Sea. We'll make it an informal question-and-answer session." Danai glanced at the high priest. He didn't look surprised, so maybe this had been discussed beforehand. "Please take notes. There may or may not be a test in the near future." There was a flurry of activity as novices got notebooks out and poised with their pencils to take notes.

"I'll go first," said the instructor as he rubbed his hands in barely suppressed glee.

The high priest nodded. "Please do."

"The Alkynaia. How long have they existed in the Heldiar Sea?"

"Before I answer, what do your books say?" asked the high priest in turn.

"Roughly three thousand years, give or take a few centuries."

High Priest Myltan's smile was sad. "Multiply that by ten and add a few more millenia to that."

Instructor Solars gaped as him and Danai noticed her fellow classmates were also stunned. She already knew, though, from the verbal history handed down by the Weltonians that what was written in the school library about the history of this continent and the surrounding waters was wholly inaccurate.

But who was she, a Weltonian—and novice to boot—to correct them?

"You have proof of this?" asked an intrigued Instructor Solars.

"Fossils that date back tens thousands of years and the tales of our ancestors lend credence to the duration of the Alkynaia existence," explained the high priest politely.

Instructor Solars looked eager to ask more questions but seemed to recall that his students were yet to ask their own.

"Who would like to go next?"

Lexia raised her hand.

"Yes, Novice Detran?"

"Sir, how fast do Alkynaia travel?"

Danai gave her friend a puzzled look.

"That depends on the purpose," began the high priest. "If it is to stalk prey, they can take their time and chase their intended food for days on end."

"Why?" asked another student, raising his hand.

"It's hard to say why. Perhaps they enjoy the chase, but there have also been instances when they have attacked suddenly and without warning." He glanced at Lexia. "As to your question, they can also travel quite fast…" he paused and turned to stare at Danai before continuing. "Some of us have seen them disappear from one spot and instantaneously appear in another several miles away."

Instructor Solars looked skeptical. "You're referring to instant travel? Isn't that just a sea legend?"

The high priest shrugged. "As I said, some have seen this, though I have not."

Danai felt a bit disturbed by the high priest's demeanor. It seemed as if he was trying to tell her something.

"Can Dyhaeri have children with humans?" blurted out one of the students at the back of the class. The instructor shot a glare at the unfortunate student while many of the students failed to control their laughter.

The high priest seemed mildly surprised. "What a curious question."

"And a thoughtless one too," said Instructor Solars angrily. "I apologize on behalf of my students, sir. The next one who asks a stupid question gets an automatic fail in that test you're all going to take soon."

The laughter died and most of the students turned irate looks on the student who had put them in this predicament.

"Now then," said Instructor Solars when he saw the class had gotten the message. "I'll ask two questions and the rest of you will follow."

"How do Dyhaeri breathe under water?"

Danai held her breath as she looked at the high priest. She was relieved he didn't seem upset about the previous question. But he had not answered it either.

"Wielding." The high priest snapped his fingers and a spark leapt from his fingers and morphed into a small ball of fire. Instructor Solars stared at the senior Dyhaeri while the rest of the class *oohed* and *aahed* . Danai bet they had never seen such wielding before. But she had, from the Weltonians who taught her as a child.

"A simple tier-one wield is what I have in my hand right now," continued the high priest to the captivated audience as he put his left hand above the fiery globe. "One starts off small and gradually increases the size of the fireball while keeping its wall very, very thin." He flexed the fingers of his left hand and began to wield-pull the top of the globe. This made the ball of flames bigger as the red hue of the flames faded.

"Then you cool it down until you get a lukewarm or slightly cool flame and keep expanding this ball until you have one large enough to encompass you. Remember, it has to contain enough air for you to breathe."

No one made a sound.

"However, I've had lots of practice, so I can do that quickly." He outstretched his hands in a quick motion and then flung the barely visible reddish globe of warm air around his body. Everyone gasped when he started levitating several feet above the floor. Then someone started clapping and the whole class joined in. Even the instructor was clapping.

Only Danai did not clap. She struggled to keep her face neutral as Lexia clapped excitedly beside her. Wielding to breathe under water was a secret art among the Dyhaeri. Danai had asked her parents once how it was that the Weltonians knew this particular wielding skill, and they always brushed off her questions with the same answer: "It was handed down to us by our ancestors."

That answer had frustrated her even more as she had gotten older, so now she was utterly puzzled right now about why the high priest was so eager to tell them about certain Dyhaeri wielding lessons she had thought were forbidden to the landlocked humans.

Why now and why like this?

The high priest nodded and slowly came down. He twisted his right hand, pulling the globe of air off his body and shrinking it down to a small ball of fire innocently levitating above his right palm.

"Do not try this at home, novices. As I said, one needs teaching and years of practice in a safe environment to pull this off."

Several students raised their hands. Instructor Solars grinned and pointed at a student.

"I'm Novice Mel," said a student excitedly. "Water is my element, so can I do that too?"

The high priest and the human instructor exchanged an amused look.

"Only with permission from your wielding instructor, who will probably ask the high priest not to do that again," replied Instructor Solars with a smile. The class groaned in dismay.

The instructor simply chuckled at their dismay. "Next question!"

#

"Welcome to third year dancing and etiquette, Prince Mat!" announced the female instructor loudly.

Mat hid a wince and was tempted to cover his ears. The collective curious gaze of the gathered female students was just as disturbing as the instructor's grating voice.

"I am Instructor Helene Droye! Are you familiar with this class, Your Highness?"

"No, I'm not, and please, just call me Mat."

The instructor was taken aback by the informal address but smiled after a moment. "Splendid!" she said with a delighted squeal before turning to address the students in that same shrill tone.

Mat was beginning to think the woman thought he was deaf. A quick glance at Harto showed the Malaquey officer was just as uncomfortable.

Good. He had been quite irritated when he and the others had found Harto waiting in the corridor outside their private dining rooms. That irritation had turned to anger when the Malaquey officer had stated he would be accompanying Mat to his classes today. Mat looked at Harto again now and was a bit puzzled to see the human officer studying the students with a worried expression.

Mat frowned at that. *Why was he studying the females so intently?* He followed the direction of his gaze and realized who was in this class.

Novice Britea D'Tranell and her friend, Pearl. Britea looked nervous, and Pearl was exchanging glares with a familiar dark-haired human girl.

Another thought entered his mind. "Instructor Droye, I've noticed there are only girls in this class. Where are the boys?"

Some of the students giggled as if they found his words amusing. Mat resisted rolling his eyes.

"Oh, you shall be attending that tomorrow your high—I mean, Mat. We separate the boys and girls for this class as the learning requirements differ."

Mat tilted his head. "In what way?"

"We ladies are bound for the court, and we must demonstrate the proper decorum, which is vastly different from the boys," said the girl who had been staring daggers at Britea's friend earlier.

"And you are?" asked Mat.

"Lady Lianne Arkei," offered Instructor Droye with a huge smile and an affectionate pat on Lianne's right shoulder.

"She is the best student in this class and is absolutely right about the difference in curriculum. The boys learn about diplomacy and the fine art of politics. It's vastly different than what the girls need to learn."

"So, apart from decorum, what else are the girls learning?" asked Mat curiously.

"How to dine, run a household, and dance." Mat blinked and stared at the female instructor for a long moment before turning to face Harto to determine the officer's reaction.

Harto was a bit surprised by the attention. "Can I help with you something?"

"Yes, in fact you can. What is the difference between a human female and human male?"

Harto looked puzzled for a moment before smiling arrogantly. "If you need me to describe the structural differences then we—"

"I'm referring to their minds, Lieutenant Flay," cut in Mat. "What is the difference?"

Harto narrowed his eyes as the entire class and Instructor Droye watched their interaction. "I guess there is no difference when you view it that way. Why?"

Mat studied him for a moment and turned back to address the class and one worried-looking instructor.

"I say this as an observer. I am Dyhaeri and thus don't know much about your culture. However, I find it odd that girls are taught less than boys about diplomacy. Back home, we're all taught the same things to better prepare us for interactions with..." he wanted to say "humans," but instinct warned him not to. "...other cultures and in life in general. So, my question is this: why would you hamstring half your students based on their gender?"

Silence greeted his words. Most of the students looked confused, but a few students, including Britea, had thoughtful expressions on their faces that indicated they agreed with him, or were at least open to considering his point of view. Mat still found the situation mystifying. The combat and defense class was somewhat similar to Dyhaeri society, but even then, he had seen concerning aspects. But the discrepancy with this class was baffling.

Instructor Droye tried to smile as she cleared her throat. "We...we do things differently here."

"I see," said Mat with a neutral expression. This assignment was getting confusing. Beside him, Harto kept quiet.

"If you gentlemen would like to take a step back, we shall begin pairing the students."

Mat said nothing as he and Harto and took two steps back.

"You don't seem to mind ruffling feathers, do you?" whispered Harto.

For a moment, Mat was tempted to ignore him. "As I said, I'm here to observe."

Harto looked at him for long time. "So you say." Mat turned to face him and their eyes locked.

"Gentlemen?" called Instructor Droye in a voice so loud it forced them to break the deadlock.

"We're about to start."

"Please carry on, Instructor Droye," said Mat with a polite smile.

#

Lieutenant Commander Peras Nell waited until his nephew had entered the unmarked stationary coach before he reached over and shut the door. The coach was parked in the courtyard of Syla College, surrounded by ten mounted Malaquey Naval Intelligence officers who would ensure no one eavesdropped.

"So, how were your first days observing the Dyhaeri?" asked Peras.

Harto let out an infuriated sigh. "Frustrating, and to my dismay, I have realized I cannot do it alone."

"Why not?"

"The high priest has asked that Mat and Kahl be assigned to different classes while he either observes a class or meets with the instructors. Simply put, I cannot be in three places at once. This debriefing is only possible now because it is currently lunchtime for the college."

"What is the solution?" asked Peras.

"I suggested to the headmaster that he allow two more officers to assist me and he refused."

There was silence for a moment. "Hmm," mused Peras.

Harto raised an eyebrow. "You expected this?"

Pears sighed. "You saw how upset Headmaster Clayre was when the king told him the Dyhaeri were coming to inspect Syla College. He had no say in the matter, so put yourself in his shoes. How would you feel?"

Harto was forced to agree. The headmaster had no control over what the king wished, but he could still try to dictate who else came to his college.

"We could take this matter to the king," said Peras thoughtfully, but Harto was already shaking his head.

"And risk alienating the instructors and their headmaster because we went over his head? That would only worsen our relationship with them. Plus, the Dyhaeri would see we are not united."

Peras nodded approvingly. "Well done for deducing that. But we don't have a choice. Like you, I agree we need more eyes in that place. I've even tried to get our people hired in the kitchens."

Harto looked up. "We have spies there?"

Peras shook his head. "Unfortunately, no. Apparently Warden Asteros oversees the hiring and has stated they do not need any more staff. I haven't even been able to bribe those who already work there. They're quite unreachable."

"The head chef certainly doesn't like me," said Harto dryly.

Peras tilted his head. "What were you doing in the kitchens?"

"The high priest wanted to speak to the cooks about Dyhaeri dietary requirements, and who did do we happen upon in the kitchens? Britea D'Tranell and a second novice. They were on a punishment detail."

Now Peras was intrigued. "What rule did they break?"

"I'm yet to find out. The instructors aren't overly chatty, especially with me. But give me time, and I'm sure a student with loose lips with give me the full tale."

"Anything else about Britea D'Tranell?"

Something in his uncle's tone made Harto stare at him. "Like."

"What are her classes?"

"I saw her in the third-year etiquette class—"

"And her dorm room?" pressed Peras.

Harto was wondering why his uncle needed this information. "I have no idea."

Peras gave him a withering look. "Well, I attended a ball at Lady Arkei's residence last night, and her daughter Selina told me Britea is still in the junior wielding classes."

Harto tried not to roll his eyes. He could tell his uncle was in a scolding mood.

"A socialite was able to give me more intel about Britea D'Tranell than you, and you're supposed to be an intelligence agent. Maybe I should hire Selina and her sister, Lianne, to do your job for you."

Harto fought to keep his voice polite. "I apologize, uncle. I will strive to do better."

Peras glared at him for a moment. "What news do you have about the skills of Prince Mat and Prince Kahl?"

Harto hid his relief at the change in questioning. "Mat is a good fighter. Staves are his weapon of choice, and Kahl is a skilled wielder."

His uncle narrowed his eyes. "Elaborate."

Harto went on to describe the sparring match between Mat and Danai Riverun. He also told his uncle of Kahl's spat with the senior wielding instructor.

Lieutenant Nell was quiet for a long moment. "I find this situation quite curious and full of one too many coincidences. One, Britea D'Tranell just happens to be have been trained by Kahl on her journey here. Two, Lanead Riverun just happens to transport the Dyhaeri contingent to us, and three, Mat just happens to be spar with Danai Riverun."

Harto nodded reluctantly. "Put it that way, and it does sound suspicious." Then he noticed the pensive countenance on his uncle's face. "What's wrong?"

"There is something about Lanead Riverun that rubs me the wrong way," said Peras. "Each time I spoke with him, he didn't sound or behave like a Weltonian. He's way too proud for starters, and he's certainly not afraid of authority. And don't get me started on his apparently close relationship with the high priest."

Harto nodded.

"By the way, what do you make of the captain's daughter, Danai Riverun?"

Harto hid his discomfort at his uncle's sudden interest in Danai. "I haven't had the chance to speak at length with her. Following the Dyhaeri around all the time takes all my time."

"You need to get close to Danai Riverun and determine the extent of her father's involvement with the Dyhaeri," said Peras.

But she's not the enemy here! "What? How?"

Peras gave him an exasperated look. "You're a young, handsome, rich officer. Two thirds of eligible girls, and even their mothers, literally fling themselves at you at every ball you attend. Ask her out to dinner or buy her something nice. I'm sure you can think of something. Just get the information we need."

Harto felt uneasy. Despite what his uncle thought, he suspected Danai was not easily influenced by the trappings of the wealthy. "Anything else?"

"Keep an eye on Kahl and Britea D'Tranell. Those two seem to be the weak links. And for the sake of us all, please avoid a confrontation with Mat. I really do not want to hear you got into a duel with a diplomat."

I can't promise not to hurt him too badly when I get the chance. "Yes, sir."

"In the meantime, I will certainly get those extra eyes you need."

Harto gave his uncle an alarmed look. "But I thought we had decided not to alienate the instructors."

"I have an idea that might just get us what we need without disturbing the still waters. I'll see you in a week for another debriefing."

Harto knew when he was being dismissed. "Yes, sir."

As he moved to the door, there was a loud knock. He and his uncle shared a look. The other officers knew not to disturb the debriefing unless something important had happened.

"Come in," ordered Lieutenant Commander Nell.

A young officer opened the coach door. "Sir, you wanted to be alerted about anything unusual. An Arkei family coach just pulled up. It's Lady Adria Arkei."

Harto muffled a curse while ignoring the mildly disapproving glare from his uncle.

This mission was about to get a lot more complicated.

CHAPTER 21

"Thus, I believe it would be in the best interest of the college to host a ball by next week, ensuring the most prominent houses with students at this school are invited, of course. This will show the Dyhaeri the influence you have in Malaquey government."

Warden Asteros closed his eyes briefly and quietly asked the Lords of Light and Shadow to give him strength as Lady Adria Arkei finished her spiel.

He had been going over the numerous preparations for the fast-approaching Wielder Trials when he had gotten an urgent message that Lady Arkei was at the school and needed to see him at once. Instantly, he knew it had to do with their new guests. The headmaster had refused to see her, citing important matters to attend to, which was why it had fallen to him to see the esteemed noble lady.

It was days like this when he hated being a moderator. He steepled his hands under his chin and turned his attention on Lady Arkei, who was clearly expecting a favorable answer.

"Lady Arkei, I'm afraid the answer is no."

The noble went still, clearly surprised by his reply.

"May I ask why?" she asked softly, but the warden was not fooled by the smooth façade hiding a razor-sharp mind.

"The Wielder Trials are in four weeks, and the students are also preparing for end of term examinations. This is certainly not the time to hold a ball. Besides, the Dyhaeri are here to observe training practices. Having a ball will give them the impression we take a wielder's education for granted, and I know King Wilhem wants us to put our best foot forward. Nowhere in his letter did he state we were to have parties to accomplish that goal."

Lady Arkei paled, clearly not accustomed to not getting her way, but the warden was not in the mood to care.

"That is indeed unfortunate. I did, however, stress this would improve your patronage if you did so," said Lady Arkei.

"Indeed you did, Lady Arkei. However, as I said, we are following the king's order, and there was no requirement to include what you just suggested. Also, it is not appropriate at this time."

Lady Arkei sat back and stared at the warden, who didn't flinch.

She nodded slowly after what seemed an eternity. "After the Trials and examinations then? Would you be open to a ball as a reward for the students from all three colleges?"

The warden smiled politely at the change in negotiation tactics. "That depends, Lady Arkei, on the other colleges as they may have different policies than Syla College. However, at that time, we may be open to reasonable suggestions."

"Fine," Lady Arkei said, standing abruptly and briskly pulling on her gloves, a display of her displeasure. "Until later, Warden Asteros."

The warden was already on his feet and bowing as Lady Arkei left his office.

He waited until the door had closed before collapsing back into his chair.

The warden suspected he had not seen the last of her, and fully expected other nobles to also suddenly take an interest in Syla College in the next few weeks.

#

Britea looked around the training area as she and Pearl walked through the doors of the outdoor combat and defense class. It was a mite colder today, which made her dread the outdoor training.

"Look!" said an excited Pearl. Britea turned, and to her combined fear and surprise, Kahl was already in the class talking animatedly with Weapons Master Caren. He was also dressed in the school's training uniform, with a blue line on the front and back of his outfit.

"Are they going to keep sparring with us?" whispered Pearl.

"I have no idea, but why are we whispering?" asked Britea in a murmur as well.

"Seemed appropriate," said Pearl with a mischievous smile.

"Let's go change before Instructor Talios yells at us," said Britea.

"Hey, Britea!" called someone loudly behind her, which made Kahl turn in her direction as she tried to acknowledge the caller.

A tall boy with walnut hair and almond-shaped hazel eyes was looking at her. His tunic displayed earth-brown lines on the cowl.

"Yes, and you are?"

"Dariuz Solarn. You're Weltonian right? Like Danai Riverun?"

Britea blinked.

"Whatever gave you that idea?" demanded Pearl confrontationally. "She's from a village in Weldaros, so she's not Weltonian!"

Part of Britea wanted to mention her Weltonian ancestors, but she realized this was neither the time nor place for an argument. "What do you want Dariuz? We're about to start class."

Dariuz held up both hands. "I meant no offense. I was hoping you could put in a word with Danai for me."

Now both Britea and Pearl stared at him.

"Danai is right over there," said Britea. "You can speak to her."

Dariuz seemed a bit uncomfortable. "Um...I don't know her very well. I just need you to tell her I really need to speak to Prince Mat or Prince Kahl."

"Hey, she's not your messenger," protested an annoyed Pearl before Britea could speak.

"Is everything all right?" asked a familiar voice.

Britea froze. The she forced herself to turn and face Kahl.

#

Kahl had made sure to arrive to this class early, before the students arrived. Because he had been at the school for only two days, he was still trying to memorize the layout, so he had known it would take him longer than it should to get there. On his arrival at the outdoor class, he had been greeted warmly by Weapons Master Caren and his instructors.

Based on what he had heard about Mat's experience, he had asked if he could also partake in the class. Master Caren had been a bit startled but had agreed.

It wasn't long after Kahl had changed into a practice uniform before Master Caren had begun to quiz him about Dyhaeri combat training. Kahl had been careful with his answers and stressed most of their training concerned avoiding the Alkynaia, fighting them only when absolutely necessary.

Then he had heard someone call Britea's name. He had turned instinctively to see she and Pearl were talking to a young male student, and Britea's body language was defensive. He had excused himself then and walked over to find out what was going on.

"Hey, she's not your messenger!" protested Pearl, annoyed.

"Is everything all right?" asked Kahl.

The young male novice gave him a startled look, and Pearl spun around with a stunned expression on her face. Britea though, appeared frozen and only turned after a long moment. She seemed a bit apprehensive...*surely not of him?* This he had not expected. By the Mother, this was awkward.

"It's good to see you again Britea, Pearl," said Kahl when no one answered him.

The male novice gaped at him, then glared at Britea. "Wait, you know him?!"

Kahl frowned at the accusing tone. "And you are?"

The boy snapped his attention back to Kahl. "I'm Dariuz Solarn. My uncle is Lord Nalin Solarn, the minister of finance."

Ah, the minister who kept inviting us to his home. "I am familiar with the name," said Kahl politely.

"Good," said Dariuz as he stepped forward. "There is much you and I need to discuss, from access to Alkynaia eggs and the vert-silk trade. My uncle believes my family would be better trade representatives than the Weltonians, who currently control the trade." Kahl saw Pearl narrow her eyes as she watched Dariuz. Britea looked flustered, and that bothered him, so he held up a hand, halting Dariuz's approach.

"If you wish to discuss matters pertaining to trade, please do not do so here. I doubt Master Caren would approve of that," Kahl glanced at the weapons master, who was still watching them from a distance.

Kahl turned back to a now apprehensive Dariuz. "Also, I am here to observe the training of wielders and not negotiate trade deals. Please, remember that. Now, if you would excuse me, I would like to speak to Britea about her training." He looked meaningfully at Dariuz. Fortunately, the young noble took the hint and darted off.

Kahl turned back to Britea and Pearl, and the latter gave Britea a guarded look.

"I'll be fine," said Britea, and Kahl hid his pain. *Was she scared of him?*

"I'll be close by," said Pearl, giving Kahl a warning stare before walking a few feet away to lean against the wall.

Kahl watched her go, wondering what he had done to upset her. Then he turned back to Britea, and they stared at each other for a long moment.

Then he noticed the circles under her tired eyes and the thinness of her face. She had lost weight. *What had this school done to her?*

Breaking the awkward silence, Britea smiled shyly and said. "You look good in that Dyhaeri uniform. Even in our sparring gear."

Kahl found his face heating. "I appreciate the compliment." He paused. "Are you thriving in this school, Britea?"

She sighed tiredly. "As well as one could, I think. I'm learning a lot here."

It was on the tip of his tongue to ask if she was happy, but he was too afraid of a negative answer.

"That's good." Silence fell yet again.

"I..." she began.

"You..." started Kahl at the same time, then both stopped.

"You go first," said Kahl and Britea almost simultaneously. For some reason, this made the two break out laughing.

Kahl finally shook his head, his heart a bit lighter after hearing her laugh and motioned for her to go ahead.

"So, you're sparring with one of us today?" asked a curious, bolder Britea. This was the version he remembered, the one who wasn't scared of bargaining with an Alkynaia.

"I sure hope not. Mat is a lot better than me."

"I refuse to believe that," said Britea firmly. "You're wonderful in your own way."

Kahl felt his heart beat a bit faster at those words. "Thank you. Those are kind words."

A loud warning cough from Pearl had both them turning to see Weapons Master Caren approaching.

"Kahl, I'm glad to see you interact so well with the students, but these two need to get changed as the class will soon start in earnest."

"Of course," said Kahl, hiding his chagrin. He stole a look at Britea, and she was smiling wider now. Even Pearl gave him an approving look. "I hope to speak to you again later."

"That would be nice," said Britea shyly before she and Pearl left for the change rooms.

Kahl turned to see the weapons master watching him.

"An old friend of yours?" asked the instructor.

She's more than that. "Yes," answered Kahl simply while he waited for a sign of disapproval.

"Splendid," said the weapons master with a kind smile. This startled Kahl.

"If you don't mind, I do have more questions about Dyhaeri training."

Why this sudden interest? You didn't ask Mat this yesterday. "How can I help?"

"Do you have competitions between the different Dyhaeri factions?"

Kahl raised an eyebrow. "We don't have factions, but we do have competitions in singing, music, and sports."

Master Caren stared at him in surprise before recovering. "Forgive me, I meant wielding competitions."

Now Kahl was a bit concerned. "Not officially." The weapons master gave him a questioning look. "Wielding, to us, is as simple as breathing because we need it to survive underwater. Therefore, we don't challenge each other with it. However, at family gatherings, we do have impromptu wielding games that children or young people take part in." Now, he felt he had said too much. "Why these questions if I may ask?"

"Fair enough," said Master Caren. "Have you heard of the Wielder Trials?"

Kahl took a moment to search his memory. "Only a little. It's a contest between your wielding schools isn't it?"

"Correct. It's a competition dating back to 1934 AC. Every two years, the best wielder students from the five colleges of Namira and Malaquey would journey to a chosen college for a week-long competition. The winners of each event would earn significant coin while honoring their respective colleges." Master Caren paused. "But since the situation changed in Namira more than forty years ago, only the three Malaquey colleges attend the event now. This year's Trials will take place in four weeks."

Kahl was speechless for a moment, wondering if the high priest had been aware of this. If so, why had he not told him and Mat? "That sounds intriguing."*But were these Trials dangerous?* He sure hoped Britea was not a contestant.

Master Caren smiled. "I thought you and Mat may be interested. That's why I'm curious about Dyhaeri training. I would love to give my students an edge in this competition."

"Is that allowed Master Caren?" asked a worried Kahl.

"There are no rules against it. It would just be friendly advice from you and Mat. I would, however, first discuss it with the high priest as well. I wouldn't want you to break any of your laws. Now, let's show you how our students train in this class."

Kahl's smile hid how uneasy he felt.

#

Lanead felt a strong urge to pace as he waited for the transfer of the Namiran refugees from his sister ship, *Mother's Star,* to be complete. It was late evening, and the sky was filled with a fog that crept over the slightly choppy waters. He would have preferred to do this transfer in the dead of night, but they had received an urgent message borne by a seahawk that the *Star* was damaged and needed assistance. Apparently, they had run into a Namiran Emerald Raider warship. One look at the burnt starboard side made him wonder what miracle had prevented the *Star* from being holed. Thank the Sea Mother the warship had been an ancient model of the Namiran warships or the Weltonian ship would not have been able to escape. They had just lashed the undamaged portside of the *Star* to the *Peacekeeper* 's starboard side.

"The last of the refugees has been transferred, captain, and we're settling most of them below deck, but it will be a bit cramped," said First Mate Tanet.

"At least they're alive." Lanead had seen the all too familiar worn, thin faces, eyes filled with despair, and hoped some of them weren't contemplating suicide. He didn't even want to think of the hell they must have experienced in Namira. "We've spent more than enough time in this region."

The first mate nodded; the two ships were near the water border that divided this section of the Heldiar Sea into Namiran and Malaquey territories.

"Make sure the lines are reinforced on our starboard side. We have to tow the *Star* to the closet friendly dock for repairs—"

"Vessel inbound starboard!" The shout from the lookout in the crow's nest had Lanead and the first mate rushing to the aforementioned side.

"Where is it?!" asked First Mate Tanet as they both searched the fog covered waters.

Lanead thought quickly. "Laria!" One of the female Weltonian air wielders ran forwards.

"Improve our ability to see, please."

The Weltonian nodded and released a powerful tier-one funnel of air, and it cleared the fog right in front of them to reveal a behemoth, which appeared to be hovering above the water.

"By the Dark Sister," breathed Tanet in disbelief.

The floating metal contraption was less than two kilometers away, but from this distance, Lanead could appreciate its immense size. Its overall length was roughly three hundred meters long and had neither flag nor insignia to designate its origin. However, it seemed a bit similar to a Namiran warship in design. But how was this mountainous hunk of metal levitating above the Heldiar Sea? But more importantly, the more he stared at it, the more his instincts were telling him to start running in the opposite direction.

"It's coming about!" cried out the lookout.

"Laria, use the fog as cover!" The air wielder obeyed instantly, once more obscuring the view as Lanead ran to the steering wheel and shouted orders at his first mate.

"Tell Captain Blaze of the *Star* not to touch his wheel!"

By connecting his wielder earth power to the seabed, Lanead began to steer both ships deeper into the fog while using his instincts to avoid any obstacles. It didn't take long for a headache to begin at the base of his skull. He knew he could only hold this tier-five wield for a short time or he would collapse.

It was fortunate that icebergs were yet to float this way. That was one less obstacle to worry about. He had the water wielders to thank for that. It wasn't long though before he heard the wooden sides of both ships groan in protest as he tried to steer the ships faster. His headache rapidly grew into a migraine.

"It's still following us!" warned another crew member looking out from the port side.

"Tanet!" yelled Lanead through his pain. The first mate was at his side instantly. "Get the water wielders to ease the passage." First Mate Tanet nodded and dashed to the deck while yelling instructions to the various wielders ready and waiting.

Three positioned themselves on the port side and the other three on the starboard side. They gauged the speed of both ships, then wielded tier-one forms to calm the sea. Once the waters had calmed, they switched to a tier-five form that shaped the waves to make for a smoother, faster ride. But still, the sides of the ships lashed to each other continued to groan in protest, and Lanead thought he heard a board crack. He prayed he had not just holed a Weltonian ship.

"It's gaining!"

Lanead felt cold sweat form on his brow as he tried to maintain their speed without sinking both ships. His migraine was now akin to a hammer slamming the back of his skull.

"Captain Riverun!" yelled First Mate Tanet, who had just run up.

"Not now, Tanet!"

"Captain Blaze is going to cut the ropes and veer off sharply to starboard!" That almost made Lanead stop steering.

"Tell him no!"

"He insists! He and a few of his wielders will stay on board and try to draw that thing away from us. He said we must save the refugees!"

Lanead looked at the desperate light in his first mate's eyes and knew Captain Blaze was right. But it was so unfair.

"Captain, what is your decision?!" asked Tanet.

Lanead knew he had to say it, but he felt like he was condemning a friend and fellow Weltonian brother, to death.

"Cut the ropes."

The sailor closed his eyes briefly but ran off to do his duty.

Lanead forced back his tears as he concentrated on steering. All too soon, he noticed the creaking had stopped and the steering was much smoother as the *Peacekeeper* moved faster with the help of six experienced water wielders. The pain in his skull had also reduced considerably. Then a streak of fire flew off the starboard side as a fire wielder on the *Star* sent a fire ball towards the floating contraption.

It fell short of hitting the pursuer, but the response was immediate. The floating vessel quickly sped up until it was hovering over the *Star* . He saw several streaks of fire emerge from the undercarriage of the metal behemoth and strike the exposed deck of the *Star.* The Weltonian ship erupted in fire. With tears freely streaming and his heart full of anger, Lanead kept steering forwards while swearing to avenge his fallen brethren.

#

"Hmm, that was very good," said Queen Kallesa as she gazed at the burning Weltonian ship below them. They had been fortunate to glimpse the ship when the fog had parted briefly. And to think they had tried to outrun her ship.

That was one less Weltonian ship to worry about. A pity about the wielders though; she could have used their essence for her armlet.

"Any other ships nearby?" asked Minister Lensworth. The Namiran marine standing beside him shook his head.

"Only this one was sighted, sir, Your Majesty."

“Splendid,” said Queen Kallesa. She signaled to two of her Specialists, who began to close the hold.

“It might be best if we return to base, Your Highness,” said Minister Lensworth. The queen glared at him. Her guards did likewise.

“Why is that?”

The minster forced his voice to remain calm. “We’re just about out of fuel, and the serpent looks unwell.”

He saw the queen’s eyes blaze before she brought her emotions back under control.

“Of course,” smiled the queen brightly. “I appreciate the concern. Inform the captain we are to return home at once.”

“As you wish, Your Majesty,” said Minister Lensworth while hiding his unease. He kept his head bowed until he was the only one left in the cargo bay.

CHAPTER 22

Headmaster Clayre read the letter with the Malaquey royal seal a second time before carefully placing it on the desk before him. Then he took a deep breath to control his anger before looking at the bearer of the message.

Lieutenant Commander Nell smiled brightly at the head of the college. "I trust you will do your best to be ready within the next two weeks." He got up to go.

"You did this to get more of your people inside this school to spy on the Dyhaeri, didn't you?" growled the headmaster.

The commander sighed and turned. "If you had listened to my nephew and simply agreed, you would have had more time to prepare for this ancient competition. But you decided to nurse your wounded pride and here we are. This situation was of your making, headmaster. Now, I shall take my leave as I'm sure you have an awful lot to do. I hear the other colleges were thrilled to have the games moved forwards. It shall certainly be entertaining."

Headmaster Clayre remained silent until the Malaquey naval officer left. After several moments, the headmaster wearily walked out of his office in search of the warden. They needed another emergency meeting of the college faculty—today.

#

Kahl tried not to yawn. Today was Quintusday as the humans called it. To him it was the fifth day of the week. No need for outseaish names. So far, the Dyhaeri delegation had been at the school for the last five days. It was all he could do not to fall asleep in the middle of this social studies class run by Instructor Teron Dawn. The students were taking a test, and waiting for them to finish was mind numbing.

He was seated at the back of the class, and it was too quiet. All the novices were hunched over their papers as they tried to answer the questions within the time limit. He searched for Britea, and she was close to the front of the class. Beside her was Pearl, and they were scribbling furiously. Kahl was disappointed it was always so hard to talk with her in private. The students had so many tasks and classes to get to, and their time was strictly overseen, so he didn't want to get her into trouble. And he still didn't know why she and Pearl were serving a punishment detail in the kitchens.

Kahl glanced at the unanswered list of questions before him. Instructor Dawn had given him a copy, though she had told him he didn't need to answer the questions.

Kahl was grateful for that because the questions looked difficult.

Question one: What is the most important role of the elected minister and lords at the Emergency Conclave, which may occur once in a generation? Kahl had racked his brains for the answer to that one. Didn't it have something to do with voting on whether the current heir was fit to be king? Then again, the Malaqueys only allowed male heirs to rule. Kahl thought that was stupid.

Question two: Name all the current elected ministers and their responsibilities. Kahl scoffed silently. The only minister he recalled was Lord Nalin Solarn, and that was only because his nephew had already approached them twice about the trade commission. Kahl had met the nephew in combat and defense class, and Dariuz had approached Mat in the one of the hallways. Needless to say, Mat's response had been far less polite than Kahl's.

Mat had asked Dariuz if he intended to harvest the vert-silk materials himself or hire others to do it. When Dariuz stammered he was still in school and thus could not harvest the materials, Mat had interrupted him by saying, "Then you're wasting my time. I'm here to observe, not to increase the amount of coin in your coffers."

That had been two days ago, and ever since, Dariuz had kept his distance.

Question three: What occurs if the Emergency Conclave cannot reach a decision on who is to be king? Kahl frowned at the placement of the question. It should have come after the first question. *And what was the answer anyway?*

Question four: What treaty does the Kingdom of Malaquey hold with the Dyhaeri?

Kahl smiled. This he knew…or so he hoped. The only treaty in place now was the Sea Treaty Agreement. For every vessel that sailed on the Heldiar Sea, a wielder had to be present. That was the same treaty they had shared with the former Oldenarian Empire and had thus passed down to Malaquey and Namira after the Human Civil War in 399 AC.

"You have five minutes to drop your pencils!" Kahl looked up at the warning. Some students cried out in dismay as they tried to write faster. He glanced over at

Britea, and she was calmly rereading her answers. With a sigh of relief, he folded his incomplete test. He was going to show it to the high priest and Mat.

"Time!" The students dropped their pencils, some with a groan.

The instructor collected the completed tests. "Your assignment for the weekend is to write about the previous political structure in Namira before Queen Kallesa took the throne." The students stared at him in shock, but he was not done. "And you are to compare it with her current rule. Lastly, you will compare both to the current Malaquey rule. I want advantages and disadvantages written in a tabled format." This elicited loud mutters of protests, but the instructor simply smiled at their displeasure.

"Remember, the library is your friend in this situation. Have a good weekend." The instructor left the class before the students began to trickle out, most of them in a grim mood, but Britea and Pearl looked excited. She turned to smile at him as she left with Pearl, and Kahl jumped out of his seat. The next class, which was the last of the day, was wielding. Surely, he could walk them to Instructor Shelley's junior wielding class. To be honest, he found the students in that class the nicest. Probably because they were still so young and not yet disillusioned by the real world.

Kahl left the classroom, and his smile disappeared when he saw an angry Pearl and an irritated Britea surrounded by four girls. One of them he recognized as Lianne Arkei.

"What's going on here?" he asked immediately.

Novice Lianne Arkei turned to face him. "It's a school matter, Prince Kahl. Please move along. This does not concern you." Kahl glanced at Britea and saw her curl her hands into fists. His instincts told him this was a fight about to happen.

"I'm afraid it does concern me." Everyone turned to him. "You see, Britea and Pearl are friends of mine. What is the problem?"

Lianne arched an eyebrow in disbelief. "Friends of yours?"

Kahl disliked her tone. She made the word "friends" sound like a disease.

"And did these friends of yours tell you they were almost expelled for dueling on the school grounds?"

"Lianne, you have no business telling him that!" hissed Pearl.

The brunette wielder laughed at the surprise on Kahl's face. "Oh, they didn't tell you that? Now, what kind of friends hide secrets?"

Kahl glanced at Pearl, who was bursting with rage, while Britea looked embarrassed as she stared at the floor.

"You haven't answered the question, Prince Kahl. Now you can see how distasteful it would be to be friends with two lawbreakers such as these—"

"You're just like your sister," interrupted Kahl to the astonishment of all present. Lianne gaped at him.

"Where did you meet Selina?"

"Vindictive and cruel just for the fun of it. Tell me, what pleasure does one derive from that?" continued Kahl. "How do you live with yourself? And who are you to speak to me in this manner?"

Lianne's stunned expression was soon replaced by one of anger. "How dare you question—"

"What is going on here?" boomed Instructor Dawn's voice. Everyone turned.

"Aren't you all supposed to be in class?" His glare included Kahl.

"We were just chatting," said Lianne in an innocent voice that grated on Kahl's nerves.

"I was offering to escort Britea and Pearl to their next class," he said in a somewhat calm voice.

The instructor narrowed his eyes and stared at each of them for a long moment.

"Thank you, Prince Kahl. Please do so. The rest of you will remain behind to answer a few questions." The look Lianne shot Britea and Pearl was pure malice.

Kahl waited until his two new charges began to trudge away before following them.

"Thanks, Kahl, but you didn't have to—" began Britea.

"Why did they ambush you, and what is this about dueling?" asked Kahl.

Both girls looked uncertainly at each other. Then Pearl sighed. "I'll walk on ahead, Britea. You should tell him before he hears an exaggerated version from Lianne or one of her friends. I know what she's like." Pearl quickened her pace as Britea hugged her books to herself.

Kahl kept pace with her and forced himself to wait.

"Lianne and her friends don't like me very much. I have no idea why, but it started on my first day. I tried to avoid her and not get into fights, and that seemed to work for a while…then two weeks ago, she tricked me into a duel." She paused.

"How?" asked Kahl.

Britea told him everything. At the end, he was left speechless for a long moment and could only stare at Pearl, who was walking far ahead of them.

Britea placed a hand on his arm. "I think she's changed now. She's been awfully helpful since she didn't get expelled."

Kahl calmed and much of his anger left him after she touched his right arm. "You told her about the Seers?" Actually, it was that part of the tale that was worrying him the most."

"No, I didn't want to be seen as being insane." Kahl gave her a startled look.

"I didn't even know the Seers existed until they…they spoke to me. Even Danai was worried about their involvement, and she didn't want to tell the school authorities either," whispered Britea frantically.

"Good point," conceded Kahl. Now it was his turn. "The Seers picked Mat and I for this assignment, Britea."

She stopped and gaped at him. "What? Why?"

"Mat and I aren't exactly sure, but we think it has to do with a prophecy. We don't know exactly which one, and the high priest isn't telling us everything."

Britea had to start walking again when Pearl looked backwards and motioned for them to hurry.

"This all sounds scary."

"Tell me about it," agreed Kahl. "However, I'm glad I'm here…with you."

Britea's smile brightened and Kahl felt much lighter. They walked in a companionable silence until they reached Instructor Shelley's class.

#

"This can't be happening," said Master Pietor Caren as he read the royal missive. He and the others involved in preparations for the Trials were currently huddled in the private meeting room for senior faculty members. He passed the letter on to another instructor to read.

"Can't we file a protest?" complained Instructor Droye. "My girls haven't finished learning the new dances for the After-Trial Ball!"

Several instructors groaned. "Seriously, Helene? The After-Trial Ball is what you're concerned about?!" shouted Instructor Lexar.

"I know this has come as a shock to you all," began the headmaster, "but we cannot go against the king's will. He has already stated that the two naval colleges are happy to do the Trials early. We truly have no choice."

"Oh, those last two words again," growled Instructor Charl Melvin. "First, we get the honor of being chosen to be inspected by the Dyhaeri, and then we get the Trials moved up two weeks on the king's whim. Since when did Syla College, the oldest of the three, become the doormat of the royal court? If I had known this would be the norm, I would have taken up a position at the Royal Malaquey Naval College."

"It's not too late, Charl," said Eowise Shelley dryly. This was met by laughter from the other instructors while Charl stared daggers at her.

"Order," called the warden, and the noise died down.

"I understand your frustration, but we have to move forward," continued the headmaster. "Please work on proposals as to how we can speed up preparations, and hopefully, the Wielder Trials won't be a disaster after all."

#

Minister Lensworth stood, frozen, as Queen Kallesa set a second antique chair on fire with a scream of rage.

A few minutes ago, he had delivered an update from his spies in Malaquey.

Apparently, the Wielder Trials had been moved forward by two weeks. Clearly the queen was not happy.

"Why was it moved forward?" asked the queen in a deceptively calmer voice as she put out the fire by absorbing the flames back into her hands.

"The reason is unknown, Your Majesty," said the minister calmly, blinking furiously in the acrid, smoky atmosphere.

The queen sighed and collapsed in one of the two unburnt chairs. She didn't seem bothered by the noxious environment she had created.

"We'll have to move faster, Minister Lensworth. My original plans required four weeks, but now I have to cram them into two weeks!" She paused, thinking. "Get me more cows for the serpent. Malie will have to be put back to work sooner than we expected. Now get out of my sight."

"Yes, Your Majesty," said Minister Lensworth as he bowed and fled before the irate queen set him on fire too.

CHAPTER 23

Mat sighed happily to himself. It was the sixth day of the week and there were no classes to attend. Finally, he could explore. Kahl had left earlier, saying he wanted an early start because he wanted to do some research in the school library.

Truth be told, ever since Captain Riverun and the high priest had started training him and Kahl, he had been sure their interactions with humans would be disastrous. And it had come close a few times. He may even end up fighting Harto one of these days. But at the same time, being at Syla College was becoming interesting.

Especially after meeting Danai.

At first, he had been shocked and somewhat frightened, or at least intimidated, when he had realized who her father was, but she was such a formidable fighter he just could not resist her. Sparring with her had brought back memories of training with his fellow marines. Had she been trained by her father? If so, then who had trained Captain Lanead Riverun?

Mat's mind returned to the present when he found himself in the central gardens. They were currently empty. He wondered if the students who had stayed back for the weekend were still in their dorms. Sitting down on one of the stone benches, he tried to appreciate the quiet as he closed his eyes.

At first his mind drifted aimlessly, and then he found himself thinking of his distant ancestors, who had once lived and thrived on land more than forty thousand years ago. The ancient tomes stated a great cataclysm had forced them to take refuge underwater; thus, the Sea Mother had blessed them with wielding abilities so they could survive.

Being under the open skies had been torture at first. However, Lanead had gradually helped him and Kahl adapt; he had a lot to thank the grumpy Weltonian for.

After several moments, he opened his eyes. Now, he was bored. Maybe a trip down to the library to see what his cousin was up to was in order.

#

Danai glanced at Britea, Pearl, and their fourth unlikely study partner, Kahl.

Danai had an assignment in history due next Primeday, so she had woken up early on Septday morning to get a start on it only to realize Britea had the same idea. Danai had even managed to keep a polite smile on her face when Pearl had joined them; she still didn't fully trust the noble.

Then she was stunned to find Kahl waiting for them outside the school library. She had been proud of how she had hidden her surprise when Kahl had greeted Britea and Pearl like old friends. But what she had not expected was his reaction when Britea had introduced her.

He had stared at her. "Mat told me about you."

"Oh," was all Danai had been able to utter for a moment. "What…what did he say?" She had tried to ignore Pearl and Britea's inquisitive looks.

"That you fight very well," Kahl had said.

Danai was silent for a moment A Dyhaeri thought she fought well. That was high praise indeed.

"That…that's very kind of him. Did you need something?"

"Ah, yes, I wish to join Britea and Pearl as they study."

Danai had scrutinized the two younger novices; they had clearly planned this.

"Fine. Just don't speak in the library. It upsets Custodian Mitra. You don't want to get thrown out."

Kahl's green skin had turned rather pea soupy. "Duly noted."

Now Danai was curious as to what the three of them were working on. She had been planning on sitting at a different desk but had then decided to stay with them to ensure no one got into mischief.

Once they had checked in with the custodian, Danai had picked a large desk in a corner of the mostly empty library for their group to study at while Britea and Pearl took Kahl on an almost silent tour of the big library. Danai saw his eyes shine and recognized a fellow book lover.

She wondered if his cousin liked books as well.

Danai shook her head; she had to work on her history assignment. She grabbed the books she needed and stacked them on one corner of the desk, then she pulled out the questions the history instructor had given the class.

"Is this seat taken?" asked a familiar voice that almost made her jump out of her chair.

She looked up into the handsome face of Prince Mat.

"I…" she began when she finally found the words.

"Shh!" both turned to face an angry Custodian Mitra, who had approached them unheard. The custodian pointed to a handwritten sign mounted on the nearest wall decreeing, "QUIET!"

"I'm sorry," mouthed Mat, bowing deeply.

The custodian glared at him for a moment before making a soft scoffing noise and walking silently back to her post.

"Is she gone?" whispered Mat, who was still bowing.

"Yes," whispered Danai, trying not to laugh. "What are you doing here?"

Mat sat down beside her. "I came looking for my cousin and just happened to see you sitting by yourself. Why are you in an empty library on the sixth day?" His voice was barely above a whisper.

"History assignment, due on the first day. I just wanted to get it done as soon as possible so I could relax this weekend."

"Relax?" queried Mat with a smile. "And how exactly do you do that?"

Danai found herself amused by his flirting tone. "By reading a good book or going for a walk by the sea behind the school. We're allowed to do that on the weekends."

"Sounds exciting," said Mat. "May I join you on such a walk?"

Danai stared at him, sure he was jesting, but though he smiled, his eyes were serious.

"Um…sure…"

"Mat?" Kahl's startled whisper made them look up to face the three stunned younger wielders.

"What are you doing here?" asked Kahl.

"I was bored, so I came looking for you," whispered back Mat. Pearl and Britea shared a look and struggled not to giggle.

Mat's eyes went to the books they were carrying. "Assignments as well? On what?"

"Yes," whispered Britea she sat down. "It's about the previous political situation in Namira before Queen Kallesa took the throne. We have to compare that rule with her current rule and then compare both to the current Malaquey rule."

"With a tabled list of advantages and disadvantages," added Pearl in a low tone.

Mat glanced at Danai. "Mine is different. It's about the last days of the Old Olderian Empire, particularly the biggest factor that brought about its conclusion."

"The Human Civil War," said Mat.

Danai shot him an impressed smile. Mat grinned back at her. "I'm not completely ignorant after all."

Kahl gave his cousin a startled stare.

"I might as well use the opportunity to explore your library for something to read," whispered Mat as he stood up. "See you all soon."

Danai watched him go, then turned back to see the three younger wielders staring at her.

"What?"

Britea and Pearl shared a quick look. "Nothing," said the two at the same time as Kahl dove into his own book, his face a darker green than usual.

Danai felt a bit self-conscious now, but she had to force herself to concentrate on her work.

#

Mat was true to his word and came back with a book. A quick glance at the cover told Danai it was a copy of the one she was currently using. She couldn't help but wonder if there was another reason why Mat had chosen it. She was relieved when he concentrated on his reading, yet part of her missed his attention.

Get a hold of yourself, Danai! She mentally scolded herself as she continued with her work.

The group was silent as they pored over their books until Britea and Pearl glanced at the chronometer on the wall, and without a word, started packing up their books.

Mat glanced up from his book with a questioning look.

"Time for our punishment detail in the kitchens," whispered Pearl.

Mat frowned. "Why the punishment?"

Britea shot Kahl a silent look. Kahl raised his hands. "I didn't tell him. It's not my story to tell."

Mat's frown deepened. Danai felt the atmosphere grow tense before Pearl sighed softly.

"I did a stupid thing and forced Britea to duel me. I should have been expelled, but Britea tried to help me, so we both got punished with seven months of kitchen duties before most meals."

Mat's eyes widened and he stared at Britea and Pearl for a long moment before looking at Kahl, who nodded silently.

"We really have to go," said Britea shyly.

"I'll escort you both," whispered Kahl. Britea gave him a long-suffering look.

"Please?" pleaded the male Dyhaeri.

"All right," said Britea with a sad smile. Mat watched the three of them prepare to leave before realizing Danai was also packing up her work.

"Assignment done?"

"Almost, but in just over an hour, it'll be time for lunch. I want to hit the beach before that. Care to join me?"

Mat was already on his feet. "Gladly."

CHAPTER 24

Dear Lords of Shadow and Light, I beseech thee. What did I do to deserve this?

That was the warden's silent prayer as Lady Adria Arkei and Lady Rose Ceres walked into his office. He stood and bowed slightly, waiting for them to be seated. Their stern expressions told him this was not a social call.

It was currently midday on Solisday, his favorite day because he usually got to relax.

The last thing he had expected was a forced audience with nobles. But the two women before him weren't just any nobles. Warden Asteros had already had an unfavorable run in with Lady Arkei earlier in the week when he had refused to host a ball, and now she was here with Lady Ceres.

He was sure the purpose was going to strain his patience. "Lady Arkei and Lady Ceres, how may I help you today?"

Adria glanced at her friend. "Rose, I'll let you speak."

Lady Rose Ceres glared at Warden Asteros. "I have heard my precious Pearl has been forced to work and study with a criminal, and I demand to have this addressed."

The warden kept his expression neutral. Lady Rose Ceres may be speaking, but he knew who the puppeteer was.

"Could you please explain?" asked the warden.

Rose stared at him. "I need to explain?! Where is Headmaster Clayre? He should be here right now to answer for this travesty!"

Warden Asteros kept his face sympathetic. "I'm afraid you missed the headmaster by a few hours. He is currently attending a meeting with the king at court." From the corner of his eyes he saw Adria frown. Apparently, she was annoyed at the headmaster's absence.

"If you wish to wait for his return, which will be tomorrow evening, then you can speak to him yourself." *With me hovering in the background to prevent you from badgering the poor man.*

Rose seemed uncertain, but she looked at Adria, who almost imperceptibly shook her head.

Ah, the strings are being pulled .

"No," said Rose coldly. "You will fix this mess right now!"

"Once again, could you please explain what, exactly, I am supposed to fix," continued the warden as politely as possible.

Rose glared at him. "I'm talking about Britea D'Tranell! That tramp pulled my daughter into a duel that almost got her expelled. And now, instead of that peasant being kicked out, she's been allowed to stay, and my precious Pearl is being punished for it. I demand that Britea D'Tranell be arrested and expelled from this school immediately! If this is not done at once, I shall take this up with the king, and he will be alerted as to how poorly this school is being run!" She exchanged a triumphant look with Adria, who smiled at her as if praising a well-trained pup.

Warden Asteros looked at both women for a long moment. "Ah, now I see the problem." He rose from his desk and walked to a cabinet pulling out a folder before returning to his desk. He sat and opened the folder.

"Lady Ceres, I have no idea who gave you that version of events; however, I must inform you that they are, in fact, lies."

Rose gasped in shock and stared at Adria, who was coldly observing Warden Asteros.

"It's the truth!" demanded Rose as she turned back to the warden.

He turned the signed documents around to face the two noble women.

"I have here signed accounts from reliable witnesses who stated that Novice Pearl Ceres, with two of her friends, held a younger novice wielder hostage to force Novice Britea D'Tranell to take part in a duel. Novice Pearl Ceres later went on to confirm in my presence, and that of two other senior faculty members, that she did indeed challenge Britea to a duel."

He paused waiting for the information to sink in.

"So, as you can see, your precious Pearl was one of the instigators of this mess." His tone became colder as he continued while ignoring their shocked expressions.

"She also refused to name the two accomplices even though they were named by the witnesses as standing nearby and supporting Pearl Ceres. Their names are—"

"That won't be necessary," cut in Adria with a loaded glare.

Warden Asteros continued regardless of the interruption. "—Novice Lianne Arkei and Lady Valerie Mern." He watched Rose go pale and send Adria a startled look.

"So, Lady Ceres, you never did mention who gave you those alternative facts. Who was it?"

Rose searched Adria's face and something in the noblewoman's expression made Rose redden in anger.

"It was Lianne and Valerie—"

"Rose!" hissed Lady Adria Arkei.

"My daughter is not taking the fall for this, Adria!"

Warden Asteros smiled internally. Apparently, Rose had a brain after all. She had just realized she was being used.

"Lady Ceres, Novice Pearl Ceres was to be expelled from the school once she was discharged from the infirmary. However, Novice Britea D'Tranell pleaded on her behalf. It is due to the mercy of a girl of low birth that your daughter still has a place in this school." He paused and stared at both women. "It certainly wasn't due to the assistance of her two noble friends who abandoned her the moment she got caught."

By now, Lady Arkei's eyes were promising murder, but Warden Asteros didn't give a damn. He had the Trials to organize, the Dyhaeri to accommodate, a Malaquey naval officer to watch, and a college to run. Right now, becoming Lady Arkei's enemy was the least of his problems.

"Do you have any more concerns?"

Lady Rose Ceres was flustered. "I...I would like to see my daughter."

"I'm sure that can be arranged," said the warden with a smile while ignoring the fuming Lady Arkei.

#

Pearl waited nervously in one of the family visiting rooms. It had come as a complete shock to find out her mother was here. Just a few minutes ago, she, Britea, Kahl, Danai, and Mat had been in the library working on their assignments for the second day in row. If someone had told Pearl a month ago that she would be friends with Britea and Danai and doing schoolwork with two Dyhaeri princes, she would have declared that person insane.

That idyllic moment had been broken when the custodian had handed her a note on her way out of the library.

"What's wrong?" Britea had asked.

"My mother is here," she had whispered, terrified.

"Is that a problem?" Kahl had asked in a whisper. Danai and Mat had stayed silent but had listened intently.

"I…I don't know. I have to go now," Pearl had said shakily. Danai and Britea had shared a look and nodded.

"We're coming with you." Danai had said resolutely, crossing her arms. Kahl and Mat had shared a glance, shrugged, and followed suit.

Pearl had gaped at them. "You don't have to do that."

"It's all right," Britea had whispered reassuringly. "We'll be nearby, just in case you need us for after."

"My darling, baby girl!" Her mother's voice brought her back to the present. Pearl turned and was soon enveloped in her mother's warm arms. For a moment, Pearl let her guard down and just enjoyed being loved…even if it was just a façade.

"Let me look at you!" Her mother gently pushed her back and frowned a bit. "You seem to have lost a bit of weight but could stand to lose a bit more!"

And so it begins, the never-ending obsession with my weight. Pearl smiled and suppressed her anger.

"Mother, you look well." A cough behind them made her turn to face Lady Arkei.

Pearl felt a moment of panic before etiquette training took over and she bowed.

"Lady Arkei, forgive me. I had no idea you were here."

The noble lady smiled. "My child, do not apologize. It is so lovely to see you. I had so hoped to see you at one of our balls this weekend. I wondered why you hadn't traveled home as you usually do."

Pearl kept her face passive. "I had so much schoolwork to do."

Adria touched her shoulder gently, and Pearl forced herself not to recoil from the touch. "But child, all work and no play isn't good for the soul. I—"

"Adria, dear, I would love to visit with my only daughter in private if you don't mind," said Lady Rose Ceres in an overly sweet tone. Pearl froze in shock. She had never heard her mom interrupt Lady Adria Arkei before.

The lady in question glared at Rose for a moment, then seemed to recall they had an audience. "Of course. I will wait in the lobby."

Rose kept her eyes on Adria and a smile on her face until the noblewoman had gone. Then she turned to glare at Pearl.

"Mother…" began Pearl as dread grew in her chest.

"Would you like to know how last night went, my daughter?" Her voice was cold, and she didn't wait for Pearl to reply.

"Your father and I attended a ball at the Arkei family winter lodge, and while I was there, your dear friend, Lianne, decided to regale the entire ballroom with a tale about how you got tricked into a duel and are now being punished for it by working in the school's kitchens."

Pearl felt herself go cold then hot in turn. Her dread gave way to fury.

Her mother continued. "Then Lady Arkei began to describe how low the standards at Syla College had fallen lately, especially now that they're letting all sorts in here, and how poorly you were being treated. Your father and I had to stand there for hours listening to everyone's asinine suggestions as to the actions we should take, and that, dear Pearl, is why I am here today!"

Pearl said nothing. In moments like this, it was best to become part of the furniture.

Lady Rose Ceres began to pace in the parlor. She lifted a finger. "You had one task: finish wielding school with acceptable scores and without getting into trouble, and then do your Year of Discovery in the Arkei home—"

"I'm never going there again!" hissed Pearl before she could stop herself.

Rose stopped in her pacing and glowered at her daughter. "You're damn right about that! Thanks to your antics, our family is now the laughingstock of the royal court!"

Pearl pressed her lips together tightly to prevent a retort from escaping.

Rose continued talking and pacing. "I came here to do some damage control…only to find out Lianne and Valerie had been part of the plot, and they lied about what happened. They all tried to use us for their own amusement!"

Pearl stared at her mother. *Was she just now realizing this?*

"But there is another rumor I heard that I hope is false." She stopped pacing right in front of Pearl. "I heard from Lianne and Valerie that you are now close friends with this peasant girl, Britea D'Tranell. Tell me this is also not true."

Pearl thought carefully before responding. "She and I got the same punishment detail. The punishment included being paired in all classes and the punishments for the duration."

Rose watched her daughter for a long moment. "That is all?"

Pearl kept eye contact with her mother. "Why are you concerned, mother?"

Lady Cere's expression softened as she gently touched her daughter's shoulders. "I always told you to pick your friends with great care. You must surround yourself with those who will aid you in your rise to the top. Not with peasants that gain us little."

Pearl could not help but recoil from her mother's touch. "You don't know Britea."

Rose's demeanor became stern one. "Pearl—"

"She pled on my behalf for me to stay in this school. It's because of her that I still have a place here." Pearl paused and narrowed her eyes. "You knew that, didn't you? And yet you despise her, even though you've never met her!"

Rose's expression was icy. "That settles it. I will speak to the warden and ensure this does not continue. I will also have to meet with this Britea to make sure she gets the message, won't I?" Lady Ceres stormed out of the visiting room.

Pearl panicked. "No, wait!" she yelled as she ran after her mother.

She caught up with her mother, who was marching purposefully down the corridor…in the wrong direction. Then Pearl saw Britea, Danai, Kahl, and Mat emerge from behind one of the large columns. Her mother's steps faltered when she caught sight of the two Dyhaeri. Pearl nearly ran into her.

"Pearl, is everything all right? We heard you yell," said Britea as she stepped forward wearing a worried expression.

"Who are…" started Rose as she stared at the two Dyhaeri. Britea answered before Pearl could warn her.

"Good morning, my lady," said Britea as she curtsied perfectly. "I'm Britea, and this is Danai, Mat, and Kahl." Danai lowered her head respectfully while Mat and Kahl nodded slightly.

Pearl watched her mother's face undergo a parade of expressions, from disbelief to cunning to charming as comprehension dawned.

Bet you didn't expect the peasant girl to be friends with the Dyhaeri, did you?

"Friends, this is my mother, Lady Rose Ceres," said Pearl in a tone that was calmer than she felt.

Rose stared at her daughter for a long moment before her own etiquette training kicked in as she turned back to the others with a bright smile.

"Pearl is yet to tell me about you; however, I am delighted to meet you all."

#

"You were wise in your choice of friends this time," said Lady Rose Ceres reluctantly.

Pearl rolled her eyes as they strolled back to the lobby. Her mother had insisted on talking with her friends for some time, making her and Britea late for their punishment, though the warden had intervened on their behalf. Though Pearl had been relieved at that, she had just prayed her mother wouldn't embarrass her, and to her relief, disaster had been averted. Now she breathed a sigh of relief as she walked her mother out, leaving Britea and Kahl waiting for her so they could head to their punishment and Danai and Mat to their walk on the beach.

"I now see why Lianne and her mother are jealous. Do you know how many lords and ladies have been trying to get close to those Dyhaeri? And you're practically best friends with their Weltonian friend!"

"Mother, Britea is not Weltonian. Danai is the only Weltonian in this school," groaned Pearl wearily.

"Well, Britea certainly looks like one. And Danai seems quite close to Prince Mat," she said, giving Pearl a speculative look. "I need you to keep an eye on them and find out all you can about—"

"No," Pearl said firmly to her mother's surprise. "I'm not spying on my friends, mother. Don't ask me again."

Rose stopped walking and stared at her daughter. "Well, one good thing has come out of this duel disaster. You appear to have grown a spine."

Pearl was taken aback by her mother's reaction. "Um…thanks?"

Rose chuckled and resumed walking. "I will come to see you again. Until then, stay out of trouble. Is that clear?"

"Yes, mother," replied Pearl, resigned.

#

The air was crisp and cold, yet the sun shone brightly over the blue waves that crashed against the shoreline. Mat saw the water and suddenly yearned to be back home in Light-Under-Sea.

"Do you miss the sea?" asked Danai softly. They had been walking in companionable silence for the last five minutes. This was their second walk in two days.

"Yes, I do," said Mat. Then he looked at Danai. "You?"

The Weltonian smiled sadly. "I think of it every day."

"Why are you training here, Danai? I know your people have more than enough teachers to train wielders."

Danai snorted elegantly. "True, but I have my own, personal, reasons for coming here."

"Ah," was all Mat said.

Danai gave him a quizzical look. "And this is the part where you ask me what those personal reasons are, am I right?"

Mat smiled. "The word 'personal' indicates it's not my business, so I won't ask."

"Wise decision," said Danai with a laugh. The two walked on for a bit in silence.

"Mat, how do you know my parents?"

The Dyhaeri nodded as if he had been expecting that question. "Captain Lanead Riverun was kind enough to transport the high priest, Kahl, and I to Port Trident."

Danai waited as if expecting more. Mat wondered momentarily if she was authorized to know about their mission, but his instincts advised him to tell her more.

"Kahl and I also stayed with him for more than three months to learn more about human culture."

Danai stopped in her tracks and stared at him. Mat grimaced at the shock on her face.

"Are you here to spy on the Malaquey government?" whispered Danai as though they were still in the library.

Mat rubbed his face as he warred with himself about how much to tell her. "We're here to assess Malaquey's readiness to take on Namira if war were to erupt tomorrow."

Danai's pretty face went ashen, then after a long moment, she resumed walking. They walked side by side in silence once again.

"Thank you for telling me, though you didn't have to," finally said Danai.

"You're welcome."

Danai cleared her throat. "I'm not supposed to talk about this yet, but Master Caren wants to ask you about helping the Syla team prepare for the Wielder Trials."

It was now Mat's turn to stare at her in surprise. "The Wielder Trials? But aren't those a month away?"

Danai gave him a pleased smile. "You know of them?"

"I've only read a bit about them, thanks to your father. To be honest, they seem interesting. Are you a contestant this year?"

Danai scoffed. "Not really. Master Caren wants me to be a strategist. I've agreed thus far, but I'm still of two minds about it."

"Why?" asked a curious Mat.

"It's just that they're a mixture of politics and just plain intimidation tactics. I prefer a simpler life. So, what do you think of the offer I really wasn't supposed to tell you about?"

Mat was silent for a moment. "I must admit it sounds intriguing, but I'm hardly an expert in the games. If I agree to it, will you help me?"

Danai looked at him for several moments. "Sure, I'll help." She gulped. *Would she come to regret this?*

#

Mat rubbed his hands with glee as he looked at the spread before him. The chefs had outdone themselves: delicately spiced small crab cakes with a cool vegetable salad, a stewed rice dish, and a sugary fruit concoction on ice. The aroma was making his mouth water.

"About time you showed up," said High Priest Myltan dryly. "Where have you two been?" he asked as he gestured for Mat and Kahl to take a seat.

"We were in the library doing some research," said Kahl before Mat could say a word.

"All day?"

"Oh, Mat also went for a walk on the beach with Danai, and I accompanied Britea and Pearl to their punishment and then to their lunch," continued Kahl calmly. Mat tensed and glanced at the high priest, expecting disapproval.

"What did you learn at the library?" asked the high priest casually as he helped himself to two crab cakes and salad.

"The research was interesting," continued Kahl. "Danai even knows their history texts are incomplete about certain historical events. For example, their history speaks only briefly about the reason for the war between Dyhaeri and humans. There were barely six lines. I could have blinked and missed that passage. Why was that account so short?"

The high priest sighed. "History is usually written by the victor, and even when the defeated do write, they tend to minimize their role in the poor outcome or erase it from their history all together rather than admit the truth."

A disturbed silence fell.

"I found something about the Time of Persecution in 1392 AC," said Mat gravely. Kahl sent him a puzzled look while the high priest said nothing.

Mat continued. "Weltonians built this college in 1384, and the two military colleges soon after. Many Weltonians were the first novices to enroll. But in 1392, a political movement began that branded them spies for the Dyhaeri or enemies of Malaquey. This led to riots and unrest, and many Weltonians died."

Kahl stared at him in shock, but the high priest didn't seem surprised by the revelation.

"It lasted over a year before the late King Adren Cen-Taros brought a stop to it by arresting the politicians involved and having most exiled and the rest executed. Most of the exiles settled in Namira, which also had a low tolerance for Weltonians."

"That's why the Weltonians stopped attending the colleges, isn't it?" asked Kahl.

"Which makes one wonder why Danai Riverun is a student here," said Mat. He kept his gaze on the high priest.

The elderly Dyhaeri smiled sadly. "What happened to the Weltonians was unfortunate. They didn't deserve such treatment." Then his expression changed. "Have you asked her why she's here?"

Mat felt his face flush. "I did, but she said it was personal."

The high priest nodded as if that was to be expected. "Well, on to a lighter subject. I received an interesting request from Weapons Master Caren today." Kahl looked at him expectantly. "He has asked for you two to be advisors for the Wielder Trials."

Kahl's eyes widened in surprise.

"I accept," said Mat immediately. Now it was the others' turn to stare at him.

"I...I mean it sounds like a good idea."

Kahl looked at him skeptically.

"Is Danai a contestant in the Trials?" asked Kahl innocently. Mat glared at him.

"I have no idea," said the high priest. "However, I agree this is a great opportunity to observe how the best students from the three colleges have been trained and how they react under stress. Oh, one more thing. The contest has been brought forward by two weeks."

Mat blinked. "But it was supposed to be a month away."

"Master Caren apologized for the short notice. He seemed quite upset about the change in schedule."

"Why was it moved up?" asked Kahl.

"That wasn't explained," said the high priest. "Now, Mat, how was the walk on the beach?"

Mat was speechless for a moment. "It's a pretty beach, well maintained."

The high priest waited as if expecting more. "Is it secure from an attack by sea?"

Mat flushed as he recalled what they were here for. "No. There was only one guard at the back door. He wasn't even there when we returned for the second walk today."

The high priest looked disturbed. "We need to talk to the warden about that."

"Of course," said Mat quickly, ignoring the odd look his cousin gave him.

CHAPTER 25

"All right, everyone, have a seat," said Master Caren to the gathered students in the combat and defense class. Britea sat between Danai and Pearl and snuck a quick look at the back of the class. She smiled when she saw Mat and Kahl. The two Dyhaeri stood at the back of the class with the other instructors. This time, the cousins were dressed in their own sparring outfits made from a cotton-like seaweed material. They were jade green and took the form of a short-sleeved tunic and long pants. They still wore their thigh-high, walnut-hued leather boots. The students had given them startled looks when they had both showed up to class. Only the instructors weren't surprised. And even better, Lieutenant Harto Flay was absent today.

Master Caren waited until the students were all seated on the lawn before beginning.

"By now, some of you may have heard the Trials have been moved forward by two weeks." Britea and Pearl shared a startled look while the other students murmured angrily at this. Master Caren waited for them to get it out of their systems.

"And many of you present here today have been chosen to participate in the Trials and make our school proud. However, I have asked Prince Mat and Prince Kahl to observe and advise us during our final preparations." The students' expressions ranged from quizzical to hopeful.

"Will they be competing on our team, sir?" asked an excited Navos. Britea's smile echoed his own. He had gotten his confirmation a week ago that he would be on the reserve team for the sparring event. He had been so excited that even his girlfriend, Lexia, had been happy for him though she wasn't a fan of the games.

"No." This was met by disappointment. "They aren't students. However, their advice will be welcome." This was met by hearty cheers. Pearl grinned, but Britea felt a bit nervous for Mat and Kahl.

"Also, Novice Danai Riverun will be joining the strategy team to help our Dyhaeri guests learn the rules." Everyone stared at Danai and murmured, surprised but impressed. Britea shot her roommate a stunned look and saw she looked grave.

"Today, we're going to hold mock Trials." This was greeted with shocked cries.

"Better get used to it, class. When the real thing starts, you need to be prepared." Master Caren looked at Instructor Talios. "Create the teams."

"Yes, sir," said the female instructor as she stepped forward. "Anyone not competing, get off the field and sit in the stands. Today, you're spectators!" There was a ragged cheer as the suddenly freed students ran for the elevated benches.

Britea turned to catch Kahl's eye, but he and Mat were already surrounded by the excited students who were going to compete in the upcoming Trials.

"Come on!" said an excited Pearl as she tugged at Britea's hand. "Let's grab a seat before the best ones are gone!"

"You seem pretty happy," said Britea as she followed her friend.

"Are you kidding?! For the first time in, well, ever, we don't have to run! Instead, we get to watch other people run!"

The two reached the stands as Instructor Talios began to divide the competitors into teams.

"What are they doing now?" asked Britea.

"She's properly pairing them up for the simple race, wielding race, simple spar, wielding spar, and endurance wielding. I bet she'll leave the pairing for the rapid-answer knowledge competition for Instructor Dawn." It took a moment for Pearl to notice Britea was staring at her.

"Oh, you've never seen this competition before. Silly me. I've seen it twice. It's exciting!"

"I never took you for one to like such contests," said Britea with a smile.

Pearl grinned back. "I am more than I appear, my friend." That last word made Britea happy.

"Hello, ladies," said Henrick wearily as he sat down beside Britea.

"Hey, Henrick," greeted Pearl casually.

"You missed the big announcement!" said Britea.

"Blame Dariuz," said Henrick as he glared at a certain male novice sitting far away from them.

"What did he do?" asked a curious Pearl.

"Complained about you two, his uncle, and Kahl all night long." Britea gave him a questioning look. "Apparently his uncle isn't too happy about his lack of progress in nabbing the vert-silk trade deal. He talked for so long I barely got any sleep, which made me late for breakfast, exhausted for most of my morning classes, and then I eventually fell asleep in Instructor Felgreen's class. She was not pleased, and she gave me a quiz to do on the spot, so I barely made it here."

"Ouch," said a sympathetic Pearl.

Britea grimaced. She had noticed at breakfast that he was exhausted, but she had not had enough time to ask him why because by the time he had arrived, it was time for her and Pearl to head to dancing and etiquette.

And there had been no opportunity during the rest of the day to talk to him either because most of their instructors had placed Britea and Pearl at the front of the class since their punishment had begun. She wished she had been able to sit near Henrick in history class; maybe she could have nudged him awake.

"But Dariuz is just a kid like us," complained Pearl. "How exactly does his uncle expect him to negotiate a trade deal with the Dyhaeri?"

"I have no bloody idea," groaned Henrick. "I just pray he lets me sleep tonight, but first, I have to survive Instructor Melvin's wielding class. So, what did I miss?"

Pearl and Britea took turns in updating Henrick on the latest developments. He blinked several times when they were done.

"The Trials were brought forward by two weeks? Does anyone know why?"

Britea shrugged. "If they do, they didn't tell us."

"Hmm." Henrick was thoughtful as he gazed at the field. "And Kahl and Mat are going to observe and advise us. Master Caren must be delighted."

"Can you blame him?" said Pearl. "I bet the other schools campaigned to bring the games forward when they realized we had three high-ranking Dyhaeri inspecting our school. So now, maybe the Dyhaeri may help us balance the scales and even win."

Henrick sighed sadly. "The last time Syla College won was more than twenty years ago. Ever since then, we've come last every time."

"It'll be different this time, you'll see," countered Pearl.

"Attention!" the amplified voice of Instructor Talios made the watching students fall silent.

"The first competition will be the simple race between Novice Belle Dright representing group A and Novice Elvira Moors representing Group B!" The two girls took to the racetrack and crouched down.

"Silence in the court!" The entire field fell quiet, and after what seemed an eternity, a loud bang went off, and the two girls were racing around the track.

Soon, the students in the stands began cheering the girls on. Britea found herself getting caught up in the excitement.

"It's a lot louder at the real Trials!" happily shouted Pearl.

The race was over in less than two minutes, and Novice Belle Dright of Group A was the winner. An assistant instructor placed a mark on the huge scoreboard mounted close to where the competitors were gathered.

Students and instructors then ran onto the track to place large obstacles. It took Britea a few moments to see the pattern. The first three obstacles were a pile of wooden planks, a bonfire, and a huge pile of boulders. The next three obstacles were again wood, fire, and rocks, and the last three were the same as the previous two sets. Troughs of water were also placed near the fire obstacles. "Next up is the wielding race!" announced Inspector Talios.

"This is going to be fantastic," whispered Pearl. Britea sent her an inquiring look. Her friend hastened to answer.

"Two racers like last time, but this time with barriers. They have to use their wielding abilities to either go around the barriers or through them. The first to the finish line wins."

"In the first lane is Novice Vran Lhanell, representing Group A, and in the second lane is Novice Thom Meldson, representing Group B!" The instructor paused as the two novices crouched down, ready to race.

"Silence!" The spectators complied immediately. After a long moment, another loud bang went off, and this time, Britea saw who created it. Weapons Master Caren had a pistol that he fired into the air when it was time to race. Britea had read about such weapons, but they were rare and quite expensive to make. This was the first time she had ever seen one.

"Here they come!" said Henrick excitedly. Britea turned back to the race.

The first twenty meters of the track were clear, and then the two runners encountered their first obstacle: two piles of wooden planks almost the height of a full-grown man. Vran got to his first and began to air wield the planks off the track, but Thom simply ran around his. Britea saw the frustration on Vran's face as the spectators laughed. Vran stopped wielding and ran after Thom. The next obstacle was fire, which was lit as the runners appeared. Thom got there first, and he tried to use his water wield to try to put out the flames while Vran released a tier-one air blast to blow his way through, but it only fuelled the intensity of the fire, making the flames leap higher. Britea was so shocked by this turn of events she found herself standing up with the other spectators.

The two novices couldn't even run around the blaze. It was too big and too dangerous. Fortunately, the two assistant instructors who had been watching nearby used their water-wielding abilities to put out the flames. Some of the students who were waiting to compete ran onto the track to help. Britea was alarmed to see Danai was one of them. It took some time and a lot of wielding, but the flames were eventually extinguished. Poor Vran and Thom looked quite embarrassed though.

"No score!" announced Instructor Talios to the disappointment of the crowd.

"At least no one got hurt," said Britea as she returned to her seat.

"Oh, the day is still young," commented Pearl grimly. Britea gave her an odd look.

"The real thing is a lot more intense than this, and a lot more dangerous."

"How so?" asked Britea.

"Students have died during the games before," said Henrick somberly.

That left Britea speechless.

#

Earlier, Kahl had felt nervous when he had realized he and Mat were going to be advisors to Syla College for the Trials. What if he said the wrong thing and made them lose? In contrast, Mat had been eager to get started. Kahl wondered if his cousin was just bored and looking for some action or if a certain Weltonian lass was to blame.

However, as the mock Trials started, Kahl found his nervousness replaced by excitement until dread crept in when the wielding race failed.

"Are you seeing this?" asked Kahl softly in Dyhaeri as they watched the two novices fail to go through the first fire barrier. Danai had already run onto the track to help her peers put out the fire.

"Uh huh," said Mat, his eyes narrowed as he watched the fire eventually be extinguished. "Kahl, forgive me in advance, but I'm about to suggest something a bit crazy. Support me please?"

Kahl shot his cousin a worried look. "Of course. I'm at your side always."

"I appreciate that," muttered Mat with a grateful smile before he turned to Instructor Talios.

"My cousin and I would like to run the wielding race with the same obstacles."

Kahl's jaw dropped. *What was his cousin up to?*

Instructor Talios and the nearby students stared at Mat. "You wish to compete?" finally asked the stunned instructor.

"Just in the mock Trials. I have an idea that I'd like to try out with the fire obstacles. Kahl will be my opponent." The instructor glanced over at Master Caren, who was standing far away talking quietly with the two downcast novices.

"Let me have a word with Master Caren first."

"Of course," said Mat. He looked at Kahl. "Got your running boots on, cousin?"

"Wait, you're related?" asked Navos. The giant of a novice had been limbering up for his turn in the sparring competition.

"Yes," said Kahl as the other students watched. Navos seemed bolder than the rest.

"Nice," said Navos. "I hope I get to train with you two sometime."

"Anytime," said Mat in a friendly tone.

Kahl gaped at his cousin. *Who was this imposter?* Apparently, he genuinely wanted to spar with the humans at this school. Part of Kahl was glad, but he was also worried it was all an act.

"Master Caren agrees," said Instructor Talios as she returned. Kahl looked over at the weapons master and saw the two students beside him looked less despondent.

"We'll prepare the course, and then we'll restart the wielding race."

Mat rubbed his hands with glee while Kahl tried to hide his concern about his cousin's strange behavior.

"Kahl, I have an idea about how we can get through those obstacles," began Mat as the two cousins walked to take their places at the start of the track. "Listen carefully..."

#

"What's going on?" asked Danai when she noticed the instructors were resetting the course and relighting the first fire obstacle.

"The Dyhaeri princes want to have a go," replied one of the instructors.

"Wait, what?" exclaimed an alarmed Danai as she turned. Sure enough, Mat and Kahl were taking to the field as Instructor Talios spoke in an amplified voice.

"For the wielding race, we have in lane one, Prince Mat, representing Group A!" This drew a surprised cheer from the spectators. "And in lane two is Prince Kahl, representing Group B!"

"This can't be happening," muttered a concerned Danai.

#

"I thought you said they weren't going to compete!" Henrick was on his feet with everyone else trying to watch the two Dyhaeri.

"That's what Master Caren said!" Pearl's face was flushed as she stood. Britea on the other hand, was far from being excited. After learning students had died in this race, she was more worried about Kahl getting hurt than Syla College winning the competition.

"Everyone, sit down!" roared one of the instructors standing below the stands. The response was immediate, but the air was still filled with tension.

"Silence!" Then a long moment later, Master Caren shot his pistol into the air, and the race was on. The crowd cheered when Kahl reached the wooden planks first. He didn't even bother wielding. He ran around it.

"Hey, why didn't he do something? Like wield or something?!" complained someone behind Britea. She turned to glare at the novice.

"Pay attention!" said Pearl as she grabbed her friend's arm.

#

Kahl glanced behind him. His cousin had also run around the pile of wooden planks. Forcing himself to concentrate, Kahl ran towards the raging bonfire and pretended he was underwater, then he wielded a tier-one bubble from the nearby trough of water. He kept running as he encased himself in the watery bubble, instantly dulling the roar of the crowd to a mere mumble before he leapt into the bonfire. He missed the cries of alarm that became loud cheers when he emerged on the other side unscathed, still hurtling forward while elevated in the bubble above the ground.

Now, that was interesting. That was the first time Kahl had done that on land.

A quick glance to the side showed Mat had done the same with a tier-one air bubble. The bonfire also seemed a bit smaller. Mat had probably used the right amount of air to suppress the fire instead of fanning it on. Once clear of the blaze, both Dyhaeri shed their bubbles, landed on the track, and kept running.

The third obstacle was a twelve-foot pile of rocks.

"Race you to the top, cousin!" yelled Mat happily as he pulled ahead, and instead of running around the rocks, he used a tier-one wield to create steps of air, which he used to run up and down the pile of rocks.

Kahl grinned in response and reached behind him to wield bubbles of water from the trough of water at the first bonfire. He heard the stunned reaction from the spectators as the bubbles caught up to him in time to wield watery steps that he used to race up and then down the pile of rocks. Then he was running after his manic cousin. By the time they got over the last trio of obstacles, he and Mat were almost neck and neck. Kahl heard different groups chanting his name and Mat's, but he kept his eyes on the finish line.

"Time!" boomed Instructor Talios. "And the winner is Prince Kahl for Group B!"

Kahl almost collapsed on the ground, but he managed to stagger to a seat while the students and instructors of Group B clapped him on the back. He glanced over at Mat, who was still standing, though breathless. Kahl watched as Mat walked over to Danai.

"What did you think?" Kahl heard Mat ask as he tried to catch his breath.

"Impressive," said Danai, though she wasn't smiling. "But you lost."

Mat shrugged. "Win some, lose some, but at least I got you to watch."

Kahl's eyes widened. *Was Mat flirting with Danai?*

"That was remarkable, Prince Kahl!" said a smiling Weapons Master Caren, drawing his attention away from Kahl's oddly behaving cousin.

Kahl quickly rose, still trying to catch his breath. "I…I… the track is something else."

"From your performance, it seems Dyhaeri childhood games are similar to some parts of our Wielder Trials."

"I believe so," agreed Kahl. *But why was that?* Maybe he could ask the high priest about it.

Navos raised his hand. "How did you do that bubble-encasement wield?"

Kahl had finally got his breath back. "I used a tier-one bubble and gave it an extra thick layer. Then I leapt into it as I opened it up and encased it around me." He demonstrated by forming a small bubble and then opening it up without collapsing it. Then he closed it again.

The water wielders among the novices began to try and mimic what he had just done.

"Thank you, Prince Kahl," said Navos, and several students echoed him.

"Please, just call me Kahl." He was so tired of the "prince" title.

"Sure thing, Kahl," said Navos with a smile. Some air wielders drifted over to Mat to ask him to demonstrate, and Kahl hid his surprise as his cousin did just that.

It was time he had a chat with Mat about his abrupt change in behavior.

#

"Navos has an impressive swing," groaned Mat as he soaked in the warm pool in the Dyhaeri guest quarters. "Not surprising, though. He has the build of one who can swing an axe. He just needs to work a bit on his footwork."

Kahl nodded in agreement. "I'm sure he appreciated the advice, though he did get in some good hits."

"Tell me about it," groaned Mat as he let the warmed waters treat his sore back.

It was evening. Today had been a long day and the high priest hadn't returned yet. He had mentioned earlier he was going to attend a series of meetings with the headmaster, the warden, and a few instructors, which was why Lieutenant Flay had been missing from combat and defense. He must have stuck to the high priest like a leech all day.

That must have been excruciating for them both.

Kahl brought his mind back to what was bothering him. "Mat, what is your intention towards Danai Riverun?"

His cousin froze in the pool, then turned to look at his cousin. "Excuse me?"

"You've been flirting with her."

"Why are you concerned, Kahl?"

"Two reasons. One, she's the daughter of Captain Lanead Riverun and Captain Sonei Riverun. They're good people, but they won't appreciate it if you're toying with her. Two, Danai is Britea's friend and roommate."

Mat blinked. "You're taking this very seriously."

"As should you," said Kahl, squatting outside the pool to be at eye level with his older cousin. "What is your intention?"

Mat was silent for a long moment. "I'm actually glad you brought this up. I don't mean any harm. She seems like a level-headed person, and her fighting skills…well, they're just as good as any Dyhaeri marine."

Kahl raised an eyebrow. "You only sparred with her once."

"And I would love to spar with her again," said Mat in a dreamy voice.

Kahl stared at his cousin. "You like her."

Mat's green skin flushed a darker green. "I just said I like sparring with her! That doesn't mean I like her!"

"Yeah, right," said Kahl, unconvinced. "Fine, be that way."

"What is that supposed to mean?" asked Mat, glaring at his younger cousin.

Kahl smiled mischievously at him. "I'll wait for you to realize it, my dear cousin." He leapt out of the way when Mat wielded a large soap bubble at him.

#

Britea knocked on Pearl's door.

"Give me a moment!" came a muffled voice from within.

Britea nodded even though no one could see the gesture. This was the first time she had come to Pearl's dorm room. Once Pearl had given her the directions after the first day of mock Trials, she had been surprised to realize it wasn't far from hers.

The door swung open, revealing a flustered Pearl. "Come in while I tidy up."

Britea gingerly entered the room. It was much smaller than the one Britea shared with Danai and was currently a mess. There were clothes thrown helter-skelter on the single bed, and dozens of books were arranged haphazardly on the desk and chair.

Pearl took one look at the expression on Britea's face and sighed. "Lianne used to get some of the juniors in our corridor to clean our room. Now I have to learn how to do it myself."

Britea stared at her. "Using juniors as servants? Surely that's not allowed?"

Pearl shrugged. "It probably isn't, but Selina used to do the same and no instructor ever called her out on it." She went back to tidying.

After a few moments, Britea couldn't help herself. "Let me help you."

Pearl gave her a relieved smile. "Thanks. By the way, is Danai all right with me coming to your room to work on our biology assignment?"

Britea smiled cheerfully while hiding her uncertainty. "Of course, she is."

#

Britea tried to hide her nervousness as she and Pearl approached the room Britea shared with Danai, a little unsure of how Danai would feel about Pearl entering their shared space. She had invited Pearl so they could work on their biology assignment. It wasn't as if Danai couldn't help, but Britea suspected Pearl was lonely. And the state of Pearl's room had confirmed that.

Britea had also noticed how the other highborn students snubbed Pearl, and it hadn't taken long to guess who was behind that.

To Britea's surprise, even Vindell and Chelton had gradually warmed up to Pearl. It had come as a surprise to Pearl as well, and it had all started when Pearl had tried to show Vindell how to improve her tier-one wielding. At first, Vindell had been hesitant to learn from Pearl of all people, but over the last two weeks, the junior wielder had become less afraid.

But Britea was still nervous about how Danai would react when Pearl showed up at their room because Britea had to wonder if Danai was still a bit suspicious of Pearl. She had asked Danai yesterday if Pearl could come to their rooms, and her Weltonian roommate had agreed to her request. But ever since the mock Trials, Danai had been gloomy at dinner. Britea could only wonder why Danai was in a bad mood. As the study partners reached Britea's quarters, she decided not to ponder it anymore.

"So, this is my room. Would you like to come in?" asked Britea.

"Sure," said Pearl as she yawned. "Though I doubt we'll get much work done, I'm so sleepy."

Both girls walked in only to see a fuming Danai pacing the room while Lexia, who was perched on the desk by the far wall, watched her, looking worried.

"Oh," said Britea as she wondered if this had been the wrong time to arrange a visit.

"Is this a bad time?" asked Pearl. Lexia gave the two girls a concerned look; for once, she didn't seem agitated by Pearl's appearance.

"Yes, it is—"

"What was he thinking?!" blurted out Danai. "Wielding steps of air to run up a pile twelve feet high and getting his younger cousin to do the same thing? They could have fallen and hurt themselves, and then we would all have been in trouble with the Dyhaeri monarchy!"

Britea and Pearl stared at each other, then at Danai.

"Prince Mat?" asked both girls at the same time. Lexia sighed and closed her eyes as Danai stopped to face them.

"Who else would I be bloody talking about?!"

Pearl shoved Britea into the room and shut the door behind them.

Danai resumed her pacing. "Yes. I admit, he's an accomplished wielder, but the Trials are nothing to trifle with. I know I've always disliked what the competition has become, but to show off like that?!"

Lexia opened her eyes and folded her arms, tracking Danai's pacing.

Britea was unsure of how to proceed. Words escaped her because she was still unsure why Danai was so angry. But Pearl smiled as if she knew a secret.

"Oh, you like Prince Mat." That stopped Danai cold. Lexia shot Pearl an irritated look.

"No, I don't!" protested Danai vehemently, and her face reddened.

Pearl laughed softly. "I knew it. In the library, he came looking for you. He also stayed back to read a book by your side two days in a row. And let's not forget that when my mother," Pearl grimaced, "came to visit, you and Britea wanted to support me, and Prince Mat followed."

Lexia shot Danai a surprised look. "You didn't tell me that."

"But…but Kahl was there too!"

Now it was Britea's turn to flush.

"We both know Kahl is sweet on Britea," said Pearl.

Lexia's jaw dropped. "Wait, what?" asked the petite redhead.

Pearl continued to address Danai. "And Prince Mat may be sweet on you too. I think he was trying to impress you, and it seems to have worked."

"No, it didn't!" insisted Danai through gritted teeth.

"Then why are you so upset?" asked Britea calmly.

That took the wind from her sails. The Weltonian novice collapsed backwards on her bed.

"I'm an idiot," she groaned at the ceiling.

Lexia gave Britea and Pearl a firm look. "I trust you two will keep this to yourselves."

"Of course," said Pearl as she returned the same look. "I don't run with Lianne and her group anymore if that's what you're worried about."

Lexia smiled coldly. "I'm glad we understand each other."

"It doesn't matter," said Danai, resignation in her voice. "I'm human and he's Dyhaeri. I don't care if anyone talks about it. Nothing will ever happen."

That made Britea think of Kahl. *Was that their fate as well?*

Pearl gently put an arm around Britea as if sensing her despair. "Who knows, Danai? You may be wrong about that. Come on, Britea, let's work on our assignment."

But as Britea opened her textbooks, she kept wondering if there was any future for her and Kahl.

CHAPTER 26

Lanead tried not to fidget as he waited for the Weltonian Elders Council to summon him. He was currently sitting on old tree stump on the outskirts of Glenning Forest. It was one of the few places on land Weltonians could safely meet since they owned this piece of land in the northern icy regions of Malaquey. He wrapped his cloak tighter around him and blew warm air over his hands before rubbing them together. By the Lords, he hated winter.

It had been a week since he had brought the refugees to safety, but because a Weltonian ship had been destroyed, he had requested an emergency meeting.

A meeting that had taken a week to arrange. Some may say that was not a long time, but Lanead disagreed. A flying ship had destroyed the *Mother's Star* and its crew. That was enough reason for urgency. The meeting should have been held the night they had docked at a friendly harbor, but no, they had to wait for a certain member of council to be present. Lanead took deep breaths to control his temper.

"The council will see you now, Captain Riverun." Lanead sprang from his seat and followed the young female Weltonian deeper into the snow-covered forest. He kept his eyes on her back to prevent getting lost. That would be beyond embarrassing.

Eventually they came to a clearing with a large tent in the center. Lanead was relieved to see several guards around the tent and hidden in the tree lines. Since the Time of Persecution, it never paid to be too cautious.

His single escort stopped by the side of the entrance and silently bade him enter.

Lanead's nervousness returned as he entered the cavernous tent. It took a moment for his eyesight to adjust. Seated in a semicircle were thirteen elders representing the different factions of the Weltonian people. He recognized them all, and their expressions were stern.

Well, at least they're taking this seriously.

He entered the circle that had been drawn on the floor and faced the elders.

"Council leaders, I am here." That was the cue for the meeting to begin.

"We see you," came the answer, confirming him as a Weltonian. The reply made him feel more at ease.

"Before we talk about the main reason for this meeting, I would like to discuss a few things first," began Elder Brett Skylight of the Second Faction. He was in his mid-sixties and the captain of the *Majestic Wind* . He was also the member who had demanded the meeting not take place until he had arrived. Lanead counted to eight in his head to control his temper.

"Proceed," said Elder Naleen Summers of the First Faction.

"Trade is down in the last quarter, and we need to increase sales of vert-silk to make that up, or it will be harder to provide for all the factions."

Lanead blinked. The faction leader wanted to talk about trade *now* ? When lives and freedom were at stake?!

Elder Crane Starflame of the Thirteenth Faction held up a hand to object. "Harvesting the raw materials for vert-silk is not a simple swim in the lake, my dear Brett." His tone was icy. "Besides, you well know it's a seasonal material as Alkynaia only lay their eggs twice a year. That gives us but a narrow time frame to reap the gel from their hatched eggs!"

Lanead closed his eyes briefly and asked the Sea Mother for patience.

"Do you have any other suggestions?" asked Brett dryly.

"Why don't you lot expand your farming to include more land, so we have more spices to sell to the people of Malaquey?" retorted Crane.

"Elders of the council!" growled Lanead before he could stop himself. "I didn't come all this way to listen to you bicker about trade and profits! Several of our people died last week when a flying—I repeat, *flying* — Namiran ship obliterated the *Mother's Star.* " Most of the elders watched him silently, looking displeased, and Brett glared at him. Frankly, he didn't care as long as they all listened.

"If we do not address the problem right now, the seas will no longer be safe for our kind. And the humans certainly aren't going to just hand over their land. This is why we need this meeting today."

The thirteen elders simply looked at him for a long moment.

"We are aware of the unfortunate incident," said Elder Naleen Summers calmly. "Despite what you desire, we will address that matter once we discuss why your daughter, Danai Riverun, is still at Syla College."

Lanead stared at her, speechless. *Why would the elders bring up Danai now of all times?*

"She has been there for four years now, has she not?" asked Elder Dren Wind. He represented the Tenth Faction.

"Yes, but what does that have to do with—" began Lanead when he finally found the words.

"Why is she still there?" demanded Elder Brett Skylight. "Most Weltonian youths know where they wish to stay before completing even a year of the Time of Seeking, but she has stayed at Syla College for four years."

"She has one more year left," said Lanead through gritted teeth.

"No longer," said Elder Naleen Summers. "Due to current circumstances, we are reducing the Time of Seeking to four years. Your daughter has less than four months to sort out her affairs and return to the fold, or she will be exiled."

Lanead took a step back in shock. "Why are you doing this?"

"We have lost too many of our own, Captain Riverun," said Elder Rhedd Frost in a kinder tone. He represented the Fourth Faction. "Even at the age of sixteen, your daughter had the makings of a natural born leader. I was saddened when I heard she had chosen to spend her Time of Seeking at Syla College. Our ancestors built those colleges, and today the people of Malaquey and Namira have forgotten the part we played in the establishment of all five wielding schools. She will not be appreciated by the people of Malaquey, and she has no place there."

The other elders nodded. Rhedd continued. "We need her back amongst us because it may not be long before she has to wield the reins of leadership."

Lanead tried to ease the mounting pressure in his chest. "But you have to give her time to decide."

"She has four months," said Elder Naleen Summers in a voice that said the decision was final.

"Now, about the Namiran attack. What more can you tell us about the vessel?" asked Elder Val Night of the Fifth Faction.

Lanead wanted to rage at the council. *They had just threatened his daughter with exile, and now they wanted to discuss the attack?!* He took a long moment to compose himself before he replied. "The flying ship's length, overall, was roughly three hundred meters, and it had neither flag nor insignia to designate its origin. I had no chance to accurately estimate the height of the ship as we were fleeing at the time."

"Weapons?" asked Brett.

"They certainly had wielders on board, but as I said, we didn't stick around to find out if there were additional mounted armaments." Lanead forced himself to keep his tone civil.

"You saw only one ship?" asked Elder Pran Timelock of the Ninth Faction, Lanead's own faction. Elder Timelock was one of the more militaristic members of the council, and her faction had more wielders than the rest. She had also been one of Danai's teachers before his daughter had left for Syla College.

One ship was all we needed to encounter, thank you very much! "Yes," replied Lanead.

"It may only be a prototype," said Elder Crane Starflame.

"That works quite well," commented Elder Dren Wind.

"Is there any word from our people in Namira about this flying ship?" asked Elder Val.

"A few months ago, we got whispers of a new project initiated in the renovated shipyards at Port Fearless," said Pran gravely. "They were bringing in prisoners to do the work; thus, we were unable to get anyone inside. The prisoners have not been seen since, and little food was delivered to that shipyard." This was met by silence. It didn't take a genius to know those prisoners were dead.

Pran continued. "It would have been a one-way trip for an agent anyway. What I do know, is that those covered shipyards can hold more than one ship of the size Captain Riverun just described."

There was further silence as they absorbed that information.

"We need to warn the Malaquey government," said Lanead, and everyone looked at him.

"They probably already know," said Elder Stev Tremors of the Sixth Faction.

"Then it won't hurt if we make sure of that," countered Lanead.

"I agree," said Pran to the surprise of the other elders. Lanead gave her a look of gratitude.

"We will put it to a vote at the end of the meeting," said Elder Naleen Summers.

"What about the Dyhaeri currently at Syla College?" asked Elder Melody Timeless of the Seventh Faction. "How long do they plan to stay there?" Now everyone turned to look at Lanead.

Lanead had made no secret of the fact that he had taken the three Dyhaeri to Malaquey; he had told them almost everything.

He had left out the prophecy though. The Seers had warned him not to let that slip; it wasn't time yet. "They failed to mention exactly how long they would be staying, and I saw no need to ask them." He was a bit amused to see most of the elders were disappointed in his reply.

"I still wonder why, out of all of us, King Jahlaniin picked you to grace with his presence," said Elder Brett Skylight, a skeptical expression on his face. "Come to think of it, didn't he and the high priest visit your ship the day Danai was born?" The elder looked around at his colleagues. "None of us have been so blessed by his royal presence, and yet he has been in your company several times, before her birth and after. Why is that, Captain Lanead Riverun?"

Lanead could detect the hidden jealousy and wondered if the others had heard it too.

"You'd have a better chance of getting an answer from the Sea Mother, Brett," said Elder Pran dryly.

"Who visits whom does not concern us as long as such relationships do not endanger our people's safety," said Elder Naleen Summers firmly.

Brett held up his hands in mock surrender. "I was just curious."

Yeah, right, thought Lanead.

"Does anyone have anything thing to add?" asked Naleen. She was greeted by silence.

"Then we vote."

In the end, they unanimously agreed to send an urgent report to Malaquey Naval Intelligence about the new flying vessel.

#

Harto gritted his teeth in frustration as he forced himself to remain calm.

He had been waiting outside the headmaster's office once again for the past thirty minutes. This reminded him of the times he had gotten into trouble at the Royal Malaquey Naval Wielding College. It had only happened a few times.

All right, make that more times than he would care to admit. However, it had just been innocent fun, just some pranks that had gotten out of control.

But this time, he had not been playing a prank. He was trying to do his best to defend Malaquey as he had sworn to when he had joined the navy. So, why in the Seven Hells was he made to wait outside as if he was still a wet-behind-the-ears novice?

This wasn't the first time he had tried to gain an audience with the headmaster.

Ever since he had found out five days ago that Mat and Kahl were helping the students train for the games, he had demanded an audience. The result? He had been turned away several times.

The reasons? Oh, the headmaster is at court. Oh, the headmaster is having an afternoon siesta. Oh, the headmaster has gone to bed for the evening. Oh, the headmaster is busy. Oh, the headmaster has gone to obtain more materials for the Trials that were moved forward without any warning. He had thought that last excuse flimsy when he had seen how the instructor who had delivered the message had smirked at him, and Harto had realized he was being punished.

To keep his frustration at bay, Harto turned his mind to the rest of his plans for today. His uncle had recently asked him how his second mission was going. To be precise, the one involving the Riverun family. As expected, his commanding officer—his uncle—was disappointed he was yet to get any intel. To be honest, Harto didn't see the point in questioning Danai. What if she was innocent? But he had promised his uncle he would try, and soon. He already had a plan on how to do just that.

The sound of the door opening had him rising from the backless bench in the hallway.

The tall, thin-faced warden regarded him with a grave expression on his face. "You may come in now, Lieutenant Flay."

Harto tried to keep a polite expression on his face as he walked into the headmaster's office. The man in question was behind the desk. Several papers were strewn before him. "Good morning, Headmaster Clayre."

There were bags under the headmaster's eyes, and his eyes looked bloodshot as if he had not slept for days. "Best of the morning to you," said the weary headmaster. "Please, have a seat. How may I help you today?"

The warden positioned himself close to the desk and remained standing while facing Harto. The young naval officer wondered who he should be more concerned about.

"I discovered five days ago that Prince Mat and Prince Kahl are helping Master Caren train the students for the upcoming games."

The headmaster and the warden looked at him.

"And?" asked Headmaster Clayre.

"Is that wise? Having the students learning unconventional methods of wielding just two weeks before the Trials may put their lives in danger."

Headmaster Clayre pushed back from his desk, his face flushed with anger. The warden remained neutral.

"So, you running to your uncle so he can whisper into the king's ear and bring the games closer by two weeks doesn't also increase the risk to our students?"

Harto felt his face heat up. "That had not been my intention…"

"Yet, here we are," said Headmaster Clayre in a calm voice that belied the rage in his eyes. "Do you know what these papers are on my desk? Pages and pages of special supplies we have to buy to accommodate all three colleges. Now usually, the prepaid orders would have come in a week at the original Trials date. But because the Trials were moved up, I have to pay extra to get the supplies even sooner. Do you know how much that's going to cost the college, hmm?"

Harto wisely kept his mouth shut.

"You have no idea, do you? Our coffers are not as endless as those of the Royal Malaquey Naval Wielding College, so believe me when I say your careless antic has drained our treasury before it was time for the quarterly stipend from the royal court. I'm sure you're aware that of the three colleges, Syla gets the least funding from the court, yet we have to host the Trials every blasted two years." The last two words held a current of bitterness.

Harto had the grace to look at his feet in embarrassment. He had not known his uncle would suggest moving the games. When he had gotten word, he had rejoiced, knowing that now he had the excuse he needed to bring more Malaquey agents to Syla College under the pretext of providing security for the Trials. But even if he had known of the consequences of his uncle's actions, would he have done anything about it?

"Was there anything else?" asked the warden in a monotone.

Before Harto had entered the office, he had been prepared with a list of questions, but now he didn't have the heart to say anything more.

"No, that will be all. Thank you." Harto quietly left the office, feeling once more like a chastened novice instead of the confident naval intelligence officer he was.

#

Pearl knew something was wrong the moment she and Britea walked into combat and defense several minutes before it was to begin.

Lianne, Valerie, Daphne, and Theresa were also there, still in the usual school uniform.

"What are they doing here?" asked Britea. The four girls were chatting with a few students who had also arrived early. Each day this week had consisted of brief exercises for the class before a repeat mock trial for the real games, and some classes were allowing non-competing students to come watch and encourage the competitors. The real draw, though, was Mat and Kahl, who were coaching the competing students.

"I'm not sure, but I don't like this," said Pearl as she felt dread mount in the pit of her stomach. At first, she had disliked combat and defense class, but in time, she had actually begun to like the class. Here, no one cared if you were highborn or lowborn. Besides, Lianne and her ilk disliked physical exertion of any sort, so they would never join such a class.

But if they had changed their minds, then Pearl's only safe zone was gone.

"Let's go change before they see us," said Pearl in an urgent whisper. "We can hide in the locker rooms, and by the time we come out, maybe they'll have gone."

Both girls hurried to the change rooms for the girls, passing the bold sign that read "Only for Female Members of Defense and Combat Class.' Pearl and Britea each grabbed a freshly laundered uniform with their wielding colors. The two girls were the only ones in the change rooms for the moment.

"Do you think they came to join our class?" asked Britea in a worried voice as she entered a stall to change.

Pearl snorted in disbelief. "No, they probably came to watch the mock Trials." She sat down on a bench to exchange her boots for softer running shoes. Pearl was unlacing the left boot when she heard a sound from the doorway. Britea was still talking.

"Wait, I heard something. Let me check."

Britea fell silent as Pearl went searching and fatefully running into the last four people she wanted to see.

Lianne Arkei smiled at her. She was, of course, flanked by Valerie, Daphne, and Theresa.

"Oh, there you are. Someone saw you duck into the dressing rooms. Are you here all by your lonesome?" asked Lianne.

Pearl backed into the change room and raised her voice, hoping Britea would take the hint.

"Yes, Lianne. I'm the only one here. What do you want now?" Pearl sat down and casually began to remove her boots.

Lianne looked at her followers. "Wait outside and prevent anyone from entering." Daphne and Theresa left, but Valerie stayed behind. Lianne shot her a dark look. "You too."

Valerie blinked in surprise, and her expression turned to anger when Pearl smirked at her. The blond stormed out of the change room.

Lianne began to pace around the room. "My, how far you've fallen." She sniffed as if smelling something foul. "How can you stand rubbing shoulders with the peasants?"

Pearl's heart rate rose when Lianne got too close to where Pearl could see Britea was hiding. "Enough with the posturing, Lianne, what do you want?"

Lianne turned back to face Pearl and stepped away from the changing stalls.

"I hear that, somehow, you've become friends with the Dyhaeri." Lianne's expression was calculating.

Pearl folded her arms. "That's why you're here? In the combat and defense class you've always looked down on since you and I started as the most junior of novices?"

Lianne sniffed again as if uncomfortable with an imaginary scent.

"Circumstances make strange bedfellows, don't you agree?"

Pearl raised an eyebrow. "What's that supposed to mean?"

"Last weekend, your mother was only too happy to tell everyone you and Britea are friends. I sure hope for your sake that part isn't true." sneered Lianne. "I also heard the pair of you were quite close to the Dyhaeri princes." She stepped closer and glowered down at Pearl.

"So here I am, unable to get close enough to them to even have a simple chat, and you've managed to become friends with them!"

Pearl pointed three fingers in the air. "That's the third time you've mentioned the 'friends with the Dyhaeri' part, yet you still haven't told me why you cornered me in the change room." She paused to tilt her head and raise an eyebrow. "We eat in the same dining hall, and we attend almost all the same classes apart from combat and defense. Are you so ashamed to talk to me that you had to catch me alone?"

Lianne closed her eyes briefly as if trying to contain her anger, then she took a deep breath.

"I am here to offer you a chance to return to my circle."

Pearl blinked. "Excuse me?"

"My family needs information on the Dyhaeri, particularly why they're here and what trade ventures they might be willing to negotiate on—"

"This is about the vert-silk trade, isn't it?" cut in Pearl.

Lianne made a face as if she had tasted something vile. "Perhaps. However, if you can get me a meeting with them, or even better, convince them to attend one of my family's parties, all will be forgiven, and I will let you move back in with Valerie and I."

Pearl stared at her for a long moment. "Why did you abandon me, Lianne?"

Lianne was taken aback by the question. "I don't understand."

"Do you remember the night of the duel on the Forever Bridge? I fell over the side and thought I was about to die. But someone wielding water pulled me to safety. For one precious second, I was sure it was you, saving me. But it was Britea. I looked for you and Valerie, but you had both fled and left me alone to die!" Pearl rose and walked towards Lianne, who took a step back.

"But your betrayal didn't stop there, did it? I sent you a letter from the infirmary begging for your help while I kept silent about your part in the sordid affair. Do you remember the reply you sent back? I do. It was, and I quote, 'I do not associate with breakers of the Wielder Creed and breakers of academy rules. Whatever punishment she gets is one that she deserves, and the warden's decision of expulsion has my blessing!'"

Silence reigned in the dressing room.

"I stayed in that infirmary for three days while you and Valerie partied at your home. That was followed by ridicule and then lies to my parents when they attended a ball at your house two weeks ago! You think I didn't know about that? Read my lips, Lianne, the day I help you is the day the Seven Hells freeze over!"

Lianne's expression turned cold. "If you don't help me, I'll spill the reason you hate going home so much."

Pearl took a step back.

Lianne looked triumphant. "You know, like how you were such a fat slob, how embarrassed your parents were of you, and about the slimming classes you had to take in secret. Oh, and let's not forget about your cousins."

"Stop," hissed Pearl as she tried to resist the urge to wield an air orb into Lianne's sneering face.

"You *will* help me, Pearl or I will…"

"Do absolutely nothing," said Britea, stepping out of the stall in her sparring gear. "Leave her alone."

Lianne stared at her in surprise, then back at Pearl in disgust.

"So, you are really friends with this peasant rat?"

Pearl responded by shoving Lianne. The girl took a few steps back with a surprised cry, but she didn't fall. Pearl stepped forward, rage in her eyes, only to find her path blocked by Britea.

"No! Don't!"

"You'll pay for this, Pearl!" yelled Lianne, who had instantly wielded three spears of water from a nearby bowl of water. Britea reacted by instantly forming a water shield made up of several tier-one oval shapes.

"Stop right there!" bellowed Instructor Talios. The force of that shout had Lianne dropping her wield, but Britea kept her shield up.

"Britea, drop your shield right now. No one will hurt you or Pearl," ordered the instructor. It took a long moment for Britea to comply. Pearl stayed silent behind her.

"Oh, Instructor Talios, thank the Lords you got here in time," said Lianne, sounding distressed. "These two attacked me—"

"What are you doing here, Novice Arkei?" demanded Instructor Talios sharply.

Lianne's eyes widened as she continued acting like the victim.

"I was just looking at the change rooms—"

"Did you not see the sign outside? It says this room is only for female members of the combat and defense class. I know every one of my students, and you are not one of them."

Lianne tried to protest, but the instructor was not done. "Plus, I arrived at this class a few minutes ago to find my students not in their gear. Would you like to know why, Novice Arkei?"

"How does that concern me?" Lianne replied, irritation lacing her voice.

The instructor smiled coldly and walked right up to Lianne. "Three students also not in this class were telling my students the change room was being repaired. That's why no one could go inside. Do you know anything of this?"

Britea saw Lianne go pale before she predictably began to deny her involvement. "I have no idea what that has to do with me."

Instructor Talios nodded. "I see. Regardless, you, Valerie Mern, Daphne Kellen, and Theresa Chade just earned yourselves a trip to the warden's office."

"But they attacked me!"

"What I saw was you wielding spears and Britea trying to shield herself and Pearl. I will swear in a court of law that you are the attacker here, Novice Arkei, and in addition, you're in a restricted area."

Lianne's face went red with rage. "Do you know who I am?"

Instructor Talios raised an eyebrow. "Do you want me to add insubordination to the growing list?" Then she signaled to the two female instructors who had been waiting silently in the doorway.

"Please escort her and the others to the warden's office for the offenses I just mentioned."

Lianne opened her mouth to protest, but the grim looks on the faces of her appointed escorts rendered her silent. She shot a vengeful look at Britea and Pearl before being forced out of the change rooms.

Instructor Talios snapped her fingers at Britea and Pearl. "You two, get into your gear and meet me at the end of the track." Both girls gave each other a frightened look. She glared at them, and Pearl and Britea dove into two stalls to finish changing.

"Do not keep me waiting!" yelled the female instructor before she left.

#

"Why did you come out? I was handling it!" asked Pearl as she and Britea ran towards the irritated Instructor Talios. The instructor had gone to the end of a track not being used in today's mock Trials. The rest of the class had arrived and were being divided into competitors and spectators. Kahl and Mat were also present, and Britea hoped Kahl never heard about what had occurred in the change rooms.

"She sounded like she was trying to hurt you," replied Britea.

"You should have let me beat her up," growled Pearl.

"Then you'd be facing expulsion again," countered Britea.

"About time you two showed up," the instructor said, staring intently at them. "Before we go any further, you two *will* tell me what happened in the change room."

Britea and Pearl shared a quick look and kept silent.

The instructor's eyes flashed. "I'll keep you two here until tomorrow morning if I don't hear exactly what happened!"

Another long moment passed before Pearl finally deflated. "Lianne wanted me to get her close to the Dyhaeri delegation."

Instructor Talios looked puzzled. "Why?"

"Because of the vert-silk trade," ventured Britea. She wasn't going to let Pearl do this alone. "The Arkei family wants in on it."

"And what pull do you have with the Dyhaeri, Pearl?" asked the instructor.

"I don't have any. They just happen to be friends with Britea, and they've been nice to me too," said Pearl.

Instructor Talios gave an embarrassed Britea a questioning look. "I met them months ago, before coming to Syla College." The instructor studied Britea for a long, uncomfortable moment. When she finally turned her attention back to Pearl, Britea released a sigh of relief.

"So, what happened when you turned her down?" The instructor crossed her arms. "I assume that's what you did since she wanted to murder you two."

The casual way Instructor Talios was talking about everything was making Britea feel very uneasy.

"She threatened to say things about me," said Pearl in a subdued tone. "Stuff I'd told her years ago."

Instructor Talios narrowed her eyes. "This stuff…is it that important?"

Pearl shot her head up; her eyes were blazing with anger.

The instructor wasn't moved. "So, to you it is. Well, let me give you some advice. It's up to you to accept it or not." The harsh angles of authority on her face eased, and she uncrossed her arms, letting out a sigh. "Take whatever baggage you're carrying from the past, empty it all out on the floor, sort out what you can still use, and get rid of what will only hold you back."

Britea blinked. She had expected an epic, scathing, scolding. Certainly not thoughtful advice.

Instructor Talios continued. "Former acquaintances that only use you to get ahead are the baggage you throw away. The shared memories those acquaintances would use against you need to be excised and defanged. So what if you were considered fat as a child?"

Pearl went pale while Britea gaped at the instructor. Apparently, she had listened for a while before intervening.

"You are not the first, nor shall you be the last, who was a bit plump. Do not let someone use that against you. Forget about them. However, friends who would throw up a shield to protect you at the first sign of harm," She looked at Britea before continuing. "those are the ones you hold on to till the end of time."

Britea looked at Pearl, who was staring at Instructor Talios thoughtfully.

"I understand." Pearl looked at Britea and smiled wanly. "I guess you're awesome baggage then." Britea couldn't help but giggle, and soon Pearl was laughing too.

Even the usually stern Instructor Talios was smiling. "Now, I still have to punish you two." Both girls groaned.

"So, drop down and give me twenty push-ups."

Both girls complied, smiling the whole time.

#

Kahl scanned the outdoor class as he warmed up. It was now seven days until the Trials, and the last six days had been busy. Ever since he and Mat had showed the competitors a different way to race, they had taken to it like ducks to water. The adaptability of the humans was both amazing and frightening. He and Mat had attended every practice session and found themselves offering advice on everything, even sparring. Some had been accepted, some had not. There had been fourteen sessions so far, two per day: one during the combat and defense class and a second one in the evening for only the competitors and the instructors. Danai had been assigned to the cousins to guide them through the rules of the Trials. Kahl still noticed the tension between Mat and Danai, and he wondered if each was also aware of it.

Apart from all that, Kahl found the training sessions interesting. He would never have imagined that training Britea while onboard the *Windrider* would eventually lead to this point in time.

By the way, where was Britea?

This brought him back to the present. Kahl was feeling anxious as he was yet to see Britea today. Then he saw three people walking towards the group from the other end of the unused track.

One of them was Instructor Talios and the remaining two were Pearl and Britea.

His heart lighter, he made to go towards them.

"Hey, Kahl!" called an excited Navos. "Wield sparring is about to start!"

Kahl turned and the everyone was already heading to the elevated combat square, which was twelve feet by twelve feet. Three corners held three glass cauldrons. One held fire, another water, and the third earth. No cauldron was needed for air as it surrounded everyone.

Kahl glanced behind him, and he saw Britea and Pearl had separated from the instructor and had headed to the stands, which were already teaming with eager spectators.

"On my way," said Kahl before reluctantly joining an excited Navos and the others.

#

Mat watched the two male competitors warming up outside the combat square. One, Novice Llane Kato, had a light practice spear, while the second, Novice Sol Timus, had a pair of daggers. Some would have thought that uneven odds, but Mat knew either weapon was equally deadly in a skillful pair of hands.

"Any questions?" asked Danai softly from beside him.

Mat glanced at her. "Why aren't you competing?"

Her face flushed at the unexpected question. "I believe I've answered this question before. I don't wish to."

Mat wasn't about to let her off the hook. "You're a skilled fighter Danai. Having you as a competitor in the Trials would give Syla College an edge."

The pretty Weltonian sighed. "Now you sound just like Master Caren."

Mat turned back to the contestants as they entered the rectangle, ready to begin wield sparring.

"He's not entirely wrong."

The instructors positioned themselves at the four corners of the rectangle. They were there to shield the spectators from stray fire balls, deadly water orbs, or out-of-control air projectiles. He missed the pensive look Danai gave him.

"Representing Group A is Novice Llane Kato, and in the B corner is Novice Sol Timus!" Instructor Talios's shout had everyone cheering in the stands. "We will wait the usual three minutes while the combat area is inspected!"

Mat recalled this odd rule. The instructors would be acting like the judges, who in the real Trials, would check the rectangle for any traps or oddities. They didn't do that for the races but only for the combat events. Mat thought the whole procedure was strange.

What were they trying to prevent? Cheating? Humans were confusing.

Kahl nodded at Mat and Danai as he came to stand beside his cousin.

"Well, hello, Danai Riverun," said a familiar voice. All three turned to face Lieutenant Harto Flay. He had walked up unheard and planted himself besides Danai.

Mat saw Danai stiffen, but she answered politely. "Good day, lieutenant." There was definitely something about the Malaquey officer she didn't like, and Mat had to avoid giving into the temptation to push Harto away from her.

"Lieutenant Flay, we haven't seen you in a while," said Kahl mildly. Mat shared a look with his cousin. For the last week, Harto had been sticking close to the high priest instead. When asked about it, the high priest had shrugged and stated he was unsure about the sudden interest in him.

"I had preparations to make for the upcoming Trials," answered Harto.

"Such as?" asked Mat in a calm tone.

"Oh, you'll know soon enough," said Harto smugly. Mat curled a fist and tried not to envisage smashing it into the blond officer's face.

"Contestants, enter the ring!"

Mat forced himself to concentrate on the fight about to take place.

The two combatants faced off.

#

Danai was relieved when combat and defense class was over. For the entire duration of the wield sparring and physical sparring, she had been forced to stand between Harto and Mat. Harto had tried to talk with her, and she answered him politely, but Mat had spent most of the time glaring at Harto. The tension had been so thick one could not have cut through it even with a knife. She also wondered why the officer was just showing up in the class after a week's absence.

Danai had thought he would have been more concerned about Mat and Kahl's help coaching the students for the Trials, but the officer had failed to appear at first.

To be honest, she had been relieved at Harto's absence. The last thing she wanted to witness was a battle of egos between Mat and Harto. The few times she had seen them in the same room, they stared daggers at each other while continuing their painfully polite façade. Even Kahl was wary of their interactions.

She sighed and patted down the storm-grey school uniform she had changed back into. She preferred the sparring gear; it was far less restrictive.

Danai exited the change rooms with the other female students and saw Kahl chatting with Britea and Pearl as the three left the outdoor classroom. Then she saw Mat waiting for her near the double doors. He was looking at her and smiling.

Danai felt her heart flutter and couldn't help smiling back in return. He was a bit brash, but that only hid a gentleness she had always detected in him. Besides, he was a magnificent fighter.

"Novice Danai Riverun! A word please!" She froze at Harto's voice and saw the smile disappear from Mat's face. *What in the Deep did the Malaquey officer want with her now?*

She turned to her right to see Lieutenant Harto standing several feet away. She didn't think he was aware of the glare Mat was sending in his direction.

"Lieutenant Flay, I was about to head to class," said Danai as the officer walked towards her. From the corner of her eye, she noticed Mat go still, then a heartbeat later, he too started walking towards her, keeping his eyes on the approaching Malaquey officer.

"I know," smiled Harto while ignoring the admiring looks he got from some of the students, both female and male, who passed him.

"I was hoping you and I could chat. Are you free this weekend? We could have dinner in town."

Danai was speechless for a moment. Where was this coming from? Did he not recall how rude he had been to her several months ago in the market? Did he think she had forgotten that? Mat's determined march towards her had now turned into a hurried gait, and his eyes were flashing at the oblivious Harto.

"I'm afraid I must decline," said Danai quickly. Harto stared at her in surprise. Clearly, he had not been expecting that response.

"May I ask why?" His tone was just this shy of demanding.

Oh, that's how you want to play it, huh?

Danai lifted her chin defiantly. "I have a prior engagement this weekend."

The Dyhaeri came to a screeching halt just beside her, forcing Harto to finally notice him. "Prince Mat." His tone was cold, and his expression was furious.

"Harto," Mat said just as frigidly.

Danai looked at their stances and knew a fight was brewing.

"Why, look at the time!" Danai announced loudly as she entwined her right arm into Mat's left. That stopped the staring war for a moment.

"Mat, there is much you and I need to discuss about the upcoming Trials. Lieutenant Flay, I must get going to my next class. It was a pleasure talking to you." She turned and had to physically pull Mat along with her. The Dyhaeri shot one more glare at Harto before walking away with Danai.

Lieutenant Harto Flay stood watching them leave, his jaw tightening in anger.

#

"What was all that about?!" demanded Danai once she and Mat were safely away from the outdoor class. She let go of his arm, but they remained close enough to touch. Half of her was worried he would run back to duel with Harto. The other half of her just liked having him close to her.

"I don't like him," said Mat tersely.

"Why?"

Mat was silent for a long moment.

Danai sighed. "I suppose it's none of my business..."

"What do you know of how Britea and Kahl met?" he asked softly.

Danai hesitated before answering. She had not discussed any of what Britea had told her even with her parents, so why did she feel she had to answer Mat?

"Only some basic facts."

Mat waited for her to elaborate, but that was as far as she was willing to go. The Dyhaeri nodded as if he knew what she was thinking.

"While on board the *Windrider* , Britea and Kahl had to help the ship flee four Namiran warships. To discourage their pursuers, the *Windrider* sailed into the Sorrows Pit."

Danai nodded. This she already knew, but it was nice to have Mat confide in her.

Mat continued. "Well, due to Britea's courage, the Alkynaia were all too happy to bargain with her, and the result was three destroyed Namiran warships. Malaquey Naval Intelligence tried to pin what happened in the Sorrow's Pit on the Dyhaeri. Lieutenant Flay even accused us at court."

Danai felt her anger return as she recalled how Britea had told her of her interrogation by three Malaquey officers, one of whom had been Lieutenant Flay.

"I see."

"You obviously don't seem to be a fan of Harto either. May I ask why?" asked Mat, smiling.

Danai sighed. "Britea and I met him in Carlellis Market some months ago. He demanded to know why she was outside the school and tried to dismiss me as some busybody, an unworthy Weltonian when I tried to intervene. He didn't even believe I was a student here. His ignorant, pompous attitude towards Britea and I that day really annoyed me."

Understanding dawned on Mat's face at first, but then suddenly, strangely, he looked awkward and uncomfortable. "Ah. I see."

Both walked for a few moments in silence before Mat took a deep breath. "I have a confession to make."

Danai gave him a questioning look.

Mat seemed to have trouble finding the words. "I grew up hearing tales of humans, most of them not good. Then I became a marine and my perception of them worsened."

Danai kept quiet.

"I saw them as ignorant, selfish, warmongers." He paused to gauge her reaction.

"You're not entirely wrong there," agreed Danai. "Just look at the ongoing humanitarian mess that is Namira. That place makes Malaquey seem holy in comparison."

Mat grimaced at the mention of Namira. "Be that as it may, recent events have shifted my perception to realize some of you are…different. Some of you are kind and brave and good."

Danai tilted her head. "What made you change your mind?"

Mat smiled reluctantly. "Kahl and Britea's friendship for one. It seems like the Sea Mother is trying to beat some sense into me."

Danai grinned. She knew how she felt. Never in a million years would she have thought she would see a blossoming relationship between Britea and Kahl, a human and a Dyhaeri.

"Then there's your father, who did his best to teach Mat and I about the human world, and…and then there's you." The last word was said so quietly it almost stopped Danai in her tracks.

"That's awfully nice of you, Mat," said Danai awkwardly as she prayed he didn't see her embarrassment.

Mat looked shyly at her, an unusual behavior for him. "Thank you, Danai."

"You're welcome. By the way, are you coming to observe my next class?"

"Yes. Um, what is it?"

"Bloody Dancing and Etiquette for Fifth Years," said Danai in a resigned tone.

"Oh, that sounds downright delightful," groaned Mat, and Danai laughed at his misery. It didn't take long for before Mat too was laughing.

CHAPTER 27

Pearl and Britea stood frozen and silent in anticipation of an important speech about to start.

For this morning, Chef Trey Blane was going to address the entire kitchen staff. The diminutive chef was standing on an overturned cauldron that had been dragged to the center of the kitchen. How he had gotten up there, only the Lords of Light and Shadow knew.

The minute Britea had seen him on the cauldron, she had the strongest urge to laugh. She dared not and even stopped herself from looking at Pearl because she suspected her friend was having the same difficulty.

"This is it people," said the chef as he placed his knobby fists on his hips and glared at his attentive staff. "Another Wielder Trials is upon us, another non-stop mayhem-filled event to endure for the next seven days. The contestants from the other two colleges will be arriving this afternoon. They will be hungry, thirsty, and demanding. I trust you all to be on your best behavior." His glare included Britea and Pearl. "But if anyone mistreats you, be it with words or wielding, I want to hear about it immediately. Do you understand?!"

"Yes, chef!" roared the kitchen staff, and for one moment, Britea felt as though they were about to head into battle.

The chef beamed and rubbed his hands.

"On the notice board are assigned groups for tasks. Study it well every morning as adjustments will be made. I expect you all to not disappoint me. Is that clear?!"

"Yes, chef!" Britea winced at the roar and wondered if the chef was a drill sergeant in his spare time.

The chef nodded with satisfaction at the loud response. "To your stations, everyone!"

Pearl and Britea promptly went to their corner of the kitchen. This morning's task was peeling carrots.

"I cannot believe it's finally here," said an excited Pearl as she dove in. Britea took a moment to watch her and was relieved when Pearl succeeded in peeling a carrot without cutting her fingers. It had been astounding how fast the noble had adjusted to working in the kitchen.

It did prove that, once one puts their mind to something, they can do anything.

"The days went by too fast," agreed Britea.

"But that's not even the best part," said Pearl. Britea sent her a questioning look.

"One of the benefits of the Trials is that classes tend to get cut by at least a week just before they start because of the number of people involved in the Trials."

Britea nodded. The last seven days had seen a flurry of activity at the college. Competitors were practicing feverishly; even Danai, Mat, and Kahl had their hands full. The other non-competing students had been given tasks such as cleaning the halls and the guest dorms for the visiting students. Strangely though, Britea had not spotted Lianne and her hangers-on during the massive clean-up.

Pearl continued. "However, the very best part is that during the Trials themselves, there are no classes because we all have to attend the events!"

"Do you think we'll get time off our punishment duties to see the procession?" asked Britea.

Pearl sent her a dismayed look as if she had just realized the impossibility. "I sure hope so. I love looking at the different uniforms, and let me tell you, the Royal Malaquey Naval male novices are absolutely dashing in their navy-blue outfits."

Britea smiled as she picked up another carrot to peel. "Then we better hurry, and as the chef says, be on our best behavior if we want even a shot at going."

#

Britea nervously patted down the front of her storm-grey uniform then looked in the mirror once more. After kitchen duty and a hurried breakfast, she and Pearl had dashed back to their rooms for a quick wash and to change into clean uniforms. She had wrestled her curly, chocolate-brown hair into a single braid. Her crisp white cotton blouse was spotless, and the water-blue lines on her skirt and cowl were vibrant. She wasn't competing, but she still felt nervous. She wondered how Navos and the others were doing.

A loud knock on the door brought her back to the present.

"One second!" She walked to the door and opened it to find an impatient Pearl in her own immaculate uniform. The only difference was she had let her long raven-black hair down.

"You ready yet? It's almost time!"

"Yes. Where do we go?"

Pearl grabbed her hand and pulled her out of the room so fast Britea almost forgot to close the door. Once in the corridors, Pearl let go of her hand. Both girls walked briskly. Other students were also leaving their rooms and rushing in the same direction.

"The headmaster and the senior instructors will meet each contingent in the front courtyard. Then, once they exchange greetings, the contingents will go to the dining hall for a meet and greet and food!" She paused.

"And then?" asked Britea.

Pearl smiled brightly. "Then the real fun begins. The rivalry, the snide whispers, the subtle hints that we of Syla College are not worthy. Then someone loses it and swings a punch before the competition officially starts."

She turned to catch Britea's horrified expression.

"That's…that's terrible!" finally said Britea.

Pearl laughed. "I know, but it's fun to watch."

#

Kahl tried not to fidget as they waited for the contingents from the Royal Malaquey Naval Wielding College and the Artra Army Wielding College to arrive. He glanced at the others standing in a semicircle formation facing forwards, and he had to admit they looked impressive. He and Mat wore their indigo-blue leather marine uniforms, minus their spears, and the high priest wore a black tunic, long black pants, and knee-high leather boots. Of course, he also carried his ceremonial staff. The outfit was eerily similar to the outfits worn by the combat and defense students. Kahl had seen a few of the instructors and students stare when the high priest appeared.

Danai wore her usual storm-grey uniform with the fire-red lines on the cowl and the hem of her full-length skirt. She stood between Mat and Kahl so she could explain the procession. The competitors also wore the same grey uniform as Danai and they stood with Weapons Master Caren, Instructor Talios, and three other instructors. The remaining faculty members had been positioned either in the corridors inside or in the Great Hall. The headmaster and the warden occupied the center of the courtyard, looking official and regal in their usual black robes. They would be the first to welcome the contingents.

Then Kahl realized someone was missing.

Where was Lieutenant Harto Flay?

He was about to ask his cousin when he spied the Malaquey officer standing to the far left of Weapons Master Caren and the competitors.

"Here they come," warned Danai in a whisper, and Kahl looked towards the open metal gates.

Three full, open carriages drawn by two horses each appeared. They stopped outside the gates, and the passengers dismounted. Each wore water-blue robes, some with fire-red lines on the hems or cowls, some with navy-blue hems, and some with earth-brown lines. He surmised the ones with white hems were the air wielders.

Two people approached Syla's top officials. The first to reach them was a middle-aged woman with iron-grey hair plaited in a single row down the back of her head. Her uniform was a darker blue color, and she had a white hem on her cowl. She strode confidently towards the headmaster, smiling as she shook hands with him and the warden.

"Lieutenant Commander Marya Helsliff," said Danai softly. "She's the warden of the Royal Malaquey Naval Wielding College."

Mat nodded. "And him?"

Behind the female warden was a stately middle-aged man who walked with a slight limp; he wore the same darker blue uniform but his came with an earth-brown line on the hem and cowl. He also sported a scar on the left side of his face. His suspicious gaze scanned for threats as he approached the senior members of Syla College. He shook his colleague's hand, a stern expression on his face.

"Commander Brann Zelon, headmaster of the Royal Malaquey Naval College. He lacks a sense of humor and gets easily irritated," said Danai her tone cautious.

"Good to know," whispered the high priest. Danai shot him a stunned look. Kahl hid a grimace; he had forgotten how legendary the high priest's hearing was.

After exchanging greetings, the female warden beckoned the blue-clad group to approach. Kahl counted at least twenty-six; sixteen of them appeared young enough to be the competitors, and the rest had the confidence and gait of experienced teachers. Kahl glanced at the competitors on the Syla welcoming committee, and he was concerned to see most of them looked apprehensive. Tension already filled the air, and the games were yet to start.

At a signal from Warden Asteros, Instructor Talios stepped forward.

"Please follow me," she said courteously, and the Syla group parted so the Royal Malaquey contingent could enter the school. The Royal Malaquey students strutted like peacocks as if sensing the distress of the Syla group, but then one caught sight of the high priest.

"Wait, is that…are those Dyhaeri?" exclaimed a Royal Malaquey student.

The procession almost came to a halt as the visitors, including Commander Brann Zelon and his warden, gawked.

Kahl was surprised at their expressions. Had they not known the Dyhaeri would be present?

"Please, we must move along so as not to hold up the procession." Instructor Talios said calmly.

Commander Zelon was the first to recover. He gave a piercing whistle that almost made Kahl cover his ears and did make some nearby wince.

"Come on, Royals! We have a job to do. Follow Instructor Talios!" bellowed the naval headmaster.

"Yes, sir!" answered his students and instructors before dutifully following Instructor Talios into the building. But as Commander Zelon passed them, he gave the Dyhaeri trio a piercing stare.

"Well, he certainly looks friendly," said Mat dryly. Navos, who was standing nearby, nearly choked trying to suppress his laughter. Danai sighed as she heard other students hiding their laughter behind their hands. Even Master Caren was smiling.

"The Artra Army is here," warned Danai, and everyone became serious once more.

Kahl looked to the front and saw three open carriages had replaced the other three, which had been quietly removed. These occupants wore varying shades of olive green. Two officials in dark olive-green buttoned tunics and pants stepped forward. Both had water-blue hems. The first was a man in his mid-forties with bronze skin and curly mahogany hair; he saluted the headmaster and the warden first and waited for them to extend the same greeting before extending his right hand.

"Lieutenant General Piotr King, the youngest warden in the history of the three colleges."

Behind him was a smiling older gentleman with a ruddy-red complexion; an iron-grey, bushy mustache; and a completely bald head. At first glance, he seemed a bit rotund until one saw the bulging biceps now hidden by his dark olive-green robes.

"General Ravh Welbrick, Headmaster of Artra Army Wielding College." The bald headmaster saluted briefly before enveloping a stunned Headmaster Clayre in a hug that almost lifted him off the ground. He repeated the same act with a solemn looking Warden Asteros, then laughed at something Headmaster Clayre said.

"He's clearly the life of the party," noted Mat to the amusement of those around them.

"You could say that," said Danai in a cautioning tone. Kahl gave her an odd look, but then he had to look forward again. The Artra group was approaching.

"Ho, ho!" said Headmaster Ravh Welbrick. "Dyhaeri, as I live and breathe." The jovial headmaster stopped in front of the high priest.

"I'm Ravh Welbrick." He struck out his hand as the students and teachers of Arta and Syla looked on.

The high priest smiled and shook the human wielder's hand. "High Priest Myltan."

Kahl noticed Warden Asteros and Headmaster Clayre rapidly approaching and their looks of alarm.

"What brought you here?" asked Headmaster Welbrick, ignoring his warden, who appeared a bit anxious about the impromptu conversation in full view of everyone during the procession.

"We're here to observe and enjoy the Wielder Trials."

Kahl noticed that though Ravh smiled, there was a cunning glint in his eyes.

"Absolutely splendid. I look forward to chatting with you soon, Old Boy Myltan."

Danai went pale at the causal insult while Mat's eyes widened. The high priest however, kept smiling as if amused.

"As do I, my dear child Ravh."

There was silence for a long moment until Ravh laughed. "Oh, I like you." He clapped High Priest Myltan heavily on the right shoulder and finally walked through the gap. The high priest kept smiling as if he was not bothered by the lack of respect.

Danai released a sigh of relief. "And now we follow them to the Great Hall."

Kahl noticed his cousin giving her a worried look. He was sure Mat had questions, as did he. Why was he getting the feeling the Wielder Trials were not that amicable?

#

The noise level in the corridors grew as the first contingent appeared, and the instructors made no move to silence them. Britea and Pearl had found a good spot by a pillar and stared as the blue uniforms of the Royal Malaquey Naval Wielding College came into view. Some Syla students started cheering and exchanging greetings. Britea was pleasantly surprised by the camaraderie.

"This friendship isn't going to last," said Pearl cheerfully. "Wait until the rest of their schools and their parents arrive tomorrow for the first event."

"What do you mean?" asked Britea.

"Tonight, we host only the competitors and their instructors, but for the next nine days, we'll host much of Malaquey. On top of everyone I've already mentioned, many students from the other two colleges will also come to watch the Trials, plus their parents. And who knows, we may even be lucky enough to be graced with the presence of King Wilhem. At the last event in 2182 AC, he sent one of his ministers to represent his house instead."

"But now of all times is when he should come," said Britea, puzzled. "The high priest is here observing. Imagine the impression the Dyhaeri will get if it appears the king doesn't care about such an important event."

Pearl gave her an approving look. "You know, for a farm girl, you're definitely picking up on the intricacies of politics."

Britea shrugged and turned back to watch the procession. She was just in time to see the Artra Army Wielding College appear.

Compared to the Royal Malaquey team, the Arta contestants were far more boisterous, and where the Royals seemed polished, Artra appeared a lot more rugged. Some exchanged greetings with nearby Syla students, but some also threw insults. Instructors from Artra and Syla had to step in when the insults got too mean.

Pearl sighed at Britea's shocked expression. "See what I mean?"

The procession ended in short order. "What happens now?" asked Britea.

"We follow them to the dining hall, which has been spruced up and decorated. We might even be lucky enough to catch a fight!" said Pearl gleefully as they joined the other Syla students heading to the dining hall.

"You seem to like conflict a lot," pointed out Britea.

Pearl shrugged. "It helps with the boredom of school."

As she had predicted, the dining hall had been completely transformed, the rectangular tables replaced by round ones covered with snow-white cotton tablecloths. Black, water-blue, and olive-green ribbons hung from the ceiling, and though the colors should have clashed, it looked oddly breathtaking.

Britea saw several of the kitchen staff she had come to recognize standing close to the buffet line. They were smartly dressed in ironed-white uniforms and had polite smiles on their faces.

"I must admit, the food smells heavenly," said Pearl with a sigh.

Britea had to agree. Breakfast had been ages ago.

"Welcome, one and all," boomed the headmaster's voice behind them. Everyone turned as the headmaster of Syla College and it's warden entered the hall with the Dyhaeri delegation not far behind. Britea caught a glimpse of Danai walking with Navos and the rest of Syla's team.

Headmaster Clayre continued as he positioned himself in the center of the full dining hall.

"Today, we shall meet and greet new and old friends. We shall be as kin, and there shall be no rivalry. May the Lords of Light and Shadow smile upon us all. Please, eat and be merry."

This was greeted by cheers as the three headmasters, their wardens, and the Dyhaeri left. Britea noticed the instructors from the three schools left as well. She gave Pearl a questioning look.

"Them leaving is normal; we're supposed to bond with the other students," said Pearl dryly. "Which hardly happens."

For a moment, Britea took the opportunity to observe how the students from the three colleges interacted. At first, they kept to their own groups, then a few brave souls from each side tried to make friends. There was laughter as the mingling increased, and Britea even saw Danai, Navos, and Lexia speaking with three Artra students. For the moment, it appeared peaceful, the atmosphere light.

"Ugh," exclaimed a daintily dressed girl in the water blue of the Royal Malaquey College. "Is this what we're supposed to eat? It smells awful." The two other Royal students with her agreed.

"And so, it begins," said Pearl while Britea stared at the visitors. She looked at one of the kitchen staff who had served them. It was Alandra. Britea knew her. She was quiet and shy. The young maid looked dismayed at the Royal Malaquey student's reaction.

"I demand to speak to your cook at once! This rubbish cannot stand! How dare you serve us this?"

Before Pearl could stop her, Britea was already walking over to the Royal Malaquey trio.

"What seems to be the problem?" She paid no heed to Pearl, who had run after her.

The Royal Malaquey girl glared at her. "Are you the chef in charge of this school's sorry kitchen?"

"I'm not, but I don't think you should talk to Alandra that way." Some students started gathering as if sensing a fight was in the making.

"Who in the blazes are you?" demanded the Royal Malaquey student.

"What's wrong with the food?" asked Pearl, now standing beside Britea.

Britea gave her a grateful look before turning back to the angry Royal Malaquey girl.

"It's food only fit for peasants! Spicy boiled rice with fried chicken and plain vegetables?! We demand to have certain delicacies—"

"Such as soup a la crème with marinated pork cooked in rare vintage wine?" cut in Pearl dryly. "What do you think this is? A resort or a college competition?"

Some nearby students of different schools laughed.

The Royal Malaquey novice glared at her, and Britea thought she was about to explode.

"Please ignore her, Sheila," said a familiar voice Britea was beginning to hate.

"Pearl Ceres will eat anything, which explains her obese appearance." Britea saw Pearl stiffen at the last two words. "After all, she just loves to eat despite what it does to her figure," Lianne emphasized the last word. "Thus, she does not possess the self-restraint that has been gifted to us," said Lianne as she drifted to the Royal Malaquey group.

Sheila's anger gave way to a smile. "Why, Lianne, it is so delightful to see you. I find it so hard to believe you're at this pathetic school. Why aren't you at our school?"

"Oh, it's nothing really. My family wanted us to uplift this sorry establishment—"

"I can tell you the real reason why," said Pearl loudly. Everyone stared at her, and Britea saw panic appear on Lianne's face before being replaced by anger.

"That is, if anyone cares to listen," continued Pearl as she stared steadily at Lianne for what seemed an eternity. Finally, Lianne dropped her gaze and turned to the Royal Malaquey student.

"Come Sheila, let's get some real food and talk about the upcoming season," Lianne led Sheila and her friends away. Sensing there wasn't going to be anymore drama, the other students dispersed.

"Are you all right?" asked Britea in a low voice.

Pearl took a deep breath. "I will be. Come on, let's grab a meal and disappear."

#

Harto walked into the common room that had been reserved for the Royal Malaquey Naval College. He had barely gotten his bearings before someone yelled his name.

"Well, if it isn't Lord Harto Flay!" bellowed one of the assistant instructors, a young man with piercing grey eyes and espresso-brown hair that reached his shoulders. His water-blue uniform was lined in fire red. The other instructors shouted greetings as Harto walked over to them, smiling.

"Keep your damn voice down, Therry," said Harto good naturedly as he hugged his old classmate and fellow agent.

"Good to see you too, rascal," said Lieutenant Therry Welspring. He clapped Harto on the shoulder, and they stepped away from the other instructors still partaking of a light meal. There had been an opening ceremony in the Great Hall after lunch before Headmaster Clayre formally opened the ceremonies and gave the guests leave to head to their accommodations. Harto had decided to give his alma mater some time to settle in before seeking out Therry.

"So, now you're an instructor?" asked Harto as he and Therry passed by the buffet tray and grabbed a few spiced delicacies and two glasses of wine.

"Assistant instructor. Naval intelligence thought it best one of us was inserted with the Royal Malaquey group. I was the natural choice given I mentored students for the games in our final year."

"Good to know," said Harto. They were now in a far corner of the common room, away from eavesdroppers.

"So, what can you tell me about the Dyhaeri's time here?" asked Therry, keeping a casual expression on his face. Anyone observing would think they were just two former classmates exchanging tales.

"They're interested in the students' training and have even helped with the preparations in the last two weeks."

Therry paused mid-sip. "The Dyhaeri are training the Syla team? Is that even allowed?"

"I checked. There's nothing in the rule book about it, and there's even a clause that says the colleges can invite former students or other wielder groups to coach." Therry gave him a surprised look.

"From what I can surmise, it has only been used once, which was more than ninety years ago when the Namiran colleges still attended these events."

"Hmm," was all Therry said for a while. "Are the Dyhaeri a security risk?"

Harto sighed. "I honestly don't know." His friend shot him a sharp look.

"You've spent more time with them than anyone else in intelligence. Tomorrow more agents will arrive to inspect the grounds for the king's visit. You'll have to tell them in definite terms if the Dyhaeri are a security threat."

Harto frowned. "Wait, the king is attending this year?"

Therry glanced around to make sure no one was watching. "Yes. His ministers and naval intelligence are against it, but he made a compelling argument. How would it appear if he didn't attend when a high-ranking member of the Dyhaeri was present for the games?"

"It would appear that he doesn't give a damn about the Trials or the wielding colleges," said Harto.

Therry raised a glass to him. "I knew you had brains."

Harto was silent for a long moment. "They're not a security threat."

Therry looked at him cynically. "And to what reason do we owe this speedy reversal from 'I don't know'?"

Harto was reluctant to reply, but he didn't have a choice. "They only seem interested in two particular students, Britea D'Tranell, a late wielder, and Danai Riverun, who is the first Weltonian in the school in the last eight hundred years."

Therry stared at him. "That wasn't in your report, Harto."

To get more agents, Harto had been forced to deliver a hastily written report on the reason for the deployment. He had only stated that the Dyhaeri were staying for an indefinite amount of time, and he was unable to watch their every move.

"I had to be sure and now I am," said Harto.

Therry's face showed he wasn't convinced. "Do you know why the Dyhaeri are interested in these particular girls?"

"Not yet, but I'm working on it." *And failing spectacularly at it.* Danai declining his invitation a week ago had shocked him and affected his confidence. He was used to noblewomen constantly vying for his attention, but this Weltonian lass was clearly not impressed by his status.

And that was fascinating. He had to talk to her again in private…once he got the courage and opportunity to do so.

Therry sighed, disappointed. "So, these…unique students. They wouldn't happen to be a security risk to the king?"

"No. They're harmless," said Harto with absolute conviction.

Therry scoffed. "For your sake, I hope you're right about that."

CHAPTER 28

Instructor Shelley stepped onto the stage and faced the packed stadium. "Good morning, everyone, and welcome to Syla College and the One Hundredth and Twenty-Fourth Wielder Trials!"

Her announcement was greeted by a loud cheer. The crowd in the packed stands consisted of the entire Syla College student body, many students from the other two colleges, and just as many parents, relatives, and friends of all the students. They were all packed into what was ordinarily the outdoor combat and defense classroom, which was truly a stadium in itself with its marked tracks and bleachers. Filling center field was a variety of items to be used as obstacles for the races. They had, however, added an enormous white scoreboard at the south end of the field. On its face were three empty rows. Atop each were the flags that represented the colleges.

Black for Syla, water blue for the Royal Malaquey Wielding College, and olive green for the Artra Army Wielding College. The scoreboard was currently unmarked, a situation that would change very soon.

"Today is the official start of the competitions. In ten minutes, we will commence with the sprints."

This was met by another cheer.

"May the best college win!"

Britea could already feel herself going deaf at the roar around her. She was sitting in the east stands with Pearl, Lexia, Shran, and Henrick. Everyone was excited. She looked towards the Syla contingent and could make out Mat and Kahl by their distinct indigo-blue Dyhaeri marine uniforms.

Britea looked at her program. "So, Novice Belle Dright is representing us in the first four hundred meter race. I sure hope she wins."

"How in the Abyss did she manage that?" queried Lexia.

"What's going on?" asked Britea when she realized her friends weren't listening and were looking elsewhere.

Pearl scoffed and pointed at who Lexia was staring at. At the south end of the stadium were stands built lower and closer to the tracks, giving the occupants an excellent view of the starting position. It was known as the Prime Box and was reserved for the most senior faculty members of the three colleges and visiting dignitaries. However, Lianne Arkei was seated in one of those coveted spots, and beside her were two older versions of her.

"Her sister, Selina Arkei, is the one in the middle, and the other is their mother, Lady Adria Arkei. I guess the Arkei family is representing the royal court today," said Pearl in an exasperated voice.

Lexia gave Pearl an odd look. "They didn't sit there two years ago. What's changed?"

"Maybe they're trying to impress the high priest," said Shran.

Britea's gaze drifted towards the high priest, who was seated beside Headmaster Clayre. The Arkei family sat directly beside the Syla college headmaster. On the other side of High Priest Myltan was Headmaster Zelon and Headmaster Welbrick. The three wardens of the schools sat in a row just below, and Lieutenant Flay sat to the right of Warden Asteros.

They really want that vert-silk trade," said Lexia. Britea and Pearl had told their friends about the confrontation in the change room.

"Where's Lianne's father?" asked Henrick. Britea had wondered that herself.

"He rarely attends the first few days. He's more interested in the Grand Ball at the end of the competition. That's when he likes to rub elbows with the winners and make business deals," said Pearl bitterly.

"You really don't like them, do you?" asked Lexia in a gentle tone that surprised Britea and Pearl.

Pearl recovered quickly. "What's done is done. I'm in a better place now. Hey, I wonder what Kahl and Mat think of all this." She looked at Britea.

Britea shrugged. "The last few days have been quite busy for them. I've hardly seen them. Danai would be in a better position to answer that question. She's been at every last-minute training session and sometimes gets back so late at night, she just falls into bed."

"Yeah," agreed Lexia. "I've barely seen Navos myself. I just cannot wait for these Trials to be over." Britea gave her a close look. Underneath her bored tone was concealed worry.

Britea turned back to the track, dread now in the pit of her stomach. She hoped the presence of the Dyhaeri would forestall any misfortune.

#

Kahl couldn't help but feel keyed up by the palpable tension. He watched as the first runners stepped out. One female wielder from each college would race. The first to reach the finish line would get three points, the second two points, and the last one point.

The accumulated scores at the end of the Trials would determine the winning college, which would get a huge cash price that would be divided between the competitors and kept in a trust fund until they graduated.

Kahl thought it odd they were competing for money. Humans were odd.

"Runners, get in position!" yelled Instructor Talios, who was now on stage with two other instructors, one in olive green and the other in water blue. Each would oversee a competition.

The three female runners took their places at the start of the track.

"Anyone who goes before the shot will be disqualified! We shall now have absolute silence!" continued the Syla instructor. A hush fell over the entire stadium as all eyes turned to the three frozen wielders.

Kahl felt his heart rate increase.

After what seemed like an eternity, Master Caren fired the starting shot into the air. For a moment, it looked like the runners were still frozen in place, but then they were off. The crowd was on its feet, cheering like maniacs. Even Kahl ran to the edge of the track, and Danai and his cousin were not too far behind him. Kahl found himself yelling at the top of his lungs, trying to urge Novice Belle Dright on. Once the three runners passed the halfway mark, the girl in the olive-green uniform began to pull ahead.

"No! Come on!" yelled Mat in dismay.

With just a few meters to go, no one could catch the Artra runner, but Belle took second, while the Royal Malaquey runner came last.

Kahl and Mat were stunned at the loud cheer from the Syla students, and both looked at Danai. She was also smiling.

"Trust me, this is a good start compared to the last three Trials."

Numbers began to appear on the scoreboard as an instructor in Syla black with a wind-white hem wielded a white marker above his head to write down the score. Three points to Artra, two to Syla, and one to Royal.

"Ten minutes for the next competitors to get ready!" announced a Royal Malaquey instructor.

Three male students representing the three colleges stepped forward.

#

Danai sighed as she looked at the latest score results. The second race had ended with Royal in first, giving them four points in total. Artra had come second, keeping them in first with five total points while Syla College came in last, ending up with three points and putting them at the bottom. She had been irritated when the Royal Malaquey and Artra Team had pointed at the dejected Syla competitors, making snide remarks and laughing. No sportsmanship at all, just outright bullying.

"You all right, Danai?' asked Mat softly. She looked at him and noticed he was also glaring at the Royal Malaquey and Artra teams. Surprisingly, they were yet to notice his disapproving look. Danai appreciated that Mat was taking Syla's side.

"Yeah, I'm doing fine. So, what do you think of our fine tradition?" Try as she might, it was impossible to keep the scorn out of her voice.

"Too early to tell, though I sure hope this day gets a lot better."

"Five minutes until the wielding race!" yelled the male Artra instructor overseeing this race as Instructor Talios and her Royal Malaquey colleague stood behind him.

Danai glanced at the Malaquey and Artra teams; their female contestants were limbering up and appeared confident about the coming race. She turned to the Syla team. Novice Aaliya Dune, a water wielder, was already heading to the track. She appeared nervous, and Danai ran up to her.

"You've got this. Just wield and run like no one's watching."

Aaliya gave her a shaky smile.

"Take your places!" yelled the Artra instructor. The Royal Malaquey contestant strolled over to the track as if it was a leisurely event. Even the Artra contestant seemed just as confident.

"They are quite confident, aren't they?" mused Mat as he watched.

"Royal Malaquey has won this particular race in the male and female categories for the last five competitions," said Danai in a low voice that carried only to Mat and Kahl. "Artra came second, and we came last, so yes, they're far too confident."

Danai knew Aaliya was the fastest female runner Syla College ever produced. But her weakness was lack of confidence. She just hoped Aaliya wouldn't overthink the wielding race.

The Artra instructor walked a few feet along the track to ensure the obstacles were ready. This was going to be almost identical to the mock races. The first set of obstacles would be three rock piles twelve feet high; the second set, three bonfires with two large tubs of water nearby for extinguishing the flames; and the third, a large pile of logs.

"Ready!" The field fell silent as the runners took their positions.

"Get set!" After an eternity of silence, the gun went off, and the runners dashed down the field.

Danai held her breath as Aaliya stayed in first place for the first one hundred meters. Then she reached the first pile of rocks. She was still in the lead as she ran around the first set of obstacles. The other runners weren't far behind.

Aaliya's long strides ate up the second hundred meters as she reached the second fiery set of obstacles. Her opponents were already slowing to start wielding to douse the flames. But the crowd began to murmur with concern as Aaliya picked up speed instead and simultaneously wielded a tall water bubble that she jumped inside of and used to sail through the first fire obstacle.

The stadium erupted in pandemonium when she appeared on the other side unscathed. She dropped the water wield and kept running full speed at the second fire obstacle.

The Artra and Royal runners were stunned and stared at each other briefly before redoubling their efforts to extinguish the flames. Clearly, they had no idea how to imitate that wielding trick. They had just put out their bonfires when Aaliya reached the wooden logs. She glanced behind briefly and saw no one was behind her, so she did the wise thing and ran around the wooden obstacles. By the time her opponents began the last hundred meter dash, she was first past the finish line.

The Syla watchers screamed in joy, and Danai found herself grabbing hold of Mat and hugging him. Beside them, Kahl was cheering himself hoarse. The Artra and Royal contingents wore identical shocked expressions.

"She won!"

Mat grinned at her. "Indeed, she did!"

A weary Aaliya was given a heroine's welcome when she got back to her teammates. The Artra and Royal Malaquey contingents were visibly upset.

"Ten minutes until the next wielding race!"

Danai made sure to congratulate Aaliya then looked at the scoreboard and froze. The scores were yet to be posted. She looked at the Prime Box where the headmasters, the wardens, Lieutenant Flay, and one Dyhaeri high priest sat. It looked like the headmasters were arguing.

#

"What your girl did was unconventional and should not be scored!" hissed Headmaster Zelon as he pointed an indignant finger at Headmaster Clayre and looking at Headmaster Welbrick for support. "Ravh, you agree, right?!"

The Artra headmaster looked reluctant to weigh in.

"This is a wielding race, is it not?" interjected the high priest. They all stared at him. "Did Novice Dune not wield to pass the bonfire and win?"

"Yes but—" began Warden Helsliff of the Royal Malaquey team.

"So, what is the problem here? She wielded through the fire while the others wielded to suppress it. I see no fault in her methods."

The senior officials stared at him. Then the Arta headmaster smiled at the frustrated expression on Headmaster Zelon's face.

"Novice Dune's race stands. She wins," said Headmaster Welbrick. Headmaster Zelon glared at him while Headmaster Clayre seemed stunned by the unlikely support from Artra.

#

Danai let loose a breath of relief when the scoreboard finally reflected the scores she was expecting.

"You were anticipating otherwise?" said a too-perceptive Mat.

"Something like that."

"Contestants for the next wielding race, step up to your marks!" yelled the Royal Malaquey instructor.

Mat, Danai, and Kahl gave Novice Thom Meldson encouraging nods as he passed them. The male runners from Artra and Royal Malaquey were now looking less confident. If anything, they looked anxious.

Danai hid a smile. Good. It was high time they were kicked off their pedestals.

"Get ready!" The runners knelt. "Set!"

The shot went off and so was Thom. For the first one hundred meters, he was in second position, but when they reached the pile of the rocks, the others ran around while he wielded air steps over the mountain of rocks. He darted up and over and reached the bottom before the others, nabbing first place. The audience stood to get a better glimpse, shouting in disbelief, but he kept running, his eyes on the next hurdle. He repeated the air steps with the second and third rock piles.

He reached the fire obstacle, and just as Aaliya had, he wielded an air bubble, jumped inside it, and sailed through the bonfire as people yelled in alarm. Thom came out the other side unharmed, dispersed the bubble, and kept running as his two opponents tried to extinguish the flames. He reached the pile of logs and ran around it. His long strides ate up the last one hundred meters in a heartbeat, and then it was over. He'd won. The stadium was on their feet shouting as he collapsed to his knees, exhausted.

In the Prime Box, the high priest watched as Headmaster Zelon gaped open-mouthed in disbelief for a long moment before glaring at Headmaster Clayre and Headmaster Welbrick.

"This calls for an emergency meeting. Right now."

"The first day's events are over, so that can be arranged," said Warden Asteros calmly. Headmaster Zelon transferred his fiery gaze to the Syla warden before storming out of the observation box.

#

Britea was thrilled. She smiled and listened as Pearl recounted everything that had just happened. Right now, the students and faculty of Syla College were riding a high.

They had beaten both the Royal Malaquey Naval Academy and the Artra Army College in the wielding races for the first time in ten years. There was a lot to celebrate. For the first time in a decade, they were the leaders on the scoreboard.

That may not last, but at least for tonight, Syla College was King of the Wielder Trials.

"Never in a million years could I have envisioned this!" exclaimed Pearl as both girls walked to the kitchens. Lunch was a few hours away, and Trials or not, they still had their punishment detail to fulfill. "What do you make of it?"

"This is my first Wielder Trials, but I'm just as over the moon as you are," said Britea as they rounded the corner and entered the kitchens.

To find Mat, Kahl, Danai, Lexia, Navos, Henrick, Shran, Vindell, and Chelton waiting for them with a crowd of kitchen staff just inside the door.

Britea's smile disappeared. They all looked so serious. "What's going on..." She stared at Pearl, who was no longer smiling. She was waving her right hand at the gathered group.

"One, two, three...go!"

"Happy birthday to you! Happy birthday, dear Britea, happy birthday to you!"

Tears sprung to her eyes as the entire kitchen staff—including the chef—two Dyhaeri, and her friends sang happy birthday to her.

At the end, they were all smiling.

It took a while before she could find her breath. "Th...thank you. Thanks so much. How did you know?"

Pearl pointed at Danai.

"I noticed you were a bit quiet this morning, pensive even. Then I remembered what today was, and I asked Pearl to help me out."

Britea looked at Pearl and felt like crying again. Pearl hugged her. "Happy birthday, Britea."

"As my gift to you, no punishment for either of you today. Plus," the chef and kitchen staff parted to reveal a table full of treats at the far end of the kitchen. "A table of delights awaits you all." The tiny chef waved dramatically in the table's direction.

"Thank you so much, Chef Blane," said Britea through her tears.

He nodded in response. "Now you lot, go eat. I only do this once for you children," said the diminutive chef as he shooed them towards the awaiting feast.

#

Danai smiled as she watched Britea chat with Kahl and the others. When Pearl had suggested this, Danai had misgivings and had been surprised when Chef Blane had agreed. Everyone knew the kitchens were off limits. She just hoped the chef didn't get into trouble for this gift. She was even more surprised to see Vindell and Chelton chatting easily with Pearl; no one would have guessed that less than a month ago, the noble had terrorized the two junior wielders.

"An emerald for your thoughts?" asked Mat as he sat beside her, a pile of delicious-smelling fried fish and vegetable spring rolls on his plate.

"Forget an emerald, I'd settle for some food."

Mat bowed his head respectfully. "As my lady commands."

Danai felt her face go warm at his words and laughed to hide her expression.

"You are quite the charmer, Prince Mat-rallenin." She took a vegetable roll, and they ate in silence for a moment.

"We did well today," said Mat.

Danai nodded. "And I bet the Royal Malaquey headmaster isn't too happy about that right now."

Mat gave her an inquisitive look.

"I saw him storming out of the Prime Box earlier. I bet our poor headmaster is getting an earful from him right this moment."

"We didn't break any rules."

"Yeah, but I have a feeling that in a few days, a lot of people are going to get bruised."

Mat's eyes narrowed. "What do you mean?"

Danai hesitated before answering. "In three days time are the wielding maze run, the endurance wields, and the sparring competitions. Artra usually rules in those three categories, and Royal is a close second. I expect to see a lot of displaced aggression in a few days."

#

Harto tried to keep his expression neutral as Headmaster Brann Zelon yelled at Headmaster Zalei Clayre in the spacious office where Harto himself had gotten scolded a few weeks ago.

The sprints had ended two hours ago, marking the end of the first day of events. At this moment, the schools were eating lunch. But Harto had been forced to follow the high priest to this emergency meeting because Headmaster Zelon had demanded the presence of the Dyhaeri high priest.

Harto had been surprised and a bit alarmed when High Priest Myltan had meekly complied. This had the makings of a diplomatic disaster.

"What I want to know is when were you going to inform us the Dyhaeri were training Syla students for the Trials?!" shouted Brann.

"That is incorrect," interjected Weapons Master Pietor Caren. "I simply asked them for advice in the last two weeks, and they were kind enough to give it. As for the training, only I and my team of combat and defense instructors had that honor. If you wish to lodge a complaint about our methods, please recall there is a clause in the rules that permits teams to hire outside advisors provided those advisors do not compete."

Silence met his calm words. Brann looked incensed. He opened his mouth to shout something yet again but was forestalled by his colleague.

"He's right, you know," said Headmaster Ravh Welbrick before slurping from his mug of beer. Harto wondered when and how the Artra headmaster had been able to snag a pint of beer on the way to the meeting.

Brann gave the Artra headmaster a disgusted look.

"You say that now, but will you be spouting the same words when your carefully chosen fighters get trounced in a few days?"

Harto glanced at High Priest Myltan. The Dyhaeri was leaning against a table, his arms folded as he calmly watched them all.

Ravh belched before answering. "Tomorrow is on its way, and today is about to expire. As far as I'm concerned, the race scores stand. I have no problem with Syla College winning. They deserved it." He grinned widely at Brann's furious expression.

The Royal Malaquey headmaster scoffed and turned to face the high priest.

"In that case, to keep the competition fair, I demand High Priest Myltan and his princes use the next week to train my students, and we halt the competition for that duration."

Ravh froze and gave Brann a stunned look. Harto was speechless and saw his feelings mirrored in the faces of Zalei and the Artra and Royal wardens. But Warden Sammel Asteros and Pietor were closely watching the high priest.

"No," said the high priest calmly.

Brann blinked, clearly not expecting that response. "What—"

But the high priest wasn't done. He pushed himself off the table and walked slowly towards Brann. "I was sent here by my king to observe your colleges' training methods. I was specifically told by *your* king that I would only be allowed to visit Syla College. Ever since we arrived, the faculty and students have treated us with kindness and respect, and when they asked out of friendship for advice, we were only too happy to provide it."

The high priest stopped less than two feet from Brann. "But you, instead, try to order me, the second in command to King Jahlaniin, son of Queen Mother Zaleria of the Dyhaeri, to teach your students? How dare you?!"

He spoke slowly and softly, but that just seemed to make the accusation more pointed. The chagrined headmaster tugged at his collar with one hand but clenched the other in a fist.

Harto's eyes dropped to the headmaster's fisted hand, realizing the stupid headmaster was about to wield.

"High Priest Myltan is here as a guest of King Wilhem and at the behest of King Jahlaniin," said Harto loudly, diverting the attention to him though the high priest continued glaring at Brann.

"We already know that, boy," said Ravh, irritated, as the Royal Malaquey warden approached Brann and placed a calming hand on the fuming headmaster's shoulder. He only shook it off, leaving Lieutenant Commander Helsliff standing there awkwardly.

At least Harto's interjection had eased the tension somewhat, but he knew he had to do more before things got out of hand.

"I am glad you are all aware." He stepped forward and bowed deeply to the high priest.

"Sir, I apologize for my senior's poor behavior." Harto felt the moment Brann shifted his furious glance in his direction. "Please have mercy on him."

"Harto, what are you—!" The Royal Malaquey headmaster's outburst was cut off, and Harto risked a quick look to see that Sammel had stepped to Brann's left and had applied a crushing grip to the headmaster's hand. The pain on his face was almost comical.

"I accept your apology," said the high priest, pretending not to see the drama playing out beside him.

"Rise, my child. Come walk with me, for we have much to talk about."

The high priest left the room. Silence reigned momentarily as everyone stared at Harto. The Malaquey intelligence officer ran after the high priest.

#

Harto quickly caught up with High Priest Myltan. For a few moments, they walked in silence down the wide, empty corridor away from Headmaster Clayre's office.

"You must be wondering why I wished to talk to you," began the high priest.

Harto nodded but kept silent.

"Back at court, I suspected you wished to know more about your homeland and about King Olnanier, yet you have said nothing."

Harto nearly faltered but forced himself to keep walking.

"It didn't seem appropriate at the time. Nor has it yet."

High Priest Myltan smiled sadly. "Maybe so, but what if time runs out for some of us sooner than later? Would you not wish to make the most of your time?"

Harto felt a chill at the sadness on the high priest's face. "What does that mean, sir? Are you ill?"

The high priest laughed softly. "Who was your father?"

Harto stumbled at the abrupt change of subject. "I…why do you wish to know?"

"You share a close bond with Commander Nell, yet I know he is but your uncle. What happened to your father, and who was he?"

Harto struggled internally. This Dyhaeri had no right to enquire about his family! But Harto had been plagued by unanswered questions since he was old enough to know about his true heritage. He glanced at the high priest, who simply watched him patiently.

"His name was Revan Flay. He was a lieutenant commander in Malaquey Naval Intelligence, but he was originally from Namira."

The high priest stayed silent, expecting more.

Harto nodded. "He and my uncle went on a mission to Namira just before I was born. My uncle made it back. My father died."

"Please accept my condolences."

Harto nodded and felt the back of his throat burn and his eyes sting. He had always found it odd that he grieved for a man he had never met. Maybe it was because to this day, his mother still mourned. That could explain her alcoholism.

"What did you know of King Olnanier?" asked Harto, trying to change the subject.

The high priest smiled gently at him, acknowledging the tactic. "He was a good man, but he was extremely stubborn. His ministers had a tough time trying to guide him in certain matters." His expression darkened. "Especially when the Pirate Queen Kallesa caught his eye."

Now Harto was paying attention.

"At first, King Olnanier's goal was to capture her and put her on trial for crimes against the people of Namira and for the numerous ships, mostly Weltonian, that she had sent to the bottom of the Heldiar Sea. But something happened upon their first encounter—no one knows what—and suddenly she surrendered to him and disbanded her pirate gang. Within months, their wedding was announced. The Dyhaeri and the Weltonians tried to warn the king, but he refused to listen, and the rest is history."

Harto was silent for a long moment. "Why are you telling me this now?"

The high priest shrugged. "I felt it was time. I suspect someone else has told you some of this tale before. There is something more, however." The Dyhaeri stopped walking, and Harto realized they had reached the Dyhaeri guest quarters.

"This morning, I received an urgent message from Captain Lanead Riverun about a strange, hovering metal ship that attacked his ship and a second Weltonian ship."

Harto blinked, speechless for a moment. The high priest tilted his head.

"He swore it was of Namiran design, and I am inclined to believe him."

"Namiran design? Surely, he was wrong. I have heard of no such thing," said Harto in disbelief.

The high priest narrowed his eyes. "I find that odd considering Lanead also stated he sent a similar report to your uncle."

Harto had no idea how to respond. If his uncle was in possession of such news, why hadn't he told Harto? He soon realized the high priest was waiting for an answer. "I will look into it."

The high priest smiled sadly at him.

"Soon enough, there may come a time when you may find yourself in the same position your late father found himself in on his mission to Namira. My advice would be not to give in to sorrow and anger but to use those emotions to help others less fortunate than you."

Harto stared at him, concerned at how the high priest had jumped from one topic to another without warning. "Is this a divination, High Priest Myltan?"

That sad smile appeared again. "And now, I must rest. I will see you later." The high priest slipped through the door to his quarters and was soon out of sight.

Harto just stood in that empty corridor for a long moment, trying to work through his troubled thoughts.

CHAPTER 29

Day three of the Trials had started off so…calmly.

Britea couldn't help but yawn as she waited with Pearl in the crowded Great Hall for the general knowledge portion of the Trials to start.

First, however, she and Pearl had worked in the kitchens as usual. Thank the Lords, the punishment detail this time had been washing pans and pots. That had gone quickly, and then they had downed a quick breakfast with Lexia and Henrick before heading to the Great Hall. Danai, Shran, Navos, and Henrick had eaten breakfast with the Syla team instead. Henrick went because he was hoping to be considered for the next games two years from now, so he was observing. Britea hoped Shran wasn't too nervous; this was going to be his first Wielder Trials. If it had been her, she was certain she would be scared out of her mind.

"I'm surprised you're bored. I thought this would be your favorite part, especially since you've read all the books in the library," joked Pearl. Lexia chuckled.

Britea smiled wearily at her. "I stayed up a bit too late last night."

Pearl's eyes sparkled with mischief. "Oh, do tell. Did it have anything to do with a certain handsome Dyhaeri prince?"

The sleepiness left Britea's eyes when she realized what her crazy friend was implying.

"No!" Students nearby sent her startled looks, and she lowered her voice. "I was up reading because I was too excited to sleep."

Lexia and Pearl exchanged skeptical looks. "Yeah, right."

"Hey, you can ask Danai. She was with me last night!"

"Fine, we believe you," said Pearl with a wink as Instructor Shelley stepped onto the raised dais and clapped her hands loudly. Silence fell as everyone turned their attention to the senior faculty member.

"Good morning, everyone, and welcome to the general knowledge round of the Wielder Trials. Each college will have a team of four students. Our panel will pose a question to all three teams, and the first to ring their bell will have thirty seconds to answer." She gazed over the audience. "There will be two rounds, each consisting of twenty questions. Each correct answer gets a point, incorrect ones, zero. At the end of the two rounds, the college with the most points will get three points for winning."

Instructor Shelley turned now to address the teams. "Contestants, please make your answers audible and clear, or you will not be scored."

Britea's gaze went to Shran. He appeared much calmer than his three teammates.

"Shran's got this," said Lexia confidently. "If anyone in this room has a bigger brain than his, I'll eat my purple hat."

Pearl frowned at her. "You have a purple hat?"

Britea rolled her eyes, then realized Pearl was trying to lighten the atmosphere.

"Contestants, to your stations!" announced Instructor Kacia Felgreen.

The three groups of students moved to the center of the floor to cheers from the audience. Britea searched for Kahl and saw him sitting with Mat, Danai, and the Syla team across the room from her. Beside them was the Artra contingent, and to the right of them was the Royal Malaquey group. Britea could not help but notice the dark looks the Royals were casting in the Dyhaeri's direction.

She tore her gaze away. The senior members of the three colleges and High Priest Myltan were seated on the podium, seemingly oblivious to what was happening a few feet in front of them. But then Britea saw something else that made her blood boil. Lianne and her mother and sister were also seated on the podium, to the right of the high priest. Lady Adria Arkei was talking to him, and even from this distance, Britea could tell the high priest was working to maintain a neutral expression. She bet he was bored out of his mind, maybe even a little irritated.

"And guess who's once again close to the center of attention?" asked Lexia dryly. Pearl harrumphed her agreement.

Suddenly, there was a flurry of activity on the podium as Lieutenant Flay ran up the stairs and straight to Headmaster Clayre. He whispered into the headmaster's ear, and his expression went from annoyance to shock. After a few moments, Headmaster Clayre clapped Harto on the shoulder, then stood up and walked to the center of the podium. Harto looked determined as he approached Lady Adria Arkei. Her smile disappeared when Harto briefly spoke to her. Britea was now very curious.

"Everyone, please rise for His Majesty, King Wilhem of House Taros, Crown Prince Wiltran, and Princess Crystal."

Murmurs of surprise filled the hall as everyone stood, including the Dyhaeri high priest.

Everyone—the headmasters, the wardens, the instructors, and the students—bowed, but Britea noticed before she followed suit that High Priest Myltan, Mat, and Kahl remained standing.

"The royal court has honored us," continued Headmaster Clayre, still bowing.

"Please rise," said King Wilhem. Britea stood and realized more people had entered the hall in addition to the three members of the royal family. The additions all wore the navy-blue uniform of Malaquey Naval Intelligence. They had to be his bodyguards.

"Oh my. Look who just got told to get off the stage," whispered Pearl gleefully. Britea shifted her gaze to see Lady Arkei and her daughter quickly vacating the seats while the king and his children waited to reclaim them. The red hue on the faces of the Arkei family told all those assembled they were embarrassed. They started looking for seats in the general audience, and it took some time before they found a place to sit.

Britea covered her mouth to hide her laughter.

"As you were," said King Wilhem as he sat next to the high priest, who nodded at him and his children in greeting. Britea noticed Prince Wiltran and Princess Crystal were more interested in the Dyhaeri sitting by their father than in the Trials.

The headmaster signaled to Instructor Felgreen to continue, and the history teacher turned back to the audience.

"Joining me on the stage will be Instructor Brett Katos of Royal Malaquey Naval College and Instructor Waris Dragen of Artra Army College." The two male instructors walked onto the podium and bowed to the king and then to Instructor Felgreen before standing on either side of the history teacher.

Instructor Felgreen turned to the contestants. "Are you all ready?"

"Yes, instructor," chorused the three groups of contestants.

"First question: in what year did the Olderian Civil War start?"

The bell for Syla College rang first, and Shran stepped forward. "399 AC."

"Correct," said Instructor Felgreen before stepping back as Instructor Katos stepped forwards.

"Who was the First King of Namira?"

Shran rang the bell before the instructor had even finished speaking and answered. "King Val."

"Correct," said Instructor Katos as Instructor Dragen took his place.

"In what year did Namira create its first wielding college?"

This time there was a slight delay as the other colleges mulled over the answer. Shran rang the bell a third time and earned some hard glares from the other two teams. "1394 AC."

"Correct," said the instructor.

"You're right. Shran does seem to know it all," Pearl said to Lexia while Britea watched in wonder. The hall was completely silent.

"Mmhmm."

"What is the Sea Treaty, when did it come into being, and what does it signify?" asked Instructor Felgreen.

This time Royal Malaquey beat Shran to it. "The Sea Treaty is an agreement between the Dyhaeri and the humans that peace will reign provided a wielder is aboard every ship sailing on the Heldiar Sea. It signifies the end of the Dyhaeri-Olderian Empire war in 184 AC." The girl who hand answered sent a smug look Shran's way, but he was too busy watching the three instructors as he and his team waited for the next question.

"What is the percentage of wielders in the general population?" asked the Royal Malaquey instructor.

"Less than seven percent," whispered Britea as she recalled her first meeting with Danai's friends.

Artra rang their bell first and answered. "Nine percent!"

The instructor shook his head.

Shran lifted his bell and rang it before answering. "Less than seven percent."

"Correct," said the instructor and some in the crowd cheered.

Instructor Felgreen frowned at the crowd. "Silence please."

The Artra instructor stepped forwards. "Who is the Malaquey minister of finance?"

Shran was ready before the other two colleges. "Lord Nalin Solarn."

"Who is the Malaquey minister of health?"

Britea's gaze automatically went to Shran when once again he beat everyone to answer. "Lady Celess of De'Were." The Royal Malaquey instructor looked impressed, but the Artra and Royal Malaquey contestants were staring daggers at Shran, who simply ignored them.

This was followed by six more questions about other ministers and certain laws, and Shran got them all. By the end of the first round, it was a forgone conclusion.

Syla College was well in the lead.

#

"Here he comes!" bellowed Navos as he bowed and announced Shran to the small group of Syla students waiting in the corridor. They cheered as the slim, bookish student appeared, his cheeks flushed. Shran obviously wasn't used to this much attention.

"Thank you all…please, have a good day," stammered Shran. His fellow students clapped him on the back for putting their college in the lead. Syla was ahead with twelve points, with Royal behind them with ten points and Artra in third with nine points.

"Congratulations, Shran, on boosting our scores," said Lexia.

Shran gave her an odd stare. "I thought you didn't like this competition."

"I still don't but mostly because of the maze run and combat trials coming up in two days." She shot a concerned look in Navos's direction. Fortunately, he didn't notice because he was too busy chatting with Henrick. "The general knowledge part is okay, though. And besides, you killed it."

"In two days?" asked Britea.

"We get one day's grace to prepare, plus it gives the organizers time to build the maze," explained Danai as she yawned. "However, the most important thing is that I get to catch up on my sleep."

"Mind if we join you?" said Mat from behind her. That wiped the fatigue from her eyes.

Pearl smiled mischievously. "You wish to join us for sleep?"

Danai glared at her, and Mat looked confused. Kahl too made his way to the group, exchanging casual greetings with nearby Syla students along the way. Navos and Henrick drifted over to join them too.

"I'm sorry, did I miss something?" asked Mat.

Pearl tried but failed to look innocent. "Danai was just talking about how she was going to—"

"Rest tomorrow," cut in Danai. "However, we still have half a day left to do nothing…or we could all go to the market today?"

Everyone stared at her.

"It's Triday after all, and it's possible the coaches aren't being used. We can grab two and dash into the market to show Mat and Kahl the sights."

There was silence for a moment.

"We'll have to ask the high priest first," said Kahl eventually, though he seemed excited about the idea.

"But we have punishment detail this evening!" said a disappointed Britea.

Danai glanced at the chronometer on the wall. "Well, since this morning's competition extended into lunch, pushing back dinner, we have at least four hours to kill before supper. We can get to the market and be back before then. You two will still be on time for your punishment."

But Pearl gave her an odd look. "Who are you and what have you done with the rule-abiding Danai?"

"Good question," added Henrick.

Danai chuckled. "She's still here. I just want us to get out of here for a bit. Let's get permission and meet in the courtyard in an hour. I'll get the coaches." She hurried off.

The others looked at each other briefly before scattering to get ready.

#

"Danai, I can't believe you managed this!" exclaimed a happy Pearl as they bounced down the road in the carriage. They were halfway to Carlellis Market. Danai was in the first carriage with Pearl, Britea, and Lexia while the boys were in the second carriage.

Danai smiled at her, hiding her concern. She had an ulterior motive for this outing. For the last two days, she had been worried sick about her parents. Oh, she had hidden it well during training for the Wielder Trials, but now she had to know if all was well.

Every week, at least one Weltonian ship was docked in the harbor. Port Trident was favored among most Weltonian captains because of the easy access to the diverse, bustling Carlellis Market. She was sure her parents were keeping things from her. Usually she would let it go knowing they would tell her in time, but since the last visit from her parents, she could not help but feel that something dire was about to befall her parents.

Danai felt guilty dragging her friends into this and doubly guilty for breaking her promise to her parents not to venture to the docks, but she had made that promise weeks ago. Surely the danger had passed by now.

And if it hasn't? asked a little voice Danai decided to ignore.

#

Though it was Triday, thus the middle of the week, Carlellis Market looked as busy as ever. That was both reassuring and concerning. Reassuring in that many people were about, concerning in that the bustling crowd suddenly made her feel confined.

Matters got worse when folks sighted the two Dyhaeri. At first, the roadside merchants were stunned and pointed at them, whispering, but when Mat and Kahl showed interest in their wares, many began pestering the Dyhaeri cousins, trying to get them to buy their goods at outlandish prices. Danai rolled her eyes when she and the others had to act as a barrier between the Dyhaeri and the merchants. For this outing, they had worn their distinct storm-grey wielder uniforms.

Mat was enjoying himself, and even Kahl was curious about Carlellis Market. Britea stayed close to him as if protecting him. Danai shook her head in amazement. There was a bond between those two that defied explanation. It was a quiet, solid relationship she envied. But she was rather concerned about their future. Britea and Kahl came from two vastly different worlds. Dyhaeri lived for several centuries. Her father had told her that Queen Zaleria had gone to the Sea Mother when she was more than three thousand years old, though no one knew exactly how old she had been when she had passed. Then there was King Jahlaniin, who had become the leader of the Dyhaeri even before the Olderian Civil War more than seventeen hundred years ago. He had been ruling for centuries before King Wilhem was even born.

Danai wondered if the human leaders ever remembered that.

"Can we go to the bookshop?" Danai came back to the present when she realized Britea was asking her a question.

"What bookshop?" asked Pearl before Danai could answer.

"*Carlellis Books and Writing Materials.* It's on Fashionista Lane," replied Britea. "Erina Seaworth owns it."

Pearl's eyes went wide. "She has a shop here?"

"You didn't know?" asked Henrick. Pearl gave him a startled stare. "Britea told me about it the first time she went there."

"What? Oh, please, let's go there!" said Pearl.

"Sounds like a grand idea," said an interested Shran.

"Anyone else wish to do otherwise?" asked Danai.

Navos raised a hand. "I want to check out the armory section."

"I'm going with him, so he doesn't get too excited and go broke," said Lexia. Navos grinned at her before the two set off.

"All right, that's those two settled. I have to head to the docks first myself, just to drop a letter off," said Danai.

"Fashionista Lane is close to the docks. We can all go there together, then head to the bookshop after," said Britea.

Danai was relieved at the show of support. "Thanks so much."

The docks were busy as well, and she hung back, letting the others get ahead. Before long, there was a sizable distance between her and her sightseeing friends. Danai glanced at each ship, hoping to find a Weltonian one.

"Danai, what are you really doing at the docks?" She turned to find Mat at her elbow. His beautiful jade-green eyes were too knowing.

She made a decision. "I need to get a message to my parents. I just want to know if they're all right." She kept her voice low enough to reach only Mat.

The Dyhaeri glanced ahead at their companions, who seemed oblivious to their discussion. "If there is any way we can help, please don't hesitate to ask."

Danai was surprised by his offer to help. "I appreciate that, but there's no need—"

"Danai Riverun?" She and Mat turned to face two male Weltonians she didn't recognize. Only one addressed her, and he kept stealing glances at Mat. His partner was equally stunned.

"Yes, and you are?"

"Aidenn and Brien. We're the crew of the *Majestic Wind*. Our captain, Elder Brett Skylight, would like to speak to you."

At first Danai had been relieved she had been recognized, but that was soon followed by concern. *Had they been waiting for her to come to the docks? And if so, why?*

"Has something happened to my parents?"

Aidenn blinked, clearly taken aback by the question. "I have heard no news."

"So, why does your captain wish to see me?"

Aidenn and Brien exchanged a guarded look that was beginning to worry Danai.

"Please, come with us."

"I'm coming along as well," said Mat behind her. Danai looked at him and nodded; she was more than happy for the company. Him she knew, these two Weltonians, not so much.

"Which way is your ship?" asked Danai.

"It's about three ships down. Your friends are near it," answered Brien.

"Please," said Mat with a smile. "Lead the way."

Once the two Weltonians had put some distance between them, he spoke in Dyhaeri. "Is aught amiss?"

Danai shot him a startled look. *How had he known she spoke the language?* "I'm not sure," she finally answered softly.

Mat nodded as if she had just confirmed something for him.

They reached a large ship in due course, its bright sapphire sail tied down. From the look of things, they were about to depart. At the foot of the gangway stood a distinguished Weltonian with snow-white hair and a trimmed beard. He wore a pure white tunic and pants with pale brown leather boots.

On the short walk over, Danai had been racking her brain to remember the names of the different faction heads. She recalled hearing about Elder Brett Skylight from her father, and what she remembered had not been in the elder's favor.

Elder Brett smiled genially when he saw her and Mat, but unease began to build in the pit of her stomach when she noticed the smile didn't reach his eyes.

"Daughter of the Sea Mother and of the Weltonian people! It is good to see you." He held out his arms for a hug, but Danai was reluctant to step forward. Brett's smile dimmed a bit.

"Ah, even as a mere child, you were always so cautious." At Danai's questioning expression, he added. "The last time I was a guest on your father's ship was when you were just beginning to walk. Time has gone by too fast." Then he turned to Mat. "Please forgive my rudeness, Son of the Sea Mother and of the Dyhaeri people." He bowed deeply before arising. "I am Elder Brett Skylight of the Second Faction and captain of the *Majestic Wind*. I must confess, this is the first time I have seen one of you on land."

Mat smiled and waved a hand. "I am Mat-rallenin, friend to Danai Riverun."

Danai fought to hide her surprise. Friendship with a Dyhaeri was not usually publicly declared, so for Mat to say this meant he was also informing Elder Skylight he was her ally.

For a brief moment, the look in elder's eyes was uncertain, but the faction leader recovered quickly.

"That is good to hear. Please come aboard for a brief visit. We have some time before we cast off." Brett turned to walk up the gangway, fully expecting them to follow.

Do not get on that ship. Danai had no idea where that thought had come from. However, she was in agreement. Something about this meeting felt off. "No."

Brett froze on the gangway for a moment, then slowly turned to face her. Though he kept a puzzled smile on his face, she saw the glint of anger in his eyes.

"Danai Riverun, did you just decline an invitation to board a Weltonian ship?"

There was a hidden warning in those words, and she knew she had made the right call. Danai would not be giving him any messages to pass on to her parents.

"Please, tell me what you wish to discuss. I have to be back at Syla College before long."

Brett stared at her and then at Mat. "I also extend the invitation to you, Matrallenin. You can accompany her."

Mat crossed his arms. "As Danai said, we really don't have much time for a prolonged visit. I am happy to stay here with her."

This time Elder Skylight didn't bother to hide his anger.

"Fine," he said through gritted teeth. "I was trying to help your father, but now you leave me no choice but to pass on a Final Warning to the one known as Danai Riverun."

Danai felt Mat tense beside her, and without thinking, she put a calming hand on Mat's forearm. "What are you talking about?" she asked in as cool a tone as possible.

Brett's smile was cold and malicious. "Three weeks ago, your father received a proclamation stating that you must return to the fold within four months or risk being exiled."

Danai felt the blood drain from her face. She could barely acknowledge the shocked look from Mat.

"Ah, your father is yet to tell you? I bet he's still at sea trying to save more wretched Namiran refugees."

Danai's shock was instantly replaced by anger. "Don't you dare talk about him like that!"

Brett laughed mirthlessly. You're just as quick to anger as he is." His face became stern. "You now have just three months and one week to tidy up your affairs. You have been warned." He turned and walked up the gangway onto his ship. Once there, the gangway was withdrawn, and the ship pulled away from the dock.

Danai watched them go. Her suspicions had been validated. If she and Mat had boarded that ship...

"Why are your own people threatening you with exile?" asked Mat in a soft, worried tone.

Danai felt a terrible ache in her chest as she herself tried to understand, and she was yet to come to terms with the fact that her father had known for more than three weeks!

"I don't know. Maybe when my parents return, I'll ask them."

Mat wisely stayed silent as they watched the *Majestic Wind* depart.

#

Britea stole a look at Danai, who was walking beside Mat. The group had turned and begun the return to the market only to find Mat and Danai waiting for them near one of the empty berths. When Pearl had asked if Danai had been successful in her search, the Weltonian student had responded with a strained smile.

"Yes, now let's go to Fashionista Lane."

Mat had given Danai a worried glance before following her. Britea hoped the two had not quarrelled. She was happy Danai and Mat were friends.

"Are all markets in Malaquey this busy?" asked Kahl. Britea was grateful for the interruption in her racing thoughts.

"I don't think so. The market in Weldaros is so much smaller than this place. It's also a lot friendlier."

The hustle and bustle of Carlellis Market reduced noticeably when their small group entered Fashionista Lane.

"Why 'Fashionista'?" Mat asked.

"Because of the types of shops here," said Danai, who had brightened a bit. "The latest in attire and jewelry is found in this part of the market."

"As well as Erina Seaworth's bookshop," said Pearl. "Oh, that reminds me. We need to get outfits for the After-Trials Ball."

Pearl raised an eyebrow at Britea's puzzled expression, then sighed when she saw how disinterested Danai and Shran were. Mat, Kahl, and Henrick, on the other hand, seemed intrigued.

"Come on!" she said to her girlfriends. "It's the most important part of the Trials!"

"I already have an outfit picked out," said Danai wearily.

But Mat narrowed his eyes. "So, what is this After-Trials Ball?"

"It's an opportunity for both match making and hiring potential top-tier wielders…for after they've finished their Year of Discovery of course," replied Pearl.

"Don't forget that the Malaquey Navy and army also use these games to hire future recruits," added Henrick.

Shran snorted in agreement.

"It all sounds quite…odd," said Kahl with a frown on his face.

"We might as well check out clothes first before we go to Madam's Seaworth's shop, so we have time to chat when we get there," said Danai. "We have to hurry though, so Britea and Pearl don't get in trouble."

That was how they found themselves in front of *Lara's Attire for the Frugal Wallet*. This time, the two guards, Boren and Kliev, were stunned when they saw Mat and Kahl.

"Good day, Boren and Kliev," greeted Danai, but they were too starstruck to answer. Danai shrugged and walked past them into Lara's shop. Britea was close on her heels with the others close behind her.

There were a few people in the shop, but they stopped what they were doing to stare at Mat and Kahl.

Lara had just finished accepting money from a customer when she turned to greet them. This time she wore a fuchsia flowing gown, and her robin-blue hair was thankfully down this time and hanging loose around her shoulders. Her chestnut eyes widened in surprise.

"Danai! Britea!" She did a double take when she saw Pearl.

"Oh, hello, Lara," said Pearl as her face flushed.

Lara narrowed her eyes for a moment, but then she turned to smile at Henrick, Shran, Mat, and Kahl.

Danai took care of the introductions. "Everyone, this is Lara Firbright, a wonderful friend of mine from back when I roomed with her in my early years. Britea, Pearl, and Shran, you already know."

Lara hugged Shran, who seemed quite happy to see her.

"Please meet Mat-rallenin, Kahl, and Hendrik."

"Nice to meet you all. Welcome to my shop."

After a brief discussion about the purpose of their visit, Lara took Henrick, Mat, and Kahl to the men's section while Shran perched on a stool and brought out a book he had been hiding.

Danai laughed. "It sure took you long enough; I knew you had at least one book on you."

Shran shot a sly grin at her. "I'm surprised you noticed, especially with how captivated you've been with Prince Mat."

Dania groaned. "By the Lords, not you too!"

Shran smirked. "It's just an observation."

While she watched Danai and Shran, Britea began to notice shoppers were lingering, trying to catch another glimpse of the two Dyhaeri.

"I bet Lara still hates me," muttered Pearl beside Britea.

Britea frowned and looked at her. "Why do you say that?"

Pearl hesitated, then looked at the floor, ashamed. Britea waited. "Lianne's sister, Selina, hated Lara's guts because she protected Danai, so a couple times, the other girls and I helped Lianne make trouble for Lara." She looked up to see Britea's disapproving expression. "It's not something I'm proud of."

"Then maybe you better tell her that," said Britea gently.

Pearl stared at Britea as if she had asked her to jump off a cliff.

"Do you ladies need anything?" asked Lara brightly as she approached them. She bestowed the same smile on each of them.

"I'm good, thanks. I still have that lovely green dress I bought here," said Britea while Pearl stayed silent.

"Have you worn it yet?" asked Lara.

"No, but I will to the After-Trials Ball at the end of the week."

Lara sighed. "I wish I could be there to see you all decked out." Then she winked and tilted her head in Kahl's direction. "Especially with that young Dyhaeri hanging onto your arm."

Britea felt her face go red and warm.

"Lara, can I please talk to you?" asked a nervous Pearl. Britea and Lara stared at her.

"Of course," said Lara politely. "How can I help you, Lady Ceres?"

Pearl winced and gave Britea a pleading look.

"I…it looks like you two need to be alone. I'll go bother Danai and Shran." Britea fled towards the two older novices.

#

"What's going on over there?" asked Danai as Britea reached her and Shran.

"Pearl wanted to talk to her."

Shran closed his book to watch Pearl and Lara. The two women were talking in muted tones, their expressions solemn. "Seems serious."

Danai moved to stand up, but Britea placed a gentle hand on her arm.

"I think we need to leave them alone for a bit." Danai stared at Britea for a long moment, then nodded.

The unheard conversation seemed to go on forever. Then Danai saw Pearl wipe at her eyes, and to the astonishment of all, Lara hugged Pearl warmly then patted her shoulder before walking away.

Danai, Shran, and Britea shared a stunned look.

"I've got Pearl," said Britea as she stood up from her chair.

"We've got Lara," said Danai as she and Shran went after the smiling shop keeper.

When Britea got closer to Pearl, she noticed her friend was crying softly and trying to dry her tears.

Britea's heart sank. "What happened?"

"I apologized, and she…. she forgave me," said Pearl. Britea realized these were tears of joy.

"She just made me promise not to be an idiot in the future. I thought she hated me!"

Britea was beginning to wonder what Lianne and her friends had done to Lara. For Pearl to feel guilty about it, it must have been awful.

"How do you feel?" asked Britea.

"I…I feel better, lighter," said Pearl after a long moment.

Britea smiled at her.

Eventually the boys' shopping came to an end, and by then, Pearl had regained her composure. She had even picked out a beautiful black and silver scarf she said would go well with her dress for the ball. After they had all paid, they headed to Erina's shop.

Britea was relieved when they entered and found the shop empty apart from Erina, who was up on a rolling ladder, stocking the top shelves.

"I'll be with you in a minute!" said Erina without turning. Once done, she climbed down.

"Welcome to my shop…" she began as she turned. The smile froze on her face when she saw Mat and Kahl.

Britea was concerned. Erina appeared frozen in fear.

"Hello, Erina. This is Mat and Kahl. I wanted to show them your shop and your books…" Beside her, Pearl and Danai shared a worried look.

"By the Sea Mother!" gasped Erina Seaworth as she came forward and gazed at Mat and Kahl, who were at this point looking a bit alarmed.

"Never did I dream to have you four standing in my shop!" Her stunned gaze included Britea and Danai.

"But there are seven of us," pointed out a puzzled Shran.

Erina blinked and tried to compose herself. "Of course, there is! Forgive me. Long has it been since I last saw a Dyhaeri standing a few feet away from me. Please, make yourselves at home."

Pearl smiled and stepped forwards. "I'm a big fan of your books. Would you please sign the books I buy today?"

Erina was pleasantly surprised by her request. "Definitely. It would be my pleasure."

Thus began a tour of the modest book shop. Shran was intrigued, and he spent quite a bit of time picking out books. Kahl's face also lit up when he saw the rows and rows of human literature. Before long, he and Erina were chatting about her books. Pearl filled a basket with only Erina's books, and poor Henrick soon found himself carrying said heavy basket!

Mat and Danai hung back, watching Kahl and Erina. Britea was relieved the two were less moody. She still wondered what had upset them earlier though.

Danai glanced at her chronometer. "Miss Seaworth, thanks so much for showing us around. We do have to go soon though."

The writer stared at them in dismay. "But…but I've not yet offered you tea and cakes!"

"We will try to come again," said Mat with a gentle smile.

"We promise," said Kahl, his arms full of books. He missed the wry smile Mat sent his way.

When it came time to pay, Erina tried to give the books as a gift to them all. However, everyone, including Mat and Kahl, insisted on paying her. With unshed tears in her eyes, Erina accepted. Pearl gave a squeal of delight when Erina signed her books.

But when they were about to leave, Erina grabbed Britea's arm. The writer's eyes flashed silver for a brief moment before resuming their natural walnut color.

"In days to come, thou shall find thyself in a perilous situation on a bridge, though fear will ambush thee. Thou must use the fear itself to flood thy troubles away."

Fear clutched at Britea's heart. "Wait…what is that supposed to mean?"

Then Erina shook her head and rapidly withdrew, looking dismayed. "Please, don't hate me. That…that happens at times."

"Britea?" She turned to see the others staring at them. Kahl was concerned.

"Is all well?" asked Danai, giving the cowed Erina a cautious look.

"Yes, we're fine," said Britea, trying to keep a calm look on her face. Maybe loneliness was making Erina behave oddly. Britea gave the older woman a gentle hug to show her she bore no grudge.

"We'll see you again." But as they left, Britea turned in time to see tears begin to fall from Erina's eyes.

#

They met up with Navos and an exhausted Lexia, who had just finished touring the armory shops, and they all agreed it was time to return to the carriage, but the main street was busier than it had been earlier, and they soon found their pace slowed.

"Maybe we should take a short cut?" asked Henrick.

Danai sighed. "You do realize the short cuts around here are a lot shadier than the main streets?"

"Henrick is right," said Shran. "We need to find a shortcut or Britea and Pearl will be late for their evening punishment. There's plenty of alleys."

Danai looked at the other six members of their group.

"I don't mind taking a shortcut," said Britea.

Lexia yawned. "Yeah, I'm for whichever route gets me back to my dorm room faster."

"It should be quicker that way," said Navos.

Pearl wasn't comfortable with the idea. "Alleys? What about…" She glanced looked around before lowering her voice. "Unsavory characters?"

Danai knew she meant thieves and scoundrels and the like. Part of her agreed with Pearl, but it was getting late and the crowd on the main streets was going to be difficult to get through.

The others looked at Danai as if she was the designated leader. But Navos spoke first.

"There are nine of us, five hefty boys and four talented girls, and most of us in wielder grey. We should be fine. But we'll have to move fast."

Mat gave Navos an odd look. "Sounds like we'll be going through enemy territory."

I sure hope not! thought Danai as she tried to stay calm.

"Nah, anyone seeing our wielder greys knows we shouldn't be bothered," said Navos confidently. "I've taken the alleys plenty of times in the past and was absolutely fine every time."

"Seems like the majority is for the alleys. We'd best get moving then," Danai said, leading the way.

They may have made a different decision had they seen the several hooded individuals who blended into the walls lurking several feet behind them. They pushed themselves off the walls and began to stalk the unwitting group.

#

Mat tried not to gag at the stench of the alley behind the shops on Armaments and Armor Lane. Lining one side of the alley was the high port wall, against which leaned small, ramshackle structures, torn and dirty rags covering broken windows and puddles of filth littering the entrances. It was from those buildings miserable, unkempt people emerged clothed in bedraggled garments to shuffle aimlessly down the alley. So, this was where the poverty-stricken population scraped by. It saddened him deeply, but the worst was still the stench.

By the Deep, he had thought he was becoming immune to the smells of human surface dwellings, but this was the worst he had ever come across. He wondered why the denizens and homes of this area were so unkempt and without when the well-kept shops of rich merchants lay just on the other side of the alley. Mat hid a shiver at the hunger in the poor souls' eyes as they stared at the two Dyhaeri and seven wielder students.

He glanced at Danai and was glad to see the wariness in her gaze and her gait. Mat turned to check on Kahl, but his cousin was chatting with Britea.

He rolled his eyes. Of all times, when Kahl should have been alert, he was courting.

"How much farther?" asked Mat in a quiet voice that only carried to Danai.

She gave him a sharp look then went back to observing their surroundings as they walked.

"Not much further. Is something wrong?"

"I'm not sure yet, but I don't like this place. It feels…" his voice trailed off as six tall ruffians in blood-red tunics abruptly blocked their way. In contrast to the poor residents the group had encountered thus far, their clothing was well made and emphasized their muscular frames. Mat stiffened as their hands drifted towards their weapons: a combination of staves, long daggers, and at least one pair of dueling swords.

"Kahl, trouble of six in front," called out Mat in Dyhaeri.

"Mat, we have six behind," replied Kahl, also in his native tongue.

"Hey, what's going on?" asked Navos angrily. "We're just students at the college."

"We just want the two girls," demanded a female thug as she stepped forward, her face concealed by a matching hood. Mat thought her intonation sounded odd, like she was about to sing. "Her." She pointed to Danai. "And her," she said again, pointing to Britea.

Mat saw Danai's face go pale as Pearl gasped and Lexia held on to Navos for dear life. The others shifted behind him, and he hoped they were getting ready to fight, diplomacy be damned.

Mat cursed himself for not bringing a weapon along. He relaxed his hands but was stunned when Danai grabbed one of them.

"Let them strike first, then we defend." She raised her voice so the entire group could hear her.

"So, I take it that's a no then?" asked the apparent leader of the ruffians. Her voice turned hard. "Take the targets and kill the rest!"

The students, and Dyhaeri, dropped their bags.

Mat bounced on his feet as steel was bared, and the gangsters charged with a shout. Three of them went for Danai and three came his way. He waited as they swung their swords, and then he wielded the air out of their throats and upper lobes of their lungs. Their eyes went wide, and the six thugs grabbed their throats and went down to their knees, gasping for air. It would take several minutes for them to recover and even then, they would be in no state to fight. Yet if he had wanted to kill them, he could have done so.

"More incoming!" yelled Danai as six more spilled out from the buildings. Before Mat could move, Danai wielded fire from a barrel of fire housed in a street corner. With a wave of her hand, she set the thugs' feet on fire.

Mat's jaw dropped as the would-be kidnappers were turned into dancing, howling humans.

"Let her go!" shouted Pearl. Mat turned to see her using one of her new hardcover books to hit a thug on the head. The attacker was trying to drag a frightened Britea away, but Pearl was persistent, and each swing hit the hoodlum's head like a ton of bricks. By the fourth thud, the attacker fell to the ground, unconscious.

Kahl, meanwhile, was fighting hand-to-hand with another attacker, who had the advantage of daggers. Navos had grabbed a plank to use as a stave, and Lexia was cowering behind Navos. Shran had been knocked to the ground and looked on the edge of consciousness. Henrick dragged his friend out of the way and ran back into the fray, his hands balled up into fists.

Why in the Deep weren't Kahl and the others wielding? Mat wondered, confused as Danai let loose a blast of fire that lit the red jackets of three thugs on fire.

"Use your blasted wielding, people!" bellowed Danai like a drill sergeant. The response was immediate as she continuing wielding tier-one forms to set the thugs' feet on fire.

Danai's order snapped Kahl back to his senses, and he remembered his water-wielding ability. Taking muddy water from a pothole, he flung it into his attackers' eyes. They yelled in pain. Mat promised himself that, provided they survived the fight, he was going to take his cousin aside and scold him to within an inch of his life for his lack of response.

Navos knelt to the ground and used air to create a whirlwind that knocked his attacker off her feet.

"In front of you!" yelled Britea to Mat and Danai.

They spun to see two hulking brutes with sledgehammers running towards them. Mat's eyes widened. He had not known humans could grow to these proportions.

"By the Sea Mother," muttered Danai as she tried to draw more fire from the barrel. But before she could wield, the back door to one of the armory shops on the left burst open to reveal an alarmed Lieutenant Flay. The intelligence officer immediately aimed his palms at the ground beneath the feet of the charging brutes, and the earth began to buckle and heave before caving in. With frightened shouts, the attackers fell in.

Harto glared at the other ruffians. "Cease or be arrested by the order of Malaquey intelligence!" He turned and called over his shoulder as if to some unseen backup. "Over here! I found the princes!"

The leader of the gangsters whistled, and the remaining attackers fled.

Suddenly, it was just Harto, the two Dyhaeri, and seven weary novices in the alley. Mat looked back at the group and saw Kahl with one arm around Britea, who was quite pale.

"We have to leave, now," said Harto. He walked towards Danai, and Mat moved to block his path, fixing him with a glare.

Harto stared at him then turned and saw suspicion in Danai's eyes as well.

"Wait, you think I had a hand in this?"

"Why are you here?" asked Danai, stepping around Mat.

Harto sighed. "I was following Mat and Kahl. My job is to keep an eye on them. But it would be best we discuss this back at the school before the thugs realize I'm on my own."

"He's right," said Danai reluctantly.

"Then let's get moving," said Mat as he went to help Henrick with the unconscious Shran.

#

Mat tried to stay calm as Danai was assessed by Healer Storm. The entire group was being cared for in the infirmary now that they had safely made it back. High Priest Myltan, Warden Asteros, Weapons Master Caren, Lieutenant Flay, and Lieutenant Welspring hovered nearby, anxious for details of the attack. Harto had wisely advised them to wait for explanations until the healer had checked the group for wielding fatigue. Danai was the last of the humans to be examined by the healer. The high priest took care of Mat and Kahl.

Mat knew the signs of wielding fatigue: rapid heart rate, breathlessness, and profound lethargy, at times followed by unconsciousness and in some extreme cases…death. He had only wielded once to the point of collapsing during his endurance training. He didn't think Danai would be affected from this battle, but he still could not help but worry.

"Novice Riverun's vitals are stable," said the healer. Mat hid his sigh of relief. A glance at the high priest revealed the easing of tension on his face. Mat was curious as to why the high priest had been so concerned. Perhaps it had less to do with their welfare and more to do with having to explain to an irate Captain Riverun that Mat and Kahl had gotten his only child killed in the market.

"Good," said Warden Asteros. "Now, I want to know exactly what led to the attack by the Red Rats gang."

Mat blinked. *The ruffians had a name?*

"And what was Lieutenant Flay doing in the market at that precise time?" asked the high priest mildly. Mat smiled coldly when he saw Harto flush.

Danai raised a hand. "The outing was my idea. I just wanted to visit the market and drop a message off for my parents. I had no idea it would end up like this."

"Please continue," said Syla's warden.

Danai described their route from the central market area to the docks, past city hall, and then to Fashionista Lane.

"You didn't see them on the way in or out of that district?" asked Weapons Master Caren, who had been standing by silently with Lieutenant Therry Welspring. Mat had been suspicious when the Royal Malaquey instructor had appeared with the weapons master, and that suspicion had only grown when he had discovered the lieutenant just *happened* to also be Malaquey intelligence.

What a coincidence.

"No," replied Danai. "When we went to leave, the market was overcrowded, and we couldn't move very fast. We needed to get to the departure place on time so Britea and Pearl wouldn't be late for their punishment detail, so I led them through the alley."

Mat frowned. She had not been the one to make that suggestion.

"Because I insisted on it," added Navos, and Mat's respect for the human grew.

Danai shot Navos a warning look, but the others spoke up too.

"That's right," said Lexia wanly. "Most of us voted to go through the alley. Danai was the only one who didn't want to. But the rest of us thought that because of the size of our group and our wielder uniforms, no one would bother us."

Mat looked at Lexia, concern evident on his face. He doubted any of them would *ever* take a shortcut again after this experience.

"That was when we ran into the Red Rats," continued Danai. She proceeded to describe how they had defended themselves. Mat saw the warden nod approvingly when she stated their group had waited for the kidnappers to strike first before defending themselves. Lieutenant Therry Welspring looked at Mat sharply when Danai explained that Mat had stopped the first six attackers on his own.

"How?" Therry cut in.

Mat smiled politely. "I performed a tier-one wield near their faces." Therry frowned when he realized Mat was not about to explain further.

"What happened next?" asked Warden Asteros. Danai briefly explained how everyone had contributed to the fight, and what Harto had done to stop the two brutes in their tracks. Mat saw the high priest's eyes narrow when she mentioned the brutes, but the high priest stayed silent.

Then everyone looked at Lieutenant Flay.

"I guess it's my turn," said Harto.

Mat folded his arms as he stood beside Danai.

"Another agent informed me that Mat and Kahl were in the courtyard, so I went to do my job. By the time I got there, they had left with the students. So, I borrowed the Royal Malaquey coach and set off after them. When I got to the market, I discreetly followed them. I saw nothing suspicious and certainly didn't notice the Red Rats until, of course, this group decided to take that shortcut behind Armory Lane. I was so far behind the students the Rats didn't see me, but when I realized the seriousness of their intent, I knew I needed to intercede. So, I ran around and into one of the Armory Lane shops, barged in, waved my badge, and ordered them to show me the back door to the alley. Thank the Lords we're all still standing."

Silence greeted his words.

"We thank you for the assistance," said Kahl. Mat tried not to roll his eyes.

"Kahl has the right of it," said Navos. "Thank you for your help, Lieutenant Flay."

Harto stared at Kahl and Navos in surprise. "You're welcome."

"Well, all that aside, why did the Red Rats want only Danai and Britea?" asked Therry.

Mat was glad someone was finally asking the right questions.

"I truly don't know," said Harto before pausing and looking at Danai. "Unless it has something to do with Weltonian criminal activity. Danai, do you know of any Weltonian Red Rats members?"

Oh no, he didn't just say what I thought he said. Mat saw Danai go rigid with anger.

"Because I was a target? You think this was my people?" Danai practically hissed the words.

"From our reports, Britea is also of Weltonian descent, and she's your friend and roommate. Being Weltonian is the only real link between you two," said Lieutenant Therry Welspring.

Danai glared at him. Mat's chest tightened and his vision blurred. Ignoring the warning stare from his high priest, he prepared to verbally blast the two Malaquey officers.

"Hey, Henrick and Shran," suddenly called out Pearl. The two boys gave her startled looks. "Between your two brains, there's a lot of knowledge. Are the Red Rats Weltonians?"

Shran blinked as he searched his brain. "No, historically Red Rats members are locals from Raven's Fall. The gang is at least a hundred years old, and none of the prominent members in the history books were Weltonians or wielders."

"Thanks, Shran. Henrick, any thoughts?" asked Pearl as she turned to her next target.

Henrick's brow furrowed as he answered.

"The Red Rats are notoriously territorial and extremely wary of outsiders. They don't like Weltonians and would never admit one into their gang. Besides, those attackers were too tall to be Weltonians, especially those two hulking brutes."

Everyone stared at Pearl as she turned to the two Malaquey officers with a cold smile.

"Did it occur to you two geniuses that maybe Britea and Danai were targeted because they *look* like Weltonians? The Maker knows that throughout our history, Weltonians have been largely discriminated against and killed, which is why for centuries we didn't have any Weltonian students until these two. So, instead of you trying to pin this on Danai and Britea or Weltonians, why don't you look for the miscreants who tried to hurt us?!"

"And you are?" demanded Lieutenant Welspring.

"Novice Pearl Ceres of House Ceres," said Pearl with a calculating smile.

Mat watched the officer's countenance change to one of respect and wariness. Mat shook his head in disgust but silently applauded Pearl for how she had handled the situation. Left to him, he would have exploded by now.

"I trust the investigation has been shared with local law enforcement?' asked the warden, staring steadily at Harto. The blond Malaquey officer hesitated, and the warden's expression turned glacial. Mat was so glad that was not directed at him. The warden was so similar to the high priest in his mannerisms.

"I'll get right on it."

The warden nodded at Weapons Master Caren. "Master Caren will accompany you to headquarters to submit your report."

The warden turned to the students. "Britea and Pearl still have their duties in the kitchens this evening. I have already told Chef Blane to expect you to be a bit late due to a visit to the infirmary. Speak of what happened in the markets to no one. The last thing we need is panic." He looked each of them in the eye. "You're all dismissed."

Mat turned to speak to Danai, but she had already gone. From her stance, he knew she was still seething at what the Malaquey officer had implied. Mat took a step to go after her.

"Kahl and Mat, I will speak with you," said the high priest.

Mat wondered what more the high priest wanted from them. Danai had already explained what happened!

The walk to their quarters was silent. Mat glanced at Kahl, who was oddly subdued and looked a bit shaken. He wondered why. It wasn't like Kahl had never seen battle before.

Once in the privacy of their quarters, Mat noticed fruit and pastries on the table nearby. His mouth watered.

"Please eat as we talk." Mat didn't hesitate to heap food on his plate and only paused when he realized his cousin was morosely picking just a few treats for his own plate.

The high priest, in the meantime, filled a glass with water and sipped it as he watched them eat for a few minutes.

"I would like you to describe the attackers for me and spare no details." Mat gave the high priest a puzzled look. Even Kahl perked up a bit when he realized the high priest was acting oddly.

Mat put down his untouched plate and launched into a detailed description of the would-be kidnappers. Several times during the retelling, the high priest made him repeat certain details, especially about the Red Rats' leader. Mat told him repeatedly she had been a female and she spoke as if she was about to break out in song. That seemed to disturb the high priest greatly.

The next detail of note was the high priest's reaction when Mat had stated the Rats' outfits had seemed new and well sewn. And when Mat got to the size of the two hulking brutes that had appeared at the end of the encounter, the high priest put his glass of water down and stared off into the distance.

"High Priest Myltan, what's wrong?" asked Kahl.

For the first time in his life, Mat saw the second most powerful Dyhaeri of the Heldiar Sea look uncertain, afraid even.

"The kidnappers…they were not of the Red Rats Gang. Those were the Namiran Death Squad."

"What…who?" asked Mat. The high priest rubbed his face with one hand.

"This is not common knowledge, but Weltonian spies have, at great cost, obtained intel for the Dyhaeri people." Mat and Kahl stared at him. "In the northern mountain regions of Namira once lived the Calif Nomads. The mountain air and the minerals that ran into their spring waters made the indigenes grow tall and bulky."

"The brutes?" asked Mat, trying to hide how the word "lived" made him uneasy.

The high priest nodded. "And believe it or not, their language makes them sound as if they are about to sing. The Calif Nomads were fiercely territorial and over the centuries ran skirmishes against the Namiran Royal Infantry. Over three hundred years ago, a truce was reached, and the nomads were left to their own devices while the rest of Namira promptly forgot about them." The high priest ran a hand through his hair before continuing. "But shortly after Queen Kallesa murdered King Olnanier and took his throne, she went up to the mountains to have a chat with the Calif Nomads."

The room was silent as the cousins waited for the rest of the tale.

"She razed the entire region to the ground, killed the adults, and took some of the surviving children as slaves."

Mat suddenly lost his appetite and had a brief urge to throw up. His cousin's green face had gone pale.

"The intel we got from the Weltonians revealed those children and their offspring were trained and conditioned to become her Death Squads. They're known as assassins but also act as shock troops during territorial disagreements. Somehow, she's gotten a group into this city, and now they're posing as the Red Rats."

"Surely, the Red Rats would have protested that," said Kahl.

Mat had a sinking feeling he knew why they hadn't.

"They would have, but it's likely they're all dead," said the high priest solemnly.

"High Priest, with all due respect, why didn't you mention this to Malaquey intelligence?" said Mat, trying to keep his voice even and polite.

The high priest smiled sadly at him. "They aren't ready to listen…yet."

Mat stared at him. *What kind of cryptic answer was that?*

"So, why did they want Danai and Britea?" asked Mat, feeling his anger build. He was fast running out of patience. "Did Queen Kallesa send them?"

The high priest hesitated before answering. "That will be a question for another day. Try to get some rest. We have busy days ahead of us." He left before the cousins could ask any more questions.

Mat frowned at his plate, not sure what to make of what he had just heard. But this incident had confirmed one thing: he and Kahl were *so* unqualified for this spying business. *So, why in the Deep had they been chosen?*

"I don't understand. Why would Queen Kallesa send her assassins after Danai and Britea?" muttered Kahl from beside him.

Then Mat recalled something else he had to discuss. He had two approaches open to him: shout or speak gently. His instincts advised him to go with the latter.

"Kahl," he began calmly. "Why didn't you wield right away?"

His cousin went silent and guilt flashed across his face. Mat waited. "I…I just wanted to beat them to pieces with my hands. They wanted to take Britea away from me!" The last few words were said in the heat of anger.

Ahh.

Mat could only understand too well what his cousin had experienced. But he had to point out a few things. "Kahl, you're my cousin, and I love you very much." His cousin gave him a wary look. "But the next time you're in the heat of battle, I need you to take a step back for a brief moment, assess the situation, and wield like Britea's life depends on it." *Especially now that it appears her life may truly depend on it.*

Kahl went pale. "You think they'll be back?"

Mat leaned forward. "A queen who didn't hesitate to attack her own father and kill her twin sister is hunting Britea. And then there's everything else she's done, from killing the Namiran king to exterminating the Calif Nomads and enslaving their surviving children. Do you really think she'll stop at just one attempt?"

Kahl remained silent, and Mat knew he had gotten the message. "We can protect her as much as we can, but there are only two of us," said Mat as he dropped his untouched plate on the table.

"And Danai and her friends need protection as well. Don't forget, she's a target too," Kahl pointed out.

"Fair enough," said Mat after a moment. "I'll tell her about this."

Kahl sent him a stunned look. "Shouldn't we clear it first with the high priest?"

Mat shook his head. It had become increasingly clear to him the high priest was keeping a lot from them. At first, he had reasoned the high priest must have a good reason, but now he was tired of waiting for more clumps of information to drop.

"No. We need to do this on our own."

#

Danai picked at her food. Strangely, she had no appetite. Though given what had happened just less than an hour ago, she should not have been surprised. She recalled Harto and Therry's arrogant expressions as they accused her and Britea of being involved, or knowing others involved, with the Red Rats gang. She clutched her fork in anger.

"Danai, are you okay?" asked Henrick.

She looked up to find Pearl, Britea, Shran, and Henrick watching her with worried expressions. Lexia had retired early to her room, and Navos had escorted her there.

Danai relaxed her grip on her eating utensil. "I'm fine, just not very hungry."

"That's understandable, but..." Shran's voice trailed off as he gaped at someone behind her. Danai also heard startled murmurs from nearby students, so she turned to see Mat and Kahl stroll into the dining hall.

Danai was worried when the two Dyhaeri headed to their table. "What's wrong?" she hastily asked when Mat and Kahl reached them.

Mat smiled kindly at her. "Kahl wanted to visit your dining hall since we've not had a chance to experience it." He looked at his cousin.

"Yeah, what he said," said Kahl nervously.

Danai narrowed her eyes. "What's going on?"

Mat kept smiling, but the light in his eyes was solemn. "Danai, please, may I have a word? It's about tomorrow's games."

"And this chat can't wait?" pointed out Pearl as she frowned at Mat. "The poor girl is drained."

Danai had an inkling that Mat had something important to tell her though, so she stood. "Sure, I'll be right back, guys." Then she left with Mat, glancing back once to see most students staring at Kahl, who was now seated with her friends and chatting loudly with them.

Ah, Kahl was the distraction.

Once in the corridor outside the dining room, she turned to Mat. "Okay, what's going on?"

Mat glanced around to ensure they were alone. "There's something I must tell you. The Red Rats are not what they seem. They're the Namiran Death Squad."

Danai couldn't believe what she was hearing. "Wait, what?"

Mat went on to relay what the high priest had told him.

For a long moment, Danai was speechless. "What does the Queen of Namira want with Britea and I?"

"You don't know why you're a target?" asked Mat in a low tone.

Danai gave him a stunned look. "Of course, I don't!" Then she narrowed her eyes in suspicion. "Do you?"

"I don't and when I asked the high priest, he refused to say."

"Why are you telling me this?" asked Danai.

Mat's green face flushed, and for a moment, he was at loss for words. "I just thought...I think you need to know."

Danai raised an eyebrow. For a moment, she had been sure he had been about to say something else...certain, special words she realized she wanted to hear. But who was she kidding? He was Dyhaeri and she was human. Surely, he wasn't interested in her no matter what Pearl said. "I appreciate the information, but shouldn't we be discussing this with Lieutenant Flay?"

Mat's expression turned bitter. "I'm not sure he'll listen."

"That doesn't mean we shouldn't at least try to talk to him about it. We're not qualified to handle this mess!" pointed out Danai.

"Tell me about it," muttered Mat. He signed as if resigned to his fate. "If you think we should tell Harto, then I'll support you in this."

Danai was warmed by his trust in her. "It's too late to go looking for him now. We can catch him first thing in the morning."

CHAPTER 30

Harto was hungry. His day had begun earlier than usual to accompany Weapons Master Caren to the local militia. Submitting the report about the attack on the wielder students had taken hours. As he had expected, the local militia hadn't taken it as seriously as he had hoped. Harto knew the locals weren't qualified to undertake this investigation, but protocols had to be followed.

He was on his way to the dining hall when he ran into Kahl, Mat, and Danai. From their solemn expressions, he assumed they had been waiting for him.

Harto had to tamp down the jealousy he felt when he saw how close Mat and Danai were standing to each other. "Can I help you?"

Mat glowered at him while Danai sighed. "We need to talk to you about the attack yesterday." Kahl stayed silent.

Harto's stomach growled, and Mat's glare turned into a smirk. "But I suppose it can wait since the lieutenant is starving."

The officer tried to keep his expression neutral even though he wanted to punch Mat's handsome face.

"We can grab some snacks from the buffet in the dining hall and talk in one of the empty classes," suggested Danai.

Mat stared at her and Harto smiled. "That sounds like a marvelous idea."

Several minutes later, after a few small sandwiches and coffee, Harto felt sated enough to pay attention. They were sitting in an empty class, and Kahl was keeping watch outside, ensuring they were not disturbed.

"Okay, we've got privacy and I've eaten. What's going on?"

Dani glanced at Mat and nodded. The Dyhaeri began to speak in a solemn tone. "The Red Rats that attacked us yesterday are not the real Red Rats, they're the Namiran Death Squad."

Harto froze and stared at them.

"Is this some sort of joke?" He didn't bother to hide his anger.

"No, it's not," said Danai. "The proof is in their accent. The leader sounded like she was about to sing when she spoke, just like the Calif Nomads of Namira."

Harto stared at her. "You're aware I'm Namiran."

"Mat told me."

Harto glared at the Dyhaeri. "But unfortunately, I was born here, so I have no idea who the Calif Nomads are." He saw Mat grimace as if he had tasted something terrible, but a voice inside warned Harto not to lash out at the Dyhaeri. He forced himself to keep calm. "What do you know?"

Mat took a deep breath. "I told the high priest about how the Red Rats looked and spoke. He believes they're Calif Nomads due to their unique speech and impressive build. The high priest also told us what happened to the Calif Nomads about forty years ago. Queen Kallesa slaughtered them when they refused to submit to her rule, and she took the children as slaves and turned them into her personal assassins. We believe the original Red Rats were killed, and the Death Squad took their place."

Harto stared at him in shock for several seconds. "How did the high priest obtain this information?"

Mat's countenance was grim. "I am not at liberty to say."

Harto glared at him and then turned to Danai.

"I didn't tell her either," said Mat.

Harto tried to keep his tone even. "Why didn't the high priest mention this last night in the infirmary?"

"I doubt this is the kind of information you want more people to know than is necessary," pointed out Danai. Harto had to reluctantly agree with her. There had been at least ten people in the infirmary last night, most of them not cleared to know such sensitive information.

"So, what now?" asked Harto. Danai and Mat stared at him.

"You're supposed to be Malaquey intelligence. Shouldn't you investigate the Red Rats' disappearance?" finally asked Mat. Danai kept quiet, an expectant look on her face.

"On the say so of an easily duped Dyhaeri marine and a naïve Weltonian?" Harto didn't bother to hide his scorn. "It would make me look like a fool."

Mat stared at him with rage in his eyes while Danai sighed. "And I thought you might actually be reasonable," said Danai.

"Well, unless you tell me who your source was, I cannot proceed."

Mat looked at the ceiling and scoffed. "The high priest was right. You're not ready to listen."

Harto was taken aback by that, but before he could reply, Kahl walked in.

"We have to leave now. The afternoon session of the Trials is about to start."

Danai nodded and tapped Mat on the arm. "Let's go. We've done our duty."

Harto just smiled at Mat as the Dyhaeri glared at him once more. But his smile faded as he thought of what they had just told him.

He knew of the Death Squads, but none of the reports had identified them as Calif Nomads. Harto had not been lying when he had told Mat and Danai he didn't know who they were. To be honest, most of his knowledge of Namira he had learned from his mother and uncle.

So, if the Calif Nomads had existed once, why hadn't his family told him of them?

#

"Welcome back, everyone! Welcome to the afternoon session of day five of the 126th Wielder Trials!" Instructor Shelley's amplified shout was answered by cheers from the crowd.

The instructor smiled at the crowd. "I can tell many of you enjoyed the morning session of endurance wielding, which now has Syla College and Royal Malaquey vying for first place. Now, let's see what the wielding maze brings!"

Along with the rest of the Syla fans, Pearl whooped with joy and turned to Britea, but her friend only gave her a tired smile.

Pearl's enthusiasm ebbed. She knew what was bothering Britea. The incident in the markets had happened only yesterday. Thankfully, they had not been hurt, but Britea had been subdued since then.

"Hey, what's the matter?" asked Pearl leaning closer to her friend.

"I'm just finding it hard to enjoy this," said Britea as the instructor continued her speech.

Pearl frowned. This was not Britea at all. Pearl had thought of approaching Danai with her concern, but the senior novice was busy with the games.

"I hate going home because of how often I get told I'm too fat," said Pearl abruptly. Britea looked at her, alarmed, then glanced around to see if anyone was listening.

Pearl continued. "But being told I'm fat isn't the worst part. No, no, no, it's what comes next: purging drinks and concoctions, special diets, and oh, let's not forget the constant shaming my cousins treat me to when they come to visit—which is all the time. I have experienced such…treatment since I was little." Her voice sounded calm, but Britea could fell the deep undercurrent of pain. "It's no joy being called a pig by my own family."

Britea's eyes widened.

"You see, all that stopped when Lianne befriended me. My cousins were scared of upsetting her, so they kept their opinions to themselves. And stupid me, I told Lianne everything, and she promised to protect me." Pearl laughed when she realized how light she felt now that she had spoken those words of shame into existence.

"I…I'm so sorry," said Britea.

"It's fine. It's not like it's your fault. But talking about it, out here where anyone can hear…" she looked around, and sure enough, some nearby students were openly listening. "…is actually liberating. I should have done this a long time ago."

Britea's smile was now a lot brighter than earlier. "Then I'm happy for you."

Instructor Shelley had completed her spiel on the podium, and the audience was applauding.

"So," began Pearl. "What's really eating at you?"

Britea's face went dark for a moment, and Pearl was worried she had regressed into her moodiness.

"Back in that alley, I didn't wield," said Britea reluctantly. Pearl waited for her to continue. "I froze, and Shran got hurt. Kahl, all of you, almost got hurt, all because I froze." There was so much guilt in her voice that Pearl winced.

"We're not warriors, sister," said Pearl softly. "We're just students, and we were lucky the others were with us. I'm sure if there's a next time, Maker forbid, you'll outwield us all."

They sat in comfortable silence for a time.

"I never did say thank you for fighting off that thug with your new book," said Britea. "And I'm sorry it got damaged."

Pearl laughed softly and gently nudged her with her elbow. "Are you kidding? I love that book, battered and all. It's even signed by Erina Seaworth, which only makes it more precious! Hardcover books are the best, but I never knew they could be that effective as weapons. We should get Instructor Talios to add it to the curriculum and title it, 'How to Knock Out an Opponent with a Hardcover Book!'"

Britea tried to contain her laughter and failed, and soon the two girls were laughing their heads off, not caring who looked their way.

#

Danai rubbed her hands as she stood in the crisp midday air and studied the map of the maze that had been erected over the last two days and covered the entire field.

Thank the Sea Mother the endurance wields were over! Syla had come last in that contest, with Artra in second place and Royal in first place. At least Syla and Royal were tied for first place now with thirteen points each. Now everything was on the line.

It was time to take on the wielding maze race.

It was a timed event where a contender from each college would run into the roofless maze and try to get to the end in the shortest time possible. While it seemed like another version of the first wielding race, it was much more complicated.

While running through the maze, the contender would encounter ten opponents from the other schools and would have to battle to get past them without hurting them too badly. Danai knew this maze well because she had trained continuously with Navos and Aaliya over the last four months. They had alternated the role of runner between the three of them, and one would run while the other two would block. Unfortunately, Navos had not been chosen for the maze; Aaliya had beaten him, and Danai had never had any intention of tackling it.

Aaliya was their best chance to win this event. The last time Syla College had won the maze run had been when there were still five wielding colleges between Namira and Malaquey.

At that moment, for some reason, Elder Brett Skylight and his Final Warning of Potential Exile suddenly came to mind. Danai shook her head; she couldn't afford to think about that right now, especially after the disastrous discussion with Lieutenant Flay the other morning.

By the Sea Mother, why did she have to deal with such idiots?

She had been grateful the Dyhaeri cousins had agreed to put the discussion with Harto behind them. Danai had more than enough on her plate right now, and at times, she caught Mat watching her with a worried expression.

"Oh, that looks like fun," said Mat as he came up beside her. She shoved a smile on her face before looking at him. Despite her concerns, her heart felt lighter now that he was near.

"Tell that to the battered and bruised contestant and blockers who come out the other end." She had taken the Dyhaeri on a tour through a mock maze before the games had started, and even they had been impressed by the complexity of the maze.

"Artra is going first, with Syla blocking," said Kahl, reading his program. "What I don't understand is how the audience or the instructors see what's going on within the maze? Anything could happen in there."

Danai sighed and gave Kahl a wearied look. "We have to trust the contestants will be honorable and try not to hurt each other too badly."

Mat raised an eyebrow. "Why does that sound like wandering into another back alley? Oh!" He protested when Danai elbowed him. "It was just a question!" protested Mat when she glared at him.

"Have students been hurt in the maze?" asked Kahl solemnly.

Danai rubbed the back of her neck before answering. "Yes, it's the most hazardous part of the games, at least until the sparring events."

"Then why is it a part of the games?" asked Kahl.

"It's to prepare the novices for the military," said Weapons Master Caren, who had walked up silently behind them. "Surely your own exercises must be that taxing too," said the senior instructor as he addressed Mat.

"More or less," answered Mat. Master Caren smiled as if he knew Mat wasn't about to spill the secrets of Dyhaeri marine training.

"Well, I hope you all enjoy the maze run." The weapons master nodded at Danai before heading over to join two assistant instructors from Syla.

"What are those instructors doing?" asked Kahl, pointing at three people in the different college uniforms who spoke briefly before entering the maze.

"Inspecting it to ensure it's identical to the mazes at Artra College and Royal Malaquey," explained Danai.

"Ah, to ensure no one has an unfair advantage?" asked Mat.

"Correct," said Danai.

A few minutes later, the instructors from the three different colleges emerged and each gave a thumb's up to the crowd.

"The maze run has been approved," announced Instructor Shelley to the cheers of the crowd.

"And now, let's meet the contestants." She turned to gesture at the students. "The first runner will be Novice Deric Holms of Artra College!" Instructor Shelley's voice rang out as Danai and the two Dyhaeri turned to see a lean, young male in the typical olive-green sleeveless tunic, similarly colored pants, and thigh-high leather boots of Artra College. His shaved head only served to accentuate his coffee-colored, almond-shaped eyes and caramel complexion. Unfortunately, his good looks were overshadowed by his grim expression. A brown slash on the front and back of his uniform proclaimed his earth element. He began to warm up on the starting line, staring straight ahead and ignoring the cheers from both Artra students and King Wilhem's group. Today, the king was again in attendance with Crown Prince Wiltran and Princess Crystal.

Hmm, Deric probably doesn't want to be distracted, thought Danai.

"The second runner will be Novice Thran Oslor of Royal Malaquey College!" A lanky, flaxen-haired novice with his hair in a ponytail waltzed onto the field and waved at the Royal Malaquey fans, who cheered loudly. Then he bowed towards King Wilhem, Crown Prince Wiltran, and Princess Crystal. His sleeveless water-blue tunic—with a white slash to represent his air element—matching navy pants and thigh-high navy leather boots highlighted his physique. He was good looking, and he knew it.

"The third runner is our very own Novice Aaliya Dune." The home crowd roared as she appeared in her storm-grey sleeveless tunic with a blue slash for her water element, storm-grey pants, and thigh-high leather running boots. Aaliya bowed first to the king and then to the rest of the audience. Danai clapped along with Mat and Kahl, but as she turned, she caught Thran eyeing Aaliya closely. There was something about his smile that sent a chill through Danai.

Instructor Shelley waited for the crowd to quiet before she continued with the next set of announcements. "As a result of the earlier coin toss, Artra will run first while Syla blocks, Royal Malaquey will run second with Artra blocking, and Syla will run third with Royal Malaquey blocking."

Danai couldn't take her eyes off Thran. His smile turned colder and more calculated as he studied Aaliya.

"Runners, you have three minutes to prepare!" shouted Instructor Talios from the starting line.

At that, Thran's smile widened, and he stepped towards Aaliya, holding out his hand. "May the best of us win!" Danai saw the friendly greeting startled Aaliya, but she held out a hand to clasp Thran's in the spirit of good sportsmanship. Then the Royal contestant clasped her bare right arm before apologizing and properly shaking her hand.

Danai felt worry prick at her.

"I didn't know Royal Malaquey was that friendly," said Mat, who had materialized at her side.

"Neither did I," said Danai as she watched Thran walk over to Deric and hold out his right hand.

"May the best of us win—"

"Get lost, Royal," growled Deric, jogging past Thran without touching him. Thran shot a venomous look at the Artra contestant's back, and that set alarm bells off in Danai's head.

"One minute left!" bellowed one of the Syla instructors.

"Mat, could you excuse me a moment?" asked Danai. Mat nodded. He looked concerned as if he had picked up on her feelings. She ran to Aaliya, who was warming up.

"Aaaliya, are you all right?" asked Danai.

The Syla runner gave her an odd look. "I'm a bit jittery, if that's what you mean, but I'm always this anxious before a race."

Danai stared at Aaliya's bare right arm and hand. There were no marks, but she couldn't shake the feeling something wasn't right.

"Syla blockers will enter the maze now!" Navos gave Danai and Aaliya a happy grin before he ran into the maze with the other nine blockers.

"Silence in the field!" yelled a Royal Malaquey instructor who stepped forward to start the race.

Deric crouched low as silence enveloped the field.

Then a shot went off, and Deric shot to his feet and started running. The stadium began to shout and chant as he dashed into the maze, and a huge, suspended chronometer began to count down. The noise only grew when the occasional yell and shout of pain escaped the maze whenever Deric ran into his blockers. Danai's eyes drifted to the chronometer, and she wondered where the Artra contestant was.

From time to time, fire or water would ooze from one part of the maze as Deric made his way through, parts of the structure cracking as the wielding continued. At the same time as Danai heard the crowd erupt in cheers, bells ringing pierced the air, which meant the chronometer had stopped.

"Novice Deric is out in two minutes and thirty-five seconds!" Danai whooped with joy. She couldn't help herself. Aaaliya's best running time was two minutes and twenty-six seconds. Maybe this year, Syla College had a chance.

She watched as Deric sauntered back to his teammates; he seemed somewhat despondent. Maybe he had expected to do better. Then Danai saw Navos and the other Syla blockers stumble out of the maze. Navos looked better than the rest, but they were all grinning.

"How can you lot smile even though it looks like you all had the living daylights beaten out of you?" joked Mat as he walked up to the Syla blockers.

Navos grinned at the Dyhaeri. Ever since the incident in the market, Navos had become closer to Mat and Kahl. Being in close combat had a way of bringing folks together.

"Oh, you should have heard him swearing when we kept blocking his path. He was definitely not happy with our antics."

"Yet he seems none the worse for wear," said Kahl. Danai had to agree. Deric didn't have a scratch on him, but he seemed to have wielded enough to physically exhaust the Syla blockers.

"But we slowed him down, didn't we, mates?" Navos asked the other tired blockers.

He got a tired chorus of "ayes" in response. Mat just chuckled.

"The course is being reset now. Royal Malaquey, you have five minutes to prepare!" announced the Artra instructor who had taken over for Instructor Talios at the starting line.

Thran walked over to the starting line and began to warm up. Danai looked at Aaliya, and the novice was still stretching and preparing for her own maze run.

Maybe I'm being paranoid, thought Danai.

"Artra blockers will enter the maze!" The ten blockers in olive-green uniforms ran silently into the huge wood and stone structure.

"One minute left!" bellowed the instructor. The crowd fell silent.

Thran crouched and waited. After what seemed an eternity, the gun went off, and the Royal novice dashed into the maze to the cheers of the crowd. The chronometer began to count down, and it didn't take long for shouts to fly out of the maze. This time, Danai even saw two bodies clad in Artra colors fly into the air only to fall back into the maze and land with a dull thud.

"Ow," said Kahl sympathetically as Danai, Mat, and Navos collectively flinched.

Then they heard more yelling amidst more cracking.

"Deric wasn't that forceful," said a worried Navos, echoing Danai's thoughts. Whatever was going on in the maze sounded a lot worse than what Navos' team had gone through. Eventually Thran emerged.

"Novice Thran finishes with a time of two minutes and thirty-one seconds!"

Danai let out a sigh of relief. It was still slower than Aaliya's best time. Syla College could win this. All Aaliya had to do was—

"Aaliya?!" yelled Navos. Danai turned in time to see their peer drop to her knees wearily. Danai, Navos, Mat, Kahl, and the other Syla blockers ran to her.

"What's wrong?" asked one of the Syla blockers.

"Don't crowd her!" shouted Danai. "Give her room to breathe! Aaliya, what's wrong?"

"I…I don't feel so good." Aaliya was sweating profusely, and her usually chocolate-brown skin now looked washed out. Before Danai could touch her, Mat crouched down.

"With your permission, may I touch your brow?"

Aaliya nodded wearily and Mat touched her forehead. He frowned. "She's burning up."

Thran did something to her.

"What?' asked Navos with a growl and Danai realized she had spoken aloud.

"Aaliya needs a healer," said Mat, who was now supporting the runner. Two of the Syla students reached down to help them, but the Dyhaeri shook his head.

"No, get the healer first. If she has something, then I probably have it already. I would prefer if no one touches us until we're both assessed by the healers." Mat looked at one of the Syla blockers. "Go." The novice scrambled off in search of a healer.

Danai stared at him. That was why he had run faster than her. He had recognized what was happening and hadn't wanted her affected.

You beautiful idiot!

"What exactly happened, Danai?' asked Navos, a thunderous look on his face. The remaining Syla blockers mirrored his expression.

"Syla has five minutes to prepare!" shouted a Royal Malaquey instructor.

Danai jerked her head up. *Wait, did the instructors not know something was wrong?*

"Not now Navos. We need to tell Master Caren what happened first and put a stop to this competition." Ignoring her common sense, she looked at Thran.

He was standing with a large group of Royal Malaquey students. They were all looking in their direction and smiling smugly.

"Thran did something to her, didn't he?" growled Navos. He stepped in the Royal's direction, and Danai grabbed his hand.

"We find Master Caren first."

"Hold the countdown!" yelled their weapon's master's voice. Danai turned, relieved she didn't have to go searching for Master Caren. The weapons master was hurrying towards them with two healers and the Syla blocker who had ran off on Mat's orders.

"What happened?" asked the weapons master after he had taken one look at the Mat kneeling beside Aaliya, supporting her. The two healers quickly assessed Aaliya and Mat.

Danai explained everything to the weapons master, leaving nothing out. Master Caren's face darkened when he heard how Thran had clasped Aaliya and how he had attempted the same with Deric before the Artra contestant had rebuffed him.

Weapons Master Caren opened his mouth to speak, but then his frown darkened when he saw someone over Danai's shoulder.

"I knew that Royal Malaquey bastard was up to something."

Danai and the others turned and came face to face with Deric and some of his Artra teammates who had bruised faces and arms. Danai recognized them as the blockers. They all seemed just as angry.

"Aaliya won't be able to be able to run now," said Deric. Danai was surprised that he seemed worried as he stared at the nearly unconscious Syla runner. Then he turned to glare at the openly smug Thran and his Royal Malaquey teammates. He took a step in their direction, and Weapons Master Caren immediately blocked his path.

"Getting into a fight with Thran will disqualify you and lose your school points."

Deric stared at the Syla weapons master in shock. "That piece of shite just poisoned one of your students, and you're just going to let him get away with it?!"

Some of the Syla students began to mutter angrily in support of Deric.

Before Master Caren could reply, someone else spoke. "What's the holdup?"

Danai turned and her eyes widened when she saw Headmaster Welbrick approach. *Wasn't he supposed to be in the observation box with the king, the high priest, and the other two headmasters?*

"Thran just poisoned Aaliya and tried to do the same to me!" shouted Deric before Weapons Master Caren had a chance to reply.

"This is all speculation and needs to be investigated first," said Weapons Master Caren calmly, trying to be diplomatic.

"Well, at least it's not an infection," declared one of the healers.

"Then what is it?" asked Danai.

The healer hesitated before replying. "It's more like a sedative. I'm afraid some of it would have transferred to Prince Mat when he touched her."

Danai felt her heart turn to ice. She glanced at Mat, whose forehead was shining with tiny beads of sweat. He smiled cheerfully at her.

"I feel fine. Don't worry about me."

"Is there a reason for the halt to the countdown?" asked Lieutenant Flay, who was also approaching the group now. He was flanked by Lieutenant Welspring.

Headmaster Welbrick shot the two Malaquey officers a jaundiced look.

"It appears one of your boys in training may have had something to do with this."

"It is yet to be confirmed," warned Master Caren.

Headmaster Welbrick snorted. "Yeah, right." He turned back to Harto. "So, now Syla's short a contestant for the final run."

"Who was her backup?" asked Therry.

"I was," said Navos through gritted teeth. "But I was Deric's blocker."

"And he's in no shape to run after what I put him through," pointed out Deric.

Therry plastered an insincere sympathetic smile on his face as he turned to the weapons master. Harto on the other hand looked truly disturbed.

"Which means Syla will have to forfeit this run." This was greeted by cries of rage from both Syla, and oddly enough, the gathered Artra contestants.

"No," said Danai loudly. "I will run."

Silence fell, and they all looked at her. She was pleased to see Therry's smile falter and Harto surprisingly give her an encouraging nod.

"You can't take just her place!" said Lieutenant Welspring.

"Yes, she can," countered Weapons Master Caren in a hard tone. "Danai is on the team's roster as support. And you know as well as I do that all support staff can double as a substitute if the need arises."

"Agreed," said Headmaster Welbrick with a wicked smile that dared Therry to argue with both the Artra headmaster and the Syla weapons master.

Therry nodded reluctantly after a long moment. "I will alert my instructors."

"I will inform the king and the other officials of the development," said Harto, before glancing at Danai. "Good luck, Novice Riverun." He dashed away. Danai blinked in surprise.

"Well, girl, I wish you the best," said Headmaster Welbrick. "We'll leave you lot to prepare." The Artra headmaster nodded at Deric, and with a reluctant sigh, the Artra contestant and his colleagues followed their headmaster.

"All right, Danai, you have six minutes before you have to go in," said the weapons master.

"I need to change," she replied and turned to leave.

"Wait," said the weapons master. "Syla blockers, go with her. And Kahl, would you please accompany them and act as an observer, so no one tries this stunt again?"

"Yes, sir," said Kahl, a solemn expression on his face.

Danai was stunned at the sudden requirement of several bodyguards. Part of her wanted to argue, but she realized there was no time, so she nodded curtly and hurried off to the dressing rooms. As she passed Thran and his peers, she could not help but notice the looks of consternation on their faces.

Once in the changing room, she quickly changed into Syla's storm-grey sleeveless tunic, matching pants, and black running boots. Her tunic, though, had a fire-red slash on the front and back.

Danai emerged to the sound of cheers from her teammates and the audience, but she refused to let it affect her concentration. She had run this maze countless times while helping Aaliya and Navos train. She kept her eyes forwards as she strode to the maze amongst her appointed guards.

All she had to do was finish the race.

"Novice Danai Riverun will run in Novice Aaliya Dune's place."

As she got closer to the starting line, she heard jibes from the Royal Malaquey group. She ignored them and prayed her guards did the same.

She released a sigh of relief when they too did nothing. Once at the starting line, her guards peeled away. Danai remembered to bow in the direction of King Wilhem and his children, then turned and did the same for the audience. The Syla crowd's cheers grew louder.

Despite herself, Danai looked for Mat and was surprised he was still on the field, though he was sitting beside Aaliya, who looked somewhat better. Both healers were still with them. *Why hadn't the healers taken them to the infirmary?*

Mat and Aaliya saw her and waved, smiling their encouragement.

"Royal Malaquey blockers will now enter the maze!" yelled the Artra instructor now overseeing the final run.

Danai began to stretch and warm up as they all waited for the ten blockers to assume their blocking positions.

"Two minutes left!"

Danai began her Weltonian breathing exercises. She ignored the puzzled looks she was getting from the nearby contestants of the other colleges.

"One minute left!"

She waited a few heartbeats, then got into position.

An eternity seemed to pass before the shot went off, and the crowd cheered as she erupted from the starting line and ran towards the maze. Danai entered the only entrance and kept moving, trying to listen for telltale sounds, but her heart was beating too loudly in her ears.

Use your eyes.

During their maze training, Danai had told Navos and Aaliya to always remember to use their eyes to check for shadows. They would give away the blockers' positions. In the first room of the maze were three cauldrons of water, fire, and earth. Danai ran across the room, grabbing an orb of fire without stopping and creating a tier-one rope of fire that she wrapped around her bare left forearm. Her skin remained unburnt.

As she turned left around a corner, she saw a shadow move just a split second before a large air orb flew in her direction. Rather than dodge, Danai tore off a small part of the fire rope and turned it into a fire arrow, which penetrated the orb of air and set it on fire. She wielded the new orb of fire to her and threw it up into the air. It rose above the maze, and an involuntary, startled gasp pinpointed Danai's blocker. Danai ran after her target, only to find a male Royal Malaquey blocker staring up at her orb of fire in surprise.

By the time he realized he was not alone, Danai had blasted a smaller ball of fire at his feet. The novice tried to jump aside, but she kneed him in the chest at the same time, and he crashed into the wall behind him as she ran past him. Danai didn't stay to see if he was unconscious. She just knew he would not be following her anytime soon.

She turned right then into a long corridor and swore under her breath. This was the usual second ambush point. Danai looked above; her orb was still following her as it should. She tore a piece from it and used it to form a form-fitting fire-laced bubble. This was a technique she had learned from her Weltonian teachers, and this was her first opportunity to try it since she had been at Syla. Ordinarily, she would have refused to take part in the Trials let alone perform this particular wield, but right now, she was too angry to care. She had to do whatever she could to make things right.

She ran down the corridor. The attacks came as she was halfway through. Water orbs dropped from above, so she made her bubble much hotter just before the water hit her. Before long, the corridor was filled with steam, obscuring everyone's vision but hers. Her fire bubble cleared the air around Danai, allowing her to see. Curses filled the air as the blockers yelled to each other for someone to reveal her position. Danai ran as fast as she could, keeping her hand on the wall on her left. Thankfully, she didn't run into anyone until she emerged into a room with less steam within. Two Royal Malaquey blockers were still coughing though and trying to dry their eyes. Danai was still in her fire-laced bubble, so she could see clearly.

She whistled to draw their attention, and when they turned, she forcefully wielded two medium-sized fire orbs that knocked both blockers to the ground. Then she broke into a run yet again, her enormous overhead orb keeping her company.

Danai turned left again at the next corner and heard voices ahead of her. Usually, she would slow down to take stock of the situation, but she didn't have time. She ran towards the voices and discovered three blockers. One wielded watery ropes to bind her while the other two began to wield the earth beneath her feet. Danai responded by taking half the floating fire orb above her and wielding it up to the fifth tier to create a fire-bubble platform, forcefully pushing and lifting the three opposing wielders off their feet. Their bodies flew into the air as they screamed in fear.

Danai ran on as she snapped her fingers above her head, bringing the three wielders down with a loud thud. Their answering groans were a testimony to the hours of pain that would follow as they recovered.

She turned right this time and found herself in another long corridor. This time, there were two grim-looking blockers between her and the exit. Danai paused for a moment, and they smiled, mistaking her pause for fear.

Danai simply looked up, flung her left arm at the remaining fire orb above her. The fiery rope still around her arm turned into a whip that hooked onto the floating orb. Danai tugged, and the blockers stared in disbelief as she sailed over their heads before alighting on the other side of the corridor. She tore out of the corridor before they recovered, and her heart almost burst with relief when she glimpsed the welcoming light of the exit.

Danai ran out to thunderous cheers. She extinguished the fiery rope and the floating orb above her head.

"Novice Danai Riverun emerges with a run time of two minutes and twenty-nine seconds!"

Danai felt her knees go weak. She stared, unbelieving, at the board. Syla was back again in the lead again with sixteen points. She was soon mobbed by cheering Syla *and* Artra contestants. For some reason, Artra didn't seem to care that she had beaten them. She wondered if it had to do with what Thran had tried to do to Deric and what he had done to the Artra blockers.

She felt immense satisfaction at the mixture of disbelief and anger on the faces of the Royal Malaquey contestants, especially Thran, who looked like he was about to burst with rage.

"Congratulations, Novice Riverun," said a beaming Weapons Master Caren. "I always knew you had it in you." A smiling Mat was now standing beside him with Aaliya and a relieved-looking Kahl. Danai was reassured to see Aaliya and Mat looked stronger.

"Three cheers for Noble Novice Danai Riverun! The Wielder Queen!" shouted Navos as he pointed to Danai. He motioned with his head, asking her permission to carry her, and she agreed. Navos beamed and lifted her onto his broad left shoulder as the cheers continued around her.

"Hip, hip, hurray! Hip, hip, hurray! Hip, hip, hurray!"

Danai smiled and found herself crying as well. She knew this was a moment she would treasure for a long time.

CHAPTER 31

"Prince Mat is well, but he should rest for the next twelve hours," ordered Healer Thomena Storm.

"But I feel fine!" protested Mat as he sat on the bed in Infirmary One. He and Aaliya were being reassessed by the chief medical healer. High Priest Myltan was present, along with Headmaster Clayre, Warden Asteros, Weapons Master Caren, Danai, and Kahl.

"I feel all right too," said Aaliya. "Why can't I go back to my dorm?"

"You both may feel well, but the sedative is still in your system. Had you both not insisted on staying to watch Novice Riverun race, I could have purged it out of your systems sooner."

Everyone looked at Danai, who felt her cheeks burn from the scrutiny.

Headmaster Clayre cleared his throat to get the healer's attention. "May I speak to the three now?"

The healer looked at the headmaster sharply. "For a few minutes. I need these two to rest, and I also expect Novice Riverun to stay and relax. Her wielding maze run would have exhausted her."

"Duly noted," said Headmaster Clayre before turning to Danai, Mat, and Aaliya.

"Weapons Master Caren told me some of what happened to Aaliya, but I'd like to get the whole story from you three."

They spent the better part of an hour relaying the interaction between Thran and Aaliya from all three perspectives. At the end of it all, the headmaster looked grave. He looked at the high priest, who had been silently watching him.

"While Thran's behavior does seem suspicious…it does not indicate without a doubt that he tried to sedate Aaliya."

Danai's jaw dropped in shock. "What?"

"I don't understand," said Mat while Aaliya just stared at the headmaster.

"Thran was checked after the maze run," said Weapons Master Caren. "We couldn't find any trace of the sedative on his uniform or his hands."

"He…he must have washed his hands when he ran into the maze," said Danai. She was thinking of the large cauldron of water that had been in the first room of the maze.

"Maybe," said Warden Asteros, shrugging. "But we have no proof."

Danai felt her heart sink. "You're just going to let him go?"

"We have no choice," said a grim Weapons Master Caren.

"Surely, you can't be serious!" exclaimed Mat incredulously.

"Mat-rallenin," warned the high priest, but Mat was having none of it.

"Danai and I both saw him approach Aaliya and clasp both her arm and hand unexpectedly. Even, though I've only been here a short time, it's clear to me the Royal Malaquey Naval College thinks Syla College is beneath them. Thran's so-called act of *friendship* was a clear act of deceit and treachery, and you're saying there is no proof?!"

"Enough," said the high priest firmly. Mat sighed angrily before directing his glare at the floor.

Headmaster Clayre was clearly embarrassed, but the warden wore a grave expression, and Weapons Master Caren seemed just as frustrated as Mat.

"It's politics," said Master Caren to everyone's surprise. Mat looked up at him.

"It's just vicious human politics, so I agree with you, Mat, that Thran needs to be dealt with, but this will take time. So, please, I implore you, leave this to us."

Danai stared at the weapons master. He was explicitly asking Mat not to get involved.

Mat held the human weapon's master gaze for a long moment, then reluctantly nodded. "I'll stay out of it."

Master Caren released a sigh of relief, then he looked at Danai ruefully.

"Everyone was impressed by your last wield, using the orb of fire as a lift. The king and his daughter, Princess Crystal, would like to talk to you about it."

Danai felt the blood drain from her face. "I…I…but why?"

"Not just them," added the warden. "Royal Malaquey and Artra recruiters also want to speak to you immediately."

Kahl and Mat shared puzzled looks.

Headmaster Clayre came to their rescue. "The Wielder Trials are used to find new recruits for the Malaquey Army and Malaquey Royal Navy. The best performers and those who think quickly on their feet are usually snapped up for enlistment after graduation. It comes with good pay and benefits. Novice Riverun's performance in the maze run has the recruiters eager to talk to her."

Danai took a deep breath. "But I'm Weltonian. We don't serve in the army or navy. That's been our rule since the colleges were founded centuries ago."

Master Caren sighed. "I told them the same thing, but I'm afraid they still want to try and recruit you. I've already told the king and the recruiters that you're in the infirmary, so you at least have your freedom until after the games tomorrow. Please let the recruiters down gently."

Danai nodded.

"Who taught you that last wield, Novice Riverun?" abruptly asked the high priest, who had been silent besides the warning he had issued to Mat.

Everyone stared first at him and then at Danai as they waited for her reply. "My father."

To Danai's surprise, the high priest smiled sadly. "Did he ever tell you who taught him that wield?"

Danai stared at the high priest. The elderly Dyhaeri was behaving as if they were the only two people in the room. "He said…he said it was someone he'd met long before. He never said who exactly."

High Priest Myltan laughed softly. "King Jahlaniin and I taught Lanead that wield when he was much, much younger than you are now. I'm glad to see he passed on the knowledge to you."

Danai forgot to breath for a moment. Everyone else, including Mat and Kahl, stared at the high priest, and her, in shock. The warden was the first to recover. He opened his mouth to speak, but the high priest yawned.

"It has been a long day, and I must turn in. Kahl, you're with me. Let's leave Novice Dune, Novice Riverun, and Mat to rest. We'll see you all in the morning." High Priest Myltan waved at them and left with a flummoxed-looking Kahl.

Stunned silence followed their departure until Aaliya cried, "Your father was taught by the Dyhaeri king and the high priest?!"

"I…I didn't know!" protested Danai. She glanced at Mat and saw the way he was staring at her with equal parts concern, hurt, and caution as if she had been keeping secrets from him. That made her feel awful.

A discreet cough from the corner of the ward had them all turning. Healer Storm tapped her chronometer.

"Ah, we're being kicked out," said the headmaster. "Please rest, you three, and we'll see you in the morning." The headmaster, the warden, and the weapons master left the infirmary.

"Now, settle into your beds. Supper will be here in a few minutes," said the healer, turning to go until she saw Aaliya frantically waving her right hand. The healer sighed. "Yes, Novice Dune?"

"Please, can I chat with Danai? I promise I won't tire her out."

"Fine, but please keep your voice down."

Danai saw Mat give the healer a disbelieving look before looking up and down the otherwise empty infirmary.

Aaliya nodded before running over to Danai's bed, practically bouncing onto it. Danai winced internally as she braced herself for the questions from the excited fourth year.

"Mind if I join the conversation?' asked Mat casually. Danai looked at him, and for a moment, thought of refusing, but then she shrugged.

"Sure."

Mat smiled thinly before dragging a chair to her bedside, turning it backwards, and sitting astride it while resting his arms on the back of the chair. Behind him, Danai saw the healer throw her hands in the air in exasperation.

"So," began Aaliya excitedly. "How old were you when your father taught you that wield?"

"I was fourteen." Aaliya's eyes went wide while Mat kept silent, watching them.

"How long did it take for you to learn it?"

"Just a few times before I got it right."

"How long did your father take to learn it?"

Danai laughed softly. "To this day, he refuses to tell me."

"Oh, maybe it took him a long time, which is why he wouldn't tell you," said Aaliya. Mat raised an eyebrow at that assumption and gave Danai a look that revealed how comical he found it all.

Oddly, enough that made Danai feel more at ease.

"Maybe, but he sure didn't give me any details about that wield, especially about who taught him." She spoke the last few words with more heat than was necessary.

Aaliya's smile faded, and she leaned back and pulled her legs up to rest her folded arms on her knees. "You're upset with him?"

Danai blinked. "I…I don't know."

Aaliya nodded, understanding. "I'm sure he had his reasons. But enough about that amazing wield. What I really want to know is what happened in the maze run."

"I second that," said Mat, curious.

Danai was only too happy to oblige. She would rather talk about anything else than dwell on the fact that her father had kept yet another secret from her.

#

"I have to sleep now," said Aaliya before she yawned. Dinner had been brought to the ward an hour ago, and the three of them had been talking about the Trials ever since. Mat in particular had asked a million questions and had given his own opinions about what he thought of the games in general.

"See you two in the morning," said Aaliya before rising and sleepily heading to her bed in the far-right corner of the ward. Danai watched her go and then turned to find Mat watching her intently. That made her very nervous.

"You're not sleepy?" She regretted the inane question the moment she asked it.

Mat tilted his head adorably and smiled. That certainly made her heart beat faster as she wondered why a smile from him affected her this way.

"No, I'm not," he finally replied. "Are you?"

Danai shook her head. "One would think after the excitement of today that I'd be ready to collapse, but I'm not." She glanced at Healer Storm's desk and was surprised to find it empty. Maybe she was in the washroom. "I never got to say thanks for helping Aaliya, but you really shouldn't have touched her. You got sedated by whatever Thran used on her."

Mat smiled at her scolding as if he found it cute. "But I got to watch you beat Royal. Trust me, being a bit sedated was worth watching their frustration."

Danai chuckled. "Oh yes, I bet it was."

"I've been meaning to talk to you about what happened at the docks," said Mat as his smile turned to a serious expression.

"Yeah, no matter how you look at it, being ambushed in the alley was my fault—"

Mat raised a hand. "I'm talking about what happened earlier when we met Elder Brett Skylight."

Danai tensed. "What about him?"

Mat brought his voice down to a whisper. "What did he mean by a Final Warning? Why do your people threaten you with exile?"

While Danai was grateful for his low tone, she didn't appreciate his question. "That is a Weltonian matter I'm afraid I cannot discuss with you."

Mat appeared hurt at her words, and she wanted to take them back, but ever since she was little, her parents had told her repeatedly she must never discuss certain parts of Weltonian culture with non-Weltonians.

"Please, understand. I'm not allowed to."

Mat sighed and nodded. "I do. I apologize for putting you in that position. I will endeavor not to do it again."

Danai was sad rather than relieved. She felt like a distance was growing between them.

Mat looked at the floor for a moment and then at her. "However, I'm glad you're all right. But remember, if you ever need help, please don't hesitate to ask me."

Then Danai understood the reason for his odd behavior. Mat's own high priest was keeping secrets from him…just like her own father had kept secrets from her.

"Mat, why did you really tell me about the real identity of the Red Rats?"

Mat's green face flushed, and for a moment, he seemed at a loss for words.

"To be honest, I don't know why. I just felt compelled. I know too much is being hidden from us. I'm tired of secrets and…and I don't want you hurt." The last sentence spilled out so fast Danai barely heard it.

Her jaw dropped as she realized Pearl and Lexia had been right. Mat did like her.

While part of her wanted to shout for joy, the rational part made her take a step back.

"But you're Dyhaeri…and I'm human." She left unsaid the fact that it would never work, but they both heard the unspoken words.

The pain in Mat's eyes made her gasp. She opened her mouth to reassure him.

"Excuse me?" Both turned to face an irritated Healer Storm. "You both need to sleep right now!"

"I'm sorry, Healer Storm," said Mat as he stood. "Our conversation is over." He bowed to Danai and the healer and retreated to his bed directly opposite Danai's. She watched him go, her heart hurting.

"Danai, are you all right?" asked the healer, worried.

It took her a moment to realized she was being spoken to. "I…I'm just tired. I need to sleep." She turned her back to the concerned healer and tried to deal with the fact that she may just have accidentally broken a Dyhaeri heart.

#

"Welcome, everyone, to the sixth and final day of competition!" shouted Instructor Shelley. Today, the games were being held in the Great Hall, which had been transformed over the past few days. The stadium bleachers had been moved into the hall and shoved against the circular walls, and the center had been turned into a ring for the fighters.

Overheard hung the distinct flags of the three colleges, and on the north wall was the hovering scoreboard. Syla was leading with sixteen points, Royal was second with fifteen points, and Artra was last with eleven points.

The crowd, which was the biggest so far, roared their approval as the contestants appeared. The hall was packed, for today was the duels, both non-wielding and wielding. Danai always found the name of this final event odd considering duels were banned at all three colleges.

Danai glanced at the crowd while she tried to gather the courage to talk to Mat. When she had gotten up this morning, he had already left the infirmary. When she and Aaliya had been allowed to go to their dorm rooms, Danai had found Lexia, Britea, and Pearl waiting for her. They had pelted her with questions Danai had tried to answer as she quickly as she could as she got ready for the sixth day of the Trials.

Her three friends had escorted her to the meeting room where the rest of her teammates were…as well as Kahl and Mat.

Mat had greeted her politely, but there was a reserve there that had been absent before. Kahl quickly greeted her and rushed off to chat with Britea. That Dyhaeri only had eyes for one human in this college. Danai noticed how amused their other teammates were at how Kahl treated Britea. No one found it odd or considered it taboo.

So why had she acted like an idiot last night?

She never did get a chance to talk to Mat because Master Caren had called her aside to discuss the plans for the day. Now that she had participated in the maze run, Danai was now on the active roster for the wielding duels and was taking Aaliya's spot because the healer had advised her against any more strenuous activities for the next two days. Navos was tackling the non-wielding duels.

And it didn't get more strenuous than dueling wields. Danai got a thumbs up from Aaliya as she caught the sidelined contestant's eye. Danai nodded. She could do this; she knew what she had taken on when she had volunteered the day before.

Her mind returned to the task at hand as they announced the first set of contestants. The non-wielding duel was scheduled for this morning. Each contestant would have a chance to land three would-be fatal blows within five minutes, but the first to land the most blows would win.

The coin toss had determined that Artra would fight Royal first, and the winner would fight Syla. It would work the same way for the wielding duels as well.

Navos walked up to Lexia and planted a kiss on her cheek before he ran off to wait on the side of the ring. Something about that suddenly made Danai figure out what to do about Mat.

She found him talking with Instructor Talios; they were discussing the points system for this bout, and Danai was hurt he had not spoken to her.

"May I interrupt?' asked Danai. The instructor and Mat turned.

"You needed something?" asked Instructor Talios.

Danai froze for a moment. Then she decided to take the plunge. "I need to speak to Prince Mat in private, please."

Mat stared at her while Instructor Talios raised an eyebrow. Then the instructor smiled. "Don't forget, you're up after Navos." She left them alone.

By now, Mat had recovered. "How can I help you, Novice Riverun?" His voice was courteous, and Danai searched his face for the pain she had seen the night before, but it was either gone or well hidden.

"Last night, I didn't say something I should have."

Mat's expression turned guarded.

"I'm Weltonian. Our ancestors survived by keeping secrets. Some of those secrets have been passed on to my generation. But it does not excuse how I treated you last night."

"You don't have to apologize. My people also have their secrets," said Mat.

"I'm not done," said Danai. "Mat…I…I really like you." Mat blinked. "I just think maybe we could be friends for now, and then we could see what happens. It's how my parents began…as friends."

Mat's jaw dropped and she saw a mixture of hope and longing appear in his eyes.

"Novice Riverun!" yelled Instructor Talios. "Report to the side of the ring!"

Danai smiled at him and turned to go. Then on impulse, she turned back, walked up to him, stood on the tips of her toes, and planted a kiss on his right cheek.

Whistles erupted when her nearby teammates saw. She left a stunned Mat and ran to where Navos waited by the ring.

Kahl strode over to his speechless cousin and slapped him on the back.

"You still alive?"

Mat finally found the strength to speak. "She just…she just kissed me on the cheek!"

Kahl looked at him knowingly. "And how do you feel?"

Then Mat smiled dreamily. "I feel good. Really good."

#

"About time, Danai!" teased Navos as she ran to the ring.

"What are you talking about?" asked Danai with a laugh.

Navos shook his head. "You and Mat? Everyone who has eyes saw that."

"You two, stay focused on your upcoming duels," warned Instructor Talios.

"Yes, instructor!" chorused Danai and Navos.

Instructor Shelley stepped up to the podium. "First up are the non-wielding duels. Representing Artra Army College is Novice Deric Holms." The earth wielder stepped forwards, once again ignoring King Wilhem's box and even his own cheering schoolmates and their families. He was clad in Artra's olive-green uniform once again.

"He will battle Novice Sunrise Belford of the Royal Malaquey Naval College." A tall, blond, muscular female novice dressed in Royal colors stepped forwards.

The contestants bowed to each other.

"Choose your weapons," ordered Instructor Talios, who pointed at the three tables. Each table bore a different flag representing each college and displayed various weapons of wood to limit the extent of the injuries. Each college had brought their weapons of choice with them.

Deric picked a wooden stave from the Artra table while Sunrise grabbed a wooden broadsword from the Royal Malaquey table. Danai's eyes narrowed when she noticed Sunrise testing the weight of her weapon. Wooden weapons weren't supposed to be heavy, so she wondered why—and how—the Royal

Malaquey weapon would be heavier than typical practice swords. That wasn't allowed.

Danai folded her arms and watched as both contestants entered the ring. Deric was casually flipping his wooden stave as if it was weightless.

"I hope Deric beats her arse," said Navos beside her. Danai nodded but said nothing. She suddenly felt as if someone was watching her and shifted to find Thran staring at her intently as if trying to intimidate her. Given the result of the coin toss, there was every chance she might meet him in the wielding duel.

She decided to ignore him for now and turned back to watch the two novices in the ring. They were facing each other as Instructor Talios addressed them.

"There shall be three rounds. The winner shall be whoever makes close and non-lethal light contact to the neck, chest, abdomen or upper or lower back or whoever lands the most hits at the end of the three rounds. Remember, no wielding. Contestants, to your corners," shouted Instructor Talios from the center of the ring.

Deric and Sunrise each walked to the opposite corners of the ring, and the instructor left the ring completely to stand next to Instructor Shelley.

"Silence, everyone." Almost immediately the audience went quiet for what seemed an eternity.

"Begin!" yelled Instructor Shelley, and the two novices charged each other.

Sunrise grasped her broadsword with two hands and brought it down with lighting speed on Deric's head, but the Artra novice was no longer standing before her. He had danced to the side so fast she had not seen it happen. He spun his stave and tapped her on the flank.

"First strike goes to Artra!" yelled Instructor Talios as an Artra instructor made a mark on the clipboard she held, and the crowd cheered.

Danai blinked. By the Sea Mother, Deric was fast.

Sunrise roared in anger and spun around to attack Deric. But the deft Artra novice was already elsewhere. He began to jab at her defenses as he danced around her, tapping her knees and feet lightly. Those taps didn't hurt, but they were clearly frustrating his opponent. Sunrise tried to move as fast as Deric, but that potentially heavy broadsword was slowing her down.

Then Deric feinted to the right, and she fell for it. He dashed behind and to the left before tapping the middle of her upper back.

"Second strike goes to Artra."

Sunrise's face went red with rage as she screamed and spun around again, aiming her broadsword at Deric's face. He threw up his stave to parry, and there was a resounding crack as she split his stave in two. Deric took several steps back. Danai's arms dropped to her sides as she stared open-mouthed. Beside her, Navos swore. Startled murmurs emanated from the watching crowd.

"Halt!" shouted Instructor Talios. Danai expected her to stop the fight entirely. Clearly Sunrise's weapon was unconventional, if not dangerous and illegal.

"I'm all right!" shouted Deric without taking his eyes off the furious Sunrise. "Let's continue!" He now gripped both pieces of his staff in such a way Danai suspected he was also proficient with batons.

The instructor watched them with narrowed eyes for a long moment before nodding. "Proceed."

Danai's hands curled into fists. Something was wrong here. Deric must realize that, but the Artra novice was determined to continue fighting.

Sunrise was already charging across the field before Instructor Talios had even finished speaking. Deric danced out of her way.

"Stay in one place, damn it!" roared Sunrise. Deric just kept dancing.

Danai nodded approvingly. Deric knew what he was doing. Sunrise would come close enough to hit him, and then he would dance out of the way. Danai chanced a glance at the chronometer and was stunned to see he had less than a minute remaining. When she looked back at the fighters, she realized Sunrise had become desperate and was trying to hack away at Deric, but he never stayed close enough for her to make contact. Then she overreached and Deric took advantage. He bounced to the side and tapped her twice on her neck.

"Third strike goes to Artra. Artra wins!" shouted Instructor Talios. The crowd roared.

Deric turned his back on Sunrise, and Danai saw the novice's face twist in an angry snarl as she raised her broadsword, but before Danai could shout a warning, Instructor Talios jumped between Deric and Sunrise.

"It is over, Novice Belford!" The broadsword stopped mid-swing as Danai held her breath.

The crowd gasped and one of the Royal Malaquey instructors ran into the ring and reprimanded Sunrise.

Danai watched the battle rage leave the novice's eyes as she allowed her instructor to escort her off the field. Instructor Talios calmly watched the defeated novice leave before handing over the ring to the next instructor.

"I always knew Instructor Talios had nerves of steel," whispered Navos in awe.

Danai nodded. She was worried. "Sunrise could have split the instructor in two with that sword."

"A sword that never should have broken Deric's stave," said a familiar voice at her elbow.

Danai turned to face Mat. "What are you doing here?"

Mat exchanged a friendly smile with Navos before replying. "I am simply observing while recovering from the kiss you planted on my cheek."

"Now's not the time to distract our Wielder Queen," said Navos playfully.

Danai growled. "Will you stop calling me that?"

"Nope," said Navos with a cheeky grin.

"Navos, you better focus and beat Deric," said Mat.

The muscular giant clapped his hands gleefully. "I've got this."

#

"But I got in two hits," moaned Navos as he stared at the scoreboard.

"You did well, brother," said Danai as she stood on her tiptoes to rub the space between his shoulder blades.

"I can assure you he felt each hit and will be terribly sore until their healers treat him," said Mat. Navos beamed at the praise from the Dyhaeri.

The non-wielding duels were over, and Navos had lost to Deric. However, because he had been able to get in a couple hits, unlike Sunrise, he had scored two points for Syla.

Syla College still led with eighteen points. Royal had sixteen points, and Artra had fourteen points.

"You know Royal is gonna be desperate now, right, Danai?" added Navos gravely.

Danai was only too aware. And the coin toss had decided that Royal would battle Artra first, and the winner would battle her. This was the last chance for Royal Malaquey to pull out a win.

"I know."

"Now, for the last event of the Trials: the wielding duels!" announced Instructor Shelley to the cheers of the packed audience.

"First up is Novice Thran Oslor of Royal Malaquey Naval College." The blond novice stepped forwards. He looked dashing in his water-blue uniform complete with the air-white slash across the front and back of his torso. He bowed to King Wilhem and his children and then to the adoring crowd.

"And his opponent is Novice Narl Montree of Artra Army College." A stocky male novice stepped forwards wearing Artra's olive-green tunic, a blue-water slash across the front and back of his torso. He too bowed to King Wilhem and the cheering crowd. Thran watched him with disdain.

"Choose your weapons!" called out the instructor from Syla College.

Thran picked up a wooden axe from the Royal Malaquey table while Narl chose a wooden rapier from his college's table. Danai frowned. Narl's weapon may not stand a chance against an axe unless he was fast on his feet.

Danai noticed once again that Thran, like Sunrise, checked the heft of his wooden axe and seemed satisfied. That made her nervous for Narl.

Both contestants entered the ring and waited for the Syla instructor to give them the order to begin. This time, the ring held four transparent cauldrons containing sand, water, and fire, with the last empty to represent the air all around them. Behind the cauldrons were four instructors from all three colleges. They were there to counter or neutralize any stray wields that may endanger the audience.

"As seen in the non-wielding duels; these wielding duels shall be three rounds. The winner is the contestant who makes three close and non-lethal light contacts to the neck or chest or abdomen, or upper or lower back of their opponent. The contestant who uses a wield to knock their opponent to the floor also scores a point. You may only wield up to tier four. Contestants, to your corners," ordered the Syla instructor overseeing the duel.

The instructor waited until they were in their respective positions. Silence filled the hall as all watched.

"Begin!" yelled the instructor, and the two charged each other.

Thran used a tier-one wield to create a water whip, and he quickly wound it around Narl's legs, yanked it, and tripped up the Artra novice, who landed flat on his back.

"First strike goes to Royal Malaquey!" yelled the instructor. Danai felt her jaw go slack with surprise. That had happened so fast Narl hadn't even had time to react.

Narl dusted himself off with a look of frustration while Thran grinned mockingly at him.

"Proceed," ordered the instructor.

Narl ran at Thran, who stood completely still. However, as Narl got closer, Thran made a motion as if to fling his whip again, and Narl tried to sidestep, but at the last moment, Thran revised the motion of his arm and the water whip went to Narl's neck.

The Artra novice tried to raise his rapier to counter, but Thran jumped into the space that left and forcefully rammed the side of his wooden axe head into Narl's chest. The crowd yelled as Narl went flying backwards with a cry of pain. As he lay on the floor, Danai could swear she saw him cough up blood.

"Halt!" yelled the Syla instructor, glaring at Thran. "The rules clearly state a light, non-lethal tap, Novice Oslor!"

Thran shrugged and smiled as if he had done nothing wrong. "Oh, sorry. I guess I don't know my own strength."

The instructor stared at him for a long moment. "Second strike goes to Royal Malaquey. We shall wait while a healer assesses Novice Narl Montree."

Danai bit her lower lip to keep from swearing. Thran should have been penalized for that stunt, but apparently it was going to be business as usual. This was why she hadn't wanted to take part in the Trials in the first place!

"Is this normal?" Mat asked Navos, worried.

Navos sighed sadly. "Unfortunately, it is. This happens at every Trials. Royal cheats and uses unnecessary force, and for some reason, no one calls them out on it."

Mat was silent for a long moment. "I see."

Danai stayed mute. She had to focus. At this rate, she was going to be next. The healer checked Narl and shook his head. The Artra novice had sustained far too much damage to continue. With the help of a fuming Artra instructor, they carried Narl out of the ring.

"The duel is over." Thran was incensed and marched up to the instructor to complain.

"Oh, someone isn't happy at not getting his full three points," said Navos.

That made Danai wonder. *Was that really why Thran was so upset?*

The expression on the Syla instructor's face showed he was running out of patience. He cut Thran off mid-sentence. "If you hadn't hurt Narl so badly, you would have had a chance to get those three points. I suggest you prepare for your next duel."

Thran turned to glare at Danai for good measure before walking out of the ring.

Danai took a deep breath. By the Sea Mother, she was nervous.

"Mat and I believe in you Danai," said Navos, fierce determination on his face.

Mat nodded. "You almost beat me, so you can beat this pompous idiot."

Danai couldn't help but smile at the two wielders. "Thanks for your votes of confidence."

"And now on to the final wielding duel! Novice Thran Oslor of Royal Malaquey will be meeting our very own fifth-year student, Novice Danai Riverun of Syla College!"

The crowd cheered, and some started chanting her name. That took Danai by surprise.

"Everyone still remembers you flying above the maze yesterday. The whole school is behind you, Wielder Queen," said Navos.

Danai closed her eyes as she tried to absorb all the good wishes. "I'll do my best." She opened her eyes and mentally shook off all stray thoughts as she walked towards the side of the ring.

She waited until a new Artra instructor beckoned for her and Thran to step forwards.

"Choose your weapons."

Thran kept his wooden axe while Danai went to the Syla table. Her hand hovered over the batons, then she drifted to the double wooden long swords. Their reach was longer, and she felt engaging in close combat with Thran would be to her detriment.

She turned to face her opponent, who smirked at her.

Danai maintained eye contact with Thran as the Artra instructor repeated the rules again, stressing that only light taps were acceptable, and wields could be used to knock opponents to the ground. Once again, the warning to only wield up to tier four was repeated.

"Proceed."

Danai didn't rush in. Instead, she began to circle to the right while Thran moved to the left.

"So tell me, Weltonian tramp, who taught you those pathetic wields in the maze?" taunted Thran.

Danai ignored him while keeping her eyes on his feet.

"What? No words? Did a cat cut out your tongue, or did kissing that Dyhaeri trash rob you of your speech?"

Danai said nothing. Thran's face twisted in anger as he suddenly rushed her while flinging his water whip at her. Danai was now closer to the cauldron of fire, and she called the element to her, letting it engulf her swords. She ignored the gasps from the spectators as she crossed her arms and formed a tier-four blast that knocked Thran off his feet.

"First strike goes to Syla College!" The crowd was cheering, but Danai paid them no heed. She dampened the fire on her wooden swords. She had to end this fight quickly before her weapons turned to ash.

Thran was back up on his feet, and he was even more incensed now.

"Does Novice Oslor need a healer's assistance?" asked the Artra instructor. Danai thought the instructor sounded rather gleeful.

"No, I'm fine," said Thran through gritted teeth as he began to circle Danai, who continued to do the same. He pulled more water to his water whip, and she suspected he was about to change tactics.

Suddenly, he rushed her and flung out a water net. Rather than dodge it, Danai spun, holding her fiery swords away from her body. The swords cut right through the net. Unfortunately, the net had only been a diversion because Thran was now in her personal space, and he tried to repeat the same attack he had used on Narl. However, Danai darted to the side and then used her right elbow to knock him away from her.

She cursed inwardly as she had not hit him in an area that would have earned her points. But she had no time to waste as Thran wielded three large water orbs and flung them at full speed at her face. Using the two fiery swords again, she sliced each orb in two as s Thran rushed towards her.

She went down on one knee as the axe went over her head. Then reversing the thrust of both long swords, she hit Thran in the middle of his lower back.

"Second strike goes to Syla College!" Danai could now see from the corner of her eyes that the audience was on their feet. She shifted her gaze back to Thran.

He was beyond incensed now. His face was red with rage. With a roar, he emptied the large cauldron of water and performed a tier-five wield even as the instructors yelled at him to stop. He brought the tier-five orb down on Danai, who dropped her swords and used a tier-one maneuver to wield several arrows of fire. She shot them into the orb of water, transforming the water into steam and obscuring her vision—and that of many nearby.

She heard Thran yell again in rage as he charged her last known position. She slunk to the side and closed her eyes as she heard him pass her. Then Danai reached out and her fingers brushed the back of his tunic. She grabbed hold with both fists and yanked downwards as someone wielded air to clear the steam.

The air cleared just in time for everyone to see her plant Thran on his back with a loud thud that echoed throughout the hall. The Royal Malaquey novice groaned in pain and seemed incapable of standing up.

The Artra instructor looked at the defeated Thran and this time didn't bother to hide his satisfied smile. Then he turned to the crowd.

"Third strike goes to Syla College. Syla College wins the wielding duel and the 126th Wielder Trials!"

The crowd erupted.

Danai felt weak with relief but kept her eyes on Thran, just in case. The shady Royal contestant was in too much pain to notice her though.

Only when he was carried away did she allow herself to relax. Suddenly Mat, Kahl, Navos, and the rest of the Syla contestants swamped the ring.

This time, Mat and Kahl lifted her on their shoulders as Navos took up the chant. "All hail the Wielder Queen, Danai Riverun of Syla College!"

Danai found herself laughing and crying as they shouted. "Wielder Queen! Wielder Queen, Wielder Queen!"

CHAPTER 32

The fisherman sighed with contentment as he looked at his catch. Two bass, well-grown and bound for the pot. He rubbed his hands in glee and began to roll in his fishing line. Then a strange sound made him freeze in his task. He glanced up and down the river. It was early morning and not a soul was in sight, but he could have sworn that he had heard what sounded like an engine.

Finally, he realized it was coming from above him. He frowned at the darkened clouds, but unfortunately, his sight was unable to penetrate the grey mass high above him.

Suddenly, he felt a terrible foreboding and had a sudden urge to get home. He hastily pulled in the last of his line and began to row for the shore, praying to the Maker all would be well.

#

"Wakey, wakey!"

Britea opened her eyes to see an excited Pearl beside her bed. Yawning loudly, Britea sat up slowly. "Oh, my days. What time did we go to bed last night?" She glanced at Danai's bed. It was empty.

"Danai's in the washroom," said Pearl as she sat at the foot of Britea's bed. "She gave me the task of waking you up for the exciting day ahead."

Britea leaned back on her pillow with a tired smile. "What could honestly beat last night?"

For the first time in twenty-four years, Syla College had won the Wielder Trials. Though many had contributed to the win, everyone was talking about how Danai had won the wielding maze run and the wielding duel. She had pushed Syla College into a comfortable lead, so now Danai Riverun was the Wielder Queen of Syla College, and best of all, Britea's roommate.

Last night, Danai, Lexia, Britea, and Pearl had stayed up way past bedtime talking and laughing as they reminisced on the events of the 126th Wielder Trails. Britea would certainly not forget a bit of it any time soon.

"The After-Trials Ball tonight will be amazing," said Pearl dreamily.

"Why?" asked Britea.

Pearl raised an eyebrow. "I heard the high priest of the Dyhaeri, his two princes who just happen to be our friends—the king, and his family are attending…as well as every noble house that managed to score an invitation!"

Britea stared at her, still not comprehending the importance.

Pearl sighed in exasperation. "It's bound to be the most heavily attended ball in ages. It'll not only beat Lady Arkei's parties, but even those at the royal court. And we both get to go!"

Now Britea was wide awake. "Doesn't everyone else get to go?"

Pearl shook her head. "Not the first or second years."

"But I'm a first year!"

"Not really," said Pearl in a reassuring voice. "After all, you were moved to the third-year wielding classes, and you've been taking third-year general studies."

Britea released a sigh of relief. "Okay, now I feel much better."

Danai emerged from the washroom in her robe with a towel around her short, wet hair.

"Good morning, Wielder Queen!" chorused Britea and Pearl at the same time.

"Ugh," grimaced Danai, but then she smiled. "Seriously, you all have to stop calling me that."

"Not in a million years," declared Britea as she got up and walked into the washroom. Behind her, Danai and Pearl began to chat like old friends.

That more than anything else made Britea smile.

#

The rest of the day was spent trying to get ready for the After-Trials Ball. First, she and the Pearl had to finish up their kitchen duty for the morning and afternoon. However, Chef Blane had been kind enough to let them off early that afternoon to get ready for the ball.

Which was how Britea now found herself in the elegant new emerald-green dress she had bought from Lara Firbright's shop what seemed like forever ago. It was form fitting and flared slightly from midthigh to ankle. The embroidery on the skirt created an extraordinary peacock.

"You look stunning," said Pearl, who wore a two-tone velvet gown. Black sleeves flowed into a deep blood-red bodice, and the night-black skirt flared from the waist to the ground. Pearl had let down her hair but kept her chestnut-brown locks off her face with a headband encrusted with diamonds. The final touch was the black and silver scarf draped over her shoulders. "Now we just have to tackle your hair."

Britea groaned. "It's no use. I've tried a million times. Nothing can help this mess."

Pearl guided her to the dressing table. "Have a seat and let me try."

Danai chose that moment to come in with Lexia. "Oh, just let me freshen up and change." She dashed into the washroom. Lexia, on the other hand, was already clad in a lilac blouse and a plum skirt that ended just below her knees.

Pearl gasped. "Lexia, if I must say, that is one beautiful, daring outfit."

The petite redhead grinned mischievously. "I know. That's why I picked it. So, what are we doing to Britea's hair?"

"Trying to make it presentable," said Britea gloomily.

"Oh, I'm sure between Pearl and I, we can make something work," said Lexia as she picked up a comb. Britea couldn't help but smile to herself.

"Not too long ago, you two were enemies."

Lexia and Pearl looked at each other and chuckled. "People change, dear Britea," Lexia said.

"Definitely," said Pearl as both girls tried to tame Britea's brown mane.

#

Kahl tried to keep a polite smile on his face as he casually scanned the entrance while he waited for Britea. He ignored the admiring glances from many of the guests. He and Mat had shed their military garb and wore indigo vert-silk tunics, matching pants, and dove-grey suede shoes. Tonight, they were supposed to be celebrating at the After-Trials Ball, but he couldn't stop thinking of what the high priest had said to him and Mat that morning.

"Tonight, everything changes. Make sure to have fun while you can my sons." Mat had tried to get the high priest to explain, but the elderly Dyhaeri had stayed silent. Eventually, Mat had given up.

Kahl could see the high priest's cryptic words were beginning to wear on his cousin. Kahl understood. He was also worried that now that the Trials were over, they would have to leave.

So, what had they achieved? Kahl was unsure of what the goal had been in the first place, so he could understand Mat's frustration. And he didn't want to leave Britea, but how could he stay here without disobeying the high priest?

"Prince Kahl!" He turned to face Harto, who was heading towards him with his uncle, Lieutenant Commander Nell.

By the Sea Mother, not now! He smiled and met the two Malaquey officers halfway.

"Lieutenant Commander Nell, we haven't seen you in a while."

The senior officer smiled thinly. "Matters of state kept me away from the Trials. Though I hear from my nephew that you and Mat contributed a great deal to the victory of Syla College."

"You heard wrong," interjected Mat before Kahl could say a word. The two intelligence officers turned to find Mat behind them. "Any contribution we made was small, especially when one considers the exceptionally talented and humble individuals who made up the Syla team."

Lieutenant Commander Nell stared at Mat. "You must mean Novice Danai Riverun. I heard her maze run and wielding duel were particularly spectacular. The recruiters are fighting each other for a chance to interview her." Kahl stole a look at Harto, and to his surprise, the younger Malaquey officer seemed uncomfortable.

Peras continued. "In fact, her wielding was so unique that the question on everyone's lips is, who *actually* taught her?"

Mat maintained eye contact with the lieutenant commander. "Why don't you ask her yourself?"

"Did you teach her?" abruptly asked Peras.

"No," replied Mat.

Peras studied him for a long moment, then nodded. "I shall take your advice to heart." Then he looked at Harto. "A word, nephew?"

Harto seemed a bit disconcerted as if he preferred to linger with Mat and Kahl. "Of course, uncle." He left with the senior Malaquey officer.

"What was that all about?" asked Kahl.

Mat was still watching the two Malaquey officers. "I don't know, but I don't like their interest in Danai…oh, my word."

Kahl wondered why his cousin's voice had trailed off until he followed his gaze. Danai had just entered the hall with Lexia, Britea, and Pearl.

Danai's short, curly, raven-black hair gleamed as if lit internaly. A molten caramel form-fitting gown with long, fitted sleeves and a slit that reached from midthigh to the floor created an unforgettable image. He also saw a flash of chocolate leather leggings that ended in sensible flats, and Kahl nodded his approval at the effort to ensure freedom of movement. Then he turned his head and saw Britea and was struck speechless.

Her shining dress of emerald green made him think of the way the sun shone on the green algae of the Heldiar Sea in the summer and made it sparkle so bright it hurt to look at it. She had left her curly walnut hair loose to frame her enchanting heart-shaped face, and her coffee-brown eyes shone as she approached him.

"Evening, Kahl," said Britea shyly.

Kahl was still speechless until Mat stepped on his right foot. "You look spectacular!"

Britea's face brightened. "Thanks. You look really nice too."

"We'll leave you four. Be good," said Pearl with a twinkle and a smile as Lexia led her away to where Navos, Shran, and Henrick waited.

#

Danai had been worried about Mat's reaction. At first, he had stared at her in shock, and his cousin had displayed the same reaction when he had seen Britea.

She stifled a laugh when Mat stepped on Kahl's right foot to get him to say something.

Then Mat walked over to her, smiling broadly. "You are an absolute vision." He bowed over her right hand to the stunned murmurs of several onlookers.

Danai now felt very embarrassed. "Mat, stop that."

He gave her a cheeky grin before offering her his right arm. She entwined her arm in his and they sauntered over to a corner of the crowded Great Hall.

It had been decorated with the three colleges' colors: Artra army green, Royal Malaquey blue, and Syla black. The round, hovering lights cast circles of light on the ballroom floor that made the whole atmosphere look surreal. Placed in several areas were old wine barrels that had also been painted with the colleges' colors. The barrels had polished tops that attendees could place their used plates and empty glasses on. It gave the hall a rustic feel, and Danai liked the effect.

There were so many attendees Danai wondered how they had fit so many people into the Great Hall.

"So, how do you find this day, Wielder—"

"Don't you dare call me a queen," cut in Danai gently. "I'm just me."

Mat snorted. "There is more to you than meets the eye, Wielder Warrior Danai Riverun."

She gave him an exasperated look.

"Well, you didn't want me calling you a queen."

"Ah, there you are." They turned to face Weapons Master Caren. "It's time you met the king, Danai."

She gulped and tightened her hold on Mat's arm.

"Is something wrong?" asked a worried Mat.

"No, no. It's just that…well, I had hoped he had forgotten about me," said Danai in a low tone.

The weapons master gave her an odd look. "Being sought after by the king is a rare honor. He won't hurt you."

You don't know what the Malaquey royal family did to my people! Danai forced her anger aside. The Persecution had happened centuries ago; this was neither the time nor place to bring up that ugly part of history.

"All right, I will attend."

"And, I'll be with you," said Mat. Danai sent him a startled stare. *Had he sensed her distress?*

"That's splendid because he wants to talk to you as well." For a moment, the Dyhaeri looked nonplussed, but he recovered quickly.

"Oh, well that's fortuitous."

#

Harto found himself distracted from his report when Danai appeared. She was a vision of rare beauty and grace, and she was smiling at Mat, who appeared just as thunderstruck.

"Harto, have you finished?" demanded his uncle, and he forced himself to return to the task at hand.

"Oh yes, uncle… um, I mean no, uncle."

Peras frowned at him. "What's wrong with you boy?" He followed Harto's gaze until he saw Danai and Mat and said, "Please, don't tell me you're attracted to that Weltonian trash."

That made Harto's blood boil. "Don't call her that. She has more honor than those Arkei sisters mother keeps throwing at me!" He saw his uncle's eyes go wide.

"I'm not your enemy, nephew."

Harto felt bad when he saw the hurt look in his uncle's eyes. "I'm sorry. Watching over the Dyhaeri hasn't been easy, even with the extra agents."

Peras gave him a fatherly smile. "That's all right, my boy. So, what else have you learned about the Dyhaeri? What do they have planned next?"

Harto thought briefly of telling him what Mat and Danai had said about the Red Rats being infiltrated and taken over by the Namiran Death Squad. He discarded the thought instantly; there was no point in spreading insubstantial rumors.

Harto shrugged. "Only the Maker knows. The high priest isn't exactly forthcoming about his future activities."

Peras nodded distractedly before glancing at the giant chronometer on the wall. Harto realized that was the fourth time his evening he had noticed his uncle looking at the chronometer.

"Are you expecting someone, uncle?"

Peras gave him a startled look. "No, not really. It's just that I promised your mother I'd be home early tonight and that I would bring you with me."

Harto was already shaking his head. "I have to stay here and watch the Dyhaeri—"

"Leave it to Lieutenant Commander Trent." Peras gestured at their female colleague standing to the far left of the king and his family. "You've done more than we asked of you. It's time you rested, my boy."

Harto was torn. Then he recalled something that had been bothering him. "Uncle, did you read the report I sent you last week?"

"Which one?" asked his uncle as he glanced at the clock again for a fifth time.

Harto frowned. "The one about the high priest stating that Captain Riverun sent you an urgent message about a flying Namiran ship that had attacked his and another Weltonian ship?"

Peras scoffed. "I'm sure he was drunk or hallucinating. The Immortal Queen does not have such outlandish vessels."

Harto was starting to feel something was wrong with his uncle's behavior. "So, either the high priest or Captain Riverun was lying?"

His uncle shrugged. "What does it matter? Let's go home and rest."

Harto tried to suppress his anger. If the high priest had lied to him, then there was no way he could leave without getting an answer as to why. Harto could not overlook the possibility that the high priest had used Mat and Danai to spread a rumor about Namiran Death squads posing as the Red Rats gang. This had to stop now.

"No, I need to stay for a bit. I'll see you in the morning, uncle. Please send my regrets to mother." He turned and left, missing the fear on his uncle's face.

#

Harto was almost to the high priest when someone called his name. He turned to face a stern-looking Warden Asteros.

Oh, what now? "Warden Asteros. How can I help you?" Harto tried to smile.

The warden glared at him. "I just heard from Chef Blane that Malaquey intelligence refused to let the kitchen staff decorate the Great Hall for the ball."

Harto hid his surprise. "I'm sure they were just conducting a threat assessment. After all, there are many important people here at the moment."

Warden Asteros frowned. "But to insist on decorating the hall? That's the kitchen staff's job. Your officers were downright rude to the staff and threatened to arrest them!"

Harto blinked. "I…well, such behavior was uncalled for." Warden Asteros opened his mouth to protest, but Harto held up a hand. "Please, let me find out what happened, and I will ensure Chef Blane receives an apology. I have to go now though. I have to speak to the high priest on an urgent matter."

"Then I will wait by your side until you are done," insisted a fuming Warden Asteros.

Harto tried not to grimace as they strode towards the Dyhaeri high priest.

#

Danai's heart sank when she saw who surrounded the king and his family: the Dyhaeri high priest, various ministers, the headmasters of all three colleges, the army and navy recruiters, and of course Lady Arkei, Lord Arkei, and their two daughters, Selina and Lianne. The girls glared at her with disdain, their eyes narrowing when they noticed her arm entwined in Mat's. It was the sisters more than anything else that put her defenses up.

Whatever was between her and Mat was none of their business.

"Your Highness, I present Prince Mat and Novice Danai Riverun," announced Weapons Master Caren.

Danai let go of Mat's arm briefly, so she could curtsy. Mat lowered his head respectfully in the king's direction.

King Wilhem stood and walked over to them, his arms outstretched. He placed one gentle hand each on Danai's right shoulder and Mat's left shoulder.

"To see you two walking side by side gives me hope for our two races. Please, sit with us." Some of the ministers frowned as they moved out of the way so Mat and Danai could sit in the two empty seats to the king's left. Lord Arkei and the other ministers, however, soon surrounded the Dyhaeri high priest and began to bombard him with questions. Danai distinctly heard Lord Arkei ask about the vert-silk trade.

King Wilhem turned to Danai. "I watched you fly over the maze run. It was the most spectacular thing I have ever witnessed. I had to search our history books to see if anyone had ever wielded like that, and lo and behold, Queen Zaleria did during the Dyhaeri-Human War."

Danai gulped and laughed nervously. "Is that so, Your Highness?" Beside her, Mat stayed silent.

"Who taught you that wield?" asked a child's voice and Danai turned to face eleven-year-old Princess Crystal. The child stared at her with guileless aqua-blue eyes.

"My father did."

Princess Crystal's eyes widened. "Will you teach me when I start school here?"

It took a moment for her meaning to register.

"Wait, you're a wielder?" asked Mat, surprised.

Princess Crystal beamed at him. "Yes, I spontaneously wielded air a month ago. My mama wants me taught at court, but I want to go to Syla College!"

"She decided that after watching your maze run," said Queen Ariande.

Danai looked at the queen, who wore a weary smile, and then at the king.

"Please, please, please will you teach me?!" begged the princess.

"Now wait, Crystal. First you have to learn the basics," said King Wilhem. "And only when you have learned control will you be allowed to learn the difficult wields like what Novice Riverun did."

Crystal bit her lower lip as she sulked. "Okay."

King Wilhem laughed. "She will be the first wielder in our direct family line since Headmaster Lance Cen-Taros." Danai blinked, wondering how the Arkei family felt about competing with young Princess Crystal.

"That is wonderful news, Your Highness."

The king smiled. "Her brother doesn't think so and has been praying to the Maker and the Lords of Light and Shadow that they turn him into a wielder too, but there's no chance of that happening."

Danai suddenly thought of Britea but kept her mouth shut and smiled.

"Ah, here come the headmasters of Artra and Royal Malaquey, along with their recruiters. Brace yourself, Novice Riverun," encouraged the king with a smile and a wink.

Danai felt a bit overwhelmed at how relaxed and friendly the king of Malaquey was. This was the first time she had ever spoken to him. His cordial behavior was at odds with the tales of how the Malaquey royal family had stood aside while her people had been persecuted and killed several centuries ago.

"Novice Riverun," bellowed Headmaster Ravh Welbrick. Danai stood immediately. "Congratulations on your impressive win!" He engulfed her small hand in his massive paws. "Never before have I seen such skill displayed at the Trials. I hope we will see more Weltonians enroll at all three colleges."

Headmaster Brann Zelon of the Royal Malaquey Naval College gave Headmaster Welbrick a dour look. Danai suspected the Royal headmaster would not approve of Weltonians *staining* the reputation of his college, but he sure would be eager to use their knowledge!

"Well, Your Highness," said Headmaster Zelon with a respectful bow to the king. "We would like to start the recruitment interview, if it pleases you."

Headmaster Welbrick rolled his eyes, not caring who was watching, while Headmaster Clayre kept silent, though his smile was filled with pride.

King Wilhem looked amused. "Please, do continue."

Headmaster Zelon beckoned his warden, Lieutenant Commander Helsliff, who stepped forward promptly.

She bowed first to the king before turning to Danai. "The Royal Malaquey Navy has a long and outstanding history of serving the people of Malaquey. Upon joining the Malaquey Navy after graduation, you would be entitled to benefits that far exceed any of the Artra Army, and you would have the advantage of traveling to unique locations; thus, you would be richly rewarded for joining the Royal Malaquey Navy."

Behind her, Headmaster Welbrick wore an expression that Danai translated as, *Do you actually believe this rubbish?*

"Join us and continue the illustrious legacy that is the Royal Malaquey Navy."

Danai tried to keep her expression neutral; she had the urge to gag but decided such behavior would be rude.

"I thank you for the invitation. Please give me a few days to decide."

Headmaster Zelon smiled thinly at her. "You have twenty-four hours." Then he and his lieutenant made way for Lieutenant Commander Piotr King.

The Artra warden stepped forward. He went down on one knee to the king and on rising, he bowed to a stunned Danai.

"Novice Danai Riverun. I bow to the prowess of such a skilled wielder. You won two events, propelling your college to the top of the scoreboard."

"It was a team effort," hastily added Danai, and the Artra warden paused.

He smiled at her. "Be that as it may, the Artra Army did not fail to notice that you were not originally supposed to race. But when the call came, you didn't hesitate to step up and take your fallen colleague's place."

Behind him, Headmaster Welbrick smirked at Headmaster Zelon, and the Royal Malaquey headmaster looked as if he was about to explode.

Warden King continued in his dulcet tone. "That kind of forward and adaptive thinking would be nurtured to its full potential in the Artra Army. We do not waste time trying to impress the people of Malaquey with our titles or riches; instead, we defend all of Malaquey from all enemies, external and domestic. Join Artra Army and fulfill your destiny of becoming an honorable warrior."

Danai blinked. Wow, that speech had been so impressive that for a split second, she had been tempted to say yes. Then she remembered that Malaquey had used the Artra Army to round up Weltonians from the streets during the Time of Persecution.

"I thank you for the invitation; please, give me a few days to decide."

The warden smiled with compassion. "Please, take as much time as you need."

The king rose. "Thank you, both Artra Army College and Royal Malaquey Naval College, for investing your time and effort in keeping Malaquey safe."

"It's our job, ain't it, Your Highness?" said Headmaster Welbrick jovially. Then Danai suddenly noticed a faint acrid smell, and beside her Mat stiffened.

King Wilhem began to sniff the air as well. "What is that awful smell?"

"Papa."

Danai turned to see a sleepy Princess Crystal. "I don't feel well…" The girl's eyes rolled back in her head as she fell forward. Danai was quick to catch her as a female guest began to scream. And then pandemonium erupted in the Great Hall.

#

Britea and Kahl watched as the others danced. She was not comfortable dancing and was relieved when she discovered Kahl felt the same way. Everyone was having fun tonight, especially Navos, Lexia, Henrick, and Pearl. They danced with abandon, not caring who was watching as they laughed and made fun of each other. Britea had been surprised to see Deric Holms of Artra dancing with Aaliya. From the looks on their faces, they were enjoying each other's company.

Even Pearl's mother, Lady Ceres, looked happy as she watched her daughter dance.

"Your friends are nice," said Kahl.

Britea smiled at him. "So is your cousin." They stared at each other and laughed at the awkwardness of their words.

They stood side by side in comfortable silence for a time, watching the dancers twirl by.

"I hope you had a good time while you were here," said Britea.

Kahl smiled. "It was much better than I had expected." Then the smile left his face.

"What's wrong?" asked Britea.

Kahl hesitated for a long moment. "The Trials are over, and I have no idea what the high priest has planned for us."

Britea felt her heart almost stop beating. "What do you mean?"

He gazed at her for a long moment, then opened his mouth to answer when someone screamed.

They turned and noticed the polished barrels in the hall were emitting an acrid-smelling orange gas. But more alarmingly, wielders from all three colleges and their guests were collapsing on the dance floor. Britea saw Pearl looked bewildered as she tried to prevent Henrick from landing on the hard floor.

Britea was about to run to her when she heard someone yell her name. Both she and Kahl turned to face a frightened Vindell and Chelton.

"What are you two doing here?!" Britea exclaimed.

"We need to hide!" hissed Chelton as he grabbed Britea's hand. Vindell dashed onto the dance floor.

"Vindell, no!" cried Kahl. The girl ignored him, covered her nose with a piece of cloth, and grabbed Pearl's hand, tugging her in Britea's direction. In that moment, Britea realized the gas had reached her, and she began to feel light-headed.

"Please, come with us!" urged Chelton, who was also covering his nose with a piece of cloth. Britea noticed Kahl stumble as if he was going faint, and she grabbed him with her free hand and followed the two first years and a frightened Pearl. Vindell led them to a cleverly hidden side door that concealed an ascending staircase. The group climbed to a darkened balcony. Once there, the clean air free of the orange gas cleared the fog from Britea's head. Even Kahl looked a bit better.

"What in the Abyss is going on?!" demanded a distraught Pearl.

"We're being invaded," said Vindell. They all stared at the two first years.

"What are you two doing out of your dorm?" demanded Britea.

Chelton and Vindell shared a guilty look before Chelton answered. "We wanted to watch the ball. We'd heard there was a way to sneak here from our dorms, so we tried it, but we saw some strange people in the dorms for the first and second years."

Britea felt a chill in her chest. "What kind of strange people?"

Chelton replied, "Some wore dark-purple uniforms, but the rest wore Malaquey naval uniforms. They were opening the dorm rooms and flinging in small sacks that gave off this smelly orange gas when they hit the floor. They ran off as soon as the gas started coming out."

"Solarian dust," muttered Kahl darkly. They all gave him startled looks. "I've heard of it in our history books. Humans used it on us during the war in Queen Zaleria's time. As part of the treaty, its manufacture and use were banned by both humans and Dyhaeri. But who would use it on the colleges? And why now? Why would the Malaquey Navy attack everyone at this ball?"

"Vindell, what happened after they dropped the dust and ran off?" asked Britea.

"Chelton and I were already hiding in one of the side corridors when we saw other students dropping like flies. We didn't think they were dead though, so we tried to get here to warn everyone, but we're too late," said Vindell, visibly scared.

Pearl's scared expression became determined. "You saved us, guys. You have our thanks." Then she looked puzzled. "I stood in the midst of that gas and didn't pass out."

Kahl gave her startled look. "Either you're immune, which is extremely rare, or you inhaled tremendously little."

Pearl shook her head. "I was coughing and wondering what the stink was, but I didn't feel sleepy at all, and Henrick and the others dropped with one sniff."

Britea went pale. "By the Maker! What of the king and the others?!" They crept to the balcony to look down on the Great Hall. The air was now hazy with an orange mist that appeared to be rising, but they also spotted the unconscious figures of the Malaquey royal family. Next to them were Danai, Mat, several ministers, and the high priest. Even Warden Asteros and Lieutenant Flay lay unconscious.

"Where are the attackers? Why aren't they here yet?" asked Pearl.

"Even if you don't breathe any of the gas in, any exposed skin still absorbs the dust and renders one unconscious eventually," said Kahl grimly.

"So they're waiting for the mist to clear," said Britea, her dread mounting.

"Correct," said Kahl gravely. "By then, the gas will be well in the lungs of everyone here, and then the invaders can enter and do as they please."

"The orange mist is rising. It'll get to us soon," warned Chelton.

We said you would need her, the chorus of Seers said in Britea's mind.

"But not Pearl," said Britea as she gaped at her friend. Pearl noticed everyone was now staring at her.

"What are you lot looking at me for?!"

Kahl stared at her. "You could save us all."

Pearl was speechless for a moment. "Excuse me? Have you lost your mind?!"

"You're immune. You need to get to the high priest. Just drag him to the door, and I'll wield the gas out of his lungs."

"I thought you said that was dangerous!" exclaimed Britea.

"Cool!" said an impressed Vindell and Chelton.

"It's all part of the resuscitation and healing we learn as scouts." Kahl turned to Pearl. "Can you do this?"

"What if the attackers see me?" asked a terrified Pearl.

"Pearl, you can do this. Please," pleaded Britea.

Pearl stared at her for a long moment. "Fine. Tell me exactly how to do this."

#

Britea tried not to bite her nails as she watched Pearl nervously hug the wall as she tried to get to the unconscious high priest. The orange mist was getting thicker as the barrels continued to emit the sedative gas.

"I just checked the entire balcony; we're alone up here," said Kahl as he crouched down beside Britea. "What's her status?"

"She's almost to the high priest," said Vindell in a low whisper.

Kahl nodded grimly. "I'll go down and wait at the door to help her drag him in."

Britea wanted to scream "no," but she forced herself to keep her voice down. "I'm coming with you."

Kahl gave her a worried look. "I can hold my breath for long periods."

She ignored him and began to tear long strips from the hem of her gown. Oddly enough, destroying her only ball gown didn't bother her. "Wear this over your nose and mouth so you don't have to."

Kahl gave her a resigned look. "Thanks, Britea. But masks will only limit the effect. All it has to do is touch enough skin. You should stay here—"

"We're wasting time," hissed Britea as she hurried to the stairs still tying her impromptu mask. Vindell and Chelton shot each other a worried look and silently followed her.

Kahl had no choice but to run after her. Britea tried to control her breathing while praying the masks would work long enough for them to help Pearl.

They finally got to staircase and already the gas was beginning to creep upwards.

"We wait here," said Kahl as they stopped. "Once she's out of the mist, we run down and help her, but please hold your breath. Chelton and Vindell, stay back where you are."

Britea nodded silently, as did the scared first years.

The next few minutes felt like hours before the door banged open, and they saw Pearl's back as she strained to pull the high priest up the stairs with her tier-one air ropes.

Once she had breached the rising orange gas, Kahl and Britea held their breath and rushed forward to help Pearl drag the unconscious senior Dyhaeri up the rest of the stairs.

"He is bloody heavy!" cursed an exhausted Pearl.

"How do you feel? Sleepy?" asked Britea.

Her friend shook her head. "Not in the slightest. So, what now?"

Kahl was already bending over the high priest, his hand on the unconscious Dyhaeri's midriff. "Solarian dust is highly soluble, so I'll wield a small amount of water into his lungs first and then—"

The high priest suddenly sat up and vomited violently. Britea and Pearl jumped aside to avoid getting hit by the spray.

"High priest!" exclaimed a relieved Kahl, who hugged the dazed holy leader.

"What…what happened?" asked the high priest hoarsely.

Kahl filled him in with Vindell and Chelton's help.

As they spoke, the high priest's confused expression became steely. "We need to wake the others. Get me to where the balcony overlooks the center of the room. Quickly." Kahl and Britea helped him stand as fast as they could. "Here is fine,' said High Priest Myltan.

Britea looked over the balcony, and the gas was still oozing from the barrels.

"Novice Ceres." Pearl looked at the high priest. "Thank you for saving me. Now I need you to create tier-one orbs around each barrel, leaving the orb tops open."

"Novice D'Tranell." Britea jerked at her name. "Fill those orbs with water, and then Novice Ceres will close the tops. That will dissolve the mist."

"And me?" asked Kahl, Vindell, and Chelton at the same time.

"Stand guard, you three," ordered the elderly Dyhaeri with a gentle smile.

The high priest waited until Pearl and Britea had done as he had ordered, then he wielded seven small orbs of fire before multiplying them until there were hundreds floating in the air. He pushed with both hands, and the orbs descended to hover over the unconscious bodies. "Water dissolves Solarian dust, but fire destroys it even faster. It will draw the gas out of every afflicted person without harming them, but there might be lasting side effects in the older humans."

Britea watched in wonder as the orange gas began to dissipate and the remaining tiny orbs were inhaled by the sleepy guests. A few seconds passed before a few began to stir.

"Let's get down there. They'll still be groggy, and we need to keep them quiet while we explain what's going on. I'll start with the healers because we'll need their skills before long." The high priest led the way as the human wielders started at him in amazement and Kahl beamed with relief.

#

Danai woke up to a pounding headache and the worried face of a tired High Priest Myltan.

"Are you well, child?"

"What…what happened?" Then she saw a groggy Mat being attended to by a healer. Before she could say a word, the high priest took her right hand in his massive hands.

"Daughter of the Sea, will you let me impart the blessings of the Sea Mother?"

Danai blinked. To be blessed by the high priest was an honor usually reserved for Dyhaeri. She now wondered how her father had been privy to that piece of knowledge before putting that thought away for later as her instinct told her the high priest meant her no harm.

"I would be honored, Holy One."

He smiled at her and placed a gentle hand on her forehead. The headache and fatigue disappeared instantly. She felt much better, but one thought persisted.

The high priest was also a healer?

"Stay seated for a while," advised the priest when she tried to stand.

"What happened?" asked Danai.

"We were attacked with Solarian dust," but the reply came from an angry, exhausted King Wilhem. A nearly drained healer was looking after his family, who had just been woken up.

"Who…why?"

"Two first years saw the attackers. Most wore Malaquey naval uniforms, but some wore violet outfits," said Warden Asteros, the lines under his eyes etched more deeply now. He glared at a dazed Lieutenant Flay as he spoke, but the Malaquey intelligence officer looked just as shocked as everyone else. Still, those nearby began to regard Harto with suspicion.

"Namira is behind this," said the high priest in an urgent whisper. "This would not be the first time that subterfuge was perpetuated using fake uniforms or fake flags."

"Agreed," said King Wilhem. "So, what now?"

"We get you and your family out of here—" said Headmaster Clayre before he broke off into a wheezing cough. Headmaster Zelon slapped him lightly on the back to help him breathe better. The Royal Malaquey headmaster didn't look well either; he was deathly pale.

"I agree with that plan," said Headmaster Zelon in between his colleague's coughing fits.

"But first we have to find out where the attackers are. Why haven't they come in yet?" asked Harto, becoming more and more alert as time ticked on.

"They're just waiting for the dust to clear. It usually takes effect in just a few minutes but takes up to thirty minutes to naturally dissipate from the atmosphere," explained High Priest Myltan.

Headmaster Welbrick looked at the high priest curiously. "Speaking from experience?"

The high priest smiled thinly at him. "Of course. It was used on my platoon several times during the Dyhaeri-Human War." Danai saw the respect in the headmaster's eyes and realized the Artra headmaster was finally appreciating that the high priest outranked them all in age and experience, even combined.

"We had better disappear then," said King Wilhem. He turned to Lieutenant Flay. "I trust you to get my family to safety."

"Sir?" asked a stunned Harto.

"You still trust him?" asked a shocked Headmaster Zelon. The king looked at the Royal Malaquey headmaster.

"Yes, I do." The king turned back to Harto. "So, suggestions?"

Harto tried to answer but was thwarted by a coughing fit. It took a while before he was able to speak, and even then, his voice was raspy and weak. "We need the strongest wielders to protect the royal family while the next strongest need to scout out the halls and shoot a danger flare into the sky to alert the troops stationed in the courtyard to the danger."

"And if those troops are in on it as well?" demanded Headmaster Welbrick.

"Then we all fight together," declared the high priest rising. He helped Danai to her feet. She was feeling much better now, but her mind was racing.

"I volunteer as scout."

Headmaster Clayre stared at her. "No, you are one of the strongest wielders Syla College has ever produced. You will defend the king!"

Danai opened her mouth to argue, but High Priest Myltan put a gentle hand on her shoulder and spoke for her. "She's right. She needs to be out there, scouting with the others—quickly. Look at your senior instructors." He paused and stared at the other wielders in the hall.

Danai and the others followed his gaze, and to her dismay, many of the senior instructors were leaning weakly against the walls or sitting on the floor. Several were coughing and were clearly in no state to even defend themselves.

"By the Dark Keeper," cursed Headmaster Zelon softly. "They wouldn't last three minutes in a fight against a first year."

"Exactly," agreed the high priest. "We of the older generation know what Solarian dust can do to both the Dyhaeri and human physiques. The older ones usually experience lingering effects that last for days."

Danai felt he was talking to her more than the others.

"But Danai doesn't have the experience I have," started Harto before a coughing fit took him again. This time it was so violent that the king himself had to help Harto to a nearby seat.

The high priest glanced at him. "I could offer you the blessings of the Sea Mother—"

"No, thank you!" vehemently declined Harto. "Um… no offense."

The high priest smiled in understanding. "None taken." He turned back to the king, the headmasters, and a silent Warden Asteros. "Danai knows the layout of the college and will lead the scouts. I will stay by the king's side. I have centuries of wielding experience."

Headmaster Clayre opened his mouth to protest but changed his mind. No one could argue with that.

"I'm going with Danai," said a determined and angry Mat. His eyes were clearer now. Danai was relieved.

"Are you all right?" she asked.

Mat came to stand beside her. "I asked for the blessings of the Sea Mother, and She answered."

Danai noticed how uneasy those nearby were at those words. The king alone seemed relieved there was a plan.

"Splendid," said the high priest. "Do get Kahl, Britea, and Pearl to join you. Oh, by the way, Novice Pearl Ceres is immune to Solarian dust."

The headmasters, Harto, and the king gaped at High Priest Myltan.

"That's impossible," finally spluttered Headmaster Zelon.

"Not impossible, just extremely rare. I believe it occurs in one in twenty thousand people," said Warden Asteros wonderingly.

"Yes, we got quite lucky, didn't we?" said the high priest as he gave Danai a knowing look. Somehow, he knew of the Seers and the warning they had given Britea.

A warning, that if ignored, would have left them all at the mercy of the invaders.

The king clapped his hands loudly. "Time's a wasting. Let's get the scouts out and about."

#

Britea, Pearl, and Kahl were still helping a groggy Navos and Lexia to sit beside an exhausted Shran and Henrick. Britea had been relieved to hear their tiredness would pass with time because the healers were attending to the older wielders and guests, leaving many the students to recover on their own. It was fortunate the frenzied healers of the three schools had been present at the ball. Even Chelton and Vindell were worn out now that their adrenaline had worn off.

"We…we were attacked. Who would attack us?" asked a stunned Henrick.

"Namira…it has to be Namira," said Navos. Though fatigued, the rage in his eyes was enough to scare Britea. May the Maker help whoever Navos directed his fury at.

"You're all okay."

They turned to face a relieved Danai and Mat.

Britea ran to hug them both. "I'm so sorry I wasn't by your side when you fell."

"Oh, don't be silly," said Danai. "If you had been, I suspect things would have been a lot worse." She spied Vindell and Chelton and frowned. "So, these are the two first years who broke the rules to come watch the ball?"

The first years squirmed before she smiled at them. "Thanks for breaking the rules, little warriors. If it weren't for that, things would have turned out much differently."

A healer reached their group and began to assess Navos, Henrick, Lexia, and Shran for exhaustion.

"So, what's the plan?" asked Navos even as the healer placed a hand on his forehead.

"We scout out the invaders' location—" answered Mat.

"I'm coming," said Navos before Mat had even finished speaking.

Danai shook her head. "No, you stay here. As much as I love you, brother, you're not one for sneaking about."

"Hey, I can sneak with the best of them!" protested Navos loudly.

"Shh," hushed a nearby healer. "We don't want them knowing we're awake." She jerked a thumb towards the closed doors. Many weary but angry wielders of the three colleges were also watching the doors. Britea suspected anyone walking in at that moment would be the target of some very incensed wielders.

Danai raised an eyebrow. "See? Even Healer Mavian knows what I'm talking about. For this mission, I'm taking Britea, Mat, Pearl, and Kahl. We need the rest of you to protect the royal family and everyone else in the hall."

"Wait, why not take the senior instructors?" asked Henrick.

Before Danai could say a word, Shran answered. "The effects of Solarian dust are more pronouced in the older population; their co-ordination and focus will be way off, and they might accidentally hurt themselves if they try to wield offensively."

Danai waved a hand. "What he said. But we need to move fast." She turned to Britea. "I know I'm asking a lot of you, but we have to go now."

Britea dreaded what they would find out there, but she also wanted to stop feeling scared and defenseless. She stood up and dusted her hands off. Kahl and Pearl came to stand on either side of her. Taking a deep breath, she replied simply. "Let's go."

#

Harto watched Danai and her small group pass through the double doors and felt deeply shamed.

Those five were younger than him and nowhere near qualified to meet whoever the attackers were, and here he was, avoiding responsibility because he was afraid of a simple blessing from the Dyhaeri high priest.

And the security of the Royal House of Malaquey had been *his* responsibility, and he had messed that up royally too.

He forced himself to stand. "High Priest Myltan." The holy Dyhaeri excused himself from discussing their current defense plan with the king and the three headmasters.

"I apologize for refusing the blessing. Does your offer still stand?"

The high priest stared at him for a long moment. "Of course, it does."

CHAPTER 33

Danai felt her heart rate pick up as she and the others passed through the double doors of the Great Hall. Hearing the doors shut behind them was akin to hearing a death knell.

Now that she was outside the safety of the hall, she wondered what kind of insanity had made her volunteer for such a dangerous mission.

But the senior members of the college were incapacitated, the healers were running on empty, and those they had left to guard the entrance to the hall may not even be strong enough to wield to their full capacity thanks to the lingering effects of the Solarian dust.

She still felt a bit odd but thankfully nothing like when she had woken up. And she couldn't help but notice that despite his age, the high priest had recovered quickly. Mat and Kahl had recovered just as fast, just as she had.

"You all right?" asked a too-perceptive Mat.

"Yes, you?" She tried to sound confident as she led their motley crew to the Forever Bridge.

"It's been an eventful evening."

Danai stifled a laugh at his dry humor. It was a windy night, and the sky was filled with dark clouds. It would have been nearly impossible to see if not for the two massive firepits at each end of the bridge. As Danai passed one of the firepits, she wielded two ropes of fire and wound them around her forearms. Mat walked beside her, keeping his hands open and loose, ready to wield at a moment's notice. Danai glanced behind her. Britea was trying to keep a brave face while Kahl was looking at every shadow as if it hid a potential threat. Pearl looked pale, but an unwavering light shone in her eyes.

"Stay ready," Danai warned them, raising her voice to be heard over the wind. She took the lead and peeked over the side of the bridge. High tide was coming in, and the water would soon be a few feet below the suspended bridge. Danai saw four ribbons of water fly up over the side and nodded with approval as Britea and Kahl wrapped the tendrils around their forearms like she had done.

"Where are they?" asked a worried Mat.

Danai wondered too. Had the attackers been so afraid of the effects of Solarian dust that they had stayed far away? And why had they stayed away for so long?

A low whistle made them all turn. Harto was running towards them.

"What is he doing out here?" groaned Mat softly.

Danai kept silent as the Malaquey officer reached them.

"Good, you didn't get too far yet."

"Why are you here?" demanded Danai in a whisper.

Harto took a moment to catch his breath. She suspected he had not yet fully recovered from the Solarian dust.

"I finally convinced the king I should accompany you on this mission." Then he paused. "I also accepted the high priest's blessing."

Mat raised an eyebrow. "You mean the Sea Mother's blessing? The one you vehemently rejected the first time?"

Harto only acknowledged his question with a sidelong glance and then turned back to Danai.

"I have the most experience, so I should take lead."

"You're not," said Mat and Danai at the same time.

"Psst! We're wasting time and we're out in the open!" said Pearl, indicating the empty bridge around them.

"She's right. We should find cover," said Danai. She turned and strode to the other end of the bridge while she prayed their luck would hold and that Harto would not push for leadership. To her surprise and relief, he kept his mouth shut.

They finally reached the other end. Danai cautiously pushed one of the school's double doors open and was relieved it didn't creak on its obviously well-oiled hinges. She cautiously stuck her head in and was startled to find no one in the corridor. Then she heard faint murmurs. Yanking her head back out, she silently put a finger on her lips.

Then they all snuck through the doors and into the corridor. Following the empty corridor to the stairs, they descended on tiptoe towards the voices. As they got closer, they could hear the conversation.

"How much longer do your think they'll be out?"

"Hah! Did you see how much dust we put in those barrels? They'll sleep until we get them back to the ship. They just have to load the little ones first, then when they find whoever they're looking for, we can move on to the big prizes in the Great Hall."

Danai and the others shared a worried expression. The "little ones" could only mean the first and second years. And who were the invaders searching for?

"Come on, let's go find something to eat."

"But we're on guard!"

The other invader scoffed. "The sleeping beauties aren't going anywhere, and besides, none of us can approach the Great Hall until the dust has dissipated."

"Oh, all right then." The two guards wandered off, and Danai cautiously peeked around a pillar to ensure they were going in the opposite direction.

"The big prizes?" whispered Britea.

"They must mean the king and his family," said Pearl.

"But they mentioned they were looking for someone? Who?" asked Britea.

"Let's get back to the mission at hand," said Harto. "We have to send the flare up now. Where is the best place to do so?" asked the Malaquey intelligence officer.

"The gardens at the center of the school," said Danai as an idea began to take root. "We send the flare up and run back to the hall to defend the others."

"But what about the first and second years?" asked a distraught Britea.

Danai had a sinking feeling in her stomach. "It sounded like they've already been taken. We have to send for help before these guys get to the king and rescue the little ones later."

"She's right," whispered Pearl. "If we fail now, then we all fall."

Britea nodded reluctantly. They really didn't have a choice.

The group continued to sneak down the halls to the center garden, making sure not to alert the nearby invaders to their presence. Danai tried to slow her heart rate, but it was pounding so loudly she could hear it in ears.

They eventually reached the center garden, but it was occupied by a stunning red-headed woman peering into the pools, fascinated. They dashed behind a tall bush and peeked through the small gaps to watch her. They could not see her face, but they were mesmerized by the way her deep-violet velvet tunic and matching cape, both lined with gold, contrasted so beautifully with the luminous red of her hair.

Danai was wondering who she was when a voice called out nervously. "Your Highness, I come bearing bad news." *Your Highness? Oh no! That could only be…*

The Weltonian suppressed the terrifying thought and watched a trim middle-aged man in a similarly violet-hued uniform enter the garden. Even from this distance, she could see he was sweating profusely.

"Tell me you've found the D'Tranell girl," threatened the fiery-haired monarch of Namira, continuing to gaze at the calm pools as if lost in their depths.

Danai glanced at Britea, and to her credit, though she looked terrified, she did not make a sound.

The man swallowed nervously. "I've checked and double checked each of the first and second years. None of them match her description."

The Immortal Queen of Namira turned her head slowly to face him. "Are you certain?"

"Yes, my queen."

Queen Kallesa sighed, then casually lit the large central pool on fire. The man began to cough from the wall of smoke.

"Either you're blind or stupid. Take me to the brats; I'll search myself." The queen strolled out of the garden, followed closely by her coughing subordinate.

Mat had wielded a huge air bubble around them as they hid behind the bush, so the smoke just billowed around them.

"That was…" began Pearl in a scared whisper before she stopped to stare at a shocked Britea.

"Why does she want me? Why did she go after the first and second years?" Britea had to fight to keep her voice from trembling.

"She must have thought you were a first year," said Harto, worried.

"Which means someone at the school was feeding information to the Namiran queen," said Kahl, his voice hard as he glared at Harto.

The Malaquey officer gaped at Kahl. "You think…you think I had something to do with this?"

"I doubt it," said Mat to everyone's surprise. "You may be annoying, but you're not stupid."

"Thanks, I guess," said Harto dryly.

Mat nodded as she continued talking. "Whoever gathered intel for the queen made the wrong assumption. So, either the person didn't do a thorough job or is an outsider who could only gather limited information."

"Stay on target people," warned Danai. "We still have a flare to send up." Then she studied the large bonfire in the now dried-up pool. "Besides, I think the queen did us a favor."

"What?" asked Mat, confused.

But Danai was already marching purposefully to the bonfire. She added her fire whips to the fire and wielded a starburst sign that translated to, "We're in danger! Send help!" She waited until it began to pulse in time with her heartbeat and then wielded it straight up into the sky. It would continue to burn bright until help arrived…or she died.

"Hopefully if the queen's guards see it, they'll think it was their crazy queen who did it. I bet none of them will be brave enough to ask her about it." Danai wrapped fire ropes around her arms once more.

"That's a big 'if' Danai," said Mat, worried.

"So, what now?" asked Pearl.

"You lot go back to the Great Hall," said Harto, "I'll stay and gather more intel."

Mat laughed softly. "So you'll be the hero?"

"You're not doing this alone," said Danai. "We need to find out where the queen took the first and second years."

"That wasn't the mission," said Harto.

"She attacked the school because of me," said a stunned Britea before Danai could respond.

Danai gently grabbed her roommate by the arms. "Hey, hey. We don't know that. And as you so brilliantly pointed out earlier, those idiot guards we passed mentioned prizes, plural, not prize, singular. I believe she's here for more than just you. But now that we've sent the warning, we can see what we can do to save the others."

Britea nodded as a bit of spirit came back into her eyes.

"This is suicide," protested Harto.

"Then run back to the king. We'll be fine without you," said Mat harshly.

Harto glared at Mat. Danai left Britea and approached the two males.

"The enemy is out there with a bunch of unconscious young innocents. I trust you'll both remember that."

"Yes, ma'am," said Harto automatically.

"Yes, Wielder Queen," said Mat, and Danai just rolled her eyes.

#

The next part of their plan was harder than Danai had expected. It took only moments before they heard something coming from one of the dance halls used by the etiquette instructors. There were only two ways to get there: the most direct route was through the dining hall, and the second was a slightly longer route through the outdoor combat and defense class. In the end, Danai chose the latter. Her instincts warned her it was safer.

She was relieved when they came across no one in the sparring hall, but they did run into an unexpected person in the dance hall corridor.

"Chef Blane?" asked Harto suspiciously when they silently turned the corner to find the diminutive chef apparently waiting for them.

The short chef glared at them. "Took you lot long enough. One of my staff saw you sneaking out of the central garden. Where's Warden Asteros?"

"How do we know you're not working with the Namirans?" demanded Harto before Danai could reply. The chef gave him a look filled with menace.

"Who was it that told Warden Asteros that men wearing Malaquey Naval Intelligence uniforms prevented my staff from decorating the Great Hall? Who told the warden those same men were seen wheeling in barrels and when we asked why, we were threatened with imprisonment?"

The rest of the group now turned to stare at an embarrassed Harto.

"So, it *was* you," growled Mat as he shot a vicious look at the Malaquey intelligence officer.

"Hey, wait a minute! I was a target too!" protested Harto.

"And yet, Lieutenant Flay, we warned you about Namira infiltrating the Red Rats, and you ignored it," said Mat as he edged closer to Harto.

Pearl and Britea stared at them while Danai glared at both males. "Hey…"

Chef Blane sighed, and to the astonishment of all, he wielded a large tier-one square of earth between the two males. It made Mat and Harto jump back.

"You two lumpheads!" The chef pointed at Mat and Harto, and both males gaped at him. "This is neither the time nor the place, and yes, yes, I am a wielder and Warden Asteros knows. Now, where in the Abyss *is* he?!"

Danai hastily explained the situation and the chef's expression darkened.

"So, you're the calvary? It's worse than I imagined."

"But I sent up the flare," said Danai.

Chef Blane snorted. "That's only helpful if the Malaquey forces who were supposed to have been stationed in the courtyard see it in time, wherever they are."

"What do you mean 'supposed to have been stationed'?" asked Kahl, worried.

Chef Blane looked at him. "Just before the ball began, my lads were serving the Malaquey army refreshments when an officer in Malaquey Naval Intelligence gear gave them new orders. The army's commanding officer argued against leaving but did so in the end."

"What were the new orders?" asked Harto.

The chef shot a jaundiced look at Harto. "Did you know anything about this, son?" His tone was deadly serious, his eyes piercing.

Harto swallowed nervously, aware he was on trial. "I didn't, sir."

Mat scoffed. "You expect us to believe—"

"I believe him," said the chef abruptly. "The new orders stated that because the Red Rats had been sighted near the college, the army was to investigate."

Harto's face went pale. Mat stared at him, pity in his eyes.

The chef continued. "I thought the Red Rats being close to the college was unusual. They know better than to bother wielders. Even the commanding officer tried to insist that the local militia should handle the Red Rats, but in the end, he left because he saw the royal seal on his new orders."

"The Red Rats are just a distraction," said Danai. Everyone stared at her. "We need to get the Malaquey Army back here!"

The chef nodded. "When I saw the flare go up, I sent a few runners. Sea Mother willing, they'll find the army and get them here, pronto."

"But what of the first and second years?" asked Britea. She couldn't remain silent any longer.

Chef Blane's expression was grim as he jerked his hand at the dance hall. "She's laid them out on the floor. They're still asleep, and the Immortal Queen is checking their faces. It seems she's looking for someone."

"Me," said Britea guilt flooding her eyes.

Chef Blane blinked in surprise. "Oh, we cannot let the Defender of the Innocents be taken!" He rubbed his hands together, and his block of earth morphed into brown ropes of earth. They flew back to him and wrapped themselves around his forearms.

"How did the Namirans get here so stealthily anyway?" asked Pearl. Everyone stared at her.

"Check the side window and look up," replied Chef Blane. They ran to one of the big windows overlooking the beach. Dozens of small empty boats were moored offshore, but when they looked up…

"By the Maker," exclaimed Harto softly.

"Uh huh," said the chef from behind them as they gaped at the gargantuan hovering warship. Though the wind was howling, they could still hear the giant engines keeping the technological monstrosity hovering.

"Brilliant idea striking at night. That ship is barely noticeable with its dark coloring, and I suspect the guards we had on the beach are dead by now," said Chef Blane grimly.

"What now?" asked Mat once they had stepped back from the window.

"We're planning to distract the queen and her men somehow, then we'll grab who we can. You lot need to run back to the hall and hunker down and wait for the army," replied the chef.

"No," said Danai. Chef Blane stared at her in surprise. "Your distraction may cost you your lives, but I have another plan…'" Then she looked at Britea. "But I'll need help."

Britea shot her friend and roommate a puzzled look. "If I can help, of course I'll do anything."

"Hold on," said Kahl nervously. "Please, never reply with 'I'll do anything.'"

"Agreed," said Pearl and Harto at the same time. Mat just shook his head at Britea, smiling gently.

Britea looked at them all, touched by their concern but determined to help the unconscious students. "Danai, what do you want me to do?"

Her roommate looked at her for a moment as if to ensure she was making the right decision. "Ready to run as if our lives depend on it?"

#

The Immortal Queen Kallesa was aware of how silent and nervous the ninety-six individuals behind her were. They had good reason to be; she had handpicked each of them personally based on their skill and devotion. But despite planning for every contingency, something always seemed to go wrong.

She had just wasted time looking at the faces of one hundred and twelve sleeping Syla students, and none of them fit the description of Britea D'Tranell.

Rising slowly after checking the last face, she turned on her heel to face her terrified subjects.

"First, the engines of the second Namiran airship fails just before we're to set out on our mission, then we have to sneak into Malaquey under the cover of darkness, then the intel from our so-called spy is missing one salient fact." A ball of fire suddenly materialized in her right palm. "The main target is not among them!" she yelled. The Namiran soldiers flinched. "Is no one competent?!" She turned to face Minister Lensworth. "So…" The single word oozed out like poison, but to the minister's credit, he remained calm, though he was paler than usual. "Please, give me one good reason why I should not burn you to the ground."

Minister Lensworth eyed the ball of fire in her hand and opened his mouth to speak.

"Because you are a pathetic pretender on the Namiran throne!" The yell came from behind her, and she turned to face two dark-skinned girls in ball gowns. One wore a fashionable caramel gown, and the second…. was Britea D'Tranell.

And both girls were clearly wide awake.

Queen Kallesa was so stunned that the ball of fire went out. Her guards began to rush forward, but she made them wait. There was something odd about the girls.

"Ah, Britea D'Tranell." Then she looked at the first girl. "And this must be Danai Riverun."

The queen smiled evilly when she saw the girl's eyes widen. "Yes, we have heard of you. The first Weltonian to attend a human wielding college in centuries. Yes, you are of great interest. Well, thank you for making my search less tedious. Come forward. We will escort you to my ship." Queen Kallesa's smile disappeared. "But do tell me, why are you not asleep?"

Danai smiled coldly. "Because we're immune to Solarian dust, Pretender on the Throne."

The queen's anger bubbled to the surface. *How dare this girl insult her? Did she have any idea in whose presence she now stood?! She who should rule the waters below, the skies above, and every land in existence?! Why was this girl not scared of her?* Oh, she would love to see this girl scream for mercy as she sucked out all her power.

"Come here now, or watch these children burn—" but before she could wield, Danai erected a pulsing, tier-four fire shield over the sleeping children. It would stay up until either Danai was unconscious or someone with a stronger will broke the shield.

Danai sneered at her. "You have a choice. You can either break that or catch us, you worthless wielder." She tapped the silent Britea on the arm, and the two disappeared into the shadows.

"By the way, the Malaquey Army is on their way back!" yelled Danai in a singsong voice as she ran away.

Queen Kallesa howled with fury and ran after them.

"Protect and defend the queen!" yelled Minister Lensworth as he ran after his mad queen. The Namiran invaders followed suit.

#

Britea's heart rate picked up alarmingly as she and Danai fled down the corridor to the empty dining hall once they had passed through the first set of double doors. Mat used a tier-four air wield to lock the doors before he joined them in their mad dash across the vast dining hall to the second set of doors where Harto nervously waited.

The plan had been to get the enemy to chase the girls to the Great Hall, drawing the invaders away from the unconscious students. Pearl and Kahl had been given the task of locking the outdoor arena where the Trials had been held so the invaders could not use that as a shortcut.

Chef Blane had sent a runner to the Great Hall to warn them of what was coming.

"The chef is tapping on my shield with his earth element! I'm going to let go now, so he can grab the first and second years," shouted Danai as they ran. Britea wanted to ask how she knew it was Chef Blane, but she didn't want to slow down.

A loud bang and a crash behind them told them the enraged Namiran queen had broken through the first set of double doors. As they reached the second set of doors, Harto was waiting for them, bouncing on his feet. Once the three had passed him, he used his earth element to lock the doors behind them before joining the three runners.

They found Pearl and Kahl waiting for them in the west corridor to the Forever Bridge. Britea almost wept when she saw the relieved expressions on Pearl's and Kahl's faces.

"Go, go, go!" yelled Harto. "She's right behind us!"

They ran onto the Forever Bridge, and Kahl used a thick tier-four water rope to tie the handles of the double doors together to keep them locked as long as possible. Britea could both feel and smell the ocean spray as the tide was now at its highest and was more than halfway up the giant pillars holding the bridge up.

She could see the doors of the Great Hall in the distance. They beckoned her to safety.

A loud explosion sounded behind them, and the doors Kahl had locked flew apart in a fiery blaze. Unsure why, Britea stopped and turned to see an enraged Queen Kallesa. Her purple cape billowed out behind her, and the wind of the night seas waved her vibrant waist-long hair in crazy tendrils behind her. Her green eyes gleamed with evil.

"You can never escape me!" yelled the queen as she advanced with her soldiers.

"Britea! No, don't!" yelled Kahl when he realized she had stopped halfway across the bridge. The others, realizing the same, turned and started running back to her.

Britea stood frozen in place as the queen rapidly approached. Queen Kallesa smiled confidently, sensing surrender.

Then Erina Seaworth's frantic words came to her in rush.

"In days to come, thou shall find thyself in a perilous situation on a bridge, though fear will ambush thee. Thou must use the fear itself to flood thy troubles away."

So Britea closed her eyes and reached deep inside her for her fear, her simmering anger, and all her strength to use for a tier-five wield. Then she grabbed the high tidal waters. The Namirans hesitated when they saw the now three-hundred-foot waves suddenly curving over the Forever Bridge. Britea brought them crashing down on the invaders.

Britea opened her eyes and watched through a haze of pain as her enormous wield encountered a barrier. She may have been thwarted in her effort, but she still heard the invaders screaming as some were washed over the side and into the sea. Weakness settled over her in seconds, a warning that this wield had been too much for her. But she held on, determined to wash the Namiran enemies away.

"Britea, let go!" shouted Kahl, holding on to her shoulders. She realized then she had fallen down to her knees, her hands still raised as she continued to wield.

"I…I can't. I can't."

Kahl was crying. "Please." He embraced her from behind. "Please, just let go. It's over."

Britea wanted to give up, but part of her wanted to keep wielding until all spark of life was extinguished, whether hers or the queen's. Finally though, she began to gradually reduce the power of her wield, and then she stopped completely, the three hundred-foot waves suddenly collapsing into the sea under the Forever Bridge.

Britea was still looking at a relieved Kahl when Pearl gasped in horror. "That's not possible."

Britea turned her head weakly, and her jaw dropped when she realized the Immortal Queen was still on the bridge. She was suspended in a large orb of fire, and at least half her forces remained below her. Britea had only gotten about forty of them.

"How?" asked an equally stunned Harto.

Britea struggled to answer, but she was so weak. "I have to wield."

Danai and Mat rushed to stand before Britea and Kahl. "We won't let you have her!" yelled a defiant Danai.

Queen Kallesa drifted down to the bridge and began to walk confidently towards them.

"She has talent, that's for sure, but in the end, it won't save her or any of you. Give yourselves up now, or more will die for your stubbornness."

Mat glanced at Danai. "Your father trained you, right?"

Danai shot him a quick look. "You're asking me this now?!"

"The tier-six wield."

Danai's eyes widened. "Are you sure?"

Mat nodded grimly. "I am."

"What's the tier-six wield? There is no tier-six wield!" yelled Harto.

But Danai and Mat ignored him and linked their hands. Danai wielded a ball of fire that fit in the palm of her right hand while Mat wielded a similarly shaped ball of air in the palm of his left hand. The Immortal Queen halted for a moment, then her eyes widened in surprise when both wielders began to bring both elements towards each other.

"No!" she screamed in outrage as she ran towards them with her soldiers, but the two elements connected then, and a fiery, rounded barrier fed by air now separated the queen from her target.

"I will break this wall and then break every bone in your bodies!" screamed the Immortal Queen as she rained large orbs of fire on the combined barrier. The orbs failed to make even the smallest dent.

"Oh my," said an astonished Pearl while Harto stared at Danai and Mat's linked hands with a mixture of dismay and shock.

"You cannot maintain it for long!" shouted Queen Kallesa while she tried to find a way through. Her remaining Namiran soldiers looked cowed by the fiery obstruction.

Britea heard a commotion behind her and weakly turned to see a crowd pouring out of the Great Hall. The group included King Wilhem, the high priest, the headmasters, their wardens, and a plethora of weary but angry instructors and their senior students. Britea spied Navos, Shran, Henrick, and Lexia among them.

"Boost the shield!" called out the high priest as he ran towards Danai and Mat. The king and the others followed.

When she saw them coming, Queen Kallesa lost all reason and formed two huge tier-four fiery fists to bash against the barrier, and for a moment, the barrier seemed to give. But when High Priest Myltan reached them, he laid a hand on Danai's shoulder. Kahl who was still kneeling beside Britea, put his hand on Mat's right leg as if lending him strength. Pearl remained standing and put a hand on Danai's back.

Harto let go of his surprise and laid a hand on Mat's left shoulder. Mat turned to look at him and acknowledged his gift with a slight smile. The remaining wielders began to form a chain as those in front touched the shoulders of those directly supporting Danai and Mat, growing the magic chain. The barrier snapped back into place and glowed even brighter.

"Don't forget, Pretender!" yelled Danai. "The army is on their way!" The veins in Queen Kallesa's neck bulged in fury, and Danai prayed the mad queen would have a stroke.

One of the Namirans, the middle-aged man, approached his livid queen. She turned to face him, and he shouted something quickly.

Whatever it was, it calmed her. She turned back to the barrier.

"This is not over." She glared at Danai for a long time before transferring her stare to Mat, Harto, Pearl, Britea, Kahl, and the high priest in turn. She completely ignored King Wilhem.

At the urging of her minister, she turned and fled, taking her troops with her.

Despite the queen's surrender and subsequent flight, Danai, Mat, and the other wielders kept the barrier up until the Malaquey Army turned up several minutes later.

CHAPTER 34

High Priest Myltan took a deep breath as he stared out his window. It was the morning after the Immortal Queen's invasion. He closed his eyes and tried to savor the warmth of the sunlight that streamed into the Dyhaeri guest quarters.

He treasured moments like this, moments when he was just Myltan, and not the high priest. Especially when he knew what was to come.

A loud knock on the door brought him back to the present. He sighed. It was time to return to his official duties.

#

High Priest Myltan nodded to the two Malaquey Army guards positioned outside his quarters. They would stay with him until he returned to his people. Mat and Kahl were still in the infirmary; the events of the previous night had affected them all, and the high priest had been forced to order the two younger Dyhaeri to stay put. However, it had helped that Britea and Danai had also been admitted.

The high priest's expression darkened as he thought of what Britea had almost done to herself. Pulling off a tier-five wield of that magnitude was enough to exhaust anyone, but Britea had only done it once before, and that had included a gradual buildup with Kahl helping her.

This time she had done it on her own. She had almost drained herself to the point of death. High Priest Myltan was grateful to the Sea Mother that Kahl had been able to convince her to let go in time. Unfortunately, that wield had left Britea terribly weak. The high priest suspected she would have to stay in the infirmary for quite a while. He had even tried to heal her, but she needed more care than he could offer.

He and his escort reached Headmaster Clayre's office in short order. Six Malaquey officers stood outside: two in Malaquey Naval Intelligence uniforms and the rest in army green. They all wore grave expressions, but they saluted the high priest as he approached. High Priest Myltan hid his surprise as he acknowledged their sign of respect with a nod and the blessings of the Sea Mother.

This was the first time he had ever been acknowledged as one of their own military leaders.

The situation was grave indeed.

He walked into Headmaster Clayre's office. Those within—King Wilhem, the three headmasters, and Warden Asteros—turned, all with grave expressions. The high priest wondered where the other wardens were.

King Wilhem rose from his chair, still clad in his outfit of the evening before, and now it looked as if he had slept in it.

"High Priest Myltan, I hope you slept well," said the king as he indicated a chair for the high priest to sit in. After he had taken his seat, the king and the others also took their seats once again. All were arranged in a circle beside the huge desk.

"It was restful. What has happened now?" asked the high priest. He felt uneasy when he saw the headmasters exchange a silent look.

"Artra Army College and Royal Malaquey College were also attacked on the same night," announced the Headmaster Clayre gravely.

High Priest Myltan was silent with shock for a long moment. "She has more of those flying ships?"

Warden Asteros shook his head. "No, from what we can tell, she dropped small boats of soldiers off before heading here, and then they all struck simultaneously. Syla College was the prime target, but she still took more than ninety wielders from both Artra and Royal Malaquey Naval colleges."

Now the high priest knew why those wardens weren't present.

"How many dead?"

"More than twenty," said Headmaster Zelon in a subdued voice.

Myltan hesitated to ask the next question, but he had to. "How many taken?"

"We're still counting," said Warden Asteros gravely. Myltan had no idea what to say next.

"You do realize, High Priest Myltan, that this means war between Malaquey and Namira," said Headmaster Welbrick in a somber tone that was unusual for the jovial general.

The high priest looked at the silent king, who had been observing the exchange. "Your Highness, I am yet to hear your thoughts on the matter."

King Wilhem smiled dryly and took a moment to prepare his answer. "Yesterday morning, my children were pestering me about wielding. My young daughter, Crystal, was looking forward to learning about wielding." His face went grave. "Then the attack happened, and all I could think about was protecting them." He stared into the distance for a long moment.

"Did you know my daughter snuck out of the hall when Danai and Mat conducted their tier-six wield and everyone linked their power together to keep the barrier up? She saw it all." He laughed dryly. "I scolded her soundly when I found out because I was scared that now she was so scarred she would give up wielding. But the little warrior surprised me. She wants to wield more than ever, and she wants to go to Syla College."

High Priest Myltan saw Headmaster Clayre heave a sigh of relief while Headmaster Zelon rolled his eyes, but Headmaster Welbrick just clapped the pale Syla headmaster on the back and offered his congratulations.

The high priest hid his confusion because he suspected the perceptive king had a point to make with this narrative.

"I saw courage in my little daughter, courage I was lacking last night, and I was ashamed." The king's frank confession drew startled looks from them all.

Then King Wilhem's face hardened. "So, I agree. This means war between Malaquey and Namira. Will the Dyhaeri stand with us?"

High Priest Myltan studied the king for a heartbeat. "We will."

The humans didn't bother to hide their relief.

"By the way, where's Lieutenant Flay?" asked the high priest. He had wondered from the first why the officer had not been part of this discussion.

The king and the others exchanged a silent look.

"Last night after searching the grounds, we found the dead bodies of the real Malaquey intelligence officers. One of them was Lieutenant Therry Welspring. They had been classmates and close friends," replied Warden Asteros.

High Priest Myltan felt sympathy for the earnest Malaquey officer. "I see. He is in mourning."

"Yes, and he has been confined to his quarters," said Headmaster Zelon.

The high priest tilted his head. "Surely, you don't suspect him of espionage? He helped the others get the signal out and contributed to the barrier."

The king held up a hand. "He went into isolation willingly. Lieutenant Flay said he needed time to understand what had happened. I placed guards simply to ensure he does not try to kill himself. He's taking the death of his friend pretty hard."

Now the high priest understood. "A failure of this magnitude is enough to make anyone doubt themselves. I imagine he blames himself as an intelligence officer for not having more information and heading off the attack in the first place?"

"Precisely," agreed Headmaster Clayre.

A knock on the door made them turn, and the warden went to open it. A scowling Chef Blane rolled in a trolley laden with aromatic plates.

"Breakfast is ready, everyone!"

The king rose eagerly and walked over to Chef Blane. "May I shake the hand of the chef who helped rescue the entire first- and second-year classes?"

The chef was stunned for a moment, then took the king's hand. "Just doing our part, Your Highness."

"And the food is splendid as usual," said Headmaster Welbrick as he heaped his plate high. "Compliments to you and your staff."

"Thank you, Headmaster Welbrick." The chef smiled and left them.

The king stood staring at the closed doors as the others chose food from the breakfast buffet. "Headmaster Clayre, I had no idea the kitchen staff was Weltonian."

One could have heard a pin drop in the silence that ensued until Warden Asteros cleared his throat. "Yes, Your Highness, they all are. Is that a problem?"

Everyone stared at Warden Asteros It sounded as though his tone held a challenge.

"I knew," said the high priest calmly. "And I absolutely love their cooking." He ignored the stares as he picked a pastry.

From the corner of his eye, he saw the king smile.

"No, I don't, Warden Asteros. I only wish I had a chef who could cook half as well as this as well *and* wield like a warrior."

High Priest Myltan turned and caught the relief in the warden's eyes. The warden nodded silently at him, grateful for his support. A weary Headmaster Clayre returned to his seat with a small plate of food. He still seemed a bit out of breath. Warden Asteros gave him a worried look, and the headmaster waved away his concern.

Then Headmaster Zelon stepped right in front of the high priest, forcing him to look at him. "With your permission, since we're going to be partners and all that, I really wish to know more about that tier-six wield."

"Say, high priest," Headmaster Welbrick jumped in before High Priest Myltan could say a word. "Can you help the Artra Army recruit Britea D'Tranell?" Warden Asteros glared at him, and he hastily added, "Not right now, folks!

Later, when she's fully healed and closer to graduation. She would be a fantastic addition to the army! Also, I would love your boys to visit Artra College and spend some time teaching my students in our combat and defense class."

Behind them, King Wilhem was clearly holding in his laughter with great difficulty as he watched the two headmasters pester the high priest.

#

Malie kept his single good eye open as he tried to ignore the pain that wracked his serpentine coils. They had used his essence to bring this cursed contraption to this place.

And now they were flying away to the Deeps knew where!

But what scared the alkynaia most was the mad red-headed monarch staring at his watery cage.

Queen Kallesa had been in a dreadful rage when she had returned. Once they had set off, she'd had them bring in ten captives in olive-green and water-blue uniforms. As she had ripped their powers from them, their pleas for mercy and screams of pain had angered her even more.

Now the corpses lay around her, and she was still behaving oddly.

There were days Malie wanted to die, especially when she did experiments on him. But strangely, the serpent had been feeling...hopeful recently.

Now, why was that?

Right now, though, all he felt was fear.

"Danai Riverun, a backwater Weltonian of no importance, called me the Pretender on the Throne," suddenly said the Immortal Queen in a subdued tone. She stood and walked towards his glass cage and pressed herself against it. It took everything Malie had not to recoil. That was when the serpent realized the queen had been crying.

"She doesn't have any idea who I am. Who is this Britea that she inspires such loyalty from humans, Dyhaeri, Weltonians...and even Alkynaia?"

Malie's inner ears perked up. Alkynaia helping humans? Had the Immortal Queen finally gone completely mad?

Queen Kallesa turned away from the glass and leaned on it.

"I will see Danai Riverun and Britea D'Tranell again." A fiery ball appeared in her right hand and she stared at it. "And then I will tear the truth from their bodies."

Malie remained silent and suppressed a shiver at her dark promise.

THE END

List of characters, places and events…

WIELDING (Fire, Water, Air and Earth.)

First Tier (Stability) = A single shape = repeat 7 times

Second Tier (Flexibility) = Two types of shapes; repeat 7 times; rotate around each other

Third Tier (Concentration) = Three different types of shapes; move them in different directions at increasing speed.

Fourth Tier (Perseverance and Defense) = For shielding but requires a lot of effort. Use simple small tier one shapes

Fifth Tier (Strength) = Force oriented. Use it to push an object. Example use air to fling a body away or towards one

Sixth Tier (A Blend of 2) = Only Dyhaeri and weltonians do this

Seventh Tier (Unity) = Very very rare (in the next book)

PLACES

Weldaros (a village in Malaquey)

Port Xanthos (nearest port to Weldaros)

Light-Under-Sea (Dyhaeri underwater home)

Raven's Fall (capital of Malaquey)

Port Trident (of Raven's fall.)

Port Fearless (of Namira)

Carlellis Market (in Raven's Fall)

Syla College (Wielding college)

Royal Malaquey Naval Wielding College (military)

Artra Army Wielding College (military)

Flintwood Castle (Namira)

Virtoria (Capital of Namira)

Arder's Heights = Pearl's home

Flay Estate = home to Shalina, Harto, Nell and other namiran refugees.

PANTHEON

Maker = *humans*
Lords of Light and Shadow = *humans*
The Dark Keeper = *humans*
Seven Hells
Land of Peace (paradise)

Sea-Mother *(dyhaeri)*
Dark Sister *(dyhaeri)*
By the Deep
By the Abyss
Gentle Seas (paradise)

DAYS OF THE WEEK

Primeday
Duoday
Triday
Quartusday
Quintusday
Septday
Solisday

CURRENCY

A day's pay is 45 silvers. (minimum wage.)
A yard of vert-silk cost 15,000 silvers (6 to 7 yards to make an ensemble.)
A yard of vert-silk cost 150 gold or 1.5 titane
100 silvers = 1 gold
100 gold = 1 titane (very rare metal.)

PEOPLE

The D'Tranells (*The Novice Wielder*)
Britea D'Tranell (water wielder)
Valden D'Tranell (Britea's father)
Samera D'Tranell (mum)
Carlina D'Tranell (Britea's older sister)
Mama Chloe = (Britea's great aunt)

The Dyhaeri
Kahlazetanin (water)
Mat-rallenin (air)
Almeita (earth)
High Priest Myltan (fire)
High Commander Neilara (fire)
Queen Zaleria (former queen mother-deceased.)
King Jahlaniin (water wielder)
Sle'niazza (missing presumed dead-air)
Kallesezza (transformed-fire) also known as Immortal Queen Kallesa of Namira
Dyhaeri Marine Corps

Wind-rider crew (The Novice Wielder)
Captain Thadeon
First Mate Melina Aldell
Daria (chirurgeon)
Ken Lanfor (water wielder)
Nathan (ship artist/recorder)

Night-flyer crew (The Novice Wielder)
Captain Drakor Moore
Lady Selina Arkei (water wielder)

Peacekeeper crew (weltonian ship)
Captain Lanead Riverun (earth wielder)

Co-captain Sonei Riverun (non-wielder)

First Mate Tanet

Mother's Star crew (Weltonian)

Captain Blaze (dead)

Weltonian Elders.

Elder Naleen Summers = 1st faction

Elder Brett Skylight = 2nd faction (captain of the Majestic Wind.)

Elder Rhedd Frost = 4th faction

Elder Val Night = 5th faction

Elder Stev Tremors = 6th faction

Elder Melody Timeless = 7th faction

Elder Pran Timelock = 9th faction, Lanead's faction

Elder Dren Wind = 10th faction

Elder Crane Starflame (farms vert-silk material.) = 13th Faction

Others

Malie (male) a half blind alkynaia serpent held prisoner by the Mad Queen Kallesa

Lara Firbright = former air wielding student she owns *Lara's Attire for the Frugal wallet.*

Erina Seaworth = writer of wielder stories; author of the following:

Lost histories of the Deep Vol 1 and 2

Wielder's Tales Vol 1 and 2

Doomed Love stories of Time and Legend

Syla College...

Senior Staff

Custodian Mitra (librarian.) earth wielder

Warden Sammel Asteros (fire)

Headmaster Zalei Clayre (earth)

Instructor Eowise Shelley (air)

Weapon Master Pietor Caren (earth)

Instructor Talios fire = 2nd in command to Master Pietor Caren

Instructor Lexar (defense class) water

Instructor Kacia Felgreen (earth) History

Instructor Teron Dawn (fire) Social Studies

Trevor = coach driver

Chef Trey Blane = short chef with a large mustache and short fuse.

Healer Thomena Storm = Chief Medical Healer

Subjects being taught.

Social studies = Instructor Teron Dawn(fire)

History = Instructor Kacia Felgreen (earth wielder)

Arithmetic

Economics

Geography

The Sciences = Engineering and Biology

(The above are in the Educational topics.)

Three types of Instructors = Educational, Wielders and Combat

Biology = Instructor Yanny Solars (fire)

Defense and Combat = Weapons Master Pietor Caren and Instructor Talios (earth)

Wielding Junior Division = Instructor Eowise Shelley (air)

Wielding Senior Division = Instructor Charl Melvin (water)

Dancing and Etiquette = Instructor Helene Droye (air)

Students

Danai Riverun (weltonian student and fire wielder) = 5th year student

Navos Odell (student –wind) = 5th year student

Lexia Detran (student-air) = 5th year student

Shran Alton (student-earth) = 5th year student

Henrick Walters (student-air) 3rd year with Britea

Lady Lianne Arkei (student-water) 3rd year

Lady Valerie Mern (student-air) 3rd year

Lady Pearl Ceres (student-air) 3rd year

Lady Daphne Kellen (student-earth) = new hanger on 3rd year

Lady Theresa Chade (student-fire) = new hanger on 3rd year

Novice Chelton Blade = grade 1 wielder fire

Novice Vindell Masters = grade 1 wielder fire

Daiuz Solarn = classmate/roommate of Hendrick

Novice Aaliya Dune of Syla College = water wielder and 4th year contestant

Novice Thran Oslor of Royal Malaquey = air wielder and 6th year contestant

Novice Deric Holms of Artra College = earth wielder and 5th year contestant

Novice Sunrise Belford of Royal Malaquey College = fire wielder and 5th year contestant

Novice Narl Montree of Artra College = water wielder and 4th year contestant

The Wielder Trials 126th edition.

It consists of a general knowledge testing with rapid fire quiz before a large audience; running, running while wielding past obstacles; sparring with weapons; then sparring via wielding and endurance wielding.

Royal Malaquey Naval Wielding College

Lieutenant Commander Marya Helsliff—Warden (air wielder)

Commander Brann Zelon—Headmaster (earth wielder)

Lieutenant Therry Welspring—(fire wielder and also agent and Harto's friend.)

The Artra Army Wielding College

Lieutenant Commander Piotr King (water) youngest Warden in all three colleges

General Ravh Welbrick (water) bald; has a moustache; drinks everyone under the table and is jovial.

Malaquey Naval Intelligence

Lieutenant Commander Elizea Trent

Lieutenant Commander Peras Nell

Lieutenant Harto Flay (Earth wielder)

Lady Shalina De'tre Flay (Harto's mum and sister to Peras Nell)

Lieutenant Commander Revan Flay (deceased.)

Malaquey Monarchy

King Wilhem of House Taros

Queen Ariande

Wiltran = heir = 16yrs old

Crystal = princess = 11yrs old

Aren = princess = 7yrs old

Government = Elected Ministers and Lords, they could support or veto the Monarch's orders. Like a Parliament.

Malaquey Military = Navy, Army and Wielders Division

Lord Nalin Solarn = Minister of Finance. His nephew is Dariuz Solarn.

Lady Nara Gedea (member of the court)

Lady Adria Arkei

Lady Selina Arkei

Namiran Intelligence

Minister for the Namiran Intelligence Agency = Nathan Lensworth

Master Engineer Tresh Stamets

Other notables…

Natia (one sassy alkynaia/sea serpent) = *The Novice Wielder*

Lieutenant Commander Dariv Fhon (namiran) = *The Novice Wielder*

The dead and gone…

Commodore Zachary Wolfen

Captain Rian Meldron

Chronology

-578B.H (before humans) The 1st Alkynaia War Vs Dyhaeri (Queen Zaleria of the Dyhaeri is victorious)

A.C = After the Crossing

Current year = 2184A.C

184A.C = Dyhaeri Vs Humans War (The former Olderian Empire) Dyhaeri win and the Sea Treaty Agreement seals the peace

305A.C = Jahlaniin becomes King of the Dyhaeri

399A.C = Human Civil War

The Continent divides into the Kingdom of Namira to the South and the Republic of Malaquey to the North

King Laren Cen-Taros, (1st king of Malaquey and ancestor of Headmaster Lance Cen-Taros)

King Val of Namira (1st king of Namira)

699A.C = The second Alkynaia War Vs Dyhaeri. King Jahlaniin is victorious.

1384A.C = Syla College founded by Headmaster Lance Cen-Taros.

The first of three colleges of wielding

King Adren Cen-Taros, brother to Headmaster Lance Cen-Taros, King Oltair of Namira and Queen Mother Zaleria of Dyhaeri attend the ground breaking.

1392A.C = Time of Persecution when weltonian's were driven out or attacked.

Then the weltonians split from the colleges and refused to be students.

The Wielder's Creed was amended.

1394A.C = Namira creates its first wielding college, the Olderia College. The first of two.

1934 A.C = The first Wielder Trials is held in Syla College. The event is every two years. Namira takes part as well.

2132A.C = King Jahlaniin banishes his daughters Princess Sle'niazza and Princess Kallesezza

2142A.C = King Olnanier marries Kallesa, a 'commoner'. Lanead is 9yrs old

2147A.C = Queen Kallesa resumes control of Namira, the two colleges close indefinitely and diplomatic relations between Namira and Malaquey worsen.

2150A.C = Queen Kallesa attacks the northern mountain regions of Namira and razes the Calif Nomads home to the ground while taking their children to become her Death Squads. They are very tall and talk as if they are about to sing.

2184A.C = Britea begins to wield at the age of 16yrs. *The Novice Wielder*

Lanead is now 51 yrs old. Sonei is 49 yrs old
His daughter Danai is 19 yrs old.
Mat is 19 yrs old
Harto is 20 yrs old.
Kahl is 17 yrs old
THE 126TH WIELDER TRIALS

CPSIA information can be obtained
at www.ICGtesting.com
Printed in the USA
LVHW111726090221
678834LV00003B/746